THE DEFENSELESS

Novels published by Midnight Fire Media

Your Own Fate
Night on Earth
Dreams Belong to the Night
ShadowWalk
Alarums of Reality
Afterglow Dust
Black Dragon
Falling
Thunder Road - Ice and Fire
Season of the Witch
Afterglow Rain

Anthology: Red Shadow and Other Stories

The Janus Clan series:

The Defenseless
The Slaves
Birds Flying in the Dark
At the End of the Rainbow
Lewis of Modern York

Poetry:

Amos Keppler: Complete Poems 1989 – 2003
Secrets - Descriptions of what cannot be described

(A few of the) novels to be published:

Afterglow Fire
The Werewolf of Locus Bradle
Fangs and Claws of the Earth
Forsaken

For a «complete» list of current and current future Amos
Keppler and Midnight Fire Media projects see the back of the
book and the Midnight Fire/Midnight Fire Media web pages.

The Janus Clan, Book One

«The first twenty years - Book One»
The years 1968 - 1974

The Defenseless

By

Amos Keppler

MIDNIGHT FIRE MEDIA
2019

Midnight Fire Media

http://midnight-fire.net/mfm
For more about The Defenseless and the Janus Clan:
http://midnight-fire.net/sw

E-Mail:
amos@midnight-fire.net
manofhood@yahoo.com

Cover, text, design, premedia, art and photos Amos Keppler

ISBN 978-82-91693-26-2

From the foreword to Eric Carr's novel, «The Defenseless» (excerpt):

I sit here looking at two photos, one old and one a bit less old, on the surface two ordinary photographs of groups of ordinary people… and they're giving me the willies.

Why? You ask.

Let me put it this way: Are you willing to believe the unbelievable, the utter and absolute horror, the wildest joy?

You do that to an extent anyway. You believe we will all be saved or condemned by entities beyond human ken. You pretend life is basically fair…

You deny the shadows because they don't fit into your perception of what life is about.

The world is never as you see it. It's safe to say it's never as anyone sees it… because one single human being will never see more than a tiny bit of the whole picture.

Perhaps every human alive, every being alive in the entire universe together can't grasp it all, can't grasp more than a tiny fraction of Infinity.

What is really going on in any given situation? Do we know? Can we know? Will what we thought we knew be completely and totally turned around many years later, when more facts are known? And is even that sufficient to even see a glimmer of what goes as truth? The only truth is, as I've learned only too well that there is no truth. Everything depends on viewpoint. Do we find a kind of approximate to it all by standing back, attempting to look at the big picture? Perhaps. But in my opinion, there is always something to be said for being in the middle of it all, in the thick of the experience. If one of our main purposes is to learn, experience is surely the key to it, to gain insight, independence, gain Life. And if pain is a necessary part of it, Ted Warren and the others must have truly gained profound insight.

I would have wanted to speak to Mike. He's an essential, missing part of the puzzle. There is more, but he's surely one of the most important. Did something change him in his early teens? Did someone… or something reach out to transform him, or was what happened inevitable, a kind of fate?

I know more about this than anyone resembling an outsider, I think, perhaps even more than many directly involved. And I still have many more questions than answers. Life is a puzzle, a riddle, a *mystery*. We're all walking The Invisible Labyrinth, stumbling in its many pitfalls.

And it's one hell of a run.

Part one:
Day and Night - The Two Rivers

Chapter One

The rivers ran from south to north, Cherry, the calm one originated on the prairie. South Platte ran from the mountains, wild and terrifying. And when they met, and South Platte continued alone on its further way north, who could say what was hiding below its surface?

The water waited for them, dark and foreboding.

The brothers went fishing. The brothers and the sister went on fishing trips often during summer, but not today.

There were flashes of images going through his mind, not going through his mind, but touching it from somewhere else, like a movie of a person carrying a camera as he or she walked forward, as she or he walked backwards. They froze him. They made him cringe and crouch standing up. He couldn't escape it. Closing his eyes made it worse. Opening his eyes made it worse. There were pain and blood and haze in a gray, ever-changing landscape. There was nothing to hold onto, except the pain, the blood, the haze, the cracks of thunder on a sunny day.

They all went fishing and never returned.

The annual local shooting contest had begun in this southern suburb of the city of Denver, Colorado, USA.

The loud cracks from guns sounded in the morning. They sounded throughout the day and early evening. Until the sun rested just above the mountains and darkness wasn't far away. Loud cracks in the fresh, warm morning air. Singing, vibrating shots in the hot summer day. By the end of the day hardly more than muted, insignificant sounds, even through the ears of the many onlookers.

These were social events. It always drew a crowd, but today it had drawn a doozy. Something had brought all the people here. Something.

The contenders wore mufflers over the ears, to protect their hearing from the many loud and otherwise deafening shots. They stood in a horizontal line, lay in line, stood on their knees in line by each other's side. The shots were fired at an uneven speed. Some finished before the others. They used rifles. On bull's eyes, on moving targets, while staying or lying still, or moving through the terrain of the contest.

The spectators applauded for each new result being called. The shooting contests were a tradition of more than a hundred years in these parts and both Denver locals and visiting travelers loyally supported the competition.

The gun smoke made Ted Cousin's nose itch. They used what was supposedly smoke-free powder these days without it helping any. The massive amount released from these events made such an effort useless. It stuck in his clothes, its taste in his mouth, in the very air long after he had left the arena, until it finally mixed with other, less identifiable smells.

He was young, just about thirteen, tall, pale and lean. His eyes occasionally flashed in red, seemingly a darker reflection of the sun above the mountain. Those who studied the boy closer couldn't say for sure what was correct. His eyes, or rather the skin around his eyes seemed swollen, in a way, too. He seemed angry, he seemed vulnerable. They couldn't read him at all and they worried. He saw their insecurity and he smelled it. They clearly felt uncomfortable in his presence. He had always had a keen sense of smell.

Iris Carson, a skinny, undeveloped teenager approached him eagerly.

– So what you're saying is that the powder from the guns is making your nose twitch, huh? I can't smell a thing, you know.

– I can smell it all, he told her, looking, not looking at the sun.

– My nose is probably fucked up by civilization, Iris joked sheepishly. – That's not fair.

That made him look closer at her, but only for a second or two.

He smelled them all. The scent of their fear assaulted his senses.

Everybody rushed to the cafeteria inside the clubhouse, filling it quickly. Ted didn't really know what he was feeling, sitting tense in the chair, surrounded by friends and family. He was a bundle of nerves. He always was, and it sickened him. But by thoughtfully pondering his situation, something he also did quite often, more complicated emotions surfaced.

The winners were called to the stage one by one. He was called last both the first and third time. Now everybody knew

10

and the raging emotions within intensified further. He stood
and raised his hands above the head. The smile felt strange on
his lips. He had won his class and also the entire competition,
no matter the competition category. He had won.

On the stage, where someone had left a derelict, old piano
he received a number of prizes. He received them from Jeff
McCabe, the Denver police Chief. This in addition to the
cup he had been given outside. Even photographers from
the major Denver newspapers were here to honor him. Ted
descended from the stage and was congratulated by his brother
Michael and then Michael's girlfriend Tilla. She kissed him
lightly on the cheek. So did the brothers' sister Linda, though
considerably more cautious. Erazmus Coogan, his uncle gave
him a hearty handshake. His parents embraced him.

– Not the best in the world, his father grinned, – but quite fun
anyway, right?

– Great fun, Ted confirmed. He waved eagerly to everybody
who cheered and applauded.

– So, how do you feel about this, Mr. Cousin? A journalist
called out to the group. – About your boys. Your older son is
actually the runner up.

Rodney Cousin straightened and bristled.

– I'm quite proud, of course, but not really surprised. We have
always encouraged the competitive element in our family. Mike
has been the best until now. That's natural since he's older, but
this is a reminder for him to improve himself further, to step up
his game.

– You're just the perfect American family, aren't you? Another
journalist called without the slightest hint of irony.

– We like to think so, yes, Cousin smiled. – In these troubled
times I feel it is even more paramount for someone to stick to
the old well-proven ways.

Ted pulled back a bit, just a step or two, hardly visible,
without looking at his father. He knew how it must look, this
family gathering. Such harmony, such envy. As the day melted
into the eternal night every face stood out to him. The stiff,
falsely happy faces. He saw them from behind, saw from
behind their true color and himself mirrored in the big display
windows by the parking lot. The image of the parking lot faded

with the last few remnants of day, when the shining electrical, artificial lights ascended.

– They don't cheer for me or for the event, he told Linda vehemently later. – They cheer for themselves. To keep their own wretched lives from going completely to the dogs they attempt to live through me, through anybody else giving them a quick fix, to give meaning to their lives.

Linda didn't say anything. She hardly did. Did he see a small tear in the corner of her eyes? He could never tell.

He became resigned once more, allowing what would happen anyway to happen.

There occurred a lot of pretense in his life. No, too kind. He pretended a lot, that he wasn't who he was, and he wasn't where he was. He pretended a lot, at least to others. The true difficulty lay in lying to himself, but he had gotten quite good in that, too. He dreamed a lot, about the future. Usually stupid daydreams about the ridiculous and unreachable.

But also more.

He walked the road to the house through the forest. Suddenly… something happened, like a fist in the belly, a sledgehammer in the head, but worse. He knew about physical pain and this was nothing like it. This was similar to an assault, but it came from within, he was certain of that much. He saw himself as older, sometimes much older. An image full of contrasts, but little content, black and white, gray, the dark. A flash of continuing hopelessness. He ran. Not through this forest. Not this forest, but another far away. Someone ran at his side, but he could never discern whom. He saw nothing but a shadow. Bright summer nights, it did him no good, helped less than nothing. Wherever he ran darkness gathered.

***/

The last day at school. A much desired holiday waited with a slap in the face. The teacher, Erazmus Coogan studied, with a smile on his face the long line of pupils approaching him in a more or less orderly fashion, to shake his hand. He was old school, he bothered with such things. The children thought he was corny, of course, but a few returned his smile. At least he imagined they did. Old «blue eyes» Coogan belonged to the select few of the attending teachers at the school the students could stomach at all. He had a reputation as «okay», but something of a dork.

– This semester has been finished in outstanding ways, boys and girls, he chided them, admonished them. – Welcome back in the fall.

He shook hands with each of the children coming forward, those among them degrading themselves to such an act. Today's youth saw elementary polite behavior as a non-priority. Now, towards the end of the sixties the traditional generational divide had been widened to formerly unknown depths. Contempt - and even hatred - never strayed long from the surface.

The youths yearned to leave the school premises as soon as possible. That was undoubtedly one reason why so many were «forthcoming».

– I would like to give you greetings from my parents and this little gift, sir, Frank Forester greeted him and presented the gift in a somewhat eloquent move.

The gift itself had been very «tastefully» wrapped in expensive paper and ornaments. Thomas and Regina Forester did everything in «style». Or their servants did.

– Say thank you to your parents from me, Coogan said very politely.

He actually saw an even greater hatred in the eyes of the, well… well fed boy, something that rarely or never reached the surface. It didn't surprise him. He saw the boy as a born hypocrite, a trait not exactly discouraged through the first thirteen years of his life.

Some more young meat bothered the teacher before he virtually forgot Frank… and everything else. He pulled himself together with an act of will and directed his attention at the long, fiery red hair. Gray eyes stared coldly at him. Coogan noticed that he didn't quite manage to keep his composure. Tilla Stevens had always that effect on him. He was made to feel old by the patronizing look in her eyes. This time he even got a hard-on by her stance and the lack of clothes covering her luscious body and it made him depressed.

– We must improve your grades in the fall, he said and cursed the hoarse voice. – They weren't as good as they could have

13

been this year.

– I don't give a fuck, she snarled. – There's no way I could be the slightest interested in what marks you put in that fucking book.

She always managed to get to him. He was unable to fathom why… or why she behaved the way she did. Her abilities and intelligence undoubtedly far exceeded any common average. So how could she let it all go to waste like that?

The charade ended by her pulling the report book out of his hand and heading out of there with her head held high. Distraught he kept shaking his head, kept wondering what made her behave in such a manner. It wasn't her parents. He had met them. They were nice, well adapted people. She always made him doubt himself, that little bitch.

– So, shall we continue, teacher? Iris Carson looked innocently, teasingly up at him.

For a moment he looked sharply at her, too, before managing to pull himself together. Iris had something of the same impudence and lack of respect in her make up as Tilla, but contrary to Miss Stevens she was just an underdeveloped, scrawny kid, not even close to be that distracting.

He gave her the book. She took it and stumbled disappointed out of the classroom. The boys looked at him with reluctant respect. The teacher was a cool customer.

One by one they paraded by him. The line thinned. Finally, at the back of the queue only two remained. When looking closer at the two, the brother and sister he felt the usual flash of irritation, of worry.

– Now, Ted and Linda, he greeted them in a friendly, jovial manner. – What can I do for you? Is anything wrong?

They didn't reply, not vocally anyway. After receiving their report card, they just stood there in silence, staring blindly ahead. But not at him. It seemed safe to say that they hardly saw him at all, that they, in truth didn't realize they were there with him, in the same room as him.

– You shouldn't look this glum, he said jokingly. – Your grades weren't that bad, you know.

– Grades? Ted looked directly at him and Coogan started sweating instantly.

It was a hot day, but not that hot, and suddenly it felt very cold.

– Grades are important, he said defensively. – For your future and wellbeing as productive adults of the community. But yours are definitely above average and I'm confident that you'll improve further during fall.

Linda forced a pale smile, one looking more like a scowl. The boy didn't change his expression one way or another.

– So? You want to tell your favorite uncle what's wrong?

He was actually their only uncle, or their only uncle locally. Another one, by the name of Eugene Kendall, Coogan's half-brother lived farther south in the state, but they had little contact with him.

– Nothing, they said in unison and shook their head, so synchronized one would be tempted to think they were identical twins.

He didn't believe them for a minute. Something was happening, for sure, something he wasn't privy to. Once more he was overwhelmed by an unexplainable worry. Ted worried him. The dark look from the dark-haired boy burned accusingly at everyone and everything. The brown eyes almost looked black in the pale-skinned face. Coogan froze like he had never frozen before, a negative experience in every way that counted. If he never had experienced one before, he did so, now.

And he would know, after one year in Vietnam, only one year, an eternity, until being honorably discharged after being wounded twice, counting himself lucky. He had inevitably changed in that horrible place. And he had seen others change, inexplicable in that damp, remote jungle, a wilderness fit for no man. But… only in minor ways compared to these two. Before he left they had been normal, lively kids. Now, they stood as transformed before him. He had seen fear in others' eyes during the war. He saw it now, in the youths' eyes. Fear, despair and hatred and quite a lot more. Nuances he hardly felt capable of identifying. They were bullied and persecuted by other pupils, he knew that much, but not more than others, not excessively so, nothing to explain the insane uncomfortable sense of dread he experienced in their company.

The conversation slowly ground to a halt, unnoticeable a first, then obviously. He was unable to decide whether or not he or they were the cause. And that also bothered him.

– Everything okay at home?

– Everything, Linda confirmed, nodding eagerly.

– Everything. Ted echoed.

And Ezra imagined he could hear a true echo somewhere, in the hallway perhaps, but he couldn't be sure. The hallway had never been prone to echoes, he knew that much.

– I'll accompany you outside, he said friendly enough.

He didn't bother to lock the door. The custodian would take care of that, or not, later. They walked first with fast, nervous steps. He managed to keep up with them in a fairly relaxed manner.

No one spoke during the walk inside the dark hallway. The western wing, where a huge window usually lit walls, floor and ceiling had been sealed temporarily due to ongoing restoration work. Very little sunlight emerged from the convoluted web of dark tarp and added construction material.

Whoever had dreamed up the new set up, should be shot on sight, he thought grimly.

The only real daylight emerged through the double front door, opening and closing as the pupils rushed outside. Ted's skin seemed only worse in here. He walked with bowed head and bowed back, so bowed that he seemed smaller than his sister, crouched, as if in pain, like a humpback. He had been quite well-built for his age. Now, he seemed abnormally thin and pale. The constantly fresh colored skin had paled to muddy water. Something had happened. What?

Coogan shook hands with them by the exit. When he looked encouragingly at Linda he saw her mouth twitch at least once. She wanted to tell him something. The blue eyes gave her away.

She seemed transparent to him. Compared to her brother she still looked quite okay, but she had turned into a fearful and brooding girl. He saw it, even if no one else did.

He… smelled something… huge and bad, the stench of it so strong that it actually literally made his nose twitch. He felt an abyss of understanding open up below him, so wide that he could hardly see its walls on either side. But present, like a sore thumb. It made his mood deteriorate even further.

Howard Grey, the biology teacher rushed towards them and ruined any change of engaging in a confidential conversation. Ezra experienced a nauseous mix of relief and self-contempt. He hardly noticed the brother and sister slipping through the door.

– We need to talk, Grey stated in his usual pretentious, unbearable manner. – In confidential circumstances.

Linda held the boy's hand and dragged him away. She seemed far stronger than him. Coogan kept them in his sight until the end of the school's plaza. They met Mike by the gate. The older brother met them there almost every day. It had caused a few remarks at first, but now it only seemed natural. Linda and Ted obviously needed his support. And no one doubted his ability to give it. Michael looked like a bigger and far healthier version of his kid brother. He wasn't more than sixteen, but his frame and strength far exceeded the average of his age. Coogan knew they were of about the same height, approximately six feet two, but Ted's… *folded* frame made him look smaller. The muscles filled the older brother's clothes. His pride and confidence practically made him glow. Coogan wondered what had happened to Ted and not to him.

– Is there any rush? He asked Grey, not bothering to hide his indifference.

– There is indeed, Grey stated very, very correctly. – The correction of sloppy work can't wait until later and your two prodigies have in truth been even sloppier than I could have imagined possible this time around.

Coogan wanted to ask him if he could ever imagine anything, but held his tongue. An unquestionable and familiar feeling of dread rose instantly in him. He realized he knew and feared where this was heading.

– So, you mean…

– The confirmation just arrived, Grey told him, clearly gloating.

But he would have gloated even more, if he had realized what he, in truth was sitting on. But Coogan had no intention of telling him that.

– Show me, he demanded.

– Oh, I will, the other man said. – Rest assured of that…

They walked straight to Grey's office. Several colleagues attempted to initiate a conversation, but for once the two of them were completely in agreement. Coogan found himself unable to hide his eagerness, how upset he truly was. He had been very eager and also reluctant to get the confirmation Grey spoke about. He had been interested, against his own best judgment. And now his curiosity led him helplessly down the road he absolutely didn't want to go.

Grey locked the door behind them and then went straight for his briefcase. Coogan recognized the papers he pulled up and handed over. He did so immediately. The vast abyss opened up further below him as he read, as Grey added his own sarcastic spoken words.

When Ezra Coogan sometime later emerged from the office, he was deeply, visibly shaken. It was a man on the brink people saw leave the teachers' recreation room.

– Then you will talk to them? Grey called after him.

– Yes, he replied absentminded. – I'll talk to them.

He had a faint recollection of having physically assaulted Grey in there, but couldn't verify whether or not it had actually happened, other than in fevered flashes of imagination.

The dean approached him, accompanying him out in the hall.

– A good year, Ezra?

Ezra felt a sense of profound irritation. Only his friends got to call him Ezra.

– In terms of work and grades among the students…

The dean looked encouragingly at him.

– … we have had an excellent year.

The dean nodded, content in his world.

– But I can't for the life of me convince myself it was worth it.

The dean stopped and let him go on his way.

He walked through the schoolyard, left the school, left his car behind on the parking lot and started walking home. He kept shaking his head. A part of him had always wondered, wondered what was wrong, but this opened up even more than he would have ever expected. Because this couldn't be it. This couldn't be everything. He had convinced himself of that, now.

18

Nothing made sense anymore. Things had made sense once. He dimly recalled that time with a certain fondness, a shaking of the head. A bench appeared in his vision somewhere ahead. He sat down on it.

As the wind blew, as he saw it move the treetops.

Across the street two small boys were playing. The mother stood there watching. There was rough horseplay, but no malice.

Ted fell apart, inch by inch. But he didn't know what Ezra had just learned. If he had known, it would have been easily discernible. The grades weren't the worst. They were clearly above average. But that, too, was a kind of duty, a distraction. He was certainly intelligent enough, but didn't use it. He had a lot of physical potential, but failed to reach for it. Something was missing, something relevant. He didn't belong here, an outsider of outsiders. Coogan's distinct impression was that the boy quite simply was dying on the vine; that he turned to dust in front of everybody.

His self-respect had, at some crazy turn vanished utterly.

Something terrifying was happening before everyone's eyes and no one saw anything. They saw the reality of it, of course, Ted's obvious illness, his fall from grace. But they didn't have a clue why. And in spite of the fact that he knew more, far more than the others neither did Coogan. The more he knew the more convoluted and distressing the web revealed itself to be. At every turn he got sucked further into the invisible labyrinth.

Nothing made sense.

*****************/

South Platte River passed majestically the old, white house, where the boiling, enraged water made a turn. Boiling water, boiling sky, making the Earth shake. An old, tall oak grew right by the dark river. On one of its thick branches, a human length or so above the unruly waves an overly lean frame sat rocking. Skin was pale and made the long dark brown hair completely dominate the face. As if dreaming the brown eyes stared across the river and at the tall mountains rising outside the city. The branch he sat on was rocking slightly. The rhythm poured pleasantly through his body.

Ted Cousin enjoyed sitting here, like this, momentarily

distracted from his dark thoughts. With his eyes closed he could dream about other times, other places. His thoughts felt light, as if not being weighed down anymore. It was surprisingly easy, like his spirit truly took flight from the body and moved across mountains, forests and seas. Eagle flew out of the night and into… into the valley of kings.

And as ever panic set in almost instantly. He felt… a presence and he had to open his eyes. Wide-eyed he stared down, into the water, the dark and deep pool. He saw a naked face dominated by the eyes reflecting the low, setting sun. But it was only one face, one pair of mirrors. The relief he felt made the hatred and self-contempt rise to a bile inside.

The thirteen-year old boy rolled his hands into fists, into knots. Every time he looked at himself critically, like an outsider in his own body he felt ever more pathetic and helpless. He dug out his wallet, opening, looking at a photo there. It had been taken one year earlier, only one year ago, of him, Linda… and Mike. While looking at the photo of Ted Cousin, the twelve-year old, there were few or no remaining similarities. He feared he was sinking deeper and deeper into an abyss there was no way out of.

And his weary, adult thoughts kept haunting him.

Through the thick set of leaves he looked at the house. The parents relaxed in the garden with Linda and Mike. They sat in their chairs close to the house' southern wall and it was about 30 steps away. Ted had counted them once. In spite of the distance he still easily heard the thunderous laughter, thick with contempt and malice. Mike laughed because of something the father said.

– Let's leave Ted to himself for a while, dad, he said, shaking his head. – For unfathomable reasons he has decided to go through a… phase right now. It will pass, it always does.

The parents didn't notice the scorn in Mike's voice, but the twins easily heard it, sensing it cutting into them, their flesh and thoughts. The girl lowered her eyes, to keep them from betraying her. Ted dug his fingers into the bark, feeling the sickening rage coming on.

He slowly, carefully broke off a thinner branch and threw it into the river. The movement, slight as it was, made him lose his footing. Not until the very last moment did he manage to grab hold of the nearest branch above. Breathing heavily he pulled himself to safety. Sweat flowed from skin seemingly even more pale then seconds earlier.

Where he stood, breathing and sweating hard and with muscles virtually screaming in pain he had very little in common with the healthy, sturdy boy celebrating his twelfth birthday the previous year. The shoulder blades showed, even through the clothes, grotesquely free of flesh. The arms were so thin that he could reach around the upper arm with one hand. Under the worn shirt one could see the ribs. He stood with his back to the tree, but didn't use it for support. Instead he made certain that his back didn't touch any part of the tree.

The Dark traveled with the cloud traveling with the sun across the sky, covering its light, and with him as well. As he moved, it moved. He studied his hand in the sunlight, as he moved it and saw The Shadow. He hit the tree with the hand and cried out sharply as the brutal contact with the wood hurt his skin.

He looked up again, finally, after what seemed like forever. Only Linda remained by the big camping table, lithe and lean, beautiful as a mirage. Her eyes were as blue as the clear sky. Still, it was something somber about her, clearly noticeable by a second, closer inspection, nothing physical, but below the surface, festering like a disease.

She rose and walked towards the river, to him. No one else would have noticed the slight hesitation, but he did. He knew her so well.

She wasn't really that deep. He sensed none of the abysmal depths in her that he sensed in himself. Ironically, she could be said to be the mirror image of Mike, what Ted wasn't.

Her closeness, the bright smile for a moment washing away his cynicism, his dark thoughts.

Both cast a look back at the house. They saw no one there, but their happiness, their pubescent joy over being alone, over being alone together faded to gray.

She stopped just below the thick branch, resting her back against the tree.

– Do you remember the last time we went to the library? He said brusquely, before she got to initiate the conversation.

21

– Sure. She shrugged. – Why do you ask?

– Mike actually told us to go to the library to wait for him, Ted persisted.

– It was nice of him, she said automatically. – He knows how much we enjoy it in there.

– We looked through the damn newspapers, he continued unabated. – We were looking at the world, at everything happening out there.

– Yes, she said brightly. – People are claiming their freedom everywhere.

Behind the smile, the exuberant mood....

He had seen the fear in her eyes.

– Why did you come? He said, attempting to keep a light tone, but unable to not expose the bitterness in his voice.

– Don't you want to talk to m-me? She stuttered unhappily.

When he saw her like this, naked and exposed, the hatred and the fear within grew even stronger.

The hatred, the fear, the self-contempt. Sometimes he got everything mixed up, to the point where it all turned indistinguishable, the common denominator flashing before his eyes, like fire, like sweet pain.

She held hard, almost convulsive in his leg, clutched it to the point where her nails almost broke his skin. An indefinite sense of power rose in him. She needed him, as much as he needed her.

– So much has changed, he said softly, – but I'll always talk to you. That will never change.

She smiled then, but behind the smile he saw the all too familiar shame. He stiffened. She pulled down her skirt. Suddenly it was as if she couldn't stand meeting his eyes anymore and she looked down.

– Mike sent me to fetch you, she said unhappily, and reached for his hand.

Her words hit him hard. He realized, as he should have done instantly that she had not come of her own volition. He pulled away like a wounded beast, but then he stopped, resigned, looking bitterly at her.

– Go ahead, he said, his voice rasping like metal. – I can't stop you. You're far stronger than me. Mike has fed you well.

22

She broke into tears and stared at him with a naked expression in her eyes.

– How can you say something like that? She cried. – How can you be so c-cruel? You're not the only one suffering.

Sobbing she fell to her knees and hid her face in shaking hands.

Filled with regret he jumped down from the tree, to her, not even noticing how easy, how effortlessly it happened. She was right. He had nothing to blame her for. She was stuck in the mire, just as much as him. They ate, slept and lived on sufferance and vicious mercy.

– Don't cry. He choked. – I've got no one else to turn to. If it wasn't for you I would have given in a long time ago.

He glanced towards the river. Her eyes widened in shock. He nodded to her unspoken question.

– It would have been so easy, wouldn't it, he said almost absentmindedly, – to surrender to the river, let go of all problems? The thought of you has helped me resist its pull, but something *else,* too, a resistance beyond… beyond anything I know.

– You're so grown up, she sniffed, smiling. – And such a poet. I love you.

– It's his fault, he said. – The devil up there is to blame for everything. We're being hounded and spat on by our former friends *and it's his fault*.

– Don't say that, she protested. – He's our brother.

The hurt and rage in his eyes almost went beyond anything she had experienced before.

– I didn't mean it, she whispered. – I didn't mean it like that. It's what he wants me to say, what he's teaching through every single harsh lesson.

Despair jolted her when she discovered that Ted straightened. He always did that when being excited. As if to keep him down, she dug her long nails into his back.

She backed off when he suddenly crouched, his face distorted in pain. He collapsed in a heap on the ground. She saw blood flow from his lower lip. He had bit himself.

– What's *wrong?* She wondered. – What has he *done?*

Ted did his best to roll away, to avoid her closer scrutiny, but she carefully, determined grabbed his shirt and held on to it, comforting him. After a while she removed it, exposing the skin beneath.

Skin hidden under thin fabric.

The shock almost made her stumble into the river. She closed her eyes hard and hoped to awake after an afternoon nap on the twelfth birthday, to discover that it had all been a nightmare. But while reopening them she still saw her brother writhing in pain on the ground, *then* and *now* superimposed on her vision. She desperately wanted to turn away from the horrible sight, but couldn't, couldn't, couldn't.

She realized now why he had walked around like some sort of humpback recently. The entire backside, from his butt to the neck had swollen to unbelievable proportions. She kept blinking, hard pressed to convince herself that he was still alive and not a walking dead.

– Oh, my God, she whispered. – The shooting contest.

Without looking at her he rose and dressed, teeth gritting. With eyes turned towards the house he started walking. It seemed to Linda that he hadn't heard a word she had said, since his own, last outburst. Confused and frightened she ran after him.

– Cain and Abel were also supposed to be brothers, he mumbled.

The girl's eyes grew round and huge. She feared he didn't know she was there at all.

Chapter two

Denver, during the late nineteen-sixties, was far from any center of the Storm raging across the world. This had almost always been the case, but was presently even truer than during other periods in history.

It was a typical modern city, in the sense that the tall buildings were concentrated at its center and that the spread of its suburbs reached far beyond that, into the rural landscape.

One of the few things Denver currently had going for it, was that Jack Kerouac and Neal Cassady, the beat-generation gurus had grown up here. In the pool halls on Glenarm Street, in «LoDo», the city's lower downtown area they had started on their path to infamy. LoDo was changing, giving way to the so-called post modernism of the approaching seventies, but even though the change had started at this point, it was still pretty much as Cassady and Kerouac would have remembered it.

Rodney Cousin had grown up here. He had never spoken about having actually met any of the other two, but it was safe to say that his life had taken a distinctively different turn.

The smoke-filled room was also filled with shadows. Light and dust played funny tricks on the mind. Ted stood with his back to a corner coughing, observing his father. As he played pool Rodney seemed somewhat like a different person in this place, more relaxed, in a way, less rigid, reminiscent of youth, perhaps. As he played his wicked game he was just as focused as he usually was, but… happier? He was focused whatever he did.

He played Eightball against a bunch of local roughnecks. His features completely impassive, he took the game and them on as methodically as he did everything, beating them soundly. His reputation as a pool-shark had started to spread and even though they didn't say it outright it was obvious that they had come to the place to challenge him. They paid him grudgingly, but without really acting up or anything. Perhaps they did see the hint of danger at the edge of his eyes, the hint paradoxically softened in these smoke-filled halls. Cindy, his devoted wife, in a rare show of open affection, of joy embraced him and kissed his lips.

Afterwards the family sat by a table eating their burgers and fries.

– This is the last time, he said.

– Why? She asked him, taking his hand, knowing the answer before asking the question.

– I'm getting bored with it, he said, shaking his head.

Ted was used to keeping his mouth shut, so he said nothing.

– You didn't seem bored, if I may say so, sir, Mike interjected grinningly. – The way you handled those hoodlums was truly amazing.

– Just the last memories of old glory, his father told him.

Ted hadn't really looked at, studied his father, until that moment. He could do it without being noticed. He was quite good at that. Rodney Cousin had always been there, a constant presence in their lives, but never really interfering in anything. And he had seemed ordinary. Stern, perhaps, but not that much different from any fairly conservative American father. But in that moment of confrontation between him and the pool sharks, he had been far from ordinary.

They walked through the LoDo area, as the last remaining rays of sunlight touched the ground.

– I used to play in these parts as a child, Cindy said dreamingly, longingly. – The old theater, where I learned the craft, wasn't far away from here.

Ted looked at her. Even she seemed human today.

Cindy Coogan had been an actress and quite a celebrity, before she got married. Ted dimly remembered the media attention the family had endured the first few years, but it had faded in time, only to resurface a bit occasionally, like after the shooting contest.

Cousin bought a bundle of today's newspapers, those he didn't already have a subscription to. The Cousin household was one very aware of local, national and global events. It was inevitable, with all the shit lying around. Ted supposed he should be grateful for that. His curiosity about, his craven interest for the world at large had been awakened from an early age. He and Linda could spend hours in the library, devouring news and stories. They did so, in spite of the availability «at home». It was their turf, their private space.

Linda held up newspapers while she danced across the floor. Ted looked through a book, interested in spite of himself.

Modern slavery
by Sheila Ashcroft

It didn't really pertain to their situation, as it was far more international and far-fetched in scope, but it did make Goose-bumps appear on his arm.

Linda held the newspaper article closer, so he couldn't avoid seeing the headline.

CONGRESS ENACTS ANTI-RIOT ACT

He threw the book at her in a burst of surprising strength. It was a thick, bound book, but she caught it easily.

– You know, you got some reflexes girl, he said, shaking his head, wrinkling his brow.

– They are as good as Mike's, are they not? She said lightly. – Or almost as good? I've always been quite agile, too. And coordination has clearly been above average. That's why I've loved to dance, I guess.

Sadness, anger overtook them, then, once more, the sense of futility, of hopelessness. She forced a smile, and suddenly, on a whim, she threw the book back at him. He caught it, too, in a firm grip. The surprise caught them both off-guard. He looked for the usual shakes in his hand, the feeling of dread. It didn't show. Her eyes widened, too. In joy, in fear? Linda did a pirouette on the library floor, stretching her long, lithe body. This late in the afternoon not many people visited the library and she got the floor, more or less to herself and for a moment, a few short seconds she really cut loose. It was like watching an animal in motion, across a field, a forest bed; nothing like any dance he had ever seen. He swallowed hard and looked down, looked at the floor, his entire body shaking.

He looked up again, eventually finding his sister standing before him with an encouraging stance and smile.

RIOTS PLANNED FOR CHICAGO
DEMOCRATIC CONVENTION

– This is important, isn't it? She ventured. – I mean, it's practically unheard of… right?

– It's just words. Ted shrugged.

– But the newspaper, the journalist is lying, she pointed out.

– The people mentioned don't want to riot, only protest against what they see as wrong in the world.

– One thing's for sure, he said lightly, half bitter, half longingly, half anything. – There will be one hell of a show. There's always hope, right?

– Yes, there is, she insisted, taking his hand, deliberately misunderstanding his words.

1967 had been the summer of love. 1968 looked like it would be the summer of rage. Pent up frustration lingering for years was about to explode.

They read everything they could about this, and almost any subject, like people starving for days without number. The librarian looked suspiciously at them. Suspecting he would suddenly grow long hair and a beard, probably.

– Father is always taking his time, talking about this with us, Linda wondered. – He doesn't really seem interested, but he's talking about it. I know of no other parent who does.

– You're right. Ted nodded. – He's a chef, for Christ's sake, and in a snobby workplace, too, not exactly a picture of a radical. It is strange.

That, too, was. Strange.

– Nothing strange with mother, though, Linda said. – She stopped acting for marriage. Now, she's just there, like furniture, the typical housewife.

He heard an unfamiliar resentment and anger in her voice just then, and didn't like it. Her temper… her temper, too, occasionally ventured into rage. He shouldn't be surprised, though, should he… that she was her brothers' sister?

They had used to rehearse for their own theater performances here, quietly, to not disturb whatever peace there was in the library.

The walls, the ceilings melted away, gave way to the walls and ceilings in the Cousin home, without Ted really remembering the interim. He often experienced reality that way, like a series of… of transitions. Others didn't, he knew that much and couldn't tell if it was good or bad. It was one of the few things he hadn't discussed with his sister. It seemed… private, like a glimpse into a bedroom or a toilet booth.

28

He shrugged. The driving back and forth to town was boring anyway. He didn't see it as strange that he had developed a sense of selective memory. In that, too.

Anger and fear shot through him once more. He was entitled, right?

The Cousin family home by the river close to the southern suburb of Lakewood was like a cozy candle-lit cave. That was how Ted supposed it looked like to visitors, to outsiders anyway. At least Erazmus Coogan, who arrived at eight o'clock sharp for dinner seemed to ever find himself well here. He made jokes and showed his joy for being present at a family dinner in a thousand small ways. In a room where candles cast long, soft shadows. There were many candles, canceling most of the shadowy shapes around the room.

The three youths sat by the table with their mother and uncle. Their father, the family cook wandered back and forth between the living room and the kitchen, where he was bathed in steam from the hot stoves. It made his hair even darker than it was, making his Indian ancestry shine clearly through. Paradoxically so the small, round glasses made him look even more like a Chief, and a patriarch of an expanded family.

Cindy, by comparison was his complete opposite, blond and tall and bright, with none of the threatening demeanor that could be seen in him occasionally. She looked like her daughter's mother, like the boys looked like their father's sons. Everything fit perfectly.

Mike sat there with his eyes half closed, half open. At the opposite side of the grand table Ted did more or less the same. Mike studied Uncle Ezra and Ted did the same. Mike was so astute all the time, extremely aware of everything happening around him. Ted admired that, he did. He froze when he once again registered the… the red glare in Mike's eyes. It was like a beast sat there, exposing its fangs and claws.

A coincidence made Ted look at Coogan then, a compulsion, something or something inside, perhaps. Just for a moment there Ted imagined he lost his joyful mask and revealed a worried, painful expression. Just for a moment. It was easy, so easy to believe he had seen the dancing fire in Mike's eyes and that he knew about, or at least suspected what was going on. Ted once more felt the irrational sense of hope rise inside, dismissing it instantly with a cold, hard thought.

– Feel free to entertain yourselves, Cousin cried from the kitchen. – This will take some time. Good things take time.

– Why don't you do your juggling, Linda? Cindy suggested.

Linda flushed. She had loved to perform.

– Oh, can I?

She looked at her mother, but it wasn't her she was talking to. Mike nodded, almost imperceptible.

The girl almost jumped up from the chair, almost overturning it, too excited to be down because she needed Mike's permission to do whatever she wanted. He allowed her to perform here, where only the closest family could observe her, experience her beauty and grace and skill.

She ran to the floor across the room and pulled forth her gear from a drawer. Five spheres, five sticks. She started with the spheres instantly, in fast, fluid moves. And before anyone really noticed the sticks had started spinning through the air in whirls of indistinct movement, like daggers of fire mirrored in the brothers' eyes. They were heavy, well balanced, more like knives than not. Only the edge was missing. Silver metal seemed to expand, the illusion of spinning metal being something solid, tangible in the air turned real. The whole room seemed to spin. Ted blinked. He saw something in the whirl; saw the dark, the shadows mix with the shining moon, saw it expand, until becoming a hole in the air, a tunnel sucking him in.

– She is good, Coogan whispered. – She is really good.

From out of the corner of his eye Ted saw Mike grab a knife from the table, saw him lift it… and throw it at the dancing moon on the floor, straight at Linda's heart.

She caught it elegantly in her left hand, without missing a step. The knife became just one more integral part of the show, as the sticks and the spheres and she was. It didn't seem dramatic at all.

Ted looked at Mike with burning eyes. He wasn't really scared or shocked or even angry. He realized he hadn't truly been worried or thought Mike wanted to kill her or hurt her. As he looked at the others, wide-eyed Ezra, cool Cindy and indifferent Rodney, he wondered what the reason, the motivation was, if there was one... beyond mean, callous boredom... if Mike had wanted to... test her.

She was sweating now, the girl on the floor, as she started picking up random objects from the room and include in the show. Ted could hear the music. He could see the audience, the outside stage she moved on, in a city where buildings had been destroyed and the streets flooded with water. He blinked and the very, very life-like images, vision faded. He saw the girl, the innocent girl he thought he knew catch the spinning knife, twisting it slightly, so effortlessly... and throw it back at her older brother.

Mike caught it just in time. It vibrated in his hand, clearly speaking of the force behind the throw.

Linda curtsied smiling and pleased. The others applauded, Cousin from the kitchen. Everything seemed relaxed and normal. Everything always did.

Coogan let out his breath in a deep, prolonged sigh.

– What's next, little rose? Are you considering taking up fencing?

Laughter. Pleasant. Fake.

Roses are white, red, violet, yellow, Ted thought. She is...

The White Rose bowed and accepted the accolades from an adoring audience.

A headache made his head throb. One small second, he was convinced it would split.

The tiny family group sat down by the dinner table and had dinner. Cousin eloquently served the food on hot plates, before joining them. Cindy, with sparks in her eyes, lifted her glass of red, red wine.

– A toast, she ventured, – to the new Chef at Hotel Colorado.

– Hear, hear. Coogan lifted his glass, too.

They all did. Glass met glass. Wine burned in stomachs loaded with spices. Ted felt it, felt the heat spread from his stomach, to his entire body.

Uncle Ezra sat on the couch, carefully juggling the book from the library. He looked strange, he did. As he noticed Ted... and Linda... and Mike... and Cindy... *and* Rodney looking at him, he turned to them with a sobering look in his eyes.

– The book is true, you know. It's not fiction, but an autobiography of actual events.

– I think I did hear about it. Cousin shrugged. – They mentioned it briefly in the news a few years ago. The news crew obviously treated it as a hoax.

– That's the way it goes, isn't it? Coogan shrugged, too. – But in this case, I happen to know for a fact that it is indeed, a fact. I know Mark Stewart, the man who helped rescue the woman from captivity, from a place where a number of human beings had been held against their will and forced to be their captors' servants… in all things. I know Mark well. I have known him for many years. He showed me evidence of extended trafficking in human cargo. Slavery, sexual and otherwise does exist in our time.

– I can believe it, Mike said. He didn't shrug. – The world is a pretty fucked up place.

Linda looked at him then, startled seeing the passion burning in his eyes.

– And it's filled with secrets. Coogan rose. – Dark, potent secrets threatening to explode into the light of day.

He looked almost menacing just then, before once more returning to his usual, jovial self. Ted and Linda looked at each other, a brief glow of hope touching their eyes.

And it died, as the conversation once more returned to lighter subjects.

After «his embarrassing outburst», as Cousin dubbed it later, Uncle Ezra seemed close to… subdued. Either that or scared. Ted could never tell the difference. The boy knew that the teacher had looked straight at Mike when his eyes had flared. Ted had looked at him, not Mike. He could always tell when his brother got angry, could sense the minute changes in his temperament. And anger, among other things made the beastly eyes flare.

Coogan had seen what Linda did, and had said nothing. Ted had sensed the jolt in him, had always been quite empathic, very good at reading people and their emotions.

With a professional cook on board they did all the courses, all the stages of a meal in this house. The first course went fast, almost imperceptible as the brothers wolfed it down, as the sister ate in slow silence. It was expected of girls that they would eat like birds, so no one reacted to this either. Ted looked down in his lap. He couldn't actually remember what it had been afterwards, the food, he never could.

Cousin took another trip to the kitchen, as he often did to check on the progress of his art. This time, however, he returned with two huge plates of hot, steaming meat, encircled in fruit and vegetables.

– Rabbit, he grinned, – roasted and tasty. Kudos to Mike who shot it.

There was applause… or was it? And no one seemed to find that strange. Ted's own eyes flared, of anger, of renewed resentment. Mike had certainly done a lot of things, but he hadn't shot that rabbit.

Nothing seemed wrong, nothing at all. Outsiders looking in, through the window or otherwise, saw nothing but the happy, modern urban family, enjoying some quality time together.

It is a theater, Ted thought. Life is a theater, a theater of blood.

– My dear Ezra. Cousin lifted his glass, snickering. – I must, on behalf of the family express my joy that you have finally found time in your busy schedule to join us for dinner…

– I have to study and encourage my students, Coogan replied in the same, playful tone. – We live in such difficult times and young people in particular need all the support we can give them.

Everybody laughed. Mike the loudest. Everyone taking even more than a passing glance at this family had to believe they were both happy and thriving and not notice the secrets bouncing under the surface, ready to emerge, to erupt.

Two pair of blue eyes met over the table. Linda's eyes suddenly flooded with tears. She started coughing instantly.

– Linda, dear, her mother inquired, – what's the matter? You haven't swallowed a bone or anything, have you?

– No, mommy, her daughter replied thickly, – I caught a bit of onion in the throat, that's all. It burns like fire.

Mike quickly handed her a tissue. She accepted it with a grateful smile and blew her nose, blew it hard.

Linda had been forced to become an excellent actress, too, as the more famous Tilla and the brothers.

The evening progressed more or less uninterrupted after that. Desert was served. Dinner progressed with no major disturbances. Cousin was a sucker for progression, for rigidity. Everything had to happen in the correct sequence, the way it was planned, set up, sometime, somewhere. It was one of his Absolute Rules.

The meal eventually, finally ended. Uncle Ezra excused himself, said goodbye, shaking Ted's hand.

– I'm convinced your grades will improve next year, he told the boy.

That was all.

He walked out the door, leaving their house, leaving their lives.

He's running, Ted thought.

That was how he felt it, and he was a very empathic boy.

He saw Coogan walk to his car, saw him putting himself behind the wheel and drive off. And he opened his eyes and wouldn't see anymore.

– Okay, kids. Mike rose. – Remember the party tonight at Forester's? As you can see I'm already dressed and you're the slackers. We're late, so hurry up.

The edge of anger, of command was evident in his voice, at least to the twins, if not the parents.

Ted did the usual, quick trip to the bathroom. The stench of the shampoo and deodorant made his nose twitch. He had always had an acute sense of smell and the modern toilet held no promises for him. On the contrary. While considering it, something he hadn't really done before, he believed he would prefer to go around stinking of sweat. At least that smell was natural.

But he didn't have a choice in the matter.

While taking the stairs to the second floor in two and two steps shame flowed through him. He was tired of it, so sick and tired. At his room he burrowed his fingernails deep into the mattress, tearing at the blanket. Curses flowed freely between his lips. Contempt, against himself, against everything and everybody made him hit the bedpost, breaking it in pieces. He froze in surprise, staring at the disintegrated material, hearing the knock on the door, quickly moving a chair; covering up the destruction.

He couldn't hold back an angry remark when Linda's slim figure appeared in the doorway.

– What is it, now? Do you bring another message from Mike?

It was stupid really. He expected her to break down and cry, and was about to go to her, to comfort her… when he remembered, *remembered* the flash of metal, of whirling movement, of a distorted facial expression unlike he had ever witnessed, a calm, cold, serene mask.

– I did try to kill him, she whispered. – There was never any conscious decision, but the moment I threw the knife I felt calm, collected, enraged and absolutely certain I wanted to. There was no doubt, no regret, only the burning desire to bury the knife in his heart and the certainty that I was… I was able to. I don't know what came over me.

– Hey, even certified saints are human, he joked, completely misplaced and completely out of character for him, and he was glad.

– Chef's daughters do such things, she smiled, paler than ever, continuing as if she hadn't heard him.

– Dad and mom must truly be out of it. He shook his head. – If they haven't smelled anything before, they should certainly have done so tonight.

She didn't comment on it, still somewhat in shock.

– And what about Uncle Ezra? Does he know something? Ted's eyes burned at her. – And if he does, why isn't he acting on his information?

– I guess he isn't sure, Linda said, groaning in silent pain. – And he wants to be. I know how that is, being cast between doubt and certainty until nothing but doubt remains.

– Or he is just a blatant coward, Ted said enraged, – afraid to do more than imply and do anything more than come up with pointed remarks, to act on anything that might lead to «unpleasantness».

– And I've just made things worse, she said painfully. – Mike is sure to make you pay for my «indulgence» earlier.

– And you will feel guilty, because of his actions. He's quite good at that, the game of shifting blame, too.

She stepped closer, comforting by her closeness.

35

That had always worked on him before. He had noticed lately that that it worked ever less, was insufficient to still the boiling rage within.

– I read something once, he said, fiercely, desperately. – It's foolish, I guess, to give so much meaning to words in a book…

– Perhaps, she said softly, touching him. – What words?

He stood there straightening. It hurt, but he did so anyway.

– «Never give up, never give in to the forces aligned against you, or they will truly crush you». Something within… responded to it.

Don't give up. Never give up.

They grabbed each other's hands.

– He has already failed. She spoke into his ear. – You used to get… weaker, more compliant every time he… fucked with you, for every new act of cruelty and oppression from his side. But lately I've noticed something new in you, a defiance. Whatever made me do… what I did tonight, I'm certain it was in part inspired by it. You seem to grow stronger for every new beating, every new attempt to crush you. And Mike knows it… and he's growing more desperate.

Suddenly her touch turned insistent. The fear showed in her naked eyes.

– You know what will happen at Frank's tonight, she cried out, in a whisper. – Even if Uncle Ezra will eventually do something, anything to help us, it won't be now.

– A year, he said. – During one year he has terrorized us, as if we, his brother and sister, are nothing to him. We can take it one more night. I can take it. I can take much more.

His intensity made her shiver. It was as if he was pushing deep inside her, his fire touching her on levels she had hardly imagined existed. She spotted the disintegrated bedpost. He saw that she saw, and there was a calm in him when he looked at her. Her eyes widened.

He grabbed her hands.

– He's waiting for us. We must go. Come

And she followed him, suddenly more afraid than she had ever been.

********/

Frank Forester's folks were loaded. On an enormous estate

not that far away from the Cousin house they had raised two luxurious castle-like villas. In one Tom and Regina Forester lived in excess. The other, smaller their son had at his disposal, something that made him far more popular than he would otherwise have been, including among the older teenagers.

Mike and Tilla, Ted and Linda on their way through the forest, heard the ruckus clearly, heard the sound of breaking glass and furniture.

– That's the thing about Frank and his parties, Tilla said. – He can always redecorate tomorrow…

Ted and Linda walked a bit behind the other two. Not because they wanted to, but because that was how Mike wanted it.

Tilla wasn't older than the twins. She hadn't been forced to repeat any years or classes at school or anything. She was thirteen, but she looked older. Where she walked tight to Mike, clinging to him, Ted couldn't take his eyes off her, he never could.

Frank, as the perfect host met them in the door. He smoked a cigar and even though he looked like a child in an adult package, there was something there in him, in them all, that wasn't quite like that of a child.

Ted wondered if his parents, if they had known what went down in their neighborhood would have cared, if they had known that the way the children spent their adolescence was far less innocent than imagined, than the celebrated official version.

– Welcome, Frank greeted them. – An excellent evening for a party, isn't it?

He strained and reached, with his shorter body in an effort to meet Mike's eyes. Ted, he ignored completely, but greeted Linda very, very heartily. The girl smiled, but only because Mike had ordered her to do so. It was sufficient. Good ol' Frank melted on the spot.

– The shebang started some time ago, he said with regret to Mike, – but there's more than enough left of both liquor and energy to last the entire weekend. We didn't want to start the music, so to speak before your timely arrival… so what's your fancy tonight, Mike?

– A Hard Day's Night, Mike grinned.

Shouts of expectation echoed throughout the room.

– He means it, someone said, Ted heard. – And not just the record title…

Ted and Linda exchanged looks.

– Keith Lampard is here, Linda whispered.

Ted nodded. He had already spotted the guy. They both knew what it meant to them; that Mike's behavior would be even more brutal and sadistic.

Lampard was a biker, a person who rode motorcycles across America with his gang, a type of people generally doing what they desired wherever they came. There was something completely insane about him, and it showed in his face beneath the red hair, in his entire demeanor. He had one blue and one brown eye, clearly, uncannily visible, even from a distance. His skin was paler than Ted's. The freckles in his face seemed black and the insane look in the eyes completed the impression of a monster. The craziest rumors circulated of what he had done with people who had pissed him off.

Looking into the two different-colored eyes, Ted recognized something in Lampard he was unable to… identify. It washed over him like a warm breeze, a horrible feeling, but there it was, undeniable.

He dismissed the obvious explanation outright. They looked nothing alike. But he had taught himself to trust his instincts and it bothered him, it did.

There were certain aspects to the bikers, the leatherjackets' way of life that appealed to him, the freedom, the open road.

But not these bikers. They disgusted him.

The contempt wasn't caused by the eighteen-year-olds outer appearance. Ted had learned to see beyond the superficial and he did so now, and he shuddered. Lampard was Leader of the local gang of leatherjackets. He had, as the rumors went, defended his position thrice with his knife. He was Leader.

But the respect he showed Mike left no doubt about to whom he, himself deferred, reported to.

Mike reached out a hand for Tilla. She lifted her hand and he took it. He led her out on the dance floor and the dance began.

– «Let the dance begin», he declared, and it did. The sixteen-year old boy dominated the room and everybody in it, utterly and completely, like he had done since he had stepped over the doorstep. He was just as good a dancer as he was at doing everything else.

Linda looked envious at the dancers, at all of them. Ted knew she wanted to be out there. She loved to dance, wild and free, but Mike had expressively forbidden her to do it in public.

Ted had been given a standing order not to sit down, but he didn't mind.

– You must find a place to sit down, she told him weakly.

– I don't mind. He shook his head. – I can stay on my feet forever.

And the pain merely spread, was distributed to the entire body. And it sustained his anger, his rage, making it glow, making it grow.

It also made it easier to keep an eye on everything that went on, went down. He had always been an excellent observer. He could stay in the shadows, keep back and… and study it all.

He studied the whirling shapes on the floor, looking beyond the smiling masks as they toasted with each other, as they danced Friday Night away. He used his skill, pulling his analytical abilities forth from forgetfulness. There was nothing he could do but think, but no one could take that away from him.

The hippies had come to Denver, at least in a fashion sense. The clothes, and the hair length weren't that far removed from the occasional short televised newsflashes from San Francisco. None dared wear flowers in their hair in fear of being ridiculed or worse, but through the music, through the pop culture the rest of America was dragged screaming in the pioneer's footsteps, a development he supported, he so desperately craved.

Betty Morgan entered the premises arm in arm with Bob Tremblay. Ted observed them, observed her as she and the boy split. As far as Ted knew they didn't join up again during the entire evening. Betty was Tilla's cousin and they looked remarkably similar. The same red hair, the same dry-mouth sexy body. The only thing keeping her from being an exact copy of Tilla was the color of her eyes and skin. Skin was paler and the eyes weren't gray, but distinctively green. Betty should have been just as popular and sought after as her cousin, but wasn't. She kept herself in the background, very much like Ted, observing, similar to him. She had arrived in the customary way, with a boy, but had discarded him easily, without a fuss. Ted studied her closely from afar. Not by matching his eyes' movements with hers, but by letting her walk into his range of vision. By not chasing her, or anybody else with his eyes, he could pull back and observe in a very non-obtrusive way. Nobody had made him yet. Not Mike, not anybody. A fact he was quite proud of. He didn't follow her as she went upstairs, even though he wanted to. If he had learned anything the previous year, in addition to pain, searing pain, it was patience.

He started his walk, tonight's walk. It didn't really diverge much from his earlier walks through the house. Mike didn't mind where he went, as long as he didn't leave. There were several levels of the house, of course, and the party proceeded to its inevitable climax in all of them, as it had done every other night. He knew the building from top to bottom. There was nothing here that truly interested him, and he didn't expect to find anything new tonight. No more than all the other nights. He «coincidentally» drifted upstairs, drifting across the entire floor above. There was no sign of Betty. She had probably walked further up or used another staircase back down. The house was *huge*, and he could only imagine the splendor in which Frank's parents resided. To «give» one's son an entire house to use and a palace to boot, exposed an extravagance so inflated that Ted couldn't relate to it at all.

Suddenly he felt a need for fresh air and headed for a balcony. There were a lot of them here, a lot of everything. Most were taken, but he finally found one of the more remote, devoid of people. Something very much like claustrophobia addled him and he started breathing heavily, in an attempt to get air, to get any air. And then, bending over the balcony, almost falling into the darkness below, he could breathe. He straightened himself slowly, feeling sick, sick to the bone.

And for the thousandth time he detested himself. The contempt he felt for himself had, for a long time been something tangible, alive, making him afraid, and sometimes he wondered if that fear was what really kept him… from letting go. And the contempt grew.

The house was formed like a half moon. From his present position he was able to observe the dance floor below. The celebration was about to take off. Out on the smooth floor the dance went wild. Tilla screamed in delight as Mike raised her body above his head and spun her in the air. Ted closed his eyes, but there was no escape from the sight of the exposed thighs, the smooth skin, the lack of panties.

Bruce Channon and his older brother Ray «The Rat» - Keith Lampard's right hand man - had occupied another balcony. Not the one beside «his», but close enough for Ted to make out what they were saying. They were drunk already and spoke a lot louder than other «couples».

– Tilla is a mighty fine girl, Bruce commented, his eyes almost erupting from their sockets.

– She's indeed a sight for sore eyes. Ray nodded dreamingly, and nodded again. – You tend to forget her tender age. Her curves are already more developed than in most grown bedsores.

Bruce nodded. There were a lot of adults here, both women and men, and they all cast long, envious stares in Mike and Tilla's direction.

The age range was all in all remarkably diverse. Bruce was the envy of his comrades and classmates because he frequented such adult circles. Or he would have been, if not most of them were present, too.

There were always some kids traversing young adults' haunts, no matter how much parents denied it, but not to the degree seen here.

– And she's hot as a cupcake. Bruce shook his head in wonder and amazement. – You don't have to take more than a passing look at her and realize that she's enjoying *doing* it.

Ray nodded, signifying agreement and also signaling obvious satisfaction.

– Don't even go there, Bruce grinned. – I'm willing to make quite a bet to the fact that you never have had her or even come close to her.

– Jesus, kid, you youths are quite the misinformed lot, ain't ya? You should know that the cunt is our mascot. We're taking turns.

– You're lying through your teeth, the other said decisively.
– It's common knowledge that first Cumbes and then Cousin took her as their own, with exclusive property rights and all, no sharing and shit.
– Watch your mouth, you…

He trailed off. Bruce, drunk as he was, grinned bravely to his face, ignoring the fear in his gut caused by Ray's position and horrid reputation. Through another strange genetic quirk he was both taller and stronger than his brother.

Though he certainly felt an unmistakable sigh of relief when Ray found it suitable to change the subject.

– I can't see Ted, the doormat brother dog anywhere. He's usually staying close to the sister like an unmoving statue. Have you seen how she's supporting him around, like she's his crutches or something? Hard to believe he can ever move on his own.

– I agree with you on that one, Bruce conceded willingly.
– One may be tempted to suspect Mike has painted him in white… Or something.

The conversation halted there. That pleased Ted somehow, as he heard the clink when two glasses met and parted, as the brothers toasted. He sensed that they didn't have a lot to say to each other. They didn't hate the other. They just didn't give a shit.

Ted stretched his thoughts. And it felt as if he was truly doing it, like he was back downstairs, standing by the dance floor, long before he rose to leave the balcony and actually made his way there. He imagined he could feel Tilla's hands in his, smell her stinking perfume through Mike's nose, experiencing her through Mike's senses. And wondered if Mike could similarly sense his whereabouts. The imagined contact sickened him, exhilarated him, as he stopped a moment to ponder, to wonder.

He shook his head, considering a moment a career as a poet, like he had already done in many a lonely moment, drying a single tear from the corner of the eye, in sadness, in rage.

The room was spinning. And he felt it. The sadness and the rage were tangible as a taste in the mouth, a distant scream so loud it could be heard anywhere. And he felt it.

Mike sensed the stare of Ray the Rat all the way from the balcony, sensed it malignancy, as if the man was standing right next to him. It bothered him, it did. He admitted that freely to himself.

– The vulture again? Tilla spoke softly in his ear.

– The rat, the vulture, the anything, he admitted. – The parasite. He has climbed the ladder by filling the holes left by those above him, as they have fallen behind.

– I can tell, she smiled enticingly to him. – I know you so well.

– Yes, you have indeed become much attuned to my needs, he told her. – That's good.

The smile didn't vanish. It wasn't even possible to spot it fading in any way. Not to others. To him it was a piece of cake. He saw through her façade, the veneer of her vanity. He saw through anything.

– Jeffrey's brother is here, she said.

Jeffrey Cumbes was the former leader of the bikers.

– I know you know that, too, she said, – but he has been staring at us, at me every fucking moment since we arrived. And he doesn't bother hiding it. I know you're not afraid of him…

– And you are?

She nodded silently, sullenly.

– Afraid for you, she said hastily. – He's even bigger than Jeffrey… than Jeffrey was.

He had to admit to himself that he could never read her completely. There was fear in her eyes, for sure, but also something that could be interpreted as excitement, as if she wanted a fight, wanted them to fight over her. He couldn't tell whether or not there was a teasing underbrush present in her voice.

– I know you turned the older Cumbes around your finger. You even tried it with me, but you won't anymore, will you?

She shook her head.

– You're a wise bitch.

The fear dominated now, as he started slapping her lightly on her cheek. At first, she shrank from his touch, but as the slapping continued and the skin began to turn red, she just stood there, as he did what he wanted with her. There was no sign of compromise or willingness to compromise in his eyes, in his body language. She had used her female wiles on him, what had worked so well on Jeffrey Cumbes, but didn't work on him at all. Instead he had turned her game around and made her his creature.

– I love you, Mike, she whimpered. – I love you so.

She leaned at him, as close as she could possibly come, offering it to him, unresistingly. He kissed her on the swollen lips, making them swell even more. He pushed a hand into her crotch making her cry out, making her moan in need, oblivious to the presence of all the people in the room.

– You have been taking liberties with my patience lately. That ends now. Understand?

She nodded instantly, assuring him with her eyes, with every part of herself she could muster, terrified over the fact that it had gone so far that he had found it necessary to candidly warn her, realizing that he had probably let it go that far, to really drive his point in.

– I'm your bitch, Mike. I'm yours. There's nothing I won't do for you. Nothing. Please, Mike.

Gray eyes pointed at him. A pouting mouth pointed at him. Erect nipples pushed against his chest.

She felt the pressure let up then, felt him let go of her. There was a rush of sound as the music started fading in once more. The rest of the room re-entered the consciousness. She once more saw what she perceived as leering faces surrounding her. No one seemed to have missed a beat. She doubted they had noticed anything at all, or that they would ever notice anything.

Mike directed his attention without directing his attention at the big biker opposite the dance floor. Rufus Cumbes had governed a biker gang over in Nevada with an iron hand for a few years. He had no opponents left. His rule was based on absolute fear. Mike shook his head. Compared to that his own, local influential sphere looked like a kindergarten.

That worried him, it did.

They finally left the dance floor. She couldn't tell how long they had been dancing, but they had been at it since they arrived this evening.

She loved it, but didn't mind that it had ended for now. She wanted to sit close to him, for them to snuggle on the couch. And More. She wanted more.

– Do you love me, Mike? She asked in that low, a bit naïve voice she knew he liked.

– You're created for loving, he said shrugging.

– We belong together, don't we?

– That's right, pretty girl. We're gonna go far.

– That's great, Mike, she said breathless. – But what if something should happen to you? Then I'm on my own. That bully from Nevada…

– No one, no one here is my equal, he snarled, unexpectedly passionate. – Not one. I'm gonna crush him. I'm gonna crush anyone trying anything, anyone opposing me.

The nakedness in his voice astounded her. He held so hard around her arm that she yelped in pain. But except for that she held her tongue. She was used to it and could take it.

And she knew where his nakedness, his *fear* came from, what… or who caused it.

Lampard sat, with some groupies on the smaller couch Mike wanted to occupy.

– I certainly hope we're not disturbing anything, Keith, Mike said jovially. – Tilla and I would like to enjoy ourselves here for a while.

– No problem, Mike, the biker said hastily. – I and bunch have for a long time now, considered a visit to the dance floor.

Tilla laughed aloud at the sight of him and bunch virtually running away. She saw how his neck crouched in anger, as a reaction to her openly shaming him, and she laughed even harder.

– Mike, she said cuddly, caressing him. – Why don't we go to one of the bedrooms instead, to truly enjoy ourselves?

– Not now, he said dismissive. – Sit.

– But…

– *Sit down.*

She realized that she had overextended her cockiness and slipped down close beside him in an effort to patch things up, to minimize the damage.

He grabbed her hand by the wrist. It started to hurt instantly as he tightened his grip on the nerve-endings in the transition between hand and arm. She gasped in extenuating pain. Her entire body seemed to go limp, unable as she was, to move a single limb. Her head fell into his lap, as tears popped like rain from her eyes. When he let go of her, she had to fight off an enormous weight of lethargy to sit up and pull back.

– You didn't have to do that. She sniffed. – Why did you do that?

The rage, the red-eyed animal scared her. That was the part of him that she couldn't control.

And his eyes were still burning at her, burning a hole right through her. They were like fire, like on fire. And whether or not she was only imagining it, it frightened her beyond words.

– Because you didn't get it, he said harshly. – You weren't open for my teaching, not wide open, but you are now, right?

– Yes, Mike. She nodded.

– Good. It isn't anything you haven't seen before, but repetition never hurts, and you didn't understand before. I know you do now.

She nodded some more. And some more. And when Mike turned away from her, turning somewhere else, to someone else, she felt the same relief, the same disappointment she always did.

– TED! He shouted it, as a command, impossible to ignore.

The boy was there instantly. Or she imagined he might have been there for a while, invisible like furniture or something.

– Fetch us two bottles of cognac.

Ted hurried off. Tilla counted the seconds, sensing Mike's growing impatience and foul mood. Ted returned with the two bottles. Tilla couldn't tell how many seconds had passed. She thought she had counted them, but she couldn't really remember. There was the characteristic sound of the bottles being opened. Ted's hand was shaking when he poured the liquor into the glasses. Incredibly enough he didn't spill any. Mike grabbed the glasses and handed Tilla one.

– Cheers, he exclaimed and raised the glass to his mouth.

He swallowed everything in one attempt, while she sat there sipping.

– Drink it all, this instant, he bade her. – It's great cognac.

She started shaking. Some of the alcohol spilled on her dress, but she didn't notice. In one, abrupt move she poured the cognac into her mouth and the strong liquor washed her already sore throat. Minutes, seconds passed. The skin of her face turned to a deeper color and she sighed as she leaned heavily on the body beside her.

– Good girl. Mike smiled and patted her cheek. – You're learning and are thereby growing more useful to me. You have much to look forward to.

An implied threat, a promise.

– Oh, Mike, she said. – I'm turning hot and cold all over.

She looked at Ted, and then at Mike, and back at Ted.

– Poor dog, she said.

She leaned back on the couch, communicating to Mike a smile of complete contentment, doing it with her entire self.

Time passed, as it always seemed to do, in boredom and non-action. Tilla writhed on the sofa, obviously performing for the man by her side. He seemed oblivious to her presence, though. As if he saw right through her, as if she wasn't there at all. He didn't seem to care about what she did or didn't do. He remained on the spot, drinking heavily, as the night progressed. One drink, two drinks, three drinks. There was no discernible effect. An hour, or perhaps no more than ten minutes or so later the bottle was half done. He sat there silently, sullenly, staring at the sister. Linda returned the stare as daggers of cold, blue fire.

Tilla sat up, shaking off the sight of those eyes.

– Mike, she offered, in a distant, indifferent manner, – are you aware that we danced three hours without break?

– Mmm, he mumbled. He had started drinking directly from the bottle.

Her heart sank. He seemed more interested in drinking than listening to her.

– There's no one but us who are able to do anything like that, she said eagerly. – We're setting the standards there, like we are in all things. I do want to be… be your woman, and I want to do everything you demand of me. Everything.

She swallowed fearfully, angrily. Just a minor twitch in the corner of his mouth revealed that he had heard her at all. Her muscles tensed, and she was about to rise, to leave him, holding her head high, eyes burning in fire and pride. Tilla Stevens looked from Mike to Keith and back. She did so again, looked long and beside herself at Keith Lampard and swallowed hard. It almost hurt. It hurt so much. She shrank back on her spot. Nauseous and shaking she had to lean her head at her knees. Pale and quiet she crouched deep on the couch, begging Mike with her eyes, waiting for him to say something, anything, but he never did. He didn't even open his mouth to drink. He merely filtered it through tightly woven lips. She knew his moods, his black, black moments signified by the bending of his shoulders, of the claw-like fingers, how his eyes started to move without the head, and this time… this time it terrified her.

Keith Lampard looked pleased at her, at Mike, at Rufus Cumbes raging silently at the other side of the room. He kept Ray Channon company. Ray was as ever quite attentive, a perfect lieutenant.

– Look at them, Lampard mused. – The two giants are moving towards each other like a meteor and the ground, inevitably. One may have to wait, patiently for it to happen, but when the impact comes it is always worth the wait. The question is merely who is the meteor and who is the ground.

Channon nodded, and by searching his expression one might be able to spot expectation there.

Frank Forester sat course for the two, staggering slightly. He had a skinny, pale hungry-looking brown-haired girl in tow.

– Some party, huh, Keith, he bawled. He was quite a bawler, the good Frank.

The longhaired redhead nodded quite convincingly.

– Your best one, yet, Frank, he generated his praise, a bit distant, once more involuntarily stealing a glance at Tilla.
– The music is great. Your audio equipment sounds totally, enormously fantastic.

The way overdone praise made the boy blush. Proud like a coq he pulled the girl tighter.

– I guess that's true, he bristled. – Everything is brand new and probably one of the best there is. It set me (his father everybody knew it was) back, temporarily, of course, ten thousand grand.

– Listen, Frankie, Lampard kept up his inflated praise, I haven't really had the opportunity to try out the dance floor yet. Could I borrow your girl for a moment?

– Sure! Frank kept bawling, and pushed the girl into Lampard's arms.

Lampard had expected some resistance in the girl, but there was nothing except the expected façade of resistance, the lie of independence. He saw fear in her eyes, he saw something else, and he saw suspicion and need. She reddened as he studied her unscrupulously.

– You have your own way of whisking girls away, she said shyly. – A very original one.

He slapped her. He kept leading her in the dance. Her eyes turned huge and wet, as the mark of his hand faded in on her cheek.

– You're just a girl, Iris, he stated. – A tiny slip of the girl with hardly more femininity than a boy. But you have a certain crude intelligence and I can use that. You will do something for me and if you do it well, if you please me, I will not punish you. I might even choose to reward you.

She tried to look around, to look for a friendly face, for anyone to come to her aid. He slapped her again, and again.

– You're *trying* my patience.

– What do you w-want me to do? She said weakly and subdued.

There was no one here willing to rescue her, willing to risk anything on her behalf.

– I want you to go to Ted over there. I want you to keep the poor guy company, that's all.

He grabbed her jaw, forcing her to look into his frightening expression.

– Do a good job, okay? Or you won't need to worry about your late developing femininity anymore.

She nodded keenly, scurrying away from him like a frightened animal.

Channon placed himself at his side once more, the ever-loyal lieutenant. Lampard experienced a slight trickle down his spine, a clear sense of revulsion. If the rat wasn't so damn useful he would have slit its throat long ago.

– Everything is proceeding smoothly, Lampard said pleased, as a reply to Ray's questioning look. – But it never hurts to plan in depth, to have insurances in terms of alternative plans in place.

Slowly he let his hand fall. He could still sense the warmth from Iris' cold and wet skin. Somewhat content he turned and left the polished floor.

– The entertainment is about to begin.

With half closed eyes he looked at Tilla again.

Mike had started on the second bottle. Tilla looked at him with despair in her eyes. He hadn't commented on her wow of devotion, of submission. He had, in fact not said a single word since she had uttered hers. Suddenly she smelled the scent of leather and sweat in her nose and she started perspiring in desperation. The man from Nevada towered above her and Mike seemed totally oblivious to what was going on, to everything going on.

– I've always favored redheads, Rufus Cumbes said with a rough, very rough smile. – Would ya care for a dance?

– No thanks, she said decisively. – I'm not available.

She collected her wits, all her bravery and returned to him a haughty look.

– I really don't think you're old enough to decide such matters. Cumbes nodded, as if there hadn't been a rejection or as if it didn't matter. – Let's ask your keeper instead, shall we?

– What are you talking about? Mike looked up and said grudgingly.

– You, my man, Cumbes replied, revealing his entire wondrous row of teeth. – I feel the girl don't have a vote here. Therefore, I'm asking you, holding her leash if I can dance a couple of minutes with her.

There was a moment of silence. Mike looked blank at the biker.

– Now, what do you say? Cumbes' voice got slightly more agitated.

The dance had stopped, as if on a cue. Everybody stared at the drama unfolding.

– Be my guest. Mike shrugged. – Enjoy yourself.

Astonished everybody held their breath and tongue. Tilla

stared at him in disbelief and fear. Even Cumbes hesitated a moment, before proceeding. He exposed his teeth in an excited grin. Without further warning he grabbed the girl's arm and dragged her off.

– Mike, help me, she cried. – You…

The leather jacket laughed in contempt and slapped her face. In spite of the music the sound of the impact was heard all the way to the front door. His hand left a swollen, a very swollen red mark, on her cheek, on the golden skin. Her head hung low as he dragged her towards the stairs. He grabbed her jaw, pushing it up forcing her to look at him.

– Kiss me, he ordered sharply.

Good girl, I'm a good girl, she thought.

She obeyed, returning his kiss instantaneously.

– That's a good girl, he said pleased. – I'm looking very much forward to teach you manners, teach you to be an attentive, lovely doll.

She sensed hardness in him, a coldness that had hardly ever been present in his brother. Jeffrey had been rough, but he cared about how he was perceived by the world and had therefore been easy to manipulate. Rufus didn't care about anything or anybody. She started moaning even before he started pinching her breasts. She screamed as he pinched them hard.

– Yes, I knew you were a screamer. Every doll is.

The tears came then, sobs of despair and deep, tearing numbness. She wanted to be close to him, to feel his hard, strong body close to her, but he held her in his rock-hard tight grip, an arm's length away.

Even as he let go of her she still felt his strong hands on her, as marks not fading on her arms.

– Kneel! He ordered casually.

She obeyed chokingly.

– *Spread your legs, cunt,* he roared.

He pushed a foot in between her legs and she obeyed, spreading them wide. She blinked. Her vision dimmed. She didn't look at him, but imagined she could see him through the others' eyes. Only him. He crouched over her, making a point of pulling the dress off her shoulders. Her breasts, swollen and sore were exposed for all to see. He grabbed the lower parts of the dress, also exposing her butt, her sex, pushing a hand into the wet, red hot nest. Shame and lust intertwined made her moan louder. She didn't see the biker pull down his pants, but she imagined she heard it, heard every possible move he made, as she saw what would happen next. How he would take her as his, how he would collar her, and carry her far away and he would treat her as nothing. She would be nothing.

Everything… stopped. That was the only way she could describe it. She sensed it. She sensed the hand on Cumbes' shoulder. She saw Mike stand there behind him.

She turned her head and there he was, and her heart swelled like joy in her chest.

– Is this what you call dancing in Nevada? Mike Cousin asked the biker in wonder, a Mike totally transformed from the indifferent, drunk kid in the sofa. – If you indeed do that, you must be pretty stupid. I would venture that you, yourself can hardly think at all.

He took a step back, deliberately, making a point of allowing Cumbes to regain his bearings, to pull his pants back up, to put in place a stiff blood-filled cock.

There was laughter. There were sounds of expectation and fear. The cry of the mob surrounded the two men, the man and the boy. Tilla pulled back, pulling the shoulder straps back up, straightening her dress.

– I realize now, that there was something essential I forgot to communicate to you, boy, Cumbes stated heavily. – You're not old enough yourself to participate in adult decision-making. Get it?

– I heard nothing but incoherent rabble, Mike snarled. – I still don't, and don't really believe it will improve with repetition, but you might wanna try anyway.

The reaction, the attack was instantaneous. The fist seemed to erupt from out of the very air. Mike's hair moved as the air pressure caused it to move. He struck the biker with a flat hand in the face. The blow, in spite of it being delivered in a very non-effective way was so hard that the big man staggered back. Blood flew from the mouth.

– You're just a bug, Mike said in ultimate contempt, – to be crushed under my heel.

He kicked the other in the ribs. The huge body was thrown at the stairs. Mike could have pressed his advantage, but didn't. Cumbes rose painfully, enraged, air wheezing in and out of his half open mouth.

– YOU'RE DEAD, he screamed.

And he didn't let his rage consume him, making him careless. He closed in on his opponent with every bit of caution, now, the only useful tactic against what he now realized was a worthy adversary. There might be a flash of fear, of insecurity in the look of consuming anger he sent Mike Cousin. Just a bit of it.

Cumbes attacked once more. This time with a blow to the jaw, and Mike was hit. He jumped away, making the other's next effort turn into a miss, hitting nothing but open air. Mike dried his bloody jaw with one hand, and then... then Cumbes saw the red, horrible light in the face suddenly frozen, frozen like a mask. The grown man staggered slightly, almost paralyzed, visibly pausing before advancing, a fatal hesitation.

The force of the blow had pushed Mike against the stairs rail. Now he pushed himself away from it, right at Cumbes. He diverted an ineffective strike with one arm and landed a devastating blow in the opponent's belly. It went so deep that the entire hand seemed to disappear into the malleable flesh. There was a sound of ribs cracking. He bent forward in one horrible involuntarily move. Mike smeared Cumbes' face against his knee.

It had happened so fast, so frighteningly fast. The leatherjacket knelt there on the floor, before the raging storm hovering above him, hardly able to raise his hands above the head, signaling his surrender.

– You pathetic worm, Mike Cousin snarled in contempt, and it was hardly a voice at all, but a snarl from the deepest pits.

He landed another devastating slap on the other's cheek. And another, from the opposite side. Then he kicked him in the face. Something gave. They could all hear it. They could *see* it, as the boot was buried in the skull.

Incredibly enough Cumbes was still able to move. To the spectators the fact that he was still alive was incredible. Mike

Cousin, the *Mike Cousin* very few of them had truly seen or experienced grabbed the grown man's hair and lifted up his head. Hairs were torn off the scalp. He lifted up the entire heavily built man, lifted him above the head and threw him through the window. The limp body landed on a mound outside, and remained there, unmoving.

The winner stood there calm, centered. There was no signal, nothing discernible anyway, but Keith Lampard rushed forward, very astute and attentive.

– I want him Gone, Mike said. – Understand?

Lampard nodded. He managed to stop nodding only with the most major of efforts.

– Put him and the shitheads keeping him company on the first bus or whatever out of the city. Keep their bikes. Tell them if they as much as breathe close to us again, they're toast. They will beg for death. *Understand?*

Several of them were present in the room. They did nothing, except freeze on the spot, allowing themselves to be grabbed and led off.

Lampard nodded, and nodded again, considerably paler, even compared to what was normal for him.

– They're all Ghosts, he confirmed hoarsely. And as if he feared it wasn't sufficient, he added: – They're Gone. We will never see them again. They will shrink in our presence to the point that we won't see them, even if they should happen to pass before our eyes.

Tilla ran to her man, pushing herself as close as she could, into his arms.

– I love you, Mike, she whispered. – I love you, love you, love you.

The ghastly light in his eyes faded only slowly. He didn't breathe noticeable harder. The only mark on him from the fight was the one on the jaw.

Ted blinked. He couldn't really recall if his brother just had been hit that once. He thought so, but couldn't be sure. Most of it had fallen into the dark mudhole he called memory.

– One can surely say one thing about Mike, Frank whispered to Bruce. He whispered very low, but everybody heard him. – He gets things done fast.

Bruce nodded in complete agreement. The fight had hardly lasted more than a minute, if that long.

The word «fight» is hardly fitting, though, he thought. I would say «butchery» is far more fitting...

Silence reigned on this corner of Forester Manor, a deafening silence lasting centuries and millennia, echoing through eternity.

Chapter three

Ted found himself in the basement. There were darker music, darker moods down here, somehow brightening his mood. Somebody had put «The End» by The Doors on an endless repetitive loop. The hammering of drums, the waves of the guitar echoed through him.

He saw Betty again. He almost missed her, as she passed by him only a few steps away. She didn't give him either anything resembling the hot, possessive feeling he (and everyone else) got when observing (gawking at) Tilla. It was as if she wasn't present, wasn't there at all, as if she... wanted it that way.

Ted was sweating. It was as if he would never stop sweating. It was hot, but not that hot. The heat originated in his boiling insides. Excitement and despair warred within him. Flashes of recent memory repeated itself endlessly in his mind. Flashing red eyes, flashing fists. The creature, the beast making mincemeat of a human being.

The music rose. The heavy drums started up. And it was as if he was re-experiencing it all, as if it all returned to torture him, to forever torment him. The image of an invincible giant burned itself on to his retina.

Then, as his eyes were wide-open, shadows began to dance around him. He blinked. The shadows disappeared. He blinked again. The shadows reappeared. He saw the ordinary people, too. But in addition to that, there were shadows dancing in the air, indistinct forms flowing more than moving in the badly lit room.

Iris Carson approached him. Even though he didn't give anything away he had seen her approach from afar.

– What are you doing here? He asked, with his teeth gritted.

– I just want to keep you company, she said softly. – Is that so wrong?

– It is a bit surprising that Keith Lampard cares, he snarled.
She shook slightly, before composing herself.

– I wanted to come anyway, she told him weakly, – but I didn't dare. You're alone. I'm alone. He pushed me into coming, and no matter his motivation... I'm glad.

He fell silent. It was obvious by just those words that she was an entirely different person from what she seemed, and he had believed. He looked hungrily at her and she bathed in his heat.

And he studied her quite openly, without the slightest pretense, to her, another of his more appealing characteristics.

– I feel like I know you, she stated, a strange expression on her face, - like I have known you my entire life, not just recently met you, and I'm not just saying it either. It's true.

He studied her thin, girlish frame. She was a girl. Only the makeup gave the pretense of a woman.

- Does that make sense? She whispered. – Please tell me it makes sense.

But when he looked at her she seemed to be changing before his eyes, becoming grown up and strikingly different. He wanted to say so, but tiger got his tongue, and he remained silent.

She hesitated, before stepping close to him.

– I'm not a virgin, you know, she said, and she didn't sound and seemed like a child at all.

He caught himself, reprimanding himself. He supposed most people thought very much the same when looking at her. And he... he was no different.

Shame once again stopped him from acting.

– After I started bleeding, my father finally gave in to temptation, one I guess he had had for years. And I... loved it. It felt a little strange at first. I knew what he was doing. I knew it was wrong, but I felt his interest, his... excitement, and it... turned me on.

Her huge, dilated eyes were close to his. As she continued, as she related her story, Ted sensed his own vocal chords constrict further, and he couldn't utter a single sound.

– And as he touched me... below, as he touched my *cunt* with his big fat hand, I couldn't help releasing those tiny, girlish sounds. «YOU WHORE», he swore while slapping my face. «YOU FILTHY WHORE»! He tore my dress to shreds and pushed me down on the bed. And then he undressed and I saw his huge manhood and I couldn't help but moaning. It was as if I had longed for it my entire life. And even though there was pain when he pushed himself inside me, taking my cherry, it was like the fulfillment of all my dreams. I didn't have any dreams anymore. They had all been fulfilled.

Ted didn't look around, to see if anybody heard her. He knew they hadn't, and he realized he didn't care.

– I just wanted you to know this, know that we're both trapped in bodies and minds we hate. I wanted you to know... how alike we are, that's all.

She kissed him on the lips. He wanted to push her away, but found that he was unable to.

– I know that you can sense my pain, she told him, in his ear. – I have studied you, seen how you are registering everything happening in a room,

– You're so astute, you know, she said, suddenly lightly. – You're very empathic.

It was true. He could sense other peoples' feelings, moods and more. What years ago had seemed like his imagination playing tricks on him, had slowly turned into a certainty, and he wasn't exactly spoiled with certainties.

He looked at her, reading understanding in her eyes.

– I wish I weren't.

– I understand what you mean, she whispered.

They found themselves on a couch somewhere. The sound of silence was everywhere around them.

She rocked back and forth, to the slow, haunting beat.

– I'm hopelessly in love with Jim Morrison, you know, she said, laughing, a shrill and ghastly sound virtually completely devoid of happiness. – I want to fuck his guts.

The girl leaned on his shoulder, as if they were a couple and he was comforting her.

– The day after my father was gone, she continued. – He had left my mother and me alone. I wanted to kill him, shoot him on sight, if he ever showed his pathetic mug to my eyes again. I've had a few... experiences after that, but they have all been bungling boys, leaving nothing but their acid tears and stinking gratitude.

She turned to him, turned to his face, leaving him nothing to see but the dancing shadow fire in her eyes.

– I have *watched* you, watched your Hunger, your burning, bottomless pit. Your passion is burning up everything around you.

Her voice was very... modulated. She had been with the theater, too, at least part time. He remembered one of the instructors say that her voice was «her best feature».

He remembered wanting to punch the guy for his blatant insensitivity. But then something had happened. Suddenly he had felt the Rage, truly felt it for the first time, and he had been too shocked, too frightened to move.

Like now. He felt the Abyss open below him.

– Hey, do you remember the theater? She said, brightening visibly.

– I sure do. Her excited words brought a smile to his face, masking the wonder, the worry behind.

– It was fun. She nodded eagerly. – We were told to express ourselves, and we did. We were told to go deep within ourselves, to express ourselves... and we did.

She frowned, turning serious again. He marveled at her, wondering why he had hardly noticed her before. She was one of those people with a very expressive face, like the waves on a rough sea, never being exactly the same. And he felt the desperate sadness and an eerie sense of loss catching in his throat.

– I... felt something, then, she said, – something opening. For a very short moment it was as if all the secrets of the world were mine to know. Then it closed, never to open again.

Her mood changed again.

– I remember how the press wrote about the redhaired girl and the two dark brothers... how romantic.

She shook her head, her mood changing yet *again*.

– Mike is nothing, you know. Nothing but a storm in a bottle, compared to you. He's afraid of you.

– Afraid? He said incredulously.

– Of course. You saw how easily he handled that giant biker. Who else could he have reason to worry about? He's afraid of himself, anybody can see that. Therefore, he's naturally afraid of you.

Ted blinked. Suddenly there was more. Linda was there by his side, or she seemed to be. The lines of worry in her face, as she looked at him, very visible. Lines of worry, lines of fear. Fear for him… *fear of him*. And in that moment, he felt as if the secrets of the world were indeed his to know.

And it felt horrible. He felt betrayed.

Linda, he said silently, looking for her, but she wasn't here.

– You're so mature, he told the girl by his side, suddenly desperate to comfort her, searching for the right words… and more. – You see so clearly, understand so much. You… should be proud.

– Yes, the mature, the responsible one, that's me, she stated bitterly.

She turned to him again (again). As if everything repeated itself.

– Remember that I came here on Keith's «request», she said, pulling back. – Remember everything.

The brown-haired girl patted his hand, a bit before pulling away.

– You will take care of your… *problems*, I know that… and then you will come to me. You will come with your sword and whisk me away, whisk us all away. Drop a single stone in the water and observe how the ripples spread.

– This isn't Shakespeare anymore, right? He joked, unable to do anything less.

She grabbed his hand, clutching it a bit, before moving, before leaving him. He was alone again.

And almost immediately the dream sequences, the vision of the recent battle returned to haunt him. His brother's blood red fists. The sound of breaking ribs. The sight of the ragged doll of a human being thrown through the window and remaining on the mound lifeless and still.

He saw Linda stand by the door, but there was no door here, only the broad stairs to the ground level. This was a sub-terrestrial level with earth all around it. The Forester houses were built into the Earth itself, quite modern. She stood by the door, but she didn't walk through. She didn't leave. And she was once more on the level, the floor above, and he didn't see her.

Bob Tremblay approached him. Bob was okay, though very focused on social status and such. Ted didn't mind. He didn't have that many friends.

60

– Very strange occasions these, don't you think? Bob commented, in this usual mix of somberness and cheerfulness.

– And why, may I ask, is that so? Ted interjected, aping but not repeating the other's manner.

They stood a bit by themselves, away from the others. They had always been able to talk about everything. In spite of their differences they seemed to have so much in common.

– A thirteen-year old boy hosting a party of this magnitude and… inclination? C'mon, that isn't strange?

Ted nodded slowly. He hadn't thought about it that way.

– I guess most people would say a lot of strange, off the wall things are happening. If they notice anything at all, that is.

– You're right, of course. Bob nodded. – Most people are sheep.

– I wouldn't put it exactly that way, Ted replied rigidly, – but you're not wrong.

This was not the place, but their discussions could go on for hours sometimes.

– Look around you…

Ted did. Often, he did nothing else. He was the born observer. The thought brought bitterness to the fore once more.

– See order in Chaos. There is no law, but you don't see the human beast erupting into disorder, do you?

– There were guards at first, hired by Frank's parents, but Mike… made them go away.

There was a bit of silence, before the harsh voice continued.

– Mike is the Law.

Bob nodded, as if he suddenly understood something.

Jim Morrison's voice shrieked once more from the speakers, crying its word of death on a sleeping world. Ted and Bob had started walking around, visiting the various hot spots in the house. The insanity of The End was far away, but Ted heard it still. He stumbled a bit, momentarily frozen in his track, before continuing his stride. He felt it building, felt the forces rise in his surroundings, of bile and horror. As he had told Iris, he would rather not possess his astute senses, his keen certainty. He had experienced what was coming many times before and knew the signs, knew them as well as the fluttering beat of his own heart. Suddenly his eyes were huge in his pale face. Cold droplets of sweat, of fear formed on his skin.

– What... Bob looked around, as if he didn't, couldn't fathom what was... what was coming.

It all happened so fast. It had all happened so fast. The fight had ended just a few minutes ago. It had just felt longer, during his rushed escape to the basement, his rushed conversations with Iris and Bob. He couldn't run, he couldn't hide. There was nowhere he could run, nowhere he could hide. He knew that now.

He saw Keith Lampard, with his eternal scheming and hatred, saw the congregation gather, as if they knew. They didn't, of course. They couldn't. It was a purely instinctive reflex on their part. They didn't know. He met Linda's eyes with a hurt expression in his eyes. She knew. And he felt betrayed. His inner voice cried to her, in anger, in despair, unheard.

There was a fog, a haze. He saw Keith and Mike intermingling, turning into one.

There was a voice, like a saw when the Monster spoke.

– I think you're turning soft, Keith stated. – Your decisive treatment of our guest notwithstanding.

No one could accuse Keith of disloyalty, of challenging the authority of the leader. He was too smooth, too cunning for that. He had balanced on the edge of Mike's sword for months now, without being cut.

– Oh, how so? Mike joined the game, not without a degree of satisfaction.

– I turn your attention to exhibit B, Your Honor...

As if on cue, everybody turned their attention to Ted.

– Look at the dog. Look how groomed it is, how pretty are its clothes.

Ted started shaking, but Linda shook visibly on her spot a few steps away.

– What are you talking about? Bob cried out. – His clothes are not...

He held his tongue, burning with shame and helplessness.

Everybody looked at Mike.

Everybody knew what was happening.

– Now, Mike, Linda heard Keith say, – are you losing it?

Even though he probably didn't, and she was just imagining

he said aloud what he was actually saying. She cried out and took one step forward. One look from Mike and she turned into a rock, stuck to the ground.

– So black and so lethal, she said aloud, as if on a stage, – like a raven predator in a darkened sky.

And the spectators heard her, like knives in their gut, before forgetting it all.

– You're not wrong. Mike nodded to Keith, seemingly very pleased. – There has been a long time since the last disciplinary action. An entire week, in fact.

In one, flowing move he grabbed his brother by the collar and raised him above the head, shaking him hard. Somewhere in the room Iris fainted and fell to the floor. No one noticed.

– No one is losing anything, Mike shouted wildly and in just a few powerful pulls he tore Ted's clothes from his body.

Several people gasped when they saw displayed the ugly swollen marks on the kid brother's body. He stood there with his eyes closed. Mike had put him back down. He desperately attempted to close himself off from reality. The pain in his back didn't go away and the crowd's excited mocking laughter felt like a whip to his soul.

Without warning Mike sent him like a projectile at Keith, returning the thrown gauntlet.

– Hey, catch. Then you can see for yourself how little fire there's left in him.

The red-haired boy didn't get away. Ted's head hit him in the belly. With a shriek he fell to the floor. The pale boy saw him fall and something changed then, on the spot. Something asleep awakened, and he pushed a knee into Keith's unprotected abdomen. Keith crouched in a very volatile move. Brown and yellow stomach contents flowed from his mouth and decorated the carpet.

– Fuck, Bruce exclaimed. – Keith has always been a pig, but this…

Ted didn't have time to react, before Mike kicked his feet away from under him. He remained at Keith's side and stared up at his brother with blinding hatred.

And he realized, too, that Mike, by giving in to the cries hungry for Ted's punishment, had showed weakness. He cared about what others thought, how they perceived him.

– The whiskey, a complete unknown offered two bottles to Mike.

– Outstanding, the dark boy grinned. – The Dog loves whiskey.

Like lions being fed, like hens in the yard the mob gathered around the helpless boy on the floor. Slowly and clearly enjoying himself Mike opened one of the bottles. He turned it upside down and the strong, burning liquor flowed down the brother's neck. The thirteen-year-old boy desperately attempted to avoid it, but by turning his head he got whiskey from another bottle straight in the face. He didn't have time to completely close his eyes. There was horrible pain. The alcohol penetrated beneath the eyelids, the humiliation burrowed under his skin. His sore cry harvested a roar of laughter.

They were everywhere, everybody taking the opportunity to grow in Mike's shadow and those carried away with the wave. A few kept back, some of them curious and frightened. Others watched with contempt the tiny creature on the floor.

– Our little rebel is unable or unwilling to accept our gift of cool shadows and forest ponds, Tilla cried out, in a horrible echo of Linda's theatrics. – May he receive it anyway.

The laughter hit Ted like huge hailstones. At first there was pain, but as the rain progressed it was relieved by an eternal, monotone thudding, until just a tiny, single area of his body remained dry.

And it didn't last long.

As they opened his flyer and yet another layer, impossibly as it seemed was added to his pain.

Later he could never say how long the torture had lasted. But he remembered his own bile on the floor and how they had forced him to lap it up, to re-digest it all. He remembered it very well.

He relived it in flashes and flashes of red, black and brown.

They were peeing on him and he imagined they had shit on him, too.

He lay there, completely at their mercy. Their ugly stares exaggerated the shame and self-contempt to a previously uncanny degree.

– He's dirty, one exclaimed. – To the pool with him.

– TO THE POOL WITH HIM, they choired.

Their grins as they lifted him up were insanely wide and horrendous. His head rocked from side to side. Their faces never appeared distinct to him. Just a forelock and eyes, that's all.

Only one face stood out to him, as it should. Brown and black hair, a nose slightly turning outwards and a tight mouth. His own face, not his own.

– Let him have it, Ray shouted.

When he hit the water in the pool the cold came as a shock. He hadn't expected it to be cold, hadn't expected it to feel cold. The cold soon to be supplanted with infinite warmth, not at all unpleasant. It surrounded him like sand, forcing its way in everywhere. He sank. And when he hit bottom, he kept sinking. There was a murmur somewhere, as his upper levels of consciousness blinked out one by one. He sank, but there was a murmur refusing to let go. And he felt it… felt the glow within. In a burst of power, he kicked at the pool bottom, struggling wildly to reach the surface. When he saw the stars he felt, for the first time in a very long time a wild, indescribable joy. In spite of the hurting lungs and the banged-up body, his mind was strangely clear, and the strength of mind only increased as he swam, as he made his way to the pool wall. He experienced, more than saw the slim, strong arms pulling him up. He looked into Linda's eyes. She was a mess, but her eyes were clear.

He straightened there, on the edge, looking at the assembly before him, his brother and his cohorts.

– You'll never be rid of me, the shaking figure cried. – I will always be here. You have to kill me, brother, because I will never kill myself. *I will always be here*.

And he stared them all down. And they looked sullenly, silently back at him.

Supported by Linda he staggered away from the pool, from the garden, from the «party». Later he could never recall more than a few, foggy details from the trip through the forest. He heard whispers and he heard the wind, but nothing more. During the entire struggle he had a fist in Linda's silver-white hair. He couldn't say if she had reacted or in what way she had reacted to his outburst, but she was there, with him. She supported him and kept him on his feet, as she had done so many times before. Never more!

– Uncle Ezra *will* help us, he told her. – Whether he wants to or not.

Linda didn't reply. She was probably afraid of what would happen if she voiced her agreement, but Ted didn't care about her silence.

They glimpsed their home between the trees, a house lit by the shimmering silver light of the moon, of the spare lights from distant nearby neighborhoods.

– There is nothing here, he mumbled. – Nothing here for us.

– This is our home, Linda protested weakly.

Ted observed the moonlight mirrored in the still river surface… until the remains of the idyllic sight were shattered for all time. He saw the two police cars in front of the gate, the lights blinking red and blue. He saw his mother cry against his father's chest and Linda's wide-open eyes. He saw it all simultaneously.

He wanted to voice his concern, his burning worry, but his constricted larynx kept all sounds inside.

– Uncle Ezra is dead, children, their mother said. – He drove off a cliff with his car. Lieutenant Clarke here wants us to come to the coroner's office and identify his remains.

Lieutenant Clarke stood there, an image of the trustworthy, stoic police officer.

Remains… Ted thought unmotivated.

The twins stood there paralyzed. Strangely enough Linda was the one who broke down.

– Uncle Ezra dead? She whispered.

Her mother nodded, reaching out to comfort her daughter.

Linda took one step back forward, suddenly furious, her face contorted in anger.

– That can't be TRUE! She shouted. – Uncle Ezra can't be dead. Did these men tell you that?

She turned a tearful face at the lieutenant.

– They're LYING, she howled and spat him in the face. – They lie to…

Cousin took one step forward and slapped her on the cheek.

– Get hold of yourself, girl, he roared in a sudden, unexpected burst of rage. – Pull yourself together.

She didn't seem to feel the burning skin. For a while she merely stood there, staring blindly at some point ahead, before her eyes was filled with a grief and fear Ted understood only too well.

– You talk as if he is dead, daddy, she sniffed. – The police want you to take a closer look at… the body. They can be wrong, can they not?

Clarke coughed when the girl looked at him with begging eyes.

– I'm afraid there's no doubt, Miss Cousin, he said while drying his face. – He has already been identified. Your parents are next of kin. It's procedure. I'm very sorry, but your uncle isn't the first person to lose his cool and his life in that curve, and he won't be the last, I'm afraid.

Ted released a moan then, through barely parted lips, and sank to the ground.

Everybody rushed to his side. Clarke cried out in surprise.

– What's happened to him? He looks like he has barely survived an accident himself.

– Ted has been very sick lately, Linda said sadly. – He fell off a cliff on the riverbank earlier today and hurt himself.

It was an outrageous statement, but nobody seemed to notice. Her growing contempt for normal people was confirmed once more.

– Uncle Ezra's fate is just too much for him, she added.

– Poor boy, one of the patrolmen said. – We should get him to bed.

– Perhaps it would be best to postpone the identification procedure until tomorrow? Clarke wondered hesitatingly.

– No, we'll do it now, Cindy Cousin stated firmly. – If you just help Linda get him to bed, everything will be all right. Everything!

The Lieutenant nodded.

– Okay, he agreed. – Doyle, you help the girl.

A huge middle-aged patrolman bent down and grabbed Ted.

– Jesus, this one is light as a feather.

He followed Linda's lead through the door and up the stairs to the attic.

– He doesn't eat a lot, she mumbled, touching her brother's forehead.

She saw her parents through the window at the top of the stairs, saw them enter the patrol car and disappear down the road.

Doyle grunted, shaking his head, looking down at the boy's deadly pale face.

He shifted his grip slightly, unnecessarily, on the back. The boy grunted in pain.

– In here, the girl told him and led him into a huge room with a double bed, obviously belonging to the parents.

He lowered the shaking body down on the bed.

Linda placed herself by the bed with the arms crossed on her chest. She saw herself look down on her brother. She was healthy. She was far healthier than him and she had to look after him.

– Is there anything more I can help you with, Miss Cousin? He asked.

She looked confused at him, as if being surprised by the fact that he was there at all.

– No. She shook her head. – I can manage from here. You may go.

– Your brother will need a strong person to lean on for a long time to go, he said hesitatingly.

– Yes, he will.

And with that, she saw him off.

Ted rested on his back. It didn't feel like his back. Not anymore. Eyes were wide open. He heard Doyle's heavy tugging steps grow distant as he left the house, kept hearing steps as the patrolman seated himself in his car and drove off. He knew that Linda knew he was awake. He stopped her hands, grabbed them in a firm grip, as she was about to undress him. And her eyes grew wide, too, as he sat up in the bed.

– I needed everyone to leave, he mumbled, as his words grew more distinct for every syllable.

He gritted his teeth as he rose completely, as he stood on the naked floor, as he stared at her. She nodded numbly and walked to the window, looking out at the yard, at the river. The silver moonlight was shattered in thousand bits as the white waves acted up and changed, into a raging river.

There was no one outside, no one inside.

He started moving, and with a trickle, a thrill down her spine she realized she moved with him. Motivated by hatred, by desperation they descended the same stairs they so long ago had ascended. He walked to the living room, and once there, to the locker in the library section. Hands grabbed the locker and shattered it virtually at impact. Inside was a collection of big bills, of money. He grabbed them and put them on the table. The last few rags on his body were left there on the floor. He took a set of clothes from a chair and started dressing, and when finished, he put the roll of bills in his right pocket. Combing his hair back did just a little to moderate his savage look.

Hands found each other. They left the house like that, holding hands.

There was a late bus, to downtown Denver. They would always wonder about that, how they reached the bus stop exactly the moment the bus appeared around the corner, without looking at any timetable. They didn't speak. The bus left the stop, proceeding to its preordained destination. None of them remembered actually entering the bus or paying the fare. One moment they were outside, the other inside, sitting in their tight seats, looking outside. The world rolled by, new and unfamiliar.

They had been to LoDo several times, but mostly during daylight. Now the crowds and the tall buildings did the best possible attempt to intimidate them. But they weren't. The worst was already behind them, far behind. The world awaited them out there, with its countless horrors.

The Denver Union Station was old. Chairs were worn. Walls hadn't been painted for a while. They weren't certain whether or not they saw it as it was, or how it would one day eventually become.

There was a train scheduled, but it was late, and they had to wait.

– This waiting is nothing, he stated. – I've waited my entire life.

The benches were of wood and that made it even more unpleasant to him, but he didn't complain a bit. His will, his unfathomable ability to keep going had always frightened her.

It was the first few hours of June 6, 1968. The seconds were ticking away towards morning.

– It is night, she whispered. – Dreams belong to the night.

The morning had come. The train had left the station. To them it still seemed like night. Even as the train left the station, as it made its way east, even as it entered the state, the plains of Kansas, hours later they weren't convinced they had actually entered it.

They slept. They were awake, but both slept, slumbering, drifting in and out of it during the occasional train shakes. As they took their jackets and covered themselves Ted felt empty. Uncle Ezra was dead. Gone! He could just as well never have lived. Their uncle was dead, but Mike lived and thrived.

– I remember, he said. – I will never forget.

Two slim bodies turned restlessly in stupor. The nightmares assaulted them like rain on the plains and there was no place to seek shelter. Like vultures the horrific visions haunted them, devoured them - until nothing but the bare skeleton remained.

Chapter four

The sun had just started rising on the sky. The long shadows still hadn't shrunk from humans and buildings. The morning mist had not evaporated above the shooting arena. But the line of sight was clear in spite of that. The sound of the fifty-four combatants loading their rifles echoed across the field. Ted Cousin had looked very much forward to this day. He noticed that some of the others cast gloating glances at him. They probably wondered how he could hold the heavy Mauser rifle. Ted grinned triumphantly in return. The gun was alive in his hands. They saw that. The shaking stopped and the pale skin glowed. They had seen him shoot, but still couldn't believe it.

– This is *the* contest when shooting is concerned, he had told Linda. – The participants are the best of the best from Denver and most of Colorado. I want to be a part of it. I want to!

– It's dangerous, she had said nervously.

– I won't beat Mike, he had assured her. – He's in the class above me. But I know I'll do well. I can shoot. In fact I'm very good at it.

The boy let his eyes wander across the field. He could see the board, the mark clearly. The distance was 200 yards.

– You have always done well, their father had told them. – Since you became members, you've shown everybody what you're made of. I know you'll continue to do so, making me proud.

They had been members since first grade and they had made father very proud.

– Some day you will need your skills for real, Cousin had said.

– Why, Ted had asked, – will we need it?

There had been no reply. Their father was like that some time.

The first shooting was fast approaching. Ted prepared, went through the various stages in his head. He did it methodically, stage by stage, calmly, measured. The headgear covering his ears was loose, was skewed. Not good. The Mauser everybody used, the 38"caliber weapon sounded like thunder when fired. One without protection would turn deaf after the first salvo, the first round of firing.

There wasn't a single breath of wind, ideal conditions for shooting. Not that it would have had a major impact on the big caliber bullets, but it might turn a ten into an eight or a seven and in this sharp competition every point counted. Now, there was no need to worry. They had the sun behind them. Temperature was about 70. Ted smiled without being conscious of it.

He heard the voice of the referee through the speakers. Everybody was told to be ready. One minute to start. The boy eagerly grabbed the rifle. He saw the chairman of the club, police Chief Jeff McCabe, receive the microphone.

– Everybody ready, McCabe shouted with a voice high-pitched enough to blow the speakers. – Good...

He stood by the window. The shooters would have been able to see his raised hand, if they had looked in that direction, but they didn't, of course.

– Ready... FIRE!

The fifty-four rifles fired virtually simultaneously. But then the speed among the shooters varied wildly. A while later the echoes died as the final shots were fired. Ted rested on his back. He needed to do that. The effort had left him weak and his entire body shook in fatigue.

He turned around for the second round. For more than a little while the sound of shots once more thundered across the field. In the silence afterwards, McCabe cried:

– Okay, guys, you have fired twenty shots. We have now arrived at the speed shooting. You will fire ten times within a twenty-second limit. When it's time the boards will be pulled down and there will be no change to fire your ninth or tenth bullet. Good look, guys, May the best shot win.

When the signal sounded this time hell broke loose. Every competitor could only use two seconds an average on each bullet. Precisely twenty seconds later a siren sounded, and the shooting stopped. Many fired an extra shot even if there was no board to fire at, and they swore because they hadn't been able to complete the round. Everybody rose and left the stands. Ted remained for quite some time. The chest rose and fell on the slim figure.

– C'mon, kid, a friendly older guy told the pale boy. – Let's go to the café to wait for the results.

Ted slowly dragged himself up. The rifle felt heavier than lead. It wasn't like that during the actual contest. The weapon felt like it was a part of him, then. He wondered why it wasn't always thus. He speculated on whether or not he was himself, now.

Robert - Bob Tremblay approached him with two cokes in his hands. He offered Ted one. Ted had to smile. Bob was the same age as himself and attended the same classes. He was tall and fair-haired and usually wore glasses. Everyone thought he was a bit strange. Perhaps that's why he and Ted were friends.

– So, how was your shooting? He inquired.

– I don't know, Ted said in his usual distant manner. – Everything is a blur.

The point counting began. Ted felt the excitement rise within as more and more results were shown. When every score was counted he had won his class, with two points more than Bob.

– We have the winners, McCabe cried dramatically. He evidently enjoyed the drama. – The winner of the junior class is Michael Cousin with 293 points.

Loud cheers.

– Then we have the winner of the main competition, Lieutenant Grant, also with 293 points…

– The winner of our youngest competitors is… Ted Cousin. The reason I'm calling him last is that he has 294 points and he will be the one representing us in the Colorado Springs competition next month.

Major cheers and salutations. Some eager beavers fired shots across the field just for the heck of it.

The two brothers Cousin stood side by side and received their prizes. Mike's façade of joy and happiness was just as impeccable as it always was. Ted felt the cold in the heat like knives in his heart.

He walked home alone in the dark. Linda had looked at him as if he had gone mad when he insisted upon doing so.

– I want it over and done with, he said, and he saw her skin turn white and gray.

He saw Tilla across the street, but not Mike. Tilla didn't seem to spot him, probably because he was walking in shadow. He was good at that, had always been good at that.

He spotted two women a few steps away. He heard them talk.

– Look at her. One of the older ladies, who weren't really that old, said disapprovingly. – Hardly more than a child and she's already a tramp. She is a shame.

Something snapped in Ted. But he waited. He waited until Tilla was gone and he had followed the two several hundred steps.

– Excuse me, ladies. Ted closed in on them. – Could I have a minute of your time, please.

It wasn't a request. They wanted to leave, but he stopped them with a smile and a slight move.

– Which one of them are you? One of the ladies asked shocked and impolite.

Suddenly they weren't really sure. He was used to that.

– Don't you go away now, he said, very politely. – When walking around slandering other people, the least you can do is to hear people out, when offered an alternative explanation of your bias…

– Or I might be tempted to gut you like the pigs you are.

He put a hand on the nearest one's shoulder and led them a bit off the road.

– Are you aware that some social-anthropologists, doing studies of modern societies, claim that those same societies are postponing adulthood with at least six years?

They looked astonished at him. Probably not because of his words, but because he dared to question accepted truths.

– It's true. They claim that adulthood and the start of sexual activity should come only a year or so after the first, initial physical signs are becoming evident, that by postponing it, we, as a society are hampering a given person's development, causing all kinds of grief.

They didn't really listen, or didn't want to, so he made them.

– And concerning your favorite subject tonight, Tilla Stevens, she was kidnapped after one of her theater performances by a bunch of brutal bikers and raped. She reported it to the police the first time it happened. And the second. And the third. In vain. Not a shit was done. And then she didn't care anymore.

She turned into a regular biker girl. And then, when my brother took control of that particular party of scum, he inherited her… So, *ladies,* for the future, I would suggest you investigate a matter before being so cock-bull sure about it.

He felt good about that, he truly did. Until reaching the forest. Until walking alone through the dark forest. On the entire long walk home, he sensed the burning eyes in his back. He noticed that the body wanted to shift uncomfortably, to shrink in the rays of the burning eyes he imagined in his back, but he forced it to comply with his wishes. He reached the house. Mike wasn't there, but Linda and their parents were. She greeted him with a careful, hopeful smile. He returned it as a favor to her and wasn't sure he did her a favor.

The evening passed. The night passed. The two of them met Mike at breakfast next morning. He was his jovial self. Linda shifted between joy and hysteria, turning more into a nervous wreck by the minute. They met Mike briefly, before he was off to some of his «errands».

– It was as if he wasn't there, she whispered to her twin in her room afterwards. – Nothing has changed.

It was Saturday night. Ted returned from visiting Bob. The forest was dark. Suddenly it turned into a flash of dirty water. A rock held Ted in place. Mike waited for him, standing relaxed with his back against a tree, a statue of cold rage. Everything hidden in daylight was now revealed.

Ted wanted to fight. He wanted it so much that it hurt. He shrank like an empty bag of potatoes being dropped on the ground, before big brother had said a word.

– Go, Mike commanded. – We're going far away, to a place where we won't be disturbed.

With his head bowed Ted stumbled forward, encouraged by Mike's stick, the lazy strokes from behind. There was no hurry, really. Ted had been to the little cabin in the forest before. He stumbled on for hours. When they finally reached their destination the minor resistance that might have remained was completely drained from the body and mind of the thin boy. Completely exhausted he collapsed on the cabin floor.

– You're not worth much, are you? Mike snarled. – No glory, no will left. You've entertained *ideas* in your head lately. We can't have that and we certainly won't.

Tilla stretched on the bed. A happy, expectant smile crossed her lovely features. Nude feet and rusty red hair flashed before Ted's eyes. He hadn't realized she was there at first. That shocked him, shocked him to the bone. Her gray eyes studied him, as if he was a gnat, as if he was nothing.

– What a cute little runt, she cooed. – What are you going to do with him?

– Teach him manners, once and for all.

Mike pulled him up by the collar and threw him on the bed. Ted landed close to Tilla. She didn't move.

– May I use the whip on him? Please, Mike?

– No. I have my own methods.

He hit the stick slowly and deliberately against the palm of his hand. Ted was put on his belly and tied to the bed.

Tilla started scratching his neck, like he had seen her do with cats.

– I heard you were defending me, she mewed. – That's so sweet that I want to eat you. You poor boy scrapping with my big man.

– Tilla, he moaned. – How can you watch this? How can you be in the company of this… maniac and his hoodlums?

– How…? It's very simple, my darling. He is a mean, bad wolf and I am his bitch.

She stretched her arms above the head, performing for him, but most of all for Mike.

– Enough talk, Mike snapped. – Time to begin.

Tilla left the bed, still performing, exposing herself, her curves and her womanhood.

The first stroke fell. Ted bit into the sheets and willed himself not to scream.

The second stroke fell. The scream echoed within the walls. Strokes repeatedly hit Ted's back. Skin cracked under the onslaught. The skirt was ripped apart. Blood soiled the sheets.

– Too bad with the bed, Tilla said sourly. – We can't use it tonight.

– This will be the-last-time you resist my will, Mike breathed insanely.

Last time. It wasn't the last time. Tilla's enormous eyes stared

76

at the unmoving figure on the bed. Mike stood by her side, with an arm around her shoulders. A timeless time later everything seemed to breathe, the walls, the very air. The figure on the bed lay dead still. Ted Cousin gasped, but didn't move.

Never give up. His own words to himself, a cry in the nothing of the void. He heard someone cry, a sore, desperate sound. The uncle in his car, with Mike in the back seat. Suddenly Mike is outside. He lifts the car and throws it off the cliff. Mike grabs another car. In it Ted and poor Linda sit. Keith Lampard sits with Tilla on a bench and watches the spectacle.

He remembers his twelfth birthday, how he saw Linda naked in the shower.

Shadows, there were *Shadows*.

– Uncle Ezra is dead.

Someone screamed something to him, at him. Hands on his chest pushed him back, holding him down: he fought against it with all his might. Nobody should hold him down. Not anymore. Nevermore.
*****************/

He sat up in the bed. It was as if his body was pulled from straight to sitting position. Linda tumbled several steps backwards. He sat up in bed, with wide and round eyes, and sweat pouring down his face and body.

He sat on the bed, breathing hard.

– You were having a bad dream, Linda said tentatively. – You were screaming, and I ran to you.

He looked strangely at her. She looked different. The way she wore her hair and the ornaments in it. Her clothes… Slowly it dawned on him… the foreign room. There were the two beds in the small room, but hardly anything else. The door was open. A lot of people, strangers looked in, also dressed… dressed like hippies.

– Everything is okay, people, Linda said, smiling her sweet smile. – It was just a bad dream, that's all.

She hushed them away with her smile, and they were once more alone.

Everything was a haze, a haze of darkness. Outside, inside, night had turned dark. First there had been a gray haze, as if he could see everything better. Then darkness had settled.

– Chicago, he mumbled. – We're in Chicago.

– Proud citizens of «Sickago», she said cheerfully, – that's us. For more than a few days, now.

– We escaped, he said. – We ran away.

– And the sky didn't fall on us.

She looked at him with her expressive eyes, the telltale face.

They had been on the move for some time, going from place to place in a search for a safety they would never feel, before settling here, before deciding to stop for a while.

He looked at her, the suntanned, glowing skin, but also the ever-wavering eyes.

– Our lives have been completely turned around, she stated hotly, passionately, not like a thirteen-year old girl at all. – This was right for us, so very, very right.

When leaving the bed, he instantly felt the heat, growing conscious of his paper dry throat. He went to the sink, drinking greedily directly from the tap, splashing water in his face. The mirror was old, derelict, like the building, full of cracks. He saw his own face and he was able to look at himself with something that probably wasn't contempt. His skin was as brown as hers. He was still skinny, but not sickly so. The marks from the beating had healed remarkably fast.

– The marks are gone, she whispered. – When looking at your back it is as if they never were.

– No need to wear pajamas anymore, he replied lightly. – Not with the Cousins' excellent healing tissue.

– I remember, remember when you cut your finger as a little boy, she said. – The wound disappeared in a day or two. For others it takes at least a week and it leaves marks.

He looked at her again, noticing the happiness, the worry in her voice, in her wavering eyes.

– Let's go have breakfast, he grinned.

She gave him an almost maternal look. He had started eating like a horse, and it hardly showed. There was no belly or fat, only added muscle mass.

He dressed, and doubted that anybody in Denver would have recognized him if they didn't at least look twice. The two of them left the room. There was no door to the room, no doors in the entire ramshackle building.

The two of them shared the room. They didn't need to do that. There were more than enough rooms for everybody to have their own, but they preferred it this way.

– The sun is so hot, she said.

Chicago was, for several reasons the destination for quite a number of Travelers this summer. When Ted and Linda had arrived here, through luck and circumstance quite a number of squatters had already moved in. They had turned it into one of many «illegally occupied» houses during the early days of summer.

– Joan and Charlie were… were fucking again, last night. She blushed as she spoke in a low voice, as they progressed down the corridor, down the rusty, quirky stairs.

– I heard them, he said. – I can hear everything. Sometimes I think I can hear what goes on in every room in the building. There is a lot of fucking going on. People are free here. They do what they want.

The words sent a thrill through her entire body. The Sun's heat no longer came only from the outside.

On the ground floor there was a hall, or rather a collection of rooms, where the walls had crumbled, where the ceilings of several stories had vanished. Birds flew up there, high above them. About thirty people gathered around the long table in the middle. A number of them were children, some even younger than Linda and Ted. They had run away from home and come here from all over America, or they were local brats with occasional visits to the freak show. And more than one stayed put.

– Hi, you two, a girl in her late teens greeted them. – Isn't it a lovely morning?

– A lovely morning it is, Margaux, Ted bowed.

Margaux actually looked a bit flustered for a moment then.

Linda looked closer at him, once again. He could be very charming. She wondered if he was aware of exactly how charming.

The women of the house served the food before sitting down themselves. Everybody sat around the table eating and conversing. There were very few distinctions between the children and the adults, and at least far less of it, far less distinctions then what was usually the case.

– MOBE is coming, the protests are still on, right? Margaux eagerly asked no one in particular.

MOBE was The National Mobilization Committee, a loose «federation» of alternative groups formed in conjunction with the upcoming 1968 Democratic Party National Convention in this city. Their existence had already created major headlines in major newspapers. The press conference held March 17, to announce their plans of a Festival of Life during the Chicago Convention had been notorious, and might have, as some claimed contributed to Congress enacting the Anti-Riot Act in April.

In addition to, among many factors, the mounting Vietnam War protests, of course.

Ted and Linda hadn't stopped reading newspapers. If possible their eagerness to absorb national and global news had heavily increased this month, this month in freedom.

Joan, sitting close to Charlie replied a bit flustered.

– I don't see why not. Everything is in place. People will come to Chicago whether or not we're granted permission to demonstrate.

– I'm not so sure all this is a good idea, Hugo Manning, a powerful built man said from the other end of the table.

– And why is that, Hugo? Joan asked.

– Well, the Anti-Riot Act can really be used to criminalize any protest. I just don't think we should make it easy for them, that's all.

– Isn't that the point?

– Huh? Hugo looked around the table to see who had been speaking.

– Isn't that the point? Ted asked pointedly. – Shouldn't we really protest exactly because of the «Act», to protest its very existence?

– I really think that is a valid point, Hugo, don't you? Margaux said sweetly.

Manning grunted something unintelligible. Even though his opinion was easily understood. Linda understood that easily, looking beneath his smile and pleasant exterior.

– You're just a sanctimonious oaf, Hugo, Charlie said, and

80

started laughing his guts out.

The laughter in the room turned very strained.

Ted and Linda rushed their breakfast, hurried into the sun.
There were no enforced rules here, no ruling body. People
came and went, and usually did what they pleased.

Out in the streets, even far from the building they felt the
same. They walked hand in hand in the big city.

– It all seems so peaceful…

She paused. He waited.

– But that's just superficial, isn't it?

He nodded.

– Everything is different, she said excitedly, embracing it with
her arms. – Look at it. It's alive.

– It's true. His face was transformed by the flowering joy. – I
can feel it, you know.

– Everything is the same, she said, in a voice suddenly low
and timid.

– That, too. He nodded darkly.

The Dark Passions, both good and bad, ruling them their
entire life, waxed and waned.

Their time as Wanderers and in Chicago had been like that,
like a rollercoaster of emotions.

– I have no sense of time anymore, she said, shaking her head.
– It might be yesterday since we left Denver. It might be years.
When… when I close my eyes I fear I will open them and still
see Mike standing there right in front of me.

I understand what you mean, he thought, saying nothing,
saying everything.

The twins walked in silence for a while. Tall as they were,
and wearing their hippy outfits they weren't easily identifiable
as children. They were just two of the increasing number of
potential rebels descending on Sickago this summer. The
heat made them sweat, but it didn't really bother them. It was
summer and everything was new. Starry-eyed they explored
their new world.

They arrived at a green area, one more green area with at least
a statue or two.

– What's this called then?

– Grant Park, she told him helpfully.

– Yet another celebration of a past «hero»?

– Probably, she replied cheerfully.

He touched his head, rubbing it.

– The entire park is filled with people, he stated slowly.

She moved her eyes back and forth. There were a few people enjoying this fine morning, ignoring the signs prohibiting walking on the lawn, but certainly not crowded.

– I can see shadows everywhere, he said aloud. – They're transparent and don't acknowledge our presence, but they're There.

– You're scaring me, she whimpered.

He didn't reply and he didn't acknowledge her presence, and he was lifted up in the vast airspace, and time and thunder took flight with him.

************/

THE CITY OF CHICAGO
UNITED STATES OF AMERICA
23. AUGUST/LATE AUGUST 1968

Lincoln Park, this was Lincoln Park. Not now, not yet Grant Park (again). Ted blinked, and the shadows turned solid, turning into flesh and blood people, becoming real. A rush of hot air and weeks and months vanished like smoke.

There were cops everywhere. One couldn't possibly avoid seeing them the moment one opened one's eyes. The presence of various security forces was probably heavier than at any time in American history, including the Civil War Washington DC scene.

The Democratic Party National Convention 1968 was afoot and the town was filled with protesters.

– Can you feel it? Ted cried to Linda. – Can you feel the rush in the air, the boiling of the blood?

– Yes, Linda cried back. – Yes.

But she couldn't. Not really. Not the way he could. She knew that, and that awareness would always haunt her.

They were moving with a certain crowd within the park, people gathered there, like them to learn karate and general self-defense. There were even courses in snake dancing. One of the instructors, a tall, lean sailor type moved like lightning while demonstrating his skill. His short-term pupils looked like statues in comparison.

– This is a very good method of knocking people's head off, he nodded, while the assembly strived to get their breath back, – of killing, of Death. But it's more than that. More than anything it's a way of Life.

He paused a bit while letting it sink in.

– Many don't get that.

Ted and Linda trained together. They knew each other so well that they could more easily avoid hitting the other while trading blows.

– Observe, after a while how fluid your movements become, how they flow from one moment to the next. And know this: This is nothing compared to what you will sense after prolonged training.

Linda saw how Ted formed a sentence he repeated time and time again:

«I feel it».

«I *feel* it».

Linda echoed his sentiment and this time… this time it wasn't pretend.

They sat down in an area called The Hill, where another statue had been raised. As they had so rightly observed earlier there was no lack of statues in Chicago parks. Not in Chicago parks either.

– I've always attempted to learn various techniques, for obvious reasons. Ted no longer spoke in his usual distant manner. The eyes locked on Linda's, burning and glowing. – But just during this first guided session I've gotten rid of some of the bad habits, bad moves, and the progress is tangible, isn't it?

– It certainly is, Linda replied, waves and the sea dancing in her blue eyes. – This feels very much like my knife juggling performance, remember? So very natural, like I was born to it.

– I certainly do… He grinned.

– And the awkwardness while training with others is virtually gone while I do it with you.

Ted nodded slowly. It felt so… right.

Not so strange really. They were twins, after all.

We are growing, he thought, seeing the flex of worry in her eyes. Growing at an alarming rate.

There was snake dancing, performances, and wild abandon. The boy and the girl pulled back a little, content with enjoying the assault on the senses. A snake was rising from a basket, engulfing a woman, a tall and curvy woman. With misty eyes she did the snake dance, raising the fervor of everybody present. Linda noticed that her brother crouched a bit. When she realized what it meant, what it signified she blushed and turned away.

Everybody had a great time, also because their reasons for coming here were generally reaffirmed, though the seriousness of it all took a backseat to what was presently happening. But Ted and Linda, perhaps because they had already seen more of life's darker side then most adults, observed what happened beneath the surface. They easily saw the obvious. They saw police officers post 11 PM curfew signs on the trees and they had little trouble recognizing civilian cops mingling and taking notes.

Most people saw the signs, of course, and eventually they reacted. Groups started to form, and the heated discussion was on. It continued the rest of the day and culminated on a major meeting the next evening. Ted didn't remember much from it later except a few words, a few faces.

– Ultimately, no government or other person can decide where we can or cannot go. That, as it is with most things, we can only decide for ourselves.

– That is Abbie Hoffman, one standing close to the twins whispered to a friend, – one of the head honchos.

The Doors, the infamous rock group was in town. Their concerts fit well in with everything. Jim Morrison held one of his most memorable and controversial performances.

– ARE YOU SLAVES OR ARE YOU ALIVE, PEOPLE? DO YOU DECIDE YOUR OWN DESTINY OR DO YOU LET OTHERS DECIDE IT FOR YOU?

So much was happening. Everything simultaneously. The mind exploded from the bombardment directed at it. Ted and Linda had never done a LSD-trip, but the way they felt fit well with how others, more experienced hippies described it. One breath was a Universe, and no time existed within the boundary of the Sickago experience, within this human cauldron.

And then it was two nights hence, the time a few minutes before eleven. Lincoln Park was a cauldron of heated emotions. Everybody present realized the obvious: People would not leave before the curfew. On the contrary. They deliberately defied it. The previous evening the police had attacked people attending a music festival and also a march to Conrad Hilton Hotel, the main convention center. Tension and rage shook the air, shook reality in the hot night.

People shouted into microphones, urging those present to «hold the park».

– DON'T LET THE PIGS TAKE THE HILL, Rennie Davis shouted wildly.

People returned his words with cheers and raised hands.

– There must be thousands of people here, Ted whispered in awe. – Thousands refusing to follow the edict of the establishment. Father prepared us for this, or something like this.

The excitement in his eyes, his entire body, washed over his sister like a tall, powerful wave.

What they had experienced in Denver seemed like a dream, a tiny wave of a distant past.

There was singing, chanting and talking, and nothing but.

– This is a peaceful assembly, where we are exercising our constitutional rights to gather and protest, Jerry Rubin said. – The eager servants of society won't drive us off and we will certainly not be intimidated by them. We will stay.

The police attacked not long after that. There was no warning, really, no clear signs of what was going to happen. Some of the protesters present in the park had certainly experienced similar actions during racial protest marches in the south or university protests, but nothing quite like this. The uniformed thugs already present came in waves, seemingly from all sides, using clubs and teargas to «disperse» the protesters. In the course of a few seconds total insanity ruled where singing had dominated a short while before. Ted *heard* bones break as clubs hit arms, legs and heads. He saw gushes of blood color the night red, turning it from dark, to dark red. He held onto Linda for dear life, to not lose her in the insanity progressing in Sickago. They ran and they ran, until they hardly had any breath left to run anymore. There was no way to tell whether or not anybody was actually chasing them. Police could be seen everywhere. The two half grown human beings jumped off a height down on a concrete sidewalk. He landed okay, but she gave away a yelp of pain and would have tumbled to the ground if he hadn't grabbed her.

– Can you walk? He asked her, his voice raised several levels in his desperation. – *Can you walk?*

– No… She whimpered and started crying. – I'm sorry, sorry, sorry.

He put her over a shoulder and started running again, hardly noticing the extra weight.

Running. And for a while there was nothing but the running. He ran through darkened streets, crossed where there were cars, and there might have been the banshee whining of breaks, but he couldn't tell. He just kept running until he didn't anymore.

– I'm sorry. He sat on a bench with his head bowed. – I didn't mean to shout at you. It was just… Everything was just…

– … insane, she completed. – I know! Please don't feel bad. Please.

Dawn, the color of rust and blood, bringing no consolation, no comfort to the thousands of distraught souls wandering aimlessly through Chicago's streets. Ted Cousin sought through garbage cans for breakfast and found it without having to strain that hard. His heart jumped a beat when he saw Linda sit on the bench, so alone and vulnerable. That image among many stuck in his memory forever.

They fed greedily. He was pleased that he had thought about bringing more than he had thought they could eat, because they consumed it all, wolfed it down like wild beasts that hadn't had anything to eat for days. This night, this night had felt like days and weeks as far as their minds were concerned, and evidently their bodies agreed.

– This is the world, he stated solemnly. – This is the Hawkworld we live in.

– Please don't say that, she countered. – Please…

One heartbeat, two, until she spoke again.

– How do you think it makes me feel to take on the stereotype role of the typical, civilized, conditioned, overcautious human female? She exclaimed, suddenly enraged. – It isn't fair, it isn't…

She hid her face in her shaking hands. They embraced and sat like that, with their arms around the other for a long time.

At long last she smiled as she tested her injured ankle.

– I think it is all right. She sniffed. – I can walk. There is hardly any pain.

And they started walking. They kept walking down the path to infamy.

Chicago Coliseum. A rally of 4000 people. There was a lot of shouting and anger. Lincoln Park again. Night again. At precisely 11.20 PM the police once more attacked, breaking bones and chasing people off. The crowd emerged into the streets. Shouts of rage and despair filled the dark night.

– This DOES it, a woman shouted. – I've had enough. I won't take it anymore. I WON'T!

And she grabbed a rock, a loose brick from the ground, and she threw it forcefully at the nearest streetlight. It hit the target head on and smashed the bulb, casting shadow over the crowd. The street… The boy saw it as a river, and the river was blood. A thousand years. The reign would last a thousand years.

– I WON'T, Linda cried, picking up a brick.

She threw it through a shop display window. The glass broke into a thousand pieces. The cry of rage rose from the crowd, as they started smashing every window and streetlight in the block, and then starting on the next and the next. When the police showed up the protesters didn't run, didn't back off, but attacked with high-pitched snarls. It went on through the night and beyond.

Grant Park the next day, the bandshell opposite the Hilton, early August 28th. 15000 people gathered to hear the people on the stage. David Dellinger, Bobby Seale, Rennie Davis and Tom Hayden, four of those who would later be known as «The Chicago Eight». Abbie Hoffman had been arrested while having breakfast for having the word «fuck» on his forehead…

The shouts and noise slowly faded, but never faded

completely, not even close to completely.

– We've done nothing wrong, Bobby Seale cried. – Nothing but exercising the constitutional right and duty to protest we are given at birth as citizens of a supposedly free country. We have been attacked verbally for months now, through media and from fat politicians seeing their «hard won» positions threatened. And now the oppressors and their eager servants have come full circle, by attempting to break every bone in our body, in last ditch attempts to finally break our spirit. People of all colors, all «creeds» are rising up against injustice, against oppression, all over the world. We are not alone, people. Our brothers and sisters are with us… In short… pick up a gun, pull the spike from the wall, because if you pull it out and you shoot well, all I'm gonna do is pat you on the back and say: Keep on Shooting.

The Black Panther Chairman held up a fist, and a lot of the people present, black, white, yellow or red did the same.

– Let's pay a visit to the fine building over there. David Dellinger bent over the microphone and raised his voice. – Where the decision-makers, the insane makers are having a fit, sweating their heart out. It's about time.

Well over a thousand people divided from the main body and followed up on Dellinger's calling, and joined him on the east sidewalk on Columbus Drive on his way to the hotel. The crowd filled the sidewalk. Not long afterwards the police stopped the march. A man several policemen would later swear was Abbie Hoffman, (in spite of him being in custody at the time) instructed the crowd to disperse into units of five and ten people and then do their utmost to penetrate any shielding, any defense put up by the police or security guards, and generally do as much disruption as human possible. Then the police attacked in force and superior numbers, once more using clubs and teargas grenades. Everything turned red and gray.

Ted and Linda had sought refuge in an abandoned building south of the park. They were both shaking in rage and turmoil raged inside them.

She touched his head with a shaking hand.

– You're injured, let me…

– No, no, it isn't my blood. Believe me, I can tell.

It was all over him, forming both spots and droplets. She led a hand to her own face, and it turned bloody red. Blood, there had been blood everywhere.

The Democratic Party nominated Hubert Humphrey as their presidential candidate. The two weary and exhausted youths heard that from two people passing them on the street later that evening.

And that was that, for now.

Chaos subsided, even though it lingered, and kept lingering in the air. They slept in a park, some park. It was an empty and silent park, devoid of evident life. They washed off most of the blood in a fountain, though it turned out to be impossible to remove completely at the time.

The next morning, they didn't even have to search garbage cans for food. They found scraps and pieces, and also steaks and cheese, and a lot more, without really looking

They sat down, feeding greedily.

– There hasn't been any lack of food for us, lately, Linda stated thoughtfully, – but I can hardly remember how often we have eaten. I don't think we did eat at all yesterday, even though I can't be certain.

They walked back towards the park. It was on their way «home» anyway, to the hippy collective in the derelict old building. It felt like ages since they had left it, not less then a week.

This park also got filled up with people. No cops openly showed their ugly mugs, but somebody had evidently called a meeting here. Linda asked a boy at her side about it.

– Some silly goat, calling himself the Bishop of California. The boy shrugged. – This is one of the few places not swarming with pigs, though, so we thought it would be fit to rest our heels for a while. This park doesn't even have a name, or at least no one knows its name, so it's gotta be a great spot.

Time slipped away, as the boys and girls were not waiting. It was quite a feeling this, to not wait for anything, and they all relaxed. Visibly exhausted as they all were, they needed to relax, to recharge the burnout in their mind, in their gut.

Ted shook his head irritably. A fly jumped back and forth to and from his left and right shoulder. He attempted to swat it, something he used to be quite good at, but now he couldn't find the energy or will to really take a stab at it.

– Hey, man, another boy said, – you must be seriously spooked by all this.

– What? He looked up, completely disoriented.

– You've got gooseflesh all over.

He looked at his arm, at both his arms, and saw the truth of it. His skin had turned into an uneven field of gooseflesh and hair standing straight up.

– We should leave, he said.

Nobody reacted, not even Linda, and he realized that he hadn't spoken up or hadn't spoken at all. He tried again, but his vocal chords didn't work. His mouth moved, but nothing else worked.

The tall man approached from the opposite side of the park, towards the height at its center. He had dressed himself in white. So had his followers, his disciples. Ted called them that in his mind instantly, without having any solid foundation or reason for it.

The man dressed in white raised his arms to shoulder height, straight out from his body.

– Sons and Daughters of The Light, he cried.

Ted noticed the long, black ponytail. Shortly afterwards things started to weird out around him.

He saw the spectators' shining eyes, and saw the same sudden devotion in Linda and everybody he could see.

Then, reality turned inside out, upside down around him. Finding himself walking in a desert, strangely familiar he struggled to not be overcome by panic. The smell of salt overwhelmed his olfactory senses. He crouched there, beside his sister Linda, in Chicago August 1968. Wide-eyed he looked around him. Suddenly, inexplicably, from one moment to the next, the world had Changed. He looked at Linda. She didn't look at him. Her entire attention was locked on the platform and the man up there.

He dragged her away.

– What did you do that for? She said irritably.

Her irregular breathing, her round, dilated eyes, the sick smile, everything pointed to something being done to her.

He didn't reply. Not with words. He was visibly shaking. She saw it, startled.

– You're afraid of him, she said amazed, and suddenly she was shivering herself.

– Just the sight of him… something inside…recoiled.

– He did something to us, she mused, angrily, – influencing our emotions, opening us up to him.

Her incredibly blue eyes looked at her brother.

– But you weren't affected. On the contrary. You saw straight through him, saw him for what he was.

She might be in denial about some things, but not this one. She looked at her brother with undeniable admiration in her eyes.

– There is so much out there, out here, waiting for us, he said.

The world had just expanded again.

– Come, she said gently, urging him on, away from there.

They kept moving, shaking nervously every time they encountered uniforms or uniformed cars, but since every second person they met on the streets also had remains of blood on them they didn't get too worried. They kept to backstreets and alleys, but didn't run. Not unless police cars or clean-cut, powerfully built men got too close. Eyes moved constantly back and forth. Their time in Chicago had marked them, marked them for life, just as much, as certain as the time in Denver had done, and more was yet to come. What would reach a terrible climax in the Australian desert forty years later had just begun to manifest.

Nothing had changed in the derelict building that had been their home for most of the summer. Nothing important. People still came and went there relatively undetected. The blood and the ragged clothes raised a few eyebrows, but not much more. Hugo Manning, arriving with his boys and girls in tow, made more than a few eyebrows rise. Ted slowed down visibly. Linda pulled him away, calming him by rubbing his back. Their room waited there for them. New arrivals had simply chosen others of the many available cubicles to crash. It was no big deal. They owned nothing, no thing in the world they feared losing.

Ted washed off the last spots of blood standing before the mirror, the cracked mirror. Linda did it before the hall mirror.

All the physical marks slowly faded. He stared at the lost horizon in the mirror. A while later he stood by the window, looking down at the street, looking at the wall in the horizon, shivering in the summer heat. She walked up behind him. He grabbed her hands and turned around before she could touch him.

– I'm okay, he assured her. – I will be okay.

They stayed in the room, until dinner, until the time of dinner, breathing sighs of relief when they walked down the stairs and found that there would be one. None of them felt like going out today.

Dinner tasted somewhat bland, like the taste didn't truly register on the tongue. Conversation was virtually non-existent, with just the smallest of small talk, of non-committal phrases.

Ted lifted the spoon to the mouth. He parted lips to digest the soup. He let the arm fall down to the plate once more.

– This has all been a terrible tragedy, Manning said. – One that should have been avoided.

The arm froze.

– Oh, Ted said. – In what way, if I may ask?

– Of course, you may ask, Edward, the grown man said. – Feel free to ask me anything.

There was a brief pause, before Manning continued. Others stopped eating, listening in.

– I just feel that the confrontational line chosen by the leaders of the protests has set us back years, in the attempt at ending the war.

– I don't agree, Ted replied icily. – And it's about far more than ending the Vietnam War anyway. As Jerry Rubin told Abbie Hoffman. The rebellion is too focused on the Vietnam War, not realizing that that particular insanity is merely one of many horrors, one of countless inevitable *results* of an insane society.

Linda shivered under his stare, in the heat of his words, realizing what they implied.

– In other words, you will not only having us continue the confrontational line of action, but even expand upon it?

Manning sat there good-humored, seemingly enjoying himself.

– I think the first we should do is to stop pretending here, Ted grinned. – Stop pretending to be other than tea drinkers, playing at being revolutionaries. Do we satisfy ourselves by playing a game or do we truly mean what we say? Are we willing to risk anything to achieve the slightest bit of anything, anything at all?

Many blinked. They weren't certain it was still a boy sitting there, but something else entirely.

– I think you're too young to make that kind of judgment, Edward, good ol' Hugo said more than a bit tight.

– Thank you for proving, my point. Ted said very relaxed. Linda shuddered. – Reacting like a true conservative when it comes to children and their perceived place in society…

– What-do-you-mean? The big man asked in a painstakingly strained voice.

– Oh, it's pretty well-known material. Too bad it isn't acted upon. As one example among many I could mention a fact that seems to have escaped everybody else here: Women are making the food. Women are serving the food, just like in established homes. A strange paradox, right?

Manning glared at him, but didn't speak.

– There's more, definitely not agreeable with an alternative lifestyle. You, with your host of sycophants are behaving more like a head of state than anything even approaching a rebel.

The Man wanted to attack the boy. One could easily discern this from his flustered face, but he held back, realizing fully that such an action would lead to an even bigger disaster.

Ted returned the glare now, far stronger than it had been sent to him. Manning started sweating. It was visible in his face. He swallowed and left, his court leaving with him, but casting uncertain glances at each other. Manning's influence had, by one stroke, been severely cut. It was remarkable that such a limited exchange of insults and words could lead to such a dramatic outcome, but it had. Some people could stand to lose face, even those who felt they had some to lose, but he couldn't. Ted remained on the battlefield, the sense of victory, of triumph swelling within him. Linda looked at him, and then looked away.

No one returned his stare, shamefully aware of their own

shortcomings in liberating themselves from the heavy chains of tradition.

The moon rose high in the sky. Ted saw himself go to bed. He saw the hurt expression in Linda's expressive eyes and features. They had exchanged words since the dinner, but he wasn't certain they had actually spoken.

He saw himself resting on the bed and realized he was dreaming.

He saw himself, The Wanderer, and his brother, The Wanderer, his brother. And yet another Wanderer, an unknown woman with a wolf's head. He knew all this was a dream. But… it was so real, so vivid… He sat by a bonfire with an incredibly old, practically ancient woman with a mole, a birthmark on her leg, in a room filled with smoke and shadows. The woman didn't move her lips, but she was speaking.

– Carla Wolf has been Wandering for a long time. That girl, that woman is Wandering still. Carla Wolf remembers everything she will never forget. She is remembering still. Wolf is walking the mysteries of the world. Hers is a legend, shrouded in mists of Time and Shadow. «Shew me a Mystery», she says. «We shan't all know an answer, but we shall all be Changed».

A dusty office room in a block. Mike sat there with a gun on the table in front of him. Ted entered the room through the front door.

Back in Denver, in the cabin. Mike raised his stick. Time and time again he let it fall on soft tissue. And Ted screamed. He SCREAMED
**********/

– Don't hit me anymore, he screamed. – PLEASE DON'T HIT ME

With wide–open eyes he stared into his sister's worried eyes.

– L-linda, he stuttered. – Are you too… Don't let Mike h-hit m-me.

Like a little child.

He sat up in bed. Linda sat still, half asleep, suddenly wide-awake.

– Mike isn't here, she said soothingly, carefully. – We're still in Chicago. Mike wouldn't even begin to know where to look for us.

– In C-chicago…

– Sickago, she confirmed again with a weak smile.

In his confused state the boy looked around the room. First at this point he realized that he wasn't at the Denver home, that the nightmare night revisiting through the dream had happened months ago. Linda rubbed him on the wet forehead. Sick and shaking he sank back into the soft bed. Sweat flowed down the skinny body.

He looked out of the window, the paper window, at the approaching dawn. He might have been suppressing the horrible memories from the last night in Denver, but this night they had returned with a vengeance.

– I had a nightmare, he said hoarsely. – I relived what Mike did to me after the shooting contest. It felt horrible.

– Poor boy, she said softly.

– But there was more, he added and she met his words with silence, fearing them more than life itself.

– Dreams, he said to her. – I had dreams that were more than dreams. I saw Mike dream, muttering to himself in his sleep. I sensed fear. We were adults and we were walking on an incredibly long and broad road.

– What are you talking about? Linda asked.

He easily caught the scent of fear in her voice.

– The future, Linda, he cried. – I saw the future, as easily as I see you now. I wasn't certain until this moment, how different, how special we truly are.

With an effort of will he managed to sit up again on the bed.

– You can't be sure of that, she said, shaking her head. – You're not sure, are you?

– I'm sure, he said.

He saw her red eyes, eyes red from lack of sleep.

– You haven't slept much tonight, have you, now?

Before she managed to give a reply, he grabbed her hand and pulled her tight. She gasped, surprised by his strength, knowing fully well that she shouldn't be. And she sat willingly down by his side. Earlier, a long time ago she would have done it to comfort him, to encourage courage in both of them, but now she was overwhelmed by the notion, the certainty that he didn't need it anymore. It was a new, scary emotion to her.

– You're a fantastic girl, he praised her. – You don't know how many times I've caught myself wishing you were not my flesh and blood sister.

He smiled, but she wasn't fooled. She couldn't say for sure if she liked his newfound confidence.

– Mike has told me the same thing, she said shuddering. – You're very alike.

She held back, too late. The moment she looked at him, she realized she had made a horrible mistake. The remaining soft smile faded from his features. The darkness seemed to thicken around them both. The cold reentered the boy's body. She looked at him with desperation in her eyes.

– I didn't mean what I said, she whispered aloud. – You must forget it. *You must!*

He stared hard at her. She didn't recognize him. In despair she put her head against his shoulder and her tears rained down on the still pale skin. As certain as she had spoken those ten words, she had plotted the course for him. She had put in motion a process that couldn't be stopped.

Earlier her tears had filled him with regret. Now, he felt nothing.

– I can't forget, he said very excited. – Neither should you. We can run, but we can't hide.

– We can stay away...

– For how long? We will encounter Mike, somewhere, somehow. The question is when and who chooses the battlefield, setting the stage.

She didn't comment on that, biting her lip, holding back with an effort.

– I can tell you one thing, he continued unabated. – I swear, to you, here and now, to myself that from now on, I will never bow down before anything or anyone. I will never be anyone's servant, anyone's slave.

Ted Cousin's face was just a mask, now. He didn't look at Linda anymore. He had his attention turned to the wall, to whatever he projected there. The voice remained low and intense.

– You must not blame yourself. Nothing of what will happen

is your fault. It would have happened anyway.

Linda stopped crying. With tear-filled eyes she stared into his tight face. He seemed so confident, a confidence independent of the skinny body.

– That must not be, she said desperately. – I'll lose you, too.

– You won't, he assured her.

Then she glared furiously at him.

– You don't care what happens, she snarled. – You're really envious of Mike's power and want to take his place. I hate you. It's sick. I *hate* you.

She searched his face in despair, to if possible discover a reaction, any reaction to her outburst, but he was just as unmovable. Filled with the horrible sense of loss she turned away from him.

– I don't want to lose you, too. Don't you understand? You will lose no matter the outcome of the struggle.

He kept his silence. With a resigned sob the girl rose and stumbled towards the door. Then she abruptly stopped in her tracks. Her mouth opened in a silent scream. From the hall two bulging, red gleaming eyes stared at her. In the darkness out there she could just about make out the figure the eyes belonged to.

– It's Mike, she screamed in panic. – He has come to punish us for our rebellion. MOTHER, FATHER, HELP

She was back in Denver, as if she had never left.

And in truth they hadn't. Not really.

– It isn't Mike, Ted said quietly. – It's the hall mirror.

Slowly it dawned on her. The fear, rooted as it was in the girl's deepest self, grew and festered even more. Throat had turned dry as sand and her heart fluctuated wildly. He had left the bed. She heard the sound of the naked feet across the floor. The smell of blood hadn't vanished. She felt his hand on her shoulder. Her skin turned to ice.

– Don't turn away, he bade her. – I want you to look at me.

Driven by a power beyond herself she obeyed. She could see his face. Then her eyes widened in shock. She didn't see his face. The strange eyes dominated it completely. They seemed to stare straight through her. *It was Mike's eyes*.

– You see, he nodded. – You understand.

– What if I get Mike times two? She asked him, so very much like an adult woman. – Is that what you want? Is it?

The two last words she cried out, but it didn't faze him.

The glow in the eyes turned even more intense and his hands tightened the grip ever harder around her shoulders. The stranger, with his inner resolve and hard core terrified her.

– It won't be, he stated in a raspy voice. – It will be him and me, and no one else. I will be his equal… superior in everything. Everything he does, I will do better. I'll train myself to be stronger, harder, more resilient and sneakier than him, and when I do…

Linda couldn't stand it anymore. Desperately she freed herself from his grip. Blindly she ran to the stairs, feeling the heat from the glowing eyes in her back. She heard his voice unexplainably clear.

– … Then he will pay for everything bad he has done to us. No matter how long time it will take, I'll overcome and crush him. *That is my solemn promise.*

Chapter five
DISTANT BUTTERFLY WINGS
Denver 1967

Tilla was the star of the local theater. Even the newspapers in central Denver had published articles, reviews about her, and about her co-stars, the two dark brothers.

The old theater stood on its shaky legs not far from the highway. The distant sound of cars passing by a few hundred yards away never really let up. Aside from that the area was fairly quiet. There had been talk about tearing down the old building in favor of a new, modern shopping mall, but so far it had remained talk.

Winter had not yet let go as the five youths made their way to the evening's performance. Two dark brothers looking like twins, two fire-haired cousins looking like twins, and one tall silver haired girl.

A small group of fans had gathered outside the building. There were always some, in a modest sort of way. They studied the five with keen interest and curiosity, almost like they were movie stars.

That the two redheads were related were quite evident. They looked very much alike. But while Betty was moody, withdrawn Tilla was exuberant and easygoing, and extroverted.

The brothers looked very much alike and they also behaved that way. Period.

– Look at it, Tilla exclaimed in her usual feisty way. – It's got class. What's a fucking shopping center compared to something like this?

– A money machine, Mike commented. – A place that could just as well print money.

– A lot of monetary value, Tilla corrected him. – And not much of anything else.

Laughter echoed between the naked trees.

The instructor and his crew of one greeted them in the door.

– Hello, children. Once more I welcome you to this place of imagination and wonder.

– Hello, Jonas, they greeted him in chorus. – Hello, Martha.

Martha was a lean, tall woman in her fifties.

Jonas had been a sailor and many things besides since he had left Norway, his native country at the start of the century, never to return. That would make him about seventy, but he did look younger than Martha.

Most immigrants spoke with a heavy accent, they had been told. But if he had ever done that, it was gone now. He spoke and acted fluently, like music.

He closed the heavy doors behind them, making the prospective audience stay out in the cold.

The five children sat in the front row, watching him as he stood on the lower stage. He had placed one candle on the table in front of him. Aside from that, the room was dark. A thrill shot through Tilla.

– Our new play will soon be ready, he said. – I have earlier, many times, stressed the importance of letting out your inner Self, of expressing yourself, of finding your center, your Core, and by doing so letting out the creativity and mysteries within us all. The world is mystery and imagination and nothing but. Perception is reality.

The room had now been filled with people. All the seats were taken. The candle and the table remained, but the figure appearing out of the darkness was the tall, dark boy. Already before he started speaking talk died and faded among the audience. His voice rose, flowing like ravens in the night.

– A storm starts very small. It doesn't come into the world fully grown. Nothing does. No one does. It's said that far away, as a butterfly is flapping its wings, it's starting the first few, critical movements required for the storm to be created. And from then on nothing can stop it. It must continue its course, all the way to its fiery, horrible end.

The dark figure seemed to shimmer, to melt into the background, into the night, and in his place appeared the sun, in all its brilliance.

– Fate, she said. – Are we our own masters or are we victims of Fate's whim?

– Puppets of Fate's plan? Another sun appeared briefly by her side.

The Moon appeared on her other side.

100

– We're masters of our own destiny, right? Isn't that what makes us Human?

A row of candles started burning, from nothing, out of nowhere. The other, the one faded. The sun and the moon faded. The Shadow rose. One dark human sat in a chair.

– We're not puppets on strings, he insisted. – I'm not.

He rose from his chair and started moving around, started walking in a very deliberate fashion. New candles were lit as he moved, as others, on the places he had left put themselves out. It seemed downright uncanny and made people gasp. Everything seemed normal at first, for a long time, but then his arms and legs started twitching and jumping in a very strange fashion, and the audience gasped as they spotted the thick, strong strings attached to his ankles and wrists. He performed a dance on the stage seemingly completely orchestrated by whoever was holding the strings.

And finally, when he stood there on his knees, exhausted and downtrodden his mirror image appeared from nowhere with a gun in his hand. The Other fired and the puppet screamed and fell to the floor. Everything turned dark, until the sun once more stood there, by the front table.

– The world is constantly throwing the dice on our behalf. The sea may look calm, but from below the monster is coming for us. There are forces out there that at any time may choose us, descend upon us from friendly skies and tear us *apart*. This is food for thought, you wage slaves, you puppets, as you return to your cubicles and believe you're living your lives. Have good dreams in your Sleep and a hearty Good Night to you all.

There was more, much more, but this was what they always remembered.

The applause lasted forever, ringing endlessly in the actors' ears as they bowed and curtseyed, as everything turned night.

Euphorically happy Tilla parted with the others and started out alone on the short way home.

The three older boys walked towards her as the most natural thing in the world. They were all dressed in the characteristic leatherjackets. She had seen them often enough around town lately. Even when they stopped and blocked her way Tilla wasn't really worried.

– Hi, sweetie, one greeted her with his different colored eyes.

– H-hello.

– Come with us, sweetie.

Wasting no more time he grabbed her in one arm and dragged her off. She wanted to scream and to shout her fear to the world, but her lips and larynx felt as numb as the rest of her, her face a stiff, unmovable mask unable to express anything. Snow. The snow on the ground strangled all sound. Even the roar of the motorbikes as they started the engines sounded muted and hardly traveled more than a little through the air. The boy placed her in front of him on the bike, making her sit still with a light slap on her butt. It burned, and a tear formed in her eye. She saw no one. No one saw her, saw what happened.

– And they don't care anyway, Keith Lampard told her, and she heard him amazingly clear through the noise. – And if you tell them they'll blame you, for disturbing their precious illusion, their storybook view of the world.

Her eyes widened as she realized the harsh truth in his words, as she grew up in an instant. Something horrible twisted and turned inside her, clawed at her innards, drawing blood. The very real pain made her gasp and moan. Keith laughed and the contempt in his laughter made her shrink even more in his ruthless grip.

They drove off, taking her with them, taking her away from everything she had known.

She shook subjected to the cold, cruel wind created by the winter and the speed, but the biker didn't care. And thinking about it she couldn't imagine how she could have thought he would.

They arrived at the tents by the river. Not exactly the run of the mill tents, but huge and expensive. Tilla kept shivering. She could no longer tell whether or not it was caused by the physical cold, or the ice growing inside.

There was movement inside the tent. She saw the giant frame move in there. The cold penetrated her to the depths, the depths of hell. She forced herself to dismount the bike before Lampard shoved her off. Jeffrey Cumbes stepped through the small opening, brushing the heavy cloth of the tent aside like nothing. She recognized him immediately. He wasn't exactly an unknown quantity in and around the Denver and Boulder extended area.

– Ah, there you are, fresh meat, he grunted. – Come here, fresh meat.

And he didn't really have to say anything. His presence overwhelmed her, like the pinpricks of ice she imagined she sensed all over her body, within her previously so active mind. She walked to him, joined him as he returned to the tent, his own private tent. This was his place. He shared it with no one. She saw evidence of other female presence, a brush, a lipstick or less, faint, inconsequently. He ruled here. He was God here.

He grabbed her without further delay, crushing her in his huge paws. She stifled a scream as he started to touch her, to squeeze her like grapefruit.

– Feel free to scream, he told her. – I like it when you scream.

He put her down on the huge bed, where there was room for far more than merely two. It made her feel even smaller. He undressed slowly, lazily, without hurrying the slightest. There was a flash somewhere, inside those dead eyes, as he paused to appraise the crouching creature below. She saw his big thing and bit her lip. It was fully erect, and from the very first moment she hated, she loved the sight of it. He entered the bed and lowered himself on her, utterly inconsiderate. She scolded herself for expecting anything else. It hurt when he put his weight upon her, when he started tearing off her clothes, as he was ruthlessly exposing her. And then she cried out, helpless to stop herself.

– I like the fire in you, fresh meat, he grunted. – I saw it from far away the first time I laid my eyes on you. Most other chicks are dead as doornails, but you're bursting with life.

He squeezed her tits. She screamed then. Just this one overt, audible time, but to her the scream continued indefinitely. He started to move on her, first a few, probing trusts, before forcefully penetrating her shield, her womanhood.

There were pain and shame, and utter denigration, and she couldn't claim, in a backwards sort of way she didn't enjoy it all. Darkness fell on her, never to ever more truly let go.

He gave her new clothes afterwards. They weren't really that much different from the ones she had worn previously. No one would see the difference. She kissed him shyly on the cheek. He laughed and slapped her on her butt. When he led her out of the tent Lampard was there, waiting. She didn't realize until much later what passed between the two men. She did see the flash of anger in the two strange eyes that Cumbes, her dear Jeffrey perhaps missed.

The bikers returned her to the exact same spot they had picked her up, abducted her. Then they drove off, leaving her alone. She walked the short, remaining distance back to the house. The snow muted all sound. She hardly perceived the sound of the door opening and closing.

– Ah, there you are, her mother said from the kitchen, the typical mother. – Is everything all right, dear?

– Yes, mother, she replied calmly. – I got a bit delayed, that's all.

She did as she usually did, went straight to her room, and started playing her Beatles albums. Which one of them she couldn't tell. She didn't return to the kitchen for evening supper. After remaining on the edge of the bed for a while, not listening to the music, she crawled fully into the soft nest, put her head on the pillow, and, before long fell asleep.

The next day, after school she walked straight to the nearest police station. She wanted to turn and go home, but she forced herself onward. The police station was drowning in pure, white snow, just like the rest of the city. The reflection of the sun in all the white made her eyes hurt, even through the sunglasses. She had always had light-sensitive eyes.

The reception area of the police station turned dark, very, very dark. She approached the desk sergeant, stood there shrinking before his considerable frame.

– Hello, missy. Is it anything I can do for you?

She had always hated to be addressed in such a manner, but she held her tongue.

– Yes, she said, – I would like to speak to an investigative officer, please.

– Okay, he said, suddenly very drawling. – Is there something in particular I can tell him in advance?

– I would like to tell him everything in person, she said quietly. – It's very important.

She was led into a room where the window had been covered in drapers. After she had waited there well over an hour a man entered the room and sat down by the opposite side of the table.

– Hello, young lady. I'm Lieutenant Petersen. What can I do for you?

That was another title she didn't much care for.

– I was raped last night, she stated, without raising her voice significantly.

– Raped, you say? Suddenly he swallowed hard, as he saw a pleasant afternoon go down the drain. – What happened?

He made himself busy, procuring a notebook and a pen from his pocket.

– I was on my way home when I was dragged off and then he d-did it to me. He tore off my clothes and raped me. Afterwards he gave me a new set of clothes before releasing me.

He nodded, wrote a bit in his book, before looking warily at her.

– Did you get to take a good look at him, he who did this to you? Did you recognize him from somewhere?

– Yes, she replied. – I saw him as clearly as I see you now. I did recognize him. His name is Jeffrey Cumbes.

He stopped taking notes. As she watched him he put down the book and pen and left it there on the table, as if it was contaminated or something.

– So, what happened? He asked again.

He leaned forward, resting his jaw on top of folded hands, while keeping his attention on her somewhat. It looked ridiculous.

– The bikers kidnapped me and brought me to his tent by the river. There he pulled me into the tent and then he raped me.

He paused a bit, making a very deliberate study of the back of his hand before proceeding.

– Did you resist him?

– Of course, I did, she replied, the signs of distress now clearly, finally entering her voice. – But he was big and strong and…

– Do you have any physical marks anywhere?

He asked the question very casually.

– I was afraid, she whispered. – I was so very afraid.

He nodded.

– We will certainly look into the matter, he stated absentmindedly. – And then, after the investigation is concluded we will come back to you.

That, to her, sounded more like a threat than a true assurance.

He left the paper and pen on the table as he escorted her out of the room.

She shook her head. That was all she managed to do. Inside, where everything hurt, everything hurt more now. She found herself on the street outside the station, as she kept shaking her head, as she wandered aimlessly through the streets. After a while she just sat down in the snow and remained there until she realized that her butt was cold. She returned to her home, to her room, to her records.

A few days passed. Then they picked her up again. She was taken to the tent, to Jeffrey. This time she fought physically against him, to no avail. She was driven home and released a few hours later. This time she went to the police the same evening, showing them her bruises and wounds.

She started skipping the theater practice. She didn't have the passion for it anymore. It didn't seem of much importance. Let it go. On a day on her way home from school she noticed the whispers and stares for the first time. She stopped abruptly, suddenly gripped by a powerful need to explain everything to them, explain it in explicit ways. Her shoulders sagged, as she saw before her the endless years ahead, where all this wouldn't go away, but on the contrary increase, in both frequency and strength. Everything had changed so fast, and it seemed so long ago. The time since before they had first come for her... it seemed like years, and it was only a few weeks. She lifted her head, a bitter taint lighting her eyes, as she turned and headed for the river.

It was day. She had always seen the camp in the evening, at night. They didn't notice her, not at first, but then they did, and they proceeded with their own form of whispering, of staring. She didn't care. Ultimately, they didn't matter. Only Jeffrey mattered. She saw him with several half-naked girls, all wooing for his attention. He had fucked them, too, at first, but then left them to his gang, his entire gang. He spotted her. She smiled to him. There was no discernible reaction in his features, but she felt his interest. Heat rose in her like fire for the first time. She walked to the tent, never taking her eyes off him. He didn't take his eyes off her. Her smile broadened. She waited for him just inside the tent, taking him into her embrace, kissing his lips.

– Hello, Jeffrey, she whispered. – Lovely Jeffrey.

– Nobody understands you, he said, – but I do.

– Yes, you do, she said softly, rewarding him with huge, moist eyes.

She walked to the bed, shaking her hips, but not overdoing it. It felt so natural, like she had always been doing it. She smiled sweetly, enticingly back to him, as she crawled into the soft, huge nest, her nest, as she undressed, slowly, deliberately. The young, growing body appeared from its chrysalis, and she knew he wanted her, wanted her bad. She could always tell.

The next day he gave her her own leather jacket. She wore it with pride. Everybody could see that. The bikers, as she sat behind Jeffrey (beloved Jeffrey) on his bike, as she walked around town alone. Nobody dared touch her, even though the whispers and stares naturally persisted and grew. She treated them all for what they were worth - nothing.

Snow dissolved around her, ground, air and sky.

The theater was closed. Without her, it hadn't been the same, they told her. She kept her contact with the sister and the two brothers, without being able to tell why. They did of course represent something she had left behind, a link to her past, but she didn't really want that. So she couldn't tell why. She accepted it with a shrug, the same way she accepted everything.

Some days all her time was spent with the bikers, but there could be weeks without contact with them. She realized that Jeffrey wanted to keep her to himself, and that he did so by keeping her away. The thought brought a warm thrill to her spine, and caused her to snarl contemptuously at herself in her shame.

Spring arrived. May could be cold, but this year it grew hot. Dust and soil spiraled through the air. In the schoolyard there was, like there was everywhere kids and adults taking stock, gathering in groups, sticking to their chosen tribe. She saw that easily now, seeing it from the outside. Tilla spoke briefly with Ted and Linda, humoring them, humoring herself.

– Mike is angry about something, Ted said, shaking his head. – He won't say anything, but I can tell.

– No wonder, Linda scolded him. – His anger is certainly justified.

She stopped, blushing a bit, a tall, scrawny girl.

– It's isn't my fault, Ted protested. – I didn't hear the sound of running water because of the infernal sound of the lawnmower, and you hadn't locked the door to the…

Tilla smiled. He was such a sweet boy.

–… to the bathroom, he completed lamely.

– So, you were actually spying on your sister taking a bath? Tilla mused. – And you don't expect your brother to be angry with you?

He turned very red then. He was so easy. They were all so easy.

They met Mike later that day. He was his usual smiling self. Tilla could sense the anger in him. It had been there for quite some time, she realized, but she hadn't been astute enough to see it before. She hadn't been astute before.

Unreal, she thought. Everything is unreal. Everything here.

The river ran by them, as it made a turn, as they passed the siblings' home. She looked at the two brothers just then. They looked at the waters, and its whirl reflected in their eyes, cold as ice.

There was a diner close by, or something that had been a diner once, but really had transformed into something new and unrecognizable. Adding to that there had been trouble in the area lately, and the place had two huge uniformed cops placed by the entrance table. Aside from that everything looked peaceful, very peaceful.

The four bought ice cream. Mike paid for it and they sat down by the table in the corner. A bit later Bob Tremblay and Frank Forester arrived. Bob tall and with quite a nice build, Frank obese beyond words. The two boys sat down by their table. Frank bought the next round of ice cream. There was talk. The afternoon cast a pleasant light in the street and inside the diner turned café, and caused the ugly white light in the ceiling to fade a bit. There was music. Tilla couldn't later say what tune. Elvis or something, she gathered. Nothing threatening. She didn't look that way, but in the other corner Absalon Falwell, called Abe, sat with his gang. He was the local bully. One year older than Mike, he dominated the younger population in the entire suburb. And so far he had been smart enough to leave the adults and the kids with more influential parents alone. And certainly smart enough to not muck around with policemen present.

Or with me, she thought proudly. He would have to be insane to do that.

No one fucked with the bikers or their girls.

The sister and the brothers seemed virtually oblivious to his presence. She studied Mike. With her experience she could do that, without him realizing she was doing it. There was nothing to study really. She thought he spoke a bit loud, but she would guess he just had reason to be excited about something and would probably share it with them eventually.

– That's a nice ring, she said to Bob. – Where did you get it?

– It has been in my family's possession for generations, he replied proudly. – Father says it symbolizes our standing in society, our elevation above the huddled masses.

– Sure, Mike laughed, a bit more than harsh.

Bob looked more than a little wounded, but he also evidently rethought his words.

It was nice ring, a very special one. It had the image of a millipede engraved in its stone, its black stone. Tilla cast it an admiring look.

– My father is a bit old-fashioned, he shrugged.

– Aren't they all? Ted suggested.

– Yes, Linda snickered. – Ours are still talking about the pool games in Lo Dow in the fifties as if they were something heavenly… and he never even played with Kerouac and bunch.

Mike rose from the chair. It seemed relaxed and all, but Tilla wasn't certain.

– Let's go, he said.

– Why? Linda asked innocently. – It's sort of nice here.

– It's such a fine day for a walk, Mike grinned.

– A typical Mike-remark. Bob emphasized his teasing with a

smile.

This would never have worked with other older boys. They had a tendency to take their frustrations out on the younger kids, but Mike wasn't like that. Tilla caught herself casting long, adoring looks at him.

He's just a boy, she thought. A sweet boy. Nothing like Jeffrey.

Mike chose the route by the Interstate. Cars passed by, and they couldn't talk without virtually screaming to each other, so they didn't try. They figured Mike had something in mind, and left it all to him. Mike turned to Tilla and parted his lips in the midst of the worst traffic noise. What had he said? Something about «innocent»? The others had certainly not heard him. She turned cold all over. Her heart was hammering, like a ticking of a clock.

They realized they were on their way to school, to the schoolyard. Ted protested loudly.

– Hey, don't you think we're spending more than enough time here as it is?

– Humor me, will you?

And they did, of course. He could always get them where he wanted them.

He's so charming, Tilla thought dreamily.

Not long after that they found themselves at the center of the yard. They were alone there.

– Doesn't it feel different? Mike asked them sheepishly. – It sure does to me. I remember fairly well how it used to feel. Can you sense the space, how big it is without teachers, adults or crowds of gawking kids?

– You're right, Bob said. – The «feel» is completely different. How come we've never tried this before?

– It just didn't occur to you, Mike said, suddenly absentmindedly. – We're taught to obey, serve and please. Not to think. We're raised as slaves, fit only to grovel at the master's feet.

The redhead's skin… crawled. She looked at Mike, followed the line of his sight. Abe entered the yard in front of his court. The gate squeaked this time. It hadn't done so when they had entered through it just a minute or so earlier. Mike nodded and nodded, like he was humming a melody only he could hear, moving to a rhythm only he could sense.

– Be calm, he admonished them. – There's a lot to be frightened about, but not now. I saw him at the cafeteria. I knew he would come for me. He has wanted to do it for some time, but he has been distracted, with that pig-brain of his. I wanted to choose the time and the place.

Ted looked at him. Linda looked at him. They tried to speak, but couldn't.

– W-why didn't you tell the t-two policemen? Frank stuttered.

– That would have taken care of it then, but merely postponed the inevitable. I figured I would just take a few hits and be done with it.

Bob and Frank pulled away from him. Ted, Linda and Tilla remained. Tilla heard the rush of the river in her ears, the loud noise of passing cars and trucks on the interstate.

The other group reached them. Most stopped a few steps away. Abe took two more, stopping right in front of Mike.

– Hello, he said.

Mike hit him in the abdomen. It happened so fast that none of the onlookers had seen it coming. Abe crouched violently and released a loud gasp. Mike slapped him on the cheek and he was thrown backwards in the dust.

– I could have pressed my advantage now, and finished you, he said in a rather relaxed manner, – but I want to make a point.

Abe dried the blood from his mouth, as he rose and started to circle the other boy. He was grinning.

– So, you do have guts, after all, he said pleased.

He attacked with a familiar viciousness, well known and feared among the youths. Tilla knew he didn't underestimate the other, inexperienced boy. She had seen enough of stuff like this now, to see that. He moved deliberately, hitting Mike with a heavy, rock-hard fist on the side of the face. Mike staggered back, blood flowing from his mouth and nose. Abe struck out with his left hand, another crushing blow to the opposite side of the other boy's face… and he missed. Mike struck him in the belly. It was an ill-delivered blow hitting hard muscles, but Abe still gasped out aloud, though it didn't keep him from lashing out with a wild blow directed at Mike's genitals. Mike jumped backwards, and the fist merely brushed against his thigh.

– What's the matter with you, boy, are ya chicken?

Mike didn't reply. It could hardly be said that he reacted at all. If anything, he seemingly showed no interest in what was going on, as if he was watching something boring on television, as if he would rather do something else.

The two circled one another. Abe nodded, as if he had just confirmed something to himself. They circled, steadily closing in on the opponent. Abe primarily used his fists, but he was fast on his feet like a price fighter, a boxer. Suddenly he was very, very close. He gave Mike an uppercut. It didn't miss Mike's jaw completely, and he fell backwards. Abe could have pressed his advantage, but didn't. He waited, shrewd and canny, but was still completely ill prepared for what was to come. Mike jumped up and threw himself at the enemy, kicking him in the chest. Everybody heard it, the sound of ribs breaking. Abe cried out in pain, but stood his ground. He hit Mike on the side of the head, just as Mike was straightening from the kick. Mike shook his head, but seemed totally unaffected. He struck the other close to the eyes, causing the area of the face to swell. He struck again. The others watched dumbfounded, shocked. It was like an onslaught of fury and wind. Mike was, suddenly transformed from the boy they had known, to something… alien. Abe returned the blows, but started to miss, and to miss often. He staggered backwards, as he was defending himself, only defending himself. Mike struck him with a right swing, a hard, harsh blow. There was a crack as the bone in Abe's nose broke. The big boy backed off using his considerable technical prowess to keep the other at bay, only at bay. Suddenly his eyes widened. He discovered that he had backed all the way into a corner, the corner where the walls met, and he yelped in horror.

Tilla relived a few moments at the diner, then. She saw Mike look at Abe. She heard Abe say something seemingly totally unrelated.

– People surely are talking loud today.

She was back in the yard, in the corner, with the two boys.

Mike, with a mighty roar shoved Abe at the wall, and held him there and lashed out with his fist. The wall shook. They could all hear it. They could all see it. Pushed against the wall nothing protected Abe from the full force of the blow. The fist sank deep into his belly. All air wheezed from his lungs. He would have doubled over and fallen if Mike hadn't held him in place. Mike struck him again. His face was seemingly moved from one place to another in an instant. Mike struck again. And again. The fight had long since ended, but he kept at it. Abe wasn't unconscious, but getting there. All fight had left him. But the pain kept him awake, and he screamed. Mike kept going, as if he would drive home some point or another to exhaustion. Those watching, unable to look away started to wonder if he wanted to kill the other boy.

And then he stopped. That was almost the most frightening part of all. One moment he was the incarnation of rage, and then… nothing. It had all vanished, returned to where it had originated; his smoldering inner cauldron.

The time was far from midnight, but the dark clouds above made it turn dark like Night.

It chilled Tilla to the bone.

Abe slid down the wall, left there in the corner like a heap of garbage in a sack.

During the nights, in her sleep, in the months to come, she would slumber with this smoldering anger, this overwhelming rage rolling within her, like it had become a part of her, as if he had transferred it or shared it somehow.

Ted took one step forward and said quietly:

– Anybody else have anything to say?

There were no takers.

Mike stood there, victorious. His eyes flashed in red and fire. Tilla compared it to the color on photos after the use of flash. She could never have dreamed it would look so frightening in reality.

– Leave us, he ordered. – I will call upon you at a later date, at my convenience.

They left the schoolyard the same way they had arrived, through the gate. It didn't squeak this time. They left Abe, their former so fearsome leader there in the corner, in the dust.

Mike looked at Ted. Tilla and Linda looked at them both.

– It is such a fine day, the oldest of the dark brothers said, drawing breath. – Such a fine day for a walk.

They walked for hours.

They walked to an old, abandoned industrial area. Some of the buildings had roofs, some didn't. There was a mill there. Water was running. Green nature had reclaimed most of the place. There was just an occasional spot of gray left.

– You got some nasty bruises here. She touched his head carefully, tenderly.

– Leave it, he said. – It is only pain.

Tilla lifted her head with a start. She had fallen asleep, hadn't she? She couldn't really remember much afterwards, of the time they spent at the old mill, but she remembered this. She sat on the ground in the ruin a bit removed from the others, but she felt the heat from the fire. It burned and hurt her.

– The dance, the ancient dance begins, he told her.

She woke up with a start in her room, she knew she did, but she was still in a desert, and the Mike standing in front of her was transparent, ethereal. And very different from how she had previously experienced him.

There was fire rising from the ground and the sound of a thousand feet dancing.

There was a fire somewhere, in the biker camp, somewhere outside the Chief's tent.

– You know, I do value your advice. Jeffrey snickered. – You're a tough little cookie.

He paused a bit, before continuing.

– And if you repeat that to anybody outside this place I will kill you.

She smiled her soft smile, and stretched pleasantly on the bed, her huge, pleasant bed.

He swallowed hard.

She never said anything, but she let her displeasure be known in smaller and bigger ways.

He came to her one day. She welcomed him, as always with her kisses and her embrace, but something was clearly... amiss. He didn't notice it immediately, but just before he was about to enter her, he realized that her response wasn't as it usually was. He fucked her anyway, but it was strangely unsatisfying. He sat on the bedside afterwards with a frown in her face.

– Is everything all right? He asked, not realizing how

uncharacteristic that was for him.

– Everything is perfectly all right, beloved Jeffrey, she wooed.
– I love you, Jeffrey.

Later that night. She sat around the campfire with the other bikers and girls, enjoying herself, drinking beer, drinking wine, sensing the pleasant warmth spread from her stomach. He sat down a while after that, on his reserved spot.

– You know, what we were discussing earlier today, he said to them. – I have thought about it and changed my mind. It's no big thing really.

They nodded and thought nothing of it. He was known for occasionally changing his mind.

The two of them were in bed. The fires outside burned, burned higher than he could recall they ever did. She moved under him, moved as she had never done before. He gasped aloud, as he let himself be devoured by her cold and hot embrace.

She sat before the mirror, brushing her hair, the mirror he had procured for her. There was a swelling inside her, like that of a swamp expanding when exposed to water. She knew this was the smile her grandmother had baptized «ugly». The realization made it grow even wider.

The summer waxed and waned, like a tiny, tiny, full, full moon, the red, red moon. Nobody knew it, and nothing was ever revealed, but Jeffrey Cumbes no longer ran the bikers. In small and big ways, with hints and with hardly ever needing to actually say anything aloud…

She did.

– It's strange, she told Linda in one of their private moments, girl to girl. – It's all so ephemeral, but then, suddenly I can feel it. I can feel the entire world in my hand, and I can squeeze it like the rotten apple it is.

Linda didn't speak. She just sat there, frozen and silent. Tilla smiled and patted her cheek, leaving her, leaving herself.

Autumn came, with its fall and cold. She stood outside the tent in her morning gown, and received the dire news. Jeffrey was dead. He had driven off a cliff and had been crushed to a pulp by the rocks far below. All her efforts had been for naught, and the realization hit her, perhaps for the first time, how illusory power was. They looked at her. They all looked at her, Keith Lampard most of all. His features revealed a very possessive expression. The others might not see it, but she did. She walked back into the tent. She stayed there and waited. He would come. She knew how it worked. He would wait until he held all the cards, had gathered all the necessary threads in his hands, but eventually he would come.

There was a commotion outside, hardly noticeable at first. She lifted her head from the bed and rose, walked outside. Her eyes caught Mike instantly. He entered the camp walking. She didn't see him until he had almost arrived, but the others had surely discovered him far down the road. Tilla Stevens looked at Mike Cousin. She had hardly seen him since that day in early spring, but now she saw him, saw him for the first time.

It said a lot about the reputation he had gained the last few months that nobody even attempted to stop his ascent to the camp. Perhaps it also had something to do with the fact that he came alone, and fully in the open, without even the slightest attempt at hiding. Perhaps.

He stopped on a spot, a place that fit him, not anyone of those he spoke to. He spoke to no one in particular. The people in the camp all felt included in his embrace. He spoke, and they listened.

– I hear you're in dire need of a new leader, he said. – I'm happy to accept the job.

That was all. He didn't say more. He didn't have to. Keith Lampard crumbled in his tracks, sliding into the background, the chorus line from which he had come.

Tilla took one step forward. Mike turned slightly and looked at her. She yawned, stretching her body deliberately and clearly enjoying herself doing it, letting him see her for the first time. His eyes started flashing, slowly, in interest and burning desire.

That was all. He turned and left the same way he had arrived. Nothing more needed to be said really. They all knew the score. Tilla was left completely alone in the tent. They brought her food, but didn't disturb her in any way. She didn't see Lampard at all anymore that day.

Words are often unnecessary, she thought.

He came to her early in the evening. She heard him outside, and knew it was him, long before he actually appeared in the tent.

She sat on the bed, practically naked, with only a thin scarf hiding her shoulders and upper body. As he started to walk towards her she let it slip from her fingers. It slid down on the bed. There was a sudden gust of wind, and it vanished. To where she didn't know.

– You have never looked at me this way before, she said huskily.

He didn't reply. Not in words.

– Don't worry, I kinda like it…

– I'm not worried.

Even his voice had changed, had turned harsh and accentuated by the edges. She shivered there in the warm tent.

He undressed there before her, casually and indifferently. She saw how his cock grew and kept growing and she crouched there on the bed. He descended on her and his shadow covered her like night. The fire outside didn't reach her anymore. The fire was all here, with her, like a black sun burning.

She sat behind him on his bike. He stopped it on a dusty road at the top of a cliff. They were alone. He turned the engine off. They sat there a while, in silence looking at the sunset. The twilight crept into them. She observed how he involuntarily shuddered, and understood why instantly. She understood him so well.

– I thought I understood power, she whispered. – But that was before I saw you, the real you… before you bloomed. You *are* Power.

Flashes of reality. She saw herself grow, change from the girl she had been.

– So strange, she mused, standing before the mirror, letting him see her. – The biggest difference isn't the body at all, but the eyes. Have you looked into your eyes?

– They say they are windows to the soul, he said dryly.

And then gooseflesh broke out all over her body.

He patted the bed. He didn't encourage her to come.

He ordered her.

Her eyes narrowed, narrowed as she turned towards him, as she with a sweet smile walked to him. She steeled herself, determined to close herself off from her raging insides, the human cauldron boiling within her.

– I take my cue from you, she said. – Control yourself and you control the world.

She crawled into his lap, smiling as she took his head in her hands, kissing him with cold lips.

He's just fifteen, just a boy.

And I am…

I am twelve. I'm still twelve.

She touched him, touched his cover. He always used rubber. Jeffrey had never bothered with that. She freed herself from his embrace and placed herself on the bed, on her back, allowing him do as he wanted, but no more than that. He pumped into her and she felt nothing, except the familiar, exhilarating triumph.

He leaned on his elbow, looking down at her. His eyes… She suddenly found herself breathless. The fire was dancing in their depths. His face seemed to expand above her, covering her entire field of vision. He started to caress her left thigh. He did so casually, indifferently, like he was touching a piece of meat. And he was. She realized that he was.

– Stop, Mike, she said sourly. – Please, I'm not in the mood.

He slapped her on the cheek. Not hard. It was hardly more than a touch, but it burned nevertheless. She looked astonished at him. He grabbed her hair, pulling her to him, pushing his own lips at hers so hard that it hurt. His free hand was all over her body now. She was completely at his mercy and knew it. She had known it all along. He… *touched* her then. She gasped out aloud, fighting the cauldron inside for one heartbeat, two, then surrendering to it, writhing on the bed, moaning, begging him with moist eyes. So fast, it had happened so fast. It had always taken her such a long time to be aroused. And now aroused was hardly the correct word anymore. She whimpered, attempting to pull him close to her. He slapped her, first on one cheek, then on the other.

He rose, leaving the bed.

– If you're even close to playing with yourself, I'll beat you senseless, he warned her.

She believed him. The truth of his words sank deep inside her, and stayed there forever.

He dressed, evidently intending to go outside. He left her. She looked at him through wide and haze-filled eyes.

– You shouldn't attempt the ice-maiden tactic too frequent with me, you know. I can't stand icicles. It might be a pleasant diversion, but no more than that. Too much of a good thing may lead to… unpleasant results.

She understood. Understanding was hammered into her like nails.

Keith Lampard's face appeared in her inner vision. His different looking eyes never gave her rest.

She remained alone there, in the tent, there in the darkness, burning with a need that made her cry in despair. Tears, huge and wet flowed down her cheeks. And it didn't fade, but grew as the hours passed slowly by.

It was almost morning when she heard the sound of the characteristic steps outside the tent. She stopped breathing in anticipation, scared to death that he would change his mind and turn back. He appeared in the opening, a sun in a human body. He just looked at her.

– You don't n-need me, she said haltingly, sniffing hard. – You don't need anybody. But I need you. I need you so much. Please, Mike.

And by those words everything was forever defined between them.

She had told herself once, in a distant past, that he was nothing like Jeffrey… and she had been right.

The next day, when she woke up completely spent, hot and in a haze of pleasure, he was already up and around. She focused on his face, concentrating on being astute, because that was what he wanted of her.

– I have a present for you, he grinned.

– A present? Joy and apprehension warred within her.

– Yeah, get dressed. The place in question is quite a distance away.

A long trip somewhere was the last thing she wanted now, or ever for that matter, but she just smiled and started dressing in his presence. They emerged from the tent, the sharp light of the sun blinding her. He didn't seem to notice. For a moment her eyes flooded with tears. She dried them as she often did, in quick, short draws. The camp, this early had a quality of silence. She didn't look at the others, at the bikers and their female ornaments. She never did. The look of utter contempt didn't leave her features.

The two of them walked. They often did. She had noticed how firm her body and limbs had grown the last month. He trained her in combat, too, as if he was grooming her. In a backward way he trained her to be self-reliant, even though she knew she would never be. Just another of his wiles, she gathered. He did it because it pleased him, as he did all things.

They walked far, to a place where there actually was a forest, not just a few withered trees. She hit the trees with her knuckles.

– Harder, he ordered. – Much harder.

She obeyed in a blind rage. When she long afterwards looked at her knuckles they were bleeding.

– So, do you think your little bandoleer girl can take on big bad hulks of men, now? She asked subdued.

– Not yet, he replied, – but you will.

– Where have you learned, anyway? She asked defiant with her hands on her hips, knowing that he loved it. – You've never been to any sort of practice or one of those martial arts schools so popular on the west coast these days.

– You, like most people are deeply rooted in insecurity. His voice, his eyes smothered her like mist a dry night. – You're unable to believe humans can learn on their own, without the «benefit» of teachers. So, I'm gonna teach you. I'm gonna force you to teach yourself.

Cold. So cold. She saw the cabin ahead, and it brought all kinds of emotions to her.

– You're not making sense, she said exasperated. – Why are you doing this, all this?

Power, a sweet inner voice replied to her. Sweet, sweet power.

He didn't bother replying, and she lowered her head in that confused well of emotions.

A present? What kind of present? Anticipation and fear still raged within her.

– No, I'm not playing with you here, he said, as if she had spoken aloud. – I *will* truly give you a present, a gift you *will* most certainly appreciate. You're a bright girl, you'll figure it out.

Figure out what?

A gift? Perhaps something not actually physical, but more like…

A boon. A bone to be thrown to the loyal bitch.

He waited, letting her open the door, letting her walk inside first.

And then the world completely stopped making sense to her.

Ted hung from a hook in the ceiling. He was tightly bound, and blood and bloody skin remains were seemingly spread around everywhere. Tilla Stevens saw Ted Cousin for the first time. Truly saw him. She saw the rage, the despair, the black abysmal hole somewhere in his eyes, the bottomless pit of fire.

And then she understood.

Part two: The Road Back

Chapter six

Man and Beast stared attentive at each other. The large, brown bull stamped viciously with its forelegs, blowing steam from its nostrils. The human felt the nervousness like a thousand crawling ants in his guts. He knew that the heavy meat on two legs could attack at any moment.

– Your horse is inexperienced, Butch Davison commented.

– He has never handled more than yearlings before. The bull senses that.

– And to top that off, Kevin Davison, the twin brother, grinned big, – we're smack in the middle of the mating season. The guy is brimming with testosterone…

The rider staring at the beast knew it to be true. The half-grown calves usually pulled back when the horse and rider approached. It was completely different for a horse to meet an adult, fully-grown and enraged animal. Terrified the young stallion attempted to back off. The rider needed to use all his power to make it remain in position.

In the valley there were several others - both men and beasts. Yet the rider could see nothing more than the bull, the horse and his own diluted features. Everything else vanished in a daze of red and black. Thoughts drifted for a second. The image of the meat straight ahead turned indistinct, changed into a human face…

Then the bull jumped.

It happened so fast that the rider was taken by surprise. And the animal didn't jump at him, but bolted in the opposite direction, exactly like a frightened animal. He hadn't expected this, but collected himself pretty quickly. Clenching his teeth he spurred the horse. The young stallion turning braver the instant it saw the «enemy» running away. With a loud shriek, sounding nothing like a horse at all, the stallion galloped after the bull. Signifying a calm he didn't actually feel, the rider loosened the lasso from the saddle. He knew, by experience that the heavy animal hadn't completely put off the idea of an attack yet. If it reached the end of the valley and the cliff-like rocks it would be very dangerous following it further. The young, powerfully built boy knew that and used all the skills he had attained as a rider to catch up with the bull before it reached the end of the pasture.

He heard the thunderous hooves of the horse against the ground and felt free, free as a bird, to the point where he actually imagined he could sense the flapping of wings.

Then the bull was only a few stretches away. With a strange glow in his eyes the boy swung the lasso above his head - and threw it. The bull turned its head violently to avoid it, but the rope inevitably fell around its neck. The rider made the horse halt abruptly, and the meat on four legs, taken totally by surprise fell hard enough to make the ground shake.

The rider instantly jumped off the horse, and grabbed the bull's legs.

– The iron, fast, he shouted.

Several people approached the boy and the hard-breathing beast on the ground. Experienced hands held down the animal while the brand was burned into its butt. The bull bellowed desperately. The stink of burning flesh made the men's noses itch.

– Let it go... NOW!

Everybody rose abruptly, simultaneously, but the beast wasn't far away. It snorted and carried itself like an enraged bull in an arena. All its fury turned towards the humans who had hurt it, but it was too late. Everybody who had held it down, who had burned it, who had taken part in its humiliation, had returned to horseback, and if there was anything it had quickly learned to respect there was a man on a horseback. Depressed and heavily carrying its wounded pride, it slunk away.

– Damn me, Teddy, a freckled kid said. – You did it. I didn't think you could.

– You own me ten bucks, Linsey, Ted grinned.

Linsey Kendall returned the grin tenfold. He had long red blond hair sticking out in every direction, confirming the unruly impression.

A ten-dollar bill discreetly changed ownership.

– I could feel its rage, you know, Ted said to him later as they rode side by side, away from the two other boys and the adults.
– Its humiliation and despair, as if we virtually castrated the

126

poor fucker.

There was silence, before Linsey finally replied.

– I felt it, too initially, the first few times, he confessed. – It fades after a while. You get used to it.

– You get used to everything, you mean. Ted said, clearly agitated.

This time there was no reply. They didn't speak as they joined the rest of the hunting party.

There were more bulls, more noise and animal screams. Ted could sense how the horse grew more confident, more aggressive, as it convinced itself there was nothing to fear.

– Your horse is still behaving in a shitty way, the older, experienced Scott Thompson told him.

– I hadn't noticed, Ted shrugged.

– Usually they're okay after the first few try-outs, but this one has been nervous already from the moment we left the stable this morning.

– Almost as if it knew what to expect, another one joked.

The others laughed. Ted did, too, even though the solemn expression didn't completely leave his face.

He sat on the horse, on a hill a bit later, breathing hard. The animal kept moving, as if it had an itch somewhere it couldn't scratch. He gave up the attempt of making it stand still. There had been more bulls, more screams, more dust. He looked at the valley below, the scene of cattle grazing, the smoke rising from the cluster of buildings on a rise somewhat at the center, the main ranch houses and the barn. He studied the strangers below, his comrades in arms for more than two years, knowing they looked at him, shaking their head and wondering about what they deemed his «brooding», but he didn't care.

Two years. He could hardly believe it. Two years since he had arrived here, at the home of his uncle and aunt, his cousins, in the southern part of Colorado. Almost three years since he had left Denver. He touched his arm, hard and swollen with muscle. The fabric of the red-squared pattern shirt was like woven tight around the skin, not only on the arm, but all over his body. The muscles had been slow to show at first, but then they had seemingly appeared all over him like a growth independent of the body, of his old body, filling his clothes to the max. The shirt would have looked posy on most boys or men, including everybody of the well-trained cowboys on the ranch. It had been on him, when he first wore it.

The main building had been raised on a low hill, a round top distinct from the otherwise flat land.

– Nothing beats a Colorado sunset, Eugene Kendall said to Lex Barker.

– True, boss, Barker agreed. – Very true.

– Your favorite slogan again, father? Elizabeth said.

Kendall looked sharply at his daughter.

– Explain yourself, young lady.

– Well, she said shrugging. – In this case that's fairly easy. I'm sure many sunsets elsewhere in the world can favorably compare to your famous Colorado sunsets.

Elizabeth was not yet twelve, but well developed for her age, very well developed.

– Well, I should head back and see how the guys are doing, Barker said nervously. – Be seeing you, boss.

Coward, Kendall thought sourly.

Elizabeth smiled blindingly as her father turned his complete attention to her.

– I don't appreciate you bothering us after a long hard day, he told her sternly.

– Okay, daddy, she said lightly. – I'll keep my highly intelligent observations of the Universe to myself today.

She remained there, by his side, basking in the awkward silence.

– I agree with you, by the way, she stated. – It is a beautiful sight. That's why I don't understand why it's necessary to demean it, by attempting to elevate it above all the other beautiful places.

She was tall, already reaching him above his shoulders. All the three children were, taking after their mother, but she was tall. She had always been well developed for her age, he thought, straight from the cradle. She reminded him quite a lot of her two dark cousins, with the dark brown hair and the less than fair skin tone, darker than even her mother. He had always wondered where that had come from. He had.

– Can you feel it? She asked abruptly. – Feel the abundant life under rocks, between bushes and below the water, the whipping of the branches as the horses and riders move through the bush by the river, hear the river itself as it runs across the land?

– I think I can, he nodded.

– I can, she said dreamingly. – It is like I'm there.

– One thing, he said abruptly, very abruptly.

– Yes, daddy? She turned to him, with her wonderful big, blue eyes and innocent expression.

– I've wanted to talk to you for some time, now, he began.

– About what, daddy?

– Well, for one thing you only call me «daddy» when you've got something to hide or want to mellow me… Actually, there's a number of things I've wanted to talk to you about.

He turned his head a few times, looking closely at the surroundings. There was nobody else around. This was the ideal opportunity, if there ever was an ideal opportunity.

– For some time now, I've told you that we don't lock doors here, but still you do that. I don't know why you persist in this. It is important that you stop. We don't need keys out here. We never have, and we never will.

– But it is not I locking doors, she grinned. – You are.

– Only because you ring the bell far too early every day, he said with a pointed stare. – I have to lock the door to the cabinet to keep you from having access to the bell. And since you were clever enough to bypass the lock somehow, I had to lock the door to the shed, too.

He was about to become the laughing stock of the entire area because of this. People had certainly reminded him about it often enough.

– I had to do it. You work your servants too hard, father. They don't have a life of their own because of that.

He glared at her. They had often, to frustration on his part discussed the «realities of economics». She had a mind sharp as a whip, and he failed in the task of enlightening her about the way the world worked.

– They receive a handsome salary for that «hard» work, he said firmly. – But you seek to avoid the subject here once again and I won't have it. And don't call the workers for «servants.» You will not ring the bell anymore, do you understand?

– D-daddy, you're purple blue in the face…

He saw her scared expression through a haze of red, and forced himself to relax. She often had that effect on him. He could hardly believe how fast it had happened this time, like the turning of a switch.

– I'm sorry, daddy. I won't do it anymore, honest. I'm *sorry*.

He calmed down slowly, only with the greatest of efforts.

– It's all right, he breathed. – It's all right.

He saw the children playing down in the valley with sheets covering them. He saw it again. It always served to distract him.

– Do you know who they are? She asked with undeniable curiosity evident in her voice. – I don't either.

He kept shaking his head. She did that a lot, too: Answering her own questions.

She was a bright kid.

Perhaps too bright, but he would never say that thought aloud.

– The very sight of them gives me the funny feeling, she said.

She caught herself, before saying more. She knew very well he didn't exactly enjoy any subject touching «funny feelings».

She pulled back, removed herself from him, the hurt very evident in her eyes. He wanted to say something, anything to break the silence, but he couldn't bring himself to do it.

Elizabeth Kendall hurried to her room. The room was on the second floor. She saw it as her private space, even though she shared it with her sister June. June wasn't there right then. Of course, she wasn't, in the middle of the day. Elizabeth was alone. She stood there, on the middle of the floor, rigid and tense, fixing her eyes on the poster on the wall. There were no pictures on it, only text, handwritten text. It was homemade. She smiled.

FATHER'S WORDS

Thou shall not speak back to the teachers
(even though the teachers are
impolite, intolerant, ignorant shites)
Thou shall not lock any doors
(even though poor servants need rest, too)

Thou shall not bathe in the river
(even though nudity is perfectly natural)
Thou shall not question thy parents' word
(good girls don't do that)

She pondered a bit, before grabbing the pencil and adding more on the poster (where there was yet a lot of room):

Thou shall not speak disrespectfully
of our country's leaders
(even though they have not earned any respect)

She read it aloud, in a hasty, mumbling voice, repeating it like a mantra. The smile faded. She walked, wandered aimlessly, endlessly back and forth across the room. There were shadows in the room. Clouds drifted across the floor. The dark sunshine shadowed the girl's face. The Sun was about to set. The girl finally halted her restless march by the window. She looked outside. Mother and Father stood in the yard, arguing about something.

– Three guesses, the girl said bitterly.

She lifted her head slightly, looking at the five children playing in the valley below. The valley was shrouded in shadow. The rays of the setting sun didn't reach down there. But she could still see them, see the sheets they covered themselves with shake in the wind.

There was something… She… heard the wind, even though it was not very strong today. She heard it. It felt like she was the wind, riding the airwaves down in the valley. She stood before the mirror, studying herself, looking into her own eyes, drowning in their remote, desolate quality, trembling, tearing herself away as fear grabbed her and shook her like a doll.

She stood trembling before the window, attempting to embrace herself with her arms, her way too short arms.

Everything turned dark, very dark, and it was like hours, like days passed by her, there, in her loneliness. And whatever made it turn dark, whatever turned seconds into hours made her shiver and moan.

Something outside… distracted her. There was shouting,

and noise, the sound of hooves on the ground. She looked up. Ted and Linsey returned from work, far too early. A moment she stood there, frozen in place, before leaving the room and running down the stairs.

There was dust, shimmering in the dying sun's rays, loud, overwhelming noises assaulting her senses.

Suddenly a whole crowd assembled there in the courtyard. Linsey more hung than sat at the back of his horse. Ted was already on the ground to help him down. Linsey's features were contracted in pain. More willing hands arrived. In the commotion it could be described as a miracle that something actually got done, but they managed somehow to lift Linsey off the horse and lower him to the ground.

– It's the shoulder, Linsey gasped. – It's broken. Nothing serious. Don't worry.

But the pain was so strong that it seemed to emanate from him in waves they all could sense. Nobody noticed, but Elizabeth turned white, white as milk.

– What happened, son? Eugene asked, as the commotion was slowly fading, and a kind of normality was restored.

Linsey blushed, looking at Ted, strangely enough, before proceeding.

– I fell off the horse, he said, clearly ashamed. – It was one of the fucking young studs. Ted and I searched down by the river for a calf, and the maniac charged us. I'm willing to bet his grandfather or something was on an arena. Ted rode a horse used to such behavior, but mine was young and inexperienced. It panicked and threw me off like a rag doll. It happened so sudden, daddy. I've never seen anything like it.

Kendall senior froze a moment then, before shrugging.

– Don't worry about it, son. The main thing is that you're not seriously wounded. You'll probably be all right, with nothing but wounded pride to mark the memory in a month or so.

Laughter, not unkind, spread through the assembly.

– Enough talk, Trudy Kendall said. – You have all enjoyed yourself long enough. Let's get him to bed.

Lex Barker and Scott Thompson, the only two cowboys, except the family with a steady employment on the ranch, lifted him carefully, until he stood on his own shaky legs. Elizabeth,

June and Mother gathered around him, giving him comforting touches.

– You shouldn't make such a fuss over it, he mumbled. – I've just broken the shoulder. It's not like it's the end of the world or anything.

Elizabeth grabbed him around the shoulder, grabbed him hard. He cried out in pain.

– Sorry, she apologized, but as he looked at her, through waves of blinding pain, she didn't look very much like she was sorry.

More laughter, a bit more subdued and uncertain.

– This could be quite a complicated fracture, Kendall said. – Doc Kennedy should take a look at it, and since that old geezer refuses to have a phone installed one of us have to go and get him.

– I'll go, Thompson said.

– Okay, take the car and…

– I'll take the horse, boss, the other man said quickly.

– That old wreck, Scott? Elizabeth said teasingly.

There was more laughter.

– My Blackie is of a long line of royal horses, I have… My family has been breeding them through generations.

Thompson was quite a humorless man.

– It's just a horse. Elizabeth shrugged.

She stopped haltingly, before looking back at Ted, who hadn't said a word and hardly moved since he had helped Linsey down from his horse. She walked to him.

– You should freshen up and change clothes, she told him huskily. – Don't worry about the horses. I'll take them to the stable. I'll groom them and take care of them as if they were my babies…

– You're right, girl. Ted smiled. – It has been a hard day and I am tired. I think I'll go to bed just after the evening meal.

Kendall stopped for a moment on the threshold of the house, listening to the short conversation, the brief exchange of words, but it was already over before it had started. Ted joined the rest in the kitchen. Elizabeth ran like the wind to the stable with the two beaten down horses.

Still, he couldn't help but keep running the conversation

through his head for the rest of the evening.
**********************************/

The tall body on the bed was Ted Cousin. He was fully dressed under the quilt. His eyes were closed, but he didn't sleep. As always, in his frequent moments of loneliness unwelcome thoughts buzzed through his head like angry bees.

Sometimes he wondered how different his life would have become if he had stayed in Chicago, if he had remained there throughout the coming year, during the «Days of Rage», where autonomous rebels and members of the revolutionary movement The Weathermen had clashed with units from the police and the army. Sometimes he couldn't understand why he hadn't.

He thought about Europe, where the first, initial news had started to emerge about freedom fighters, about the new age of urban guerillas, from Germany, Italy, Belgium and elsewhere.

He had unfinished business here, here in Colorado, but still he wondered.

Sometimes he looked down the road from the main building, expecting Mike to come. And rage and fear would almost overcome him.

The night came. It came early in this house, as they rose before sunrise. He didn't feel tired. He wished he did. Waves of energy surged through him, and with it all the unwelcome thoughts. He lived in a basically distant, and except for in the season deserted part of the house. The sounds the family made were always muted. «Family»… The sound of that word would always sound strange to him. Coming here represented a new beginning to him, the beginning of his Change.

No, the twelfth birthday had been the beginning. The dream visions came easy. His right arm shook, and his eyes opened with a start. He realized he had been tired, after all, and that he had been sleeping. He heard steps on the stairs. The sense of Mike being close ravaged him instantly, like a suddenly open and painful wound.

But he knew it wasn't Mike. There was female humming and light steps. He would recognize those steps, that scent anywhere, even before he heard the humming. He closed his eyes, pretending to be asleep, in the hope that she would leave

134

quickly. He heard the sound of the door opening, the draft it created, the light from the hall illuminating his face. He sensed the heat on his skin.

She didn't turn and leave, but slid across the floor in a very quiet and foreboding way. He saw her before his inner eye. She walked barefoot, and stopped right by him. The door was closed now. But the moonlight covered most of his face and upper body. He kept his eyes closed, using his other senses, smelling her and sensing her breath in his ear.

– Sleepyhead, she mumbled.

She shook him. He let himself be shaken, concentrated on letting his body stay limp. She shook him some more. There was a break. He would have been tempted to believe she had left, if it wasn't for the very audible sound of her breath. The excitement in that breath was very evident.

He sensed her lips pushing against his then, hesitatingly, tryingly. She uncovered his body, and it didn't surprise him, didn't surprise him at all. She stroked his chest, lightly moving her hand up and down. He wondered if she was deliberately teasing him, convinced he was awake, or if she just suspected it. She touched him in the crotch. That bitch. Even before she started to fumble with the zipper in his pants he knew she wasn't going to stop, and he gave in.

In a spontaneous move, he grabbed her around the wrist, holding it in his grip.

– Hello, Liz, he greeted her.

Elizabeth Kendall met his burning eyes, totally relaxed, and with no signs of her being taken by surprise. She made no attempt to free herself. Instead she used her free hand to turn on the lamp by the bed.

– Teddy, she said with surprise in her voice. – I thought you were sound asleep…

– I just bet you did…

– Oh, I'm just having a bit of fun, she shrugged, smiling blindingly. – You know fun, don't you?

She was posing for him, clearly. Her hands behind her back, she revealed whatever there was to reveal of her front. She was casually dressed, very casually, as she had unbuttoned the upper part of her shirt, revealing the top part of her growing breasts.

He didn't say anything, but he kept his burning eyes on her. She didn't flinch a bit.

– You know, you didn't say a word the entire time out there, in the yard.

– I figured there wasn't much to say, he said.

Her mask fell, he saw it, at least a glimpse of the pain beneath, and he shuddered.

– Can you sense them? She asked. – Can you sense the ravens?

He didn't reply this time either, but this time it was because he was unable to. His throat had suddenly, seemingly tied itself in a knot.

– I can. She took two steps closer, but was still two steps away. – There is one on the roof when I go out in the morning, one outside the window in the stable when I go for a ride. They're dancing in the night. I can hear the flapping of their wings.

He realized that he was moving his lips, but there was no sound.

She brushed a strand of dark, dark brown hair away from her left eye, her left eye twinkling in blue.

– You know, when Linsey, the crown prince, the heir got wounded I felt the jealousy like a stab of pain in the gut, and I didn't like that feeling. In fact, I hated it, and it made me feel even worse.

She was sharing with him, sharing her innermost feelings, those she had never revealed to anyone, and he felt a catching in his throat, one he was certain would be revealed if he uttered a single sound.

– Eventually, even though I still felt terror, it was like everything was shrinking further and further away, like it didn't concern me at all. I only looked at you, I only had eyes for you, and it was like I was sucked into your night, your fire eyes.

She smiled again.

– I'm drawn to you, she intoned in a ghostly voice, – exactly like a moth to the flame. I know I'm gonna burn anyway, so I can just as well do it in your fire. And I want to. I *want* to.

– I love your poetry, he said, finally able to speak, to say

136

something. – I've read some of it, and it is like a river on a spring night.

She laughed throatily, the blue water of her eyes washing over him like that river in spring.

– Daddy doesn't like it, she said, suddenly enraged. – He finds most of what I do fucking unpalatable.

– Your father is an honorable man, of the old school, he said.

– You're so mature, she said with admiration in her voice, her voice slowly turning menacing. – But you can be such a child sometimes.

She stepped close to him, her face changing again. She had an extremely expressive face, as if all of her insides were visible there.

– You used to write poetry, too, didn't you… before everything?

– Yes, he replied hoarsely.

– I read it, she said, shrugging. – Linda sent it to me.

– L-linda?

– Yes, Linda. She grinned. – Sweet little sister. It was dark even then. You always have had an intuitive sense of how the world works, even if you won't admit it. She sent it to Linsey, of course, but I read it.

Her expression and stance shifted slightly.

– I saw you in a dream, she sang to him. – I saw your face contract in a rage and you hitting Linsey in the face, making him fall off the horse, causing the fracture.

The shock rattled him like bones. She hadn't been out there, he knew that. But it was like she had been. He could see everything being replayed in her eyes, her deep blue eyes.

– And you were riding the inexperienced horse. Everybody knows that. You insisted on it, even though everybody warned you before riding out.

She counted on her fingers, clearly enjoying showing off her intelligence.

– There was no mud on your horses' feet. I've seen other horses returning from the riverbank and they are full of it… like Linsey was when he told his poorly crafted story…

She took his right hand in her smaller two, rubbing fingers against his sore knuckles. The wounds there were still raw, still almost open, with remains of blood on the surrounding skin.

– This must hurt. She licked the wounds while staring intensely at him, never taking her predator eyes off his.

He couldn't bring himself to say anything. Shame and fear still raged within him.

– I want to form an… an alliance, she said formally, jokingly, but he easily heard the catching in her throat, the underlying tone of maturity, of horrible certainty.

– An… alliance? He said it puzzled, incredulous.

– Precisely. We can be of much use to each other. You know that. I know that. We have common interests and common goals.

– What *are* you talking about? He said it exasperated.

– Please, my Lord, she smiled enticingly. – I love the game, too, but don't play too much of an innocent with me. I *know* you, you see, as I know myself.

She kissed him, right on the lips, closing her eyes, opening her eyes. In those waterfalls he read boundless curiosity, acceptance…

He pushed her away. She pushed back, covering the distance between them in a heartbeat. He looked away, no longer able to hide his shame.

– I can't do this, he said.

– Why? She challenged him with her hands on her hips.

– The… Beast is inside me. I carry it with me wherever I go.

– And in me, the girl added eagerly.

The pain and the hunger… Ted thought.

– The pain and The Hunger are part of us forever, she said, Liz said.

Ted eyes widened.

Her eyes turned moist. She kissed him again, moderately standing on her toes, to push up and forward as much as possible. Hesitatingly at first, but the moment he responded the slightest her kiss turned insistent, demanding, hungry, slowly overcoming her, his inexperience.

He pushed her away, and this time he used sufficient force to keep her away.

– You're so strong, she breathed, her face flushed, not like that of a girl at all.

– This isn't right, he breathed. – Your father…

– No one is bossing us around, she breathed, equally hard. – I feel sorry for the bastard attempting that.

– You're only eleven, he blurted out, knowing the moment he said it that it was a mistake.

Two pair of burning eyes met. The cat was out of the bag.

– Ah, you're such an outstanding member of society, sir. She said it in an overwhelmingly obvious insincere tone of voice. – Little I am overwhelmed by such a show of gallantry.

She was prodding him endlessly, the bitch.

– So what? I'm ready. I don't care about society's stupid rules, and you don't either. Sexual power is postponed in a useless attempt to control it.

His own words in Denver returned to him.

– I like you, she whispered. – I can help you. I want to help, you know.

– Help me? With what? Suddenly his anger erupted into the open, and he caught himself in almost shouting.

She smiled again. He wondered how many times her face had changed expression these few minutes, from one extreme to another.

– We are cousins, she said, speaking with distinct, parted lips. – But we could just as well be twins, you know this. Or… perhaps I should say… triplets?

She took one step closer again. He didn't stop her.

– Linda, Linsey and June… they don't matter. Not like we do. You know that.

He stared at the eleven-year-old girl, not knowing whether he was shocked or interested or what.

– He will come for me, too. Sooner or later he will come for us both… if we don't come for him first. I have considered going to him voluntarily, but I prefer you. I *like* you.

The challenge was evident in her eyes when she touched his cheek.

– And what if I say I want nothing more to do with him, that I will be happy if I never see him again?

– That's okay with me, too. She shrugged. – We can stay here. There is a lot we can do here. And if the day should come that he does come for us we will be ready for him.

– You've got me all wrong, he said. – All wrong.

– Why did you come back here? She asked it softly, like a breeze. – Back here in his backyard? Why didn't you stay in Chicago? There was a Life for you there, exciting and terrifying. I'm not stupid, Teddy. I can put two and two together. You can, too. We can be good for each other. I'll help you, you'll help me, and together we'll be invincible. I know you want to. I can feel you, you know, feel how you're pulling the chains binding you, crying out for release. I do, too.

– Okay, he said hoarsely. – *All right*.

She smiled. The eleven-year-old girl smiled.

– Lovely, lovely Ted, she said weakly. – Please don't get the impression that I'm threatening you. How can I threaten such a big, bad beast like you? I love you, and I want to do everything for you. It's just so hard. It's been so hard here, alone…

She unzipped her pants, pushing both them and the panties down her thighs, slowly to let him see.

– Your turn, she said huskily. – I want to see. Please let me see. We're not alone anymore. None of us are.

He slapped her, feeling the pain in his flat hand as it hit her cheek.

She looked astonished at him, the horror finally evident in her eyes.

– You do as I say, do you understand.

She crouched in front of him, like a wounded beast, never taking her eyes of his, her huge opaque eyes.

– Yes, Ted. In all things, Ted.

She pulled the panties and the pants back up, zipping it, closing it.

He wanted to say he was sorry, wanted to scream it at her, to the world. There hadn't been much rage in the blow. It had been more a calculated one, for the effect, the result.

– Don't worry, she whispered. – I love your rage. I can sense it like a storm within myself, sensing it assaulting my senses, conquering like the wind. I'm yours now, My Lord. You have made me yours. And you did it so easy, like swatting a fly. I love you.

And the result was excellent. She had been transformed from a free-spirited girl into a sullen creature, awaiting his every command, one he could mold like clay.

– Leave me, he said coldly. – I'll give you your instructions later.

Everything had happened so fast. He hadn't had time to think. She curtseyed, pulling back, leaving the room.

She smiled, a look of mischief in her eyes.

– I can see us, you know, she said dreamingly. – We're adults, and we're together. It feels so real that for a minute or two I can almost imagine it's actually happening.

She stopped in the doorway, just a tiny moment.

– Good night, my dreaded master, she said softly. – Good night, Janus.

The thickness in his throat intensified. He sat on the bed.

Long after she had disappeared up the stairs.

She had called him Janus. Janus was, had been, a Roman god with two faces guarding the crossroads. Janus had known, in moments of clarity, all facets of life, not only good and evil, but all the facets, the entire rainbow, all the levels of complexity.

And she... had opened his eyes to all of them. Damn her.

The air vibrated around him, as if alive, alive with thought and concepts.

In an abrupt move he slapped the lightbulb, cutting himself on the sharp glass. He saw the air filled with blood the moment before the entire cellar turned dark. An infinite berserker rage filled him to the brim. He stood there for seconds, minutes shaking. Filled with frustration he threw himself on the bed.

There was a storm outside. The force of the wind had increased seemingly by a quantum leap just the last few minutes. Rain drummed against the windows. Ted registered it with a paradoxical, dull fatalism. In a way the weather was an excellent mirror of his mood.

Figures floated in the air around him. He had no idea whether or not they were real or imagined or something else. The insane laughter, loud as thunder didn't seem very convincing. He thought he saw himself, Mike and a host of others, male and female, but he wasn't sure. There were sparks, unbelievably enough from the destroyed lamp. He didn't know whether or not it was the charged atmosphere, a short circuit or something else... and didn't give a fuck. Perhaps it would make a huge and nice fire. Ted's laughter turned ugly.

– A fire, he said aloud. – Just a little fire.

The muscled, slim figure on the bed writhed and suffered.

A tiny spark on the dry carpet, and everything might end.

***/

Kendall escorted Doc Kennedy to the courtyard, where Scott Thompson waited with his horse.

– I'll put some money on your account tomorrow, he said.

– Don't bother, Kennedy said brusquely, smiling. – I consider this a friend's service.

Kendall did, too. At least he and Kennedy had common interest in the valley. And that wasn't unimportant, considering those that had not.

Kennedy stopped then, hesitatingly, glancing around.

– The matter you asked me to investigate...

A moment then Kendall drew a total blank. He just couldn't recall what the other man was referring to.

– The blood, Doc Kennedy offered discretely.

A nod, a fear in the eyes. How could he have forgotten? Kendall understood. He nodded. Scott was still too far away to catch anything of the conversation, and no one else was around.

– It checks out. There are no... anomalies.

Eugene nodded, a mix of both relief and shame flooding through him. He had sent a sample of Elizabeth's blood to a lab for checking. He had actually suspected that his daughter wasn't his daughter.

The moment his thoughts had started spinning they had just kept at it, like they were something independent of him, with a life of their own.

– You're sure? He forced himself to say, wanting to banish all doubt.

– Well, we're not talking about an exact science here, in this day and age. In the future, as I've understood it, we will be able to check on a genetic level. But yes, I, and the technicians are as sure as we can ever be.

– Good, Kendall nodded. – Thank you.

– My «pleasure». The Doc nodded, too, even a bit more tightly.

Eugene heard the neighing of Blackie, Thompson's horse, much closer than he had thought it would be. The mood turned even more awkward.

– It's late, Kennedy said. – It's time for me to return home.

– Okay, have it your way, Kendall joked, taking the other's outstretched hand. – You're welcome back anytime, of course.

They took the final, decisive steps out in the yard. Blackie grazed close to the door. Thompson stood a bit further away, overlooking the valley.

– Give Trudy and Elizabeth my regards, will you, and thank them for me, for the delicious dinner.

– I will, of course. They will probably grow lax from all the praise, but we should risk it, I guess.

Thompson walked across the yard, approaching them.

– You don't have to take me back, Kennedy cried. – I'll walk. It's such a fine evening.

Thompson stopped, grinned, and signaled that he had received the message.

– Are you sure? Kendall looked at the gathering clouds in the south, heard the distant thunder.

– I'm sure. A little rain has never hurt anybody.

– A little, Kendall emphasized.

Kennedy walked to the end of the yard, as the ground started to tilt and turned around.

– And don't worry about your unfortunate son. The fracture will most certainly heal nicely.

Kendall stood still for a while, observing the slightly crouched figure descending the ranch hill. It was open land that way, for quite a distance. Kendall turned in the other direction, to the other, bare, slightly higher hill, where there were no buildings. He walked inside, as the first drops of rain started to fall.

Trudy stood by the end of the hallway, outside the bedroom, beckoning him with her eyes, her posture. He ignored her and walked directly towards the children's bedrooms.

He went straight inside, without knocking. The room was dark. In the light from the hallway he saw the boy on the bed. Linsey lay still, with his eyes closed. His chest moved up and down in quite a regular motion. Every impression told the visitor, the intruder that he was sound asleep.

– I heard you turn off the lamp, Kendall said casually, sharply.

Linsey opened his eyes and sat up in the bed, not even attempting to continue the deception. He rubbed his eyes a bit. The sudden, sharp light made tears flow. Kendall sat down on a stool, not far from the bed.

There was a silence, prolonged silence, stretching into minutes.

– Something is bothering you, son. Spit it out.

There was silence, as Linsey spoke volumes.

– The world is full of it, you know, the boy finally said, the painkillers making his eyes and voice drowsy.

– Excuse me?

– It's full of psychobabble, father, full of bs, both in thought and action. People speak a lot of fine words, while they're committing unspeakable atrocities in the dark of the night. The night is the true world, in both good and bad ways.

And outside there was thunder and lightning in the night.

Kendall nodded, while studying his son, in fact not taking his eyes off him.

– Most youths see it that way, son. It's a natural… and good reaction to the world's horrors. We all go through a phase of rage and rebellion in our youth, until settling down, basically accepting that society is basically good, with a few… major flaws.

Linsey smiled, his feverish eyes seemingly glowing even a bit more.

– So, he said, – what did Doc Kennedy have to say? Did you and he bet again?

– Oh, he gave me quite an optimistic view of your recovery, and, no, we didn't make a bet this time. Both the shoulder and the slight dislocation of your jaw should set nicely and quickly.

Linsey touched his jaw, carefully touching the bruise there. It all happened almost subconsciously, as if he didn't notice doing it.

– So how did Ted do today? Kendall asked carefully.

Linsey smiled. He smiled broadly.

– Very well, he said excitedly. – He just keeps getting better. Sometimes we just sit there, openmouthed, observing him. The progress he has made is just astonishing, father. Especially concerning how he… he started out.

Kendall nodded.

– But that just makes his other, more hard to understand ways, even harder to understand, doesn't it?

– Yes. Linsey nodded.

They smiled, and shook their head. The boy kept talking.

– But I guess he's entitled somewhat. Linsey said.

A statement greeted with silence.

– I can remember when he first arrived here. He could hardly sit on a horse, and look at him now.

Don't look now.

They laughed, drying tears.

– What he did out there today…

Suddenly there was naked anguish, well hidden in the boy's voice. Kendall waited.

– I don't understand it, Linsey cried. – I don't understand that at all.

– Neither do I, son. But even though we must continue struggling until we do understand it, it's not something we can allow to continue.

Linsey nodded, with eyes huge and uncomprehending.

He was about to say more, something crucial, blurting out everything he had kept silent about, something Kendall wanted to hear spoken aloud, that was fairly obvious… when there was a knock at the door. Linsey once more put his face into a carefully concealed masked mode.

– ENTER. Kendal shouted irritated, ignoring Linsey's puzzled expression.

Liz stood in the door, the door already open. She stared at her father and brother with a strange, melancholic expression in her face. She was dressed in a light blue nightgown that neither hid nor displayed her bodily forms. Her hands were hidden, though, behind her back.

– Sorry if I'm interrupting anything, she said softly.

Kendall wanted to say something, and he knew that much was evident in his expression, but he kept silent. The sight of the innocent looking girl made him hesitate.

He heard Trudy upstairs, heard her play the piano, somber, haunting tones making him shiver inside.

Liz entered the room, obviously smug and secretive.

– I have a surprise for poor, unfortunate Linsey, she said, smiling meekly. – I initially thought to wait until tomorrow, but then I heard you guys talking.

She grinningly revealed her hands and what was in them.

– TA DAAAA

She held out the big plate with its huge piece of chocolate cake.

– Your favorite, as I recall, she said sweetly. – I baked it myself, sweating over recipes and the hot stove for hours. Enjoy.

She put it in his lap. He accepted it with quite a stunned expression.

Kendall wasn't looking at him, but at the sister.

– That is certainly a mighty big piece, he said lightly.

– Yes. Elizabeth smiled broadly. – I thought I would start big. And tomorrow, two even bigger pieces are waiting for my dear brother, before the cake is gone. And I'll be sure to feed him properly in the weeks to come, don't you worry. He will be fat before leaving this hospital…

– That is awfully nice of you. Kendall looked at her again, and this time he made no secret of it.

– Linsey can be an irritating boy scout sometimes, but I love him, daddy.

He was about to say something more, when he halted, thunderstruck. To his surprise and shock he saw tears in her eyes. She swept her hands hastily over her face to dry it, to cover it up, but he saw it.

– I'm so honored, Linsey grinned, – over having sole rights of Elizabeth Kendall's world-renowned chocolate cake…

– You're such a dumb ass, brother, she told him affectionately.

She bent down and carefully embraced him. He lifted his healthy arm and patted her back.

The girl departed with a flamboyant greeting, seemingly replying to Kendall's unspoken question.

– Tomorrow is another day.

The piano music stopped as Kendall ascended the stairs. Thoughts kept wandering as he walked into the living room. The fireplace was still hot and seething. Trudy stood by the window, quite far from the fireplace, from the yellow and red flames, but it still seemed like the night and the fire warred for dominance around her, that she was bathing in it. She turned as he stepped close to her, turned and embraced him, giving him sultry kisses on the lips. There was much about her reminding him of their oldest daughter then. She didn't really look like her. The similarities were in the behavior, in the body language, in the promising smile centering around the thick Slavic lips, as the fire danced on the dark, non-Slavic skin. She wasn't Caucasian, not really, not only. He saw all creeds imaginable in the seemingly young woman standing before him. And also, he added in his thoughts, many creeds unseen and unimaginable, everything present in all the children.

– Is everything all right? Her voice sounded in his ears like a soft breeze, pleasant as always, very worrying, with his now increased fears.

– Liz did a priceless number on me just now, he said. – It was quite evident, in a very non-evident way.

– But on the other hand, she grinned, – if the non-evidence was a true sign of a lack of evidence, perhaps there is no reason for you to keep worrying?

– It was a number, all right, he stated. – The reason for it isn't instantly apparent, though. Perhaps she really wanted, wants to show that she has changed, show her desire to change, I don't know.

Trudy brushed a strand of hair away from his forehead.

– Or, as I keep telling you, there is no need for her to change. On the contrary. I think you're not giving her credit for her uniqueness, her independence. You want her to be like everybody else, even though it is apparent that she isn't, and never will be.

He looked at his wife, as if seeing her for the first time.

– So, what is she, then?

– Now, that is also very obvious, isn't it? Trudy Kendall looked teasingly at her husband, crouching slightly, displaying herself. – She's a human being, a young girl attempting to find her footing in a world where everybody, by default is thrown off balance.

He stepped forward, grabbing her around the arms, almost

shaking her.

– Dammit, what is she?

– You told me you would never ask that question, she said, suddenly very serious minded. – That you would never ask that question about your own children.

She shook herself free of him. He knew she was strong, but this was like he hadn't held her at all. She started to pace before the fire, and in many ways, there was no clear distinction between her and the fire, between her and the shadows.

– I told you, told you what I am, she said, very pointed, very deliberate. – What I am, what my entire family is, doesn't change in the next generation. There is no regression, no turning back to what we once were. I told you that our children, *all our children* would be special, and walk unforeseen paths. You didn't believe me, not really, you didn't understand, and swore an oath of non-interference. I'm holding you to it, Eugene. I'm *holding* you to it.

– All our children... he repeated, swallowing hard, as he sensed the abyss opening up beneath him. – And Ted, is he...

She nodded, smiling again, an insane smile, sucking him in, drowning him.

– You can't stop what's going to happen, she said. – Nobody can. What you *can* do is to aid in the destruction of your own children. You can light the fire on their pyre if you don't wise up soon, and purge yourself of your fucking racism.

Her voice had risen steadily, and cracking slightly with the last few words she spat, like venom at him.

– That is what I want you to do, Eugene, she spat, the fury. – Is that too much to ask? It's about time, you know.

He looked astonished at her, shocked beyond words.

– I... care about you Eugene, she said softly. – At least about the man you were, or can be. But for twenty years I have held myself in check, bottling up my emotions, my Self, but no more. Never more!

She kissed him lightly on the cheek, then, suddenly very calm. And then she left him, left him there to burn. He heard her light steps as the sound of them faded, as she left the room, as she, herself grew distant.

Kendall remained there, for a long time.

148

– Your mask is finally falling, he said aloud. – Because of
Ted?

He imagined he had seen tears in Trudy's eyes there, for a
moment. Insincere, he suspected. Like daughter, like mother.
He didn't care.

The fire stretched a bit, as Trudy closed the door to the
bedroom. The farmer's eyes were fixed on the flames, but he
hardly sensed the light from the dancing tongues. He put a
hand inside his jacket, and when it reemerged there was a letter
there, the jagged edge of an opened envelope, of two opened
envelopes. He read through the letters once again. The reading
seemed to last an eternity. Slowly, with his teeth exposed in
a grin he let go of it. The pieces of paper floated on hot air an
endless moment, before being consumed by greedy fire. The
vulnerable material smoldered and disintegrated in the heat,
turning to ashes, disappearing through the chimney, into the
cold February night.

Finally, the house and its inhabitants rested. Every one with
their smaller and bigger secrets that everyone and all knew.
Elizabeth and the sister shared room. June slept soundly. Liz
sat on the bed with her legs pulled up, her head resting on her
knees, her face a study in contradicting emotions.

– Have you seen me like this, baby sister? She wondered. –
Have you ever seen me like this? I can see myself in the mirror,
and the mirror is staring back. Would you be terrified by this
look into hell?

Outside the two girls' room a passing customer would notice
an unmistakable smell of garlic.

Linsey and the father slept soundly. On the bed beside
Kendall his wife sat, and cut her fingernails with a huge knife,
doing it with unmistakable skill.

Liz fell back on the bed, closing her eyes, falling asleep,
dreaming the world and seeing it all. She saw Ted Cousin
writhing under the quilt. She saw the destroyed bulb, blood
flowing from the boy's right hand.

He gulped and something thick and musky erupted from his
half-opened mouth. Liz knew a random person passing by,
looking in, would have turned seriously scared. Liz stared
absolutely fascinated, unable to avert her eyes, knowing that

the random accidental tourist would have wondered about the red gleaming points. Beneath all the sparks and embers he or she would have seen where they belonged, and become absolutely terrified, terrified of seeing directly into another human's soul.

Liz saw it all, heard the horses, saw the bull, the bull and human being stare at one another. The bull was on the ground, being marked, on its feet again, marked and beaten.

Everything happened slowly, but still with a speed resembling inevitability. Liz trembled.

– Damn it, Teddy, a freckled kid laughed with a touch of admiration in his voice. Liz saw her brother as she had never seen him, through a red haze of rage. She gasped. – You did it. I never thought you could do it.

– You own me ten bucks, Lin, the other grinned.

And Liz saw his exposed bloody fangs.

Linsey returned the grin. His red blond hair stood up in all possible and impossible directions. He procured a ten dollars bill.

– You're far too greedy, Teddy, he stated. – Don't you agree, guys?

The other two «guys», Butch and Kevin Davison laughed themselves silly.

– Don't be too hard on him, Lin, Kevin said. – If he wants to *keep* chasing Maria Jimenez the way he has been doing recently he may need all the cash he can get his hands on. Her family is loaded.

Ted said nothing. The other three nodded with telling expressions in their face.

Ted stared back, and Kevin's horse started backing off a little. Everything turned quiet, very quiet.

Then the first ringing of the bell sounded from the valley, signaling the approaching end of the working day. A sigh of relief rose from the group, as if they had just been given a reprieve, been saved from something very bad happening.

Liz lay in bed, mumbling and protesting loud and low. This wasn't how it had happened. Ted had taken down many bulls after the first one, with an ever-greater ease, making the older cowboys nod and send him appreciative glances. She knew this was a dream, and she wanted to wake up, but she couldn't, couldn't.

Ted and Linsey parted with the two brothers where the river turned, where the road turned and turned sharp.

– I'm sorry. I am SORRY. She heard him repeating it in her head again and again. She wanted to turn off the whimpering voice, but she couldn't, couldn't.

Ted and Linsey remained there by the river, the seconds turning to minutes. They didn't speak for some time.

– What a day. Linsey drew breath and exhaled in an atmosphere of well-being.

– Linsey, Ted said sharply.

– Ted, Linsey acknowledged, a more somber mode clearly, finally penetrating his veneer of good spirits.

– Why don't you speak what's on your mind? Why don't you speak your mind?

Linsey didn't speak. In Liz' dream, at least he didn't.

– Very well, then, Ted said, like a thundercloud. – Then I will speak mine.

He moved his horse closer. Linsey moved his a bit back, backed off so far towards the edge that he could move no longer.

– I think you should seriously consider a change in behavior, Ted shouted, his voice hardly audible. – The innocent lost little boy style went out of style ten years ago.

– I think you're totally off your mark, Linsey managed to say.

Ted just kept talking, as if the other hadn't spoken at all.

– The world is just laughing its heart out by such a pathetic attempt to placate it. And the world has enough to worry about if it shouldn't also bother with a snotty little boy in a big, bulky body.

Thunder exploded. There was a snarl, as Ted went totally nuts. His suddenly raised fist flashed forward, almost too fast to see, and thunder exploded, as it connected with Linsey's jaw. The red-haired boy tumbled off the horse and fell off the small edge in the terrain, down the step below. She heard a loud crack as the shoulder-bone broke.

Ted didn't move at first. His face was a study in contradicting emotions, hatred, fear, shock. He dismounted the horse. The frightened little boy on the ground attempted to crawl away, but couldn't move, pain painted in his face. Ted quickly closed the distance between them.

– I'm sorry, he said dully, waiting a few seconds before repeating it. – I'm sorry.

And his laughter echoed through Liz' ears. And she sat up in the bed, wide-eyed and with a scream stuck in her throat, with sweat pouring from all over her body. Even though there was no sound…

She woke up screaming.

********************/

Liz jumped out of bed. June sat up, blinking sleep out of her eyes, brutally roused from her dormancy by the banshee howl.

The entire room or house or very air seemed to shake, vibrate, shiver and shimmer. The scream seemed to go on, to continue long after she felt it leave her throat and feverish mind.

- Go back to sleep little sister, Liz heard herself say, hardly able to speak. – This doesn't concern you.

Then she found herself rushing through the hallways and stairs, still in a somewhat dreamlike state, knowing beyond knowing where she was headed.

Linsey was there, the painkillers keeping his eyes hazy and dull. The door to Ted's room was ajar. They both stumbled inside. Ted lay on the bed, soaked in blood, dead pale and still. Shadows danced in the air before Liz' wide-open eyes, impossibly visible in the darkness of the room. Linsey rushed forward to the unmoving figure and checked his pulse. Liz just stood there, just as unmoving as her kin on the bed.

– He's alive, Linsey breathed in relief. – His pulse is strong. He frowned.

– Very strong.

– Like a hammer at the skin, Liz said.

– We must call the hospital, Linsey said agitated.

– There is no need, Liz said with a ghostly voice. – You know that, don't you?

Eugene, Trudy and June appeared in the door behind her. She didn't have to turn around to know that they were there.

– Call the hospital, Eugene told Linsey curtly.

Linsey ran off, to the phone upstairs, the dull pain in his eyes

152

virtually gone.

Liz walked forward, as if sleepwalking. She stopped right before the bed. A hand grabbed her, a strong hand, squeezing hers. It didn't hurt, didn't hurt at all.

– The *mouth,* Ted hissed, – it's hissing at me from the darkness.

Liz felt it, not only in her ears, but in her body, the razing all over her skin.

– I'm all right, he said to her, in a strikingly normal voice. – There is no need to be afraid.

– I'm not, she said. – Not anymore.

She felt very lightheaded, almost like she was floating.

Trudy stepped forward, too, looking at her daughter and nephew with visible fondness and excitement.

– The shadows are speaking to you, she said, - as they should and will. You're growing up.

– TRUDY! Eugene shouted.

– It was an accident, Ted mumbled. – I… slipped.

Liz giggled darkly.

Ted wanted to say more, but he couldn't. He lay there gasping, as if he couldn't get enough air. His heart hammered in his chest, outside his chest. Liz heard it, as if it was actually beating in the air surrounding them.

His hand fell down. She bent down and grabbed it, lifted it to her lips and kissed it, feeling the boiling blood in there caress her lips.

Kendall grabbed her and attempted to pull her away. She shook herself free of him and stood her ground, stood there, on that exact spot, holding onto the hand.

The song of the shadows faded slowly as the noise of the sirens rose in their ears.

Chapter seven

The May sun cast its light and heat at the huge gathering. Major banners swayed in the wind. The slogans written on the banners were steadily repeated by the masses:

– AMERICA OUT OF VIETNAM. WE AMERICANS ARE FED UP WITH OUR SONS SACRIFICING THEIR LIVES FOR A DICTATORSHIP.

And then:

– PRESIDENT NIXON IS CORRUPT, PAID FOR AND BOUGHT BY THE MILITARY/INDUSTRIAL COMPLEX. GET RID OF THE PRESIDENT AND WE GET RID OF THE WAR. KICK NIXON OUT OF THE WHITE HOUSE.

Several men and women stood on a platform in the midst of the seething humanity and screamed through megaphones. In the background one could glimpse the White House, surrounded by policemen and units from the army. A small, brown-haired young woman screamed:

– Behold the Commander in Chief in his house of cards, protected by his soldiers. He doesn't dare come to us, to descend from his throne. What a poor, pathetic coward.

– COWARD, COWARD, COWARD.

The TV-cameras were instantly directed at the Oval Office in the White House. Behind the impossible to break glass the familiar, wrinkled face of Richard Nixon appeared.

In a classroom, on a TV-screen, half the country away they could all see every furrow in that face.

– Damn, Linsey Kendall said very pleased. – That girl certainly gave him a nice slap in the face. Too bad we're not there with her, with them, don't you agree?

Ted Cousin grunted something unintelligible, but another boy, who couldn't avoid hearing what Linsey said virtually jumped from his chair, his face red in anger.

– So, you would have wanted to be there, huh? He asked furiously. – So, you're siding with those freaks?

– They're not freaks, Linsey protested. – They're...

– Linsey, Paul, the teacher interrupted them sharply. – We'll discuss this broadly and thoroughly afterwards. I think most of those present want to see everything first. Till then: Shut up. *Sit down, Paul.*

Paul Cornwall obeyed, clearly insulted. He made his opinion known by staring out of the window. Just a few students joined him, no matter how much money his father had amassed. The majority stared at the screen. More than one had brothers and sisters or/and friends who had traveled all the way to Washington DC, to participate in the giant protest against the Vietnam War. More than one had a brother in Vietnam. Linsey glanced at Ted, half irritated, half curious. In his opinion his friend and cousin paid no attention whatsoever to what was going on there on the screen.

Ted turned then, and Linsey got overwhelmed by the uncanny impression that the dark boy could see straight through him.

– I can hear the cries with my ears covered, he said, – see everything with my eyes closed, sense the boiling of the blood thousands of miles away.

The teacher didn't comment on him breaking the prohibition against speaking. Both she and Linsey froze in their chairs.

– I can see with my eyes closed, Ted continued. – My brother taught me to do that.

– That's right. The teacher felt she had to say something. – You were there, weren't you, in Chicago three years ago?

– I was there. Ted nodded distantly, so very close.

– You were so young. It had to make a major impression on you. What did you feel through it all?

– Freedom, the boy stated, the burning eyes staring at them, through them all. – Boundless, uncompromising Freedom.

The rest of the class stared curiously at him. They knew he had a past, so to speak, knew he had been to the end of the world and back, in spite of his youth. Envy, fear and hatred coursed through them.

– Daddy's boy doesn't want daddy to lose his toys, he added abruptly, pointedly. – If daddy loses his, daddy's boy will lose his, too.

Paul's eyes were hard as glass, his face distorted, his skin white as milk. He didn't move. Not an inch.

The ruckus slowly died. Calm was somewhat restored to the classroom. The teacher, Miss Bernstein picked up her pace hesitantly.

Time, Ted thought. Timing.

The opportunity he had been waiting for finally came half way into the hour, when it was almost too late. He couldn't tell whether or not he was glad or not, if he had been relieved as long as the opportunity didn't present itself. Now it no longer mattered.

Butch Davison returned from the restroom, with the wet blackboard swamp in his hand. Miss Bernstein didn't cast more than a casual glance at him, before returning her attention to the TV.

NOW!

Just as Butch passed him Ted put forth his leg. Grunting Butch stumbled forward, waving his arms wildly in an attempt to restore his balance, in vain. He fell, and crashed into Paul. Paul had just opened his mouth to laugh when the swamp hit him in the face, and he got a lot of chalk between his teeth. His anger had been building since the wordy exchange with Linsey and Ted, and now it finally found an outlet. At least as enraged as a blind bull he stared at the confused Butch.

– You damned peasant, he spat. – You thought you were being quite funny and clever, now, right?

«The damn peasant» blew his fuses instantly. He had clearly been about to apologize, but Paul's harsh words changed that. Furiously he gathered his wits.

– What the fuck do you mean? He shouted. – Fucking warmonger. You weren't much of anything yourself, until your traitor of a father revealed his plan to turn the entire valley into an industrial area.

The older Cornwall's illustrious plans were a very sore spot in the valley and had created a lot of tension between the fractions, its supporters and opponents.

– Don't speak of treason, Paul returned the scream. – You're just a damn communist who wants to leave Vietnam to the Russians.

Deeply disturbed the tiny Miss Bernstein placed herself between the cocks.

– Dear boys, she whimpered and repeated, – can't we all get along?

Ted truly enjoyed himself when Butch brushed her aside. The dark boy quietly left his desk. Nobody noticed. Everybody present gathered in a circle around the cowboy and the rich boy. There was an abyss between them, widened by the Vietnam War.

– What the fuck did you mean by that? Butch kept shouting. – Are you accusing me of being…

– A damn Bolshevik, Paul completed the sentence. – That's fucking right.

The right hook sent him straight into the canvas (the gathered circle). Hands eagerly pushed him back towards the opponent. Paul struck back. Butch struck again. And again. Blood flowed from bloody noses.

The teacher's scream lingered in the room. Nobody seemed to notice. Ted left the room, almost shocked. The result of his initial minor contribution had exceeded all expectations.

The hall was empty. Ted had expected that, but he kept his eyes open anyway, as he progressed quietly towards the natural science area. He stopped by the door and listened a few seconds, before opening the door and slipping inside. The auditorium was empty. Dark curtains covering the windows made it dark and foreboding. This was quite a setup. You didn't find such variety and quality of equipment in the average American high school. The county had enjoyed the fruits of the increasing Cornwall fortune for at least the last decade.

Ted hesitated a moment before proceeding to the section, opening the lockers where the school's lab chemicals were stored alphabetically. He didn't need to waste time looking, knowing exactly what to fetch and where to look. The bottle marked with the word CHLOROFORM flashed blindingly before him. With both hands he grabbed it and placed it on the nearest desk. He could suddenly, as he glanced at his watch, and also at the clock on the wall, smell his own sweat, sense the increasing, gnawing worry inside.

It took a while of frantic searching, opening most of the lockers, before he finally found an empty bottle. It was much smaller than the one with the Chloroform. He took it and thoroughly closed the lockers. Without spilling a single drop, amazed by his own calm he filled the smaller bottle. The empty space on the bigger one, he filled with water. He left the room as quietly as he had arrived less than a minute ago, taking one last look. No one would know that anything had changed. It looked no different.

The hall again. He headed straight for the toilets. He heard the sound of water, continuously running. The door to the boys' room was open. He walked through it, through the entire room and opened the door at the back. To a dusty and dark room, the school's storage space, and what it stored was hardly anything but dust. There was no wind here, but the dust blew and ripped through the air.

Liz stood by the deepest shadow, a shadow illuminating her face. She smiled radiantly to him, her long, dark brown hair blowing in the wind. He couldn't take his eyes off her.

– Such a beautiful witch…

He wanted to both curse her and sing her praise.

She laughed thrillingly, exposing her long canine fangs. He pulled the bottle from his pocket. She rewarded him with silent applause, hardly audible clapping her hands.

– It was easy, he told her, as a reply to her silent question. – And no one will ever know. The slight mixing of water will only cause the poor rabbits to fall asleep a bit later.

She slipped into his arms, acting like she belonged there. He gave her the bottle. She took it and slipped it into a pocket of her wide jacket.

– I must return, he said. – Even though I have been away just a few minutes it might be too long already. Butch has probably mopped the floor with Paul by now.

– You fooled them… into fighting? Her eyes lit up like a christmas tree.

– It was easy. He shook his head. – Those guys are almost like natural enemies.

– I wish I could have seen it. She sighed, like she just had missed an important TV-event, a visit from the president or something equally essential. – But I'm just a child, so I guess they would have sent me to a shrink or something afterwards.

– Your time will come, he told her.

She smiled again.

– Have I told you, you say the nicest things…?

They separated. She walked to the door leading outside, waving to him a single time and disappearing in a burst of light. He pulled himself backwards, returning to whence he had come. When he returned to the classroom everybody's eyes were still directed at the fighters. He placed himself behind Kevin Davison cheering at his brother. The teacher stood pale as milk by the two boys on the floor, unable to move anything more than her eyelids. Ted convinced himself no one had witnessed his excursion, and a sense of triumph rose in him.

A low roar among the spectators, a cry of disbelief from Kevin interrupted his thoughts. Incredulity dominated the students' faces as they witnessed Paul rise, with Butch remaining on the floor. Both had bloody faces, but Butch did look decisively worse. There was no doubt about whom had mopped the floor with whom.

Ted didn't really care, but he admitted to himself that he felt a certain surprise.

The bell rang. Everything dissolved and rearranged. The students left the classroom, even more excited than usual after the ending of a class. They chatted eagerly, while casting long looks at all the blood and the rain. Butch fought his way up from the floor. Paul turned his back on him in contempt. The teacher remained frozen, her skin whiter than that of a dead body. Ted turned his back on them all. He hurried outside, suddenly very excited himself.

In the hall there was the whirl of faces and bodies dancing before his eyes. The electrical lights had, as usual not been turned on, and the light of day from the two exits created a world of indistinct faces and moving shadows. He saw the girl stand by the stairs, in a circle of other female classmates. He walked straight there, without any visible hesitation. Several of the yapping chicks cast long looks at him, of interest and condemnation. She did, too, but her ice-cold stare didn't waver a moment.

– Hallo, Maria, he greeted her.

– Hallo, Ted, Maria Jimenez said easy going, but certainly also haughty, indifferent.

– I would like to take you out a night, he told her, straight out.

The other girls started giggling. Not overtly, but giggling

nonetheless.

– So, you would that, would you, Senor? You seem awfully sure of yourself.

Maria was of blue-blooded Spanish/Mexican ancestry. It was evident in all her moves, the way she spoke and behaved.

– So, does that mean you *will* go out with me?

– Sure. She shrugged. – Why not?

The buzz in the hallway grew even louder and more pronounced. Ted smiled, and imagined he saw the first glimmer of insecurity in her brown eyes. The buzz and the glimmer both haunted him for the rest of the school day, in the classroom, where the TV was still on, and yet showed the same scene, from Washington DC. Linsey sat by Ted's side and looked at the show, the ruckus, obviously interested and excited.

– By damn, he shook his head in admiration. – Look at that, it's the same lady again, the one who gave Nixon the blow below the belt earlier. I wonder what she has in store for us now.

Ted yawned, resulting in a disappointed look from his friend. He yawned again, striving to appear indifferent. It was hard. The exuberant mood from Chicago remained within him, no matter what he did.

Maria sat between him and the screen. He studied her, and he studied the screen. The same brown-haired girl who had cursed the President earlier spoke again.

– Look at the soldiers, she cried. – They're increasing in numbers. Why? What have we done? They're treating us like criminals. How can they, how dare they? We're just ordinary American citizens, doing a nonviolent protest, exercising our *constitutional* right to protest, and they, the masters and their servants are replying with violence. I say they're the ones who should go, they who are terrorizing us free Americans. THEY - SHOULD - GO.

– YES, THEY SHOULD GO. THEY SHOULD GO. THEY SHOULD GO.

The thunder of the crowd rose to an even higher pitch, causing the cameras, the image on the screen to shake and quiver.

A woman with hair very similar to Linda's silver blonde took the gauntlet.

160

– Don't forget the man on the pedestal, she roared into the microphone. – In an attempt to be elected to his folly one more time he has offered certain concessions, promises, but he's always making reservations… and I'm not talking about him renting a hotel room here…I'm quoting from one of his many fine speeches: «You may trust me on this. If, I, Richard Nixon am reelected President of the United States… Then you can be confident in the belief that I will fight for an honorable peace, end rapidly our war in Indo China, and bring our boys home». Unquote.

The rough laughter of the crowd bathed the White house in its acid.

– He'll bring them home, all right, a man spat loud and clear, long and wet. – The way he keeps doing it… in body-bags.

Ted had to admire the blonde. She didn't look much older than him, but she was a brave one.

She continued. Her voice rising another pitch.

– Don't let the hypocrite in there fool you anymore. Don't let his smooth talk spin you this time. Get the hypocrite off our property.

– GET HIM OFF. GET HIM OFF.

Cameras were once more directed at the oval office, but now Nixon was gone.

– What a fucking coward, Linsey said in contempt. – He can't even watch.

Paul leapt from his chair, but before he could open his mouth Elmer Caufax, one giant of a teacher coughed a warning, and the boy had to be content with slipping back into his chair with a pointed expression in his face.

A reporter appeared on the screen. The crowd in the background was thrown off focus. The reporter exposed his teeth in a classic toothpaste moment.

– That's it from us for now, folks, he exclaimed. – But trust me when I assure you we'll be back, and back instantly if there is another dramatic turn of events.

He and the background faded out, and the studio and a female newscaster faded in.

– We will now take a short break, folks, but will be back right after this message.

A buzz of sound, a whirl of images filled the screen. Americans were subjected to the relentless barrage of advertising, of television «commercial spots».

The teacher turned off the TV. Suddenly there was an awkward silence.

– Now, Elmer Coufax told them, in what they experienced as a very intimidating manner, – the floor is open for discussion. What do *you* think of all this?

The discussion wasn't very successful. It turned out to be, all in all a screaming contest between Linsey in one corner and Paul in the other, with the others caught somewhat in between.

At one time something Linsey said made Paul laugh out aloud.

– You won't laugh anymore when the Vietnam War is over, and your father loses his income stemming from arms production, Linsey screamed. – You ass kisser.

Paul seemed to consider this, for quite a while, at least a few seconds, before shrugging.

– There will always be arms production, he stated, suddenly very relaxed.

And Linsey paled, and suddenly Ted saw something in him he hadn't seen before, something making his eyes widen in amazement.

Afterwards, during the next break he kept studying Linsey, in the hope of seeing it again, but there was nothing. Linsey seemed somewhat calm again. He never stayed angry for long. And this time he noticed Ted's look.

– I was angry, he admitted. – Mostly because Paul is right. The world is like that.

– That's right, Ted said, to his relative, to all the others gathered around them. – Even if the Vietnam War does end, and sooner or later it will, nothing will really change. It will be the same world, the same world leading to, encouraging such stuff.

The others looked away, not willing to concede or even acknowledge his words.

– I noticed something, Maria said.

They all looked at her.

– I studied you when Coufax, the Iron Fist turned off the

TV during the advertising. Many of you actually had a disappointed look in your face.

Silence met her words.

– I guess you're right, a boy finally said. – We're all brainwashed zombies, eagerly awaiting and anticipating our next fix of obedience and servitude. Shit, girl, you're not telling us anything we don't know.

There was laughter, hard-edged and sore.

The swimming pool later. A whirling sea of bodies, of heat and teenage exuberance.

Ted followed Maria, in an obscure, non-obvious manner. As he swam back and forth the entire length of the artificial waters he cast her a short, long glance every time he passed her in the raging stream. The dark skin, the swelling, fine toned muscles flashed in the shadowy room, in the light of the sunlight shining through the large windows. His eyes were locked on her swelling thighs, her round breasts, and he had to swallow hard and often to keep spittle from filling his mouth.

Maria kept swimming. She didn't seem to notice his ever-closer scrutiny. There was nothing overt revealing her awareness of being looked at. She kept swimming her heavy, forceful strokes, seemingly completely unaware of the eyes burning her skin.

But Ted, trained in observation during the long, lonely time he had been Mike's plaything had learned a considerable amount of people's behavior patterns in various, the most varied of situations. He saw the pulse beat on her neck, noticed her more erratic breathing - having nothing to do with her exercise. All of it becoming increasingly clear when she stopped not that far away in front of him, and started to stare deliberately at him. She expected him to avert his eyes in shame, like most boys did, after having given in to their natural urges, but he didn't. He returned the stare. She froze. He grinned. She shifted position, clearly restless. And not many seconds later it was she who had to look down. Suddenly she was blushing from head to toe. He saw it, everybody saw it, as she rose in the shallow parts of the pool and revealed her entire tall, hot body. She gasped and started fighting her way out of the water, step by step stumbling on, hitting several of the passing swimmers with her waving arms. She ran off, crying, towards the locker room.

Ted remained there, on his spot, for a while, also breathing hard. The surroundings shifted in flashes, from one moment to the next, as if reality itself constantly changed.

He had started to walk away, out of the pool, when he felt a pat on his shoulder. He turned, and suddenly found himself surrounded by Paul and his cronies, all his supporters among the students, everybody eager to benefit from his exalted place in society.

– Nice one, Paul grinned. – Truly a pass to remember. A bit too subtle, perhaps, but still…passable.

Laughter, full of poison and scorn. A very tight group, united against the beast in their midst.

Ted struck, swiftly and lethal. His left hand hit Paul precisely on the jaw and pushed him backwards. His upper body made a loud splash, as it met the water surface. Strung out and paralyzed the rich man's son lay still and drifted away. Nobody lifted a hand to help him. The gathering of people stood there, completely frozen, no longer a group, but a collection of scared individuals desperately attempting to disassociate themselves from the virtually unconscious boy in the water.

– *Hasta la vista,* Ted said. He walked calmly towards the edge of the pool and left it. No one attempted to stop him.

He walked to the locker room, to the showers, looking neither left nor right. It was still early. The gym class wouldn't be over for another half an hour. The showers were empty. He pushed the trunks down his thighs, leaving them behind on the floor. Some time later he stood before the mirror, staring into it, having no recollection of having showered.

– I DON'T want to be like you, he shouted at the sparkling eyes in the mirror. – I will CRUSH you like the insect you are.

When the other boys entered the wardrobe a considerable time later he was still there. He stood on the same spot, still naked, whistling cheerfully. They didn't speak to him. Not necessarily because of what had happened in the pool. Some had been outdoors, playing football and hadn't witnessed or even heard about that. But they kept their silence and fear riddled their eyes and features, as they looked at the dark boy, as they averted their eyes. The cheerful whistling was just as scary as

164

the rest of his appearance, the still wet hair covering most of his face, a hidden expression, twisted and lurid.

The mirror before him was broken, the pieces on the floor bathing in rust and tomato juice.

**************************/

The embers floated in the air, the sparks from the campfire sounded between the trees, throughout the forest. Dry forest. Dry soil, dry trees, juices in its veins flowing, flowing like a waterfall in red.

He stood close to the campfire, surrounded by the embers, by the sparks. Skin felt like it could start blistering any time. The sound of the axe hitting the dry wood, the sound of it echoed inside him. He breathed the clean air, the hot air of the fire.

Ted picked up the distant sound of hooves against the ground, distant no longer. He stood there with a naked chest heaving, contracting and constricting after his hard, physical labor. He felt fine. In fact, he felt good. His eyes widened in surprise when he saw who was approaching him on horseback. It was definitely Maria. Her Spanish/Mexican features were clearly distinctive from Liz. He couldn't say if he was disappointed or intrigued, or if he cared at all. He knew she could see him, see him as he was virtually embraced by fire.

– Hear the CALL OF THE WILD, he shouted at her.

Maria Jimenez pulled the reins. The horses halted abruptly. She dealt with the sudden forward momentum admirably.

– Is it cold? She asked it with a clearly pointed look.

– It is hot as hell. He cried it out, with something at least resembling happiness.

There was something resembling pain in her eyes. She was sweating after the ride and carried in her features a haunted, rigid quality he very early in his life had learned to recognize.

That same frozen look was present when she dismounted and approached him the last, few steps on foot.

– I came here to talk to you, she said straight out.

He was taken aback, caught by surprise. His attention was inevitable drawn to her clothes, the tight riding pants, the round thighs, and her entire curved body.

– Well, talk, he said, shrugging.

– I spoke to Liz, she said. – She told me where to find you.

– She did, huh? That snotty, little bitch.

She stumbled in a root. He caught her before she fell. She released a cry of pain. He looked surprised at her. He hadn't really grabbed her that hard.

– Seeing you there, embraced by fire… She shook her head. – It was the most fantastic sight I've seen in my entire life. It was almost… like you *were* the fire, like you were giving it form and substance.

He looked at her… again. There was something very driven, intense and determined about her, a characteristic she had always kept well hidden, the fire that had always attracted him.

– My father, he…

She held back, lowering her eyes, looking at the ground.

– Come, he said. – I'm willing to bet you've never tasted, far less eaten meat roasted over a fire before.

He signaled for her to follow him, like an eager kid. He walked so fast that she had to run a bit, just to catch up with him. Just then, he caught her in his arms, giving her, stealing a hasty kiss on the lips. Her skin around the mouth was cold and still.

He had made the actual camp, with its smaller fire by the entrance to a small mountain cave. The tent, the sleeping bag, the rucksack and gear were close by, just inside the shadows.

– Do you live out here? She asked him breathlessly.

– I try to, he replied. – Some day I will.

He held back, suddenly just as hesitant, as she had been.

– Everything is… raw here. The savage, primitive Earth is still here, you know, just as untouched as it has always been.

– I understand what you mean, she commented. – There are no considerable human settlements here.

– The tent can be kinda cold during the nights, though…

He looked at her, suddenly completely lacking shyness. She felt his fire burn her, and it warmed her and hurt all over her body.

– I saw the campfire from far away, she whispered. – I feared the entire forest was burning.

The light and shadow from the big fire further out washed over them, as it mingled with the smaller closer to them.

– Have you hunted? She asked him. – Have you killed?

He looked closer at her. She was still sweating, sweating profusely. He was hot, too, but he didn't sweat. There existed a kind of dry air in the vicinity of the fires, especially between them, a warm, pleasant breeze making him feel strangely peaceful. But she looked downright… disturbed. He felt the unrest, even something resembling insanity within her like needles in the gut.

They sat down by the smaller fire. He took a knife and cut a piece of meat from the steak over the flames, giving it to her. She took it carefully with both hands.

– It's hot, she giggled.

– Wait a bit, he admonished her. – It will cool quickly.

She did, and never taking her eyes of him, she took a big bite. There was a light in her eyes. She looked at him and her curiosity wasn't really hard to spot.

And neither was something else, not easily definable and clearly disturbing.

– My father is a very old-fashioned man. The two of them remained by the smaller fire, as the world darkened around them. She sat there, staring into it. – One advantage of this is that he is very much opposed to Hunter Cornwall's extensive real estate plans for this area.

The bitterness and the rage were easily discernible in her voice, in her entire demeanor. He nodded.

– My father is doing his utmost to keep me a prisoner in my own house. It's my house, you know. I inherited it from my grandmother on my mother's side. My mother died many years ago.

– I didn't know that, he said with a rusty voice.

– Of course, you didn't. How could you? No one outside the inner circle of the family has ever before been told the truth.

– There must be something you can do, he insisted.

– There isn't anything. *Papa* keeps a tight household, never allowing anyone to break his hold on absolute power. He has to keep up a certain pretense, though. That's why I'm allowed to go to school, and everything.

School actually worked as a kind of liberation for her. Amazing!

He saw the fire dance before him. He saw the Shadow, its

eternal dance. He shook his head, both scared and intrigued.

When he once more caught the girl's eyes he imagined a thousand years had passed.

– You are Wild, she told him. – I have looked at you, studied you, a Beast pretending to be human.

– You are very beautiful, he said, lightly touching her jaw.

– Even your words, soft as petal wings are Wild.

She pulled back angrily, not once averting her eyes, her eyes like open wounds.

And when she looked at him, he felt a hatred almost paling his own.

– I have to be a virgin, she said straight out. – At least until the day I'm eighteen and get control over my inheritance. There is a kind of tradition in my family, centuries old, about... inspection of a girl's *cunt*.

She spat out the last word, as if it was a curse.

– Akin to that done to prospective queens and daughters of noblemen in the middle ages. «Loose» birds are disowned, *disinherited*.

Her accent was virtually flawless. Many of Mexican ancestry retained a kind of accent, almost hereditary, no matter how many generations they had spent in the United States. She was a strange mix of both the old family ways and the modern, kind of sophisticated society. He was helplessly fascinated by her. There was an increasingly painful pressure in his pants slowly spreading to his remaining body and mind, a rush of wind, a waterfall roaring in the forest.

– That's absolutely bullshit, he protested. – You can't possibly let yourself be ruled by it, you just can't. If you do that, your father, fuck him to hell, will have won, even if he loses.

She touched his cheek lightly.

– You're such a sweet boy. Will you help me... against my father?

– Sorry, Senorita, only you can liberate yourself. You should be able to see that, easily, for yourself. Don't you see what's happening in the world? Women, men, anybody are liberating themselves everywhere. Nobody should put up with shit like that anymore.

– The world is so far away, she whispered, – so very far away.

– I know, he said. – I know…

He pulled her head to him and then he kissed her, kissed her lips, hungry like a wolf.

– The world is here, he said. – Right here. Nothing else matters.

He felt her resistance, felt her giving in. He released her.

– That's easy for you to say, she said accusingly. – So typical a male, pretending to be free of all constraints.

It hurt somewhere inside him, even more so, than it usually did.

– So typical a female, he snarled, – using her sex as an excuse.

She stared at him, with eyes opened wide, dilated in shock. The venom in his voice froze her, as effectively as a cold, cold winter.

He grabbed her head again, pulling her to him, grabbing her body, pulling the entire her close. He kissed her on the lips. Hard. The crescendo inside, the flow of blood intensified to a roar, undeniable. He sensed her, sensed the protest, the giving in. He put a hand on one of her breasts, felt it contract with his touch.

She pushed him away with incredible strength, and rose, backing away from him, from the fire. The music inside him turned savage, chaotic and he couldn't say he didn't enjoy it.

Her voice, when she spoke was like poison.

– If you absolutely need to get in somebody's pants, why don't you go to your sweet *diablito* cousin? She is certainly willing enough, that tramp.

He sensed it inside, the viciousness, he sensed it rise. What he had feared his entire life, what he once, in a terrible moment had discovered in his brother, in himself. It felt so long ago.

– You're fond of games, aren't you, Senorita? Well, as you will discover, I am, too…I will make certain that closed gate of yours is opened wide. Your father will have difficulties removing all the blood when I return you to him.

There was thunder. The hoarse, contemptuous grin was like an echo from the past - from Mike after the shooting contest. It made an alarm clock start chiming in his brain, but it was faint, unimportant. He hardly heard it. There was the soft-skinned brown face in front of him, and that was all. He grabbed her arms, hard. She attempted to scratch his face with her long nails. He laughed and struck her hard in her ribs, blowing air from her lungs. She gasped, and her body turned completely limp, malleable. He dragged her to the tent, releasing her just in front of it, where there was a soft, natural mattress of green grass. He let his eyes burn over the still, breathing body. Her pants had slipped quite a bit down, on her hips, revealing the tight skin. She tried desperately to calm herself, to gather air to speak, shaking like a leaf.

– Ted, listen to me. Please, listen.

He loosened his belt in front, deliberately taking his time, savoring it all. There was a twitch at the corner of his mouth that perhaps could be mistaken for a grin.

That was all.

– I know. *I know.* Liz… told me.

He stopped, the twitch, the grin widening to an insane degree.

– She… *told* you?

– Yes, she gasped. – And I instantly felt… a kinship with you. I wanted to know you better. No games. Please.

And now you shall.

He didn't say it, hardly even thought it. Slowly, standing by her knees, he pulled out the belt, lifted it up, to strike. She closed her eyes, waiting for the inevitable. His chest heaved, as his breathing pace increased. He threw the belt away, with a contemptuous laughter.

– Look at the arrogant, aloof *Dona,* now, he spat. – Not much pride left, is there? A little more, now, and you'll be broken like a *twig.*

Grinning he registered how his rock-hard erection showed on the pants, a huge throbbing bulge. She saw it, too, as he began pulling the cover down his thighs. And as he did so, he seemed like an adult, experienced man. He kicked her, a bit clumsy, because of the obvious hampering his pants caused his feet.

– Please, she gasped. – Please.

– Spare me, he said coldly. – It isn't me you're interested in. You're just seeing a wild animal, something that might be of some limited use to you.

She opened her mouth.

– Just scream. He laughed at her. – No one will hear you. It will just make it more fun.

Something… something in his voice, when he said that last word made her snap completely. She started whining. Hardly hearing it, or anything but the roar in his ears, he threw himself at her. The noises coming from her stopped abruptly and she just lay there, as a rigid doll and absolutely frozen. Filled with expectation he pulled down her tight, tight pants. The panties and something resembling cotton, too. A… *scream* erupted from the girl, one unlike anything he had ever heard, so heartbreaking and insane that it would possibly cut through steel. So spontaneous and so shocking that Ted, even in his prevalent approaching, undeniable ecstasy, almost stopped in his task, but it didn't take long for him to practically forget it, forget everything.

This is fun, he screamed, his voice completely drowning in the unearthly sound erupting from the girl.

She continued screaming. Her eyes almost left the sockets. They were that wide.

Let her scream, he thought feverishly. Let her, too, feel pain.

There was a tree close by. She grabbed it. In her panic she dug her nails into the bark, attempting to drag herself free of him, of his overwhelming weight. He just grabbed the arm and pulled it back, pulled it hard. Nails were torn from her fingers.

He slapped her several times, until she lay still once more, all the time moving, moving closer to his goal, the hot, moist nest down below on her body.

Moaning hard, he stroked her back. Wow, she truly did sweat. Skin was strangely rough. Otherwise her skin in no way looked like sand paper. The roughness reminded him of

GOD

With a fear only Mike had been able to instill in him he jumped up and away from the screaming, hysterical girl, finally realizing what his thoughts had tried to tell him, what it all meant. His eyes were just as wide as that of the girl when he stared at his hands, shocked beyond words. They were soaked in blood. He stood there frozen, staring blindly at her skin. Her round butt stood out as a wound. They looked like it, a single huge wound, as a grotesque example of brutality. From parts of her back four blood-red lines glowed at the shocked boy. Ted knew way too well what the lines meant.

Maria had been whipped.

– Who d-did t-this? He asked stuttering. – In heaven's name, why?

– My father, of course, she sobbed. – He wanted to teach me a lesson, to once and for all mark me as his.

- But that is completely insane.

Images danced through his mind, and each step was pain, of the past, of a nightmarish future. Clutching his clothes in his hands he stumbled away, not caring where he went, not caring at all.

She said something, a sound, unidentifiable, making him turn, making him look back at her.

– Do you see now? Do you SEE?

Still sobbing, drying her eyes, drying saliva from her mouth, still screaming inside she dragged herself up on her feet. He wondered what kind of willpower she could possibly possess for her to ride all the way out here, ridden with the sort of pain that had been inflicted on her. Supporting herself on the tree she looked triumphantly at him.

– You knew something was wrong from the start, she said accusingly. – Still, you pressed on, caring naught for anything but your unsatisfied desire.

She closed and opened her eyes once and when she once more spoke her voice was dull, even.

– You're even more like Papa than I thought, she said. – That's good. You will crush him.

And the sign of revulsion in her eyes hit him far harder than the worst slap in the face.

And he stood there, with his body pushed against the rock, unable to say anything, unable to move. He stared blindly across the foggy hills, seeing nothing.

Chapter eight

Harsh, brittle guitar-sounds echoed through the uneven Colorado landscape.

Linsey's shoulder had healed fast, uncannily fast. He had been up and going after just a few days, almost good as new already then. And now, ten weeks later, there was no trace of the injury, no trace at all, as if it had never been. In fact, as he sat there without clothes on his upper body, he seemed to have developed a visibly more powerful frame. The muscles, previously merely suggested, were not just a suggestion anymore. And his over the top mood was almost overwhelming.

He was playing acoustic guitar, hesitatingly, exactly like a baby learning to walk.

Elizabeth stood a few steps away, listening to it, to the words. She studied him with intense, burning eyes.

> Tears are a rage
> I can't, won't deny
> Nothing is right in this world
> Even what's right
> Is wrong
> In a world
> Where everything
> Is upside down

After a while he stopped, visibly frustrated, putting the guitar down.

– So, what do you think? He asked his sister

– About what? Her teasing smile spoke volumes.

– About me, as a future musician?

– I like the lyrics, she replied. – I do. I agree totally with it. And the playing wasn't bad either. At least not considering the fact that you've just played for a few weeks…

He smiled, but there was impatience somewhere there in the sharp eyes, demanding answers. She could relate to that. She most certainly could.

– Tell me the truth, what do you think?

– It's awful, she said.

– Mrs. Barker enjoyed it. A huge, ironic grin. – She stood here for ten minutes, listening to me, looking at me as if I was the second coming or something.

– She was just being polite, don't you think? His sister pointed out, very pointedly.

He nodded solemnly.

– That can be a very annoying «quality» in some people, he said with regret.

– You shouldn't give up yet, she said encouragingly. – Rome wasn't built on a single day… Or so they say.

He applauded by slowly beating his palms together, in a mock salute.

– So young, and already a master of ambiguity…

– Thank you, good sir. She curtsied. – I try. I try my very best.

She walked closer to him, until there were just a couple of steps between them. He looked at the sunset. He looked at her.

She tilted her head a bit, as if listening, straining to hear something not easily heard, looking at him. He looked away, shivering visibly.

– What is it? She wondered, and when he hesitated: – You can tell me, tell your sweet sister.

– I dreamt about Ted this morning, he said. – dreamt about him being dead. I thought he was when the two of us found him that night. There was so much blood and he was so pale. I was completely frozen, shocked to my bones. I can still see him, seeing him lie there, dead and cold, while the socket of the broken lightbulb, impossibly sparked and flared.

She tried putting up a brave front, but it wasn't very convincing.

– It did look bad, she conceded. – I was totally beside myself at first.

– It was a good thing that you woke up from a nightmare, he noted. – Or we might have not found him until next morning, and it would have been too late.

– A very good thing, she whispered, hardly audible.

She still recalled it vividly, the total horror that had overwhelmed her, paralyzed her.

Then, amazingly, shockingly to him, she smiled.

– But he didn't spend more than two days at the hospital,

though, his wounds healing even faster than your shoulder. There was just a lot of blood and looked worse than it was.

The horror had itself been overwhelmed by a sense of intense curiosity and purpose and destiny.

Linsey didn't know what to say and didn't reply, not with words, didn't even try to put his feelings and raging thoughts into words.

– Play some more, she said softly. – Play to make heaven cry.

As she studied him, he studied her.

– Thunder is coming, she said.

He reached for the guitar, seemingly not hearing her words.

– Can you feel it? She asked him, suddenly. – You can feel it, can't you?

An almost imperceptible nod she wasn't sure she saw. She felt the chill in the hot spring air, she felt the joy.

She felt it. She actually felt the first quivering tone in her gut, and she started swaying and then humming. Down by the enclosure the horses began pacing, testing the fence, their boundaries. Those in the stable cried out their neighing. Liz imagined she could see the cows and bulls far away stop their grazing, lift their heads, and stamp their feet. As the girl sensed the first flapping of wings she started dancing.

– Oh, brother thy sting is here, she cried in the wilderness.

He stopped playing. She stopped, a huge smile, akin to ecstasy suddenly illuminating her face. Brother and sister froze. She smiling. He with a stunned expression in his face.

Hens surrounded them. Hens and other birds, from the wild, had gathered in a circle, an honor guard around them.

She stood in the middle of her room, dancing. The music from the speaker made the walls shake. Ted stood by the door, never taking his eyes off her.

– Listen to Quinn the Eskimo. She hummed, as she swayed from side to side. – He's dancing through the night and everybody hears his song. Look at the shadows moving in dark corners.

He could hardly hear her speak over the loud music, but he could hear her speak, as if there was silence, silence everywhere.

– Come, dance with me. She reached out a hand, reaching for

him.

And he did. There was no sense of elation, only of fact. And they danced.

– Are you okay? She whispered in his ear. – Please tell sweet Liz that you're okay.

– I am, he assured her. – Whatever brought on what happened it's behind me, now. There is no need to worry.

– I do worry, she said. – And I feel guilty. I think about it often. I pushed you, made you vulnerable.

– It had nothing to do with you. It could have happened at any time, really.

She sniffed in gratitude, briefly a little girl again.

– If anything, you forced a resolution.

– I d-did?

– You made me face myself, he acknowledged. – I needed to do that, needed it badly.

They danced, swaying in a matching pattern, holding hands, and no more.

– One thing's for sure, she sniffed some more. – That's yet another «incident» the family speaks about without speaking about

«The family» was Eugene's part of the family tree.

– I heard them, daddy and uncle and auntie circle around the subject for at least an *hour*. They spoke about your mother, «the famous American actress» disappearing in the South Asian jungles in the early fifties and presumed dead for five years, until showing up with a husband and three children. They wondered what had happened during that time. It was hardly more than classic gossip, really, but not without some potential usefulness.

She grinned, regaining at least some of her devil-may-care attitude.

– They also discussed, again without really discussing anything the rumor that my mother fainted the first time she saw Michael. Now, I don't think mother would have fainted for anything, that the story is a bit exaggerated, but I do believe she was visibly shocked. I guess she recognized him, recognized his features at a glance, right?

– The first part does seem far-fetched, he nodded. – Your

conclusion does not.

She laughed happily, suddenly approaching something akin to euphoria, her mood swinging at least as much as his did on occasion, as she snuggled in his arms.

– An inquisitive mind can find out a lot, she whispered in his ear. – There is nothing hidden from truly inquisitive minds. Please let me help you, aid you in any way I can.

The music stopped, its echo fading slowly from the room. The moment ended. They heard steps in the stairs.

– «Behold, the pale thunder approaches the gathering, the gathering of mist», Liz quoted. From where, Ted didn't know.

They both recognized the steps, and they would have known who it was anyway, without sound, without sight.

– Finally, Eugene Kendall snorted. – The house was about ready to come crashing down.

– I just wanted to feel it, you know, Liz stated, unusually meek and sober. – Just wanted to feel it in my bones. Can't you feel it? I know you can.

– You've got a lot of nerve, young lady, claiming to know what's on my mind.

– Why not, you're doing it to me all the time. Except for your «open door policy» you've never had much in your favor, in my eyes.

– That's NO WAY to talk to your father, he warned her.

– But you can say what you want to me, with impunity, without me being allowed to defend myself? I don't think so... I may be a child, but I'm not a sheep, going meekly to the gas chamber. Get used to it.

Trudy showed up then. Liz hurried out in the hall, behind her back, peeking sheepishly up from behind her mother.

Kendall looked at them, just looked at both.

– You're always seeking protection within your mother's arms.

– Are you saying I need protection? Do you want to fight me, is that what you want, daddy?

– You're quite the little devil, aren't you, twisting everything I say?

– Funny, that's what I wanted to say about you.

Ted stepped forward. Everybody froze.

– I think you're obviously wrong in this, Eugene, Ted stated, very decisive.

Kendall stood there, one second, two, before leaving. But it was as if everybody still stood there, frozen. They could see each other's faces.

Kendall knew, they all knew from that moment on, that if Kendall had ever had any control in this place, it was gone now, gone with the wind.

*********************/

The days had been short, like bits and pieces. They remembered them like moments from a life, nothing more.

The rain dug huge holes in the ground. Water flowed over the fields and formed ponds in every low spot. The floodgates in the sky were wide open. Lightning flared, and the first cracks of thunder had started to run in all directions.

It was May eighth, 1971, Ted's sixteenth and Liz' twelfth birthday. There was celebration, on the ranch and later in a community house connected to and used by the school not far away. Ted didn't really enjoy the added attention much, but he saw how Liz thrived on it, indeed blossoming like a flower in spring.

He hadn't really celebrated anything in four years, and he didn't now.

– Ten cents for your thoughts, Senor, the girl by his side said to him.

He looked sharply at Maria. Giggling she sat down on the other side of the table. Crossing her legs, she studied him intensely.

– Ten cents? He grinned. – You must be kidding. They're worth far more than that.

There were just the two of them in the room, a loft three floors above the festivities in the hall. The sounds from downstairs stayed loud, but inevitably muted. The sound of the rain hitting the windows was far more pronounced.

– You promised me dinner, she said, – but I haven't seen anything but words so far.

– Coming straight up, he countered.

He walked to the kitchen. She sat there, humming and keeping the beat of the below music by clapping her hands and swaying back and forth in the sofa. The laughter in her eyes warmed him.

When he returned with the tray her eyes turned huge and disbelieving.

– A pheasant, Ted Cousin, she said aloud. – How did you manage such an expensive feat, if I may ask?

She kept looking at the big bird, as if she couldn't exactly believe it.

– This is actually the Principals office away from home, away from his loving wife, Ted replied. – I'm told he takes selected students here while working long evening hours. He's got excellent taste in food…

– You are crazy, she whispered incredulously.

– Thank you, my dear, you say the nicest things.

Maria laughed to the point of shaking. They both did.

– I honestly don't feel bad about it, he said, shaking his head decisively. – The principal is a prick.

And they laughed even harder.

– Dig in. Everything is on our friend, the principal.

She hesitated momentarily, before cutting off two pieces and giving him one. He also brought two bottles of soda from the room's substantial supply and opened them, giving her one.

Down below, from the dancing hall they heard the music thundering through the speakers. Ted knew that Liz was down there. The thought irritated him a bit, but he didn't really care much for dancing. That was one of the few venues he hadn't pursued the last few years.

He touched Maria's hand slightly. She looked at it, at both hands. His skin was substantially darker than hers.

– You struggle so, you struggle so, she said, in a mantra kind of way. – Why do I both fear you and am attracted to you?

– That one is easy, he said, – we're all attracted to what we fear, fearing what we're attracted to.

And when she looked at him, she didn't really see the boy at all, but an ancient creature of both light and darkness, shadow and fire. She smelled the forest once more, the pines, the fire. She whimpered inside.

– When I first saw you, she said, – you were kind of a pathetic creature, with a shirt at least three sizes too big. You're wearing the same shirt now. Now, it's too small. But even though you were pathetic then, you projected strength, resolve. You projected hatred. I could relate to that, I knew I could. We're both damaged goods. I love you. You're so damn fascinating. How boring everybody else is, compared to you.

There was insanity in her eyes, a cruel sanity, and everything in-between. Her outburst rattled him, but he revealed nothing.

He sat there, with a mouth dry as desert sand and couldn't tell whether or not it was the girl or her tale that was to blame, but joy and expectation did rise within him. She handed him another slab of meat, and he accepted.

– Oh, boy, she exclaimed a while later. She stretched, a pleased expression in her eyes, pushing the chair away from the table with her feet. – Am I full or what. You have been so clever. Something like this would never have occurred to innocent little me.

She reminded him of Tilla, of Linda, or Liz, and he couldn't decide whether or not it was all a front and it frustrated him.

– Aren't you gonna thank me?

He didn't bother to walk around the table. He merely pushed away the heavy furniture, removing the final obstruction between them. His hand closed around her arm. Without resisting she allowed herself to be pulled into his arms. Before she managed to say anything, express any misgivings he had pushed his lips against hers, kissing her hard and fierce. He had to bend down and because of that she had to lean back.

– Hey, she said reddening. – Wasn't I supposed to give you your first poker lesson tonight?

He stopped a bit grinning.

– Are you any good? You have to be, you know, to teach me anything of consequence. Mike is very good.

– My aunt taught me. And she was very good. A man called The Gambler had taught her, and he's world class. He gained third place in the World Series of Poker in Las Vegas last year.

– I've heard about him. Ted nodded.

She freed herself from his grip, slipped from it like a snake. She sensed the savage inside him, so hungry, so eager to break out. One didn't need to be very sensitive to sense that. It was noticeable, almost visible in every little move he made. With steady hands she grabbed her purse and pulled up a deck of cards. It was twice as big as any he had previously seen.

– I like 'em. They remind me how much I like a certain tall man.

He started laughing. As she had expected, as she had desperately hoped.

– No, he said.

– What do you mean, «no»? She asked it weakly, miserably.

– I want you. You're a lot prettier than any deck of cards.

He grabbed her again, and instantly started fumbling with the front of her shirt. He attempted to be careful, but still tore loose two buttons. Shaking his head, he lifted her up and carried her off to the bedroom. She stroked his cheek, while talking, talking fast, desperately fast.

– There is a way we can both get what we want, she said, she insisted.

He stopped, giving her his attention.

– I can… help you, you know, she said sweetly. – You know what I am talking about, don't you? I know how. My aunt told me how. She told me many things.

He knew indeed what she was suggesting.

– No. He shook his head. – I don't want that, I don't want half measures, half-life.

He looked intensively at her.

– I want everything.

The waiting is over. The waiting is over. He called and recalled it like a mantra when he carried her to the bed, when he let go of her and threw her on the bed, the very large bed.

– … don't want to? Don't you realize that I can't?

He stood with his arms hanging down on the other side of the bed, breathing heavily, unable to tell how long time had passed, taking one more step forward, then another.

– No, she said. – No, no, *no*. Which part of that word don't you understand?

Hair covered one of his eyes, giving him a scary look, even without what scared people the most… the glowing eyes. He saw a small part of an exposed breast, and couldn't fathom how he managed to hold back.

– Why? He asked flatly.

– You *know* why, she cried at him. – Don't you care about anyone else, except yourself?

He felt the pain in his back, then, for the first time in months. It was still there. The scars never disappeared completely.

– You can keep your precious virginity, he spat. – I don't give a shit.

He pulled back, backed off, out of the bedroom, crossing the living room. In the hallway he dressed in swift, furious moves.

– Do you hear what I'm saying, he shouted. – I don't give a shit.

He turned in a rage, tore open the door, charged through it, and closed it so hard behind him that the crack made everything shake and rattle. Maria shook on the bed, unmoving. The sound of the door signified something to her, to them both. Something decisive. A crack, a warning of...

The approaching, impending Doom.

*****************************/

The dance hall was filled with people, and smoke drifted under the ceiling. Music was so loud that everything and everyone was constantly shaking. Thud, thud, thud. Ted sensed how the thudding disrupted his mind, disrupting the flow of thought, of blood, shaking him to shreds.

He sat by a table close to the exit. Perhaps it was his foul mood, perhaps no one truly saw him as they passed by, without approaching, without coming close. A hand closed around his. A female hand. He knew instantly who it was, but still shook when staring into Liz' innocent, blue eyes.

– What are you doing here? He growled sourly. – Didn't I tell you to stay away?

– I'm lonely, she whimpered. – Everyone else here is so light, so ephemeral that I can't really say they're present at all. And I *am* worried about you, my darling boy.

He looked at her and knew she was sincere. For what reason or purpose were harder to decide.

– As stated, you don't have to be, he assured her.

– But I am, she insisted, – but more than anything about you not living up to your potential. What you saw... in your «fever visions», and I only glimpsed when everyone else thought you were close to death was so terrible, so beyond exciting. I *want* that, for both of us.

He shivered, in the same ambiguous apprehension and excitement ravaging her.

She moved herself closer to him, smiling to him, so needy, innocent and sweet.

Only slowly, very slowly the reality of the hall, their immediate surroundings re-imposed itself on them. She shook her head in regret and despair.

– This is truly a strange custom, isn't it? She grinned. – The adults arrange a birthday party for the children, inviting the entire area. But it soon becomes clear that the party isn't really for the children, but for the adults, an opportunity for them to come together and discuss what's on their mind. Many of the adults aren't even here anymore, but have «retired» to the backrooms, where they can do their thing in peace. Not that I'm complaining. I just find it strange, that's all…

They turned as one, and spotted Kendall and Hunter Cornwall having a «conversation» by the stage. It was clear that they didn't like each other very much. They kept up appearances (appearances are everything), but to the boy and the girl, more easily seeing beneath appearances, the truth was evident.

Liz lifted her glass to the mouth and drank, drank a lot.

– Ah, Brandy is such tasty shit, she marveled.

Her challenge was clearly projected across the room, as if she dared any adult to come and chastise her. But no adult came.

– You shouldn't drink that shit, he said, shaking his head. – It's pure poison. It causes nothing but harm.

– You're wrong, she replied dreamingly. – It causes no harm, but quite the opposite. You can achieve so much with its gentle touch. Forgetfulness, freedom, like the bird, a giant bird flying through the night…

She discovered how deeply her words affected him, how they echoed within herself. She shook herself, fighting to emerge from a trancelike state.

– Isn't that what you want? She asked.

– Is that what *you* want?

She froze, too. Suddenly there was thunder. Slowly the smile reemerged in her features.

A bunch of younger kids called her name.

– COME, LIZ. TIME FOR CAKE, LIZ.

She smiled some more as she was rising.

– I must go. Duty calls. Enjoy yourself, okay?

She left the glass, half full.

He waited a bit, until she was well embodied within the flock of kids by the table on the opposite side of the room, before abruptly rising, and leaving the hall. He made his way out of the building, moving like a sleepwalker, his attention directed straight forward.

The door was open. He was able to stare directly into the wall of water, the raging storm. Rain had already flooded much of the hallway. He heard approaching voices. Recognizing them, he hurried behind the corner, hiding. A few steps away he heard Butch Davison and Claudia Cornwall in a heated embrace, the kisses, the passionate whisper.

– Not here, Ted heard her mumble. She whispered something. Ted glimpsed Butch's grin. Laughing they walked straight out, into the rain.

Ted waited until he could no longer hear their steps, before following them.

The wet storm hit him straight in the face. He instantly turned wet to the bone. The wind was so strong he had to cling to the banister all the way down the long stairs. His grip slipped once or twice, and he almost fell.

In the soft gravel there was no problem picking up the trail of Butch and Claudia. The footprints were quite deep. He saw them at some point ahead, clinging to each other. The rain hit him like a velvet fist. He ignored it. There was nothing on his mind, except what was ahead. He heard the girl's sensual laughter through the darkness.

Then, suddenly, he lost his footing. He hit the ground with his face down. The mud was pushed into his mouth. He didn't dare draw breath. Desperately he wavered and attempted to turn. He started sliding down the slope, literally floating downwards. The ground stayed soft, malleable. He struck the ground, to no avail. It was just water and dirt. Helpless, he could do nothing but let himself slide all the way down. There wasn't anything to hold onto, was nothing solid anywhere, nothing but darkness and shit. Lightning flared, illuminating nothing, blinding him to his surroundings, as he slid down, down, down. After a long, long slide he finally stopped, coughing and desperately attempting to empty his mouth. He spat many times, filled the mouth with dirty water and spat again.

He *screamed*. A shattering shout of despair and rage. A fist struck the mud, sinking to the elbow. Swearing and cursing he pulled it back up and fought himself back on his feet. He stood still for a while, his chest heaving and sinking.

He felt the hostility of his surroundings, palpable, like stabs in his body, and returned the snarl, the stabs with a vengeance, against the land, against creation itself, sensing how satisfying it was.

In silhouette against the darkening horizon he could see a structure, a shack of some kind. His eyes locked on to it. It was the only place Butch and Claudia could seek shelter. Ted knew it was an old barn nobody used much anymore. They stored some hay there, if there was a lot of it, as there had been last year. Except for that it was just used for marking the corner of four major family estates, the properties of Kendall, Davison, Cornwall and Jimenez.

He started on the climb up again, but was far more cautious. It took time that way, but he got up without further incidents. He breathed heavily in and out, as he made his way to the shack-like barn.

They had turned on the light in there. He carefully made his way to a window, looking inside. The two of them played in the hay at the other side of the room, snuggling under a blanket. He saw two plastic bags on the dusty floor and grinned. They had planned a picnic, planned it well in advance.

Wet as he was, the wind turned cold and menacing. He walked to the door. It was locked. He had to really pull himself together. He wanted to shake the door, shake it off its hinges. The temptation was overwhelming, but he resisted it.

He sensed a movement in the wind. Looking up and to the side he saw a rope swinging from side to side from a point up there in the dark. He saw the light from below reach a small, open window upstairs. Looking down at his hands he saw them covered in mud, probably making them slippery as hell. The rope, too, would be wet. It was an old rope, covered in moss. He tested it, grabbed it and pulled hard. It seemed solid enough. Then he stopped caring and started doing.

The rope was indeed slippery in his hands. Every move, every inch up cost him enormous amounts of power. It hurt, just after the first, few seconds. He climbed on. Glancing down his feet didn't seem to be farther above the ground than minutes, hours ago. His entire body was rigid with concentration. His vision filled with a sky of red, red stars. One more hand above the other, and another. He climbed on.

Finally, he reached the level of the window. Breath was labored and every muscle in his body hurt, hurt, hurt. He started swinging the rope, swinging his body on the rope. There was a distance of the length of his body between him and the window he had to cover, no more. It felt like hundred times that. He held on with one hand, while attempting to grab the low frame of the window with the other. His outstretched hand struck open air. He swung back, and again and again as he gathered strength for one, last expenditure of power, not looking down once.

And as he felt his grip slip he threw himself at the window, grabbing, holding on to the frame with both hands, resting of sorts, one second, two, before pulling himself up and climbing in, almost blacking out in the process.

The hay was soft and dry. He rested there, dreaming he was there, and not in the mud far below. Pain riddled him as he kept staring at the ceiling, at the unchanging patterns above. He heard Claudia's voice, heard her hum a tune, one he didn't recognize, a valve on wounded beasts. Her body, her smile appeared before him, dancing before his eyes.

She is just a selfish bitch, he thought happily. A selfish rich bitch.

The building didn't have a complete upper floor. One could look down to the ground floor from the wide opening at its center. Hay covered the floor all the way to the edge of the floor. He carefully crawled there, easily able to see without being seen. He saw Claudia, swallowing hard.

She sat in the hay, alone for the moment. He saw she was about to unpack the food. Her moves were gracious, enticing, the way he had seen her do gymnastics. The brown hair reached below her shoulders, a cute contrast to the green dress, one so low-necked that most of her breasts were uncovered. And to add to that effect it was at least partly wet and transparent because of the rain, in spite of the protective vests they had used. Ted started growing, hardening below. The pain almost made him cry out.

Claudia performed for Butch, that much was obvious, turning and twisting as she was, obviously wanting him to go to her. How the fucker could stay away was beyond Ted's understanding. He didn't speak, he didn't move from his current position. He had to be completely addled by arousal.

And then, in a flash Ted understood, too late. He managed to turn, just a bit, get a glimpse of Butch's triumphant expression, before he was pushed off the ledge. In a state of shock, without being able to resist he fell towards the bare floor.

He landed on his back. Air was pushed out of his lungs. He attempted to scream, but couldn't make a single sound. The pain was so intense that he thought he would never breathe again. Butch descending the stairs sounded like thunder in his ears. His vision was distorted. He saw nothing but humanlike shapes seemingly dancing towards him. Not until Butch and Claudia stood straight above him did he manage to focus on them. The old fears returned, abruptly, sickeningly. They always did, with his sense of inferiority and these two had suckered him completely, played him like an old fiddle.

– The evening will not be dull, after all, sweetheart, Claudia exclaimed happily. – Tonight's entertainment just dumped into our lap.

– You're absolutely right, girl, Butch replied just as happily. – And we must thank this fool for the effort he has made on our behalf.

A well of negative emotions revealed themselves on Ted's face. There had been a long time since he had been confronted with something he couldn't easily deal with, but now the table had been turned. This time it was he who was at Butch's mercy, and not the other way around. And Claudia was Paul's sister. Ted had also tarnished Paul's pride. The dark clouds were gathering.

Butch spoke, his voice filled with venom:

– Look at our king. Not much to look at anymore, is he?

Butch seemed to kind of slip away, turning darker in hair and skin. In Ted's eyes he suddenly looked like Mike.

Ted didn't say anything. He just lay still, desperately attempting to breathe evenly, conserving energy, in an attempt to get the strength back in the weak, exhausted muscles.

Then Butch kicked him in the belly. The heavy boot pushed deep into soft tissue. For the second time in a very short time Ted got the air kicked out of him. He screamed aloud and crouched on the floor. Tears erupted from his eyes.

– You're finally getting what's coming to you, Butch snarled, grabbing him in the collar. – You come here and play king, and expect us to put up with it.

– You see, Ted, Claudia grinned, – I and my brave protector here made a wager with Paul and Kevin, the other team, about who would capture you first… We hadn't really expected to succeed tonight, we didn't even try, but you dumped straight into our lap and you get no complains from me. To lure Paul and Butch into fighting, that was not very nice. You'll pay for that. You'll pay for a lot of things.

Ted couldn't even look at her. He could hardly move and heard her cold voice through a cascade of pain. He felt bad, truly bad. The fall and the kick, added to everything else, the emotional rollercoaster he had gone through the last few hours made the nausea stick in his throat like a ball. Once more he crouched violently. Vomit rose from his mouth like a geyser.

– God damn, Butch exclaimed disgusted, – what a pig.

– I think you can safely fetch the rope, now, darling, Claudia laughed. – I don't believe our captive will be able to move much the next few hours.

The captive… Ted looked at Claudia with water-filled eyes. She noticed, and bent down to him.

– I can see you think, she whispered. – Your regrets because you rejected me.

He looked uncomprehending at her, comprehension dawning in his eyes.

– You don't even remember, she cried. – Fucking asshole. You'll pay. PAY!

She kicked him. And kicked him again. The second time he

hardly felt anything. It was delegated to some distant part of his mind. He wondered if she had killed him.

Anger gripped him. His eyes narrowed, and he felt pain, felt hatred once more.

– I don't like you when you're angry, Claudia told him. – You're not so pretty then.

And the venom in her voice poisoned him, filling him to the brim.

She grabbed his hair and pushed his head down in the puke, dragging the head back and forth in it. Not content by merely dragging him through the mud, she also opened his mouth and put the puke back in. He attempted to shut it, but she closed his nose, forcing him to keep the bigger opening open.

– Swallow, she said cheerfully.

He desperately attempted to lift his arms, but she easily and triumphantly forced them back down.

– You should eat, you know, she giggled. – You'll need all your strength, believe me.

He looked at her with his swimming burning eyes, attempting to focus, once more showing off his helplessness.

– We can keep you locked up as long as we want. No one will suspect a thing, I promise you that. You will need all the strength at your disposal.

Butch returned. He laughed so hard that he almost lost the rope he carried.

– I heard about your dramatic hospital visit, Claudia spat. – When you disappear, disappear from the face of the Earth, they will all just believe you've made another, successful attempt at what you attempted that night.

This is real.

Ted felt fear gnaw at his bones, paralyzing him even further. He released an involuntary, weak moan, couldn't help it.

Butch placed himself above him, a study in sadistic pleasure and equal perplexity.

– I don't understand how you could have kicked my feet away from me, especially without anybody noticing. You were so far away. But it was you. You did it!

– So you can't take a joke and you're gonna tie me up, Ted gasped. – You're bonkers, totally gone.

– You're gonna *pay!*

Butch grabbed him and brutally turned him around on his belly. It hurt as one muscle gave away. Ted cried out in sudden, paralyzing pain.

– I'm an expert in doing knots, Butch bragged. – I'm sure you have noticed that. You'll never get free, you freak!

– I know you're trying to stall for time, sweetheart, Claudia told him softly, – but as you can see, my big, ruthless man is much too smart to allow that.

Butch grabbed Ted's weak hands and tied a knot around them, putting the feet on them, tightening the grip instantly, expertly, *brutally*. Ted screamed. Butch laughed, truly enjoying himself, enjoying being the top guy.

– Fetch the food, woman, he grinned. – This wet blanket won't give us any trouble.

Ted lay still on the floor, slowly, painfully abandoning hope. He wanted to move. There was no strength left in his limbs. He wanted to think. No thoughts remained. He heard Claudia's step on the floor, as she crossed the room. But…

He also heard lighter steps, heard the sound of them vibrating close to his ear. They heard nothing, but he did, not just because he was closer to the floor, he suspected, but because of his suddenly extremely acute senses, almost frightening in their power.

They didn't hear anything. Not even when Elizabeth Kendall charged from her hiding place in the dark, in the shadows. She assaulted Butch from behind, pressing a big, wet cloth over his nose and mouth.

The chloroform, Ted thought in a flash.

Butch attempted to throw Liz off his back. She hung on. One, two, three attempts. She hung on. He snarled and threw her brutally into the wall. But by then he had drawn breath several times. He attempted to shake off the approaching dizziness, but it was no good. He fell to the floor, his head hitting it with a thud.

Claudia saw what happened. Indecisive she froze a couple of seconds before charging screaming towards the door. She didn't get far. Ted jumped forward and kicked her feet away from under her. She hit the floor and remained there, shaking and still. The scream changed into a horrible, squealing sound. Ted stood above her like a statue of cold rage. With a face rigid as a mask he freed himself. She was absolutely terrified and with saliva flowing from her mouth she attempted to crawl away from him.

He grabbed her in the throat and started slapping her. Left right, left, right. The squealing stopped, and she started sobbing, loud and sore.

– It wasn't me, she mumbled. – He forced me. It wasn't me. It wasn't me.

– HAH! He cried out in utter contempt, his outburst containing all his pent-up aggression. She shrunk to nothing below him.

He pulled her up and half dragged, half carried her to the heap of hay not far from where she and Butch had planned their party. He threw her brutally down on it.

– If you know what's good for you, you'll stay here, stay put, he snarled. – And not move a fucking inch. Understand?

She nodded to him, with a timid, tiny smile of assurance and subservience.

He turned towards Liz. Her dark hair was wet and tangled. She supported herself on a beam and blood flowed from her mouth, her face just as contorted, as ugly as his own. She pointed at Butch who stood on all fours and kept shaking his head.

– He HURT me, she shouted. – Get him. Strike him down.

Butch lifted a hand in a desperate attempt to protect himself. Ted grinned wickedly and kicked him in the belly. He fell and before he had landed Ted had kicked him again. Payback felt so good and was, he knew so very evident on his face. Liz joined in, too. Kicking. Kicking. Kicking.

He stopped eventually. She, too, sinking completely spent to her knees.

– More, she gasped. – Give the swine MORE!

– Use the chloroform, he ordered her coldly. – Use it on him. Make sure he won't bother us.

She wanted to spit out some challenging remark, but stopped because of the chilling subtext in his voice. She obeyed without a word and put the cloth to his face, holding it there, until he lay still.

– Leave him here, she spat, her musk, blood and saliva hitting his face. – Let him rot!

Ted stared at her, kept staring at all the red, flowing from her mouth. She noticed, and her lower lip started trembling, her sudden smile shaky like a feather.

The loud moan distracted them. They turned as one towards the shaking figure in the hay. Ted studied her, the revealing, half torn dress, revealing round boobs, most of the wet thighs. He swallowed hard.

– YES. Liz shouted. – Fuck the two-legged bitch. She's in heat. It's your right, Make her yours, make her ours.

He covered the distance to the trembling Claudia Cornwall in a second. All dignity was gone, now, from her pose, from her eyes. He felt a savage, horrible joy because of this. He grabbed the dress, and tore its remains off her, removing everything, removing it completely.

– Please, Claudia whimpered. – Don't do this. Please don't do this.

– Teach her, teach her who is the Master, Liz whispered in his ear. – Domesticate the pet. I've always wanted a domestic maid.

Ted didn't hear her, hear them anymore. He tore his belt in two and let his pants fall. With a mix of longing and ruthlessness he fell on the helpless Claudia. She fought initially, but one hard fist made her soft and pliable.

For a while he was merely lying on her, rocking back and forth on her thighs, probing. There were glimpses of her face, of fear and longing, of sickness spreading. He sensed, unbelievably clear her hips tightening around the hard limb that now had found its way. An insane melody played in his head, as he felt himself sinking ever deeper into the mud, the mud overwhelming him, as he plunged deeper into her, into the black well.

The light in his eyes exploded in a rain of sparks. Heat spread to his entire body and the world disappeared. He moved rhythmically up and down, and sensed something flowing from him and into her.

Over. It was over. What he had wanted for months and years

had finally been accomplished. Empty. He felt empty. He looked up, meeting eyes, points of embers in a vast sea of blue.

– I can feel your discontent, the girl woman said. – It wasn't good for you. She wasn't an active participant, and she wasn't good for you.

He looked at her, incomprehension dominating his features.

– I, however, will be.

Comprehension dawned on him and his eyes widened, as he was shaking his head.

– And her? He heard himself say, nodding towards the shaking figure between them.

– She will indeed be the maid, the servant I've always wanted, Liz grinned, – and you will be good at it, won't you, dear?

She grabbed the other girl's hair and pulled hard, lifting the other hand.

– Yes! Claudia whimpered. – Don't hit me. PLEASE. I'll be attentive in all things, learn to anticipate your thoughts, obey your every wish.

– See? Liz pointed out. – So fitting, so eager, so much wagging her tail for the strongest.

– Hold her, he instructed.

He reached for the cloth and bottle. Liz had dropped it, put it close by, as if by accident.

– Yes, Liz exclaimed, happy as a little kid, – let her sleep while we're enjoying ourselves.

She was a little kid, damn it.

Claudia crouched there in the hay, not really fighting against Liz' grip, not fighting at all. She stared at the two cousins with a sick, inviting smile filled to the brim of naked fear. Saliva flowed constantly from her mouth.

– Hold her...

Liz held her hard, while the dark boy pressed the cloth at her mouth and nose. She looked at him with huge, scared eyes. He feared he would never forget the sight of them.

– You live in me, dear, dear Ted, she mumbled. – You... can... not...

The body relaxed. Eyes closed. He let go of her. Liz, too. Head fell to the side.

– The liquor bottle in your pocket, Ted instructed, – give it to me.

Liz hesitated just a bit, before obeying. Her skin was suddenly covered in goose bumps.

– Undress Butch and get him over here, close to his beloved.

He spat out the last word. His voice so harsh that she obeyed without thinking. He smiled bitterly. She, too, would become an excellent servant. And so valuable, so extremely valuable. He observed how she strived to remove Butch' clothes and drag him across the floor, but she was strong and stubborn, and managed. The soft bodies of the puppets called Claudia and Butch met in the hay, completely limp.

He opened the liquor bottle.

– What are you going to…

She held her tongue when he turned the bottle upside down and the content splashed over the unconscious boy and girl. The raw stench of the fluid shook his nostrils. Liz couldn't quite hide her fear. When push came to shove she feared this side of him, the side she couldn't control.

Ted threw the bottle at the wall, so hard that it disintegrated upon impact, into thousands of pieces.

He rose, heading for the exit

– Hey, she called to him, anxious now, – where are you going, now?

– I'm leaving, he declared

She looked at him with a puzzled expression, understanding both failing and succeeding to illuminate her eyes.

– You feel bad about doing *that,* to *them?*

– I raped her, Ted replied flatly. – There is no excuse for that.

This time, after a series of almost successes he had succeeded completely, failing miserably.

She wanted to run to him.

– Stay away, he snarled, his eyes red and burning.

She stopped, she froze.

– Where are you going? She asked, whimpering, timid and small.

– Far away from here, from you.

He turned and began the walk, the long walk.

– Teddy, you can't make it alone, she cried after him. – Admit that you need me.

He picked up speed on his last few steps inside the barn, suddenly colliding with a beam. Pain shot through him, oh, so dull, compared to what he felt within. An old, dusty sack of flour fell from the loft, just missing his head. Still looking back he opened the door. A gust of wind instantly shook it out of his hand. Not caring he stumbled outside. Before the door slammed shut Liz threw herself at him. She attempted to grab hold, but he slapped her, and she fell on her head in the mud. The door closed like thunder behind him.

She stood there on her knees, desperately cleaning mud from her face. She wanted to say something, but he was already far away. He slid down the slope, fell, fought himself on his feet, fell again, and rose once again.

– So, GO TO HELL! She shouted it after him, spat it at his back, like a curse. – You're WEAK, just like the rest. You *coward!* I'll make it without you. Go to hell!

Gasping she deliberately stuck her head deep into the mud. With tears and water flowing down her face she followed him with burning eyes as he slid more than walked forward. Thunder seemed to emanate from him, from her, and not from the surroundings. Eventually he vanished into the storm, the dark, the rain and the mud.

*********************/

They gathered the runaway cattle. They did so for days, as the storm kept raging. Days and nights were the same, nothing more than a gray, eternal twilight of lightning and thunder.

The boy sat by a fire, still gasping for breath, with a heart still beating hard, only slowly, very slowly, slowing down. He saw insane glimpses in the air, of himself and the world many years from now, where storms like this were commonplace, where the mighty sea flooded the land on all coastlines. It faded with the storm, like he faded, as he kept gasping for air, and never seemed to get enough of it.

The sky in the east started brightening. Eventually the sun was glimpsed above the mountains and its rays started penetrating the morning mist. The most visible signs of the storm remained and would do so for a long time. Enormous scars in the landscape, soft and muddy soil. Rivers flooded their banks, creating new paths at every minor turn.

195

A huge campfire made of fairly dry twigs lit the morning twilight. Around the heat sat a dozen men in quite a miserable condition, totally exhausted as they were, wolfing down warm soup. Among them Eugene Kendall, Scott Thompson, Lex Barker and Ted Cousin. The echo caused by the cattle's bellowing rolled through the mountains. Across the plains the smoke of other fires rose towards the sky. Totally exhausted Ted kept seeing red dots both when opening and closing his eyes. The men sat still. Limbs and muscles didn't hurt. They were the hurt, were the very pain emanating through them in waves. They were just about able to lift an arm, a shaking hand to put the spoon in the mouth and still at least a tiny bit of the gnawing hunger.

Later. Thompson played something on the guitar. He sang, too. Ted heard nothing, just the sound, signifying nothing.

Thompson's hands did not shake, his voice did not waver. And then something did dawn on Ted, through the haze filling his mind.

The big man put away the guitar and silence reigned once more.

– I think he may have learned something this night, Kendall said to Thompson, in a low voice, close to his ear, both glancing at the boy. – That he might be coming along to a more normal way of thinking.

Ted heard him. He didn't comment on it, but just remained there, on the spot, totally exhausted.

He saw himself from the outside, knowing fully well he looked the worse of them all. Bad as they all looked, he was a notch worse. Blood and dirt dominated. Hair was covered in mud. Clothes were merely rags. An old coat, seemingly devoured by moths covered his shoulders. He just sat there, unmoving.

Surviving rats appeared from their holes in the ground. He studied them without studying them. They strived to rebuild their lives, to keep surviving. Many were injured and just collapsed there, on the ground, dying on the spot.

And there were birds, ravens, singing to him, about the deeds of the night. One of them had a morning bath in a dirty pond, flapping its wings, squeaking loudly.

There was movement, eventually as the men fought themselves up, attempting to move, to soften rigid bodies. He did, too. His body healed, as it always did. He walked with the others, back to the houses, the soft beds, removing himself from them with every step. A flash of a blinding shadow, and he was alone, walking alone, through a desolate, remote landscape.

Kendall took him aside one of the next few days, placing a fatherly arm on his shoulder.

– I know, know well you've had your share of trouble, the older man said. – I also know you have dealt with it. The world can be such a big, wonderful place, you know.

– I know, the boy shrugged.

The bus stop was just a single sign by the road, nothing more than that. Ted was the only one waiting to get on the upcoming bus. The father, mother and the three children Kendall were there, saying goodbye. They all kissed and coddled him, as if it was the last time. He knew that the impressions he got from them this first June morning would remain for all time. It was like on a stage. They filed past him. Like specters they were, with just the occasional glimmer of color.

Kendall shook his hand. The man's hand was wet and unpleasant. Linsey embraced him, a Linsey whose body had grown considerably the last few months. Liz just stood there, a few steps away, shy, distant and unreachable. June kissed him on the lips, suddenly and shockingly. He looked at her briefly, looked at her for the first time.

Trudy had always kept her distance before, but she didn't hold anything back anymore, she no longer held herself back, and there was unmistakable heat and affection in her eyes.

– There's a wild beast inside you, Edward, Trudy said. – You must learn to master it, somehow. And you don't do that by denying its existence. You have a wonderful gift, you know. By being to such a degree in touch with your deeper parts, you're something unique among present day humans.

Ted hesitated. Then the smile transformed his face.

– Thanks.

It was the first summer day. It was raining. He entered the bus, without being able to recall the actual moment it had appeared around the turn and stopped.

He did turn his head, as he sat down in the backseat, seeing the small, vulnerable form of Elizabeth Kendall wave to him, seeing the wet dust whirl around it, her bigger form shadowed in the dust and the sand.

The bus was entering the rural area of Denver. The rest of the trip had been forgotten, or at least misplaced somewhere he couldn't reach it. Hours were lost to a black hole hiding somewhere within.

Something, a movement, something caught his attention, made him raise his head, and he felt himself awakening, rising from yet another slumber.

A girl entered the bus and he couldn't help but staring at her, all the time she was making her way back in the bus.

– I know, she said to him, she actually spoke to him. – You know you know me from somewhere, but you can't actually recall from where. Don't worry. I get a lot of that.

And she sat down in the available seat beside him.

– My name is Diana McKenzie. She shook his hand. – Nice to meet you.

– Ted, he heard himself say. – Ted…

She wasn't much older than him, and she was traveling alone. She was traveling. The rather heavy rucksack was a telltale sign.

– I've been a lot on television lately, she grinned.

Understanding dawned on him.

– Yes, she kept grinning. – I am that Diana McKenzie.

– You spoke outside a certain white house in Washington DC…

– And I just looooovvve that admiring look in your eyes, she said. – That I don't necessarily get from most people.

– I would have known you were a free spirit even without recognizing you from television, he said. – Your clothes are a dead or should I say a live giveaway.

– We «flower children» don't really dress the same, she said lightly. – We're just recognized because we all dress differently from most other people. That's our common denominator.

Denver… He was back on his old haunts, even though this was LoDo, and not the dangerous territories where he was headed. He felt strange, profoundly strange. No one had done any refurbishing on the old Union Station. No one had painted the walls or changed the old seats, resembling church seats, where no one would want to sit. All of it felt so familiar, and the horror rose in him like bile.

It was the first time he was actually dating a girl. The heat in his head was certainly not caused by the rather cold weather. It dawned on him, after a while in her company that he was actually dating her. Horror and profound interest warred within him.

– I'm here to meet people, she said proudly. – A lot of people. Ol' Dick must never be allowed a single breather. We're far from done with him.

– So, what's gonna happen?

– There will be people on several trains. Then there will be a meeting in town tonight. I have sort of been preparing it with local forces the last few days.

– And in the meantime? He asked it with unfamiliar, yet familiar mischief in his eyes.

– It's well over an hour before the first train arrives. She blushed visibly. – We've got time.

They walked to a restaurant nearby.

– The streets feel so strange, he said. – I feel like I've been away forever, like I've never left.

Grinning demons lurked in the corner, and he couldn't keep himself from sweating. The ravens danced their crazy dance, and that both comforted and scared him.

– Are there always so many birds here? She asked innocently and incredulously.

– Only when I am here, he replied lightly.

And he spotted the scared and intrigued expression in her eyes.

They sat by a table in a restaurant, as far away from the streets outside they could possibly come.

– To the Demons. He raised his glass. – To the Shadows.

– To us, she whispered.

She knew indeed what he was hinting at, what he himself hardly understood, and he knew that it scared her.

The music played in the restaurant was ordinary, boring. It

didn't matter. He heard something far different. They both did.

– You were actually in Chicago, she exclaimed after a while, with stars in her eyes. – I wish I had been.

– We were runaways. He shook his head. – It wasn't altogether pleasant. Besides, you've experienced quite a bit yourself.

– I won't deny that. She blushed again. – But most of the people in the anti-war movement are so trite, so… limited. They have given no thought about anything beyond the war and Nixon. They don't realize that it is society itself that is… *wrong,* the society creating ideal conditions for such things, for injustice, inequality and for the crushing of the human spirit.

And he knew, when she looked at him, that the fire danced in his eyes, knew that she was helplessly fascinated with him, and that created the heat burning pleasantly inside, a sensation full of lust.

He saw Mike's face reflected in a window. He knew that Mike wasn't really there, no more than he always was here, was everywhere.

But it sent shivers through him, shivers of rage.

Suddenly he heard the sound of glass breaking and felt pain. He looked dizzily at his hand. He saw a bloody hand, a broken glass. The glass had broken because of the pressure he had inadvertently exposed it to.

– What have you done to yourself? She asked horrorstricken.

– This? He held up the hand and shrugged. – This will heal in no time.

And he knew that to be true by now. It wasn't just something he said, not anymore.

He studied her, her uncertainty and burgeoning dread in his presence.

It was as if a dark cloud had come and shadowed her positive outlook on life.

He jumped to his feet.

– Come, let's leave this crappy place.

He grabbed her with the non-injured hand, dragging her with him. There were a lot of people in the room and a long way to the exit. He pushed forward between surprised and annoyed guests, ignoring them completely.

There was a towel hanging from the ceiling above the cash register. He grabbed it, leaving a few bloody bills at the counter, not looking at the people behind it at all. He increased his speed. Air, he needed air.

– You must do something about the wound, she cried out weakly, – or you might bleed to death. *P-please!*

– Here, he ordered her outside. – Tie this around the hand.

He gave her the towel. She took it. Her hands were clearly shaking as she did as she was told.

She stood there afterwards, shaking like a leaf.

The hour was almost up. He bought a bus ticket, ready to leave for… for the old white painted house in the southern suburbs. She still stared at the hand, at the blood penetrating the cloth. He knew he had made quite an impression on her.

– Well, I'll see you around, okay, she said brightly.

– Of course, he said, staring directly at her.

She blushed again, still shaken, still ashamed.

– I'm not sure if I will join any of the protests in town, though, he said casually. – What you said about the teapot revolutionaries goes double for me.

– We should do the protest thing anyway, she emphasized, – Just for the heck of it.

– Perhaps, he said. – Perhaps not.

He kissed her on the brow. She wanted him to do more, so much more. That much was evident. He turned away from her, entering the bus. The bus drove off. He sat down. She probably waved. He didn't. Not once.

Chapter nine
DISTANT BUTTERFLY WINGS
New York 1931

Jonas Bergli saw the statue of liberty appear in the fog and the rain. There were hundreds of people standing outside, by the rail of the ship, waving and shouting, rows and rows of dirty, happy faces.

The harbor on South Manhattan was busy as usual, but not that busy, really, its energy muted, betrayed by the noticeable lack of activity. Bergli hurried away from there, as if every drop of rain, every look he cast or didn't cast around him burned him to ashes. The streets were no better, though. Everywhere he went he saw people with weary eyes and dirty faces. He had last seen this city in the roaring twenties, and even if it had never truly been the roaring twenties to him it was better than this, this... city of pale ghosts.

He was dressed in his sailor's uniform and a dark, worn coat. His face betrayed no emotion, no outward manifestation of his insides. He walked through gray streets, passing gray houses. There were screams around him, cries of pain and desperation. He usually ignored it. Except when it got too close, and he looked, just to be safe. But no one attempted to jump the tall, powerfully built man. He had walked from the harbor. It was no small feat. After the consolidation of 1898, the creation of the five boroughs New York had, with the exception of London become the world's largest city. Bergli had left his native country Norway a long time ago. Why he had ended up in New York he couldn't say.

By the time he reached Brooklyn Bridge he was drenched to the bone. Both the coat and the clothes beneath were like wet rags. He stopped a bit on the bridge, deliberately turning and looking back at Manhattan. A sight instantly drawing him in was the nearly completed Empire State Building. He had seen it on newsreels, recalling with a headshake the optimistic, overly loud mood presented on the short piece of film. It had been, was amazing, really how they had managed to avoid even the suggestion of «negativity». To him the silence had been deafening.

He wasn't cold, really. The fast walk had made sweat mingle heavily with the late winter rain penetrating his clothes. He studied the city, the low fog, the almost visible clouds of particles in the air, and he almost started coughing just at the sight of it. New York was as drenched in poison as it was in rain. He hurried on. Even if he couldn't say he was in a hurry, in a hurry to get anywhere.

People looked at him, stared at him, he knew that. With the long, thick, unbound black hair sticking out of his hat, he looked more like a Native American than any prototype of a Nordic Viking. And the fact that his face was fairly clean didn't cause fewer stares.

But nobody was insane enough or desperate enough to jump him. Not even gangs of sullen looking youths raging through the streets.

The old building in Brooklyn was still there, and he had to admit to more than his share of relief when he spotted familiar faces in the street, and in the windows. Some of them even smiled when they recognized him.

She opened the door and met him, before he could knock on it. He looked at her. There were a few premature gray hairs, that was all.

– Hello, Sara.

– Johnny, she said softly. – Welcome home.

She embraced him. He returned the gesture, a bit apprehensive.

– I'm wet, he said, grinning.

– We're all wet these days. She shook her head.

– You look good, Sara, he said.

– My Johnny, she laughed, – you have always been an excellent liar.

She dragged him inside.

– Come, she insisted, – your old room is ready.

In the roaring twenties Sara Woodward had been a sort of hotel owner, a few steps down from the glitter on Manhattan, though, but still roaring. Now, he suspected, both she and her clientele had fallen on hard times.

At least she was still here, like her clientele. Many weren't that lucky.

There were pieces of paint missing on the wall in the hallway, a big scar after what seemed to be a knife or a sword. Somebody had been quite unrestrained here, at least once. The carpet had loose threads, and pieces of wood were definitely missing from the chest of drawers.

– You are as astute as you always were, Johnny, she mumbled, not looking at him.

He remembered that he had, in fact been walking up the stairs, but not the details about it. It was just another staircase. His room was familiar. Here, too, were signs of unruly tenants, but he didn't mind. He stood there for hours, looking at himself in the cracked mirror, with clothes, without clothes. He took a shower, cleansing himself of all the crud sticking to him. At least that was the idea. He couldn't tell if it actually worked. He never could.

They sat opposite each other in her private dining room, as the gray day gave way to the early evening twilight. The heat from the fireplace singed the hairs on his hand. He didn't move it from the armchair.

– So how was your trip?

– Not that good. New York during the great depression is even more depressing than usual.

– I meant your voyage, Jonas, she reproached him mildly. – Your journey across the seas.

For once she called him by his Norwegian name, not the anglicized one. But she put the emphasis on the first part of it, not the last, as she should have done.

– Not that bad. He shook his head. – At least we got regular meals on board. I have heard that that isn't necessarily so around here, these days.

He spoke with a heavy accent, like most immigrants, breaking, emphasizing every word.

She nodded, her eyes softening a bit.

– When you look at me, you'll see the same scars that I see, looking around me here, he said.

– How old are you, Jonas?

He studied her a moment, before replying.

– Thirty-six. I was born in eighteen ninety-five.

– And you have nothing to your name?

He studied her some more. She was clearly not reproaching him. She had not been the type, and she still wasn't.

– Hardly anything, he nodded. – I prefer it that way actually.

She nodded some more.

– What is on that devious mind of yours? He grinned quietly

– More tea? She reached for the old tea can.

– Thank you. Bergli leaned back in the chair, briefly closing his eyes. – I love tea.

They sat there for a while, not speaking, enjoying the silence.

– Your timing for returning to us is quite fortunate, she finally said.

– I rather thought so, he nodded.

He looked out of the dirty window, at the dirty street. It had been like that in the swinging twenties, as well, but not that pronounced. The dust from industry, from the chimneys and the increasing number of cars covered the city like a blanket, on the ground and in the air.

Twilight came, and the city faded around him. Night came, and the fire rose from the depth. The old house came to life. The house came to life, and Sara with it. She held one of her parties. She still did, even though this was certainly more muted than the previous he had experienced. That had ended with a wall falling down. This wouldn't be anything like that. He realized it with a jolt of excitement. He recalled her face, her excited face when they had been having the strange conversation in front of the fireplace.

There was old guard present, several of them old friends, but there were also others, people who stood out, who would stand out from any crowd, and who made even his old, stoic friends cast glances and mutter among themselves. Someone was playing a guitar, he noted, but it was played in such a strange, unknown way that he hardly recognized it as such. The man playing seemed to be covering half the room, he was that big. He had long, black hair, like Bergli, but its consistency was quite different.

Sara had entered the room, but she said nothing, waited until the music faded.

– Nicholas, HEY, Nicholas, she shouted, – there is someone I want you to meet.

And the man stopped playing and put the guitar down. He turned, and Bergli sensed a jolt of electricity looking into his eyes, his burning eyes.

Sara pulled them close to each other.

– Nicholas, this is Johnny Berg.

And she turned, but Bergli, amazed by himself hardly knew she was there. Something was happening, something monumental.

– Johnny, this is Nicholas Warren.

****************************/

– Call me Nick, the other one said, shaking his hand.

– I am Jonas, Bergli replied swiftly. – Jonas Bergli.

– Jonas, Nick repeated a bit off, but obviously trying.

He did it right, by emphasizing the end of the name, instead of its beginning, like most English speaking people did. That told Bergli a lot.

Warren was young, very young. He had whiskers, but even though his hair was smooth they were curled, like that of a teenager. His face was smooth, but he had no acnes. His eyes *were* burning. At least they looked like they were. Their color was that of fire, of dark fire perhaps, but fire nonetheless. They shimmered, waxed and waned constantly, as if something did burn behind them. And Jonas noticed the ring on his finger, the ring with the strange fire-colored stone, one very much resembling the eyes.

– Let's present you for the others, Nick said casually.

Jonas followed him the five steps across the room.

– This is my son, James, and his wife Rachel, he said.

Jonas had no way of holding back the surprised outcry.

– Yes, I know, Nick laughed. – I am a bit older than I look.

– Nick was born in 1890, James said.

They looked more like brothers, than father and son. If anything, James looked slightly older, more normal, more... responsible? He had normal, brown eyes, was smaller and clearly less imposing, lacking the enormous presence of the father.

Rachel had one child on her arm, and a big belly, clearly

showing that another one was on its way. The boy on her arm waved both his arms violently back and forth.

– This is Jack, she said, laughing nervously. – He is two years old. Unfortunately, he's behaving as if he was five or something…

Virgil had blond hair, and compared to the others he looked very pale, and like he hadn't slept for weeks. Jonas had seen people like him before: the walking dead men. His movements were stiff, like that of a wooden doll.

Nancy was vibrant, alive. Her eyes burned in fire, like those of Nick, though clearly not so bright, not so shadow. She had the same hair, color and texture as Nick, and a dark beauty that smothered Jonas

April's, April Powell's eyes were green, green fire brushing against him like tall, fresh grass on a field.

Carla Wolf had dark blue eyes, and in those eyes, he experienced the ocean, the mountains and the forest.

– You're all related?

He asked the question casually, easily seeing the resemblance.

– Not all of us by blood, no, but the same heat is running through our veins.

And there were others, welcoming him, not so pronounced, noticeable at the first meeting, at least not compared to those he did remember, those he would always remember, no matter what.

And he realized what they, most of them had in common: Pride, and a belief in their own Self. No one here was bowing their head against the Storm. And certainly not to the first and best would-be «master» coming their way. They were independent and free.

And it was the sense of Destiny, like a rush outside, inside. Suddenly he had trouble breathing.

– You're the ShadowWalkers, he said astonished.

The laughter warmed him, welcomed him. The rush of cries and comments from other places in the rather large room, reacting to his outburst pleased him.

– You're like us, Jonas, Nancy said softly, hotly. – You've waited, waited and waited, until being fed up with waiting.

Her inflection when she said his name was even better than

that of Nick. It was as if she was a native Norwegian.

– I've waited my entire life, he said.

Sara Woodward stood on the small stage. Bergli looked at her, smiling slightly. She had a way around her, a way of calling attention to herself without even trying.

– WELCOME, she cried. – I want you to know one more time that you're all welcome here, in this place where you can be yourself, and not have to pretend to be someone else. We are the ShadowWalkers. We walk between worlds, walk distant worlds. Look at us dance. Listen to our song.

Virgil had a battery of drums, encircling his body. He started striking them with his flat hands. Nick played his guitar, and it wasn't even remotely similar to the way Bergli had heard it out west. It was much more an Eastern feel… Asia, the Middle East, but not that either. April started singing, or chanting was perhaps a better word. James and Carla danced to it, and it was a far cry from any dance he had ever witnessed, and it took his breath away.

– You're not dancing? He said carefully to Nancy.

– No. She shook her head. – I could do it. I imagine I have the moves, the ability… But I was forced to learn, to do it at an early age, and I swore I would never do it again.

He couldn't be certain, but he imagined he saw a tear form at the corner of her eye.

– I grew up in a whorehouse, she said straight out. – My mother was taken there at an early age to be a man's slave. I was born there, and I would, like my mother have faded away there, if Nick, Roland and my cousin Desmond had not saved me.

Jonas waited. He had learned waiting, but now he felt the stirrings of a terrible apprehension. The woman before him looked pale, subdued, not like his first impression of her at all.

– They saved me, but mother was killed. And my Master escaped. And for our transgression he kidnapped me and the brother and sister, Virgil and Susan. He took us to Africa, and sold us as s-slaves. We were eventually rescued, but Susan just withered and died, leaving Virgil in disarray. I think he l-loved her. He has never been *right* since.

She rested her head on Jonas' shoulder, crying quietly.

She dried her tears, the tears like fire.

– I'm sorry, she said. – Sorry, sorry, sorry.

– Don't be sorry, he said. – Never be sorry. Not for anything resembling this.

– I've never told that to anyone, she said, smiling to him. – Thank you.

She kissed him on the lips. And he couldn't tell if it was caused by desire or gratitude.

– We looked for my Master, she said with frozen lips. – Virgil does nothing but look for him. We haven't found him, have never seen him again. Virgil *lives* for vengeance. Everything else is incidental. We all fear he will die for it, that he left what is most valuable in a human being there, in Africa's sand.

– And you? Jonas asked carefully.

– It was different with me, she said. – I found my freedom, my Self there. My master lost his hold on me. My childhood was a nightmare, but among my own I found acceptance and joy, Life and Power. I will never forget. He will never be truly gone from my mind. But my life is my own. It doesn't belong to a specter of the past. If we ever meet again, I will kill him, and making him suffer in the process, it is that simple.

And there was hunger and boundless rage in her eyes.

He felt her lips again.

– I'm alive, Jonas Bergli, she said to him. – Alive.

And she spoke to him. But there was no sound. And she sang to him, of joy, loneliness, loss and being human. And then she did dance, close to him, to the music far and close. And he would never forget her, never let her leave his mind, in his many lonely years to come.

When he awoke the next morning, she was there in the bed with him, snuggling tight, laughing throatily, generally making her presence felt.

She stretched, letting him see her, letting him see all of her.

– Do you mind me being so… active? She wondered, with just a hint of worry in her voice.

– No, he replied, shaking his head. – No.

– Most men do, she said, tinged with sadness and anger. – Even men of courage and determination such as yourself.

– I can't imagine why.

They stayed close to each other, completely uncovered. The blanket delegated to unimportance, to a place in the shadowy corner of the room. He recalled her doing it, as she had descended on him, as she had smothered him in wet kisses. He would always remember the expression in her face the moment the hot water had exploded from her loins, of pure, unaltered joy. To him that exact moment would always be frozen in time.

She was big. Taller than he was, but not as heavy, of course, being a female.

– Nick, he is your brother, right?

– No, she replied teasingly.

– Then he must surely be your cousin. You certainly look like brother and sister, more than anyone I've ever seen.

– I and James' great, great grandfather and mother were brother and sister. That's the only blood connection between us. I and Virgil are actually one generation closer...

– In our family, we consider ourselves blood kin even if we are this many generations removed. The way I've understood it our blood stays thick even through centuries of outside influence. Just like James is far more his father's than his mother's son, I am far more my mother's daughter. And this would have been true even if I had known who my father is. We tend to look alike, to behave in similar ways, but we are still far less alike than most other people.

– Have you noticed... She looked into his eyes with her ember windows. – Noticed how most people behave the same, dress the same, look the same?

– Yes, he said hoarsely. – I have most certainly noticed.

– They may have different hair color, different skin color, being physically completely different, but still they look the same.

She kept talking, kept whispering in his ears.

– Desmond, Virgil's father went to West Point...

– A legacy from his father Joe, she hastily added. – None of us are exactly in favor of the ongoing conformity in the military, or any conformity for that matter.

– No, not that Joe Warren, she said when noticing his look. – Not the more famous gold digger, buffalo hunter and all.

She frowned.

210

– But strangely enough - again, our Joe Warren was also a gold digger, buffalo hunter - and unfortunately so - Indian killer. Anyway…

He laughed softly.

– Yes, she grinned. – I do tend to jump back and forth between subjects… I'm told it's a sign of a wide range of emotions.

– It's certainly true with you…

– Courteous Jonas, she whispered, wet in her fireeyes.

Kisses turned insistent, turned hot. And he forgot everything again. It was like a wild dance. It was a wild dance, a storm. They rested there, afterwards, quietly, in each other's embrace. He still gasped for breath minutes later.

– Tired? She asked him teasingly, worriedly.

He looked at her. Yes, there was definitely concern in her eyes, and that he didn't understand.

– Completely exhausted, he chuckled.

It was then she got that distant look in her eyes. She had wanted to say something, he knew that, but it stopped somewhere inside her. She stopped, and froze like a doll.

– I can feel life surrounding us, surrounding me, she said, in a very strange voice.

It seemed to him like she wasn't there, wasn't here, with him at all, right now.

And then, suddenly, she gasped, and her skin turned pale and wet.

– I can't do this anymore, she said.

And gooseflesh broke out all over his body. He recognized Sara's voice.

He heard the sound of a gun from upstairs. Then there was nothing. Everything was silent.

– S-sara, Nancy said with a brittle voice. – SARA!

She jumped out of bed and ran to the door. In a flash she had opened and closed it behind her. He heard the sound of her running up the stairs. When he finally managed to move, to follow her, his movements were stiff, doll-like.

He finally managed to speed up, fearing what he had heard, what Nancy in strange ways had experienced.

The door to Sara's room stood ajar. He couldn't see much of what was inside, not until he, in his fear pushed the door wide open. Sara sat there, in her favorite chair, with a strangely normal expression in her face. He saw the gun on the floor. The wall behind her decorated with blood and gray matter. There was a written note at the top of the dresser, in Sara's handwriting.

I can't do this anymore

Nick stopped in the doorway, wild and filled with remorse.

– There is nothing you can do here, Nancy said softly, mysteriously.

– I was outside, well on my way to the store, he said, in his regret, in his anger. – She knew I would take too long to return.

The three of them didn't move for a long time.

*************************************/

It was May the first. Winter had gone. Spring had come.

The Empire State Building, the tallest building in the entire world towered there above the gathered crowd. An orchestra was playing stars and stripes. This was the official opening day for the skyscraper, the building touching the sky. Everybody smiled, even the people with dirty faces gathered outside the fences and away from the invited guests.

– This is a happy occasion, isn't it? Nick told Jonas in a certain characteristic manner.

It was always difficult for outsiders to actually decide whether or not Nick was actually being ironic. He had long since mastered the fine art of irony, to the point of perfection. Jonas had no difficulty reading the underlying acid in his voice, though.

– I mean, here we see before us another proof of the United States and humanity's greatness, another sign of the times to come.

– Believe me, Jonas shook his head, – I'm absolutely speechless.

– Impressive, isn't it? A man not far away echoed what he thought was their praise.

– YES! Nick exclaimed. – That was EXACTLY the word I was looking for.

The man looked closer at him. Didn't he overdo it… just a bit?

The Warrens were inside, on the guest side of the fence. Virgil's side of the family represented «old money», wealth generations old. Grandfather Joe had earned a fortune as a gold digger and buffalo hunter, and Indian killer in the old west in the seventies. So, the ShadowWalkers had at least access to the more overt or visible inner circles of the United States' ruling body.

There were speeches, many speeches. There always were. Jonas noticed only one, really, and only because he saw how it affected Nick.

A fairly young man by the name of Prescott Bush ascended the podium, the dais of power, of empty words and gestures. He looked at the congregation with a menacing smile touching his lips.

– I will draw the big picture here. Others have successfully conveyed the joy of this day, this proud day in American history. I will take a slightly different approach. There is a need, people, for further extreme measures on our part. Gentlemen... even with the extreme designs and measures we have helped put in motion we may not be able to halt the rise of communism. The Soviet Union is here to stay for the foreseeable future, spreading its influence across the world, encouraging others to take up its cause, its attack on free enterprise, on everything making this country great, on America's manifest destiny. People, we need to be patient, to build our forces, our counterattack slowly, meticulously. We may have to ride it all out through decades, before our opportunity presents itself.

This, among other interesting things said Prescott Bush, on what would later be known as the CCC (Coalition of Concerned Citizens) unofficial, inaugural meeting 1931.

– Listen to him, Nick said softly. – He's actually saying something significant. Not anything we like to hear, but significant nonetheless, exactly because of that.

And Jonas did listen, because he heard the underlying tone of rage and terror in Nick's voice.

– They're meeting in secret, Nick said. – All the important stuff is discussed there. They've embraced the blight, the blight on our world. They're the Enemy, or rather the Enemy's most eager servants.

The Rockefeller family held a reception later that day,
and virtually every single important citizen of the nation
was present. It was a place for the important class to meet
undisturbed. Here, there were no lower classes present at all,
except far away, on the other side of the walls erected around
the vast estate. Cars arrived all evening, forming a long line on
the driveway from the gate and to the main building, the stately
mansion.

– We're in the lion's den, Nick told Jonas. – Study it well.
Learn its many weaknesses, its many cracks.

Jonas circulated, though strangely enough, there always
seemed to be at least one Warren or associate in his immediate
proximity. He didn't feel angry about it, not really believing
they did it to guard him, or even did it consciously. They were
just eager to show the new initiate the sights, the glorious
sights…

– We're sort of accepted here, Nancy told him, – because they
don't really know about us. Their imagination doesn't reach
very far outside their self-imposed, narrow perception. So, in
truth they're unable to realize how far the disgust with their
works and worldview is reaching. They have to… focus on us
to know us, so to speak. And so far, they haven't. They haven't,
or we would have known.

The two of them danced, if dance it was.

– Then there are those who have focused on you?

– We believe so, she nodded. – In fact, we're almost certain
of it.

– Who? He asked it, knowing what a dangerous question it
was.

– We don't know, she replied. They had retreated to one of the
balconies. No one could hear them out here. – But we know
one thing: All in our family have died untimely, sudden deaths.
A seemingly random shooter gunned down Desmond in 1923.
All of us, in incidents reaching back centuries have been killed
early in life, either by murder or accident, strange, often creepy
accidents. And it shouldn't be that way, it shouldn't be that way
at all. In spite of our tendency towards being self-destructive,
we're better suited to survive than most people, not less.

He didn't comment on the latter. He saw how serious she was, how it cost her to reveal this to him, an outsider. Her eyes glowed at him, warmed him.

– Nick is now the oldest living family member. If he should die, it would be Virgil, and then it would be me.

He looked dumbfounded at her. He knew she was older than she looked, but this was ridiculous. He realized, because of everything she had told him, that she was close to thirty.

– I don't understand, he said. – The way I have learned to know you, you're not exactly easy to kill.

– We're extremely difficult to kill, she said, with both pride and fear evident in her voice, in her eyes. – So, they, whoever is hunting us, must know us well, and this is our fear: perhaps better than we know ourselves.

He held her, and she let herself be held, even though he was fully aware of how she resented such a set male/female pattern.

– You have stumbled into some drama, Jonas Bergli, she sniffed.

– Stumbled it is, he said lightly.

He finally got some time on his own. He needed that. Perhaps they sensed it, too, and left him alone, to think, to ponder. There was a sense of menace here, one he had always been able to sense, and here it was stronger than he had ever sensed it. He glimpsed Prescott Bush with a group of cigar-smoking, well-dressed men.

– The uneducated, huddled masses will come to demand their place in the world, one of them said, – and sadly, gentlemen, with the glorious advances of our society, they will get it. It's our job to see to that they, that this inevitable process won't destroy important structures in the world, so that we, one day can have our reckoning.

He saw Nancy's eyes, open and deep, he saw the shudder in them, and he shivered himself.

It wasn't easy, discerning what was truly wrong with this place. It took him several hours, several walkthroughs, before he finally got it:

There was no… life here, or at best only muddled life. Everything was dead and still.

He heard Nick and April before he saw them. They didn't

necessarily speak any louder than most other people, but their conversation was clearly more intense.

– If you have a child with Virgil you'll die, Nick said softly.

And now Jonas did see them, as specters between all the pale ghosts, swirling around each other like parrots.

– Are you sure? April responded, with a voice dripping of honey, face smiling like the sun. – Are you never wrong?

– No, never, Nick stated firmly.

– Perhaps you want me for... yourself

– I have no problem admitting that, Nick said calmly, with an undertone of desperation his voice, – but I would never lie about anything like this. If you believe that, you don't know me very well.

– And you want me to know you... much better?

She touched his cheek, lightly, teasingly.

– A child between us will also be powerful, he said, – but not the goddess that will suck the life out of you.

She kissed him on the cheek, where the mark of her hand still lingered.

– You and I, we're different, she whispered. – Different even from the others. We're those with Power. We're gods. There are ways, we both know that. You'll help me, won't you, staying Death's hand?

– Of course, I'll help you, Nick said thickly.

Jonas, amazingly, had heard it all.

He walked on, listening, learning, perhaps more than he ever wanted to learn.

– It's quite amazing, isn't it? Nick approached him from nowhere, as usual. – How the world outside these walls doesn't seem to exist.

– Well, there are some measures undertaken to deal with unemployment, Jonas said, his voice a remarkable copy of Nick's finetuned irony. – To keep it high, for instance. Never say the employers don't know how to keep the workforce in tow...

Nick smiled, but he seemed distracted. There was something different about him. He looked more enigmatic than ever.

– It's rather strange, isn't it? Nick looked at him. – Sara is the only connection between us, and if you had returned a week later we would never have met.

And Jonas realized that this theme was something they had moved towards for a long time.

– I would guess she wanted to wait for you, but don't think she would have held out any longer. She didn't.

And Jonas looked into his eyes, murky and muddled. The sadness and happiness sucked him in, making him float in dark waters.

– You're one of us. Soon you will know everything about us, or at least as much as we know ourselves.

It was then Jonas realized that Nick Warren had an agenda, or at least a beginning of one.

Nick looked at him, a look hard and intense.

– I was with the Titanic, you know, on its final voyage, Nick said distantly, cold and intense. – With my wife. Before that there was nothing, no clairvoyance, no precognition, only weak echoes of what would later follow. I was told I was very much like Karl, a relative who had been killed some years before. He had been plagued by nightmares and visions his entire life. Aboard the Titanic my wife died, and countless others perished, and I saw Death for the first time. Everything… opened, like a door blown open by a gust of wind. In one moment, past, present and future became one. And at the end of it all, at its beginning I saw a birdlike creature rising from its own ashes, its own demise, leaving death and destruction in its wake.

The big man dried a bit of saliva from the corner of his mouth. Jonas didn't say anything. He couldn't. It was as if he saw everything through Nick's eyes, experienced it through all his senses.

– It faded, like dreams do, but at night, in dreams and not I experience it again, and again. And a bit more remains each time. I saw you, I saw myself. I still do.

– I still do. Jonas repeated it for himself many days later, a rainy early summer day.

Jonas and Nancy walked along Jamaica Bay. He looked out at the bay from the pier. They stopped there, at its end, with water surrounding them on all sides. There was wind, there was silence, and it was as if the sea itself surrounded them and that they were breathing underwater. He wanted to hold her hand, but she just kept him from doing so, holding on to his arm instead. She seemed happy, humming and constantly smiling at him.

– Are you all right? She asked lightly. – You look a bit pale.

– It's just my stomach acting up, and I do sleep a lot, he assured her. – I seem to be tired all the time, and I feel the need to eat insane amounts of food. It's one strange disease, all right, but it will eventually go away. Most diseases do.

She stopped and she looked at him with those eyes of hers, those eyes so easily revealing everything, and he understood. Suddenly he understood. And the cold trickle down his spine was unlike any he had ever had.

– You're crying, he said astonished.

– Quite surprising, huh? She attempted to dry her tears, in vain, in swift, useless moves. – A party girl like me.

– You must mistake yourself for another woman, he joked. – A long lost twin, perhaps?

But the unnerving feeling wouldn't go away.

– There was a twin, she whispered. – She died, died at birth.

He attempted to grab her, to hug her, to make the horrible feeling go away. She pulled back, away from him. He looked at her, visibly hurt.

– Oh, Jonas, dear Jonas, please don't be hurt, don't believe for a moment that this is your fault.

– Fault…? He was unable to say anything more. Everything just stopped inside him.

– Don't you see? She gestured helplessly. – Your fatigue, your constant exhaustion? *I* am doing this to you, draining you of fire, of vitality, of life. I've never been with one man for so long before, so I didn't know.

She looked at him with condemnation in those huge eyes of hers, begging understanding.

– But now I do, she whispered. – Now I do.

He grabbed her, turning her to him.

– I can't live without you, he said thickly.

She looked closer at him, nodding sadly. It was like her eyes… *opened,* like they saw everything.

– You'll die with me… and you'll die without me. Jesus, Johnny, life really stinks.

She only called him Johnny when she was truly upset.

– I'm a witch, she said abruptly. – We're a family of witches.

He didn't say anything, just looked at her.

– Oh, it's not active in all of us, not like it is in Nick and me, but it is there, a gift, a curse to keep us awake at night, dead to the day.

– I *know,* he said. – I love you.

– Goodbye, Jonas. She kissed him, one final time.

– It isn't your fault either, he cried after her.

But there was no response but silence.

And she left him there, on the pier.

Part three: Waterfalls clashing

Chapter ten

The river roared under the three, surrounding them. Mist and drops of water lingered in the air. Smooth rock, polished over the centuries, glistened in red. Uneven cliffs looked like knives. The sun was about to set. Day was waning. And in the light of the dying day, the water looked like fire.

Michael Cousin pulled in the fishing rod with a disgruntled growl, a sound that might be mistaken for something else. He had fished since early morning, and not caught a single fish. Ted and Linda had. They approached him with their plastic bags full. He hadn't really been fishing. He had… had seen the fire.

The brothers stared at each other. Ted let go of the bag, waiting for the brother to attack him. The sister shivered in the hot summer afternoon. She imagined the firewater rise and engulf them. They becoming the water, the boiling vapor, and still fight, still rage against the fates.

To her relief Mike turned, turned away this time, too, walking with long strides towards the main road where they had parked the car. The twins hesitatingly followed him.

– Nothing has changed, has it, nothing at all? She shouted at him, at them both. – Three years you have been apart, and nothing whatsoever has changed. You're giants walking the Earth, making room for no one else. I spit on you. I spit on you both.

She sat down with Ted in the backseat. Mike reacted instantly. He turned in his seat and said harshly:

– Move to the front, Linda.

It was a command, not a request. Linda expected that Ted would oppose it, but he didn't.

Silently and sullenly she obeyed.

She hardly noticed when the engine started up, staring at the river and lake it led to. The soft early July breeze shouldn't make the water and the lake boil, but yet it did.

Two rivers, two wings

She wrote in her notebook.

Like moths rising out of the fire

A shadow creature
As real, as sharp
As the air we breathe
The water we drink

And it was like she had written nothing, like it had all written itself, and she was just an instrument, a scalpel on the paper. That she was just the pen, led by some unseen force.

Mike pushed the gas pedal through the floor, raging through steep turns. He drove insanely fast, but Linda wasn't afraid. He was an excellent driver. At least she trusted him on that.

She laughed, a shrill laughter that made a chill run down the brother's spine.

– What's the matter with you? Mike asked.

– What is the matter with me? Linda said with a voice dripping of venom. – Do you want three guesses?

And silence reigned, and only the sound of the engine was heard.

– Everything started on our twelfth birthday, she told Helen Cumbes later that day.

The two of them hid from the heat outside in Helen's room in her parents' house.

Helen looked up with an apprehensive gleam in her eyes.

– Yes, I know, Linda, snarled. – You don't want to know, and I don't want to tell. Both of those things were true, but now I don't give a fuck anymore. I - don't - give - a - fuck.

She sat down on the bed, without looking behind her. It was pure luck she didn't dump her ass straight on the floor. She sat there a while. Helen patted her head, in slow comforting touches.

– I took a shower, she said dreamingly. – It was a warm summer's day, and windows and doors had been open since early morning. The water… felt so good. I guess I was… excited… turned on… sexually excited in plain language. I was twelve and wasn't supposed to have such feelings, not according to society's rules of acceptable conduct. But I did, and… and I felt proud. When I heard the light steps in the hallway, I did nothing. I wanted him to see me. I saw him; saw Ted, the boy, as he watched me, as I touched my wet thighs, my tits, as I performed for him.

224

– Later that day I told Mike. I fucking told him. He was bent before that, I know that, now, but I set him off. I will never forget his words, so alien, so crazy: «You are my sister. You belong to me. I'll kill anybody coming close to you without my permission». So corny, so crazy were his words, and I felt excitement, I felt pride.

– But later that day I saw his eyes, as he fixated them on me, at proud me, and I felt the first completely, illogical shiver down my spine.

The wind blew from the window. The window was closed. The wind came from inside.

– You shouldn't blame yourself, Helen tried.

– I don't. Of course, I don't. Only a stupid goose will do that, right, for other people's actions?

Her eyes hurt, her eyes burned like ashes.

– They're so much alike, she whispered. – I want to be loyal to Ted. He has suffered so much, and come through it, grown, become something wonderful and powerful. But… in my blackest moments I wonder if there is any difference between them, any at all.

Helen didn't know where to place her hands. They seemed to move all the time, nervously, even when she crossed her arms in front of her and grabbed her shoulders on both sides.

– I'm so sick and tired of it all, the ice blond girl said with her hands rolled into hard fists. – I came back to end it, because I realized it would never end if somebody didn't end it. But it keeps getting worse. I hate them! I hate them both!

She stood by the window, but didn't really stand still. Her entire body was in motion. Helen looked astonished at the sight.

– The only thing I have in common with them is my height, Linda raged on. – The idiots at school call me the beanpole. That's the reason I stick with you, I guess. You're even taller than me.

Helen was both taller and bigger. She lifted weights and ran, exercised. It was necessary for increasing the strength of her lungs. Her best feature was her voice. Everybody said that. She didn't exactly look happy for the dubious compliment. Linda didn't seem to notice. She looked out of the window, towards the house she couldn't see. And her eyes turned foggy and misty like watered milk.

– Don't worry, she said, off hand. – You worry if I'm gonna hurt you, if I'm crazy like my brothers and if I'm gonna hurt you bad. Don't worry, I won't. At least not as long as you behave.

And she smiled proudly.

She stood by the window in the small white house, looking out in the garden, at the boy sitting on the thick branch in the tree by the river, half hidden, half revealed by the tree in-between.

She watched as the brothers moved around each other, positioning themselves, moving like beasts in the forests, lurking at the prey or the enemy.

– It is like a dance, she told her parents pointedly.

– What is, dear? Cindy asked her, a worried look in her eyes.

– Life is, she shrugged, smiling innocently once more.

Of blood and cuts and thousands small deaths.

Mike seemed to be in an extravagantly good mood at the daily family dinner. He entertained the minor assembly in a seemingly endless tirade of anecdotes and chivalry.

The family was enjoying today's catch. Rodney had worked for hours to prepare and cook the three-star dinner. He had set the table, set the room, with its soft lights and well-placed shadows. There were ghosts in this room. The children felt them in every little item their father had placed here, on and off the table. He was a world-renowned chef and he was all theirs.

– Ted wasn't quite lucky today, Mike grinned. – He has worked too much with cows in recent years, evidently believing he could catch the fish with a lasso or something.

– My wise, older brother is living in a dream world, Ted countered with an innocent smile, – where he gets all the fish and the rest of us nothing.

Mike stiffened in the chair. He kept smiling, but behind his eyes, in his entire body language there was a rage encompassing the world. Once again Linda wondered how their parents could avoid noticing that. It was so stupid, so utterly, totally stupid. And she felt the rage herself, blinding, deafening her to anything, but to the rage itself.

– I loved it at the ranch, Ted continued, – But I wanted to get on with my life, get past past mistakes.

And the fire of the candles turned to ice.

– Yes, the world has so much to offer, Linda said. – It's a shame we don't take more advantage of that.

– You are such wise and spunky kids, Cousin said touched, raising his glass to a toast. – You have all turned out beyond my wildest expectations.

– To the world, Cindy said, with just a slight tremble in her voice. – To the large, terrible and wonderful world.

– TO THE WORLD

There was a meeting and parting of glasses, and there was an echo, an echo in eternity. Mike touched his left temple, as if he experienced a slight headache or something.

– I can see the world, he said darkly. – I can see all of it.

Tonight, there were fewer candles lit. Clearly a deliberate act. Ted looked at his father. Mike looked at him, too, suspecting something was afoot. The room was filled with deep and long shadows. And the flames? The flames burning the candles danced and sang. He could hear it, like the wind. The wind outside, inside. It was as if it was rising from the ground, actually rising through his body. He sensed his heart flutter and beat, the river in his vein flow.

Cousin stood up from his chair, striking his glass with a spoon. And there was a sharp, singing sound of metal against glass. A special sound the sons and daughter had heard nowhere else.

– There's no label on these glasses, Ted, the curious child had asked once, in a murky past. – Where are they made?

– Oh, it is an old family thing, Cousin had replied. – We come from an ancient line of glassmakers. They say we have been working it for thousands of years. An exaggeration for sure, but it's certainly a long time.

Tradition. Everything about this man spelled tradition.

As it did now, as he stood up, ready for one of his «ceremonies».

– It's time. He spoke solemnly, obviously corny, even though none of his children would ever say that to his face. – Time to once again honor the new generation, growing up in a hostile world.

He walked to the shelf and returned with a box, a black box.

– Tonight is the time, he said solemnly. – This won't be done as it should. Circumstances are preventing a proper ceremony. We will do what we do. Tonight is the time.

He opened the box. And in the box, there was a knife. The blade was ebony, and the shaft was crafted in disturbing, intricate patterns.

– This is yours. He held the box out to Linda. – Take it. Take your birthright.

Linda just sat there, frozen.

– I don't know, she attempted levity. – Am I the only one receiving gifts? It isn't my birthday, you know. Shouldn't the boys also have something?

– Their time will come, Cousin said. – This follows the females of the family. It's tradition.

His voice, too, had a touch of levity.

– Rise, Linda of the Shadow Blade and take what's due you.

And now there wasn't even the slightest trace of levity left.

She obeyed, rising, standing on shaky legs, grabbing the shaft with a steady hand, holding it up, studying it.

– So, is this what befalls a chef's daughter? She attempted to joke some more.

– Listen to the river, Cousin told them. – Heed its roar.

And the three of them did. Suddenly it was as if it was inside the four walls, as if they were bathing in its waters.

– The knife, Linda said. – The knife is moving in my hand.

– What is this? Mike asked sharply. – What are you doing, doing to her?

Ted looked at it all with a dreamy fascination in his eyes.

– No, it's not, her father told her. – It's just you familiarizing yourself with the blade, with its weight and balance, that's all.

– Now, her mother spoke up, – hold your hand above the glass of wine in front of you.

And Linda did.

– And cut your own flesh, wielder of the Shadow Blade.

The three children stared absolutely astonished at their parents.

– Are these two strangers, I see? Linda cried out, as if acting on the stage. – No, it isn't, as the strangers are now, they have always been.

She cut her left hand, sure and swift on its meaty side. Cousin nodded in satisfaction, as if she had just performed a satisfactory, expected feat. The blood didn't start flowing instantly. First it was just a thin line on pale skin. Then the red, shining droplets colored the white wine in the glass below. It sank to the bottom, all of it, like a sea in a sea. Cindy removed the glass and put Ted's there instead. More seconds, more heartbeat went by in eternity, as the sister and the two brothers stared at the stage, as if from outside. Cindy moved the second glass away and placed the third under Linda's pulsing hand. Finally, she produced white cloth and took care of the wound, bandaging it swiftly, revealing her expertise.

– You worked as a nurse, didn't you? Ted inquired. – In Asia, before you two married?

– Now, you do your Brothers, Cindy told her daughter. – The oldest first. Cut deep. Cut to the deep of the deep.

Hesitatingly Mike held out his hand above the three glasses at the center of the table. Linda, in a daze grabbed it and made the cut. And the wine sparkled and stirred, without actually anybody actually touching the glasses. Cindy took care of Mike's hand. There was very little blood, very little on his hand, but in the glasses, it seemed to expand like a fire. The sparkle was mirrored in Ted's eyes, as he held out his hand. Linda hesitated just a bit before making the cut, making the deep cut. The dark blood seemed to be expanding in the glass, making the wine boil like a current under the sea. In both the air and the sea, the red jewels were surrounded... surrounded by Shadow. There was some trouble making enough blood flow for the third glass. Cindy grabbed Ted's hand and squeezed and there was more blood. He let out a cry of pain, couldn't help it. Now, each of the brothers and sister had one of the three glasses placed before them, placed there by their mother.

– Blood mixed, Cindy Cousin said. – Blood united. Shadow dancing. Drink.

The fair sister and the dark brothers looked at each other, looked at each other some more, before lifting their glasses and drinking, drinking the cup empty. Linda sensed it, as the blood flowed down her throat, as it touched her. There was pain, as it exploded in her stomach, the two rivers burned in her veins. She swayed, before steadying herself.

– Now, you're three, three tied for all time, united in life, burning in fate.

Rodney Cousin's voice echoed through the old house, between the brittle walls.

Ted stood in the middle of his old bedroom, familiar like a well-used chair. He was breathing hard.

– A fucking black mass. He couldn't stop shaking his head.

– It was awful, Linda said to him. – It was as if I wasn't me anymore, but as if mommy and daddy had exchanged me with someone else, and put that one in control over my body, and worst of all, my mind.

– I guess every child is bound to find out strange things about their parents eventually, Ted joked. – That's a good thing, right? Less settled parents are less inclined to put their children through regimentation and rigid brainwashing.

They both laughed nervously.

– This is nothing new, he said enraged, changing mood from one moment to the next. – It's just one more riddle added... added...

– ... to the Mystery that is our lives, she added. – To the horror stage somebody built for us.

They stared at each other, horror evident in their eyes.

The river inside the walls faded only slowly, ever so slowly.

Ted walked to the window, looking out. Looking at the tree by the river it was as if fireflies danced on its branches.

– So, how has Mike been treating you? He asked hesitatingly, holding back, unable to believe he had been stupid enough to actually ask such a question.

– He has kept up his h-harsh lessons, she said, looking at the floor, didn't want to look at him. – They started the moment I returned, as I knew they would, and I submitted willingly to them. I knew what I was heading into.

He hadn't heard her stutter since his return.

– I can't believe you returned, he said.

Why not? You did. She wanted to say, but didn't.

That was different. She conceded that willingly.

– I wrote you a letter, Linda cried suddenly. – I wanted you to come with me. Why didn't you, you son of a bitch?

He stiffened.

– You did? He said, reading understanding in her eyes, as she nodded, the anger and hurt subsiding as quickly as it had arisen.

– I never received it, Ted said, clearly frustrated, enraged.

– I knew you lived at Uncle Eugene's place, she said mystified. – I addressed it there.

– You addressed it to Eugene?

She wanted to reply. He put a finger on her lips.

– Doesn't matter, he's the one who would've picked it up, anyway.

She shook her head, in denial, in more denial.

– He took it, Ted said. – He hid it from me and probably destroyed it in a convenient moment.

– But… why? Linda looked at him in despair, in more despair.

– I don't know. You would have to ask him. Comparing his unfathomable actions to everything else happening in our lives, it isn't really that strange, though.

And with those words he sat down on the bed, and she sat down beside him, invisible tears flowing down their cheeks.

A boy sat on the thick branch in the tree by the river. He sensed the power below, how it brought everything with it, brought stone, sand and shit, the ever-moving whirling mist of vapor in the air. He rose in the air like an eagle, stretching his thoughts across the city of Denver, his home, his damnation. He flew across the Platte, the uneven, torn landscape of buildings and roads, seeing nothing, sensing everything.

Denver, Colorado, a Mile High elevation was the envy of American cities, they said, the 600 000 people making it their home. The city had its sanatoriums, its health clinics. People sought here from all over the world to be cured for their incurable diseases. Nobody seemed to notice the steel mills, and all the other factories spewing smoke across the plain, making smoke linger in the air, making any effect of the sanatoriums and the other «health clinics» negligible, at best. The eagle flapped its wings a few extra times in contempt.

Tomorrow was July fourth, Independence Day. The

Celebration always started early, and this year was no exception, with parades, shows and parties across town, American style. Flags were waved. A lot of flags were waved. Stickers and posters and banners, big and small were put up all over the city, including two classics: IN GOD WE TRUST and UNITED WE STAND

Everything happened so slowly. People moved like puppets through the streets, with their stiff, made smiles.

The doorbell chimed. Linda went to the entrance hall and opened the door. On the stairs stood four youths smiling at her.

– Hi, you're the sister, right, a well-developed dark-haired girl said, reaching out her hand. – I'm Maria Jimenez. The others are Diana McKenzie, Todd Strobe and Arnold Vincent. We're here to meet Ted. He told us a weekend-long party would start in these parts tonight.

– I'm Linda. She took the hand hesitatingly, shaking it, shaking all their hands. – Come inside. We'll be leaving shortly.

Ted entered the living room, and as he did so images flashed before his mind, to a burning of the flag staged at 16th street. Tempers flared, as Diana held the flag high… and then put a torch to it. She had been arrested, of course, and the police station had been under siege the two days she had been imprisoned.

– Flag-burning is a constitutionally accepted form of protest, she shouted through the portable speaker equipment.

Ted could still hear her excited voice, see the eagerness in her eyes.

A while later Linda left the bathroom and Mike grabbed a towel in the kitchen. But Ted was already on his way in.

– I've been waiting longer than you, he threw at his brother. – I'm first.

Mike didn't say anything, he didn't do anything. He just froze there on the spot, completely beside himself in rage. Ted froze, too, tightening his hands into fists. They stood there for a long time, just looking at each other. But nothing happened. Finally, Ted merely continued on his way into the bathroom.

Mike walked into the living room. All the chairs were occupied.

– So, you're the brother, Maria stated.

– I'm Mike, the creature towering above her said, and her lower lip started twitching.

Mike disappeared out in the garden, out of sight, and the four guests looked incredulously at each other and breathed a sigh of relief.

Ted hadn't locked the bathroom door. Linda opened it and slipped inside, without anybody noticing. Ted was still in the shower. She could see him. She could see all of him.

She had before, and didn't let it faze her.

– What have you done? She spoke low, in a near whisper. – He will beat the crap out of you.

– Did you see him, *see* him standing there? Her twin laughed heartedly. – He didn't know what to do, didn't have the foggiest idea. Opposition is such a strange experience to him. He hasn't truly met with any for years.

He stepped out of the shower, stepping close to her.

– After last night he has a lot on his mind, he assured her, – We all do. And think about it: If anything happen on the fourth of July there will be publicity and a lot of it. And he isn't certain of mother and father any longer either, certain of their ongoing inactivity.

– He's biding his time, she spat, – And so are you.

There was a prolonged silence.

– This night belongs to us, he said, as he was walking into the parents' bedroom, dressing. – The night belongs to us. Enjoy it. Enjoy it fully and completely, Shadow Sister.

Sister of the Shadow. The trickle down her spine was a waterfall of ice.

– May I have the honor of escorting thee to the ballet, beautiful maiden?

He bowed deeply and cheerfully.

She giggled and allowed him to take her arm. He opened the two upper buttons in her dress, revealing the tops of her breasts; the same that Mike always made sure were hidden beneath clothes. She didn't protest. Instead she felt an inevitable, shameful pride.

The six of them made their way out of the house. And outside they all heard the flapping of wings and spotted the dark birds, spotted the ravens. They were on the ground and in the air.

– It is as if they've been…waiting, Diana whispered.

Ted felt the jolt inside. He felt it and rejoiced.

– They welcome me, he said flatly, – welcome me to the shadows.

A bird landed on Linda's left shoulder. She played with its feathers distractedly and thoughtfully.

They made their way from the house, through the dark forest, with the ravens in tow, towards the festivities. They didn't see Mike anywhere. The night was far from silent tonight. Horns and marches were played virtually everywhere. It filled the mind with noise and didn't let go.

– What shit, Ted mumbled.

The two other boys exchanged angry and worried glance. Diana shook her head, a bit apprehensive. Maria just smiled hotly to him.

His eyes never rested. Some of his old fears of the shadows and the dark returned, and he saw red gleaming eyes behind every bush, every flickering of shade.

They passed the place where the old theater had resided. It was now a lot of open space, a parking lot… and a big shopping mall of glass and concrete, completely dominating the area, its lights and brilliance shadowing everything else in its immediate and extended proximity.

Slowly, only slowly did the brilliance fade, and there was some more forest. But it was muted, no longer more than a small glen compared to its former glory.

Then music, deafening music reached them on their path, from a house nearby. Ted started smiling instantly.

– Jesus, Todd exclaimed. – It's coming from Jonas Bergli's house. That old geezer is playing Mighty Quinn.

– And he's playing it LOUD, Ted grinned, a rush of excitement rising in him. – Good for him.

– But isn't that one celebrating use of LSD? Todd said, a bit more cautious now.

– So what? Ted countered.

That left Todd mute and deaf, and blind. A raven flew right above his head. He ducked in something close to panic.

Ted laughed, seeing the glimmer of fire in every corner.

And there were shadows. His brother used to hide in these dark corners, to jump at him, devastate him, crush him, crush him to nothing.

– Aren't you afraid? Maria asked him, a thrill in her voice.

– The shadows and the fire are my friends, he replied. – They make me grow and live.

The ravens squeaked.

– There's a lot going on, Diana said, both excited and somber. – Not all of it good. The break in at the local school yesterday for instance…

His old school. It had made national news because of what had been scrawled at the walls, of what had been painted in blood:

FREEDOM FOR ALL THE OPPRESSED

According to the principal nothing had been stolen, but there had been «a lot of vandalism and wanton destruction».

– But that's the way all schools should go, he said teasingly to Diana, – and isn't the writing on the wall beautiful?

– It is, she agreed. – Beautiful beyond words.

And she looked at him the way she almost always looked at him; with both longing and apprehension in her eyes.

The party at the Foresters' was loud. They heard it several blocks away, overwhelming a lot of the other, burgeoning celebration.

– Whatever I say, whatever happens, don't say a word, Ted instructed, ordered them all.

His words were greeted with immediate silence, before Diana's apprehension got the best of her.

– What's gonna happen?

– We're gonna have some fun tonight, Ted replied (in a stunning reenactment of Jim Morrison's immortal stage performance).

– And is having fun your sole goal tonight? Linda asked solemnly and pointedly.

– Of course, he replied. – Why shouldn't there be? That would be anyone's sole goal, would it not?

There was a slight silence, before his voice turned menacing, before nothing was hidden anymore.

– They're expecting the Ritemaster. They're gonna have him,

a bit early.

Without further delay or interruptions, they reached the minor Forester Mansion. Todd and Arnold didn't look like they were quite enjoying themselves. They, too, had grown up in the southern parts of Denver, in the adjacent neighborhood. They knew.

Ted rested his left hand possessively on Linda's shoulder, as he knew Mike had begun to do lately. Two other couples reached the main entrance stairs simultaneously, the extremely wide and tall doorway. They froze and pulled back.

Ted Cousin arrived at Forester Minor Mansion with his five human companions and the sideshow of ravens. Some of the birds remained outside, but a few flew inside. People started chasing them. Ted lifted a hand, stopping the humans in their tracks.

– Let them be, he said.

And they did, and they kept looking around with a skittish look in their eyes, a distinctive body stance, signaling their worry, their realization that everything was suddenly and inexplicably changing.

Frank met them with his usual broad smile.

– Hello, Mike, he greeted the tall, imposing boy the moment the six reached the red carpet in the minor, open hall, the exact moment, in fact. He was good at this, at hosting. – It's so nice to welcome you and company to this little soirée.

He didn't know. Almost no one did. If anyone had heard the rumors of Ted's return to Denver, they hadn't seen him or thought they had. They still thought of him as the sickly boy he had been three years ago. Of course, they did.

Ted counted approximately fifty people in the immediate vicinity of the spacious, very spacious living room, among them Keith Lampard, Ray Channon and a few other leatherjackets. There was room for several hundred, but this was the elite, the up and coming youths in this part of town. Ted noticed Lampard's sticking eyes, but ignored them, just as Mike would have done. Frank's eyes were drawn to Linda's revealed breasts. He looked briefly and nervously at them, looking away, looking back, looking away, looking back.

Ted cleared his throat. Frank shook. The assembly laughed,

a cruel and triumphant laughter. It was always fun seeing him attempting to pull himself together confronted with Mike, ruthlessly exposing his own clumsiness.

– Eh, we have been waiting for you. – What is tonight's opening gambit?

– Whatever you may choose, Ted grinned. – I'm in such a good mood tonight.

He nodded graciously. Frank pulled carefully back towards the stereo equipment, as if he was afraid to make noise. And he was.

Ted looked for Tilla, and then he spotted her, elegantly descending the marble stairs, taking her time, deliberately slow making her way towards him, a sensual, promising smile painted on her face. The adult Tilla, no longer even remotely a child. If she wasn't fully developed physically, she sure looked the part. He swallowed hard. Her breasts danced up and down behind the velvet cloth. Her hair flowed, surrounding the curvy body like that of Medusa, the ancient Greek goddess. She looked like shadow, she looked like fire.

He took in his memories of the house, deliberately all the bad ones, everything he remembered, and it was everything. The pool, the stinking liquor, the constant fear and humiliation. It flashed before his inner eyes, and it was all he could do, to keep the rising whimper from expressing itself. The Rage, the gathering Rage kept it bottled, and he embraced it, embraced everything. He took hold of Linda and he brutally showed her towards the sofa. The empty sofa, made ready for him, for Mike…

There was a chair there. An expensive Louis XIV chair. Also his, his to inhabit as he saw fit. The entire room, the entire house, the entire world was made for him, as he saw fit. He stopped by the chair, preparing to meet the Medusa, his Goddess.

She ran to him. He took her in his arms, and they kissed. She kissed him with wet lips and a playful tongue, a body writhing close to his.

He released her. She took a step back, still with the smile in place.

She looked startled at him. He wondered if what he saw in

those stone gray eyes were fear.

– Who do you all think this is? She said contemptuously, making a turn, staring at them all.

Ted remembered her eyes, glowing in joy, as he was chained to the bed in the cabin, each time the stick fell.

Frank stared openmouthed at her.

– What do you mean? He yelped.

Ted sensed the coming of a hard-on, sweet and painful.

– Are you saying what we think you are saying? Lampard's voice and stance were a study in uncertainty and astonishment.

– Ask him, Tilla said aloud. – Ask him who he is.

Lampard turned slowly towards the dark boy, looking closer at him. He started sweating. His forehead, every piece of skin visible on his body was covered in a thick layer of sweat. He discovered the minor, practically minute differences.

– You're not Mike! He cried it out in disbelief, completely out of character.

Linda also stared at him, at her twin brother, stared in horror, as her nightmare became a horrible reality.

– Have I ever claimed I was? Ted replied softly.

The reply made the other mute. Both the leatherjacket and others looked completely thunderstruck, as if they couldn't believe their eyes and ears.

– This is a joke, right? Lampard turned to Tilla. – Tell me this is a joke.

She just laughed at him. Without uttering a sound, she laughed triumphantly, patronizingly at him.

He turned back to Ted, the younger brother towering over him, like an angel of vengeance. Everybody stared at him in fear, unable to decide what they should or could do. Ray Channon glanced around the room with his rat eyes, his features distorted by hatred.

– Don't turn on the music, he snarled to Frank, and then to Ted. – We don't want you here. Get out. More than one has come here playing big man. They have all lived to regret it.

Ted's reply was a loud, contemptuous laughter making Ray shrink to the actual size of a rat.

– Frank, turn the music on this instant, he ordered.

Frank looked from the small group of leatherjackets to the

red-eyed giant towering above them all. He was in no doubt whatsoever who had to be obeyed. He just pushed the button, starting the first, best record on the disk. Pulsing, dark music filled the room. It didn't seem contemporary at all, but like something out of an ancient past... or far future.

Ray observed what happened, observed it all from his position behind Lampard's back, what direction the wind blew. He threw himself snarling at Ted, driven by an anger, a rage completely robbing him of reason. He still saw the brother, like he had been three years earlier.

Ted struck him from downwards up, almost dividing his head from the body. He was thrown backwards and slid across the floor until the opposite wall halted the slack body. He remained there, unmoving.

– I'm not welcome? Ted spat. – Is that a common opinion? Anyone?

He stared through them all, giving them shakes threatening to turn uncontrollable. The change in him was palatable. This was no longer a frightened and timid kid, but a demon haunting them late at night, making them cry out in their fitful sleep.

Keith Lampard raised a hand, signaling quite unnecessary to his frozen henchmen not to move.

– Let him feel welcome for a short while, fellows, he said. – This is Mike's personal business. Let him fix it.

Ted saw the sly flash in the other's eyes, saw how the momentarily lost ingenuity reappeared, how he did like he always did, weighing the pros and cons of any situation, considering what benefits could be won.

– Hold on. Keith had turned half away, but stopped once again, as Ted continued, as he raised his tight fist. – You were all responsible for what happened to me, what was done, either by actively participating or doing nothing. Yes, my take on it is that even those of you who are new to this place, who weren't even physically present three years ago are responsible. You're all the same. I'll say this to you all: You'll pay. Eventually you'll all pay. That's all. Have a pleasant evening.

He reached for Linda. She took his hand, and they headed for the dance floor, dancing to the unholy, heathen rhythms, making everybody present watch. Ted still hadn't learned to dance. He had never been able to learn, and now he no longer cared about such shit, about how others may or may not perceive him.

Linda could dance. And she swung herself in her newfound freedom, and those present held their breath.

– Bright and Dark are dancing, she sang. – Let the people of the world behold and carry fear in their hearts.

Ted watched Tilla from the corner of his eyes. It looked as if she was truly worried, as if she wanted to achieve contact with him, but this he didn't understand. He dismissed it as wishful thinking and continued on his path.

Other boys and girls eventually, hesitatingly found their way to the dance floor. They had their own life to live, and not everybody felt any strong, lasting fear or felt that this, in any way was their business. Ray Channon remained unconscious. No one helped him or even cast a glance in his direction. He was just another victim of a callousness they had all perfected through the years.

Ted once more met Tilla's eyes. It truly seemed like she was attempting to communicate something to him. Perhaps he should take her out of here, getting to know her better. She filled his blood, his mind, everything he was. He had to swallow hard several times before he finally managed to take the first few hesitant steps towards her.

Then he discovered that she looked up, staring over his shoulders, and he realized he was too late. He turned around and got a glimpse of Linda's corpselike white face. The others, at the dance floor and outside it stopped moving, some in fear - others in expectation. He stood face to face with fate. Mike walked through the doorway.
***********************/

The ravens squeaked and sang, staring silently at those assembled in the deadly quiet room.

Linda dumped happily down on the couch, after having danced, danced the last dance, incidentally with Bruce Channon, who, to her surprise had been both skilled and considerate. She, too, had let herself go tonight, dancing more than all the previous years combined. Now the room turned quiet. Everything and everyone turned quiet and there was no

240

movement. Nobody moved, but the five people at the table, and a dark-skinned girl close to it. Linda saw Mike react to the raven close by, the squeaking bird resting on the top of the candelabra, saw the taint of fear in his eyes, his fire dull and muted.

– Ah, there you are, Ted had said casually shortly after his arrival. – I was going to suggest a game of poker. Are you interested?

– Sure, why not? Mike had replied. – But as far as I can remember, you can't even really play the game, so how do we go about it?

– I've been practicing, Ted had said. – Practicing good.

– I've been teaching him, Maria Jimenez told them all, with a proud look and stance.

And now they sat there at the table at the center of the dance floor. A round table, with green felt.

– My dad got this table flown here from Las Vegas last year, Frank said nervously. – It's rumored to have been used during the first World Series competition. I hardly remembered it myself, until Ted mentioned Poker. I…

His voice faltered and died, and he mostly kept his mouth shut after that.

– WHAT'S THIS? Diana McKenzie cried out fairly unnecessary, with a shrill laughter, finally sensing, realizing the tension at the place. – What's happening?

– No need to worry. Bruce attempted to soothe her. – This is just the opening salvo or gambit, if you will. You still have time to evacuate the premises…

She didn't appreciate his wit. Neither did Linda, who sent him a warning, a stare with her marble blue eyes.

– One who won't exactly make this night or its participants less infamous in the years to come, that's for sure, a voice stated from the chorus line of the audience.

– Look at this, another said. – Not even the dullest poor fucker present can doubt this is the final pretext to war.

– Poker is War, Maria stated calmly.

– I'll take your bets, now, gentlemen and ladies, another said, picking a notebook and a pencil from his pocket. – Even odds, please. As many bets you want, on the poker, and on everything following.

No one really reacted to his cruel practicality. Their complete attention was glued to the opening salvo in the drama unfolding before them.

The five gathered at the table were, in addition to Ted and Mike, Frank, Keith and Bob. The game started. All lights, except the single one above the table itself had been turned off. The single lamp shook, and the light flickered. It gave the entire stage a… supernatural quality. Many onlookers stood there shaking without really knowing why.

They played Texas Hold'em No Limit, the main game played at the aforementioned World Series tournament competition at Binion's Casino, Las Vegas, a variation of the original Five Card Draw poker game played all over the world the last hundred years. Texas Hold'em was a so-called community card game, with each player having two hidden cards on his hand, and eventually five open cards, shared by everybody at the table, seven in all, comprising a hand of five. Not to be confused with what was generally called Stud, where there were no shared cards.

Everybody started with thousand dollars in chips. The amount was incidental, really. They played single table tournament. The point was for one to remain at the end with all the chips in his possession. At least in this case money meant nothing, nothing at all.

The second game started. Frank took home the first pot, the first win, a minor amount. It all seemed very elegant, very sophisticated. An outsider might mistake the tension in the room for excitement over the game itself. No one present did.

– The first three table-cards, dropped all at once are called the «flop», Bruce lectured Diana. – If two or more players have matched their hand cards with those three it's usually followed by heavy betting. But not always. Tactics may occasionally turn the game completely around.

He kept speaking. No one listened to him.

The Raven. Ted felt its presence. He observed how Mike constantly glanced at it, how it seriously distracted him from the game, from everything. Mike Cousin was sweating. Ted Cousin sensed triumph like something tangible inside. It was happening.

Ted the Raven grinned, and everybody around the table and away from it recoiled in their waking dreams. He saw Iris among the spectators, just as skinny and undeveloped as ever. And that was the final distraction, luxury he allowed himself.

The game progressed. Nothing big happened for a while. Poker was like that, long stretches of boredom. The five still had about the same amount of chips as when they started out. Lampard was slightly in the lead, but that meant nothing in the long term. Ted raised him before the flop. Lampard called. The flop was an ace, five and seven. Ted bet after Lampard had checked. Lampard folded. The fourth and fifth card was never shown in this hand. Ted took the pot, and now he was chip leader. The players studied each other constantly to learn some crack in their facade, some weakness in their game, ways to possibly discern their hand. Ted scratched his head, but he did that fairly often, and there was no discernible pattern to it. The onlookers saw that Mike nodded to himself, as if he was realizing something.

– My compliments to your cute teacher, Mike nodded. – Her lessons have evidently not been completely wasted.

– My sincere thanks, brother. Coming from you it means a lot.

Words so sweet, so horribly insincere. Those present would never forget this evening. They wouldn't forget the foreplay, the initial gambit either. Already at that point their every hope of human greatness and nobility was crushed utterly. And the worst part of it was that nothing was really happening. The five of them just sat there, playing a game, enjoying a friendly conversation.

– It's a battle of wills. Bruce kept going. – Luck doesn't really enter into it, not in the long term. You play the player, not the cards. He who in the end overpowers the opponents will win.

– Shut up, Diana mumbled.

– What did you say, honey? Bruce turned to her with a smile on his face.

– SHUT THE FUCK UP!

She struck him with a crushing blow to his cheek. Blood flowed from his mouth. He went down like a felt tree. She kicked him a single time in the head. Dizzy and shocked he crawled away like a wounded animal.

– Now you may learn how to put up and shut up, she called after him.

Cruel laughter rolled through the room. The players hardly noticed. Mike dealt the game. Two cards to each player. Lampard was big blind, second place after the dealer, having put out a pre-decided amount of twenty dollars in chips. Ted, who was first to act, called him. The two after him also called. Bob was small blind, the player next to the dealer. He raised to sixty. Lampard called. Ted folded. Frank called. Mike raised to hundred. He did so with a huge smile on his face. Bob called. Lampard folded. Frank called. Flop was dealt. Flop was ace, eight and four.

– I'm all-in, Mike declared, after all the others had checked, pushing all his chips to the center of the table.

After a short hesitation Bob did the same. He did have less chips than Mike, and would be out if he lost. Frank folded, shaking his head.

– On your backs, Maria said, with a slightly hoarse voice.

They turned their cards. Mike had two fours on his hand, three counting the one in the flop. Bob had ace and eight, two pairs. Bob swore. He needed an additional eight or ace on the last two cards. He stood up from the table, acknowledging defeat.

– This is a game of life and death, anyway, he said. – I'm not sure I want to play with those kinds of stakes.

The turn, the fourth card was a ten. The river, the fifth card was a deuce. Bob was out.

Mike was now a major chip leader.

Bruce had problems getting up. He held his head while his face kept twisting in pain. Diana knelt by his side, completely beside herself.

– I'm sorry, she whimpered. – I don't know what happened, what came over me. I'm sorry. Sorry.

There was a kind of rough laughter, even though people's attention was locked on the drama.

Ted hardly heard her, heard it. He was totally focused on what happened on the table, around the table. The world outside hardly existed. He heard the beating of hearts, sensed blood moving through veins. There was a crack, a thunder in the very air. Everything but the table and the players disappeared.

Games were played. Hands were played. Not much changed. Mike was still chip leader. Ted gained a bit more. He was now second at the table.

Ted dealt cards. Frank raised to two hundred to the big blind prearranged twenty. Mike called. Lampard called. They all heard Maria breathe. It was strange. It was like she was a part of the game, somehow. There was nothing initially keeping her from joining the game. Frank had offered her a place. There could as many as ten or even twelve players around the table. But she had declined.

Ted called, ignoring the loud call to arms of the two «pocket» aces on his hand. Flop was dealt. Flop was ace of clubs, nine of diamonds, six of diamonds. Ted felt a breath of hot air from inside. Frank bet two hundred. Mike raised to four hundred. Lampard called. Ted, too, ignoring the screaming from his set, his three aces. Frank called. Turn, the fourth card was dealt. Turn was a nine of spades. Frank checked. Mike bet four hundred. Lampard folded with a shrug and a cold smile.

– I'm all-in, Ted said, showing his remaining chips to the center of the table.

Frank folded, sighing.

Mike called, still with quite a few chips left.

Ted showed his two aces. Everybody stared at them. Mike, too, as he turned his nine and ten of hearts. He needed the remaining nine. That was the only card in the deck that could help him.

River was dealt. The fourth ace was turned. A joint sigh filled the room. Ted had not yet won the overall game, but he was by far the chip leader.

– You can't really play the game, Mike shouted. – You were just damn lucky. Or you were cheating.

The room came rushing back in. All the breathing mouths, all the beating hearts. All the power.

– You would excuse yourself with that, would you...

The very moment those very words, the piercing scorn was uttered Lampard and Frank threw themselves backwards, away from the battlefield.

– Looks like this game has been discontinued prematurely,

Lampard cried, laughing out what went for his heart.

– You have to be first. Ted blinked, as the revelation hit him. – Or you are nothing.

Quick as lightning Mike gave the table a brutal push. It hit Ted in the belly. His chair tilted, and he fell backwards, falling gasping to the floor. Chips and cards seemed to float in the air forever, before gravity took its toll, and it all fell to the floor. Mike's face twisted in contempt, as he threw himself at his brother.

– So EASY, he shouted triumphantly.

I'll kill him with my bare hands.

Ted's right foot flew up, hard as a ram pole, almost removing Mike's head from his neck. Mike landed hard far away.

Both jumped on their feet, snarling and spitting. And so, suddenly and shocking, it began. Mike lunged a fist, but it missed. Ted struck him on the left cheek, with all the force contained in his hatred. Blood flowed in a straight line from the mouth. Mike hit him on the jaw, and he felt the sweet taste of blood in his own mouth. Already bloody and horrible they circled one another.

– You can bleed, Ted shouted triumphantly. – I knew that. I'm not surprised.

There won't be a single drop of blood left in you when I'm through.

They went in clinch, hitting and kicking each other, where they stood, without retreating, without yielding the slightest from their chosen position.

Silence reigned among the audience. There had been shouting, there had been cheering the first few seconds of the fight. Now they retreated to the corners and shadows of the room, struck mute and deaf.

– What happens out there is… Bob crouched and shook his head.

– Jesus Christ, Todd shouted. – JESUS CHRIST.

Ted knocked his head at Mike's, making him stagger back a moment, and the immediate follow up was a straight right fist into the enemy's abdomen. Mike staggered backwards, and landed on a chair. It couldn't support his weight and momentum, and it broke under him. The big boy screamed aloud when one of the chair's sharp broken legs penetrated the skin of his thigh. Ted snarled, but the expression of triumph was obviously premature, as Mike landed a foot in his face. He kept at it. They kept at it. Mike threw himself at him once more. Both bodies struck the wall. The entire building shook. Trapped in each other's hateful embrace they rolled across the floor, while hitting, kicking and biting the other at every possible opportunity. The expression in their faces exceeded any description. Satanic… without mercy, without reason. They didn't even seem to notice any of the hits they received. If there were indeed any ignorant among those who watched this, it would look like a violent ballet, but even the most ignorant, most shielded from life's harsh realities would realize that there was no choreography, no planned moves.

– They're fighting like wild animals, Bob whispered, – like the beasts they're born to be.

– What are you talking about? Iris asked him nonplussed.

– There must be order in the world, Bob stated. – There must.

– Orden muss sein, one cried out sarcastically.

Bob just looked at the man, with a look filled with such hatred that the other paled in his track.

Ted lifted Mike above his head, in one fluid, brutal move… and threw him at the wall. There was a loud crack when something, somewhere on the solid frame snapped. A rib or two perhaps, or a bone in a leg or an arm. Mike landed on one foot and kicked. Ted ran straight into the kick, and skin loosened from his facial skin. They clinched again, straining against the other, none of them giving anything. Mike threw his kid brother away. Ted landed on the floor, shaking his head, attempting to clear his vision. Mike jumped at him, attempting to land his feet on his chest. Ted rolled to a momentary safety, giving the other a cruel kick in the back. Mike gasped aloud. He struck out blindly with his arm to keep the distance while he crouched, and attempted to catch his breath. They circled once more, both bleeding freely, both breathing in desperate, labored gasps. Over half of the floor was decorated in skin, blood and tiny body remains. Cards and chips were torn apart and looked like shrapnel after a bomb strike. Black hair, loosened from sore scalps was both on them and off them, stuck to walls and disintegrated furniture. The sophistication from the poker game was no more, and it was hard to imagine it had ever been. The red glare in their eyes seemed like echoes, mirror images of each other. They kicked out, pulled back, struck, pulled back. All the time there were the snarls, and the twisted, horrible faces. Some noncombatants attempted to leave. They headed for the exit, but froze and pulled back into the corners, the nothingness from which they came, cringing like frightened to death children on the floor. Maria stared transfixed at what was going on. She was speaking to herself constantly, but not a sound emerged from between her lips. Tilla sat on the stairs, completely compromised, out in the open. Bloody bits of skin and the room itself flew past her. She didn't move, but just sat there with a frozen expression on her face.

– Call the police, Linda ordered Frank.

– What… he looked at her with eyes completely clouded and dazed.

– Call the police. Unless you want to call your parents' insurance appraiser tomorrow. Unless you want to have your own body in a casket tomorrow.

Her ice-cold eyes easily penetrated his meager defenses, and he pulled away from her, towards the phone. As if he truly saw her for the first time.

She reached for a baseball club on the wall.

– That is rumored to have belonged to B-babe R-ruth, Frank gasped.

She didn't say anything. She didn't even look at him.

Ted was thrown through the big window and landed at the mound outside. He landed on his feet and jumped right back inside, hitting Mike with a foot. The scream of pain from Mike made the entire building rattle, as if it was about to crumble. It didn't just shake, but vibrated violently. It was possible to see who was who at first, because of the difference in clothes, but as the clothes were increasingly torn and soaked in blood it got more difficult.

Mike struck Ted with both hands jammed together, as if he held a tennis racket or something in his hand. Ted stumbled backwards, but struck back the moment Mike advanced a step forward.

– Jesus Christ, Todd kept shouting. – JESUS CHRIST.

He had repeated it at irregular intervals several times the last few… was it minutes or hours?

– This is amazing. Lampard kept shaking his head. – This is absolutely amazing.

He tried to dry his forehead with his sleeve. It did no good.

Nobody had moved. Nobody had managed to escape the ongoing horror inside Forester Minor Mansion. Except for the fascinated Lampard they all wanted to close their eyes, but couldn't do it. He did close his eyes, and what he saw then was exactly what he saw when they were open. Everything was dark red, and he hummed a song, hardly aware of doing so.

Desperately Ted rolled his brother off. He managed to fight himself on his feet. Mike moved slow, painfully slow. He kicked the other in the groin. He screamed the same moment his brother screamed. Both crouched in pain. Ted held around the crotch. Mike's leg was dead and paralyzed. Linda screamed, too, when she saw her twin brother's nose be smeared on Mike's knee. Ted fell down. Mike kept standing, but his leg shook so much that it was visible far away. Linda stepped close to him. She waited, allowed him to be aware of her. He turned towards the sister and her cold eyes froze him. She swung the club. It hit him at the left temple. He went down like a fallen tree, and remained there, lying still. She kicked him in the belly. He puked all over the already ruined, no longer expensive carpet. She kicked him again. There was no reaction. He was dead to the world. Ted moved. He pushed his hands at the floor, attempting again and again to force himself up. Linda hit him in the neck with the club, and he lay still, too.

– I know you can hear me, boys, she said to them, called to them softly, through haze, through sleepy dust. – I could have killed you, now. Anybody could have. I want you both to remember this, before you ever make yourself so vulnerable again.

– I'll be damned, Keith Lampard said.

She turned to him, swinging the club. I can use this, she told him, told all the vultures in the room. The sound of sirens rose in the distance. Lampard halted the advance of his cohorts. She looked at Frank, not sure whether or not he had called the cops or if they had been alerted to the ruckus as a possible case of dramatic domestic violence or something. There was more than one car, more than one siren, penetrating the night.

She let go of the club. It dropped on the carpet without the slightest, identifiable sound. She started crying, observing the crowd of police officers storming towards the building, towards her with weapons drawn. They stopped just inside the doorway, lowering their weapons in astonishment.

– Mike did this, she said, something clearly catching in her throat. – My brother did this.

She knelt down by Ted's side. He stood on his knees, and she looked at him with fear in her eyes.

– I'm all right, he said. – I am all right, all right.

She watched him, saw how his eyes, too, widened.

She turned then, again, looking where he looked, and there was no way she could describe the nothing she felt, the nothing she saw there. The long trail of blood leading to the broken window.

Mike was gone.

*************/

When darkness surrounded her she felt the beast's eyes on her. She had the distinct impression she was heading home, running through the forest the fastest she could, with police officers not far behind, but she wasn't sure. The run hardly lasted more than a minute, she ran that fast, but it felt like hours. She collided with trees, stumbled in roots and had hair in her eyes, but finally the terrified girl glimpsed her home among the trees. Blinded by tears she threw herself through the door, pushing it hard at the wall inside, almost making it leave the hinges.

She was instantly struck by the silence, the darkness inside. She stopped and listened. Her parents were home. She was able to hear them in the living room, speaking in low voices.

– They've got the right to know, Cindy insisted.

– Perhaps you're right. Perhaps you're right…

The walk through the kitchen seemed to last such a long time, not because of her paralyzing fear of Mike, but because of what awaited her ahead. There was a modest, soft light inside the living room, the fire from candles.

– You have an agenda, haven't you, she said before entering

the room, before they could see her. – Tonight's «ceremony» was no departure from that. You've always had one. And one of your sons has terrorized the other during that time, and tonight they've beaten each other senseless. Is that, too according to plan?

They didn't say anything as she approached the room. Her eyes narrowed as she saw red hair, pale skin by their side. Green eyes. Not gray. Not Tilla. Betty.

– What is she doing here?

They just smiled to her. Betty did, too. Linda dismissed it with an anger she couldn't really focus on, but was ever present, nonetheless.

– Tell me what? She asked them from the doorway, demand evident in her voice, finally confronting her parents.

They still didn't say anything, but just looked smug at each other.

And suddenly she knew, knew beyond doubt what they had hidden from her, from them. And the hot summer's night turned cold as ice.

– There are people upstairs she said numbly. – I can hear them.

– That's just poor Mrs. Wood. Cousin grinned. – She's trying on some of your mother's dresses.

There was frantic knocking on the entrance door. Linda still felt lethargic, the horrible stiffening of limbs. Her thighs and throat burned after the run. She remembered talking to her parents just moments ago in a quiet, deadly calm voice and pose, but that already seemed so far away in time and space. A couple of steps, a few heartbeats. The parents passed her on their way out to answering the knocking on the door. She was led by their move, moved where they moved. The doorknob was pushed down and the door opened before they reached it. Frank Forester and Bob Tremblay stumbled in, with Ted supported between them. He looked horrible, even worse than when she had last seen him, as his swellings developed on his more than half naked body. He smiled triumphantly, sending shivers down Linda's spine. Bob and Frank reluctantly released him, as his movements turned impatient. Incredibly enough he managed to stand on his own. He didn't fall.

– I'm all right, he insisted, speaking through swollen lips, cheeks and tongue. – I will be all right. I've been through worse. No fucking hospital, okay?

– Okay, Linda whispered.

She recognized Lieutenant Clark and several other police officers outside.

– It was nice of you to bring him home, Cindy said.

– Perhaps we were finally fed up with Mike's sadistic game, Bob said, carefully meeting her eyes.

Ted stared at Linda.

– Do they know? He nodded towards the parents.

– They know, she stated, clenching her throat, not trusting her own voice to be heard.

Frank and Bob writhed where they stood in the doorway, glancing repeatedly at the outside night, beyond the red and blue lights down the driveway.

– You boys must be hungry, Cousin said, evidently misunderstanding. – Why don't you join us in the kitchen for our evening supper?

Everything. Everything Linda had suspected about her parents through the years was now flushed into the open, to the forefront of consciousness, impossible to hide anymore. Her eyes burned at them.

– Thank you, Bob replied with blue, shivering lips. – I think we'll take you up on that offer, sir.

He looked as if he was deep underwater, a cold, dank corpse floating around.

Linda frantically looked for Betty, but she was gone, dissolved into the nothing from where she had come. They all returned to the kitchen, to the living room, to the shadows and the dust, but there was no one there. Lieutenant Clarke followed them inside.

– Excuse me, sir, he said to Cousin. – We need a few, preliminary statements.

– Mike did it, Linda said. – My brother did it all.

– Tomorrow, Cousin told him. – Come back tomorrow, and we'll be ready for you.

Clarke nodded, shrugging, returning to his blue and red lights.

– We'll leave a patrol car here, just to be sure, if that's all right with you, sir, he said.

– That's perfectly all right, Lieutenant, Cousin replied in a very polite manner. – Thank you.

He started working in the kitchen, procuring pans and pots. Linda smiled and shook her head in amazement, as he went through old, familiar motions, a smile turning dark and foreboding.

She imagined she could see Peter Clarke walk down the stairs outside, with slow, deliberate steps. He didn't look too pleased either.

Tomorrow, Linda thought. If tomorrow comes.

Frank and Bob obviously wanted to sit down somewhere, but it seemed like they couldn't decide which chair they were supposed to choose. Ted walked around, back and forth with an energy that kept building, kept being bottled up. It was as if everything he had gone through, what others would have called an ordeal was nothing to him. Linda looked at him, swallowing hard, and swallowing hard once again.

And…

They all heard it directly in their ears, as if the shrill howl from upstairs was fed directly into their auditory canals, and not from a distance away, a sound from a scared to death human being.

There was a thud, as something was hitting the floor or something above, and everything turned quiet.

– What the hell…

They all practically collided with Lieutenant Clarke on their way up the stairs. Fear was painted in their faces for what they would discover, for what would happen to them if they stayed behind alone downstairs. Primal fear and emotions ruled them all.

Her father was the first one up and on the scene, halting in the doorway to the biggest bedroom.

– He knows, Cousin said aloud.

The others joined him there, and petrified from bone to skin they remained there. A lot of other heavy feet were on their way up the stairs, in their wake.

Ted stood there without moving. He didn't even move his mouth as he spoke. The sound seemed to come from nowhere.

– He's insane, he mumbled. – Completely insane.

Clarke carefully stepped into the room, going in a wide circle to the window, the open window. The lawn below was being filled with approaching men in uniforms. There was no sign of anything… anyone else. He looked hard and strained his ears. He had a nice view from here, but saw no one leave, heard not the slightest sound of running feet. He started sweating, then, far beyond what a short run up the stairs would result in, and he didn't stop.

– DOYLE! He shouted.

– YES, SIR? Sergeant Doyle called back.

– CALL IN A FORENSIC TEAM AND MAKE THEM COME UP HERE, ASAP.

Linda didn't hear the reply, the eager as a dog, «yes, sir».

As if the room was far, far away she noticed three things:

The very open window, the abyss behind, beyond Clarke. The bloody and limp body of Mrs. Wood on the floor… and Linda's own ebony blade stuck in the woman's back.

Chapter eleven

Ted walked through the hallway upstairs. It turned dark as he walked, as if it was still dark, still night. He passed the big bedroom, where there was still a lot of yellow tape, and printed on that telling yellow tape were words, telling words:

CRIME SCENE DO NOT ENTER

He heard people move around in there, carefully, methodically, silently, but ignored that, too. He entered one of the smaller bedrooms down the hall. Linda's room. The morning sun shone on her bed. The silver blonde hair glowed in the morning light. The pale skin was indistinct from the pillow below. She attempted a smile.

– I can't sleep, she said, writhing and suffering restlessly on her back. – Can you sleep?

– No. He shook his head.

– I can't even close my eyes, she said sullenly. – Every time I try it, it is as if the room turns cold, and I'm a statue, waiting for the shadow to come out of the night. It's night. There's always night.

She moved under the blanket, not really a move at all, but more a contraction of muscles.

– The cops, they're still here?

– Yes. He listened, and he could hear them.

– I can't hear them. She cocked her head slightly.

– That's Denver's finest for you, he said ironically. – Discreet to the bone.

– You've changed, she said coldly. – From one night to the next. You seem like a stranger compared to whom you were.

– Yes, he said simply.

– I'm not holding it against you, she said. – I've changed quite a bit myself… we both have, as we must, in this hard, cold world.

She sat up in the bed, throwing away the blanket. She wore her nightgown. Suddenly he saw her, saw her again, and he couldn't help it. She, too, had, like Tilla, grown, and wasn't even remotely similar to the skinny girl he had known. She was still skinny. These weren't the generous curves of Tilla, but this was clearly a woman, not a girl. He could easily spot her nipples under the fabric covering them. They were erect, and her face was flushed. And he easily recognized the smell coming from her... that of her sex. Attempting to hide his shock he crouched slightly there, by the door.

– Come, she called, tapping the sheet. – Sit with me.

He hesitated a short while. Then he shrugged, joining her on the bed.

– We've grown, she said, – become something better and deadlier. But so has Mike. He has grown to meet our challenge, and he will never stop, never relent. *We* must stop him. Or he will never let us be.

He could smell the anger and the fear in her, as he could in himself.

– We'll stop him, he granted.

– Good, she whispered. – Very good...

He discovered that she was sweating, smelled it, as she carefully, tenderly touched the bandages on his head, the smallest skin visible there.

– It's amazing, isn't it, how... minor your injuries are. You looked like a burger last night, quite frankly...

– I've always healed fast, you know. Mike, Liz and Linsey do, too. I don't know about you and June, though.

– Yes, she nodded, and he caught another strange look in her eyes, – but this is amazing.

Her hands caught his left, squeezing its soft meat side. It didn't hurt. She hesitated a bit before removing the band aid.

– The wound, she breathed. – It's gone!

He looked and realized that she was correct. There was no wound, and only a mark, hardly more than a mark remaining of what yesterday had been a gashing cut.

– It didn't hurt during the fight either, did it?

– It did at first. Then it didn't. I figured I just didn't feel it, in the heat of battle.

– The raw, uncompromising battle, she stated.

He studied her, suddenly excited, as expectancy rose within him. She began breathing noticeably faster. The way she looked at him when she smiled made him breathe faster as well.

She kissed him on the lips, his still sore lips, holding his head close to hers.

This is peaceful. This isn't a struggle. She's clearly horny, but… And she doesn't seem to care, care about…

She let go of him, hunger and desire flashing and growing in her eyes, as she slipped the nightgown over her head, letting him see her clearly, without distortion.

– We aren't, she told him, told him softly, – we aren't…

– Ted, TED! COME DOWN. I'VE CALLED TO YOU THREE TIMES.

He ran to the window, opening it wide. His father stood below in the garden, with an unknown man by his side. Ted felt something, something…

– I'll be right down, he shouted back. – Cool your jets, old man.

He closed the window fast, turning back to his sister. She sat there still, naked and vulnerable.

– I must go, he heard himself say. – Rodney is waiting for me.

She nodded, pulling the nightgown back over her head, covering her body, pulling the mask back on. The white rose smiled at him, using her blue, blue eyes for all they were worth.

– I understand, she said. – But never leave me, you hear. Never leave me again.

– I won't, he replied. – Never!

– Mike will die, she said to him, her hands turning into fists.

– He will die. He will come for us. He will come to us, and he will die.

He caught a last glimpse of her, the moment he closed the door behind him, a complex puzzle of fear, Hunger and desire. And felt the same ravage him, felt it throughout his entire being, and he shuddered.

Air was clear and crisp this morning. The dew had yet to completely vanish from the grass. From the city below there was the sound of horns and drums. The Fourth of July celebration was just starting in Denver, Colorado the summer of 1971.

Ted felt jittery, as he approached his father and the man he didn't know in the garden. A tall, powerful built youth, seemingly not much older than Ted himself.

257

– Ted, Cousin presented, for unknown reasons clearly a bit jittery himself, – this is Mark Stewart, a Lieutenant in the Homicide Division of the Denver Police Department. He's in charge of the investigation.

Clearly not as young as he looked then. He was probably between twenty-five and thirty.

– They call me Babyface, Stewart grinned, and added, in response to Ted's stare: – I was born in 1937. Nice to meet you, kid.

He extended his hand. Ted took it… and the world seemed to bend and shift there on the spot.

Stewart was like… Ted felt a storm of emotions, a well of impressions when looking at the grown man… What he sensed more than anything was the overwhelming impression of facing a hawk, of facing it head on. The boy experienced the sense of being comforted, he experienced fear.

Looking beyond the man's pleasant exterior Ted experienced an emotion not unfamiliar to him… that of looking into a mirror.

Stewart didn't look anything like Mike or himself, but there was the characteristic familiarity, undeniable.

He had blue, blue eyes, and hair like desert sand, a quality Ted had not quite encountered before. Ted had grown to six feet three, and Stewart was taller than that. His shoulders were like that of a football player, *with* the protective gear. He looked immense.

There were flashes in the mirror, turned off and on as the shadow clouds raged across the sky.

– Have you ever been to New Orleans, Mark? Ted asked, more than a bit distant.

– No, never, Stewart replied with a more than equally strange expression in his eyes. – Why do you ask?

– Then never go there. Never even go close to it. Death is waiting on the balconies.

Stewart let go of the boy's hand. Both arms fell down.

– There's a Book turning its pages in the wind, in the hot sunshine, casting shadows everywhere.

– Ah, you're into Magick? Stewart grinned. – My mother, too, was heavily connected to that stuff.

– But I'm not…

He looked at his father for answers, but his father wasn't really there, was leaving. He, too, laughed, and seemed to enjoy himself in the hot sunshine.

– I'll leave you two alone, Cousin said lightly. – I bet you've got a lot to talk about.

And Ted, with his suddenly acute senses caught a rare glimpse of… curiosity? in his father's face, and wondered, wondered some more.

Stewart, too, looked at Cousin with more than a slice of curiosity.

Cousin disappeared into the house's cool shadows. Stewart and Ted remained.

And thus, it began, their first meeting.

They sat by the river. The river was very frisky today. Fine water droplets rained down on them, even though they didn't sit straight in the wind's path.

– So, Mrs. Wood was trying on your mother's clothes? Stewart asked quietly.

– She was. Ted jumped a bit. – Are you saying that my brother didn't choose a random victim for his madness, but wanted to kill his own mother, is that what you're saying?

Stewart threw a rock in the water. The impact hardly showed on the rough surface.

– We can't rule that out.

There was no discernible reaction on the boy's calm surface. Some lengths below, on the river bank there was a geyser of water standing straight up, like one saw on ocean shores where the water hit a spot between two rocks, and was forced upwards. The boy narrowed his eyes just a bit, not looking at Stewart, but looking at him anyway.

– Everything is so mundane, isn't it? Even the biggest variable in daily life is so normal that it's impossible to get a grip on it. And when one gets under the surface occasionally one sees there's really nothing there, nothing but the same washed up horror and degradation.

– Tell me about Mike, Stewart offered quietly, very quietly.

Ted threw a rock into the river, too. The impact fizzled and died.

– He started beating me up and tyrannizing me, and my sister about four years ago. The voice was flat, completely even, as if the boy had never raised his voice in anger. – I never found any discernible reason why. I screamed at him, screamed myself hoarse, asking him why he was doing it, why he was so cruel, and he replied, but his answers never made any sense. They still don't. I've even tried to look at the replies beyond the answers, you know, to no avail. Fuck him. Fuck him. I even tried putting myself in his situation, looking at it all from his point of view, but it still doesn't make sense. I think perhaps he doesn't know himself, and that he desperately wants to, that he will do anything to make sense out of it all, but that the answer eludes him. The more he reaches for it the more it's slipping through his grasp.

They stayed there for a good while. There was mostly silence, silence and the river.

– I heard a lot about him from the juvenile department, the policeman said, squinting his eyes at the place where the river made a turn. – He was always crazy, but there was a method to his madness, a cold, calculating mind that made it, at best difficult for us to *handle* him. I wonder what finally made him snap. I wonder about a lot of things. As you no doubt are aware of we're talking riddles within riddles here. I can't say I studied him. As far as the department was concerned I had more pressing matters on my hand. Murder is quite common in this town, you know. But after last night the city's elite seemed to have had enough. Forester did press charges.

– Yes, he did snap, didn't he?

– He most certainly did. A murder is a clear departure from his former modus operandi. And one so overt, one such a contemptuous show against everything society holds dear, clearly shows he has thrown the gauntlet. You're correct, kid, it does seem incomprehensible.

And all the time, while the two of them were having their conversation it was a perfect calm. No waves on the surface, nothing in the immediately below.

Ted, or the «kid» as Stewart called him, walked with the lieutenant to the car. Using «kid» instead of «boy» was slightly less derogatory.

260

– That cabin, Stewart asked him lightly, as they shook hands, shook hands again, – you don't where it is?

– No. A definite shaking of the head. – Only a general direction, out in the woods somewhere. He wanted us to feel disoriented, to feel helpless. And he grew on it. As we were crumbling he was rising. The weaker we got the stronger he became. And now, when we're strong he's weak. We're the Moon together, and there's only one moon.

The two of them shook hands extra fresh, before letting go.

This time nothing weird had happened, while they were touching.

Stewart looked at the boy, very serious minded.

– Listen, kid, you might say you're off the hook by a technicality, by default because of the extension of your brother's... increased transgression the last twenty-four hours. He has become our main concern. You may still have to answer for your participation in the rampage at Forester's, though. So, stay low, okay?

– Of course, Ted nodded. – Thank you, Lieutenant.

He turned away, returned to the house, lingering on the stairs.

Peter Clarke waited in the car. Stewart hurried inside and slammed the door shut the moment he sat down in the tiny seat.

– So Babyface, any leads?

Stewart waited a bit before replying, until just after Clarke had started the engine.

– The boy doesn't want help, he said. – He wants to take out his brother by himself. As far as he's concerned... vengeance belongs to him.

– That's heavy, man. Clarke shook his head. – But concerning the few, retouched, useless witness accounts we did get from the Forester party, from even the little we got, from everything we didn't get, we shouldn't really be surprised, right?

– We shouldn't, Stewart nodded.

Clarke waited, and his patience paid off.

– We will monitor the situation closely, of course. If young Cousin isn't caught soon, and I suspect he won't be, he and the younger young Cousin will eventually encounter and confront each other, and when that happens, we will be there.

– We will indeed, Clarke agreed.

He pushed the gas pedal, and the car jumped forward. It disappeared around the turn in a cloud of dust.

**/

It hurt. Every move he made hurt his entire body. He practiced in his room, hitting and kicking air. Slowly, painfully he regained his supple and agile body. Later he and Linda circled around each other down by the river, as ozone, drifting just above the ground made the air, the twilight air spark and fizzle. There was trusting. There was parting, hands and feet moving fluidly towards and away from the opponent. Like a dance, an ancient dance. The noise from the city, the celebration of Independence Day surrounded them like a thick, thick blanket. What they did about it was basically to ignore it. It meant nothing to them.

It felt awkward at first. They hadn't done this since Chicago, but it improved visibly by the minute. He sensed it, once again sensed how they… fit.

It was strange seeing her like this, so active, so dangerous. She, like him, like Mike was coming out of hiding.

– We're becoming, he said. – Becoming butterflies.

– The butterflies we're meant to be, she replied happily.

And there were waves, wisps in the air, visible to his eyes like shadows, gaining momentum, gaining strength as he watched. He stopped and crouched a bit.

– Are you okay? She asked in a worried tone.

– It's only pain. He shook his head. – If you ignore it, if you embrace it, it will go away.

They returned to the house, to its weird vibrations and inhabitants.

– This is how it should be, their mother told them. – Moon and Fire encircling each other, becoming Shadow.

Their father stood by her side, also smiling big.

Linda panted, but waited until they had walked inside, away from prying eyes and ears.

– Did you see that? That was absolutely bizarre.

– Yes, he confirmed, – they looked at us with pride, as if we were prize possessions, or something.

– It feels right, though… working out together, even more so than earlier. I've never felt more *right* in my entire life.

She was flushing, and her skin took on a deeper tone. Startled he realized something. There was pride in her eyes, too.

The evening darkness descended on Denver. The moon rose on the blue, red-hot sky. The reduced family, accompanied by Mark Stewart gathered in the living room.

– So, is there only you, Mark, may I call you Mark? Cousin queried. – Is that sufficient to the task, in your opinion?

– It's sufficient, Stewart shrugged. – Anyway, we take turns.

– We've heard that about you, Mark, Cindy said softly. – You're never eager to leave menial work to underlings.

Ted stared at her, at his father, wondering what the fuck went on here. His parents' tone was clearly… affectionate. The mystery that was his life once again opened up like an abyss below him. He wanted to scream at them, curse them for the secrets they kept from him. That. Linda's devotion. Stewart's dancing, investigative eyes. All of it made nausea stick in his throat like a ball. He felt as if he couldn't breathe, as if someone had a stranglehold around his neck. He had to leave, couldn't stand being in this room a second more. Without saying anything or looking at any of them, he walked to the door. Nobody said anything. Sort of grateful he left. The door closed silently behind him. He didn't hear the slightest sound, and he had to turn around to see if it was truly closed. It was.

He went to his room, making his way through shadowy halls. His father had hired people to put up a lot of additional lights lately, to no avail. The shadows remained. So much more in his room, where he had refused more lamps than the two already there. The light from the moon almost overpowered them, making everything silver and dark blue.

When looking out it was as if he could see another landscape, one he recognized as the Kendall ranch. And the room, too, was different. It was Elizabeth's room. He saw her slimmer arms as he looked down on himself. He was unable to blink, to close his eyes, and they remained wide open.

He spoke, and what he heard was a female voice, so like his own, but an octave or so higher.

– «I'm looking out of the window. I can see the children with sheets over their head play in the valley».

Startled he turned, and turned again, and slowly the room

became this room once more. Something else had startled him, caused him to «return» here. And he saw, saw the white envelope on the pillow, among the white sheets. He walked there, slowly, as if in slow motion. He realized it happened incredibly fast.

He picked it up. Opening it, inspecting its content confirmed his fears. It wasn't paper, but a large part of Tilla's dress. The writing had been done with white chalk, laced... laced in red. He could smell the letters, smell the red.

He couldn't even read it. Every word just flowed like mist before his eyes. Broken pieces registered, like knives.

... I COVETED MARIA, SO I TOOK HER...

... TILLA BETRAYED ME, SO I PUNISHED THE BITCH...

COME TO THE OLD MILL ONE HOUR PAST MIDNIGHT OR I WILL FLAY THE SKIN FROM THEIR BONES

ANYWAY, YOU DON'T CARE ABOUT THE BITCHES, I KNOW THIS FOR A FACT. YOU DO, TOO. WHAT MATTERS IS THE TASTE OF BLOOD IN YOUR MOUTH AND THE BURNING DESIRE TO BURY ME UNDER SIX FEET OF SOIL. LIKEWISE, BROTHER. LIKEWISE.
**/

Ted removed his remaining bandages in front of the mirror. There were still lacerations and swollen skin, but even less than this morning, and it hardly hurt anymore, not when he touched the affected areas. or he did a few quick but careless exercises. The smile of excitement and triumph still shadowed his face when he left the quiet, dark house a few minutes past eleven thirty. He closed and locked the cellar door behind him. There was no sound from inside. None at all. He could hardly hear the sound of the city itself. Everything loud was muted, distant, and the sound of nature assaulted him on all levels. The birds' singing, their anxious singing. The wind stroking the grass, bending it slightly. The branches of the trees swaying, dancing the ancient dance. He heard the river, heard it touch the land on both sides, washing away soil, breaking pathways for itself, keeping them open, through centuries, millennia. And its waterfalls, hidden and visible digging deep into the ground, below the surface, far below. He *saw* it, like pain, like release.

264

Black clouds hid the moon, making it hard to see for most people, but he saw well enough. He had always been able to see well in the dark. The image of the sawmill, the faraway place Mike had pointed out as the «meeting place» appeared for his inner eye. In his thoughts he was already there. Just before midnight, well over an hour before the letter had «suggested» he closed in on the very familiar surroundings. Bittersweet and horrible memories raged through him. The half-vanished forest trail led all the way to the abandoned mill, but he left it well before that. He stopped, sniffing in the air. There was nothing. Nothing that shouldn't be here. If nothing else the smell of blood would give Mike away, as it would Ted himself. He could smell it on himself, but not when he sniffed in the air, when the wind blew straight in his face. He stood like that for some time. There was nothing. He could hear no sound of movement around him.

The ramshackle building appeared in his vision, a moment bathed in moonlight, before the landscape once more turned dark. He circled around the open space. Wide, wide circles. He sniffed the air. Nothing. His pulse. His pulse was beating like a heart. He saw… something between the trees, saw something in the flashes of moonlight brightening the field in front of the mill. Shock made him freeze there, on the spot. He saw the two girls strangely clear. They were tied to solid poles stuck in the ground. Both were completely nude. The boy crouched slightly, for a second mesmerized by the sight of the girl's naked skin, shining in the flashes.

– Oh, no, he mumbled, hardly audible, even to himself, – you won't get me that easily.

He shrugged, seeing no reason to postpone anything any longer, and stepped out in the open. He wanted to shout, shout a challenge in the night, but held his tongue, concentrating, and he smelled his own raw, stinking sweat. When he moved it was like one, swift, rushed movement. He concentrated on breathing, making himself ready for what was to come.

The sight of Tilla nude, and placed like that made him dizzy, inevitable. He cursed himself, to no avail. He had never truly *seen* her before, only unsatisfactory glimpses while lying half beaten to death on the cabin floor.

Their eyes were closed. Both girls lay still, giving no sign of being aware of his approach. Breathing was nominal, hardly noticeable.

His eyes moved constantly. There wasn't any place close where an assailant could hide. At least twenty steps on all sides were clear. His eyes kept moving.

He quickly drew his knife and cut the girls' bonds. They still didn't move. He slapped them in the face, pinched their skin, swallowing hard. Still no reaction. He pulled them up, putting them over his shoulders. It took little or no effort. They weren't exactly lightweights, well trained and muscled as they were, but his strength was more than up to it. He carried them off, straight into the wilderness, far from any road or path.

They did start to turn heavy after a while, inevitably, unwieldy as they were. The large bodies rocked back and forth and threatened to fall from his shoulders. So, he had to hold them in a firm grip, and his arms started to hurt. His wounds started to hurt, as they were constantly struck by limp, waving arms or sliding bodies.

– Is this your «tactic»? He said contemptuously. – I can keep this up for days, you know that.

He did take a break, but just because he was tired of sweating, tired of the endless, monotonous swaying of the limp meat on his shoulders. And he sat there listening. Nothing. Absolutely nothing. He remembered being able to actually sense Mike, sense his close proximity. Now, there was nothing. He stared at Tilla, stared at her while her chest was rising and falling. He kept sitting on his heels, staring at her, unable to help himself. His hands sought her wrists. He began massaging them, while once more alternately slapping her left and right cheek.

She released a moan, one weak, but clear. He let go of her, and pulled back. She moaned again. Red lips parted. A pink tongue appeared, and she blinked twice. He waited. Slowly gray eyes revealed itself, suddenly wide in horror. He instantly closed in on her, putting a hand over her mouth.

– It's Ted, he whispered intensely. – *Ted*.

He witnessed how her terror faded, felt how her body turned limp again. He cautiously removed his hand.

– Is it true? She whimpered. – Please tell me it's true.

– It's true, he assured her.

She reached out with a hand, tenderly touching his cheek.

– You saved me, she choked. – I'm so sorry, so sorry.

He nodded, unable to voice his joy, his contempt.

She sat up, embracing him, shivering and cold. He looked into her eyes. They were still clouded by the drug. Bags were easily visible under the gray stone. She didn't look so good. He swallowed hard.

– You shouldn't have come. She put her head close to his. – You shouldn't have put yourself in more danger, because of me.

– Mike said one o'clock, Ted laughed, – evidently expecting me to abide by it. I guess he is busy elsewhere.

– I've done so much shit, she said, – so much pretense that I'm sometimes unable to tell where the make-belief ends and reality begins. I'm so afraid of him, I always have been. But when he told me straight out he would capture Maria and use her as bait to get to you, I finally had enough. I smiled sweetly to him and pretended to be cool, as usual. And it did seem useful, because he seemed to be the same arrogant bastard. But when I sneaked away to warn Maria I never got that far. He p-punished me, drugged me, and I knew nothing more. I d-didn't exist anymore.

Her voice died. The death he saw in her eyes, the flutter in her voice tore into him. He sensed the pressure of her tits, the hard nipples in a thousand ways. Blood beat like a heart in his groin. The heat and sweet pain were overwhelming him.

– You saved me, she whispered. – I must thank you.

He felt her wet lips on one side of the neck, fingers on the other. Her brown skin was covered in sweat, to the point where it was almost greasy. She slipped away from him all the time. He grabbed her hard around the arms and held on. She laughed throatily.

– Yes, you want me. That's good, so good.

Her mouth slid up his neck to his lips. The sixteen-year old boy returned the kiss with shivering lips. He held one swelling breast and nipple in his hand, squeezing it roughly and inexperienced. Heat of pride shot through him when he elicited a moan from her. She freed herself from him, slipping away like oil, leaning back in the grass, stretching her arms back over her head, letting him *see*. She rolled on the ground, turning around once, making him see everything. With neat, experienced moves she unbuttoned and unzipped his pants. Breathing hard, he pushed the pants down his thighs, pulling them off, hardly even noticing the tearing sound when he ripped them apart. He knelt naked above her, not taking his eyes off the writhing body, the dull, inviting smile.

– Hurry, she called drowsily. – Hurry.

She grabbed the hard throbbing below and pulled him down. He fell on her. Their lips met again. Her playful tongue started playing with his, and he had to fight hard to not clench his teeth. He buried his face between her breasts, kissing them repeatedly. She embraced his cock with her thighs, teasingly, impatiently. He sensed her skin rolling back and forth over his pain-stricken, sensitive skin. Then, with a push he was inside of her. There was rhythm. Rhythm exploded in his loins. He heard her long, delighted moan, and he descended on her.

Time didn't exist. He wasn't sure when it had stopped existing, but Now was just a long, long nothing in the waters, the warm, warm waters.

– You're wonderful, he mumbled, with his head partly between her thighs, unable to tell how he had come there. – I'll take you to a distant, lonely place and keep you safe, safe from everything. You're mine, to do with as I see fit.

He covered her with his body, staring down, into the crystal-clear gray eyes.

– So, it was good for you? Her voice, sweet like honey.

His body, senses, thoughts were just stuck. He could only nod.

– Do you want to do it again?

After a few more attempts he managed to speak. There was an implication of stutter in his words.

– I'm not sure I can. He shook his head in dazed wonder.

She grabbed his now quite soft thing. It hardened again almost instantly. His eyes widened, as the pain returned, as the pain returned bad.

– Of course, you can. Silly boy, you can do it many times.

A slight move, nothing more, and he was inside her once more. He looked at her. He saw nothing but her, the blushing face, the sweaty skin, the curvy body. Everything else seemed to fade around him, fade into nothing.

– I am yours, she whispered, – to do with as you see fit. Do it. Please. *Please*.

He had dreamed about this, dreamed for years, and now the dream was transformed into the far superior reality. It was fantastic, it was awesome, it was…

He shot his seed deep into her. He could almost make it out, follow it all the way in, like he was still a part of it, as if a part of him was left inside her, left deep. Gasping he rolled off her, rolled half way round, until he was on his back, resting on the forest bed. She pulled close to him, resting her head on his shoulder, kissing him softly on the cheek.

– You're wonderful, he repeated. – Wonderful…

There was, at times the occasional glimpse of Maria, nude and still unconscious, but it didn't feel important somehow, as if she was just a doll without skin, face and soul. Red hair, gray eyes interrupted every casual glance.

They rested. Their bodies, their faces close. He sensed her heat. He was bathing in it.

– More, she whispered in his ear. – I want more…

She crawled on top of him, placing one leg on each side of his body, looking down in Hunger at his soft limb. Her face was a bit turned, so he could see the silhouette of her face in the flashing, dwelling moonlight. She took his cock in both her hands, and started petting it in slow, delicious moves.

Her skills have been beaten into her, he thought unprompted.

She bent down and started licking the exposed head, after a while taking it in her mouth, pushing at it from all sides. And then… he felt it again. And again. He moaned. She moaned, too, in expectation, an expectant smile erupting in her features. He closed his eyes, and there were stars flowing the night behind his eyes. She descended on him, rocked up and down. And then there was later, when he was on top. And then she was again. And when he came he didn't know if it was the third, fourth or fifth time. And there was a sting somewhere. Sweet pain. Sweet bliss. He sensed sleep come. Completely spent he fell asleep in her arms, still inside her, seeing the content smile brightening her face. He drowned in it, drowned in her soft curves and limbs. Dust of dreams embraced him and there was nothing more.

Chapter twelve

He awoke with a start. There was panic, absolute panic, but the lethargy smothering him like a blanket kept it from instantly expressing itself. He wanted to fumble for the woman by his side, her smell, the stench from her sex still lingering in him. There was discomfort. He attempted to reach for her, but couldn't move his arm, and discovered that he couldn't breathe properly. Something tightened around his chest and arms.

A rope. Panic struck him, and ice-cold spikes penetrated the fog smothering his mind. Eyes opening hard and wide stared at the brother a few steps away with the tight rope in his hands.

And when staring at Tilla, the tight rope in her hands, and her vicious grin all moisture left his eyes, and it turned all to sand, making it impossible for he to see. And he felt almost gratitude because of that.

– MEDUSA, he shouted wildly, insanely.

Their contemptuous laughter twisted and turned within him like a knife.

He pushed himself up with the use of his fingers, the only aid at his disposal, throwing himself at Mike. Instantly Tilla pulled on her rope, making him fall backwards. He got back up instantly, but then Mike pulled on his rope, making him fall again, fall hard.

– We heard about your skills as a lasso thrower, Mike laughed hard. – We thought we should learn it, and see how good we could be. How about it, brother, how many points will you give us? Both skill and execution, please.

– You couldn't do it without trickery, huh, Ted screamed, red faced of shame and rage. – You're two lousy chicken shits.

There was only more contemptuous laughter. And that was also what he felt he deserved. Everything faded in him, everything valuable.

Eventually they got tired of the game, and moved in on him. He fought. He kept fighting. Hopelessly the underdog. Tilla kicked him in the face, and he fell like a tree. There was more kicking, and he couldn't breathe. Miserable and breathless, and totally paralyzed he just crouched there, as they tied him up, bound him tight and ruthlessly. And then he was truly helpless. Unmoving, he stared straight ahead, looking at nothing, as down as any human could come, and still breathe. He crumbled there like a wounded beast, awaiting death.

Tilla made a point of pushing her naked body close to Mike's, giving him a prolonged, sultry kiss.

– I'll dress up, darling, she giggled. – I don't want the sack of bones to enjoy the sight of me. He doesn't deserve it.

Mike looked down on him, shaking his head.

– Unbelievable. He kept shaking his head. – She made you go for her like a panting dog, completely forgetting everything else. I wonder, truly wonder how many times the males in our line have been fucked by their lust. It's amazing, isn't it, how reason flies out the window?

Tilla returned. She was dressed, but her upper body was merely covered by a clearly too small leather jacket. Even now, at this hour Ted couldn't take his eyes off her.

Without warning she kicked him in the groin. He cried out in pain, and tears jumped from his eyes.

– I don't ever want you to look at me, she snarled. – You're unworthy of me, do you hear, as much beneath me as a snail on the ground.

Ted said nothing, did nothing, but remained on his cold spot, still and dead.

Maria started moaning, signaling that she was about to awaken. Her head started shaking back and forth, in abject denial, as her fearful eyes opened wide. Tilla stepped closer to her, a whip in her hand. She started whipping the girl on the ground, making her awaken that much faster, awaken to the horrible pain of the whiplash hitting her naked skin. Red welts swelled on it, growing quickly in number and size. Time and time again the whiplash hit her thighs, her butt, her back, her breasts, as the girl rolled and rolled in a desperate attempt to escape the pain. Eventually she stopped resisting, taking the punishment with tears flowing from her eyes, constantly shaking, begging for it to be over soon.

– You'll do as we say, Mike said to her, as she crouched beneath him, – when we say it. The slightest disobedience and you'll be punished, until you learn to obey and serve your

272

betters.

She stared uncomprehending at him, her eyes empty, her expression completely devoid of reason.

Suddenly there was this insane, enraged look in her eyes, and she attacked Mike with nails sharp as claws. She scratched him, scratched him deep before he managed to strike her down. He wiped the blood off his face with an equally insane look written in his entire posture.

– So, the little cat has claws, huh? That's not bad, not bad at all. You must just learn to use it when you're told, told by your Master.

He lifted up the half unconscious girl and with a frightening ease he tied her hands in front of her body, and carried her to the nearest tree. He stretched her arms above her head, tying the other end of the rope casually around a branch. Then she hung there, her feet just about touching the ground. He turned to Tilla, reaching out his hand, about to say something.

– The whip, give…

– Oh, YES, Tilla exclaimed, – can I give her a whipping? Please let me do it, *please*.

She looked at him, like an eager girl expecting chocolate. She struck the shaft of the whip against her boots.

– Okay, I'll let you play a bit. But just so it hurts. Don't damage her, get it?

– You're my Lord and Master, she said huskily.

She curtseyed deeply before him, with a clearly excited look in her shining eyes. Her breasts slipping out of the minor confines the jacket did or didn't provide, the exposed nipples hardening in anticipation.

Mike pushed a cloth into Maria's mouth, making it stay in place with a rope tied hard around her head. She shook her head in complete, utter disbelief, begging him with her huge, uncomprehending eyes. He stepped aside and without the slightest hesitation Tilla started on the whipping. The first stroke hit Maria's unprotected back. She tried to scream, but the gag made it into a small, low whimper. Another welt appeared on the already marked skin. Her eyes rolled in their sockets. The lash hit her a second time, and a third, and fourth, and fifth…

– That's enough, Mike said sharply, I believe she sees the picture by now.

– I believe you're right, my love, Tilla said softly, stepping close to the shaking body, hanging from the branch, – Isn't that right, Mexican bitch?

Maria nodded and nodded, and nodded, and didn't stop nodding until Mike gave her a light slap on her cheek. He removed the rope around her wrists, and quickly redid them behind her back. She leaned heavily against him, as if he was her only means of support. He pushed her down on the ground and the cry of despair even penetrated the gag. He bent down and tied another rope around her ankles, but this time he didn't tie them tight together. He clearly wanted her to be able to walk, but not leaving room for more than short, stumbling steps.

Ted watched it all with a sick, sinking feeling in his stomach.

– Don't look so surprised. You don't think we would actually be carrying her, do you?

– And me? The boy said hoarsely. – Will you kill me?

– You're as stupid as ever. Mike shook his head in disgust. – Of course, I won't kill you. Aside from the point that you're my brother it would be… wasteful. You'll be extremely valuable to me, once you've learned who is boss. And you *will* learn.

Ted's feet were given the same treatment as Maria's. And then, as if Ted's big bulk of a body was nothing more than a feather, Mike lifted him up on his feet. And he was gagged, and the tight rope was tied around his head, and his head felt big as a football, and it cried thud, thud, thud. He stood there with his head bowed, and everything turned black, black, black. He didn't loose consciousness. He wasn't allowed to. Tilla slapped him, and the sting kept him in a kind of semi-consciousness. Everything faded, but his body worked somehow. He felt the noose Tilla tied around his neck, around Maria's slim neck and he felt the lash from the whip.

– Go, Tilla commanded, the whip coiling around her legs like a snake. – We're going for a long walk. And if either of you two as much as blinks without my explicit permission you will most certainly be severely punished.

The two of them started moving, in slow, defeated moves.

Mike and Tilla kissed.

– Well, that's it, then, Mike said cheerfully, – I'll be seeing you cute girls.

Ted looked up. Eyes burned at the brother.

– Yeah, that's right brother. Mike laughed scornfully. – I'm making a slight detour, picking up our sister.

Mike's face hardened. His voice was hard and merciless. There was no longer any sort of mercy in his eyes. He hadn't been like that before. Then something had, after all always held him back. Not anymore.

– You know, don't you. You know I'm gonna get her. How very perceptive of you. You're learning. You're learning your lesson *well*.

Ted's eyes glowed in rage, and he took one step forward.

– Stand still, meat, Tilla shouted.

And now she didn't hold back. The lash cut into his back, and the pain cut his mind in two, in three, in pieces. He was struck again and again, and he fell to his knees, not unconscious, but numb and dead and numb. Defeated his eyes were like open wounds.

– On your FEET, meat, Tilla shouted triumphant, giving him a few extra, light taps.

He fought himself up, desperate to avoid more pain.

He watched when Mike undressed and changed into his clothes, changed into him. It didn't evoke any strong emotion in him, just more of the dull, unending pain.

– Yes, I'm going to get her, Mike said, – and you will all be mine. I didn't get that cute famous girlfriend of yours, though. She left town late last night. Care to guess why? Too bad, I would have loved the publicity.

There was no visible response. Mike nodded pleased. Dressed in his brother's clothes, clothed in Ted's visage he started walking down the forest path. Tilla pushed Ted the first steps forward, in the opposite direction, towards the mountains. Very slowly, every step clearly beyond painful he put one foot in front of the other. Pale as a ghost, with her head swinging from side to side Maria followed him. They disappeared, *faded* into the forest, into the nothing that had become their lives.
***/

The silver hair on the pillow was glowing in the moonlight. The white house was silent. Yet Linda was awake. The room was humid and hot. The open window did nothing to alleviate any of it. She stretched out on the bed, completely naked, plagued by chaotic and feverish imagery, a young girl's mind thrown into the vast crossroads of reality. She easily saw her own body, illuminated in the moonlight, the shadow without blood, flesh and eyes dancing in the air above it, and it grew hot.

Small rocks, like grains of sand landed on the floor. It looked like dust to her, dancing under the moon. She moved out of the bed and to the window in one, fluid motion.

– I'm here, she said, hiding behind the curtain, behind the wall.

– Come out. She heard Ted's voice and her heart jumped a beat, she felt the first stirrings of increased need.

– Where have you *been?* She wondered. – Stewart was worried when you disappeared so abruptly. He has been looking for you the entire evening.

– And he's still at it, I gather. That eager beaver…

She giggled.

– Come out, he said. – This is between us, not anybody else.

She nodded. She agreed. Anger flared in her veins. She dressed quickly, casually, and was on her way down the stairs in a flash, silently, stealthily. On one occasion she stopped and listened. There was nothing here, nothing moving. She moved through the door, and when she opened and shut it, it was like there was no sound at all.

He waited for her behind the corner. He grabbed her from behind and struck her in the ribcage, and before she could do anything to defend herself, to give voice to her fear, to her horrible mistake, she was in Mike's arms, left to his tender mercy, limbs stiff like that of a doll. He pushed her at the wall, pushing a cloth into her mouth, her open mouth, gasping for breath. He tied her up, hands and feet, using his superior strength. She fought, she did, but she was helpless, so helpless, and now, while the tight ropes kept her from moving more than a finger or two even more so. He stood behind her, laughing contemptuously in her ear.

– You're such a price, Mike said to her, patting the ice-blond hair. – I was so wrong about you.

His voice turned harsh, spiteful. She shivered.

– You betrayed me. You'll be punished for that. I own you, more now than ever before. I'm gonna train you, to a life in my service, and you'll be very good at it, I assure you.

Realization came slowly, painfully.

He knows, she thought.

He grabbed her right breast and squeezed. She wanted to scream, but the gag and the pain kept her from uttering more than a muted yelp. He roamed the place between her legs, infinitely patient, eventually making her moan in need.

In a sickening cheerful mood, he placed her on a shoulder and set off. She wanted to resist, to fight. She didn't move. They left the tight clusters of houses, moving into the forest, into the wilderness. It didn't take him that long to catch up with Tilla and her charges.

– Success, Tilla said pleased.

– She jumped straight into my arms, Mike snarled and threw the blond girl on the ground, – the stupid cow.

Linda hit the ground hard. She started crying softly and quietly.

– What the fuck are you sipping for? He said harshly. – You didn't think I would carry you much longer, did you?

He grabbed her in the legs, and pulled her to him. Soon she was bound like the other two.

Maria swayed. Her eyes were clear, but dead. Ted stared at his brother and sister with a dull look. He looked like he would collapse at any given moment.

– We have a long march ahead of us, Mike said. – Walk.

Linda and Maria moved, but Ted, which eyes still didn't seem to register anything stood like paralyzed and kept them in place. Mike laughed and walked to Linda.

– Oh, I almost forgot. You don't need this anymore.

He grabbed her clothes, and in two, three brutal pulls he had practically ripped them off her. Except for the shoes, there were just shreds left where the ropes were. The pointed breasts were pushed forward. It gurgled in Ted's throat. Life returned to his eyes.

– *Now* he reacted, Tilla grinned.

Ted took one step forward, but even before he sensed the foot against the ground the redhead was over him with the whip. This time he stopped the first time he was hit.

– Walk, Mike repeated.

With Tilla's cold laughter and whip chasing them without mercy and remorse the captives started on their long walk. Ted and Maria senseless of the abuse they had been subjected to, and Linda who had hurt herself when Mike had thrown her on the ground. They walked. And time stopped having meaning. Meaning stopped having meaning. Ted imagined they passed by the sawmill again, but he was no longer sure what was real and what was not. They put one foot mechanically in front of the other. That was their only goal. Nothing else mattered. Mike allowed them not a second's quarter. He was there with the whip the very moment they stopped or fell. It bit into their skin and showed no mercy. Eventually they no longer felt anything, thought anything, just a distant, disgusting pain worse than anything, spreading all over their body. And there was nothing ahead but pain.

*********************/

They walked the entire night. The cabin rose in their line of sight. The first glimpse of dawn threw a hellish light over the mountain landscape. Ted pictured the abyss in his mind. He didn't need to. They walked through it. The fresh green grass, the heather on the mountainsides, the picturesque scene, everything seemed hellish in his eyes.

The three of them stumbled forward, the last few steps to the cabin.

– Inside. Mike kicked and beat them through the door.

Everything spun inside, shifted and dissolved, weaving into new and crazy patterns. Ted's eyes widened, as he kept shaking his head.

They fell on the floor. Linda hit her head and started bleeding from the inside of her mouth. Blood made the gag turn red. She closed her eyes without a sound.

– Poor girl, Tilla said with something very much resembling true compassion. – The nice walk was evidently too much for her.

Ted crouched half on his back, half on his side, his head twisted almost totally around, staring at the ceiling, at the patterns changing and shifting there. Mike and Tilla took their time, freeing them, untying them. He shivered there on the floor, free of bonds, unable to move a muscle. Everything swam before his eyes and he was weak as a kitten. Mike's silent laughter rattled and weakened him further.

This was not the same cabin where they had tortured him years ago. That had not been much more than a shack. This was a huge, spacious place, almost like a house, even though there were only two rooms. There was a beam in the ceiling, covering the entire length of the living room. There were hooks fastened in it, and hooks on the floor below, a mirror image.

He noticed Maria's eyes. She looked at him, and he knew, and more shame, more despair riddled him.

– They played with you. She spat at him, in a vicious, hateful manner. – You are nothing but a boy, a helpless, sniveling boy.

She couldn't move either, but her lips moved, spitting venom at him, and her eyes moved, burning him like fire. He stared incredulous at her, unable to voice a protest.

He could move. He even managed to raise himself up from the floor a bit, before Mike kicked him back down.

– You are really quite remarkable, Mike told his brother. – And your stamina is even more remarkable than your many other traits. I wonder sometimes if you have any limits, any at all.

– The beatings you took, even as a child would have killed an adult man, Tilla said.

– I tried it out, Mike said. – Remember the other runner up in the shooting contest. I beat him to death.

Ted did remember. He remembered well. He looked at Tilla, curiously. She just smiled… in contempt?

She grabbed him and dragged him to the floor below the hooks. She was strong and handled him as if she was an adult man. Without hurrying any, she tied one rope around each of his wrists and threw the rope's other ends around two of the hooks far up there. She pulled and he was dragged up in the air. She looked completely unfazed by it all, her muscles clearly straining, but there was not even a discernable increase in the amount of sweat on her skin. He hung there and cried out in pain, and he hated himself. She fastened the ropes on the wall, and he hung there, like a butchered game. She tied ropes around his ankles, too, and tied the other ends around the hooks on the floor. He noticed how the pain, strong to begin with increased immediately and by the second.

– She's strong, too, Mike grinned, waving a hand, indicating them all. – We all are.

He grabbed the two girls on the floor, and gave them the same treatment Tilla had given Ted.

– And these two have other qualities as well.

Linda looked at him, but she didn't really see anything. Maria didn't. She didn't look at anything.

He strung them up like Ted was. They hung there, in the hot, humid room as the first rays of the Sun showed on the cabin floor. Linda's head hung, like Ted's. Maria tried to keep her head up, but couldn't do it for long.

Mike stood there, with an arm around Tilla. She crouched by his side, fondling his hand, eagerly like a pet.

– Now, I finally have your complete and undivided attention, Mike declared. – It's about time. We have a lot to do, much ground to cover.

– You're completely insane, Ted moaned.

– You're normal because of me, Mike snarled. – You should be grateful.

He gave his brother another brutal strike in the ribs. Ted gasped some more, but he was already taken so far down that it hardly showed.

– You might think that something changed last night, changed irrevocably, Mike said, – something that finally set me off. But I'm happy to tell you that what I found out, I found out quite some time ago. I just got the final confirmation last night.

– What the hell are you talking about? Linda asked, not quite convincing.

He grinned. He clearly enjoyed this, or at least he put a lot of effort into the pretense of enjoyment. His eyes glared in cold rage.

– The suspicion has gnawed in me for a very long time, even before I came to be consciously aware of it, he drawled, his very voice making Ted sick. – I'm sure it has in you as well. You're not stupid. You only pretend to be.

Ted felt claws cutting up his body from the inside.

– I don't have exhibit A, your honor. Mike nodded to Ted, ironically, cruelly. – I sent you a letter, appraising you of what I had found out. You never replied.

– I never got it, Ted shrugged.

– You never... got it?

– I would most certainly have recalled a polite appraisal from you, don't you think?

Ted eyes burned like wet paper and black smoke rose from them, a smoke like shadows in the air.

– So someone in the Kendall household... kept it from you. Mike nodded. – That's extremely interesting, isn't it?

– This is INSANE, Maria moaned. – You're both completely insane. How can you do this, exchange pleasantries like this?

Mike took one step forward. It wasn't necessary. It was a deliberate, scary act.

– The year you left, you did a practical laboratory test at school, right?

– W-what are you t-talking about? Linda sputtered.

– Ah, you do remember. He nodded pleased to her. – I rather thought you would.

He looked at Ted.

– It was a blood test, Mike said forcefully. – I got curious, and decided to research the matter. You see, our dear, deceased Uncle Ezra ordered an additional blood test. He had more than one batch.

– Why? Ted asked, his voice rasping and raw, forcing the word out.

– Simple. The first one, taken at school, by Howard Grey showed that we, the two of us and our dear Linda couldn't be brothers and sister. And Ezra found out and he was killed.

The surprise and shock were evident in Ted's eyes.

– Oh, yes, someone killed our dear fake uncle, and then went to great lengths to make it look like an accident. I saw the never published police report, too.

Ted didn't say anything. He just stared at his brother, as if he had never seen him before.

– I cast your attention to exhibit B, your honor. Mike held up the pile of papers, the files bearing the school's stamp.

– And C. In his other hand he held up the police report.

– It doesn't prove shit, Ted whispered.

– Tell them, Linda, Mike said. – They told you, didn't they? Our «parents» told you.

Ted turned to Linda. He saw her in a revealing light, saw her guilt.

– No, they didn't, she spat.

– Not in so many words, huh? Mike grinned.

– I TOLD THEM, Linda shouted. – I told *them,* you FUCKING ASSHOLE. And they looked at me with smug satisfaction in their mugs. They wanted me to find out, wanted us to *know*. Doesn't that tell you something, you stupid SHIT?

– *You're my parents. You're not Ted and Mike's. They're not my brothers.*

And they looked at her with pride in their eyes.

Mike looked at her, nodding, and nodding again.

– While approaching the room, I was approaching a well-set stage, she said, shrugging, shivering. – I recognized it as such instantly, as I should have done long ago. Fuck me.

Ted stared at her, the look of betrayal and understanding all too evident in his eyes.

– They're my biological parents, she said, looking at Ted. – Not yours.

And to Mike:

– Ask yourself this, she shouted. – Ask yourself what changed you from a nice, a bit distant boy to a FUCKING sadist.

Linda realized with a chill that her… her protection had gone. He had cared about them being brother and sister. He had clung to a sort of normal life, until now.

– So, why wasn't Grey murdered, too, you stupid shithead? Ted shouted, too, to Mike, finally reacting, tearing enraged at his bonds, in vain.

The ropes tore into his skin. He didn't seem to notice.

Mike smiled. He didn't seem the slightest bit angry.

– Because he didn't realize what he had. The idiot fucker just thought he had in his possession an example of… sloppy work. He couldn't imagine another explanation.

– And I've just stumbled onto your little family drama, Maria said sourly, said whimpering. – That's great, that's just great.

– You've stumbled onto a vast drama. Mike stepped close to her, in one fluid move. – A tapestry to end all tapestries. You should be proud. It's an opportunity of a lifetime.

She shrunk under his ruthless stare, the statue of cold rage before her.

– They raised us, Mike said, stepping back. – Raised us as brothers and sister. They taught us combat, fighting, shooting, even a bit of political knowledge, of sophistication, court manners, they even encouraged acting. They have an agenda. Whether or not it's their own or that of… others, I don't know, but I'll find out. We'll all find out.

– Everybody wants something, he finished. – Everybody has an agenda.

Linda looked at him, with eyes like open wounds.

– So now, you have an agenda, too.

– Yes, an agenda to end all agendas.

He looked at her, and she sensed the tightness of the ropes, how they rubbed at her skin, kept the blood from her hands. Dizziness and fatigue made her hang weakly in her bonds.

– We'll die up here, she whimpered, hating herself. – We'll be strangled and die.

– No, you won't, Mike assured her. – Perhaps if you tough son and daughters of bitches stayed there for days, but that won't be necessary. You'll just be more malleable, easier to teach, when the time comes. You'll learn beyond doubt that I make the decisions, that *I* decide your future. Nothing has changed. Everything has changed.

His words hammered them, made time and reality stretch and burn.

– Come now, my love… Tilla spoke for the first time in a long time, petting his thigh eagerly. – Let's love, let's kill.

He looked at her, and a look of infinite, cold interest and amazement lit his eyes. He turned to the prisoners one more time.

– You'll hang here, until I say so, he stated. – Remember that: My word is Law. You will do nothing until I say so.

He stopped a bit before Maria, grabbing her thigh, tightening his grip, hard, mercilessly, showing his incredible strength. She cried out in horrible pain.

– You *will* remember?

– Yes, she whimpered. – Yes, PLEASE!

– Good girl, he whispered.

And she imagined, like Ted and Linda that he spoke directly into her ear.

He lifted up the redhead, and carried her into the cabin's southern room. There was no door, only an open arc. Ted saw the wide, wide bed. He saw Tilla's scornful, triumphant look, as she undressed in Mike's arms. She showed him, showed what wasn't his, what would never be his again.

They heard the sounds from the bed for a while, the sounds cutting Ted to shreds. Then it turned quiet and they heard the sound of the two of them sleeping, heard their breathing. The sun rose in the sky, white hot. Everything turned dark around them. They couldn't close their eyes, they couldn't keep them open. The merciless sun turned the room hot as a baker's oven. They didn't feel their hands anymore, just a faint, dull pain somewhere. Sweat poured into their eyes and their eyes burned. Ted felt it, felt his eyes burning. And in his stupor he started to see things that weren't there, insane, nightmarish images of fire and destruction.

And then… he felt something… a release… inside. Something… something incredible formed out of thin air in front of him. He saw a shadowy figure, transparent, surrounded by dark flames. And its face… he recognized its face. He gasped. There was pain, horrible pain.

– What is it? Linda asked. – You saw something. What did you see?

The image, the apparition faded. Ted's head hung once more.

– Nothing, he rasped. – Nothing but a mirage.

She looked at him for a while, striving to keep his eyes on him, but after a while her head hung once more.

And time increased the torture, increased the dull, dull never ending pain.

– It hurts, Linda cried, she wailed. – It hurts so much. I'm sorry, I'm sorry.

Her face was wet with tears, tears of pain, of sorrow. But there were no more tears flowing. She was all dried up.

– Don't give up, he said hoarsely, almost unintelligibly through clenched teeth and lips. – Stewart will find us.

He saw the doubt in her eyes, and his eyes hurt again, hurt from the burning.

– And if he doesn't come and free us, we will free ourselves, no matter what, no matter the price, *do you hear me.*

He saw how she backed off, how she shrank from his gaze, and the hopelessness gained an even stronger foothold inside him.

His head hung low. There was no strength left to keep it high, not even for a moment. Maria started screaming in Spanish. It sounded far away, and he couldn't pick up more than a few words here and there. And then it sounded as if it wasn't even Spanish anymore, but a completely different, unknown language only she could understand. It ended in hardly more than rubbish and mumbles. He caught a glimpse of her eyes, and she looked completely gone, as if there was no one home anymore.

The heat burned them. The evening came, but brought no release. It was like a greenhouse in there, an oven where they slowly roasted to death. Maria released a wail, one sounding more like a cry of a banshee, a revenant, making it actually trickle a bit cold down the boy's spine. It enhanced the greenhouse effect. It didn't bring release, but even more nightmarish mirages, he couldn't escape it, and he whimpered in his plight.

Linda didn't notice it when she was lowered to the floor, not until she hit it with her feet and her battered body. She moaned in her sudden, endless pain, and then she felt nothing, until she got an ice-cold bath of water in her face. The shock tore her out of the unconsciousness, brought her once more brutally face to face with her demonic brother.

She blinked, looking at him through a fog of pain and fear.

– You were a sleeping beauty, he said, – lying on a bed of roses, not realizing it was a bed of thorns.

Her eyes, like open wounds, were caught by his.

She and Maria stood before him, like cattle to be appreciated. He walked around them, touched them a bit, studied them, before stopping once more, in front of them, towering over them like a vulture. They understood. Understanding hit them like pain, and didn't bring release but surrender and submission.

– You will be compliant, pliable and pleasing or I will flay the skin off your bones, do you understand?

– Yes, the girls choired, the girls choked.

– You will give me your lips, he commanded in a relaxed, merciless manner, a voice like thunder. – Your lips, your bodies, your very Self belongs to me. Kiss me, cunts.

They did. Linda first, shyly, but unresisting.

Maria looked Mike, then up at Ted, and then back at Mike again. She pushed her body, pushed herself close to him, kissing him.

– Anything, Mike, she whispered. – Anything, M-master.

He laughed, and slapped her in the face. She fell on the floor. She remained there, crying huge, horrible sobs.

Mike lifted his arms in triumph, glaring at his still stung up brother.

– This is the lesson, then, he marveled. – This is the ever-lasting truth. People are willing to do anything to not suffer, to avoid pain. Forsake their dignity, their freedom, their very lives.

Tilla handed him a glass of water. He put it before Linda's lips, and she drank greedily. He took it away, and she just accepted it, with the same, dull expression in her eyes. He bent down and gave Maria the rest.

– That's enough gluttony, he said, he laughed. – You will now accompany me to the river, and be made presentable.

Maria rose, and both girls followed him like sleepwalkers. Dully they finally noticed they were not tied up anymore. It didn't matter. The swellings were chains good enough, invisible in a way and just as final.

Ted watched them go. That was all he could do. Watch. He was changing, he knew that. They were all changing, irrevocably. No matter what would happen, what the final outcome, they would never be as they had been.

Tilla remained in the cabin. She approached him with a glass of water in her hand.

– Acid? He spat at her. – Or will you throw out the water in front of me. Don't think this will shake me. Sometime during this night, I stopped being shaken, do you hear me, you horny bitch.

She brought a stool. She stepped up on it with a strange expression in her face, the same he had glimpsed in the Frank Forester party.

– Drink, she offered, smiling strangely, to him insanely. – It's clean, refreshing water. You need it. Drink.

– Go fuck yourself! He pushed out between sore lips.

She started petting him on the head. She had done so before, quite a few times, but it felt different this time, lovingly, caringly. Unblinking gray eyes stared at him.

He started crying, abruptly, huge, desperate, uncontrollable sobs.

– So, I can touch you, she stated softly, triumphantly. – You're human, after all.

She put the glass to his lips, and he drank greedily, unthinking, filled with a sickening gratitude he couldn't stop himself from feeling.

– That's it, that's a good dog. She kissed him softly on the cheek.

She removed the glass. It was empty. He had digested every single drop. She pulled back a bit, her face a study in contradicting emotions.

– I've always wanted a dog, she said. – It would be so easy, wouldn't it…

– Why are you *doing* this? He asked bitterly and weakly, choking so much that he could hardly speak. – You'll probably get what you want eventually, anyway.

Then, to his amazement she started crying, too. He gasped. It was such an unlikely event that he in that moment forgot everything else.

– I'm sorry, she choked. – I'm so very, very sorry.

She stepped down from the chair, her face virtually dissolved in tears. He still stared incredulous at her, as if looking at a mirage. She ran to the window, looking out, drying her tears in angry, bitter swats of hands moving.

She turned back towards him.

– They're still there, she said. – We've got time.

He wanted to scream to her, to shout curses at her, but couldn't even release a low sound. Everything had locked itself inside him.

– We don't have much time, she said stubbornly, painfully, laughing a bit, a hard, accentuated laughter. – I just want you to know that I not long ago took a long, hard look at myself in the mirror and didn't like what I saw. I recalled in vivid detail what I had been, before everything… started, and I realized what I had become. This is no excuse. There is no excuse, I want you to know that. But I had let myself be formed by people and circumstances. That will never happen again. I will not allow it.

She looked out of the window again. He knew where the river was, recalled it now in vivid detail. It ran about half a mile downhill from the cabin. She looked at him, with her eyes of stone. In a way she was more frightening now, this… adult, angry being facing him.

– So when you returned, I was encouraged and ready to call everything off, no matter the consequences. To go to you or to stab Mike to death or blow up the entire biker camp, I don't know what… when something new and frightening occurred.

This is insane, Ted thought. This is truly insane.

– Mike, with sweet me in tow checked out this cabin. It was perfect for «our» needs. We spent the night here. In the early morning the owners or what appeared to be the owners showed up. I'm still not sure whether or not Mike had met them before. But I knew he recognized their leader. I saw it in his eyes. The leader was a giant Negro, African American, *nigger*. He had a patch over his left eye, and he's one of the biggest men I have ever seen. «They», Mike is always referring to them as «they», had a «proposition» for Mike. I was sent out, sent away. «Go», Mike ordered me. I don't know if he did it to protect me or what. I don't know what makes him tick, I never did. But suddenly I realized the stakes had been raised. I couldn't hear anything they talked about that day. But later on, when presumably the deal or whatever had been made they relaxed, and I was allowed to serve them… serve them all.

Ted swallowed. His throat was dry again. Bits and pieces, images revisited him, dawned on him.

– Yes, she said. – They kept an eye on us, kept an eye on us all. They referred to «the brother» all the time. They *knew* us, knew us well. They spoke of a test Mike had to go through. They taunted him, saying he wasn't worthy if he couldn't beat «the brother». Never «your brother», only The Brother.

– So, the sting I have felt in my back wasn't my imagination, Ted said with distant, but suddenly clear brown eyes.

– Three nights ago, I found a wallet on the floor, Tilla Stevens said. – In it was a FBI shield.

And then Ted Cousin turned truly cold, as if there wasn't any heat here at all, as if he was hanging suspended in dark, dark Space.

– I still intended to go to you, to Stewart, to anyone… but… I chickened out. I just fell back on my old routine of eager doormat.

– But now? Tonight? Why tonight? I don't know. Perhaps I don't care anymore… or perhaps I finally care. I don't *know*.

When she raised her bowed head and stared straight at him there was rage there, and very little fear.

– Anyway, they stated that he couldn't expect any help from them, before «this was over». Not against Stewart, not against you. One Eye knew Stewart, too, knew him well.

– Release me, Ted barked. – Release me, now.

He hardly considered what she told him, not really. It was just too much. So, he acted on autopilot, drawing on his reserves, his bottomless pit, and miracles, he felt the strengthening of limbs, of will, and it felt good beyond imagining.

She hesitated, before walking to the hooks on the wall, hesitated again when reaching for them.

– He's going to visit them tonight, she said, – to gloat, to report the success. He sees this as another, quicker stepping stone for his ambitions. He will play good dog at first, before years into the future… taking them all on.

The two of them looked at each other, communicating without words, as they had done so many times in the past.

– If you free me, now, he said hesitatingly, finally, – I won't be of any use to us. I will be too weak to take on Mike. I need a lot of rest before doing that. After hours of recuperation I will have a chance… a fighting chance. I can hang here for days, if I have to. I can take it. I will kill him.

She nodded, smiling to him through another film of tears.

She realized what the decision would cost. They both did, and it felt horrible beyond imagining.

She isn't this good an actress, he thought. No one is. She isn't playing another sick game. She just isn't.

Red hair, blood in the air embraced him while she washed and strengthened him the best she could, the best way possible under the circumstances, the horrible circumstances. The wet, cool cloth felt magical against his skin. He felt like a gladiator being prepared before the game. The harsh thought wouldn't go away, and he didn't let it either. He held on to it, for dear life, used it to sustain the anger, the bottomless rage in the coming hours.

When she was through she took blood from his open wounds and smeared it over the places on his skin she had washed. He knew he looked at least as bad as before, if not worse. He grinned wolfishly, and he saw how she shrank from him.

Good.

The last of the sun's rays vanished from the desolate landscape. The bathing party returned. The girls were washed and rubbed all over the body, and they stank of perfume. Ted got sick.

Good.

His mind had never been clearer, more aware than in that moment, aware of consequences. When push came to shove consequences didn't count.

– What great timing, my love, Tilla greeted Mike. – Dinner is almost ready.

Ted felt the sickening twists inside. He embraced them.

– Fuck dinner, Mike grinned. – Turn off the fucking plate, and join these two virgins in my bed.

She hurried to the oven and obeyed. Then she hurried back, into Mike's arms. Like sleepwalkers Linda and Maria walked behind the two, into the bedroom. Tilla sent Ted a final, desperate look.

Mike pushed the girls down on the bed and joined them. He went straight to Linda and took her, took her hard. She cried out, cried out in pain, misery and lust. Ted couldn't close his ears. He didn't want to. He didn't close his eyes, but stared at it all, watched everything.

– *Querida,* Maria moaned, as she moved, and moved helplessly under Mike. – *My vida hombre.*

The bed creaked. It wouldn't stop creaking. For some unfathomable reason this bothered Ted more than anything. He felt nothing. Only a cold determination and the desire to have Mike at his mercy. The older brother had formed him like others formed iron, like putty, when the iron was hot and liquid. With these acts Mike had almost completed the process and Ted knew that the Ted Cousin that so far had wandered the Earth was dead, utterly, irrevocably, and that another had taken his place.

*******/

Night had come. Night had finally come. Ted had no idea what time it was, and he didn't care. Every nerve in his badly beaten body was on fire. The burning spoke to him, the insistent, sinister whispers making him gasp and heave.

Mike and the three girls sat around the table. They were having dinner.

– Now, girls, Mike grinned, – now you know how great food can taste, right.

– YES, MIKE, Linda and Maria replied.

Linda bent over and kissed his lips.

– Stand straight, Mike commanded her. – Stretch your body. Display it to me.

She obeyed. With her hands above her head she writhed and stretched in her awkward position. She felt lazy, fulfilled, and couldn't help the low, traitorous flame inside dulling her mind.

– You tight bitch, Mike laughed aloud. – You loved being fucked didn't you?

– Yes, Mike. The voice was even, dull. – I loved it.

– You want more, right?

– Yes, Mike. An expectant, sickly smile transformed her entire face. – *Please,* Mike.

Mike didn't look at Ted, but Ted felt looked at, felt the triumphant scorn cross his brother's face.

There were screams somewhere, but Ted didn't hear it.

– So, do you think your parents will tell us who our real

parents are?

– Sure, she shrugged, – there would no reason to keep it secret any longer, would there?

– Especially after they see how I have roughed up their girl.

She hesitated, the smiling mask still in place.

– Speak your mind, he said. – I want you to always speak your mind, do you understand. You are and will become one of my most valued advisors.

– They don't care about me, she said. – Surely you realize that? They never did. Not as anything but your plaything. I am raised to be yours. Their pride stems from how well I relate to you. Everything else is… is immaterial.

She spoke to both of them. Ted realized that and it was as if knives, dull knives cut his insides.

– I knew it, Mike cackled. – You're one smart, valuable cookie.

He grabbed her leg, raising it a bit for all to see, exposing a mole on it. He motioned to Maria. She put her leg on the table, revealing an identical mole. He didn't have to do anything more. Tilla had already placed her foot on the table. Her mole was identical, and exactly in the same position as the two others.

Mike lifted his leg. Ted looked down on his. There was a mark there, too, but it was faint, like a shadow, just a dark discoloration of the dark skin, not a mole.

– We will rule the world, Mike said. – It will take time and effort, but it will happen. It is our destiny. Two times twenty years and we will be there.

Ted looked at him, briefly closing his eyes, in the useless attempt to hide them.

– Yes, Mike whispered. – You *believe* me.

Ted wanted to say something funny, a venomous remark, but he still couldn't utter a single sound.

The night turned quiet. There was no wind, and they could hear the sounds of nature surrounding them, even through the thick walls of the cabin. Mike opened its front door and the sounds were exactly the same. Tilla froze, and she knew Mike could see it, but she no longer cared.

Ted's vision was blurred, but he still saw his brother clearly, like an ocean of raw and frightening strength, fast and ruthless, poetry of death and destruction. Fear rattled him again. Anticipation rattled him.

– You can handle everything here easily on your own, Mike told Tilla.

– Don't be long. She kissed him eagerly on his lips, kissed them until they bled. – Mmmm, I long for your dark touch, your hot seed.

And she got to him, she knew she did. She finally did.

Mike smiled when walking through the door. The girls waved to him while he walked over the rocky ground and until he was completely out of sight.

There was a second, a century when Ted held his breath, in fear and rage, until Tilla picked up a knife and came to him, cutting his bonds, lowering him to the ground, cutting his bonds. All his pent-up suspicion, his distrust just seemed ridiculous, now. She removed the remains of the ropes. He moaned loud when the blood rushed back into his hands, almost passing out there on the floor. He felt someone massaging his mangled body, glimpsing blonde and red hair.

There was a paralyzing haze, extending to his muscles and limbs. Nothing worked. Sweat ran from every single pore as he attempted to get to his feet, or even his knees. Nothing worked. The familiar sense of despair of defeat overwhelmed him and made him draw his breath in short, pitiful gasps.

Linda's white, translucent beaten-up face appeared above him. She smiled worriedly, scared, but behind that worried and scared smile was an anger that was almost comparable to his own at its worst.

She slapped him in the face. She kept slapping him.

– We need you, she snarled. – We can't take him. Only you can do that.

– Nothing works, he gasped.

He couldn't even tell if they heard him, or if he had spoken at all.

Everything seemed unclear, unreal. The black, bottomless pit inside embalmed him like water, like night.

Tilla looked down at him in boundless contempt.

– Such a weakling, she spat. – Crawling on your belly like a baby. You're a disgrace. You make me sick.

And she got to him, like she always did.

– Nobody talks to me like that, he snarled. – Fucking whore.

She spat in his face.

Linda witnessed how his eyes changed, turned burning and beastlike.

He fought himself half way up, on his knees. Enraged he reached for the golden foot an arm's length away. She simply stepped back, still with the same scornful expression in her face, the same desperate fear. Then something else attracted his attention. Maria had been sort of in the background for a while, all the time. Ted saw in horror how she grabbed Mike's stick and closed in on the other two from behind. Linda and Tilla didn't see it. He cried out a warning. Not good enough. The moment Tilla turned to meet the attack she was hit on the head and dropped to the floor.

Maria raised the stick again, to strike at Ted. Linda attacked her, attacked her ferociously. The boy looked amazed at the two girls going at each other with everything they got, everything they were. Linda was unlucky and got the wind knocked out of her when hitting the floor. Maria used the opportunity to kick her in the belly.

Kick her hard.

Linda gasped and turned limp. All the muscles in her body softened like jelly. Maria started beating her with the stick, cruelly, triumphantly. Ted felt it. He suddenly felt the rage rise in him, as if it had never been gone. The strength returned to his muscles, the strength and the fury he thought he had lost forever. Without thought he jumped at Maria. He grabbed her brutally in the hair and threw her at the wall. Two interwoven thoughts raced through his head.

She has sold herself to him. Betrayed me. Betrayed…

He kicked her in the side. She coughed. The second time she coughed blood. A film covered her eyes and she fell unmovable to the floor. He took hold of her arms and was about to turn on her with his entire strength. A voice penetrated his mind, his red haze, irritating, annoying.

– You're killing her, Tilla said, without actually raising her voice, seemingly completely relaxed, very matter of fact, trance and ghost like.

He stopped. He let go of Maria and stopped. The two girls stared at the boy they thought they knew, the unknown in their midst. They knew. They had always known.

– Tell me about the «visitors». He grabbed Tilla's arm, grabbed it hard.

She released a whimper, but didn't attempt to free herself. She didn't fight back at all, but let herself be held, let herself be hurt.

Linda looked at them, incredulously. Tilla started speaking, hesitatingly, in an even, bland voice.

– I don't know much about them… I don't think Mike does either. He just know they are There, if you know what I mean, that they must be dealt with, one way or another. There is One Eye and three others, one white, one black and one yellow. They're mumbling something, when they think they're alone or undisturbed, choiring it like a mantra… *The Abraxas Omega* - The All and the End. I have heard them do that among themselves several times. That's what they're calling themselves, what their call is.

– Another bunch of insane Greek alphabet guys. He shook his head. – Where do they get off…

– You're crazy, she whispered, she giggled, kissing him softly on the cheek, pulling back swiftly, casting long, hard looks around her, sensing his mood, fearing it.

– Can you do it? Linda asked. – Could you have done it, even without being injured and exhausted?

The finer points of her phrasing didn't go unnoticed.

– This is war, he said. – Fighting «fair» doesn't count, only victory. Mike realized that long ago. Silly ideas of morality don't fit into it, don't fit in anywhere.

Tilla sensed it, sensed all the finer points and she said carefully.

– Shall I make food? You need nourishment. You need everything you can eat.

– You should have started on that already, he bit her off. – Are you really so stupid that you must ask that? Don't you have a single independent thought in that stupid head of yours? Get your ass going. We're not on *vacation*.

She stared briefly at him with huge, wounded eyes, before lowering her head, staring at the floor. She walked, unsteady on her feet to one of the cabinets. Her hands shook. A darkness, far more pronounced than that outside seemed to invade the room, surrounding her.

Time raced. She could hardly identify the moments until he sat by the table and she put the food in front of him. Without even a hint of recognition he started on the food, devouring it as if it was just a few crumbs. She put more before him, and it just disappeared. They witnessed him growing into a giant there, on the spot.

– Why are you treating Tilla this way? Linda asked him. – I am angry with her, too. Of course, I am. Years can't be erased in minutes, but without her we wouldn't stand a chance.

He rejected her words with a single, definite move with his hand.

– Just pure self-preservation on her part. I'll bet Mike has grown tired of her and that she knows it. She's betting on the only other winner she knows. She showed her true face when I remained on the floor and she feared she had made a fatal miscalculation.

Two candles burned on the table, casting their reddish light over their faces. It didn't help any. Linda's white skin was still pale and sickly. The two brown-skins like dirty water.

Tilla sat there, quiet and pallid. When she finally spoke, she sounded like a little girl afraid of being punished for some imagined slight or transgression.

– You know that isn't true, she finally cried, cried in helpless protest. – It was to get you angry.

– Shut up, he snarled. – You're no different than Maria, shaking your tail for he you believe has the power and can give you most advantages.

She shrank there on the spot, sobbing, unassuming, fading into the background as furniture or a painting.

– You're worse than Mike, Linda said suddenly, promptly. – If you haven't surpassed him already, you will do so soon, leave him behind in the dirt.

He looked at her. He saw the light in her eyes. She didn't sound condemning.

– You will kill him, she said.

She kissed him on the cheek, blushing, waiting. He grabbed her hair, kissing her on the lips. She cried out joyfully. He put her back on her seat, and continued his meal. She just smiled sweetly to him.

– So, you, too, have learned the rules of the game, he marveled.

– And learned it well, she whispered. – I have no shame left.

She felt naked. They were all sitting there, nude, and she felt so naked. Silent and timid the two girls sat there, staring blindly at him while he completed the meal.

He rose, completely indifferent about his nudity, about anything.

– Stay here, he ordered them. – Watch the bitch.

He made sure they saw his nod towards the corner and Maria's unmoving body.

He didn't look back when walking into the bedroom. Linda's superior, «compassionate» gloating and Tilla's submissive, sore glare yet haunted him.

The cabin was huge. He imagined he was far away, out of sight, out of mind, to everything.

– You damn asshole, he mumbled, not very convincing or with much strength behind.

There was no guilt. Power without guilt. He shook his head in wonder.

He started looking through the closet. It was a wardrobe of sorts. Mike's place, his domain. Ted felt the power swell within. This was Mike's true home, where he had planned his strategy, his moves, his conquest, his very life… and it was no longer his.

Ted looked into the closet, into the darkness. There was something there, on the floor, metal flashing. He bent down and grabbed it. A sword. He looked in wonder at the intricate carvings on the hilt. He pulled it out of the container and lifted it above his head, swinging it clumsily.

He lowered it again, shaking his head in frustration. He looked into the darkness again, further in. There was more metal. A gun. A revolver. He knew that, before he picked it up. A thrill shot through him.

The revolver was a Colt. He recognized it from the gun club magazine and from Jeff McCabe's lectures. A Colt 45 «Peacemaker». They had discussed this weapon a lot, how a weapon could be literally unchanged for hundred years and still be just as popular as it had been in the old west.

– A bullet from this will *stop* a man cold, boy. Ted recalled McCabe's words. – Very few guns today have anything even approaching this large caliber. If you're hit you won't be tempted to move much afterwards. There won't even be much to move. Today we also have the Magnum 44, of course, but much can be said for tradition, boy.

McCabe had always given Ted a strange feeling of... of displacement. When McCabe talked to Ted it was as if it wasn't McCabe talking anymore, at least not the same way he talked to others.

Another mystery, another set of riddles to solve. Ted cocked the gun. It was fully loaded.

He walked back into the living room, the torture room. They saw the gun and their eyes widened.

– YES, Tilla shouted. – Shoot him the moment he comes through the door. Shoot him *dead*.

The fire, the passion, the bloodthirst in her, resonated inside him, stoking his own flames.

There was a moan, on the edge of his attention. He turned and saw Maria move her arms and head just a bit. She was waking up.

Tilla handed him the rope and the gag, eagerly like a schoolgirl. Maria stared coldly at them, her eyes clearing.

– Why? Ted asked, a statue of rage, of contempt.

– And you ask that, she said bitterly. – You, who promised to protect me over all and everyone, if I just followed you to Denver, into the world. *Diablo*. You planned this. You used me in your war against Mike, sacrificed me as a pawn in a butcher shop.

Ted staggered, literally. Words flowed through his brain and were sent through his body in small burst, worse than a thousand electrical shocks. The hard fist inside, somewhere near his heart, his gut hardened some more.

– But Mike is Mighty, she said proudly. – He will crush you, I will be his Queen, and you will only be dust on the ground we walk.

– And you believe you will be anything more than that? Tilla said scornfully. – You're dreaming. I never was.

– You're just a nigger-whore, Maria said brightly, aloof. – You deserved whatever you got. I will be his Queen. His *Queen*.

Ted stamped a foot in the floor. His lips were just one, thin line when he grabbed her arms and twisted them around. She whined in pain.

– What are you doing? Linda asked perplexed.

– I'll show her I can be just as brutal as her lover, he said, hard as a rock.

Maria opened the mouth to scream, but Ted struck her jaw. The head was pushed backwards and struck the wall behind. She went down again, unconscious. The face hit the floor first and the blood started flowing from the nose.

– Damn me, we didn't need to tie her up.

An insane melody played somewhere. Linda shook her head, gasping, sweat soaking her forehead. She clearly wanted to scream, but failed. Tilla touched her cheek lightly, tenderly.

– There are no places to run, she said softly.

And then, if not before, it was too late. She heard steps outside, telling her that they were all out of time.

Mike walked in, his usual calm and confident self. Ted froze with the revolver raised and cocked.

– Don't move. Don't move a finger.

The girls had retreated to a corner, beyond, outside the brothers' sphere, unreal, immaterial creatures. Mike's eyes glowed when looking at Tilla, but aside from that his face was without expression, like a mask.

– So, won't you say I'm weak? Ted shouted at him. – Won't you?

– I think you're confusing the issues a bit, little brother, Mike said softly. – I've never said or meant that. You're simply not in my league.

The older boy stared death in the eye, but it didn't faze him. Ted hated him even more for his indifferent calm. The fingered tightened around the trigger. Just a bit more, now… and the crack would come. The big caliber bullet would tear a huge hole in the brother's chest.

A long while he stood like that, with both his hands clutching the Peacemaker, but he couldn't pull the trigger.

– What have you planned, you shithead? He pushed out of his mouth, at the other. – What do you want?

– I told you, Mike said grinning. – We will rule the world.

– You have snapped, Ted gasped. – Perhaps you hadn't before, but you have now. You crazy son of a bitch!

There was a kind of madness in Mike's eyes, but there was also clarity, certainty.

– You see? Even my ambition is bigger than yours. Even with equal Power I would be mightier than you.

That word, its pronunciation. Ted kept shaking his head. His hands started shaking. He stopped it with a horrible act of will. He actually sensed it, sensed how he pulled something from inside, from deep inside, and made his body work.

– Interesting gun you got there, Mike said. – Do you know where I found it? In the closet of our dear adoptive father. You have spotted the engraving on it, I trust? There is a name there, dear brother. I would be amazed if it wasn't *ours*.

Hands started shaking again. Ted's entire body shook, with the hands, with the gun. He looked down on it, inevitably. As through water he saw the letters engraved on the metal, on the barrel.

One short moment and his brother was on him. Mike struck his hand, and the revolver hit the floor with a loud bang.

The sixteen-year-old boy gasped when he got a kneecap in his groin. White yellow in the face he crouched and then a fist struck his jaw. Mike kept it up without mercy. With a hoarse laughter he kicked the legs away from his brother. Ted hit the floor hard, and lay still.

Mike threw Linda into the wall with a wave of the hand and walked slowly towards Tilla who, absolutely terrified, attempted to defend herself. Mike just grabbed her and pushed her out on the floor.

– You'll be sent away with the others, of course, he said casually, – but not before I have shown you how a whip is supposed to be used.

His eyes glowed. There was actually fire in them. She stared at them, absolutely mesmerized. The eyes changed color. If it wasn't actual fire it was close, very close. The girl screamed when the tip of the whip cut through her skin. That howl penetrated deep within Ted, and once more his insides were pulled to the outside, all of him glowing, glowing in Power, in rage incarnated. With all his inherent hatred he threw himself at his enemy.

Before Mike managed lifting the whip for the third time he was struck down. The dining table collapsed under his weight. The two candles fell to the floor. The dry timber floor caught fire instantly, and the flames started licking the walls.

– Grab Linda and GET OUT! Ted shouted to Tilla.

Mike attempted to strike, but Ted parried. His fist sank deep into Mike's abdomen. The nineteen-year-old grunted, but otherwise he seemed unaffected. Ted struck again, received a hard fist on his jaw, shook it off and struck again. This fight was, if possible, even rougher than the one fought in the Forester house. None of the brothers saw Tilla, who dragged Linda towards the door. They didn't see the figure that started moving when the fire had almost reached it. They felt only the hatred, the fear they had for each other.

Ted breathed heavily. They both did. But his rest had in no way been sufficient. He felt himself break up, collapse. Slowly but surely, he was forced to fight defensively. He continued striking automatically, like a machine, like a mindless beast, and he was. A part of him was, hammering relentlessly at the enemy. The both did. They both were.

In minutes, seconds the cabin was surrounded in flames.

– The fire *speaks* to me, he said, taunting Mike with it.

The last sentence he said aloud, desperately clear-sighted, sensing in that moment its significance… far beyond this place, these moments. Elation raced through him when he saw the naked fear in his brother's eyes.

Mike found an opening, struck a blow sending him into the burning wall, down on the floor. He screamed in pain as he landed on… as he landed on *metal*. He realized what it was and his face froze in a triumphant grimace. The revolver lay by his side. One moment the brothers stared at each other across the Abyss. Then Mike threw himself forward.

Ted grabbed the weapon with both hands, sensing how fast, how fluid his movements were.

– We're forces of nature, he said… the moment he fired, his words drowning in thunder.

Mike was hit right in the chest. Blood gushed from his wound. With a horrible howl he fell into the flames. Ted stood there, suddenly frozen, thunderstruck.

– The fire, Mike screamed. – THE FIRE

Ted could actually see the figure there, see it move inside the flames, feel the burning in his gut, as the creature of fire in front of him collapsed on the floor, in an inferno similar to that of volcanic eruption. The boy had seen it, seen and felt its Power. As he did now. And it hurt, hurt terribly, making him gasp in horrible, transcendent pain.

Smoke was oozing from Ted's skin when he stumbled out of the burning inferno. He carried Maria on his shoulder and the revolver in his free hand. His face was burned, a piece of his hair gone. He fought himself forward, the last few steps to Linda and Tilla before falling on the ground, the rock, the cool, healing rock.

He lay there, on his back, staring at the sky, silent as death. The girls were quiet, too, not speaking, hardly breathing. They watched the cabin, as it burned down. The scream from the fire could be heard for ages. The stars above Ted started changing, started burning.

It could just as well have been me. It could have been anyone.

The youths had still not moved when Mark Stewart found them at dawn.

INTERMISSION:
WASHINGTON DC

«The system should be changed, I think, to begin with. It›s very hard, really, the way our system operates, now, for a truly frank, honest man to stay in that system indefinitely without being weeded out or fired or made apathetic or in fact corrupted in the end».

Daniel Ellsberg, interview with Walter Cronkite June 23, 1971

Chapter thirteen

The Dance stopped abruptly. The Dance continues.

Washington, District of Columbia was situated between the states of Virginia and Maryland, both of which had given up land to its original formation, by the shores of Potomac River. Bigger ships had always been able to sail all the way up. In spite of this the number of ships was usually relatively small. Washington DC was not an important industrial harbor. Not that many ships arrived here, relatively speaking. Usually.

Contrary to most other major cities in the United States the political capital totally lacked the presence of skyscrapers. That and the rectangular streets gave it a distinctive stamp. Here was also, of course, The White House, the President's official home.

This building was connected with Capitol, the museum-like Congress on the broad Pennsylvania Avenue. Usually the city's many public servants dominated this street, but not today. Today they couldn't get through anywhere. Not without clearing the road first.

This early summer day in 1974 humans filled the entire wide area around the President's home. The area practically boiled in passions and numbers. Pennsylvania Avenue was filled up. In the huge park called The Mall one couldn't see any green in the multitude of people. Even Capitol Hill was blackened by the crowds.

They had come during the early and late morning, some by boat, others by bus, or they had simply shown up, seemingly from nowhere.

In front of the five hundred and fifty-five feet tall Washington Monument somebody had built a platform. People spoke from it in quick succession, passionate, angry words. Above there were speakers casting the words to the entire gathering and beyond. On the platform, a few steps behind the passionate speakers sat a row of pleased men and women. Among them was Diana McKenzie.

Fear riddled her. Ambiguity and paralyzing fear. Pride riddled her. She couldn't deny the feeling of pride. She had been picked among many to join the group organizing it all, all this. Her father's official capacity, position, made hers good propaganda for the movement, she was aware of that, but she didn't care. The main thing was she was indeed here, with the thousands that had all come here for the same reason.

Or that had been the main issue. It no longer was. She sat there, warming herself in the warm sunshine, and it was as nothing, its heat no longer reaching her, no longer helping against the cold flowing through her.

A door slammed somewhere, opened and closed constantly. She shook. She smiled to the people looking worriedly at her, her colleagues, her new friends.

The man behind the microphone raised his hands, and the crowd's salute met him like a wave of sound.

– Look up there, he shouted. – Look at the man in the ivory tower, how he's busy speculating how he's gonna increase his fortune and power, and nothing but.

– Listen to him, Diana said to the man by her side. – He is good.

The man by her side looked worriedly at her, at her pale complexion and constantly moving eyes.

– They will all forget him the moment you start speaking, he told her appraising and grinning.

– Shame on you, Daniel. I'll make sure your wife hears of your blatant flirting.

He laughed and patted her cheek.

His touch didn't feel real. Nothing did.

– It's your turn. Don't bring shame on my words, now, do you hear?

The crowd's roar rose when she walked to the dais. She imagined her father's face. He watched her on the television screen in his prestigious office, she was certain of that, of that much. Thinking about it the usual feelings of guilt and rage mingled within her, many times enhanced here, now. This mattered. Here she had found her friends, her life.

It was all utterly, completely meaningless.

She took a deep breath. It was always worst before the first word. She had stood like this before, but was always nervous. And now, the word «nervous» did in no way whatsoever cover what she felt.

– Dear friends, she began. – We are finally gathered here. We have come here from all over the nation. Everybody knows why. We have come because our first house, and so many of our symbols, the things so important to us have been vandalized, have been desecrated. We have come to express our contempt for this, and to put forward our motion, our *demand* that our nation's leader shall no longer be Richard Nixon…
******/

She heard the applause, long and hard. She felt pride boiling within, so very, very happy. The applause faded only slowly, both inside and outside. She sensed Daniel grabbing her hands, congratulating her, as she retuned to her chair and the next in line experienced the crowd's greeting.

Eager eyes sought faces in the crowd, flashes of recognition, an impossible task, of course, even when using binoculars. She looked at her watch, impatiently, driven. Daniel and the others noticed, of course. They would have to be both blind and insensitive not to. She looked at her watch again.

– Daniel, she said, clearly breathless, even though she had been sitting somewhat still for minutes, now. – When is your speech? There is a break soon, right?

– Oh, not for a few hours. It's a long list, after all. Yes, the break is after…

– Come with me, then. I want you to say hello to some friends of mine.

– Okay, where…

She practically dragged him off the platform and through the crowd. He followed her good-humoredly. Diana constantly had to slip away from lewd touches and cries, but she didn't seem to notice or to care. She was blushing, she knew she was, but she didn't care about that either, didn't care about Daniel's probing eyes, about anything… except what was ahead. Her heart beat hard and fast, virtually bumping at her ribcage.

She saw them there, by the fence, didn't see him at first. She waved frantically. They waved back. Then she saw him and her heart skipped one, two, three beats. He didn't wave. She waved even more frantic. He didn't wave.

– People, she greeted them, clearly excited. – I want you all to meet Dr. Daniel Ellsberg. Daniel, here is from left to right Bob

Tremblay, Tilla Stevens, Linsey Kendall, Iris Carson and Linda and Ted Cousin.

She blushed some more.

– *The* Daniel Ellsberg? Linsey exclaimed incredulously.

– I guess so. Ellsberg smiled modestly.

Bob embraced Diana and kissed her on the lips.

– Congratulations, he said. – That was some speech. Nixon is certainly crawling further into his hole after that one.

– Thank you. She hardly seemed to notice him.

She stared at Ted, unable to stop herself.

– You are so thin, she said, touching his cheek, swallowing very hard, – almost… scrawny.

He mumbled something. She didn't hear what. He was so changed from the dynamic, raging beast she had met three years ago that she could hardly believe her eyes. Cheeks were sunken, eyes dead and cold. This boy was reserved and… he had always been haunted, but now it dominated his features, his very being. A horrible disappointment and horror rose in her.

– We tell him to eat more, Iris said, only marginally joking. – We tell him all the time.

– Diana's speech was great, Bob said. – Don't you think so, too, Mr. Ellsberg?

– I do. She would have had a fantastic career as a speechwriter… if it wasn't for her excellent and beyond passionate delivery. But call me Daniel, okay? I'm not that old, you know.

That was obvious. The youths knew that Ellsberg had just about passed forty and he didn't even seem that «old», in spite of everything he had suffered through.

He had brown hair and was of medium height. The hair was fairly long, and he did look more like a hippie than a trusted government servant, but that's what he had been. If one looked closer exhaustion was clearly visible around the eyes and mouth. He had been one of President Nixon's most trusted employees until he stepped down from his position at the defense department in June 1971. He had gone public with the so-called Pentagon Papers, and shocked an entire world with revelations of United States' atrocities in Vietnam.

And Nixon's… How Nixon and four previous presidents and administrations had been repeatedly lying to the people they were supposed to represent. Now the US involvement in the war had practically ended, but the storm at the President had not. It had, on the contrary increased in scope and strength, and Ellsberg was one of many reasons for that.

– Now, what's the verdict? He asked jokingly.

– Huh? Linsey looked disoriented at him.

– Your impression? It can't be that bad. You're not leaving me in anger, the way many journalists do.

– It's the commotion, Bob, the fun guy grinned. – There is no room to maneuver. Do you dare join us in our tents, so we can take a closer look… Daniel?

The older man laughed, and they all started pushing through the crowd towards somewhat lesser crowded and greener pastures.

Diana walked by Ted's side. He seemed… distant, and as if he didn't really see her, see anything, as if he was dreaming a waking dream. She wanted to touch him, take his hand. She lifted her right hand, but lowered it almost instantly.

She went to Bob and started speaking to him in a low, but intense voice.

– It's because of his brother, isn't it?

Bob looked at her, not saying anything.

– Listen, I know what happened. Linsey told me. And I was there, at the party, too. I know what this is about.

– He needs time, Bob said, a bit absentmindedly himself. – He will bounce back. He always does.

– There is something I need to tell him, she said.

– Oh, what is that?

– Something important. She shook her head. – But I can't, won't, do it now. He is no use to anybody like he is, now.

– No, he isn't, Bob mused.

Diana didn't notice, but allowed herself to be sucked into the group, into their hopes and fears. She wanted to, wanted it desperately.

The two tents were raised in the cool shadows of a tree. Iris and Tilla fetched chairs and everybody sat down, gratefully, protected from the Sun's boiling heat. The sounds of nature, overwhelming even here, in the midst of the modern city, the gray fog of concrete, asphalt, plastic and glass gave relief from the crowd's cries.

– Nice, Ellsberg commented.

– Shadows are nice, Ted said, very absentminded, his voice lacking modulation, lacking passion and dreams.

Linda silently squeezed his hand, but she, too, failed to get any notable response from him.

Diana witnessed how Iris tended to display herself, showing off her impressive curves and sending him promising looks. Diana couldn't feel jealous. There was no sign of him acknowledging or even noticing her efforts.

He looked like a zombie, a walking dead.

She wanted to go to him countless times, but courage failed her. Fear of being rejected stopped her.

– I saw Scarface again today, Tilla said abruptly.

They had all entertained themselves with small talk for a while, when everything… tensed. Diana saw how even Ted shook and his eyes seemed to clear, for a second.

– That can't be right, can it? Bob shook his head. – Are you sure?

– A Chinese guy with a scarred face, Tilla replied irritated, shrugging. – Chinese, oriental, whatever. It was him. I stumbled and accidentally looked behind. There he was, not ten steps behind us on Pennsylvania Avenue. I'm willing to bet there aren't two guys as ugly as him in the entire world.

– I've seen him several times, Linsey said. – My sister, too. And our classmates have talked about him, noticed him independently of us. It's one thing for him to hide in a big city like Denver or Washington, but in a small community like ours he just can't. He's real, okay?

– I don't think he cares, cares at all, if he is being spotted, Tilla said angrily. – He just… *looked* at me.

– One-eyed Negro crooks, scarred gooks, what is it with you guys? Bob threw up his hands exasperated.

– So, you've never seen him? Ted asked him.

– No, I've never seen him.

– One-eyed? Diana gasped.

She felt it, felt the rush. They looked at her. They all looked at her. She felt his eyes on her, on her skin, and it was almost all worth it.

She grabbed her bag. In swift, nervous moves she unearthed a pile of papers from it.

They all looked at her.

– His name is David Gidman, she said. – He was supposedly killed in a shootout in San Diego in 1966.

She didn't hand the pile directly to him, but passed it around. Iris was the first one looking at the newspaper clippings.

– They were about to bury him, when he vanished from the morgue, Diana continued. – He wasn't One Eye then, but when he resurfaced a few months later he had a black patch over his left eye.

– Stewart, Iris said aloud. – He looks a bit different, but it is him. He was there.

Diana recalled the photograph perfectly. The man, the face in the shadow.

– There's a pattern here, she said hesitatingly. – I can see it, see it all…

The others didn't really listen to her. They all gathered around the picture, studying it. She wanted to say more, but held her tongue.

– It could be coincidence, I guess, Tilla said to Ted. – He could just be in town for another reason.

– No. Ted shook his head, his eyes clearing and shining like beacons in the blackest night. – It is as you told me. Gidman knew him. They know each other.

– They do, Diana stated. – They've had many «shootouts», like the one in San Diego, since early adulthood, all over the planet. Both are wanted in France on murder charges. And there is more…

– It's time for us to go, Ellsberg said to her, to them all. – Break is over soon, and as part of the organizing committee we should be there. Listen… you're all welcome to join me and my wife at home tonight. Feel free to just show up, if you've got nothing better to do.

They all laughed. They liked Daniel, his still carefree attitude towards life.

– Keep the file, Diana waved to them. – I'll see you tonight.

– Bye, Linda, waved very deliberate, placing herself very close to Ted.

Diana wanted to go back, but then a wall of people had come between her and Ellsberg, and the others.

She saw it, saw Ted pull himself up from the mud, and she felt the joy and the horror all over again.

*********************************/

– It *is* him, Tilla told Ted. – The One Eye I «met» in the cabin. He has changed a bit. His body had more muscles, a lot more muscles when I saw him, and even less hair, but it is him.

- Both Gidman and Scarface, Iris shook his head. – What's going on here?

Linsey heard it, a bit off, where he rested between the two tents, enjoying the afternoon Sun on his semi naked body. He didn't hear Ted's reply. He wanted to, but suddenly there was another roar from the improvised arena by the Monument.

He wanted to be there, too, but there were so many concerns, so much going on in his life. He just didn't know which way to go.

From the Monument, and from speakers in every other direction he heard Daniel Ellsberg's voice.

– BEHOLD, Bob applauded very sweet and sour from the other side of where Tilla and Ted stood, pointing at Linsey out of the blue. – The Cattleowner's Association's representative in the Dickie Rally.

«Dickie» was Nixon's pet name, given him by all his devoted «supporters».

– Nixon has basically aggravated virtually everybody. Linsey shrugged, grinning. – Even the Cattleowner's Association has a mad on for him, to the point of sending me to speak for them. I guess they were desperate. They're usually a very conservative body, not prone to even risk rocking the boat.

– And to not rock their own boat too much, they sent you, Linda said. – Sending a representative without sending a representative. That's brilliant.

President Richard Nixon had for years mostly done whatever he pleased with the authority his elected position gave him, and no one, or very few, were the wiser. After the ending of the US involvement in the Vietnam War the majority of the observers had made the incorrect observation that he had been through the worst. Since the beginning of this year his popularity in the polls had gone from being supported by an amazing majority to close to zero, and the last few weeks' incidents hadn't exactly hampered this, to him, disastrous development.

May 20th the commission investigating the Watergate Scandal had drawn a crucial hand. On their request Charles Colson, the president's closest adviser had been arrested and charged. After a hint of lenience, he had exposed virtually everything, how Nixon for years had given him orders to spread derogatory - and also on occasion - false comments about political opponents, from both parties, among them Daniel Ellsberg. How G. Gordon Liddy and Howard Hunt had broken into Ellsberg's home on Nixon's «request», how they had conspired to «neutralize» him with the help of exiled Cubans, and so on. Only the final drop.

Of many.

Ten days later, the thirtieth it was revealed that Dickie had earned millions on milk subsidizing. Then the large demonstration was already planned. The day after that the cattleowners, among many, decided to send their non-representative representative to Washington.

Ellsberg made his speech. Against the man he once had looked up to and admired, and as some were fond of pointing out the man who was the first American president to visit China after the revolution and «and who had done more than anyone for détente in the world».

– People ask me, Ellsberg said with a loud and clear voice. He kept his mouth close to the microphone. – Hasn't this President also done a lot of good?

He took a short break, as if to catch himself.

– And I always reply like this: Perhaps he has, perhaps not. But even if he has, are we then supposed to accept any indignity he may visit upon us? I'm convinced that no matter the good that will never be good enough to cover or to balance his crimes…

– Most of the people here are idiots, Ted said, with eyes suddenly brimming with life. – They believe totally in the illusion that having ended the Vietnam War and ending this particular janitor's term early will make everything all right, while in truth it will, as always, serve to cover up the true issues.

– This is unfortunately very true, Linsey nodded. – In a very real sense the focus on Nixon and the war is working as a diversionary tactic, a blanket hiding everything truly important.

– You two are nuts, Bob shook his head. – Here our society is on the brink of dissolution, and you're saying it needs to dissolve even further?

– Smart man. Linda applauded slowly, mockingly.

– Let me see if I get this straight. Iris smiled wickedly. – The world is totally fucked up, and you want to keep doing the same things, keep repeating the overwhelming mistakes of the past?

Bob shut up then. He fumed around the mouth a lot, but he shut up.

Iris walked to Ted, kissing him on the cheek. He relaxed, smiling at her. Then suddenly she shifted position, and kissed him on the lips. She laughed throatily and pleased, pulling back a little, allowing him a complete view of her well-developed female body. He did look. He downright stared, and she blushed, she actually blushed. Linsey looked, too, and he observed how her excitement, her heat grew there on the spot. Ted took off, and she hurried after him.

They all took off, faded away, and Linsey was alone, as alone as he could be in a place where tents covered literally every green spot there was. Sometimes he needed some time alone, to reflect and think. In that respect he wasn't so different from Ted, he mused.

Linsey had wanted to come here for so long, and now, when he finally was here, he felt… disappointment, and he didn't know how to deal with that.

He heard the expected light steps from behind, but when he turned around he saw no one there. That was expected, too. She was hiding, just out of sight. That was also a part of the ritual. He started whistling as he rose and walked into the tent. He took his time, didn't want to reveal his eagerness. Impatience rode him as he lay down close to the entrance. Her shadow grew on the tent wall. He could hear her, how she circled around the tent, only very slowly approaching. She was a cat, teasing him with her sharp claws, and that was how he would treat her.

Shock rocked him when he saw the girl lifting up the tent opening and come crawling towards him.

– L-linda, he gasped, unable to hide his confusion. – What are you doing here? I mean… where is…

– Oh, you want to know where Iris is, don't you? Linda replied teasingly. – At this moment she's still busy showing Ted her good points, another useless attempt, I gather.

Linsey looked at the slim, blonde girl who was his cousin. She stood with her hands in her back pockets… and let him *look*. Or did she? He couldn't read her, couldn't read her at all.

Even Linsey's conservative, evangelist uncle on his father's side of the family spoke about her as a «modern day Cinderella». Linsey wondered what he would think now.

– I wanted to speak to you, Linda said, almost shyly. – We are alone, now, and we haven't really talked much before, have we?

That was true. They had little or no contact during most of their childhood. He nodded.

– It's rather strange, isn't it? She continued. – We don't live that far apart. Families may live in different parts of the country, and still see each other fairly often.

That word again.

He discovered that he had trouble speaking. Throat was dry and he was drowning in the blue sea of her eyes.

– Yes.

– That my parents hid the fact that Mike and Ted were adopted may not be that unusual, but they clearly didn't do it for the usual reasons. There's much more to it than that. And your mother is pretty mysterious herself. Did you know that both Ted and I have been pushing mom and dad concerning the issue of his biological parents, that they just flatly refuse to reveal anything, even names?

– No, Linsey replied hoarsely. – I didn't know that.

The image of his mother came to him, unbidden, the way she watched him all the time, the ambiguity in her eyes.

– There's a mystery here, Linda said, staring straight at him. –

A vast and terrible mystery.

There was another roar from outside, another set of cries from the gathering failing to shake the Earth.

– The ground-shattering events out there feel so distant, doesn't it? She said. – So totally unimportant?

He nodded and she nodded, and in each other's eyes they read understanding.

A fly crawled across the ceiling. He watched it with his left eye, in a remote, detached manner. He couldn't take his eyes off the girl in front of him.

– Linsey, she said.

– Linda, he said.

– What do you think of Ted? She said abruptly.

He was shocked, was rocked in his serenity, no matter how much he had expected this.

– Ted? He's quite the lucky guy. He tried joking, laughing it off. Her words worked as a bath full of ice on him. And like a glowing forge. – He has four beautiful, irresistible girls chasing him. Three of them even travel several thousand miles to get him. Yes, I would say he's lucky.

– Don't fuck with me, she countered. – Tell me what you *think* of him.

He discovered that he had lost control over the conversation, that he had, in truth done so from its very beginning. She had an agenda, and she wouldn't be denied.

– You like him, don't you? He said softly. – Like him a lot.

She wasn't blushing. She didn't say anything, just stared at him with her penetrating blue eyes.

Without warning, unwanted the memories returned to him. Things he had seen, heard and understood. He sensed gooseflesh start marching over his skin, feeling its heavy boots.

First there was the image of Elizabeth, when he, at fifteen saw her bath naked in the river, then the conversation, the horrible conversation he had overheard between her and Ted. And Ted's bloody fist. Ted's limp and bloody body, and his own frightening intoxication from that sight.

– He is… strange, he said. – He isn't here, but yet he is more here than anyone I've known. He is carrying a rage inside that sooner or later is going to blow. And he is *scaring* people, by his very presence.

Linda nodded in agreement.

– Even Ellsberg noticed it. Did you see how he flinched when he shook Ted's hand?

Linsey found himself nodding, too. He couldn't stop himself from nodding.

– I feel the same way, she said. – He's dangerous and helpless at the same time. He's with us, but he isn't with us. He never talks with anyone, not really. I can never truly get close to him. Every time I try I see his eyes darken in irritation. Not even the art Iris is practicing is of any use, is cracking his shield. He does talk to Tilla, that fucking nigger bitch. She, who has hurt him, time and time again.

The noise from outside reached staggering proportions.

– But she doesn't come truly close either, and I am relieved.

– Cynicism doesn't become you, he said to her.

– It doesn't? She flared. – IT DOESN'T?

The calm returned almost instantly. Once more she was in control of herself, of the situation, of him.

Linsey started worrying. Ellsberg's speech would be done any minute now, and Iris would come. Linda seemed to grow ever more excited. Her cheeks had turned a hectic color of red. She was breathing hard. The nails cut the flesh in her palms. She tightened her nice little hands that hard…

– I'm a terrible girl, am I not? She smiled. – Not at all what you expected.

He wanted to say that he hadn't expected anything, but the words stuck in his throat.

Her smile widened, and it made Linsey seriously worried. He looked carefully at his watch again.

– But dear Lin, she said. – I can't be very nice company. Let's not talk about Ted anymore. There's a lot of other stuff we can do.

Linsey looked at his watch for the third time in just a few minutes. He sensed sweat erupt in his armpit, adding to what was there already.

– Iris won't come, Linda said.

– W-what? He sounded as if he was caught with his fly open. Damn him.

– You see, she grinned and laughed a bit, enjoying herself, – the two of us made a deal. I will stay away from Ted during the remainder of the trip if she stays away from you.

There was no longer any doubt what she wanted, wanted from him. He swallowed hard.

– I and Iris had a very meaningful and useful conversation. We found several points of common interest and viewpoints, of course. One was a conviction that you're very much alike Ted in a way.

Her voice slurred a bit by the last words.

– There's no one disturbing us here. She started unbuttoning her blouse.

Her bra appeared in the cleft, the two half moon sight of her breasts.

– I can't wait any longer. I need you, do you understand?

He understood, but could only nod. The shock remained, like an imagined hammer striking the insides of his skin. And after realization hit him fully he also realized he had been blind earlier. From the moment she had entered the tent she had been cold and calculating. He realized that as the conversation progressed she had turned ever more dominating. As if she had been playing a part. And she had. She did. She played herself.

– We shouldn't, he said hoarsely. – We're cousins.

– I want you, she said. – And I don't give a fuck about such trifle matters, about society's narrow view on morality.

The blouse fell to the ground. She slowly, enticingly loosened the bra and let go of it, and then she stood there, naked on the upper half of her body.

– Are you jealous? She wondered. – Do you want to say no?

He couldn't voice a reply, and wasn't given the opportunity. She fell on her knees in front of him and smiled invitingly. With a sigh she fell forward until she stopped against his body. He tried to fight her, but was in truth defenseless. She was just as dominating now as she had been during the «conversation». The answer to her query was quite simple and answered itself. He couldn't have denied her even if he had wanted to.
***/

Evening turned to early night in Washington. The summer's full moon cast a ghostly light from the sky and on the city, over all the people still gathered on The Mall. In one tent Linda Cousin writhed eagerly and aggressively in Linsey Kendall's arms.

On the other side of town their friends sat around the living room table, enjoying themselves in the company of Daniel Ellsberg and wife.

– Life goes on, Tilla insisted, looking at Ted when she said it.

– To life, Ted exclaimed, lifting his glass of sparkling wine.

He returned her stare, and she gasped when noticing the fire in his eyes.

And everybody present turned misty in their eyes and hearts. As they toasted, as glasses met and parted, and they drank.

Bob left the toilet, flushing it as he opened the door and pulled his pants back up. The phone rang the moment he reentered the hall. He grabbed it and lifted it to the ear.

– Ellsberg residence, he replied, a bit ironic, witnessing with a bit of relief Ellsberg cheerfully wave his approval.

There was a brief silence.

– Is that… you Bob?

– It's me, he confirmed, more than startled over the fear in Diana's voice.

He heard traffic noises in the background. She was calling from a pay phone.

– Tell him, tell Ted I see the Tapestry in all its horror and glory. I have proof, now, indisputable, horrible.

– Slow down, Bob insisted. – I can hardly understand you. There's so much noise.

– I should have told him everything I knew when I had the chance, she sobbed. – Told you all. But I was proud, afraid of rejection. What we have seen so far isn't the end, but just the beginning, are you listening?

– Yes, Bob said, his voice sounding very remote in his own ears.

– Bob, listen to me Bob. I want you to listen to me.

– Okay…

– Don't listen to your father, okay. Reject him, as you reject all his works.

Bob sensed ice-cold spikes penetrating him, and then the line went dead.

Diana stared at the phone in her hand, desperately wanting to hear sounds from it, any sound. But it was dead. She cried out in desperation and despair, leaving the phone booth, leaving that, too, behind.

Diana ran. She ran in utmost desperation. Her facial features twisted themselves beyond recognition and her eyes revealed pure nameless terror. Her mind was virtually disconnected. All that was on her mind was to move her legs, put one foot in front of the other, to escape the people hunting her.

Breathing hurt. Muscles virtually stiffened as she ran. She kept moving. Where, she couldn't say. She ran blindly ahead, and looked neither left nor right. Escape was her only objective. Reason had flown away. She was like a frightened little animal running from a predator, from its fate. Behind she heard *his* steps, inevitable as Death itself.

She didn't see the hole in the road. Her foot stuck, she fell, hitting the ground hard. Air was pushed from her lungs, and she nearly lost consciousness. With a throbbing head she crouched on her side, gasping for air. The sharp pain cleared her head a bit. The fear kept dominating her thoughts, but she could think, reason, remember.

– Jealous, she mumbled. – Selfish. I had no right, no right. Punished, I'm being punished. Damn me.

She gasped again, but this time because she heard the steps closer, so much closer. Fear numbed her again. She saw him, One Eye. Two white lackeys followed straight behind him. They ran through the street in something resembling giant jumps, closing the distance between them and her in strides. The two lackeys were big, too, but they were not giants, like him. He dwarfed them completely. He dwarfed everybody.

Gulping air she fought herself up and ran once more. Foot hurt, but she stumbled on. People. There had to be people here somewhere. There had to. She would never reach The Mall in time. All the idiot policemen were at The Mall.

A couple crossed the street a bit further down. An older man and a young woman. Her only hope.

– HELP, she screamed. – HELP.

She reached them. Getting the shakes she just about managed to grab the man's collar.

– Help me, she begged him. – They're after me. Please, HELP ME!

The man and the woman looked strangely at her. The man attempted to pull away. Desperately she turned towards the woman and repeated her plea, but there was no more response there. The man attempted to cover his face with his hand.

And she understood.

– FUCK YOU! She shouted savagely. – Selfish bastards.

Two pair of hands grabbed her from behind and pulled her back. She resisted, writhed with all her strength in their grip, but it was no use. The two huge men held her in arms, legs and hair, making her unable to move anything, even her head. She looked up into the brutal face of the one-eyed black man, into David Gidman's face.

– The bird flew her cage, he said softly. – The bird hurt her wings. She can fly no longer.

– Please let me go, she begged him. – I haven't said anything. I won't. I *promise*.

– I'm afraid that's impossible, little white girl. You were very bad when you ran away and must be punished. But just behave well in the future, and all will be well.

He turned towards the nervous couple, just as smiling and charming, the patch over his eye hardly seemed threatening, but more an object of pity than of fear.

– Allow me to apologize for this incident. Unfortunately, there will always be escapes from hospitals, especially since we tend to be underfunded and understaffed. My name is Noble by the way, Dr. William Noble. This girl is one of my more difficult patients. She's suffering from advanced schizophrenia. Her convalescence will be long and hard, I'm afraid.

– Don't listen to him, Diana sniveled. – I'm not sick. He's just making that up. I know too much. Call the police. Tell them that Floyd McKenzie's daughter has been kidnapped. Do it now.

– Poor girl, Gidman said. – One of her fantasies is that she's the famous Diana McKenzie. And not the only one either. She also believes she's Jane Fonda, another of the present-day barricade racers.

She shrunk there and then, knowing very well that Gidman

could just kill the couple outright, so it wouldn't do her any good to convince them. She shrunk and fell into mindless despair, crying softly.

The older man looked at her, the saliva flowing from her mouth, the madness and the unbelievable horror glowing in her eyes. Poor thing. She had to be very sick. Such a fear couldn't be natural.

– Come, let's leave, he told the woman. – It's for the best.

She nodded and followed him down the street, but after a while she turned her head.

– We won't get any... trouble because of this, will we? She asked. – I mean... We won't be called as witnesses or anything?

– No, one of the orderlies replied. – There's no need for that.

The couple left quite relieved. One Eye turned to Diana with a syringe in his hand.

– Now, little Janie, he said aloud, – we'll give you a long-relaxed sleep, and when you awake you'll be home.

Diana wanted to scream, to fight, to do all in her power, but there was no fight, no power left in her.

– I so love a good performance, Gidman said pleased, before setting the syringe.

She sensed her arm turn numb shortly afterwards, and didn't know whether it was her imagination or not, and she didn't care.

– It doesn't really matter if they believe me or not or if they recognize me, or you later on. As you know I don't give a fuck about such trifles.

– We are the Abraxas Omega - The One and The All, one of the «orderlies» stated proudly. – Now you're just one more cunt in our service.

Her muscles relaxed, her mouth started sagging, limbs turned soft and eyes empty, as they slipped close. Her final vision was of One Eye's cruel smile, and it brought one final jolt of fear to her, before everything turned black and she felt no more.

PART FOUR:
THE DEFENSELESS

Chapter fourteen

The river sang to him. Ted Cousin heard it far away, without seeing any of it, standing by the soda machine outside the deli. It was like he was staring into empty air. There was no anger, but his eyes were still filled with the red glare. They all saw it, saw it in the shadows enshrouding him.

– NO need to remain in the shadow, Ted. John Jackson shouted to him, not unfriendly. – We're about to cool down soon anyway.

Cool down in the river. Ted closed his eyes briefly. The cool, raging river.

The day was hot, horribly hot. Skin felt like paper, lacking even a minimum of moisture.

No discernible reaction, as usual. John sighed. He wanted to go to Ted when Bruce Channon grabbed him and held him back, grinning widely.

– Hold on. Let the jerk stand there and stare at nothing, if that is his wish. We won't push him into joining us, if he doesn't want to, will we now?

Bruce had grown even taller and bigger during the last few years. John forced himself into facing him, both angry and scared.

– Personally, I see it as an advantage if the crazy shithead doesn't join us, Dennis Murdoch said in a vicious voice. – We risk being chased off by the other swimmers.

– Is it your intention to block my way? John asked with red earlobes and a half-choked voice.

– Not us, Bruce grinned. – I can handle a squirt like you on my own. Hell, my little finger can handle you on its own.

Rage and fear waged war within John. He wasn't really afraid, even though he knew he should be. The boiling blood slowly, pleasantly erased any second thoughts.

He sensed a soft touch on his shoulder. He stared into Tilla's stone eyes.

– You'll just be beaten senseless, she said softly. – Let me handle this.

– Ted has stood by me when I needed it, he said. – It's only just that I repay him.

– Good, she said. – Remember that, a day, the moment it's truly needed.

Before he could protest further she had turned to Bruce and taken one menacing step forward.

– You have a bad memory, girl, Bruce warned her, obviously nervous. – Remember you're Keith's woman.

She kept turning, suddenly much faster. Kicking him on the thigh, kicking him hard. He screamed and crouched before her. She hit him with an elbow on the side of the neck. He went down, fell to the ground in an instant.

– My honest intension was to give you fair warning, she said, icily, – before doing this, but your idiotic statement made me lose my temper, lose it big. You're the one with the bad memory. I'm not Keith's woman. I will never be Keith's woman. As you know I've responded to Keith's harassment by challenging him for the leadership of the bikers, but so far the chickenshit hasn't dared responded to it. You see, I'm my own woman. NO ONE owns me. No one will EVER own me. I hope this is clear to you, now, for your own sake.

He said nothing, lying there gasping.

She kicked him in the belly.

– YES, you damn bitch. He cried out, the pain distorting his face.

– CLEAR? She shouted.

– Clear as rain, he whimpered, failing completely in showing a brave front.

A cloud covered the Sun. She shuddered, attempting to hide it, but then she didn't bother. What he and any other felt about her was in the final analysis immaterial. She gave him one, final look of contempt before walking to Ted.

He spoke, without turning, as she stopped by his side.

– I can see the river, feel its powerful roar.

He turned and looked directly at her. Surprised and suddenly breathless she returned the look. His dark hair created an edge against the blue sky, the dark clouds behind. That was what she had always thought about Mike, too, she recalled.

– You're looking strangely at me, he said.

– Touché, she grinned, with a slightly nervous laughter. He

laughed, too, and she swallowed hard, attempting to hide it from him, in vain, of course. – Usually we have to shake you out of your daydreaming, you know.

– When I'm lonely, I seek solitude. Funny, huh?

She easily heard the bitterness, the anger in his voice, even though he, too, attempted to hide it behind a veneer of placidity, of indifference.

– No, she replied, – I don't think it's funny. I don't think it's funny at all.

She took his hand, squeezing it, stepping closer to him.

– We shouldn't hide anything from each other, she whispered, very emotional. – We should share everything.

He looked at her with humor in his eyes.

– What was the *commotion* about?

– Oh, it just concerned some guys with suppositions about cute, little Tilla, she shrugged, not caring if he knew she was lying or telling only part of the truth. – They've realized their mistake by now, I gather.

She lowered her eyes, before raising them again, glaring at him.

– I do need to work at it, I know that. The misconception about me is very thoroughly rooted.

A slight pause, before a certain dark light was lit behind the soot stone.

– I'm a very good girl, you know. I've been taught from an early age what a man wants. And… and I love fucking. I really love it. I can hardly get enough.

The remote, painful look in her eyes haunted him.

The two of them walked a bit behind the others. Sometimes Tilla was allowed to hold his hand, sometimes not. She alternately made a fist and bit her lip, but most of the time she was merely sad.

– Can't we just drop this? She whispered it, hardly audible. – Can't we just go home to me? We…

There was no response from him. None what so ever. And she kept lowering her gaze, kept looking at the ground in front of her, like him, like him seeing nothing.

Linda turned often, looking at them, staring at them with her burning blue flame.

The day was hot, turning hotter by the minute. Finally they arrived at the river's shore, half dead because of the heat. At this time of the year the ice melted in the mountains and the water level in the raging river was at its highest. Heat flowed through the air, like the river's currents.

– It does seem further away today, Frank Forester moaned, settling, falling down in the shade behind a heap of bushes. – Puuuh!

– They've made a broader road especially for you, Bob Tremblay grinned. – To make room. As little as you can stand of the heat they'll have to build it even broader… so you may roll on it.

Laughter. There was so much cruel laughter. Ted looked at Bob in disbelief. His friend could be such a jerk sometimes.

Those with ties to the bikers didn't laugh, though. Frank was their mascot, sort of (and the guy who financed most of their partying), and they saw it as their task in life to guard him from unwarranted hassle.

Bruce and Dennis raised their hands, using the opportunity to turn the hassling around.

– Don't be like that, Bobbie, Bruce said. – You know there is at least one other who can't stand the heat, and his case is far worse. It has damaged that one's mind.

They hinted in Ted's direction, needing to say no more.

– What the hell are you saying? John spoke up. – You shouldn't speak about damaged minds. A worse simpleton than you we'll have to look long and hard to find. You can't even make a joke. Only idiots laugh at your jokes.

Bruce sent him a flashing, scornful look.

– Wise up, little guy, before we pay you a nightly visit.

– You're not my type, John countered.

Bruce made a fist, glowing in triumph when he saw the fear in John's face. The bully turned away, content in his minor victory. Slow enough to enjoy the smaller boy's fear, but too fast to discover the resolve in his eyes. With a speed and confidence no one had believed he was capable of John stepped close to the heavier and taller boy. He grabbed Bruce by the shoulder and pushed him off the edge. Bruce tumbled helplessly into the water.

The water wasn't that cold, but the abruptness of it and the searing heat on land made it a real shocker to him.

– It looks like you're the one less able to take the heat, John snarled. – You're cheating, too, and won't wait until the rest of us have taken our clothes off.

– Good grief, Bruce, Iris choked in laughter. – The boy is a great joker. You should see your face…

Completely enraged, his face twisted in boundless anger Bruce ran out of the water, seeing nothing but the curly head in front of him.

Without the slightest warning someone kicked him in the leg and he fell. For the second time in a short while he crouched on the ground, gasping for air. He glimpsed a foggy image of a couple of legs appearing in his line of vision.

– Only my friends may call me Bobbie, he heard through a roaring buzz in the ears. – And you're not among them.

Tremblay, the stuck-up bastard. Okay, little John would have to await his turn, until he had demolished Robert William Tremblay the third.

B-but he suddenly remembered, remembered it clearly that Bob had walked towards him just before…

The peacock couldn't have done him.

Bruce lifted his head, looking straight into Ted Cousin's dark and threatening face. *Mike's face*.

– So, you're banding together, huh? Damn cowards.

– You should be one of the last to speak about that, Ted countered icily. – Gang mentality is, after all the leatherjacket bikers' specialty. If I were you I would lay low for a while. Get it?

Bruce looked around for support. There was none to be had. Frank and Dennis shrugged, and no one else bothered to even move.

– I get it, he replied hoarsely.

With one last, murderous stare at the two friends he rose and charged into the forest.

Tilla looked at Ted. Linda, too. They all looked at him. Fear, desire, contempt and submission mingled and mixed. The dark boy thought he hated them all. Slowly, only slowly the knot inside dissolved, dissolved again.

He threw himself into the roaring river way ahead of the others. So many concerns riveted his mind that he felt he would drown. He swam a few strokes on the surface, before plunging below, three, four body lengths down to the riverbed. Flashes distracted him, images, memories covering his strange and fearful existence. A dark cloud, a mystery dominated his life, and fear and rage fought for dominance within him. He saw pictures, he saw real life images of One Eye and Scarface. He had always had a vivid imagination and even though he had never seen any of the two in real life he could recall their faces in meticulous detail.

The water was crystal clear and though they were far away he easily saw John and Linda meet in an underwater kiss. Her bright hair mixing with his brown curls. Ted gathered that Linda wanted him to see it. Poor girl. Irritation and pity fought to gain the upper hand within him.

He turned and swam further down river, deeper below, moving effortlessly through the currents. Without making any effort, though, he was swept down the stream. He sensed the first pangs of a headache. He calmly turned in the water, set his feet at the bottom, and pushed himself upwards. He broke the surface quite a distance away from the others, shaking his head in delight, breathing fast, joyfully.

John swam a bit closer to him, clearly worried, in more ways than one.

– We were wondering if you would remain down there, he joked solemnly. – Do you know you were under for five minutes?

– It's called Aquatic Breathing, John, Ted pointed out. – We breathe less and there is a blood shift when we go below the water surface. Normally, without oxygen, the blood is filled with carbon dioxide, prompting the breathing response. But in water this response is heavily muted. And blood is gathering around the major organs. A gift from the age our ancestors spent some time in the water, according to some speculations. This ability is stronger in some, lesser in others.

John was and felt corrected, felt more than a little hurt, that sniveling shit. Ted pulled himself in, in another vein hope of controlling the fury inside. What was always There, with no reason, no rhyme.

– The currents are getting stronger just around the turn, John shouted. – We should head back. Back to the others.

– They will never accept me, John, Ted said decisively, forcing himself to smile to show the other he appreciated the effort. – When they see me, they see Mike. It's as simple as that.

John looked a little better, a little worse.

– You go first, Ted shouted. – I'll join you shortly.

John nodded, saying something Ted didn't hear, the roar of the current overwhelming his voice completely. Ted dived below again, swimming upstream below the surface, enjoying using his muscles to the max. Signs of the pollution were everywhere. Garbage, dead areas devoid of life, even a chair covered by moss. And now, now, he welcomed the fury. He broke the surface above the others, not feeling the slightest exhaustion. He laughed aloud, such a powerful expression of joy that it alone made him feel better.

He saw Iris on the beach. The others had left, but she remained. She followed him with her eyes. In fact, she never took her eyes off him.

He studied her. In fact, he could hardly take her eyes off her. Her fervent wish of turning into a full-fledged woman had been realized in a way obviously exceeding all expectations. The last few years, seemingly from one day to the next her curves and limbs had grown in such a manner that it made her into one of the most attractive girls in school. It was hard even to imagine the pale, skinny girl she had been. The recent, overwhelming image blocked out the old one completely.

She welcomed him as he left the water, reaching out with a hand and a smile, showing her interest, in him in every move, every look. It made him confused and angry. He got the same «funny feeling» looking at her as he did when looking at Keith Lampard, Stewart and Tilla… and Elizabeth and guys, of course. He had learned to recognize it better, now, exploring it, dwelling on it every time he sensed something like this or similar.

– It's about time you showed up, she greeted him. – We were waiting for you.

She certainly was.

The adult, the woman met him with a prolonged, sultry kiss. He couldn't help but respond. His lips burned. He felt the first, inevitable signs of arousal, the twitching down below. The large, firm breasts almost fell out of the bikini top. She was eager, the female cat, eager like a girl. He bit his lower lip. She smiled and touched his growing hardness.

– Yes, she whispered. – That's my boy, my lovely, lovely boy…

He grabbed her wrists, and he clutched them. The first signs of pain showed in her eyes. He squeezed, squeezed her wrists hard. She whimpered.

– Damn bitch, he snarled. – Whore.

Paralyzed and dizzy by the pain she hung in his grip. The thought of what he might do to her made her shake in fear. The light died in her eyes. He squeezed some more, until she let out a cry of pain, and then he let go of her. She remained on the spot, gasping, relieved to the point of gratitude.

– I'm sorry, she whimpered. – Sorry.

She knew why her advances made him angry, and she felt sorry for him. That made him even more furious.

She walked behind the bushes, the «girl bushes», and dried herself with a towel, dressed herself. He dried himself and dressed, too, completely uncaring whether or not she saw him. But she didn't. She lowered her eyes in shame, and he felt even worse.

Her clothes, seen from an established viewpoint were even more outlandish than most people dressed these days. And if the clothes didn't manage to raise their wrath the pentacle she wore in a chain around her neck certainly did it. She had started studying pagan teachings and proudly called herself a *witch*. Completely unacceptable, of course in the eyes of the average person. Ted admired her, and was reminded of that fact when she appeared from the bushes, looking intimidated and shy, but not unfriendly at him, and his confusion increased further.

– Why are you spending all that time with the bikers? He asked hoarsely.

– That one is easy to answer, she said in a matter of fact way, tinged with despair. – They're the only ones accepting me, willing and able to take me as I am.

– They're even accepting the witchy stuff?

She shrugged, both hurt and indifferent to his insensitivity.

– They, at least some of them know the feeling of being different. They have, like me achieved contact with the deeper Self, the witch in themselves, and they have, like me a... *need* to express it.

She smiled slightly, sending him a speculative, dwelling look.

– By the way... if you want to avoid female company you shouldn't play hard to get, but rather do the «tongue hanging out» routine the other boys are doing.

Her eyes took on a glimpse of pain, one of the mind. He didn't say anything.

– I know you, you see, know who you truly are below the thick layers of dust and suffering society has imposed on you. I'm gonna do it, you know. I'm gonna fuck you one day. I know I will.

He remained silent. Her soft laughter echoed in the forest, and he admired her even more.

They walked through the forest, separately, apart, alone in their suffering.

There was a campfire on the other side of the low ridge. The others had gathered around it. A cassette recorder somewhere was playing All Tomorrow's Parties by Velvet Underground. The sound of the Sixties' Freedom reverberated through the small urban Denver forest. Some of the youths were dancing, wild dance, wild abandon. Ted sat down in a small opening in the fire's circle. Iris, unbelievably enough snuck in by his side, leaning heavily at him.

Frank was smoking something. He had the stage and he used it, speaking with an almost insane excitement in his eyes and body, waving his hand constantly. He looked almost diabolical there on his spot, and like a completely different person.

– The cabin, he repeated again, intensively, distantly, smooching them all. – The cabin is *huge,* like a hotel, and when the fog is descending around it, it's like we're all alone in the entire fucking world, and we can do whatever we want, whatever we *please*.

There was a kind of symmetry to it all, to the dancers, the

speaker doing his thing, the girl by his side and everything, and Ted relaxed, relaxed a little, taking it all in.

The word «cabin» did strange things to him. He didn't smoke anything, didn't accept the various joints being passed around. But suddenly, shockingly he saw the cabin, a black, black wound appearing in the green, fertile land, devouring it all, and he fell into that black, black hole, never to appear again.

He shook, raising his head, sweat on his forehead, wide-open eyes.

Iris smoked. Her eyes turned glassy, remote, as if she wasn't there at all. Her smile smothered him like a warm, eager body.

– It's so pleasant, she mumbled, – so very, very pleasant.

– There's a bus, Frank sang. – Four wheels rolling, and once those four wheels roll, we're practically there already.

– Where? Bob asked, evidently very confused.

There was laughter. Not of him, but with him.

– The cabin, Frank said. – So far away, so faaar away.

He sat down in the dirt with an absolutely completely *gone flying* look in his eyes.

It turned dark. The sun had vanished behind the mountains some time ago, but now it turned dark. The light from the flames illuminated them all in red and fire. Rhythm-dominated music filled the space between the trees. Iris the witch danced, and they all followed her tune.

– The world is Magick, she sang. – The world is Life.

And they all repeated her words, Ted, too, for just a moment believing it.

– Bittersweet, she sang. – Bittersweet is life.

There were some initial poisoned looks from the majority of the assembly, but they were too stoned to voice any tangible protest. So, as usual they let themselves go with the perceived flow.

Ted danced with her. They even kissed. He kissed her, too. The witch cast her cloak around him, drew him into her embrace. The kisses turned sultry, the hands started exploring. He stiffened. She sensed it and withdrew. She kissed him on the cheek, smiling in regret. Someone grabbed her, pulled her away, and she was gone. She laughed. Her laughter echoed between the trees.

The gathering, many of them remained there in the small forest for the remainder of the evening and even throughout the night. Ted remembered going to bed, the forest bed, hearing the buzz of flies and animals, listening to the sounds, automatically searching for something that shouldn't be there. He slept, but kept listening, kept his guard up, and his sleep was pitiful and shallow, and would bring him little rest.

**/

The Sun burned the mountain ridge, the high horizon as it rose on the sky. The day before had been hot. This turned even hotter. The two men, Mark Stewart and Peter Clarke faced each other over the table. They had retreated to the cafeteria, the most shadowy place on the main police station. On the table between them they had placed two pitchers of water. They were virtually constantly sipping from the huge glasses in their hands, refilling in intervals measured in minutes. Towels covered their necks. Breakfast was just done, and the temperature already exceeded 100 degrees Fahrenheit. The air-conditioner had broken down two days ago and all windows had been opened. Stewart evidently dealt with it better than Clarke, who really looked out of it. Sweat still poured into Stewart's eyes to the point of him being unable to read on the meter exactly how hot it was. He swore and threw the cigarette out of the window, glancing over at the school.

On the street outside people, young and old walked by.

– Look at them, Stewart said, shaking his head in regret.

– They're told that the world is this tiny, limited place just outside their window and nothing more… and they believe it.

– They're sheep, Peter Clarke said.

Stewart very carefully arranged his face, his mask, but the pain penetrated the shell, inevitably.

– The world is vast, he whispered, – and they don't realize it. What they're limiting themselves to experience is merely one tiny, tiny spot in the vast multidimensional reality that is the Universe, and they don't realize it, except through half remembered, unrealized dreams.

Clarke smiled politely. It was his best smile. Stewart had seen it often enough, had almost grown used to it by now.

Stewart put the big file on the table, opening it, revealing the expected pile of paper. He picked one picture, almost at the top and tossed it to Clarke over the table. Clarke looked at it, and shock was visible in his eyes.

– Yes, Stewart stated, – this is he.

The picture was of a man standing in the sunlight. A beyond powerfully built brown-skinned man with an enormous presence. He looked half away, evidently not aware of the picture being taken. Only one eye was visible. The other, if there was one was hidden under a black patch.

– But how is that possible? Clarke protested weakly. – I was there. You shot him. Hell, you emptied two rounds of lead into his chest and head. And he looked… he looked nothing like this.

– He was dead. Stewart nodded, with frost in his voice. – Now, he's alive, and has enjoyed some rather dramatic improvements.

There was another photograph. It was of a rather skinny brown-skinned man on a slab, in a morgue. He was covered in blood and bullet holes.

– This was taken in San Diego Police Department's headquarters at least an hour after I shot him to pieces. Stewart showed both his anger and incredulity in a detached manner, not really showing anything. – I know he's alive. I've felt him, the way I've always felt the bastard. I don't need the physical evidence.

Clarke didn't really know what to say, so he kept his mouth shut.

– I started hearing rumors almost immediately afterwards. Mark Stewart kept speaking, hardly audible. – I didn't think much of them then. I just figured his devoted legion of supporters had removed the body from the morgue. As you recall he had quite a few of them. It was more than probable. But then… a little more than three years ago the rumors started taking on more of a… quantifiable quality. Even before Tilla Stevens gave her detailed description of the One Eye in the cabin I had received other reports, both through official and our own unofficial channels. Francis claimed to have seen him in Vegas. He was in fact quite livid about it. He wasn't certain, though, with the changes ol' Dave had gone through. But I was.

And there were others. I knew they were right.

Francis was their old traveling buddy Francis Caine, the infamous Gambler.

When Stewart mentioned David Gidman by name his voice took on a subtle horrible quality of its own. Clarke shuddered slightly in the heat.

– I've put everything I think is connected in this file, Peter.

– Including the Cousin debacle three years ago, I see... Isn't that a bit farfetched?

– He was here, Peter.

– He... was? Clarke said, clearly worried.

– At the very least some nights before. Read Tilla Stevens' account. You'll find that good ol' Dave has found religion...

Clarke went through the pile in record speed, and pulled out one thin sheet.

– I can see a vast tapestry here, Pete, Stewart said. – A black hole, sucking in everything.

– Well, we've known each other for quite some time, now, Mark, my boy, the colleague said affectionately, – and I'd say your «hunches» are worth more than a thousand filed words.

Stewart returned the smile. They had been brothers in arms for years. He leaned back in the chair, touching his temple.

– We looked for them the entire night and day and night again. I saw the fire on pure chance and found them at dawn the second morning. The four of them just sat there, staring at nothing. The boy pointed the gun at me. At least it looked that way, but he was really just pointing it at the cabin, the burned-out cabin. All four were in a state of shock, close to unresponsive. I had to call for a chopper. They spent a month in the hospital before returning home somewhat normal. One never did.

– Maria Jimenez disappeared, Clarke stated, nodding to himself. – No one saw her leave or being taken against her will.

– No witnesses stepped forward, Stewart said. – I interviewed the staff personally. They weren't lying or being evasive in any way I could discern.

– There was truly never a trace of her anywhere?

– Not even dust, Stewart replied with closed eyes. – She has been on the missing person list all this time without tangible results.

– I remember ol' Jimenez raise quite a stink about it, practically accusing us of kidnapping his daughter.

«Us» were Denver Police Department.

– If someone took her, why her and not the others?

– I don't know. Stewart kept his eyes closed.

Clarke looked through the file some more. He put another picture on the table, one of a horribly scarred oriental man.

– And this is…

– His name is Chin, Stewart replied. – His last name, first name, neither or both. He's called Scarface, for obvious reasons. It's said he is an enforcer of some kind. That's all we know. The only reason we have a picture of him is that some immigration officers had some *fun* on his behalf five years ago.

– Enforcer, huh. Clarke smiled ironically. – For whom? And what is his connection to the case?

– Unknown…

Clarke struck out with his hand, uncharacteristically passionate.

– So, to sum it all up we know a lot, but we don't truly know anything?

Stewart opened his eyes, swollen and dull.

– That's as good a description as I have ever heard.

He leaned a bit over the table, staring into Peter Clarke's eyes.

– I probably didn't do you any favors by telling you this, Pete. Merely by knowing you might have become a target.

– That's okay, Clarke replied quickly. – Who is gonna take on us, the dynamic duo, and succeed? Won't happen, man. They couldn't do it when we operated outside the law, and it certainly won't happen, now, when we've got thousands of tin soldiers lined up behind us.

Stewart didn't close his eyes. He saw David Gidman, the deadly weapon he had been eight years ago, and as he was now, when he was clearly even more deadly. He was cold. It wasn't psychological. He was truly cold in the hot sunshine, in the greenhouse-like room.

– PHONE CALL TO LIEUTENANT CLARKE, a voice called through the speaker system. – PHONE CALL TO LIEUTENANT CLARKE.

Clarke looked strange just then, before an apologetic smile transformed his face.

– Gotta go. Duty calls. See ya soon.

The two of them belonged to different departments, but they kept themselves appraised of interesting events, both because of old times sake, and for the sheer usefulness of it.

Stewart heard his steps from the distant hall as they faded and vanished somewhere in the building. The nearest phone was far away. Clarke's office was at the opposite side. Stewart turned around, towards the open windows. Ted Cousin stepped forth from behind the wall outside.

– Did you get everything? Stewart asked, unnecessary.

– Everything, Ted replied. – I have excellent hearing. You're a thespian for the ages. The stage has lost a great asset in you.

Stewart gathered all the papers and put them back in the file compartment, and hurried outside. The desert heat hit him violently, subtle, like a hurricane where there was no wind. The kid was nowhere to be seen, a shadow in bright daylight. Pain haunted him, haunted Mark, the pain of memory. He crossed the street, a bit below from the school. There was a deli there, with dark and pleasant interior. Stewart walked through it, up the stairs to the upper floor, just above the deli. The boy sat there, crouched there like a vulture.

– You've got talent for this, Stewart commented dryly. – There was a slight chance that Pete would have seen us if we had crossed the street together. It would probably not have mattered much, but one never knows.

– Better safe than sorry, right? Ted stated.

Stewart looked around some more.

– Quite a shadowy place, he commented casually.

– I enjoy the shadows, Ted said, sending shivers down the older man's spine.

– You aren't fond of bothering frogs in the ponds, too? Stewart joked.

Ted looked at him, uncomprehending.

– Anyway, I brought this…

He drew a revolver, the revolver from his coat.

– Look at it, he prompted.

Ted took the gun. His eyes were instantly, like three years ago drawn to the engraving, to the name...

J Warren

It said.

He looked up. Their eyes met.

– Yes, Stewart confirmed, – I have heard about him. I have even heard about the gun. Both were quite infamous in their time, in the early fifties.

– The gun... Ted said dumbfounded.

– Look at it.

Ted did. He had seen many guns, even peacemakers, but none quite like this.

– Yes, it's special, Stewart confirmed. – No factory has made this. It is handmade.

Ted didn't say anything.

– It's one of two, by the way. The other had the same engraving. They belonged to two brothers, Jack and Joel. They weren't truly gunmen, mind you, not in the traditional sense, but when they happened to use their gun they were extremely good at it.

Two brothers... Ted swallowed hard.

He handed the gun back.

– Keep it, Stewart said. – Your father obviously meant for you to have it. I can get you a license easily enough.

– I don't want it.

Voice was even, flat, lifeless.

Stewart took the gun, putting it away again.

– What happened to them?

Stewart sniffed a bit, looking out of the small window, at the police station.

– I don't know. I wish I did, okay. I know no one who does. They disappeared in 1952, they and the entire family, vanished without a trace.

As if on cue Peter Clarke walked out of the main entrance of the police station. He didn't take his car, but walked on with fast, purpose-filled steps. Stewart walked down the stairs just as purpose-filled. Ted followed him. Stewart turned his coat, and it changed from being beige to pitch black. That, and a cap on his head, and he was a changed man. Ted cast admiring but also pointed stares at the broad back.

344

– Trudy didn't, Ted said.

Stewart walked on, but the blood froze to ice in his veins.

***/

They walked through LoDo, tailing Peter Clarke. It wasn't
that difficult. Clarke did glance behind him and to all other
sides occasionally, but the sense of urgency evidently made
him careless. Ted had always been good at moving in and out
of the shadows, he knew that, and by following, by imitating
the older, far more experienced man he learned it even better.

They crossed Sixteenth Street. Ted kept his stare at Peter
Clarke, his entire attention on the figure sneaking around
in broad daylight, constantly turning his head, turning his
attention in all directions simultaneously. And Ted, learning
did the same. But while Clarke was clearly nervous Ted
felt nothing of the sort. He sensed the low Burning inside
somewhere, and it felt good, so very, very good.

– He's heading for Union Station, he said not long after that,
realization hitting him softly, surely.

– He is indeed. Stewart nodded. – Or at least heading in that
general direction. Whether or not he has business there remains
to be seen.

Sometimes they only glimpsed him, as he disappeared
behind a corner or was hidden in the crowd. Ted was certain
they had lost him, but Stewart had an uncanny ability, born
of experience, Ted guessed, to shadow… to shadow a prey
through the busiest city street.

They walked, they flowed over the concrete and the harsh
ground felt like soft, solid sand. They both moved like
shadows, and Ted felt pride.

– Still no luck with your parents? Stewart asked casually,
hardly audible, eyes locked at the moving prey ahead.

The big man looked at the boy without looking at him. Ted
knew he did. He could see Stewart's eyes, he always could.

– No, the boy shook his head vigorously. – I ask them at least
once a month, once a day. The reply is the same. They refuse
to tell me who my biological parents are. They claim they have
promised not to tell anybody.

The two of them kept moving, and it was as if neither of them
had ever spoken.

The last three years he had just… thrown himself into things, Ted realized. Into physical hardship, construction work, used sledgehammers and everything until his hands bled and his entire body hurt, just to forget, or at least not *remember*.

But it was no use. He saw it, experienced it, wherever he went, in the streets he walked, in the hallways he wandered, a shell of a man. In every unknown he met he saw Mike's face. In every voice he heard the shrill, desperate shriek of pain and desolation.

Stewart stopped abruptly, as soft as velvet. The railway station loomed before them. Stewart stopped, stopping his companion with the wave of his hand.

Clarke had stopped, too. He had placed himself at the main entrance, obviously waiting for something. Ted and Stewart waited behind a corner, in relative obscurity.

– How can he not see us? Ted whispered. – How can he not have discovered us?

– Because he doesn't expect to, Stewart replied plainly, stated as fact. – Perception is reality.

Clarke walked back and forth, impatiently, glancing at his watch.

Ted watched him, watched Stewart. The big man did sweat, something the boy had never seen him do before. One would be sorely tempted to conclude it was caused by the weather, but this was a deeper, more fundamental sweat than what was caused by physical circumstances. It was visible in the eyes, in posture and every little move the hands made.

Clarke, on the other hand, wore all his anxieties on the outside. He was like that; shallow, as deep as a flea-infested pond.

Ted… felt when the car in question pulled over, seconds before it actually did. He couldn't tell why. Perhaps he realized it by watching Clarke or Stewart, even though nothing overt changed in any of them. The moment the waiting ended they both turned into the professional hide and seek machines they were.

Stewart moved, walked almost relaxed to the nearest car, out of sight of Clarke and the driver in the other vehicle.

He didn't say anything, just moved, and Ted followed him

without a word.

Ted was nervous, agitated, Stewart calm, effective. The Lieutenant wrapped a bit of his coat around his right hand, and pushed it straight through the nearest car's window.

– Get in.

Ted wasn't sure he actually said that or said anything, or if he just imagined the superfluous words.

Stewart was already inside, and before Ted had jumped into the passenger's seat he had jumpstarted the engine. The Lieutenant drove straight into the street and into the other street where the other car had just left its short-lived position by the sidewalk with Clarke in it. Ted wondered if Stewart had thrown more than a bit of caution to the wind here, but he kept his mouth shut. He knew very well how experienced Stewart was, and how inexperienced he was himself.

They followed the gray car. Usually there were several cars between them and it. It could be out of sight for a considerable amount of time when turning a corner, but it always reappeared, often after being gone tens of seconds. Stewart had done this since adolescence, and if he was a bit rusty he found the rhythm and the calm again soon enough.

– It's like a second skin, Stewart said, as if he had heard Ted's thoughts. – You might not always consciously feel it, but it's always there.

They left LoDo, left central Denver. Dry, gray surroundings changed to dry, open fields, into streets once again. Ted realized that they were heading south, in a roundabout way. The driver in the other car played hide and seek, as a matter of principle… probably.

– Yes, Stewart said. – We would have known if he had made us.

The car was hot, the air-conditioning totally ineffective with the open window. Ted still experienced the cold tingling, the tingling of fear. Stewart now showed what he was like, what he truly was behind the civilized exterior.

– Who is David Gidman?

The words came by itself, unbidden, but not unwanted. Certainly not.

– You've read the reports, Stewart replied. – You know.

– They're just words, Ted stated. – I want to know who he is… from an expert, one who knows him first hand, and you do… right?

– You're getting way too smart for your own good, kid, do you know that…

Ted didn't reply, not with words. He just stared, and waited.

– He's a slave trader, Stewart eventually said. – A man trafficking in human misery, tattooing all his victims with a red fist. My wife Jean… is his sister, or half-sister. My parents were killed. I was taken in, sort of adopted by the family. We all grew up together, in Marseille, France, a place where it is said that everything, even humans is for sale. Gidman excelled in it. I and Jean didn't.

Voice was dull, lifeless. Ted knew how that was. He said nothing. He felt very cold, even colder somewhere, but he couldn't tell exactly where. It seemed to spread everywhere, and from everywhere inside him.

– You were brothers, Ted said, suddenly, unexpectedly.

Stewart didn't comment on that, not directly.

– You remember the book Modern Slavery, by Sheila Ashcroft?

– Dimly. Ted nodded.

– I knew her and with Clarke, Wolf Connors and Francis Caine I rescued her and others from a place where a number of human beings had been held as cattle, forced to do their captors' bidding in all things. Do you understand?

The direct look in those eyes, they… stabbed him, like daggers.

– I don't know. I thought it was merely a book, a story. A work of fiction.

– Listen, kid, I tell you it's true in all its blood, innards and horror. We freed those people from what's truly a fate worse than death. We freed them from the clutches of David Gidman, a man thriving on human misery, on suffering, on spiritual death.

Ted shivered in the presence of Stewart's boiling Wrath, something beyond wrath, into a mire of full-blown, long-term hatred. This was not *work* to Stewart, that much was certain. Suddenly the familiar man seemed like a total stranger, just another beast waiting to strike with claws and fangs, one Ted wasn't sure he wanted to know.

The rollercoaster of emotions he had experienced just the last few minutes was, he ventured, a lifetime worth seen from ordinary people's point of view.

– I want to know more, he said. – Much more.

– Believe me, kid, Stewart let out a short bark of laughter, more like a snarl. – You will. One way or another, you will get to know enough to last hundred lifetimes.

The pendulum swung, swept Ted to the other side of the edge.

– Why are you letting me do this? The boy asked abruptly, moody, aggressively, cunningly. – I'm just a kid, inexperienced and surely a liability in a crisis. What's gotten into your mind?

– As you surely have noted I'm not your run of the mill policeman. Stewart shrugged, a Stewart that kept staring intensively at him, yet keeping his eyes on the road. – And you're involved already. You all are, whether we all like it or not. I'm simply applying the logical consequences of that.

A short break, before the roaring, deliberate onslaught continued.

– And you're clearly your father's son. How much remains to be seen.

Ted shuddered then, more than sensing the overall menace in Stewart's voice, wondering if the other was aware of it himself.

– A *lot* remains to be seen, doesn't it?

There was no reply from Stewart. If he was aware of the venom in the kid's voice he didn't show it. His face was, once again an impassive surface calm.

The mountains grew around them, as if they hadn't been there a second ago, as if they had just appeared. There were still cars between them and the car they stealthily pursued, but the line was thinning. This was cabin area, though, and they were still on the main road, heading west on the beyond broad Interstate 70. The road went up and down in the terrain like a yoyo, and they didn't have Clarke and his companion in a clear line of sight more than seconds at the time, which was only to their advantage, of course.

Ted saw, in a flash of panic that the other car had left the Interstate, and was on its way up a steep road. He wanted to shout to Stewart, but the Lieutenant was already about to make the turn. That cold bastard!

The boy corrected himself instantly. Whatever went on below that cool exterior was nothing even resembling calm.

He saw a castle, an actual, honest to god castle up in the hillside. The road led there, and no further. He observed the other car, on its way up. Stewart pulled over by one of the many parking lots and stopped. There were countless cabins, big and small in this area, more than enough fish to hide among.

Stewart quite simply left the car. He didn't bother to dust off fingerprints or anything.

– I have a deal with Chief McCabe, he grinned. – He made me an offer I couldn't refuse, in exchange for ignoring my insignificant transgressions.

– Does he know about you being wanted in Europe, too?

Stewart slowed down a bit, considering it, seemingly not bothered the slightest by Ted's bombshell statement, thoughtful wrinkles visible on his forehead.

– He certainly knows that, since that very crucial piece of information was the wedge he used to *employ* me. But I would say he knows more. Sometimes I suspect he knows more about me than I know about myself.

He shrugged and smiled. Ted followed him in a furious mood.

They stopped by the edge of the parking lot, by a bench and table, hidden from the looming castle above by a public restroom.

– It will be dark soon, Stewart said. – We will wait here till then, and then make our way up there.

– I won't make you into a god, Ted said, – but I'm willing to go out on a limb here, and claim that you already knew about this place and that your old friend was headed here.

– I didn't know, Stewart grinned, a gloriously fake grin. – I did suspect, though.

The boy studied the older man's mask, cutting into it like the sharpest of blades.

Stewart looked up, thoughtful for a moment.

– It belongs, unofficially to an old club, calling themselves the CCC. It stands for «Coalition of Concerned Citizens».

They were formed back in 1932, in that very house, by a bunch of wealthy and powerful industrialists, politicians and media moguls, officially to combat the rising force of communism. Unofficially to strike down any force, any person fighting for a just society, thereby threatening their position as Masters of the World. Officially they're doing mostly welfare and philanthropy. Unofficially, they're as bad as they come. Shady and dodgy dealings, horrors in the night are the rule, not the exception.

– Even though most of it, he added, sniffing, shrugging, – is going on fully in the open. They're lying by telling the truth, and they're very good at it, they and the rest of their colleagues, in similar influential bodies, all over the world.

Darkness descended around them, quick and uncanny. Ted sensed how the very air turned heavy, turned dark.

Stewart kept talking, suddenly very talkative.

– They had dealings with Nazi Germany during the Second World War. Not necessarily because they shared their ideology or anything, but because it was profitable and because they wanted to crush the Soviet Union. The plot failed... miserably so, and even backfired, and they realized what they had known in their rotten old bones all the time, that they would need to be patient, to fight their battle over decades, over generations...

They walked upwards, climbed the ground with their feet, effortlessly and not even breathing hard. Ted inevitable felt joy because he had, after all, in spite of having spent years in a mindless stupor, as a *zombie* somewhat kept in shape. He walked silently, deliberately in Stewart's shadow. They moved as one, closing in on the stately bright mansion ahead.

There were no lights lit up there. Cars, dozens of them revealed themselves on the parking lot, as they ascended and circled the dark, foreboding building, approaching it from the higher position. There was a rock fence, but no special, extensive security measures. Not anywhere. There were a couple of armed guards on the premises, walking the dogs, but it was almost ridiculously easy to outsmart and avoid them. These people were certainly careless, not really guarding their secrets well. Or... Ted and Stewart exchanged glances... they were so cautious, so secretive that they wouldn't even let any but their most trusted servants get close during the nights of the meetings. They probably had the heavy security force nearby, though, in case of an emergency.

Or they waited just inside the thick walls, with their guns and death. Ted suddenly got a veritable anxiety attack.

Stewart shook him, bringing him out of the black mire he had been headed for.

The darkness, the bottomless well was close, always close, waiting for him to fall in.

There was a door straight ahead, ajar, inviting. He stopped. Stewart signaled for him to proceed, and he did, like a good boy. He walked inside. A glimpse of light reached him from the hall. There was no attack, no people here, but himself and the mystery man by his side.

They heard voices, many voices, seemingly filling the air, the walls, the very matter of the place, growing louder as they penetrated deeper inside, like daggers into the dragon's belly.

Except...

We're the dragons, Ted thought. And the people ahead are the knights, admired and looked up to by an entire world.

They reached a hall, an auditorium, something incredibly enough resembling an ancient arena, a Greek or Roman amphitheater. It wasn't that big and the comparison failed on several counts, but that was what it reminded Ted Cousin of.

The man and the boy crouched there, hidden in the shadows, in one of many shadows created by oversized candles and oozing torches, listening in, taking in everything.

Down on the stage, or whatever it was, cloaked and hooded people formed a circle. One man, the speaker was a part of that, but had placed himself a bit inside it, clearly distinct from the others. At the circle's center was an altar, complete with a book and a cross. Ted moved his eyes a bit. Outside the circle, within a smaller square floor was a smaller group, also hooded and cloaked, but bound and blindfolded.

The leader, the ceremonial master spoke up, as he lifted his hands to the level of his face.

– We first met in this house, at this table decades ago. We are meeting still.

His powerful voice rocked the room. The amphitheater's

shape amplified it to a thunder. Ted would guess any newcomer to the cult would be impressed by that. This was indeed a stage, their scene, like the world was one. It belonged to them, their crushing fist. Ted shook violently, momentarily, barely managing to control himself.

– WE ARE MEETING STILL.

The choir filled the room.

– Communism and its implications are still an ilk in our society, an impediment to our freedom and profitable activities. But we are meeting still.

– WE ARE MEETING STILL.

– We are one arm, one finger of the hand, one foot of the thousand, the thousand real people of the world. Our symbol is the Millipede, because that's what we are, a thousand feet marching united towards our manifest destiny.

– MANIFEST DESTINY

The voice was familiar, somehow, Ted was sure of that, not one he had heard often, but he had heard it. He had, at least once, probably more, seen the face glimpsed under the hood's shadow. He scrutinized all their faces, whatever he could see of them, to memorize the features for another time, another place.

The Master lifted his hands higher, above his head. The buzz faded and silence suddenly reigned.

– We have with us tonight the few, the proud we have chosen to initiate into our fold, the new generation chosen to start as our squires, at the lower floors of the pyramid of power. We are those illuminating the shadows, shining a light in the night. We shall persevere. We were present at King Arthur's table, at the church meeting in Nicaea, at the last supper of Christ. Our ways are unchanging, eternal.

– ETERNAL

Ted didn't know whether or not to laugh or cry. These were the masters of the world?

The first initiate was brought forward. He was led, still bound and blindfolded, and placed by the altar, by the book. Ted could easily make out the letters of the giant leather-bound volume: THE HOLY BIBLE.

They undressed the poor guy, the willing idiot of a slave, and he stood there naked before them. Ted didn't know him.

– KNEEL!

He obeyed instantly, falling on his knees on the cold floor.

Silence reigned. He knelt before the master, his head bowed.

– SPEAK!

There was heard a clearing of the throat, a hesitant throbbing before the low voice rose and cut through the hall.

– I am a servant of the Cabal, he shouted. – A subservient of the Thousand Feet. I stand against the forces of darkness threatening this world and others. So, help me God!

Ted shook his head. All of it started to take on a new, inevitably sinister meaning. He didn't cry, didn't feel any need to laugh. He just shook his head.

The Master was given a sword by one of his peers and he stepped forward, walked to the center, with the blade raised above his head.

– Do you swear to uphold the Law, and to protect the Secrets? The Grand Master shouted in such a way that the air in front of him was flooded in spittle. – Do you do so, knowing that the breach of your duties is punishable by death and eternal damnation?

– So, I do, the kneeling man cried out. – So, I SWEAR!

– Do you swear to serve the light? Do you do so, forever forswearing the darkness?

– So, I swear. So, I do!

And so, it continued. «Questions» and «answers», until the man on the floor was driven beyond exhaustion, beyond reason, and he just was his voice and his knees, raw and bloody. There was no blood. Nothing but dust. Ted felt sick.

The grand master pushed the tip of the blade between the white cloth and the temple. A quick shake of his wrist and the blindfold came off and floated to the floor.

– Rise, you servant of man, and be released from your woes.

The head honcho stepped behind the naked man, and untied him, as he star-eyed and with tears in his eyes rose to his feet, doing his master's bidding.

– Welcome to the Brotherhood of the Thousand Feet, you no longer nameless one, welcome, Anton Berkowitz.

– Thank you, Berkowitz whispered. – Thank you so much.

He whispered while the cry of welcome embraced him like a

valve. And he felt pardoned.

There were more of them. Not many, but seemingly an endless line.

Later that night Ted and Stewart made their way down to the car, relieved to the point of panic, more cautious and paranoid than ever.

Stewart had signaled him. «Let's leave», he said. «We've got what we came for».

– I didn't see Gidman there…

– Neither did I, Stewart replied. – But I didn't really expect that either. It isn't really his style. He won't bow down for any man.

Admiration and hatred waged war within Mark Stewart.

– It doesn't make sense, Ted complained. – Nothing does.

– And nothing ever will, Stewart answered him.

Revealed as about number six or seven had been Peter Clarke. Ted had recognized him in advance and studied Stewart instead.

– Welcome to the Brotherhood of the Thousand Feet, you no longer nameless one, welcome, Peter Clarke.

Clarke, his features a study in triumph said nothing.

– You must never say anything to anybody about this. Stewart shook the boy with his voice. – Not even those you trust. Any of them may be acolytes or potentials, reporting to someone. They do recruit them as early as in their teens. That's the entire point.

Ted wanted to protest, but couldn't, and remained silent.

Stewart started the car, and they returned to Denver on the ghostly night road of Interstate 70.

Yes, there were a couple of things he hadn't told his old friend Peter Clarke. This was just one more detail added on the list, to present in full, sometimes in the future, one lovely morning.

The car faded into the shadows, into the lights of the city.

Chapter fifteen

He opened his eyes. The searing heat hadn't decreased any from the day before. He sensed it on his skin, heard its buzz in the air. All the windows, all the doors were wide open. It was no use. Even though he only covered his body with a thin blanket he was bathed in sweat.

Linda entered the room, carrying a tray of food.

– Rise and shine, sleepyhead, she said brightly.

He opened his eyes and kept them open, easily. There was no yawning, no sense of cobwebs, the way he usually experienced the first seconds, hours after awakening from the night's sleep. He was awake.

– Breakfast was hours ago, she said sweetly. – So, I thought I would fix you something.

He felt the first decisive contractions down below and he sat up, pulling his knees up. It would be clearly visible to her, if she looked.

And if he wasn't very much mistaken she was indeed looking.

She was dressed in shorts and a shirt, more than highlighting her tanned tall and adult body. She was beautiful.

It was obvious she had spent a lot of time before the mirror recently, applied heavier make up, brushed and painted herself. She had even thinned her eyebrows, something that would have never even occurred to her earlier.

It was a kind of ugly thought, and he suppressed it and similar notions as much as he was able.

Stewart had made him promise not to tell anybody. He wanted to break that promise, to smash it to bits, but how could he?

She put the tray on the bedside table. He was hungry, so very, very hungry and he grabbed the first sandwich, and wolfed it down as if he hadn't eaten in years.

And he hadn't.

– It's good. He praised her, attempting to keep a light tone.

– Thank you, good sire, she chided him, leaning, bending forward, kissing him on the lips.

They fell on the bed, tangled, interchangeable. He heard the fluttering of birds' wings from outside, the distant roar of the river. There was the salt taste of her lips, her huge eyes strangely in focus close to his. He realized he would always hear the river. His hardness pushed against her, and she started breathing faster. Her foggy eyes and the half open mouth invited him to descend, to drown.

He untangled and got out of bed, somewhat dignified, feeling like a jerk. And that irrational sense of hurt and shame made him boil inside.

She got out of bed, placing herself in front of him, moving very slowly.

– You want to strike me, don't you?

– No, I…

– That's okay. She smiled, a strange, repulsive smile. – I know how that is.

She stepped close to him.

– Why don't you?

He wanted to say something, but couldn't.

– Why don't you strike me?

He stood there, frozen like stone.

– Sweet, sweet Ted, she whispered, touching his cheek with a feather hand.

– I'm sorry, I… I… No.

Her hand fell. She stood there, looking angrily at him for a few seconds. Then she turned and left the room, slammed the door behind her.

He stood there for a long time, frozen, worse than a statue on a winter night. There were no more sounds from the river. He looked disgusted at the sandwiches.

But he sat down on the bed once more, and he ate them anyway. Quickly, impatiently, as if he disliked every move, every taste they made him feel.

He dressed in a hurry, ignoring the inviting sounds from downstairs. Suddenly the very thought of joining Linda and her parents in the living room, in the garden downstairs, so full of memories felt completely intolerable. Without really thinking about it he crawled through the window and jumped down in the garden. He landed fairly softly, choosing to ignore the weak, dull pain in the right ankle caused by a skewed landing, hardly even noticing it, at least not after a while. There was the sound of voices from the living room. He ignored them and walked on.

The bright day wasn't fully bright. A shadow lingered in his path, making it turn half night in the middle of the day. Half night! He tried to describe it, to describe it any differently to himself, in vain. He walked in Shadow.

He spotted three of the girls from school. They spotted him, too. They couldn't avoid to. He heard their whispers, felt their stares, and it wasn't, like before, any reach for him to know they didn't like him very much. He didn't care. They were just a few more hens in the pecking order organized against anyone weird or different. And he was as weird, as different as they come.

The bus pulled up as he turned the corner. There was no need for him to wait, or to run. It waited for him. It ran to him. The bus headed north, to central Denver, to LoDo. He hardly noticed anything from the trip itself. Taking the bus to Denver failed completely at capturing his interest.

He walked through LoDo. The sixties had changed bits and pieces here. A store played the Bob Dylan main theme from the movie Pat Garret & Billy the Kid, haunting chords cutting into him like knives. Billy had been nineteen when he had been featured in all national newspapers, and in the eighteen seventies that had been a feat of enormous proportions.

People were dressed differently, but that was about it. A Sunday in town was about the same as it had been for quite some time. There were few people. Most of them spent the day at home, either bored out of their skull or resting from a hard week at work. One could see the exhaustion in their eyes, in the way they walked. And tomorrow was school. Ted, Linda and Tilla were one year late, compared to most of the youths. He didn't know why they bothered.

Ted Cousin passed the bank. He did so several times, before shaking his head. No, not like this, on impulse, where the chance of getting caught was that much bigger.

The sound of Bob Dylan's guitar kept haunting him.

He walked around in deep thought, doing so on purpose, testing himself, to see if the half subconscious dream state bothering him for so long would return. It didn't. He didn't feel good about it. He didn't feel bad.

Thornton Chandler had a combined gas station and repair shop/store close to the Union Station. Ted approached it and didn't realize it until he was just in front of it. Chandler stood outside, polishing his 1969 Firebird.

– Looking for some Sunday afternoon work, Cousin? I got some, if you're interested. Pays extra, too.

Ted shrugged.

– Okay, I don't have anything better to do, anyway.

He saw the dark cloud form above Chandler's head, and enjoyed that.

He didn't know shit about cars or engines, and wondered why Chandler had hired him in the first place. The fact was that all technological gadgets had always confounded him. So he was usually in sales, behind the counter. Not car sales. Of course not. The kiosk and spare parts section. And he washed cars by hand. Chandler advertised the fact that he owned the only place in town without an automatic washing tunnel. That should have appealed to Ted's contempt for gadgets somehow.

It didn't.

He dressed in an overall, and started on the long line of cars in the backyard. Washing and polishing, washing and polishing.

And as sure as rain Chandler entered the backyard. He wasn't really talking to Ted. Ted knew that. Talking down to him perhaps, and certainly fond of hearing his own voice. Ted had so far, in the months he had been working here basically ignored the high-pitched voice, but today, for some reason he couldn't.

– Yes, I heard a lot about that brother of yours, I certainly did. We're usually not much interested in news from the suburbs, if you get my drift, but he was an exception, to be sure. A baaad motherfucker he was, his rep going wide and far, but you took care of him, didn't you? Took care of him good...

The sun blinded the boy. The sunrays reflected in the polished chrome made it worse. He moved his hand back and forth, dipping the sponge in the bucket, changing water every five minutes, moving his hand back and forth, back and forth, making polished chrome even more polished.

He kept it going with a burning stare finally making Chandler shut up. Eventually, when the sun was about to set behind the mountains he straightened, straightened deliberately. It hurt, hurt bad, in muscles, back and limbs.

He felt anger, and it… pleased him. When Chandler paid him in cash at the end of the day the boy grinned at him. It was time, he decided. It was finally time for better things.

No more running.

**************/

Tilla saw a marked difference in Ted's behavior during the week. Everybody did. She saw it, with his every move, every small gesture. The few people she and he called friends felt the first pangs of hope and joy. Most others, who certainly hadn't forgotten, felt the return of fear and shame. Everybody tiptoed around him, except her. He sat in the school's dining hall, reading New York Times. This was a part of his life he had regained, that she had never been a part of. She walked straight to him, and sat down by his table. There were six more available chairs. No one filled the slots.

– Anything interesting? She asked lightly.

– The usual bullshit, he replied, not unkind. – Even when reading between the lines it's crammed with lies.

The two of them sat there for minutes without speaking, afraid to break the silence.

Eventually he felt he had to say something, anything.

– Have you heard from your brother recently? How is he? Shouldn't he be back from Vietnam by now?

She stared at him, her eyes cloudy and close, very close.

– My brother Rodney died there, she almost shouted. – He was killed in battle.

– And you didn't tell me? He said shocked, knowing fully well what she was gonna say next.

– I did tell you. How can you not remember?

They had stopped moving. He sat still, shaking his head, shaking himself hard.

– I wasn't really listening.

And his voice was distant as the evening wind. But she heard it, heard it well.

She reached for one of his hands with both her own. She grabbed it, and he didn't pull it away, didn't pull away.

– I understand, she said. – Please, believe me.

She wanted to go to him, to sit close and comfort him.

– You don't need to be worry about me, he stated slowly. – Not anymore.

She kept her distance.

They both attended high school, their final days of public education. She had moved to central Denver, while he still stayed at home with Linda and his adoptive parents. She lived in a small house in the no man's land between downtown and the highway. There was less than a week left of school, before finals. They both hated it, hated the degradation of human life so prevalent there, seeing the contempt mirrored in the other, as they sat far away from each other in the classroom.

She looked at him. He knew she did. But he didn't turn and look at her. And he sensed like a scar the despair within her.

When Tilla Stevens arrived home Friday afternoon she felt sick to the bone. She had worked hard to catch up with the year she had lost, and to a certain point she had succeeded, filled her brain with useless information in one of several strategies to gain a degree of independence in life, and wasn't certain she saw the point in it, anyway.

She threw herself on the large bed. Eyelids closed, and she slept heavy and dreamless.

The sun had almost set when she woke up, startled, on the floor, with a splitting headache, and being out of it, totally out of it. Her eyes were swollen and the hair in disorder. She saw herself in the little pocket mirror on the bedside table, a distorted version that didn't look like her at all. The alarm clock kept ringing and sent shakes of pain through her brain. She grabbed it and threw it at the wall. There was a loud crack, and blessed silence reigned. She closed her eyes briefly, unable to tell what would have happened to her, to her sanity if the clock had kept ringing.

– I must not be too late, she mumbled. – Must not…

She managed to get up, and stumbled to the bathroom. She turned the taps and water started filling the tub. After ten minutes it was filled to the brim. She had hardly moved during that time, hardly moved at all. Dull eyes stared straight ahead, at the vapor and the nothing. She wondered if the water was hot, if it was scolding hot.

Without bothering to test that, or to even give it a second thought she jumped fully dressed into the tub.

**************************************/

Water splashing everywhere, drowning the floor, drowning her. She floated down the river in a glow of mist and steam. Tilla Stevens walked down 18th Street with steps slowly gaining agility, tense and eager simultaneously. She stretched her arms and body, slowly, painfully turning it supple once more. She needed to be agile and dangerous, needed it badly, she knew that, knew that well. Her clothes were a mix of practicality and fashion, seemingly clinging to her body, but yet loose and easy to *move* in. Her attention, even though constantly directed forward, in the direction she was headed, wandered back and forth.

The heat, pretty bad earlier in the week had gained a few more notches on the thermometer today, a pervasive humidity penetrating her being on all levels. She wore a sweatband, helping keeping her wild, fiery mane in place. She had braided the unruly red hair in a plait down her back, knowing fully well she looked both attractive and dangerous. She smiled, in anticipation and anxiety.

She spotted the sign ahead and stopped a bit, short of breath, before crossing the street.

THORNTON CHANDLER: CARS NEW AND USED.

A man walked towards her, towards the same goal, from the opposite direction.

Stewart.

She stopped a bit. He kept walking, passed by the shop entrance. And they met on the corner. She blushed, knew that he, with his experience easily noticed the lines of exhaustion in her face, even under the well crafted makeup. Damn him.

– Hello, he greeted her.

– Hello, she replied casually.

– It was fortuitous I met you. He nodded as he smiled. He was or could be very charming. – I have wanted to talk with you for a long time.

– Okay, she said lightly. – Ted isn't done for the day for a few minutes yet, so… fire away.

She smiled, too, very charming and enticing.

– About Mike, he said. – About your time with him.

There was a shadow passing before the Sun, and the shadow cast by the building, shadowing them turned even deeper. When she spoke, there was hardly any… unevenness in her voice at all.

– My time with Mike? He could have raped me right there on the floor without anyone noticing or caring.

– That was then, Stewart said, clearly impatiently, uncaring. – But you knew him before… before the ball started rolling. What made him tick?

And she was startled to hear the flutter in his voice. He was involved. Somehow he was involved.

– I remember when it… happened, when he *crossed over*. She said.

– There had been small signs, for a while. He insisted that Ted should play the villain at the theater. He seemed to be obsessed about it. Everybody joked about how he seemed to enjoy killing Ted every night.

– But the day he met the big bully in a fight… and vanquished him everything Changed. I remember it clearly. It looked like he was crushing him with his look, before proceeding to beat him to a pulp.

– Perhaps that in itself set him off, I don't know. To this day I don't know what did.

– And what about you? Stewart asked.

– I was very eager to perform, to do exactly what I believed Mike wanted of me, Tilla whispered. – I so much craved his attention, his approval. I thought I was a woman, but I was only his child. And to this day I can't stop feeling ashamed, to the depths of my being.

There had never been any kind of official investigation into the incidents three years ago. She had never been charged with anything. He saw he had shaken her, like he had wanted to do.

– And his gang? You broke with them, didn't you?

– Yes, she said, drying a tear, unable to tell if it was real. – I told them, in no uncertain terms that I never wanted to have anything more to do with them.

– Must have been tough on you.

Tilla didn't reply. Not with words.

On the other side of the street a biker walked by. Tilla froze. He looked like he was doing his Sunday stroll. The guy didn't look at them, didn't cast a single glance in their direction. He didn't look like he was doing anything but coincidently passing by.

– I can post guards outside your home, he said. – There is something to be said for being in an influential position.

– No, she smiled bravely and shook her head. – I'll manage. I can take care of myself.

– Tough girl, he said softly. – Don't want help from anybody, huh?

She glared sullenly at him, vulnerable as china.

– So, did Mike kill Erasmus Coogan?

And her reply to his sudden pointed question came in an instant, without thought, without deceit.

– No. And then she thought about it, and shook her head, and said again: – No! He wouldn't do that, especially not without telling me afterwards in gruesome details. Telling me, telling Ted. And he wanted information from Ezra. It wouldn't make any sense. And he wasn't like that, anyway. He wasn't a cold-blooded murderer. When he killed that lady three years later he did so in a murderous rage. And he didn't deliberately kill the other guy, the shooter either.

She was laid bare, cut open like a leaf in the wind. She hated him.

He wanted to put a comforting hand on her shoulder, couldn't help it. He knew about the suppressed fear she carried. He had felt it himself.

A long time ago…

– But he was a dominating, brutal bastard, right?

He said.

– Yes.

She said.

– You wanted to see him crawl in the mud because he dominated you in absolutely everything, and brutalized you any chance he got, but you didn't want him to die. If it had been possible you would have sacrificed your own life to prevent that. So much did you love and hate him.

In monotony:

– So much did I love and hate him.

Stewart wanted to say more, but suddenly he straightened, and something changed in his eyes. Then they heard it, the sharp sound of metal against metal. Loud voices erupted from the yard behind the building. They looked at each other and started walking towards… the disruption. Both recognized Ted's voice, and more: they recognized its growling, distorted form.

They entered the yard, and saw Ted Cousin hold Thornton Chandler by the collar, pushing him at the fence, and sensed the fence and Chandler shake in terror.

Ted released him, suddenly very calm, wiping his hand, as if he had just touched something vile.

– See the *blood* reveal itself. Chandler voice was thick in a sickly triumph. – Look at you, more beast than man. You don't fit in anywhere in the civilized world.

– My friends and sister would have been proud of such a label, and so am I.

Chandler shrank under the truth of his words, the conviction resting deep within the fiery eyes. Tilla felt a catching in the throat.

– You look at me as if I am a wild animal, and I am. One who is staring back at your pale complexion with contempt and abandon.

Chandler straightened his collar, straightened himself, turning towards the two recent arrivals.

– You saw what happened. I expect you to do something about it, Lieutenant.

– I saw what happened, Stewart grinned. – I saw nothing.

The salesman's jaw dropped. He turned mute as rain. There was just the background noise, the soft roar as the drops hit the ground. And it was distorted, disharmonic, twisted.

Ted picked up his jacket from a chair, and the three of them left. Thornton Chandler remained on the spot Ted had left him, staring at their backs with glaring hatred.

– What happened in there? Tilla wondered, using the opportunity to put a hand, in a comforting gesture on Ted's shoulder.

– I sacked him, Ted grinned wildly. – I think that aggravated him to no end. He had so looked forward to sacking me one day, after he was through hassling me.

He was upset. She could easily see that. Not because of the event itself, but because he knew Chandler was right. He would never fit in.

– The fucker is a typical «employer». Ted shook his head. – I don't understand how people can take it every day, every day of their miserable lives.

– We all must, must we not? Stewart's voice had a light, ironic tone.

The two looked at him, wondering.

– They don't, Tilla said, clutching Ted's hand. – You can see it in their eyes. They claim feverishly to be content, even pleased with their pallid existence, but you can see the wounds, the suffering in their eyes, in the very way they carry themselves. They just keep lying, also to themselves, about the *horror* that is their «life».

The passion in her voice shook the man and the boy.

– You get killed for living. Ted nodded. – This society kills you just for living. No one sees the whole picture. No one is whole. We're mere shards, pieces of what we can be.

He touched the girl's cheek in a brief, anxious move. She looked at him with hope and tears in her eyes.

– What happened in there…

– Yes? She prompted him.

– It doesn't mean shit. If it hadn't happened today it would have happened soon. And I'm *glad*. The worst scenario would have been if it had never happened.

– And now you're free? Stewart said quietly.

The red flare that never failed to amaze the Lieutenant appeared in the boy's eyes. It faded when he slowly, firmly nodded.

– It is getting late. Stewart looked at the girl. – Do you want me to follow you home, Tilla?

– I don't think that will be necessary. Tilla suddenly smiled roguishly. – Ted will do that, won't you, sweetheart?

– Y-yes…

– Oh, you're such a sweet boy, Teddy. Thank you.

She gave him a wet kiss on the cheek.

They both looked at Stewart. He smiled, seemingly unconcerned.

– You two run along. Don't think about me. Don't consider my feelings…

They returned the smile, clearly uncertain, undecided.

He saw them go, saw them disappear around a corner. He wanted to follow them. With a major effort, a degree of control he wasn't sure he possessed, he steered his feet in the opposite direction.

He whistled while walking home. People smiled when they heard it… until they saw his face. He didn't notice.

It wasn't far. Not really. To the red-painted house somehow different than all the similar houses around it.

Jean met him in the door, kissing him, welcoming him like a good wife.

They walked inside, seemingly in heated embrace. He closed the door behind them. And then she really kissed him, clinging to him as if drowning. She sensed it immediately, the reluctance in him. She disengaged herself from him. He looked around, saw the shotgun by the door, the Stengun by the kitchen drawers. The house was full of weapons, and yet, he knew it would probably not be sufficient.

She looked at him, and there was determination and fear in her eyes.

– It has begun, he said.

*******************/

A while later the two youths stopped outside the gate to Tilla's place. The house was painted red, just like Stewart's, and was located in a cluster of poplars. Ted… liked it.

– Any idea what's riding Stewart? Tilla wondered.

– On some level I do. On another I don't. He, too, is keeping secrets from us. It isn't over. Mike was right. The world is our enemy.

She kissed his hand, in fear, in need.

They stood there for a while, just talking. Darkness descended on the area. The trees shadowed the streetlights. It made it even harder to spot the figures hidden in the shadows, and Ted wasn't paying attention anyway.

– Will you join me inside? The girl asked quietly.

– Not tonight, he said, rejecting her. – I've got a lot on my mind.

– So have I, she pointed out.

She nodded, but still attempted to grab his hand. He shook himself loose, and rushed down the road, away from her. She opened her mouth to call him back, but changed her mind with a sigh. It was complicated. He was complicated, far more so than Mike had been.

He walked fast and didn't look back. He didn't want to, want to change his mind. Then he stopped. After walking straight out almost down the entire street he finally stopped, breathing hard, as if he had been running. He looked back. He stood there, for a while, indecisive. She had walked inside, but had yet to turn any lights on. He heard the wind whistle in the treetops, saw her move inside, fumble on the wall for the light switch.

And he saw movement outside the house. He really saw it. He didn't imagine it. Most other people wouldn't have seen shit. But he was able to discern variations in the shadows, shapes moving, only slightly different from the dark background. The streetlights were like blinding suns, but he didn't see them. His entire attention was locked on the figures moving in the shadows. He waited for her to turn on the lights in the house. It didn't happen. Sweat protruded on his skin. He actually felt it break through, pushing itself into the fresh air. He crouched there, in the street, looking down on his hands, his clenched fists.

He charged forward, started running like the wind. His feet touched the ground, but there was no sound. He didn't really think, but registered everything with his senses anyway. There was no conscious reasoning, but his brain constantly processed information. He saw two leatherjackets outside, guards. They didn't see him. There was no one guarding the backdoor. They didn't bother with that. Rage rose in him, and now he welcomed it. He ran into the house with savage anger burning in his eyes.

From the bedroom he heard loud moans and excited voices. *Pigs.*

The door in there stood ajar. What he saw made him glow. Four men were about to tie Tilla to the bed. Blood flowed from a wound on her forehead. She still had her clothes on, but they were not more then shreds, really. The look of her naked skin made him see everything through a red haze. He recognized Keith Lampard. Ted's remaining reason evaporated, and he fell straight into the waiting trap.

The moment he charged forward and into the room he realized his mistake. He saw the triumph, the glee in their faces, and knew they had expected him. Desperately he twisted his body, in the hope of avoiding the knock on the head. Fireworks exploded in his eyes. He was hit right by his left ear, and took a hard fall as he hit the floor. He tried to move, but nothing worked. Everything had turned to jelly.

– We expected you, Lampard gloated. – And you were just as easy to fool as we expected you to be.

The words penetrated Ted's foggy mind. He wanted to cry in despair and shame, but nothing worked.

He was brutally pulled on his feet. There were more hits to the ribs, knocking the breath out of his lungs. Light taps. They were playing with him. He tried to focus through the thick hair covering the eyes. It did no good. His vision was foggy even excluding the hair.

– We could kill you now, one snarled. Ted recognized Ray Channon's rat-like face. The biker stood there with a stick in his hand. There was blood on it. – But we want to play a bit with the little king, and display you every time the Red Queen gets ideas, stupid ideas of independence and escape.

– Did you hear that, stupid bitch? Lampard slapped Tilla on her left cheek. – If you don't do exactly as we desire, if you fail to *please* us, the boy will pay.

– Don't worry, Tilla whispered. – I'll be good, be a good girl.

She smiled to Lampard and spread her legs. It was a sick smile, completely devoid of spirit.

Ted gasped and gasped. He tried in vain to whip up a storm of rage inside, to make the body, the useless body move and act. Boy… they saw him as a boy.

– Too bad she got so little clothes left, Channon giggled. – It won't be that fun to se her strip.

In one single move Ted pulled himself free from the two holding him. He hit one with an elbow, hit him hard, and kicked Lampard in the groin.

Ted lost it then, lost it completely. There was a red haze and a lot of mangled bodies, screams and the sound of flowing blood. He could hear that, above everything else.

Shortly afterwards the room resembled a battlefield, a slaughterhouse. Two of the bikers writhed in pain on the floor. Ted had only remains of clothes left on his body and major wounds seemed to appear from nowhere. His head went thud thud thud thud, and everything was just rage.

– HOLY SHIT, one of the bikers on the floor shouted, as he crawled as fast as he was able across the floor. He jumped up, jumped through the window, straight through the glass, and pieces of it stuck in his skin as he ran from the place in utter, complete panic.

The three bikers still standing jumped at Ted from all sides. The largest struck him on the jaw and before he could regain his balance Lampard kicked his feet away from under him. He fell hard, but managed in the last moment to roll away from the foot striking the floor close to his head. He grabbed it and twisted it around, using the full force of his muscles. It pleased him to hear the naked howl of pain. He shouted in savage joy.

– Let's get out of here, Channon breathed. – Somebody might have heard the noise.

Three of them ran as fast as their legs could move. Lampard couldn't get that far because of the injured foot. He pushed himself against the wall, drawing a switchblade, with an insane expression of hatred in his face. A pale wind compared to the Storm attacking him, attacking him and tearing him to pieces. Lampard made a threatening move, but before he even managed to stab Ted Cousin was over him, hitting and kicking wildly. A fist hit him and sent him at the other window. His arm went through the glass, and he screamed aloud when the shards penetrated the skin. Ted grabbed the arm, and pushed and pulled it back and forth over the shards. The scream turned to a whine, a howl from a lost soul. The knife slipped from the destroyed hand. Ted grabbed him in the collar and hit him hard in the abdomen. A gurgling gasp and he became nothing but a ragged doll in Ted's arms. Ted hit him in the head. He hit him again. And again. There was no regret anymore. For the first time he felt no regret. He pulled Lampard by the collar to the front door, and pushed the helpless bundle of a man down the steep stairs. The feared leader of the leatherjackets stopped abruptly by its base and lay still.

– This is just a TASTE, Ted shouted to them, the children running from the bogeyman. – If I see you again I'll *kill* you on *sight!* I'll take you to a dark place and you will *beg* for death.

He meant it. He knew that with himself when he saw the bikers support their leader away from there, beaten and afraid of the dark. If he had had a weapon in his hand there would have been five dead people around him now.

And it felt good.

He stood there, at the top of the stairs, he did so for a long time, attempting to control the chaos released in his body and soul, until he didn't give a fuck anymore. The confrontation he had waited for, expected had finally come. He wondered what to do about it. There was no way he would go home. Linda's knowing eyes, and the stepparents' inquiring glances was more than he could take right now. Slowly he walked back inside, closed the door and locked it.

He locked every door in the house, all the way to the bedroom, until he stood in the doorway to the disaster area of a room. Tilla was still in bed, wearing the torn t-shirt and skirt. She had freed herself from the ropes, but made no attempt to cover herself. She just lay there, staring at him, half scared, half curious - and waited. Now the waiting was done.

– No more running, he said hoarsely.

He wasn't exactly a pretty sight when walking to the bed, but Tilla didn't care. A shaking hand touched her cheek, briefly, an act speaking volumes to her.

– Don't worry, she whispered. – I want it. I want it bad.

He went down on his knees. She went up on hers. She smiled, spreading her legs, kissing his wounds, carefully touching his swollen skin.

– I'll make you forget, she whispered, didn't have to say anything more. – At least for a little while.

He kissed her on the lips. It hurt. He kissed harder. She returned the kiss.

– It will be good, she whispered. – So good, so good…

She lay down on her back, never taking her eyes from him.
There was a spark inside him, growing to an inferno. He
wanted to put it out, he wanted to fan the flames… and he did.
He fell on her body, feverishly eager. It was just like three
years ago, as if everything between the two moments had never
happened, but it had. She grabbed his head. Holding onto it,
kissing him wildly on the lips, spreading her thighs, pushing
her hips against his. She smiled. They drowned there on the
bed, in boundless desire and the inferno of sparks filling their
every aware moment.

*****************/

The warm and soft summer wind brushed the poplars
surrounding the cemetery. There were birds. They heard the
flapping of wings.

– They did it before we entered, Tilla said.

– Huh?

– The birds flew over the graves before we arrived, she
emphasized.

– The ravens still do, Ted said.

– Now… and nevermore.

As she joked Tilla sensed the sudden cold, as if it was
something physical, something solid.

The two youths stood by a grave. On the gravestone was
engraved a simple text:

MICHAEL COUSIN 1952 - 1971

They had put a large bouquet of white flowers on it. The
priest, seemingly tending his roses often cast worried glances
their way. Perhaps on their very visual wounds, the still fresh
lesions in their faces, perhaps not.

– This is my first time here, Ted said slowly.

– My love, Tilla said lightly, – the last few years you haven't
really been anywhere. Be glad it's over.

– I am, he insisted. – And it is over.

They stood there in silence for a few minutes more. Then they
left, arm in arm. They returned to the little red-painted house,
hardly even conscious of the walk through the streets, the bus
drive back to downtown.

There was still no glass in the two bedroom windows. The
living room had a huge window facing the busy street, and

there were no curtains. So, they moved upstairs. There was only one large room there, some chairs, a table and a couch.

She looked at him, curiously. There was an expression there he still didn't get.

– So, what shall we do today? (She whispered seductively).

– I don't know. Visit the museum perhaps…

She didn't take the bait, but continued to look at him. He confessed to himself that it made him clearly uncomfortable. She spoke, with her hands on her hips.

– You do realize that finals are on Monday, and that all the other cute schoolchildren are at home studying, working their butts off.

– Yes, I guess so. He smiled.

– It doesn't matter to me, though, she stated very matter of fact. – I don't plan on attending.

– Neither do I. What a coincidence.

Suddenly they were once more close, very close.

– I guess when such dignitaries like Byron, Shelley, Swinburne, Crowley and even Tennyson, that *bore* left school without taking a degree, so can we…

– I'll leave soon anyway, she said, – So I've got no use for the shit. Not that anyone has, but I have even less use for it.

– I've thought about leaving, too, you know.

– I know, she said cheerfully.

– Nothing is keeping us here, he said. – Let's leave.

He took her hand, and now he made her uncomfortable with his direct, staring look.

– There's an entire world out there, he said, – where we can be ourselves, where we don't need to pretend.

– We don't feel differently from others, only stronger, she said softly. – And that certainly does not sit well with the rest of the present-day world, a place where the showing of passion is considered an aggressive act.

She met his eyes.

– They'll never truly accept us, but it doesn't truly matter, Tilla said. – What others feel about a person is, in the final analysis, unimportant.

And that felt so right, so right that he couldn't even express his agreement.

– It's strange. He laughed loud and hard. – I think one of Mike's problems was that he couldn't deal with that, deal with the fact that he was different, that others would always look at him as different, no matter what he did or didn't do. So, he compensated, and compensated, until he could do nothing else.

Sorrow and rage warred in his voice.

– My adoptive parents had to be close to lobotomized, he said calmer, matter of fact, – to not realize what was going on… if they were not hiding something, not doing some serious role-playing. Linda is convinced they are, but she doesn't really care.

– There's a mystery, Tilla willingly conceded, – concerning our lives, all our lives.

Words… Words were thrown back and forth. And somewhere there… was meaning.

– He could rant on, rant on for hours at the time, she said shivering. – About his visions.

His visions, Ted thought.

– I don't know why, but I… recorded it.

– You… recorded it? Ted said perplexed.

She walked to the closet in the corner and found a small tape recorder. She put it on the table. It was a battery model. She pushed the play button. Ted heard the voice from three years in the past and he started shivering, too. And then hearing the words and the way they were said he started shaking.

– *I saw everything. I saw The Phoenix rising.*

And he couldn't stop, and she couldn't avoid seeing it.

– You find it unnerving, she stated, pulling close to him, as she started stroking his hair. – I do, too.

There was more than one sentence, but that one sentence cut him deep, and he couldn't understand why.

– Let's get out of here. He started walking around aimlessly, clearly distressed.

She turned off the recorder.

– The jungle telegraph has probably already made sure everybody knows. They're probably on their way already, and I can't… take that right now.

She kissed him on the neck, calming him.

– What about a weekend mountain trip? She fingered with his

collar. – An extended trip, extending well into the week. We'll kill more than two birds with one stone…

– Yes, he said, staring out of the window, staring at the mountains. – I can see it, see it before my eyes…

Once it was decided, the second they decided everything shifted and changed around them.

And it was like the floor wasn't there, the stairs weren't there, the walls faded into thin air.

They couldn't see Denver anymore. Surrounding them was nothing but rocks, rocks and rocks. Sweat had made their t-shirts transparent long ago. Tilla had left the bra at home. She displayed herself willingly, proudly.

His wounds still hurt, and the headache didn't go away, but it didn't really affect him much. He couldn't, wouldn't take his eyes off her. This was no dream. This was a no kid's fever dream. They were together, finally and forever.

They had been walking and occasionally running for hours, but they didn't really feel the fatigue. They moved forward, driven by the bright and dark fire inside.

She walked and jumped on the trail before him, eager and cheerful like a little girl, performing for him, reminding him of the happy twelve-year-old she had been.

– Martial Arts are about balance, not only in body, but also in mind, and the necessary imbalance of it all. That's not exactly like the teacher, the Sensei teaches it, though, but my… free interpretation of it. I know well, like he does, like he won't reveal that there's a necessary darker side to it, than the so-called popular, «non-violent» self-defense. He speaks about balance, not about imbalance, about harmony, not disharmony. He isn't aware of the finer points, of the shades of gray… of the Shadow.

He reveled in watching her move, strike and kick the air, as if it was solid, tangible. She attacked him, and he barely managed to avoid her blow, to counter the attack, instinctively striking out, hitting her on the jaw. She went down, like a fallen tree.

– See what I mean, she grinned, shaking the dizziness from her head, drying the blood flowing from her mouth. – His claim is that finesse will beat brutality. We know both that that is horseshit. He would probably have fainted if he had seen you and Mike fight.

She smeared the blood on his cheeks, painting lines and symbols. He felt it, felt the fluid burn his skin. She grabbed his t-shirt and pulled it over his head, and painted some more.

– These are symbols of your stature, of your power. Betty taught me them once.

– Betty?

– Yes. Tilla giggled. – I tell you, she may behave like a mouse, but inside she's much more a roaring tiger…

He saw a pair of green eyes couple the gray, and during one, brief instance the faces seemed to dissolve and flow into one.

She loosened his pants, pulling them down his thighs. Her smile widened, the haze thickened in her eyes. He was hard and full.

– Turn around, she said huskily.

– What…? Fairly disoriented he felt like he was dreaming.

– Turn your back to me, she insisted.

He did, clearly irritable, impatient. He heard her laughter as she ran away, the sound of her undressing. The low sounds of clothes ripped off soft skin reached him like growls of thunder.

– You can come now. She called to him, a siren on the stormy sea.

And he replied.

She wasn't hard to find. Her clothes showed him the way, to the big rock and beyond… and then he stopped.

There was a pond there, on basically what was rocky ground. He sensed the heat under his soles, as he walked, as he hardly knew where he was going, as he was more aware of where he was headed than ever before in his life.

She was swimming back and forth in the pond, staying low in the water. Hardly more than her head was visible. Her body was merely suggested under the shiny surface.

– Come, she called.

– I don't see much of what may make me want to move, he called back.

With her eyes locked in his and crossed arms covering her chest she rose. Water wasn't really that deep that close to the shore. Even her thighs were above the surface. She looked like a golden statue where she stood, showing off for him, slowly letting her hands fall. She turned, revealing her limbs, her forms, her everything. He swallowed hard, and he felt pain down below, pain so sweet, so sweet.

The insecurity and distrust ruling him until a few days ago, would have kept him from surrendering to her wiles then. Now nothing kept him back. He stepped forward, took the plunge, into the water, into its depths. He touched her wet shoulders and she touched him in return.

– You're so free, she sang. – You're a different person. I can feel it. I feel so free, so free with you.

She grabbed him, pulling him with her out onto the depths.

– Let's dive to the bottom. She enticed him eagerly.

A splash and she vanished below the surface. He followed her, watching her while she swam deep, deep below. It was deeper here than he would have thought. He watched her fire, her life down below, and it was as if his pain, both within and without faded away in the undercurrents, turning insignificant.

The water pushed against him from all sides, soft as velvet. She reached the bottom and grabbed two fairly heavy rocks, much lighter in the water, enabling her to stand straight in the pond bed without floating back up. The water was so clear here. It seemed like they could see forever. They could see the walls, but Ted… when he squinted his eyes imagined he was able to see beyond that, see… more. Images on a gray wall, flashing in colors and fire, wings dancing on that wall, in the deep night surrounding it.

He grabbed two stones, too, walking towards her, having a bit of trouble keeping his balance. It felt strange. It was easier to fly then to remain on the ground. Dizzy for a moment he almost lost his footing. They met there at the bottom of the pond, the life-giving well, and they kissed. Lips met and stayed in contact. They stood there, breathing in and out, into each other. One of their eyes was right by the other's other, and they stared into the infinity inside the other human being, gasping for breath, breathing easily through the soft, soft air tunnel.

She wriggled her butt, pushing her groin at his. He stood slightly bent, to keep his head at her level. One involuntary, voluntary push and suddenly, shockingly he was inside her. They pushed, they pulled, and then they lost their footing. The stones fell from their hands and landed at the bottom with a dull crack, as they rose towards the surface tangled in each other's arms.

They broke the surface, laughing heartily, uncontrollably, *euphorically*. They splashed water on each other in a storm of movement and energy. Their arms fell to rest in the water and they floated once more towards each other, becoming one body as they embraced and floated towards the shore. They stumbled on land, falling flat after a few steps on a piece of soft grassland. He grabbed one of the breasts, fondling the shockingly red nipple on the dark skin. She wasn't as dark-skinned as he was, but clearly darker than her cousin Betty. He was inside her once more, unable to remember when he had entered her. She pushed him further inside with a foot on his butt, inpatient, lovingly. Her thighs tightened around him, tightened hard. She kissed him on the neck, where the scar was, the scar from the fire. He was thinner now, than he had been three years earlier, mirroring the tired lines in his face. She stroked his muscles, less visible, but just as hard, hidden under skin, hairy skin.

The wet skin seemed to explode in dry heat, as their movements turned rapid and the volcano erupted from its long dormancy. Muffled screams, muted by lips buried in skin, echoed softly between the mountains.

They rested on that spot, in the warm, snake-like grass, exhausted and happily satisfied.

– It's so strange, he said dreamily. – The aquatic breathing… it was like I could actually *feel* it.

– I felt it, too, she said. – Like we could have been under forever. The mole on my leg burned.

She pulled up the leg, touching the characteristic birthmark.

– It does mean something, doesn't it? She asked carefully. – Mike was… right?

– It does mean something, he nodded, suddenly frustrated. – I saw Maria's leg in the swimming pool, of course. I wasn't consciously aware of the mole, of its significance, but subconsciously… I guess I was. Now, thinking about it I know Linda has had hers for as long as I can remember, since birth probably, and I guess you have, too.

– And you have dreams, Tilla said quietly. – You twist on the bed, and you cry out in your sleep.

He didn't nod. He didn't move, but he still replied.

– Sometimes I believe I can see the Tapestry, he whispered, – the Tapestry unfolding. But then a vast and dark abyss opens up beneath me, and all is lost. I stare into the night, at what I'm becoming.

She kissed him, attempting to comfort him.

He returned the kiss, touching her wet cheek.

– Deep in the desert of your eyes I can see life.

She nodded, tearful.

– We will find the fire in the darkness, she stated, a catching in her voice. – We will find the world.

They started kissing again, slowly needy, desperately, sweetly.

A grin spread on his face, transforming it. She looked inquiringly, and also a bit pointedly at him.

– It's strange, he laughed. – I feel watched. We're outdoors, but still. Here, in the middle of nowhere I feel we're being watched.

– We're alone here, she whispered. – Alone here, too. Alone isn't necessarily bad.

She grabbed his cock, abruptly, shockingly. He hardened, and drew air into his lungs in a swift, involuntary breath.

– And I wouldn't care, not anymore, if we fucked right in the middle of 18th street. I love you.

He wanted to say something, to reply to her, and he did, sort of, pushing himself at her, making her cry out in joy. His worry faded in her smile, in her heat. There was a flash somewhere, outside, inside, as the world turned white, turned Shadow, and he drowned in her pond.

Chapter sixteen

There was a full moon this night. No clouds in the sky and the stars flared like thousands of tiny lights. The silver light made the ghostlike landscape outside supersede the modest lighting inside.

Everybody moved. Ted Cousin noticed it all from the couch where he sat by Tilla Stevens' side. There was music somewhere, even though he couldn't say from where. The house was big, even bigger than he had previously experienced it.

– We're being watched, Tilla grinned.

He shrugged, returning the grin. Everybody watched them, and they would have done so whatever the two of them did or didn't do.

– Let them, he stated. – Let them watch.

He charged her like a wolf, snarling as he kissed her lips. They both started laughing wildly as they tumbled down on the couch, snuggling and thoroughly embracing the moment.

And in the enormous living room in the house Frank Forester had been given by his parents to use, all eyes turned towards them and looked.

There were just a few bikers present this time and none of the more obviously violent members like Keith Lampard and Roy Channon. The leatherjackets present were mostly teenagers, and there were fewer than usual, and they all stared at Ted with stark fear in their eyes.

The party was quieter, and people weren't spread out on several floors. Almost everybody stayed on one floor and within the living room.

– Some show those two are making, John said helplessly to Linda.

He felt obliged to at least say something.

– Ain't that the truth, she snarled. – If they just would undress each other, too, the picture would be complete…

With her head held high she left him there, left him hanging. Boiling with a rage she didn't understand she set out to leave, leave the party altogether. Frank snatched her by the entrance.

– May I have this dance? He asked her lightly, totally lacking the stuck-up tone he usually used.

She shrugged, forcing herself to smile at him, even though she didn't really feel up to it.

People change, she thought.

– I and Ted belong together, she stated with absolute calm and sincerity.

She didn't really speak to Frank, even though he was right in front of her.

No matter what her reason told her she still felt small and betrayed. Frank was made to feel that, in every accentuated movement, step she took on the smooth dance floor. The shame she felt over the way she treated him made her feel even worse.

Frank wasn't that bad. Not anymore. He had indeed changed. The irrational rage made her impossibly astute. It was as if she could read everything happening in the room. She saw she wasn't the only one keeping eyes on the lovebirds. She saw Glory, Glory Burns look at them. Betty did, too. And Bob, not the least Bob, that sneaky shit.

Poor Linda, always alone, Tilla thought, without malice. She knew nothing about Linda and Linsey that night in Washington DC.

To Ted it was as if the entire room was spinning, only more so the moment he and Tilla came up for a bit of air.

– What is it? Tilla asked, noticing his distress instantly.

He didn't even try to deny anything. She knew him too well. It was as if they had always been together.

– It's like we… aren't here, he said slowly. – Like none of us or almost none of us are. Not in this room, but one smaller, with walls of wood and carpets.

He shook his head.

– It just doesn't make sense.

– It's the cabin, Betty said.

The two on the couch shook in shock. They stared at the girl, the girl appearing from nowhere.

– You see, she stated. – See who will be in the cabin, and who will not. You see the tribe, the future us, those of us bound by fate and circumstances, those here who will leave this wretched place and never return.

She was beautiful, radiant, completely changed. At that moment she looked exactly like Tilla and Tilla like her. Gray and green eyes flashed in the air in front of him.

– Everything is set. Betty called out, for everybody to hear. – The Gypsy is ready to do her thing.

The noise persisted for a little while longer. The hushed whisper of expectation slowly shut everybody up. Betty turned her back to the couple on the couch, heading for the stairs.

Ted noticed Tilla's stare, smelled her cold sweat.

– Betty isn't using contact lenses, right?

– No, she isn't, Tilla replied. – Her eyes are green and mine are gray, and no, we're not identical twins.

– What is it between the two of you, anyway? He asked casually.

– Nothing, she replied, just as casually.

– You hate her, don't you?

She turned and stared at him, with insanity burning in her eyes.

– Do you love me? She asked.

– Yes, he responded taken aback.

– Then you will never speak about it or ask me to speak about it *again,* do you hear me?

He wanted to say something, something intelligent and kind, but he couldn't bear himself to do it. Petrified he could do nothing but nod like an idiot.

– If you don't want to speak about it we won't speak about it, he assured her, after a long, uncomfortable silence.

He kissed her, embraced her. Slowly, only slowly her rigid body, her hard eyes softened.

– Tonight is a celebration, he insisted. – To us, and also to many others present. It is renewal and change.

– Renewal, she whispered. – Change.

– Listen, he said, fearfully, almost helplessly, grabbing her arm. Her expression remained rigid. – I didn't mean to question you, to doubt you. It's just that… something is about to happen, something important, I can feel it, feel it like ants crawling under my skin.

Her expression softened, too. She kissed him on the cheek, whispering comforting words in his ear.

Frank stood at the top of the stairs. How he had managed to get there without anybody noticing no one could say.

– LADIES AND GENTLEMEN, he shouted. – Tonight, we're in for a treat. Thalama, the Gypsy Queen will tell our fortune, she will show us our fate.

There was laughter, but also eagerness, as people rushed around the room and turned off the lights. It turned dark, dark in the fire of the illuminating candles.

Frank rushed down the stairs, joining the circle forming on the dance floor. The room turned quiet. Steps thundered silently over the floor. Not everybody joined the circle, but most did. They waited there, in cheerful anticipation.

Iris Carson beat the drum, the shaman drum. They didn't see her at first, only heard the drumbeat from the upper floor, reverberating through the building, through its floors and walls, joining the beat of their own hearts. Ted felt something. He saw the figure appear at the top of the stairs before she actually appeared.

Then everybody saw her. Veronica Greyson and Betty walked by her side, carrying torches. There was a strange dichotomy between the short, dark Vernie and the tall fiery Betty.

– Behold, Betty cried. – Behold she who walks in the wilderness.

There was snickering and snide remarks, but those few it originated from were quickly hushed up.

The three entered the circle, the circle in the sand, the dry sand whirling in the air, the dry hot, arid air. The torches were tied to sticks put on two small tables. Veronica doing it a bit clumsy, slow, Betty confident, quick, as if she had done this her entire life.

They sat down at its center. Everybody studied Iris, absolutely and helplessly fascinated. She was dressed in a kind of gypsy costume, but the hood on her head and the cloak embracing, hiding her body made her even more alien than that. Her hood and cloak were red. She was Red Riding Hood.

She spoke, and they listened.

– I won't tell your fortune or show you your fate. I'm a witch. A witch opens closed caskets, revealing worlds, bringing to the outside what's inside.

Ted felt strange, out of whack. Nothing seemed true, nothing seemed right. He looked at Betty. She and Veronica had joined the circle by now. Iris was alone at its center.

– Let go. Betty whispered in his ear. And then again, more intensively: – *Let go!*

Find what's hidden. Reveal it to the world.

– There's you and there's me, Iris sang. – I'm changing. You're changing. And we're changing the world. By the grail of hell, by the cauldron of heaven we mix what is and what isn't, a glowing pentacle in the sand, a nest of sticks and bones, and the world is revealed as it is, ashes and fire in the sand.

He saw one breast stick half out of her dress. He saw her red lips move, smothering the air. Blood let go and he was bathing in it, in the sea, the molten sea.

– She's *good* at this, a girl spoke up.

– We're going on a long Journey, Iris whimpered. – We'll meet a lot of dark men, dark women.

She had fallen into a trance, slipped into it, like an old worn hat.

He felt the stirring. He felt it, something rising from the deepest core of his being.

Suddenly he sat there, in front of her, legs crossed like hers. He couldn't recall moving.

– I'm Ouarda, Iris intoned. – I'm The Scarlet Woman.

He straightened, raising a fist above his head.

– I'm The Beast, the rough voice gave voice to the air. – I give myself power to rise from the sea, the molten sea. I give myself power. Not just for a thousand days, not merely one thousand years… But Forever.

The rush of hot wind moving through the room was tangible. Not just wind, but fire and night. He sensed it, sensed the metamorphosis take place. The terrible pain ravaged him, and he screamed.

He sat there, crouching, his face contorted in pain.

– And thus, everything is changed, she whispered.

And after having spoken Iris laid a circle of stones on the floor.

There was another pile. Ted reached for them and they moved of their own accord. Iris smiled playfully at him.

He looked at the people in the room. It was totally quiet now. Nobody spoke or disturbed the peace. Those in the circle had one hue, those outside another, not easily distinguishable from each other but There. He didn't think. Everything just happened. The stones levitated above their head. Iris laughed euphorically as she watched them circling them. They descended slowly, until they once more rested unmoving on the floor.

And the two of them rested, too, falling around each other's neck, kissing and snuggling, before Ted pulled back, the memory of her skin against his forever vivid in his mind. He was drowning in her needy, sensual smile.

He looked at the people in the circle, the shock, disbelief and downright suspicion in which they looked at the girl who dared to call herself a witch. Even in these enlightened times this was evidently a stretch. And what had happened, the monumental event that had taken place most of them just wrote off as a hallucination, a trick or something. Or they just wrote it off, because their *limited* minds just couldn't handle it.

Mark Stewart felt it, felt it in a thorough, pervasive way where he stood outside, outside in the ghostlike landscape looking in, watching it all. Sweat poured from his skin, all over his body. He hid in the bushes, silent as death, fairly far away from the window, the fairly small window giving him access to the insides of the Forester Minor Mansion, as it was called locally, derogatory, but still… it was as if he was close, very close, as if he found himself in there, among them, inside the circle. He had never experienced anything similar, anything even approaching similar. He felt the heat inside, the heat of ashes. He saw the strange light, something akin to St. Elmo's fire around Ted and the girl, what was her name… Suddenly he couldn't remember. He actually couldn't remember. And he was lost. He was fading there in the dark, and he wanted to scream.

Ted rose slowly. Iris did, too. She attempted to hold on to him, keep him in her sphere of smothering sensuality, but he let go of her, and walked to Tilla. She received him with a passion equal to, as unlimited as his own. The circle broke up, dissolved, and it was like dying. There were fleeting shadows all around him, and he realized startled that there were more shadows than there were actually people. He saw unknown faces, strangely familiar… and it…

– It hurts, Betty said. – I know. Being born hurts. And they who are not busy being born are busy dying.

Her eyes glowed like emeralds. Suddenly she was shockingly close, and he realized startled that she spoke to both him and Iris. And… in a strange way she faced the window, looking out, at the nothing there.

Mark Stewart spotted a shadow, one so much a part of the landscape that it was almost impossible to spot. It moved with the grass, the wind, the trees, but even so it moved, and one with Stewart's keen and trained eye spotted it easily. He recognized the figure easily, its face, its scarred face.

He moved and drew the Lugar in one fluid, forward motion.

– Freeze, he said, suddenly calm, even though the seething cauldron persisted inside.

His hand wasn't shaking. For one, fearful moment he had been afraid it would.

He didn't have to add anything to his order. The man stopped. He didn't exactly freeze, but he stood still. A professional. Stewart had only rarely encountered them, in spite of all his experience.

– May I turn? It will be easier having a sensible conversation that way.

The man spoke fluent English, without the slightest trace of foreign accent.

Stewart nodded. He didn't speak up, but had more than a feeling that it wouldn't be necessary.

The man turned, and Stewart finally stood face to face with Scarface, the Chinese he had only seen at pictures and through description.

– Ah, I thought that was you, Stewart. Or is that Fontaine? Or Julian Temple? We meet at last. My greetings from your friends, your… longtime friends in France.

Stewart sensed an ice-cold calm spread through his body. This wasn't unexpected. It was bound to happen sooner or later. The weapon didn't waver in his hand.

– But why the gun, Lieutenant? Have I done anything…

criminal, broken the law in some way or another?

– Well… *Chin,* isn't it? Stewart grinned. – At first, I wasn't entirely sure if I shouldn't just walk up to you and introduce myself, but that seemed pretty unnecessary, since you already know me, and because of that I think prudence is the better part of valor, wouldn't you agree.

It wasn't a question, and the other man didn't treat it as such.

– You look so much like your mother, Mark… your real mother, who has been dead for thirty-five years.

Stewart wanted to pull the trigger then, but he held back. The shock rattled him this time, rattled him bad. There was so much here, so much to learn. After all this time… After all this time… something finally happened.

Scarface said a name.

– How do you know? He shouted now, abruptly, not bothering to keep his voice low anymore. – My parents died during the Second World War, and even I only learned their names by a coincidence.

Memories from ruins, suffering and death assaulted him. He had hardly been more than a baby. He remembered. He concentrated so hard that the hand clutching the gun hurt.

– There are no coincidences, Mark. You should know that by now.

Ted heard the last two sentences. He stood close to the window, staring out, unable to decide if he should run outside or not.

– Oh, and by the way…

Scarface lowered his voice. Ted couldn't' hear him anymore, only see him move his lips. Betty, Tilla and Iris standing by his side did, too.

– Jack sends his regards.

The words hit Stewart like a physical blow. In one fluid move, swift as lighting Scarface jumped at Stewart and kicked him with both feet in the face. His first and only shot went awry, and then the gun was kicked out of his hand. Stewart managed just about to strike back, and force the opponent backwards. The Lieutenant shook his head, attempting to clear it. Chin did no attempt to pick up the gun, even though it had practically landed right there by his feet. This, to Stewart was an act speaking of an incredible confidence. The opponent balanced on his toes, in classic martial arts pose. Stewart wasn't fooled. Not anymore. This was a fighter who had far more going for him than classic martial arts.

Chin sent a hard-edged hand at Stewart's neck. If he had hit the target the fight would have been done before it had begun, but he missed. Stewart pulled the head away just in time and the other grunted when the hand hit the hard collarbone. But he still managed to elegantly avoid Stewart's fast-as-lightning fist.

Seconds passed, long as minutes, as they exchanged blows... sort of. Suddenly Stewart was hit by a deluge of fists and feet, while hardly hitting anything himself. Chin had simply increased his speed. Stewart saw stars and breathed heavily. He was furious, furious at himself for letting the training slide the last few years, since arriving in Denver. Jeff McCabe had recruited him, forcibly so, but still lulled him into a false sense of security. Which he now paid dearly for. Chin, even though he had some minor bruises looked completely unscathed. He was a machine, one of those fighters that was able to go on and on, for hours perhaps without tiring.

He stood there, grinning in his invincibility.

Stewart threw himself at him with the full force of his massive body behind the move, pushing him backwards, far backwards, through the large window Mike had thrown Jeffrey Cumbes through an eternity ago. They almost landed on Ted. The boy was pushed back and landed a few steps away from the violent fight. He, like the rest froze at the sight of the savage exchange of blows, and Ted realized that he witnessed something akin to what the others had when watching he and Mike dish it out, and he understood a bit more of what they had felt.

Stewart had succeeded in landing on top, and he took advantage of that, but it wasn't enough. An elbow in the chest almost finished him. Like a cat the opponent jumped to his feet and kicked out, hitting the big man right on the jaw. Stewart went down like a fallen tree and remained there. Ted studied the man with his burning eyes, signaling to Tilla. Here was one who had mastered both finesse and brutality.

Tilla attacked with her feet. Chin struck her and she was thrown far away. But that was just a diversion. Ted moved in in her shadow and struck with his left hand. Scarface was hit, but not hard enough, not remotely hard enough. He lifted Ted above his head, and threw him at the wall. Ted hit it hard and remained on the floor, shaking his head, struggling to fight off the paralysis.

– Old tricks, young Warren, the Chinese said. – You'll have to do better than that.

Ted managed to get up, much too late. A blink of an eye, and the man with the scarred face vanished, fading like a dream. Ted jumped out through the broken window, landed on the mound, looked around, seeing nothing, realizing the futility of it all, and walked back inside. The darkness and cold of the night moved back in with him. The short glimpse of the dragon-like face remained at the front of his memory.

Iris moved her lips, saying something. He couldn't tell what.

Everybody stared openmouthed at each other. Very few had moved at all the few seconds the small man had been in the house.

Linda knelt down by Stewart's side, anxiously checking his pulse. Nothing to it. He was knocked unconscious, that was «all».

– Will someone call the POLICE? Bob shouted, with shrill hysteria in his voice.

– Oh, what's point? Ted shrugged, drying blood from his cheek.

– Man is a cultural being, Bob said. – We should no longer be content to roll in the mud. The police are the representative of Law and Order in the world.

They stared at each other for a while, before Ted broke in laughter, a short, shrill laughter.

Stewart opened his eyes. They saw pain there, and rage.

– The police are already here, he said, in a somewhat failed attempt at levity. – And the boy is right. There's no use calling anybody. I'll file an extensive and detailed report.

They would have been quite surprised if they had known he had no intention of filing or reporting anything.

The glass, the window glass still danced in the air. Still shaken Stewart fought himself up. He was dizzy, but not really injured, not as he would define it anyway. Jean would take care of it.

She had taken care of him many times before.

– You shouldn't worry much, he told the youths. – This wasn't an attack, but more of an exercise in futility, a way of communicating, a way of saying things without really come straight out and say it.

Most of them stared incredulous at him, not understanding shit.

– The question is how much and what was communicated, Ted said, staring at him.

And Stewart wondered how much the boy had heard.

Ted followed him outside, to the mound, where the policeman found his gun, and down the road, on a path through the forest. Safely away from the others Stewart finally started speaking, at least a bit.

– Everything has been turned upside down again. Chin has no connection to Gidman or to what we witnessed in the mansion that night, at least not directly. He serves… other masters. I wanted you to know that.

In the bushes and the night, they stood rigid, watching the silver light from the moon spill across the other's face.

Ted didn't ask whom, and Mark didn't volunteer anything more.

– Have a nice trip, Mark said. – Enjoy yourself.

– Thank you, Ted said. – I will.

They nodded to each other, and Stewart walked off.

He turned once, the moment Ted reached the entrance and Tilla rushed to him, and they embraced. He saw them, for the last time.

*******/

Stewart headed straight home. His car was parked just a short walk from the mansion. He walked to it, constantly studying the surrounding terrain. He walked past it, to the nearest bus stop. The people on the stop looked completely normal, but he couldn't relax. He had stopped taking things at face value long ago, and just here, in Denver he had stopped taking anything at face value. Jeff McCabe had recruited him, almost threatened him into joining the force, implying that he would expose the fact that Stewart was a wanted man in France. And not for the first time Stewart wondered about the Chief's true motives for doing it.

The people at the bus stop stared at him, at his wounds. More to keep them from contacting the police than for any other reason he showed them his badge.

– The godless bastard got away, he grinned.

They returned the grin, looking extra hard at the badge, wondering if it had been stolen.

The bus finally arrived very late. He entered the bus. The driver shook his head when Stewart wanted to pay the fare.

– We don't charge cops on duty. The smile lit up his face like a Christmas tree.

He sat down. The seat was uncomfortable, way too small and narrow. His entire big frame of a body hurt. The bus floated on the silver moonlight towards the city. The sky was filled with dark clouds. He saw them through the ceiling. He heard the thunder.

And imagined he saw his car explode, blow up the moment he sat down inside it, turning the key.

That wasn't Gidman's style either. And not *his*. But it could very well be that of others involved in some way or another. This was a giant tapestry, a weave of unimaginable proportions, with many treads, many puzzles. He sensed it, sensed its vast size, in time and space.

He exited the bus at the corner of Eighteenth and Market, far from home. He walked the rest of the way, in a wide circle. It was past midnight and virtually no people outside. Most neighborhoods were usually quiet on a Wednesday, and the one with the red house were quieter than most. He approached the house from the front, walking normally, seemingly without a care in the world. The dark clouds now covered the entire sky. Jean had kept the lights on, as always. He swallowed hard, thinking about her.

He quietly unlocked the door, as he always did. The anxiety inside, never revealed on the outside crawled like ants under his skin. He drew the gun and walked straight to the bedroom. The bed was empty. It wasn't slept in.

– We're pointing two guns at sweet Jean's head. The voice, Peter Clarke's voice sounded completely casual, as if he was discussing the weather. – I want you to throw away your gun now, Mark.

There was a yelp, as he or the other struck Jean ribs. Stewart recognized his wife's voice. He threw away the gun, wondering bitterly if there was anything he could do, anything he could have done different. The bitter, hateful voice within told him once again, like it had so many times that Jean was his weakness, his weak link. The only chance he had at this point was to… to disregard her safety completely, and he wasn't prepared to do that.

– That's good boy. Take a slow walk, now, into your cozy little living room.

He obeyed, tense, preparing for any chance that might arise, a chink in their defenses.

Peter Clarke sat in the sofa, smoking a cigarette. By his side sat Jean, unconscious, bound hands and feet and with a fresh bruising in her neck. On her other side an unknown man pushed a barrel at her head.

– I will kill you, you know, Stewart said casually, very casually to Clarke.

– Not as long as I and Bernie here, hold a gun to your love's head, you won't, Clarke grinned.

He heard the heavy steps behind him, recognized them, as if they were his own, even if he had never heard them before. He turned and kicked out, merely able to glimpse the dark face, the giant body before a large hand swatted him, and sent him flying into the opposite wall.

– Here I am, Mark, back from the dead, in new and improved edition.

David Gidman, the man he had traveled around the globe to kill. And he had done it, too. Too bad he hadn't done the job properly. This was a David Gidman healthier than ever. Stewart easily recognized the face, even with the patch, but the body, the frame was so large that it looked like somebody had sewn the head on it. He was at least a head taller, and far, far bigger. He lifted Stewart like cordwood. A giant fist hit the Lieutenant in the ribs. The other clutching him around the throat, keeping him from breathing. Stewart was like a child in his enemy's hands.

– Do you know what a grave mistake you made, now?

Gidman snarled. – Do you?

Stewart was struck again, and thrown at the floor. He felt bad. His head hurt, and he hurt inside in a way he never would have believed possible. Pain, in all its complexities dominated his very being. He descended into a state of black, black despair, as he felt his hands were forced behind his back and nylon rope was tied around his wrists, arms and ankles, tied hard. Gidman lifted him up, without the slightest visible effort.

– I've become immortal, Mark. Kill me again, and I'll return stronger and better than before. Kill me a thousand times, and I'll rise again. Will you return from Death, like I did? I recommend it. There's nothing better in terms of an eye-opener. Before San Diego I would've said we're alike, that we're two of a kind, but now I don't think so anymore, I don't believe that at all. You're just a gnat to me, now, a pile of dust I leave behind.

He carried the large cop over his shoulder, easy as pie. Bernie carried Jean, and they walked outside, left the house, left any sense of normalcy the Stewart household had pretended to.

– I could kill you instantly. I'm tempted, but I don't just want to kill you, I want to disintegrate you, making you disappear, fade away, as if you've never existed. I could've killed you at any time all these years, but I wanted to wait, wait until everything was ready. I wanted you to know, to *suffer*.

– Don't kill Jean, Stewart gasped pathetically. – P-please…

– That's just my point, you stupid shit. I'm not gonna kill her, but she will beg me to do it, and you'll wish we had, once you get a chance to think about it.

No. *No.* He drowned in the black cloud. He knew what the bastard was hinting at. Knew!

– She will be mine, mine completely, like she always has been.

The bitterness overwhelmed Stewart. Now, when it was too late he realized fully what the Abraxas Omega or what the fuck they called themselves had in mind.

The car they stopped by was a black Ford. The color of death. With a skewed grin Clarke opened the hatch to the luggage compartment. The unconscious Jean was pushed in, and Stewart brutally made to join her.

– You weren't really surprised when I showed my true colors, Clarke stated. – I rather thought you wouldn't be. You've always been a sly bastard, and have probably been on to me, for some time. Still, you weren't *prepared,* and it will cost you. Perhaps you would want to know why I did it, why I «switched side»?

Stewart stared at him with burning hatred, saying nothing.

– I got a better offer.

The hard and accentuated laughter echoed in the quiet neighborhood.

– Enjoy the last few minutes of your life, Gidman said.

The hatch closed hard and not long afterwards the car started up, and they were all on their way. Stewart choked apathetic where he suffered on top of his wife, his beloved. He felt like a little kid again, and just as useful.

Think, he thought. Do.

And nothing happened. All kinds of thoughts whirled through his head, but nothing of value. Nothing. He choked again, and the hatred grew within him, rose above him like a magick cloud. Images, details ran through his fevered mind. He knew there was something there, but was unable to see it.

There was hardly room for two and it was tight as hell. Good. If they had been thrown in the back of a van or something Bernie the gunman, at least him would have been here, too, keeping them company, removing the last impossible chance. Bernie… something about Bernie…

He remembered. The flash on Bernie's hip, the knife. The hope, the hope of a hanging man. He had nothing now, nothing left to lose. In an insane rage he flexed his sore muscles, flexed them hard. There was nothing, no sign of the rope stretching. Exhausted and totally out of it he relaxed beside and on Jean's soft body. He cursed himself, mumbled the curses in a place deep inside, a place he had never before been able to reach, but now he penetrated deep within himself, touched parts of himself he hadn't known existed. He kept flexing his muscles, but it went far beyond that. It was as if… he was growing, as if the muscles swelled, as if his entire being swelled to become the space surrounding them, the entire car. He pulled and pulled and pulled. There was no thought anymore. He had become the pull, become the flexing, the iron hard force keeping him going. He hardly believed it at first, not until the rope fell off him, loosened around his body, soft as a spider's web. He shouted a silent cry of triumph and boundless hatred. Hands, arms and feet were bloody and sore when he collapsed, free at last. It hurt, hurt terribly. He embraced the hurt, the pain of power. Something had been released inside of him, something hidden, hidden no more. He stared at the wall, and what he stared at was desert sand and fire, a wall of fire. On one level he was exhausted, more so than ever before. On another he felt better, stronger, more powerful than he could have imagined at any time prior to this moment.

The car turned and entered a bumpy narrow road. He saw it, wasn't only experiencing it. Every new, major bump shook him to pieces. Blood flowed and made his hands wet and slippery. He was sweating, sweating profusely, as he dragged himself off and away from Jean, supporting himself on the wall, focusing on the only thing that mattered, David Gidman's death and total and final failure. He didn't think, didn't consider the odds, but acted in his head, acted out everything, every possible scenario in his thoughts, liberating himself from his useless body, the warm flow of blood in his veins making him soar and flex his wings.

Survival. Nothing else mattered. Nothing.

It was dark. Inside, outside. He hid the rope, hoping against hope that they wouldn't notice it was gone from his body. This Gidman, this monster had sounded supremely confident. Hopefully he was. He would kill them, slaughter them all. Everything was crimson in his mind. Nothing else mattered. Nothing.

The car stopped with a heavy pull. And he realized it had happened some time ago. Everything happened simultaneously. Time was now. He stared straight into David Gidman's eye. At his side stood Bernie, with a gun in his hand. And in Bernie's belt, half hidden by the jacket was the knife, the shining sword, his Excalibur to be. Clarke stood a bit further back, with his hands in his pockets, in a relaxed pose. He saw that Jean was awake, the boundless mire of despair in her clouded, no longer pretty eyes.

– Get up, Bernie snarled. – Dig your own grave. There is a ravine here with your name on. You're already dead, and you know it, don't you?

He lowered his eyes, hiding the fire in them. They laughed themselves shitless. Bernie grabbed his collar and pulled him close. Stewart grabbed his collar, grabbed the knife. It was no longer a thought, only movement, only action, only blood. He pushed the blade deep into the gunman's belly and twisted the metal brutally and deadly, gutting him like he would a pig. Pulling the blade back out. Bernie screamed very much like a pig would, and fell to the ground.

Gidman attempted to grab Stewart. Stewart ducked and stabbed. Gidman avoided it and jumped away, out of Stewart's immediate reach. Stewart threw the knife at him. With a sickening SWOP the blade was buried in the giant's chest. Stewart jumped at Clarke with a beastly snarl. Clarke's shot went haywire. Stewart struck him in the ribs, and all air wheezed out of his lungs. Stewart stumbled, one hell of a dead leg almost failing him. He swore. Clarke took a swing at him. Stewart managed to pull his head back, avoiding the brunt of the fist aimed at him. He grabbed Clarke's gunhand, pointing it at Gidman. Gidman, unbelievably enough had pulled the knife out and was about to get up. Stewart butted Clarke's forehead, and the other went limp in his grip. He pulled the trigger, shooting Gidman twice before taking a wild blow from Clarke in the temple, making him see stars. He lost his grip. Desperately he kicked the hand holding the gun, and the useless piece of metal fell to the ground. Clarke attacked him with a scream of pure rage, all of his refined sophistication gone. Stewart was pushed backwards. Suddenly he sensed nothing but air below his back and he stared down a deep ravine, standing on the precipice, the sight making dizziness dance before his eyes. He kicked desperately at Clarke, making him fly backwards through the dusty air.

Stewart jumped to his feet, and he knew, knew before he saw David Gidman, covered in blood with the big gun in his hand, supporting himself on the car. There was a crack. And then a whistling sound of a bullet not hitting anything. There was another crack. There was a loud, unnaturally high crack as

Stewart was hit, as he was pushed backwards without anything to hold on to. He attempted to regain his footing but there was nothing but empty air below him. There was one final glimpse, imagined or not, of David Gidman's face twisted in a triumphant grin, before he tumbled off the precipice. The scream was not one of fear, but of bitter disappointment and pure rage. The mountains shook under the boundless Wrath.

Gidman stumbled carefully towards the edge. Pain was written in his face, but a shocked beyond words observer would say he didn't really notice his wounds.

– That's my Mark, he said to the air, to the air itself. – A fighter to the end. If you, too, should come back from the dead, I know you will be a giant among insects.

Clarke managed to rise, clearly far more unsteady on his legs than Gidman.

– He almost got us, he gasped. – That FUCKING SHIT. I don't FUCKING BELIEVE IT

– Believe it, Gidman said. – This is the world as it is, the world of giants. Rise to it or perish.

– You're insane. Clarke shook his head. – You better tend to those wounds, or you will be a dead insane giant.

Gidman turned to him, and Clarke froze in his tracks.

– You don't understand, One Eye told him, whispered to him, shouted silently to him. – I'm immortal, do you *hear me*. Nothing can kill me. Nothing!

He turned away from the cop, dismissing him, turned away from the precipice, turning towards it, walking to the car.

– You don't understand, he said to the air, – and I guess you never will.

Bernie stared at the stars, eyes dead and gone.

– What about him? Clarke wondered, all initiative, all rage gone from his voice, his flesh.

– Nobody can trace poor Bernie to us, Gidman shrugged, – To most people it will look like he and dear Mark have killed each other. Nobody cares anyway.

Jean crumbled, face down, paralyzed in the car. A giant brown hand petted her nipple, and she kept her face down, staring at the empty void her mind had become, and looking at the world with the same, empty, tearless face. The door closed, and there was nothing but darkness.

The two men entered the seats. Clarke was driving. His hands still trembled, his eyes still wavered. Gidman sat in his way too small seat. He was sweating. A thin film of humidity and blood covered his skin, but he didn't seem to notice his wounds, didn't seem to notice them at all, not really, not as most people would. He hummed a melody Clarke didn't know.

The party had picked up again at Frank Forester's place, the broken window and all it entailed momentarily, conveniently forgotten.

A haze filled the air, of musk and smoke and ashes.

Tilla and Ted snuggled on the couch. A glimpse of worry was seen in her face.

– He called you…

– Yes, Ted said. Nothing more.

Iris danced tight to Bob, very tight. She was like an explosion of fire and passion, and that was what Ted felt like, too.

Nothing more.

Chapter seventeen
DISTANT BUTTERFLY WINGS
San Diego, California 1966

San Diego was a major city in Southern California, close to the Mexican border, close to the sea. Sailboats rocked back and forth in the harbor. There was a fresh breeze, eliminating most of the smoldering summer heat.

But first impressions are often traitorous. A short distance away, within the buildings, not far away from the lush harbor, the dust and molten, fluid-like air dominated, and one was tempted to believe this was all a desert. Dust devils turned slowly, very slowly. There was no discernible wind. The sun had descended between the buildings and burned everything and everyone.

The four men, Wolf Connors, Peter Clarke, Francis Caine and Mark Stewart dismounted the train. They walked straight forward, disregarding everything and everyone else. Their eyes didn't see what they saw, but something to others unfathomable somewhere ahead.

They exited the relatively chilly colonnaded Santa Fe train depot and entered into the smoldering desert-like heat. The desert danced around them, within them. It was their eyes people noticed, the chill in them, the determination. The long coats they wore seemed and were totally out of place here. The men seemed out of place. They were. This was southern California, at the dawn of the Age of Aquarius, the Hippie movement. People filled the street with abandon, love and stars in their eyes. The four men spoke, but they weren't really speaking.

– The natives are restless, Connors remarked.

– The natives are always restless, Clarke grinned.

Connors was a tall, red-haired Irishman with an impossibly long moustache dominating his face, making his eyes seem small, like points of ice stabbing you.

Francis Caine - the infamous Gambler was of mixed Spanish/Mexican/North European ancestry. The streak of white hair at his temples revealed that he was the oldest of them, and to those who knew these things he was clearly the leader of this small group of men.

They walked through the dusty streets, and other people avoided their gaze, and stepped nervously off the sidewalk when they approached. Nobody or very few could tell why they did so, only that a great fear caught them in its jaw, and wouldn't let go.

– Good ol' Amtrak, Caine said dreamingly. – Leading us right to the city center.

– Into the belly of the beast, Clarke supplied.

– I love taking the train, Caine said, with stars in his eyes.

They passed the Greyhound bus terminal, another cluster of people in this day of clusters. Caine took one look at the strangely clad people and shook his head in contempt.

– They love the train, too. Clarke snickered.

Caine looked pointedly at him.

– So I've heard, Clarke insisted. – And look at the scenery, here, in this picturesque, fake Mexican township…

Someone was playing a guitar somewhere, crazy, ghostly chords spreading through the noise and the heated air. Four scantily clad young girls swayed in conjunction with the music.

– I see one, Stewart said.

They all did. There was a nervous looking guy not fitting in with those not fitting in.

There, on the other sidewalk was another. During a fifty-step walk they spotted at least four others with very nervous dispositions.

– They know we're coming, Clarke said nervously.

– They've known for days. Stewart shrugged.

– But the question is will they *run?*

– No, Stewart stated decisively. – This is his place of power. He's waiting for us. Those he sent after us, delaying us, were just a diversion and hardly even that, a warm up. He figured they would fail, but hoped they would get lucky.

– Luck has got nothing to do with it, Connors said expectantly, rubbing his palms at each other, instinctively touching the cold metal under his coat.

Stewart nodded, doing the same. He was not yet thirty and looked much younger. He was the youngest and clearly the most vulnerable.

And the most dangerous, Caine thought. It was like there was a volcano walking by their side.

– The train brought us here, Stewart said, – like an arrow seeking its mark. We are its point. We are what cuts and stabs.

And his voice shook them all, spurring them into action.

And they couldn't say they didn't need it. The enemy had an army waiting for them not far away.

– So close… so far away.

– I don't know, Babyface, Clarke joked, – is this the time to turn philosophical on us? You have chased this guy all across the globe. Isn't it time to get serious?

– Yes, Stewart replied.

His war with Gidman had started many years ago, when they were still children. He had chased him. He had gathered these people, including Caine. He was the bow shooting them against the enemy.

He once again noticed Francis Caine's eyes scrutinizing him, and felt another thrill of expectation.

They moved. Not fast, not slow. They moved down streets and avenues, not stopping for anybody. People hurried out of their way. Even if the colorfully dressed people didn't know what they were on a conscious level, they knew inside, where it counted.

– Look at them, Clarke snarled. – The sheep always recognize the wolf.

They walked towards the convention center. People had gathered outside with flags and banners, protesting what went on inside.

NO LECTURES FROM THE LECTURER

A banner said.

– It's the honorable Doctor Berkowitz, a guy told them.

Connors looked at the guy, only moderately interested.

– *The* Doctor Berkowitz, the guy kept up. – It's said that even some students from his university are traveling around the country to protest against him.

They walked inside, through the crowd and the line of policemen. None of the policemen made any attempt to stop the four, and they also knew why.

The arrangement was in the vestibule, a huge hall welcoming people to the even larger center.

A man looking suspiciously like the mayor stood on the dais, on the podium at the top of the stairs. At least he had all the regalia, the chain around his neck, the pendant and honors on his chest.

– Welcome, good people, he greeted the assembly.

From the inside he received polite applause. From the outside a barrage of displeasure.

– Please join me, in welcoming Professor in behavioral studies at Harvard University, Anton Berkowitz.

More polite applause and an even louder barrage of displeasure.

The man stepping up on the platform was young, sharp and very, very confident.

He waited for the applause to fade, and ignored the more distant angry roar.

– Society is riddled with crime. He began confidently, straight to the point. – Asocial individuals are roaming the modern urban landscape, completely disregarding accepted rules and laws, upsetting the Order on which we base our lives. Behavioral studies are both about what works… and what doesn't. By going deep into the psyche of asocial individuals we can find out what makes them… fail, and then use that knowledge to teach children at an early age how to avoid the possible pitfalls, teach them how to be eager, productive members of our great society.

– What a piece of work, Stewart mumbled.

– What's that, Mark, my man, Clarke wondered. – I didn't quite hear it.

– What a PIECE OF WORK, Stewart shouted.

And the speakers released a long, wailing sound, as if the shouting was close to it somehow.

The man on the dais, the professor from Harvard University paused a bit, smiling professionally, before picking up the thread.

There was a long walk through the hall. It wasn't quite as big as a football field, but in terms of the four of them needing to walk around all the well-dressed people with their canapés it was a long walk indeed.

The audience applauded for something Berkowitz said. Stewart didn't hear what, and he didn't care.

– In preliminary closing I will say this: As we're learning, as we're putting together the puzzle of the human psyche, I can assure you that crime will soon belong to the past.

– And how many times will you be closing your argument? Stewart shouted.

Caine grabbed him in the arm, turning him half around.

– What's wrong with you?

– Nothing, Babyface replied. – Nothing is wrong with *me*.

Caine paled, in anger and other, less defined emotions.

Several men in black suits appeared in the doorway where the four were headed. They carried heavy arms and had no qualms about displaying them. The four drew their own. Distractions faded, turning immaterial. The men in black suits fired first. People started screaming. The four threw themselves on the floor, returning the fire. One of the men (in suits) was hit and blood decorated the no longer white wall behind him. Other men appeared from another angle. Stewart held one shotgun in each hand. He fired both. One he fired right into the crowd. At least three bystanders were hit. The screams started in earnest and the terrified audience headed for all possible exits, ensuring mayhem and chaos. The four fired while they ran. The eight remaining suits in the doorway fell like dummies on an arena. A bullet passed close by Stewart's ear. He returned fire. He hit the man shooting at him, but a lot of bystanders, too. He grinned wildly.

– I've told good ol' Dave time and time again, he laughed. – He has major problems finding and hiring the right people.

A man ran down the stairs. Connors shot him down with a single bullet. There were two large flights of stairs leading to the upper floor. They split and one pair ascended each. A man appeared at the top. Connors and Stewart both fired at him and blew him away. Several other guards appeared, and started shooting. The two ran to the top easily and killed six opponents in a flash. The shotguns were empty, and they threw them away, drawing their revolvers. They saw Caine and Clarke appear at the other end. There was no resistance in sight. They picked up weapons as they ran, checking the chambers. They were almost fully loaded, and they were not unfamiliar with the models. They kept them.

They advanced further, quickly, from corner to corner, door to door. Connors was hit head on, and was virtually stone cold before hitting the floor. The three others threw themselves behind a wall.

– We're coming for you, Dave, Stewart shouted. – Are you ready for us?

Stewart advanced to the next wall, firing while running. One man was hit in the head, and it exploded like a melon. Two others were hit many times, and cried out as they fell. They remained there on the floor, exposed.

– DON'T SHOOT, one of them shouted. – We surrender.

Two seconds after that they were perforated by bullets, fired by their former comrades in arms. Clarke and Caine shot several of them as they exposed themselves.

– This is insane, Caine mumbled. – Totally and utterly insane.

Connors' blood wet the Gambler's skin and clothes, making his grip slippery. On one occasion he almost lost his gun.

All three of them bled by now, but all their wounds were minor, and they were all right.

– Okay? Stewart said, eyes wide open and shining.

– *Okay*... Clarke grinned. – Those guys over there? They are wussies, children playing with guns. We can take them with one arm tied behind our back.

They jumped forward, rolled on the floor and shot with both hands at the enemies ahead. The men in suits fell like puppets on a string. Caine fired from the corner. The three of them moved constantly, while the suits seemed to be standing still. Rivers of blood wet the carpet. A distraction: Stewart observed how people ran like dogs from the convention center.

– A chopper is approaching, Clarke noted.

– Is it ours?

– Nope. Wrong markings, and it's way too early, anyway. Shuster isn't an optimist. He knows we need more time...

They were in hiding again. Stewart calmly fired at the windows. They fell apart and he fired at the chopper, hitting it many times. It stopped in the air and turned, turned away.

– You won't run away this time, Stewart mumbled.

They finally reached the office section, with bloody and torn bodies left in their wake. Some of the guards were alive. Stewart and Clarke shot them in the head as they advanced. The resistance crumbled. The remaining outer circle of guards threw away their guns, and hid the best they could, pushing themselves at the windows if needed in the hope that they wouldn't be shot at, as the three attackers walked in a fairly slow pace forward. Stewart's revolver clicked on an empty chamber. He calmly reloaded it. The suits still alive remained frozen on the floor. A while after the three had passed them they ran off, escaped as fast as they were able.

The Gambler walked in front now, filled with anger, with irritation. He listened. He observed how Stewart cocked his head. Caine could almost see how the younger man's ears were *moving*. And not for the first time since they had first met he sensed horror in his gut.

– How many do you think he has left? Clarke asked Stewart and kept ignoring Caine.

– Ten, perhaps fifteen. These are his loyal subjects. Those he has trained himself, those he has elevated to his elite guard, those willing to die for him, for their master.

– He has probably convinced them of the truth of that particular illusion, right?

– Right, Mark Stewart nodded.

Ornaments, drawings of a face, more than resembling Gidman's covered the wall confronting them. Strange writings reminding them of all kinds of languages, including ancient Egyptian and Mayan.

– He has flipped, Caine mumbled.

As if to confirm his words a low hum filled the building, originating from the path ahead. Caine looked at Stewart's eyes just then, staring at rage incarnated and turned numb and mute.

Stewart showed his hand briefly beyond the corner, pulling it back just before it was shot off. A hail of bullets raced by the three of them. Pieces of the wall loosened and flew across the large room.

The hum turned to a chant, and the chant to words. Caine almost flipped himself when listening to the alien intonations.

– «Iluso is our Master». Stewart translated in a weird, strangely disaffected voice. – «Iluso is our God. Beware his wrath».

– An understatement, to be sure, he said casually to Caine.

– Illuso, huh? Clarke chuckled, a touch of hysteria noticeable in his voice. – What fucking language is that?

– Romany, Stewart replied.

More humming, more insane words. Cold penetrated Caine like daggers.

– «We are the People of Legend, and we are mighty beyond words», Stewart kept translating.

– The people of legend? Caine wondered. – Don't the Bedouins in North Africa call the gypsies that?

– They do. Stewart nodded. – At least that's the common opinion.

– So, what's the uncommon opinion? That was Clarke, just as astute as ever.

– The true People of Legend are far older than the Gypsy. The Gypsy is merely a pale echo of what once was.

Stewart brought forth a hand grenade from his coat. In swift, casual moves he had pulled out the firing pin, and thrown the explosive across the room, into the next. The entire building shook when remains of walls, floor and body parts were bathing in plasma of red, yellow and white. Stewart threw another grenade, and screams echoed through walls and ears. Stewart was up the moment right after the explosion, Clarke right after him. Caine stumbled in their path, coughing hard in the dust-filled air.

The three fired as they advanced, advanced as they fired, guns in both hands. Shapes in the dust and mist shook and fell. Parts of the floor were missing. Stewart jumped across the divide. Clarke and Caine ran on shaky legs around it. Some of the castle's defenders had fallen through the cracks. Stewart mowed them down. One gun pointing down, one forward.

– Poetry in motion, Clarke shouted. – Poetry in MOTION!

He moved, fired, moved and fired, while striving to keep up with the hurricane leading the way. There was smoke everywhere by now, almost impossible to see through, even in the pockets of thinner gray.

– WHO IS THERE? WHO IS THERE? A man shouted, stumbling around like a madman.

Stewart filled him with lead.

The three of them walked virtually straight forward now, without seeking even temporary shelter. Shapes appeared in the fog, and fell like the dominos they were. Clarke and Caine coughed. Stewart kept charging forward, totally indifferent. Stewart's guns were empty. Caine changed position with him. He had just loaded his.

– Symmetry, man, Clarke sang. – Hell's symmetry.

Caine's eyes flowed with tears. And he coughed, and his nose and throat itched like hell. There, a shadow. He fired. The shadows dropped. Caine stumbled backwards. Suddenly there was another itch somewhere. Stewart supported him for a moment, straightening him, before pushing him further forward. Caine stared irritated at the bloody arm hanging at his side, useless. The gun dropped from his weak hand. Five men rushed out of the fog simultaneously. Fire erupted from their weapons. They shook as the three attackers drilled countless holes in them. Fog turned red and black.

A demon, Francis Caine thought. I am running with a demon.

Drums were beating somewhere. Not here. Somewhere else. Funny, the sound reminded him of New Orleans. The beat matched that of his heart, that of the pulse in the vein at his left temple. Adrenaline flowed through him. The head pounded and pounded constantly. The fog lifted slowly, no longer a putrid jungle, but a modern room filled with blood, guts and shards. Remains of a brain floated in one of the biggest red pools. Nausea almost overwhelmed Caine, and vomit filled his mouth. A man jumped from his hiding place and Stewart shot him in that very same moment, as if... as if he had known, as if he had actually known the very moment it would happen. Caine felt fear, one grabbing him, one that would never let go. They heard a voice from the next room.

– I AM McQUARRIE, CHIEF OF THE SAN DIEGO POLICE DEPARTMENT. I WILL REMAIN IN THIS CHAIR WITH MY HANDS ON THE TABLE. I WILL NOT FIRE AT YOU.

The three walked inside. Stewart first, then Clarke, then

Caine. McQuarrie sat by the table with his hands resting on the table, as he had said. Stewart shot him once through the head. The table was washed in brain fluid and mass.

Gidman, a lithe, muscular man leapt from his hiding place. Stewart fired, a bit too late and missed. Gidman fired. Stewart was hit. He took one step backwards and kept firing. Gidman was hit, several times, his body shaking violently. He lost his gun and fell to the floor. Stewart kept walking straight forward, his eyes moving constantly, and simultaneously, impossibly, permanently resting on Gidman's tall figure. Gidman attempted to move, to crawl to his gun, but he couldn't do it. He moved, but was unable to summon the strength needed to move effectively. When Stewart approached him, he crouched half on his side, half on his back.

Stewart stood above him, with his guns directed at his enemy.

– You have fucking *flipped!* Gidman gasped hoarsely, his face twisted in pain.

– More than you will ever know.

Both spoke in a beyond harsh voice, emphasizing each word.

Caine lifted a hand. His eyes clouded, his hand shaking.

– Don't do it, man, he said. – There's no need. We've gathered enough evidence to get the shitbag convicted a thousand times.

Stewart looked back at him, one brief moment, before returning his attention, his utter and complete attention to David Gidman.

He emptied one gun at his chest. The entire body shook. Hot fumes rose from the holes in the brown skin. The other gun he emptied in his head. One eye jumped from its socket. Then Stewart stamped on the head. The skull burst. It visibly burst. David Gidman's frame shook one last time before lying still.

Stewart stood there for minutes. He hardly moved, and neither did his comrades in arms.

The sound of the chopper slowly penetrated their consciousness, their ears, shrouded for so long by the sound of the gun.

– That would be Shuster, Clarke said pleased, just a little shell-shocked. – His timing perfect, as always.

It was Simon Shuster. They could glimpse his withered frame through the glass of the chopper cockpit. They walked up the stairs to the roof. The chopper didn't land. It hovered no more than half a body's length in the air. The three of them jumped up. Caine swayed a bit. He denied Stewart's reached-out hand.

The door closed. The machine ascended from the bombed out building, rose above San Diego's shell-shocked population, never to return. In a matter of minutes, it was gone, vanished beyond the horizon.

Clayton Powers, one of the survivors of the battle later told a newspaper:

– It was as if a demon from hell had descended on us, as if he had come to fetch us to his court, and he did.

– One down, Stewart mumbled, someplace far away.

Or so Caine thought he heard, but he wasn't sure.

He was no longer certain of anything.

Part five: Degradation road

Chapter eighteen

The world outside the bus didn't seem real. The wipers worked hard to get all the water whipping against the window out of the way. The bus was enclosed in a thick fog, and it was impossible to see the road more than a few steps ahead. The middle stripe set the course, but for all they knew the road could end at any time. The inside of the vehicle was propped with luxuries, like a small piece of their private heaven. Frank's father owned a share in the company owning the bus, like he did in most local corporations.

The extended class from Denver was heading west, on Interstate 70, on their way further into the Rocky Mountains. They would turn south soon, off the main road, towards the small township of Leadville.

Ted Cousin stared into the fog, seeing shapes being formed and dissolved. Iris was hitting on Bob again, making Veronica (and Bob) furious. Ted smiled. It seemed so mundane to him.

Bob told his girlfriend in a very serious manner.

– I don't care about her. I care about you.

A small television set was on or rather off and on. Reception was poor in this infinite and eternal soup of gray and rain. It was yet another report from Washington DC, and the ever-bigger snowball that was the end of Richard Nixon's political career.

– I so love this… Iris approached him with her hands behind her back, showing off again, her beauty, her smoldering sensuality, but to his surprise it was somehow muted at the moment. – I love seeing the people at the top catch at least some of their just reward.

It was amazing. It was as if she had, at least temporarily, exchanged her constant flirting with a cool and rational mindset. Perhaps it was a cleverer ploy to get him to bed. He couldn't decide if it was or not.

– But of course, the cool and detached, hot and sensual temptress added, – the system isn't dependent on persons. When one puppet falls, when one janitor is relieved another easily takes his or her place.

– What are you talking about? Bob cried out irritably.

She turned to him, turned to everyone moderately interested in her words.

– The time of the obvious dictator or dictatorship has ended. They have all been forced to get sneakier, to give people the illusion of participating in the decision-making. The modern democracies are the most elaborate dictatorships in history... because they give any given population the illusion of freedom. The need for slaves in this world persists, though. You see, there will always be that need. Various degrees of docile servants, from the wage slaves to the completely mindless. Supply and demand is, after all, the glue holding the world together...

– It speaks, Tilla said sarcastically, – but this time I actually think It is right...

– So do I, Ted said dryly. – It's fairly simple, really. The economy suffers in every overt dictatorship. So, they need the control to be subtle, to happen on the sidelines, in dark corners, in people's minds. Nixon is more like an old-fashioned dictator. That's why his days are numbered. The system that created him, that made him and a million others possible lives on.

– So say we all. Iris kissed him on the cheek.

– Speak for yourself, Veronica said, clearly on Bob's behalf, loyal and sweet.

The reception went bonkers again, and the short exchange ended somewhat.

– I need to go to the bathroom, before Leadville, they heard Veronica state forcefully a while later. – Helen should have completed «today's practice» eons ago.

Helen was studying opera. She needed to practice in the soundproof room, at least in the close confines of the bus, to not scare her mates out of their wits.

So she had to use the bathroom...

Everybody else had done their thing before Helen's announced long visit, except Veronica. She had been busy aiding Bob fending off Iris' advances.

Laughter, humor, platitudes. Ted shook his head. How long had he waited to be a part of something like this? Tilla kissed him softly. She understood.

He stared into the fog, the nothing. Everything was up for grabs. It frightened him, and he couldn't understand why.

Tilla grabbed his hand. He discovered that she was looking at him, looking at him with an expression he had learned to recognize, both in good and bad times.

She dragged him to the restroom door, to the queue forming there. They made it as the second in line, after Veronica.

Veronica knocked on the door, knocked hard, with her fist, not her knuckles.

– Hey, she shouted. – Your half hour is up, you know.

– You might as well give it up, Linda pointed out. – She can't hear you. She might actually notice the vibrations, but that isn't very likely.

Finally, they heard something, the sound of the lock turning. The door opened, and Helen appeared… with Bruce in tow. Everybody suddenly noticed the obvious that Bruce wasn't, hadn't been out here. She was taller than he was, and they were a strange couple in more ways than one. There was no laughter, no scorn following their blushing and averting looks. Everybody was basically stunned, too stunned to do much more than stand there, undignified, with their mouth open.

Veronica's errand was quickly done, and Ted and Tilla walked in. She kissed him, deliberately, before the door closed, making no attempt to hide her intention or the state she was in. The door closed and locked. They were alone.

– It's stupid anyway, she breathed, close to him, very close. – We could just as well have done it out there. Everybody knows we're doing it anyway. Everybody knows that every couple going in here is doing it, so why pretend?

– We live in an insane society, he grinned. – Such pretense or the need for it is beaten into us.

– Clever boy, she breathed, kissing him again and again. – Bright, clever boy.

The bathroom was small. It consisted of no more than one toilet, one sink… and then there was the mattress.

– We don't have much time, she kept breathing. – Just put it in. Pump me up.

She pulled down her pants. He pulled down his own, hardly conscious of doing so. She crouched slightly, sticking up her butt. He crouched, too, forming his body after hers. And there was the fire embracing him. One minute they had been out there, feeling the need build. Now, they were in here, and it exploded in them both. She turned her head, locking her lips to his. They lost all strength in their legs and dumped down on the mattress, tearing off each other's clothes. Then they were completely naked and embracing passionately on the softness on the floor.

They were front to front now, entwined, pushing at the other, breathing hard, drowning in the heat and humidity of the moment.

He gasped. She gasped. Their hips met. He sensed it. Not hard, but as soft, soft velvet. Felt her nipples draw patterns on his skin, felt her embrace him totally. And then everything he was turned hard. Hard as stone, harder than steel. He sensed her tighten. Everything tightened. Her muscles were like fine threads playing him. They gasped and sweat poured from all over them. And the moon turned red, and everything was a crimson tide throwing them into the molten sea. And everything turned soft once more, and there were kisses and touches, and everything was hot, and only slowly, very slowly the cold once more gained the upper hand.

They emerged from the restroom, through the door, their clothes in tatters, clearly torn several places, a distant haze in their eyes, their entire facial expressions. Ted remembered that clearly. He remembered the others' facial expressions. It felt good, so very, very good.

The two of them weren't embarrassed. The others were.

They reached the old historic mining town of Leadville, deep within the Rockies. It had stopped raining, but the fog remained; the thick, wet, invasive fog.

– It's cold, Helen complained, high pitched, cutting into their eardrums. – My voice will suffer terribly.

Bruce used the opportunity to kiss her, to comfort her, totally uncharacteristically. He was evidently smitten hard.

– Well, it's a ten thousand feet elevation, Frank told her. – The highest incorporated city in the United States.

There was snow on the peaks surrounding the place, glimpsed through the gray mass making it hard to breathe.

– Doc Holliday visited this place, Frank related. – Oscar Wilde and several of history's notorious scoundrels did so as well.

– And rich tyrants like Tabor and Carnegie, Jane sniffed. – Tabor and wife had one of their palaces here.

– And it isn't exactly welcoming us, Dennis said.

– I would say we're very unlucky, Frank said, suddenly sourpuss. – I've been told it has three hundred sunny days during a year.

He seemed set on playing the tour guide.

They fetched their gear from the bus, and the bus drove off, to return in a two weeks' time. Frank looked around, brightening visibly.

– Come, he said, eagerly rushing them along.

They did follow him, good humored.

The fog seemed to lift, somehow. They saw more of the streets, the houses.

– Christ, Betty said, both awestruck and ironic, echoing everybody's sentiment.

Suddenly they felt they had been sent through time, to Dickens' novels, to Victorian England. The buildings, at least in this street were almost exclusively Victorian, revenants of another time.

– Wasn't I right? Frank bristled. – This isn't exactly the typical run of the mill rundown mining town, now, is it?

– You can say that again. Dennis said, stars in his eyes.

– A truly remarkable example of human achievement. Bob shook his head in wonder.

Ted listened for a touch of irony in his friend's voice, but found none. The familiar cold trickle ran down his spine, and as usual he couldn't fathom why.

They walked down Harrison Avenue, as they suspected virtually everybody coming to town for the first time would do.

– Yeah, Jane stated, with a voice filled with venom. – A crowning statement of human greed and subjugation of both nature and other humans.

– Where do you get off? Bob shook his head in disgust.

They passed the ice palace park, a park strangely or not so strangely without the actual ice palace. The Tabor home, the one Horace Tabor had built for his first wife Augusta, now a museum. To call it extravagant was in no way sufficient to describe its perceived splendor.

– The town's income is basically tourism these days. Frank kept playing the guide, as if paid to do it. – Four thousand friendly souls welcoming all strangers.

– It's like a ghost town, Iris said frostily. – Except this town is full of ghosts.

– Thousands of workers died in the silver mines, Jane snarled.

Tilla and Ted walked a bit behind the others.

– You do notice it? She asked. – The… change?

– Yes, they've started to think for themselves. At least some have.

It did feel good, the sense of not being alone anymore. He had never been afraid to speak up, to fight to be heard, but he had rarely seen the point in doing so, in an indifferent, shallow world.

It was so different from what he was used to, and it made him sore afraid. Tilla noticed it, of course, but she was afraid to ask, to push him. Was it only a few short days ago since he had felt himself break out of his armor, felt Life swell within him?

– The Tabor Opera House, Helen gasped. – I can't believe it. In its time it was the finest opera house between St. Louis and San Francisco.

More caustic remarks, not really unfriendly, at least the hostility wasn't directed at Helen. She grinned, shaking it off.

They walked straight inside the Silver Dollar Saloon, with impunity, as if they owned it, laughing and shouting.

– This is it, Frank said, pleased with himself, – the place where Doc Holliday killed his last man.

The vicious laughter rolled through the saloon. A lot of unfriendly faces stared at the newcomers.

– Are you sure? John wondered. – I have heard it was somewhere else. And he didn't actually kill the man, did he? He just shot him. The man survived.

– Details, Frank bristled some more.

– «He just shot him», Dennis spat.

Some among them joined his pointed laughter. Others did not. Old grievances died hard.

They all made their way to the bar, pushing their way forward between drunk and difficult patrons, locals and tourists alike. Ted felt the pressure of all the people around him, all the people in the room. It was as if he was… aware of them all, of their moods and mind. He had always been slightly claustrophobic, but this was different. It didn't feel bad. Strange, but not bad.

– Drinks to all of us, Frank declared loud to the bartender.

– No way! The bartender scowled. – We don't serve liquor to kids.

– So much for the friendly natives… Iris grinned. – No wonder the population number is on its way down.

– DRINKS TO EVERYONE PRESENT, Frank shouted angrily, staring triumphantly at the man behind the counter.

The entire room quieted. Quite a remarkable event, concerning how noisy it had been just a few seconds ago.

– You can treat the entire town to a drink, the man scowled, displaying his fangs. – We will still not serve kids liquor.

– You're not being reasonable, Frank protested. – If you can just…

– If you don't stop yapping our bouncers will show you an example of our proud town's hospitality you don't want to see.

Frank opened and shut his mouth, but there was no sound.

– Welcome to Leadville, Iris cried.

A man at the end of the counter, evidently a higher-ranking guy, signaled the bartender in question. The guy obeyed instantly. Frank smirked.

They stood there whispering for a while. The higher-ranking guy approached the youths.

– We're God-fearing people in this town, he began.

– So what? Ted responded, suddenly very irritated.

– We're God-fearing people in this town, the older man said constrained, but pleasant enough. – We don't serve liquor to people under the age of twenty-one. Is there anything else we can help you with?

– We've rented the Freemont Cabin for two weeks, Betty said sweetly. – And we wondered if you guys know how to get there.

– Oh, that's easy enough, the man in charge stated. – It's not far. I can have a guide take you there.

– That won't be necessary, Frank assured him. – You sell us a map, and we will find our way on our own.

– Are you sure? One wrong turn, and you might be seriously lost out there.

– Of course, I'm sure. Frank shrugged deliberately, patronizing.

The «deal» was quickly consummated. Frank made a big deal of showing the hundred-dollar bill in his hand. He received his map, his change, and they were on their way.

They stepped outside again, and the sense of displacement didn't leave Ted.

– There seem to be a church and yet another christian denomination on every street and corner here, Iris said cheerfully. – God-fearing people indeed…

– Something inside there… wasn't right, Ted said.

He suddenly found himself alone with her, a bit ahead of the group as a whole.

– So, you sensed it, too? She spoke softly, cutting deep in him, with just a hint of worry tangible in her voice. – I'm not surprised.

– Some of the men inside… *looked* at us, he insisted. – And when doing so more like vultures than patronizing drunks. I… felt their beaks nipping at my skin.

Tilla caught up with them, very on guard and sharp. They fell silent.

It wasn't far to go out of town. This might have been a major place hundred years ago, but now it was hardly more than a typical/atypical American village. A few minutes, that was all, and they had left the place behind. By a crossroads in the forest glen they could, when looking back, hardly see the buildings anymore, except for the clock tower on one of the churches.

One sign pointing to one specific trail said MT. MASSIVE. Frank took one casual look at the map and nodded.

– This is it, he said, very full of himself.

And they set out on the trail. Soft shadows were about to darken the terrain and they speeded up, slightly in a hurry.

They walked. And walked. It started raining. An even, quiet drizzle slowly wetting their clothes, soaking them to the bone. They were sweaty and messy, and then the rain no longer mattered, because sweat soaked their clothes from inside, and they turned wet and warm, and eventually woozy from exhaustion. It turned dark. And they still walked. The cold night froze their bones, and they had to run to stay warm. They kept moving, even if despair assaulted them like spiders.

– I don't understand, Frank said. – I don't understand. I have… we have followed the map to the letter.

He almost fell. Iris supported him, and he got to his feet.

– The map must be fake, he stated, enraged and miserable. – The fucker of a bar owner gave us a fake map.

– That nice and helpful man? He offered us a guide and you were the one who turned it down. Sometimes I think all your fat has spread to the brain.

That was Bob - as usual. He used any opportunity to needle Frank. Ted started to be seriously fed up by it. But right now, he didn't exactly feel very charitable towards Frank either, a sentiment he shared with everybody present.

– Stop hassling Frank, Linda said sharply. – It isn't his fault we're lost.

But that was clearly a major misconception, and a hail of protests fell on her.

Lost. Someone had finally come out and said it, and the conscious realization of the fact made them feel even worse than before.

– You damn BRAGGART! Bruce shouted insanely and took a step forward.

And then he stopped, just stopped. Why, no one could say. The others figured he had no more juice left. He quite simply sat straight down on the wet soil, his shoulder sagging, his head lowered to his knees.

If they could only have returned the same way they had come, but by now they had backtracked and sidetracked, and tracked everything so many times that they no longer had any idea where they should go to return to Leadville. It was dark everywhere around them. They had flashlights, but that was all. At some point, before it had turned completely dark they had been able to see a snowcap, but which one of the two they had seen they could no longer say. Dark, everything was dark.

And it was cold and dark. It penetrated their skin, their very being, like daggers of ice. Ted felt them, the daggers cutting him, cutting him to shreds.

– We can't stay outside until morning, Helen moaned. – We'll freeze to death.

– We'll have to keep moving, Ted said.

– That's right, Jane said. – Stay warm by our own power. Humans can do incredible things when we have to.

She would know, being one of the school's best athletes.

– I don't know, Iris grinned (a very frozen grin). – There are definitely a couple of other possibilities we can explore.

Ted looked at her. She stood before him, covered in mud, as desirable as ever. He shook his head in wonder.

There was a sound, at the edge of his hearing. He studied the others then, very astute. Tilla and Betty heard it. And Iris. And Linda. The others didn't, not until several seconds later. The sound of someone moving through the terrain, not really making an effort at hiding it.

They saw a man move under the scrutiny of the flashlights, working his way towards them. He moved effortlessly on the muddy soil.

– Hello, there, the man greeted them, covering his eyes with one hand.

They returned the greeting, mumbling in shame and relief, staring at the strange creature with a face covered by a massive red beard.

– Shoot me if I'm wrong, he said lightly, – but you people look lost.

– We are, sir, Iris said sweetly (very sweetly). – You don't happen to be the Guide?

– I most certainly am, Miss. He straightened proudly. – The best in Lake County and perhaps the entire Rockies. The name is Fitzallan, John R. Fitzallan. The R stands for Reinhart. I am at your service.

His humor worked wonders on them. They all sensed it, how their load suddenly seemed that much lighter.

– Did you know we were lost or did you just chance on it?

That was Dennis, feeling the need to release some of his pent-up aggression.

– I admit willingly that it isn't I who am most deserving of

422

your gratitude, Fitzallan laughed. – My occasional employer at the Silver Dollar observed how you took the wrong turn at the crossroads…

– But how could we? Frank was wet and miserable, and couldn't work up much more wounded pride. – The sign pointed…

– That sign is more than a bit ambiguous, by pointing right between two trails. You're not the first people choosing the wrong one, and shouldn't be ashamed because of it. But let's go now, let's have you tucked in and warm as soon as possible.

They stumbled dog-tired after him, but filled with desperate hope.

The first hour they managed to stay somewhat encouraged, but eventually they started hurting, and vision was so hazy that they couldn't really tell how long time had passed, and the Guide just kept on charging forward. The good Mister Fitzallan had failed to tell them how far they had yet to go.

– Courage, he cried. – It's not much further.

– It's not much further to midnight either, Bruce snarled.

And virtually everybody mumbled snarls of agreement.

This told a lot about their state of mind.

– There is something, Ted told Tilla. – Something going on. Something I don't get… a detail swirling in my head. Something *wrong*.

He was so tired. His mind was like filled with air and just didn't work.

Fitzallan's roaring joyous cry interrupted his broken line of thoughts.

– That's your palace straight ahead. What did I tell ya? Mrs. Fitzallan's great son has kept his promise and led you home.

The youths hardly heard him. They ran the last stretch to the cabin. Bob nodded to him, before he, too, joined the others' feverish charge towards the dark structure ahead.

– Not much left, now, Fitzallan said, appearing straight behind the suffering pack stumbling towards the door. – Soon you will be able to enjoy the fruits of your labor.

His words cut through the haze in their brain somehow. They stopped and turned.

– We need to start the generator, the Guide told them, – to

give you heat and light day and night. May I have your keys, please?

Frank, like a good dog handed him the set of keys.

They all stood there, like wet dogs, watching the older man go to the shed a bit away from the main building and open its door. Not long after that the sound of the engine starting up and running reached their ears, and it was the sweetest sound in the world. Lights were turned on all over the building, and it lit up like a christmas tree. The youths looked at it with stars in their eyes.

Fitzallan returned the set of keys to Frank, shook his hand and waved goodbye. It was all silent. The Guide's face turned pale like death, and the red hair and beard turned liquid like blood. Everything turned silent for Ted a moment, until Fitzallan disappeared down the trail, and the engine, the rain and the hurt returned to the world, and just the memory of the dead face remained.

Frank inserted the key and opened the door, two wide doors opening, welcoming them. They walked slowly inside, devout and with tight woven faces. Liz Horton stopped just inside the door, looking ashamed at the floor, at the mud and water overflowing it. It made them all look.

– Don't worry about it. Frank shrugged. – It's just dirt, after all, and dirt can be washed off.

They kept staring at it all, with eyes just growing bigger and bigger.

– Twenty-three proud youths, Frank grinned. – Only twenty luxurious suites, but my distinct impression in the matter is that there actually will be some rooms to spare.

Tilla spotted a plate on a door nearby. It said: TED AND TILLA. She blushed, and overwhelmed by joy she embraced Ted and smothered his face in kisses.

Ted felt a strange distance to it all. For some reason he noticed Frank's face at that moment, its strange ambiguous expression, and not for the first time recently he felt worry gnaw at his bones. Something was wrong. Something was very wrong.

– This is fantastic, Dennis Murdoch said dreamingly.

They walked back outside to remove their raincoats and boots, reducing the extension of possible decoration on the floor.

– Two biiig bathrooms, Frank declared. – One for the Gentlemen and one for the Ladies.

Iris removed her outer covers without thinking twice about it. The other girls were far more reluctant, especially when they discovered how the various body parts showed through the thin and wet clothes.

– You boys don't have to look away, Iris stated proudly. – I don't mind being looked at. Nudity isn't such a big issue to me. It used to be, but isn't anymore.

– Can't someone stop that mouth of hers, Veronica said, half joking, half snarling.

Nobody commented on it, on either of their speeches.

Ted was exhausted. Limbs were sore and stiff. He hardly managed to move his arms properly while removing the wet coat. They all walked to the bathrooms, to the spacious wardrobe beside it. Ted wanted to do it with Tilla. He wanted to do everything with Tilla. But… that was a practical impossibility… wasn't it? At least right now.

The remaining clothes stuck to the body, and were even harder to remove. Some were quicker than others, and the sound of running water, its scent and humidity filled the room. The bathroom was cold, like the rest of the cabin, but as the hot water filled the room, so did the heat. The water rinsed Ted Cousin's body, and also whatever rested inside it. He felt that… inside much more these days, pushing to get out. He felt like he was going to burst.

- Hurry up. Frank admonished them. – The hot water won't run forever tonight.

And it didn't. The cold water pricked Ted's skin not long after Frank had spoken. The chill penetrated his hide. Water was turned off quickly. The boys and the girls started leaving the bathroom, bringing with them their gear to the bedrooms, not completely clean, but clean enough. The girls had the towels wrapped around their entire upper body to their knees. The boys had the towels tied around their waist. Iris looked at Ted, and he felt an instant reaction down below. He could hardly believe it. He had thought Tilla's look was direct. Iris wasn't «dressed» any different from the other girls, but her stance and the way she *moved* were totally different.

He stood in the cold, outside the bedroom for minutes until he felt ready to open the door and step inside. It was dark inside, but he took it all in in a flash and could still remember it vividly after closing the door. Tilla was in bed, covered by the down comforter, nicely tucked in, her radiant face turned towards him.

– Come to bed, she whispered.

He let the towel fall from his hips, and knew she could see it, somehow. His feet directed him, without conscious thought to the bed. He joined her under the comforter, feeling her, feeling her hands, her skin.

– You're cold.

She was, too. Her neck, her shoulder, her thigh. The air was ice, and wouldn't heat up for hours. He heard her breathing there, in the dark.

– Yeah, he said lightly. – Aren't these cabins supposed to be constantly occupied? This one looks like it hasn't been for ages.

– I guess they're reserved for rich white trash like Frank and guys, she said. – Rich people own the world. They can do what they want, and the rest of us are just their playthings.

She shrugged, and he felt her entire body move against his.

– They perceive it that way, he said.

He saw, sensed her smile. The room was absolutely dark. There was no line of light under the door. No light reached them from the hall. But he could still see her smile. See it, like nuances of darkness.

– I mean, look at this place, she marveled. – Like a hotel, and each and every room here its suite.

– It's too nice, he said, chilled in his voice as well as his body. – Like an ivory tower. Nothing is real.

A soft hand moved across his arms and she felt it. She had to.

– You got goose bumps, she said astonished.

He nodded, fully aware that she couldn't see it, certain that she could.

– And it isn't the cold, is it?

He started shivering, helpless to stop.

– The walk… here… it reminded me… of the walk through the forest at home, in Denver… when Mike w-waited there, in

426

the d-dark.

– You poor boy, she said softly, anguish in her voice.

The wind and the rain escalated outside, escalated beyond reason. It shook the cabin, shook it violently, shook the bed. The raindrops hammering against the window sounded like nails, a metal larynx screeching in the vast nothing.

She touched him, stroked him slowly back and forth. She coddled him, humming a bit, and he slowly calmed down, or rather calmed to a different form of... of unrest.

– And then there is the rage, he said, considered. – What I felt when I stood up to him, when I struck him... when I beat him... and it is as if any shred of fear is blown away.

The entire cabin seemed to shift, and the bed positively moved. They heard the legs scratch the floor.

– And then? She said, prompting him to continue, sensing his need.

– When I finally *did* it, he said, – on the Kendall ranch, finally tried to kill myself I was close at succeeding, at least I believe I was.

Her hand rubbed his head. They held on to each other, both shivering, slowly turning synchronized.

– I should have been dead, he insisted. – I don't know long time it took before they found me and started treating me, but there was a lot of blood. They told me you don't die from cutting your wrist, that you have to do a far more thorough job of it, but I could *smell* the blood. It was everywhere... and then I felt something, something different... The entire room was filled with... with Shadow, a darkness far more pronounced than the night. It spoke to me, whispered loud in my ear, nameless secrets and what I couldn't possibly know. I saw it in front of me, like I would if I looked into a mirror. It had my face, and it... smiled to me.

– Oh, baby, she said softly.

– And it was more. I knew I would survive, would live. There, in that moment, as the seconds and moments ticked away I glimpsed... glimpsed...

– You *woke up,* she said astounded. – Becoming Aware... like the god you are.

Wet kisses turned insistent, growing teeth.

She changed position slightly. Their eyes met. They saw each other's eyes and nothing besides. She saw red fire. He saw flashes of green and gray. She gasped. He did, too.

– Kiss me, she whispered. – Kiss me *hard*.

He noticed inevitably the excitement in her voice. He shifted position, too, and then he felt it, the increasing heaviness below, felt it pushing at her thigh. He kissed her. Irritated she slapped the hard thing pushing at her thigh. It hurt. He kissed her and tasted her blood.

– Ahhh, she sighed. – Better, much better.

She licked her lips, licked his. He felt her tongue's rough surface, felt it on every piece of skin it touched. It had happened slowly this time, almost unnoticeable. But at that moment everything exploded, and it was as if it happened for the first time. Suddenly he pushed forward and he was inside her.

– AHHH, she shouted.

She moved her thighs, moved them around his cock. As she had pointed out herself, she was good at this. He growled, stopped a moment, wondering if that was his voice, if it was indeed him and he knew beyond words, beyond thought that it was.

– Fangs and claws, she breathed. – Fangs and claws.

And then words didn't matter, thoughts didn't matter anymore.

Heat ruled them. The cold they had felt just moments ago was just a distant memory. I am burning. I'm burning. I'm burning…

The cabin shook in the Storm.
*************************/

Everything was silent, silent as dusk.

They awoke refreshed early next day, hot, sweaty and musky.

Early as far as they were concerned… a few minutes before twelve. Tilla looked at her watch with a huge, pleased grin on her face. They lay there entwined, under the now way too hot down comforter. She threw it off with an exalted cry, exposing them both. She turned slowly, back and forth on the bed, performing for him. Rolled one way, rolled another, touching herself. She crouched on the bed, sending him hot stares.

– You've probably heard this much more than a few times, he joked. – But I will just state the fact that you're one of the most enticing creatures in existence.

Her eyes turned huge and wet. She kissed him, a short touch before pulling back.

– The boy, the sweet, sweet boy is giving me compliments, she sniffed. – His brother never did, except perhaps in some mean-spirited way or another.

She embraced him, giving him a prolonged, lingering kiss. It tasted salt, bitter and sweet.

– My voice is hoarse as a horse, she said. – I'm thirsty. Are you?

– Like an Elephant, he confessed.

– I'll go and fetch water.

She jumped up and out of bed, grabbing a shirt and slipping it over her head before rushing out of the room, leaving the door open. His first instinct was to grab the down, and cover himself, but after giving himself time to consider it, he decided not to bother.

He had no idea of what to do if Iris or some other hungry bitch passed by, but he didn't cover himself.

Tilla walked down the long hall, passing most of the bedrooms to the living room. The living room was big (everything was big here). The kitchen, too. She had feared she would be the only light-clad person, male or female, but she was far from it.

– Wow, nice legs, Dennis cried.

And it didn't feel like one of his usual, vicious comments. It didn't feel like that at all. She wondered if he was aware of that, if they were all aware of the casual mood and behavior.

Bob, Veronica, John and Linda were in the kitchen. John was blushing, very telling.

– Breakfast will be ready soon, he gathered himself. – Fortunately, we're all very late.

– Late and great, Linda grinned.

Tilla noticed it instantly, how the ice-blond girl glowed, glowed with a warm, warm flame. She strived to keep it contained, but Tilla had always had an eye for such matters.

– Except for Liz and Jane. Bob shook his head. – They

grabbed something to go, and left early on an expedition. Or so I am told.

Tilla studied him without studying him. She wondered if he had caught himself. Caught himself in what? She shook her head. He looked at her with hunger in his eyes, but that was hardly unusual, was it? Men always did that.

– Joggers, Veronica said patronizing, always ready to support her mate. – I'm still stiff after yesterday's debacle. How can anyone think about exercise such a short time after that?

The exercise, jogging-wave had swept America in the early seventies, but it was still frowned at, still new and treated with ridicule many places.

Tilla filled two huge glasses with water, and excused herself with a smile as she left the kitchen.

Ted still lay stretched out on the bed when she returned, like he was a centerfold in a magazine. She… liked that. The heat, the guilt arose the moment his manhood caught her eyes.

She closed the door.

Eyes filled with mischief sought his. She put the glasses on the floor for a moment, picking up the comforter, carrying it to the closet, and pulling out a blanket.

- We don't need the warm covers anymore… she said huskily. Walking to him.

- … we *are* heat.

She returned to the bed, slipping eloquently out of her cover, and then she was covered no more. The fire in his eyes worried and pleased her. It always did. She handed him one glass, and they drank.

– I had a dream last night…

– You did? Eagerness and uncertainty were in her voice.

– Yes, he said. – And it wasn't really a dream at all. I was convinced everything before the dream had really happened. We're here. It's night. We're gathered in a circle. All of us are. Betty and Iris serve tea. Spiced tea. Iris sits at the center of the circle. Iris is a witch. I believe that. So do you. And Betty. I don't know about the others. She's calling a name, and a… presence enters the room. I feel a trickle down my spine. She's talking.

– Who is? Iris or the presence?

– Iris and the presence. And then I'm dreaming. I'm me, and I'm more than me. And there's more. I see a bunch of kids, see them grow older, the way they relate to each other… it's so different, so refreshing, the way kids and adults should relate to each other, the way they would, if we weren't fucked up from birth, by the world we live in. I see a place… canoes, a beach and a castle in the middle of a freshwater sea. A forest surrounds the sea on all sides. I see us. And many more. A woman turning into fire, pure and terrifying. A man turning into a wolf, then into a wolf-like dog and then back to a wolf… We're the children. We're the parents.

– And then I'm somewhere else, truly somewhere else. I see a place, not a place where giant shadows walk. And I know I'm dreaming, that I'm not dreaming.

Tilla stared amazed at the glass of water, at the remaining water. She sensed the glass turn hot.

– Spiced tea, Ted said slowly. – It tastes like life itself. The same taste emanating from you every time I smell your cunt.

She smiled or rather she grinned.

– And you're like walking fire, burning me by your every touch, she said softly, with just a slight touch of awe and fear. – You're like a hunger, eating me up, devouring me. In that sense you're no different from… him.

He just nodded, appreciating her honesty. A thrill shot through her. He sensed it, a hot, overwhelming wave on the beach. The light from the fireplace danced across the edge of the couch.

But they weren't on a couch. There was no beach here, no fireplace, no tea.

The room, the sheet pushing against his skin. Never had he felt anything more real.

He observed how her nipples hardened, how they grew.

She moved closer to him, moved close.

– I'm still thirsty…

She slipped down between his knees, never taking her eyes off his.

– I want to drink you.

And then she grabbed him, grabbed his cock, and he hardened. She took it in her mouth, slipped her lips around it, and he turned hard. He cocked his head, closed his eyes, and the eyes, when he opened them stared at the world.

He came in her mouth, and he feared he would hurt her with his crazy thrusts and pulls. After it's done she pulls back a little. Saliva and semen flow from her mouth as she looks at him, the rising tide of heat in her eyes. She rose and crawled into his lap, smiling in the expectation of the upcoming ecstasy. They tumbled back on the bed. As always when they fucked she was the leading party. As always, she was making him forget everything around him. He realized that this was the moment he was at his most vulnerable, the moment Mike would strike. He gasped, in fear, in hunger, in rage. His lips ravaged her, and she gasped, too. He wondered if he was imagining the tears behind the cheerful grin. She was enticing him with playful fingers, and he relaxed. He knew he would be ready again soon enough, ready and willing.

– I didn't get to ride you yesterday. I want to ride you, want to caress you with my spurs.

Everything turned red, turned black. He recalled them leaving the bed, recalling them finally having breakfast. And he felt the taste of food, of hunger in his mouth. The spiced tea exploded inside him. At this elevation he was even thirstier than he usually was. Everything worked, worked so much better. The world turned downside up, and everything was all right in the world.

He walked on a hill, and there was a giant dam below. The dam faded only slowly, as the world turned unreal again. The fog hadn't lifted. It clung to the ground like glue. He looked at a landscape of moss, bare rock and sparse growth. Betty approached him from behind. He rubbed his eyes. A moment there he had thought she had black hair. A moment there he had thought she had a big belly.

– When you lose control, you scare yourself sometimes.
She said.

And Betty Morgan was suddenly right there beside him. And it was something markedly different about her, like when she had spoken to him and Tilla in Denver. She had always been there, mostly a detail in the general background, but now she approached him, fully grown, smoldering desire in her eyes, her eyes filled with green fire.

He recognized that look instantly, the look of an agenda, of her carrying a spike in her gut. And it felt really strange to him that he had never seen it in her before.

She stopped there before him, displaying herself, not just her body, but her entire Self. There was pride there, and a confidence Tilla lacked.

– Have you noticed how well we all have started to relate to each other?

She said.

– How it started when you once again started taking an active interest in human affairs?

The way she said that, the way she emphasized certain words. So strange.

He had noticed, noticed small things at first, tiny glimpses of what might be, in hindsight gaining far more significance.

– Most lives are like castles of sand on the beach, ready to crumble by the first wave. But you, you're the leader of men and mice.

He stood there, unwilling and unable to comment on her words.

– I'm not, he told her.

– You're a wolf, Betty Morgan told him. – Not a sheep. Most people may be defenseless against the onslaught of the world, but you are not.

– Aren't we all defenseless? He wondered. – To a certain degree a victim of circumstances beyond our control? And isn't that true even more in this world of cruelty and injustice?

– Well, control *is* an illusion. She smiled enigmatically. – Yes, this world is shit. It needs to be changed, changed in major ways. But does the onslaught need to be afraid of itself?

– *Explain yourself.*

He hardly recognized the roar, the thunder that was his own voice. He grabbed her arm, clutched it in an iron-hard grip.

– I thought you would never ask, she said, in a strange, subdued voice.

He let go of her hand.

– You let go of my hand, she said, staring at him, locking her eyes to his. – But you don't let go of me. I can feel your claws, inside me, in my soul, feel the lust, irresistible. You're the one. You're the Storm, the Fire, the final days prophesized for millennia. I, being my own being, present myself to you, your servant in all things. As I was bred and born I belong to you.

And she was gone.

He heard her, a whisper in the wind.

– And thus, it begins.

And he couldn't be sure she had truly, ever been there.

He sought Iris, sought her out. He wasn't even sure he had before he saw her there by the pond.

– You're worried, she stated, before he had even spoken.

He had come to the right place, the right person, he sensed that, and he had started to trust his instincts.

– So, what's that witch-thing of yours?

He couldn't keep the incredulity, the skepticism out of his voice, and hated himself for that.

She smiled, a smile stung with disappointment.

– It's difficult to explain. It's a subtle thing, at least at first. The notion of myself as a witch started slowly. I treated it with ridicule myself, for a long time, before I gained the confidence needed to take it seriously. It's real, you know. To me it's real. Many are just calling themselves witches, out of religious conviction, but it's not that way with me. I am a witch, one who knows more than my Hail Mary.

– Well, that is good, he stated, he grinned. – That is, incidentally also why I have come to you.

Her entire face lit up, and he shared her joy, her fear, the fear coming from him.

He told her everything, everything he knew, also what he had only hinted at to Tilla. He related the visit he and Stewart had made to the mansion outside Denver, about Peter Clarke and the few details Stewart had provided him about David Gidman.

It lasted many long moments before Iris Carson - the Witch vocally replied to him. She did so, in a thousand subtle ways before that.

– It was evidently what is generally known as a black mass, she told him. – The way you describe it, the setting, the guys in hoods and all, if I'm not mistaken an ancient necromantic ritual. It's difficult to say whether or not it actually *worked,* other than the way you witnessed it, as a confirmation, an initiation, but that's sufficient to most people.

– Something is definitely going on, he said, shaking his head in frustration. – So much has happened. I'm sure of that. But I'm not Stewart. I don't have his experience, his ability to put clues together, to fit the puzzle.

– There is a way… She hesitated

– Yes?

– I haven't actually done it before. Stubbornly she fought what he easily identified as anxiety. – It's generally not done. In the texts I have read it's spoken about vengeful spirits, loss of identity and even worse, only hinted-at, repercussions.

– I must know, he stated.

She touched his cheek.

– There is nothing I wouldn't do for you, she said, deliberately making light of it, – you know that.

Her moving lips were curves and limbs moving in front of him.

– Hey, most of those things are bullshit, anyway. It's very rare that anything happens.

They laughed.

They stood there in silence, watching each other.

– We feel excitement, we feel fear… she finally said, very serious. – That's good. That's what we're supposed to feel.

They walked in silence back to the cabin.

The evening came. There was a mix of excitement and incredulity in the air. Most of those present displayed good-humored snickering when Iris drew the circle of chalk on the floor, but not all.

– So, what we're basically talking about here is a séance? Bob's voice dripped with sarcasm

– So what's wrong with you lately? Ted wondered.

Bob turned to him.

– What's wrong… with *me?* He laughed like a snarl. – You're going primitive on me, and have the audacity to ask what's wrong with me? What's next? Do we go back to living in caves, return to Mother Nature, and destroy ten thousand years of culture?

Ted had an eerie sense of premonition, but he didn't understand it. He could only stare in shock at his friend's hostility and twisted face.

All electrical lights in the room were turned off. Candles were lit on tables and chairs. The room suddenly seemed vast, seemed endless. The walls still seemed to be there, but the human beings gathered between them no longer felt certain about that, felt sure about anything.

Ted heard Betty and Iris talk in the kitchen, saw them just as clearly as if they were standing right in front of him.

– Have you ever actually made the brew? Betty asked softly.

– No, Iris snickered. – At least not with all the ingredients, not one actually working.

– I have. I will help you. I will be your aide.

He saw Iris' shock and curiosity, felt it tingle through his mind. None of them had truly known Betty, he realized. He wondered if that was true with more of those present here, wondered if anybody truly knew anybody.

Helen, prompted by Iris, went and fetched her drum. She sat down as one of the first just inside the circle.

– What do I do?

Suddenly Betty was there, pushing Iris aside.

– Look at me, Betty said, grabbing Helen's jaw. – Feel me, feel yourself.

She beat her drum, uncertain at first. Iris nodded encouragingly. Betty mercifully.

– You're not here anymore, Betty told her.

A gust swept the room. Helen shook. She wanted to rise, to run, but Betty held her in her grip, and Ted stared as if transfixed.

– Sing. Betty commanded. – Sing the song, Singer.

And Betty started humming, a mystical, ancient wordless song. Helen listened, and her eyes turned distant, and she started humming, too, uncertain at first, but then more confident; something so different from what she was usually doing that everybody stared at her. It didn't sound like her voice at all, and she even looked different.

Betty nodded pleased, and lowered her own hum, but she kept it going, as if in trance.

Betty served the tea. She handed cups to Ted and Tilla with a hungry, transfixed smile. Tilla didn't smile in return. The three of them drank simultaneously. Spice filled Ted's mouth, flowed down his throat, exploded in his stomach.

– What does it do? He asked lightly.

– It opens, Betty said. – Opens up everything. It's the Spice of Life.

Everybody drank, even Bob, some apprehensive, some indifferent, some eager, others smirking.

The drum beat slow, lingering, like heartbeats. There was a low rumble, like the hissing of a snake.

Iris sat down at the center. Helen sat back to back to her. Everybody else joined the circle. Dennis was the last to join, and when he did the circle was complete.

– That's good, Iris smiled. – Now, hold hands all of you. Make the complete ring complete.

Ted had Betty on his left side and Tilla on his right. It felt awkward, it felt right.

– Good, Iris nodded. – Very good. Now concentrate, concentrate on what we're doing. If you don't feel up to it or think you'll break into scornful laughter or something during the ceremony you should leave, really. Negative energies are known to disrupt Journeys, and answers we seek may be denied us.

There was a bit of unrest and shifting of positions, but nobody left. Everybody held hands, completing the circle.

– Something is happening, Helen sang with a deep voice.

The others hardly recognized it.

– We're becoming attuned, Iris said. – The spice does that, does that, too, making up for much of our inexperience. It has already started what we otherwise might have needed to fast and sweat for days to achieve. It has started, and when this night is done you will never be the same.

She giggled, and it echoed dark and menacing through the room. Betty laughed, as she looked euphorically at Ted. He remembered her words, her vocalization, declaration of independent servitude. She meant it. He saw it in her eyes, in her entire posture. The demon was his to do with as he pleased. And he wondered if this was how she wanted him to think.

Iris spoke again. Ted's attention shifted constantly between the two.

– What I will do is to call my spirit guide, and through her reach out to the shadow world. When I've done that my voice may change. This is perfectly normal, and nothing to fear.

But she was clearly afraid.

She closed her eyes, concentrating.

There was a low rumble, and the floor was shaking under them. The very air seemed to darken in the room. Ted felt like the darkness was surrounding him, and he saw it, saw the shadow close to Iris. There were sounds everywhere, strange sounds that could just as well be nothing but ordinary and perfectly natural sounds, as the wind blew and moved the walls and floor. Iris opened her eyes.

– Thalama, she called, – Thalama - Goddess of Destiny - hear my call. We are seekers, and as seekers we reach out to you in your heaven. We want to know, want to see the secrets of Time and Space unveiled.

The drumbeat had slowed to a halt, the humming had faded. Helen slumped to the floor.

– Thalama, Iris called. – Thy humble servant is beseeching thee. Please let us in in your favor. Let us glimpse the secrets, let us see behind the veil. Thalama, I offer myself, I offer

She simply stopped. Everything turned silent, silent as death. Iris Carson sat there frozen, as if someone had just turned a switch. Ted felt it. He felt the energy, well before Iris' eyes turned inside out and turned absolutely white. Her lips moved, and the voice wasn't anything resembling her voice.

– Time is not a river, but a flood, flowing fields and forests.

A bird hit the window. They heard its screech. A black bird hit the window, and they saw nothing in the dark, only heard the sound of the actual hit, and the raven calling out in a strange voice:

– Distant butterfly wings are flapping, past, present and future, affecting everything. Small events, seemingly insignificant when they happen gain importance… in time. The pages of the Book of Shadows are turning in the wind.

– The Book of Shadows? Ted said uncertain. – Isn't that what witches use to describe their experiences and their craft?

– No, Iris/Thalama said, acknowledging him with a devilish snarl. – That's one book of shadows, not *The* Book of

Shadows, the one also called the Book of Fate, where all things are written down. Everything that has been, everything that is, everything that might have been, everything that will ever be, everything that might be.

Iris moaned, as the forces ravaged her. And in glimpses Ted didn't see her, but the Shadow, gaining clarity, gaining ascendance. And these words, these notions raging through Ted's mind weren't unknown to him, weren't unfamiliar, and the forces started ravaging him, too.

– I see a sword, Iris said, – a sword of fire, shadowing the Earth, tempered in the hot furnaces of the desert.

And nothing happened for a long, long time.

Time expanded to eternity, space to infinity, as they sat there, waiting, waiting, waiting, waiting for summer to come, the axe to fall. The room changed, no longer a room. The people changed, no longer people. Ted looked at them, stared at them all, sweat trickling down his forehead.

– These are your first warriors, Phoenix. With them you will fail, succeed and fail again. You will dream, dream your resurrection dreams.

Ted gasped. He couldn't see Iris anymore. Where she had been was just a misty black hole, and she had been sucked into it. And it was the misty black hole forming words like lips, and then he realized he could see her, that the black hole was the space between her lips, and she was so much bigger than he could remember, a giant sitting in a field, in a wasteland of wreckage and destruction. And he saw her, saw her for what she was, what she truly was. In the ebony space he glimpsed her fangs. And in her eyes, he saw himself, saw himself, saw what he was.

– I'm so fucked up. It was John's voice, but it wasn't necessarily John, or at least not only him.

Ted sensed it then, sensed the twisting and turning inside.

The candles started flickering and the shadows grew longer.

The slow running river became a waterfall.

He screamed in pain, and almost fell over. His eyes were open, and he couldn't close them.

– Yes, Thalama said in her ghostly voice. – The oracle sought an oracle, sought a witch, and has found one.

He knew well what those words entailed. They were clear enough. But he couldn't grasp it, couldn't hold it in his hands, couldn't catch the wind.

Betty smiled her smile. She grabbed him.

– I know it hurts, she hummed softly in his ear. – Being born hurts.

Bob screamed like a lost soul not that far away. He ran away in the darkness.

There were no walls anymore, no ceiling, no floor.

Betty and Ted faced each other in the wasteland, a place where the ruins were only tiny rubble by their feet.

– You do see it, don't you, she whispered, looking so much like Tilla, so different from her then, – the Tapestry unfolding?

And yet again, meeting her eyes he felt frost trickle down his spine.

– Yes, you do. You do!

Her face, her entire being brightened like the sun, darkened like the moon.

She touched him, stroked his hair, calming, demanding.

– What do you see? Tell Betty, tell your muse.

Clarity swept him again. Confusion riddled him.

– There's a giant, a Cyclops, a one-eyed giant like in the Greek legends. And I see rows and rows of… of dolls. They sort of have human faces, but rigid, frozen, frozen horrible smiles. It's us. They're all us. I can see Stewart walking through streets I don't recognize. He's on fire and he's smiling. I feel the fire and it isn't burning me. I'm back at the cabin. Suddenly the door and its windows are turning into a face, Mike's face, and it's glaring at me.

– And then it is many years later. He's obviously older. He's crying. He sits in an empty room, and he's crying.

Ted grabbed Betty.

– Why can't I see? When I see so much, why doesn't understanding come?

– This is, the way I have heard it very common among precognitives, she said. – The secrets of time reveal themselves only reluctantly. Have you ever tried, while on a mountaintop to focus on details far below? You see everything, you see nothing, in an ever-shifting tapestry of confusing imagery. But understanding *will* come, I promise you that.

Iris screamed, a sound cutting through metal, through flesh and blood like that famous image of the hot knife through butter.

– JESUS CHRIST, a voice cried, one he couldn't, was totally unable to recognize, – they have flipped. They have seriously flipped.

He woke up in a middle of a nightmare, one even worse than the one he was currently living through.

– I saw it, he gasped. – I saw claws like talons reach for us and tear us apart.

It was daylight. He was in bed. Everything was strange, alien. The room was not the room, but a foreign, horrible place. He was sweating profusely. His entire body hurt. Tilla was at his side, in the bed, attempting to calm him down. She soothed him with a hum and soft touches.

Glory, Glory Burns left the circle. They all did. Chalk was spread for the four winds, and everything dissolved. But he saw her, fear and shame and hatred visible in her features.

They all fled the circle, like rabbits before the wolf.

They sat there, frozen, writhing on the floor, unable to get to their feet.

Betty was afraid of him, too. She desperately tried to hide it, but he saw right through her. He laughed to her face.

Tilla ran. She didn't know where, and didn't care. On the surface it looked like the area outside the cabin, but there was a bluish light somewhere, making the landscape very alien. The light, the brighter than dark glare, seemed to come from everywhere, both from the air and the ground.

She stopped. Her legs could carry her forever, but her mind couldn't.

There was a tree in the middle of a lake, the full moon casting the silver, bluish light, casting it on this fire lake. The color of the moon and the color of the fire were both dominant and dominant simultaneously. Everything happened simultaneously, someone said. Past, present and future were merely stones hitting the lake at the same time. They were experienced differently because they were hitting the surface in different places. But if you squinted your eyes a bit and looked at the surface horizontally everything was the same place.

The tree grew in the middle of the lake. There was no soil there, no ground. It grew in and was nourished by the water itself. There was no forewarning. Suddenly, shockingly the tree fell, fell silently, like a whisper in the night. It hit the water… and the water turned to ground, to stone, and the stone turned to glass, and the tree hit it so hard that it cracked. The older, red-haired woman walked through ruins, between buildings with walls hardly taller than that of a human, dwarfish remains of skyscrapers and giant towers.

– Yes, this is the Wastelands, Betty said. Tilla turned, and there she was. – I have heard numerous interpretations of what that actually is.

Betty walked in a circle around her. She stopped before her, and everything happened now.

– Some say it is the realm above the one where we live so briefly, one our Shadow, our eternal Self passes through on its way to the infinite Universe. Others that it is parallel dimensions, other earths, where other human species have tried and failed. Dying universes where all probabilities are gone. Or that it is quite simply the future, our future, as it will eventually become.

– How did we come here? Tilla asked frostily, rubbing her arms, attempting to warm the icy skin on her bare arms.

– We're not really here, stupid. At least our bodies probably aren't. They're in the cabin, drugged to a stupor. This is a dream, or some sort of one, where we aren't dreaming. This is real. And what we're experiencing is the future, of a sort. And that's very interesting.

Betty seemed to tower over her, her green eyes big as campfires, a demonic look in her face.

– We're the same, you and I. At least we could be, if you just got your ass in gear. The fact that I've had some teaching, and have gained something of an advantage doesn't enter into the inevitable conclusion: You're pathetic.

Tilla wanted to say something, wanted it desperately, but she had no longer any mouth to speak with.

– You see, I'm a witch, too, but one of many of those no more able to foresee the future than any of the walking dead mundane smucks pestering our lives. I know this for a fact, and that means, by default, that you can't either. Why do you think that is?

Tilla was in bed, in her house in Denver. She was lying paralyzed by the green campfire deep in the wilderness. Betty sat by her side, stroking her skin, touching her, in ways slowly turning more intrusive.

– Mmm, I know how you love this, when Teddy does it. But now it feels like the worst form for intrusion, of torture, right? Because you're completely in my power. I can do whatever I want with you, you helpless sack of dirt.

It was the day after the party. Tilla had been out shopping. Ted had been in bed sleeping when she left, and she wanted to make breakfast for him. People had stared at her, stared at the bruises and cuts, but she was used to them staring, and pretended to ignore it. She fixed the meal, put it all in the pan, (the pan being a cauldron, the thought making her twitch), and left it to cook. The first, lingering smell was already pervasive in the air. She smiled as she walked out in the garden, and lay down on the hammock, swinging back and forth in a lullaby of soft, soft vibrations. From the living room she heard the voice of Richard Nixon. Another clueless reporter was interviewing him, allowing him to speak his lies, unchallenged. She struck the ground with a hand. It didn't hurt. She hardly felt the impact.

Suddenly Betty was there, sitting in the garden chair, close to her.

– Power is the way of the world. The sooner you start dealing with that, the better you'll be off. Ol' Dickie isn't the power, though, but like all presidents, all janitors, hardly even the power's hand.

The green-eyed redhead broke off the point of the points of two vials and pushed into Tilla's nostrils. Tilla attempted to turn her head away, but nothing worked. She couldn't move, not even her fingers, not even her distant butterfly wings.

– Now, I want you to breathe, breathe deeply.

– NO! Tilla concentrated, desperately attempting to breathe through her mouth and fight off the other's pervasive influence, what penetrated her thoughts like mist.

– You *will* obey!

She gave in after no more than a few seconds of feeble resistance. At first, she drew her breath weakly, but then deeply, deeply, deeply.

– That will do. Good girl.

Ted arrived back home. Tilla finished preparing the food, with the little extra Betty had asked her to include. He fell asleep, and when he woke up hours later he just smiled and said apologetically:

– I must have been more tired than I thought.

Sweet Ted. Contempt and despair flowed through Tilla.

– Good girl, Betty told her. – He will wake up quite soon, you know. He's got a remarkable constitution. He notices us, on some deeper level, notices us hovering above him.

– Do you know what?

Betty whispered in her ear.

– I saw bikers not far from here. It would be easy for me to call them, get them to pay you a visit, wouldn't it?

She laughed out loud and viciously when she observed how the fear made Tilla shiver and shake, how she attempted to move, but couldn't do it.

– No, p-please. Tilla begged.

– Nobody will hear your piteous complaints, I can assure you of that. Besides, as you know, with my power of persuasion I can take you deep into the mountains, where you can scream as much as you could possibly want.

Betty held her, held her in her terrible mental grip. Tilla stared into the demonic green eyes, sensing that she was drifting away. Reality just faded until it no longer mattered. Her ability to think independently slowly eroded. When she once more came to her senses, it was night. She saw her own naked body in the light from the fire.

– They're here, little beauty. The bikers are here. Aren't you happy?

She was truly out there in the wilderness, deep into the mountains. Keith Lampard and Ray Channon were there, with all the other leatherjackets. They all stood in a circle around her, laughing triumphantly, and all had their fly open. Their huge, swollen cocks were sticking out, pointing at her. She

444

screamed, screamed herself hoarse. Her childhood's nightmare haunted her. They grabbed her, they punished her and made her theirs. She fought. She did, but she was helpless, like a child in their hands, in their power. The laughter from the green fires made her shake in terror. Nothing was real, and she screamed herself hoarse.

Chapter nineteen

Ted sat up in the bed, his heart hammering in his chest.

Tilla screamed her lungs out. She jumped hysterically up and down in the bed, completely beside herself. She looked so totally out of it that he had continuous and violent frost rides down his spine. He tried to grab her, to comfort her, but the moment he stepped closer she gave him a knock on the head that sent him flying out of the bed. He landed hard by the closet, shaking his head.

She stopped. She just stopped, staring horrified at him, before falling on her knees on the bed, howling like a lost soul.

He rose, and fell. He crawled back into the bed, carefully touching the girl's deadly pale skin and embracing her sweaty body.

Linda, Bob, Veronica and John rushed into the room, spearheading a regular invasion. They all gathered around the disaster area of a bed. No one seemed to notice that the two on it, and most others were nude. This was more than evident in the room's soft darkness.

Someone finally remembered the fact that there were lights in the room. Hands reached for the various switches.

– No, Tilla stopped them. – Don't turn on the lights. I'm okay. I'm okay now.

They hesitated, but did as she wanted.

– Are you sure? Linda asked.

– It was a nightmare, Tilla mumbled, without really acknowledging Linda or her words. – Just a nightmare. You may go. Thank you, guys.

They left, filed out of the room while casting curious and worried looks behind them.

The door closed.

The two of them returned to the comfort of the bed, under the blanket. The room was warm. It was cold there, under the thin cover, skin to skin.

She shivered. She trembled.

– Did you see? She said. He sensed the rigid, dead body by his side. – They looked at me. The boys looked at me. They w-wanted me.

He wanted to say something, anything, but the words stuck in his throat.

The room was dark. Some light shimmered through the window. He would guess somebody had turned on a light somewhere, and that it reflected from the ground outside and shimmered through the window. Perhaps they looked around the room like he did, at the dark that moved and breathed. He couldn't keep his eyes still. One sound from somewhere, and he had to fix his eyes at that point, to see if someone... something was there.

– Tell me about Betty, he said.

– What is there to tell? She *scares* me, okay?

– You're keeping something from me. I won't have it. *Tell me!*

He hadn't meant for the anger to be revealed, but there it was, a living thing, just like the dark.

His will against hers. It was no contest. He felt good when she shrank under his remorseless stare, when she succumbed to his power.

– She c-came to me some months ago, suddenly very, very different from the distant mouse she had always been, or at least pretended to be. I... felt it instantly, her power, her ability to take control over me. *Mind control*. She spoke a lot, even implied my brother Ronald was still alive, taunting me with it, taunting me. I don't know if she wanted me to understand or not, but I didn't. I don't. She made me p-poison you, treating it like a test. What it was a test of, of my compliance, of your endurance, I don't know. I had to do what she commanded, do you understand? There was no choice, no free will. Except hers.

He attempts to say something. He can't

– I'm sorry, Tilla sniffed. – I'm *sorry!* I'm so worthless, so fucking worthless. You should leave me, leave me behind.

He touched her cheek, just a little, just briefly.

– I've seen how... persuasive she can be, he said. – I saw it with Helen. You're wrong if you think I don't understand.

He sees it in her eyes before she speaks.

– But I didn't want to tell, she whimpered, – but you made me tell. No hocus pocus, no «Magic», only your will against mine, and I lost. You're so much stronger than me.

He imagines she grabs him, but she remains still, unmoving.

– I'm weak, she said quietly, horribly. – A weak bitch in need of protection, of shelter. Say that you will protect me, please. Please.

– The way I see it you don't really need to be protected. He attempted levity, carefully touching the growing swelling by his left eye. – I'm not very good with promises. You should protect me…

He had promised Linda, promised Liz, promised Maria.

– Swear! She said subdued and timid. – Swear you will protect me.

– I swear, he swore empty and diminished.

Silence reigned for a long time, and he felt sick to his stomach She kissed him on the cheek. She spoke with lowered eyes.

– I'm so glad you find me pleasing, pleased that you can be forgiving. I'm yours, now. I'm yours to do with as you please.

The vast Abyss he had always feared opened up below him, and he was falling. He didn't move, but he was falling still.

Everything was so silent. He was unable to hear a thing, even if he strained himself.

She pulled tight to him. He wanted, wanted badly to push her away, and worse, but did nothing.

He couldn't sleep. He didn't know if she was sleeping or just dead in his arms. Every time he closed his eyes fear assaulted him, and he reopened them in a fit of panic.

– You're troubled, she whispered. – Don't be. Tilla will comfort you. Tilla will make everything all right.

Eyes closed briefly, in the moment of explosion. He knew he had emptied himself in her, but he didn't remember doing it. She was asleep now. Of that he was certain. He was sleepy, and the ejaculation had tired him further. He should have been able to fall asleep. Eyes opened wide in a burst of panic, turning his head everywhere, at the deeper shadow in the corner, on the spot beside the bed, the open closet.

He had almost fallen asleep… when he sensed… the presence in the dark, and he once more turned wide awake.

Time dragged on, till morning, and even then, at the first light it was as if there were shadows everywhere. He remained in bed, staring at the world through swollen, sore eyes, feeling totally exhausted and out of it.

He took a shower. There was no one else there this early. Silence reigned. He hardly heard the sound of the water pouring down on him, around him. It felt good cleansing oneself, so very good. There was a smile, a bittersweet smile, a shaking of the head. He being early. That was worth a laugh. The water needles drummed against his skin. He still felt the need to constantly turn and look behind him, but resisted it, resisted it with his hands curled into fists, and blood mixed with water as his claws dug into his palm.

It hurt. It stung. He welcomed the pain, the incessant pain.

They had breakfast much earlier today. He studied the many early birds. A lot of them looked more than a little skittish. Bob looked particularly bad. He looked downright scary where he sat, scowling at everybody. Ted shook his head, wanting to speak to his friend, but held back. So many thoughts, so many images rushed through Ted's mind, and he couldn't make sense of any of them.

He kept reliving the memory of himself and Stewart visiting the castle, the initiation ceremony. Shadows and faces filed before his eyes, everything that had happened lately, since he had come out of his self-imposed mental hibernation. His power of observation, serving him so well earlier in life kept doing so. The sarcasm he directed at himself made him want to puke.

Iris hadn't left her room. He found her there, sitting on the edge of the bed, with one sock on a foot, and the other in her hand. She had been sitting still there a long while, staring at the wall.

– All things start small. Then, suddenly lightning strikes, and everything changes.

Her voice didn't sound like a voice at all, but more like sound filtered through wet paper, the way he imagined that sounded anyway. She sat there, pale and timid, circles around her eyes. Her wounded look resembled Tilla's in many ways, and the way she had looked, her eyes had looked like that of a kid.

– You and Tilla have argued.

– If only it had been an argument, but it's only death, he said, and his voice was hardly a voice at all.

She sat there, unmoving, but he saw her writhe on the floor, with dozens of pins sticking out of her skin.

– I saw a hungry gap in the dark. Her shoulders sagged even more. – Black lips moving hungrily, unseen teeth tearing me up. It... *looked* at me. The mouth looked at me.

– Perhaps it wasn't like that? He offered.

No reaction.

– We went too far, she said, like frozen over, – and paid the price.

She kept staring at the wall, unmoving. Only her lips had moved, briefly, flowering before dying. He left, walked away, and closed the door behind him.

He returned to his room, the one he shared with Tilla. She had showered and was dressing. The moment he opened the door she smiled and ran to him, kept playing the devoted wife. He punished her by not slapping her, waiting patiently until she pulled away from him.

In the corner there was an oblong package, one wrapped in cloth. He had placed it there the night of their arrival and could hardly remember doing so or even hardly recall its shape and texture. He unpacked it in stiff, mechanical movements, but with a determination clearly evident and clearly felt. The content revealed itself slowly for their eyes. It was his old Mauser rifle. He looked at it, studied it from all sides, assessing it with burning eyes. She looked at it, looked at him. He had removed the grease, and re-oiled it before leaving Denver. It was in great shape, in perfect order. He hadn't used it for six years.

The hall, dark and foreboding. He walked down it, to the living room. She remained in the room. He knew that, without looking back, not sensing her by his side.

He had said casually to those present on a seemingly random meeting a few days before leaving Denver:

– Why don't we bring guns?

Among those present were Bob, John, Helen and Bruce, «fellow» members of the gun club.

– That's a great idea! Frank exclaimed, before anybody else managed to say anything. – Lake County is supposed to be a great area for hunting.

And that had been that. Ted hadn't needed to present his thoroughly thought-out illogical reasoning.

Perhaps I have a talent for this, after all, he thought.

He entered the living room smiling relaxed and confident.

– Why don't we go outside?

They looked at him. They all looked at him, but he had expected that.

– It's such a fine day.

*****************/

With a few, notable exceptions everybody gathered outside the cabin, the cabin palace. A strange mixed mood of curiosity, excitement and apprehension flowed between them all.

It was indeed a fine day. The Sun had been heating the ground since early morning, and large parts of the less wet areas had dried. The majority of the gathering, those without weapons and more than moderately interested sat down on those exclusively dry spots. The others sat higher up, on rocks, content on enjoying the day.

These are your first warriors, Phoenix, Ted thought, looking at them, studying them without studying them. With them you will fail, succeed and fail again.

He had gotten his answer, all right, bought dearly and paid for, with pain and blood. But that was how it would always be. He had realized that, now.

They had found a kind of natural shooting course, very distinctive, just a few minutes walk from the cabin. It was like burned into his memory, and he knew beyond doubt that he would always remember it beyond clarity.

He felt the weight of the rifle. It was heavy, but not as heavy as he remembered it.

– It's more than a bit crowded here, Glory Burns commented, turning towards the three sitting close to her, Liz Horton, Betty and Linda. – How come?

– It is because of Ted, Liz replied. – Three years ago, he swore he would never fire a gun again.

– Why? Wasn't he the local champion once?

Linda only listened halfheartedly to the conversation, staring longingly at Ted under half lowered lashes.

451

– He killed his brother Mike with a gun, Betty added.

Linda opened her eyes fully.

– My apologies, Glory said quietly. – I didn't know.

– I didn't either. Liz expressed her shock in a shrill voice. – I heard that Mike was killed when that cabin burned. Nobody has told me differently, Nobody.

– It wasn't widely publicized, Linda stated, and added, turned to Betty. – Where have you heard differently?

– I just heard. The green-eyed girl shrugged.

They turned silent, watching the shooters prepare. They all looked at Ted.

– It's a strangely exhilarating sight, isn't it? Betty mused.

– What is? Linda wondered.

– To see a human being pull himself up on his feet by the hair. And it isn't the first time he has done so either.

Ted heard them, heard them unbelievingly clear from his position. He shouldn't have. It was too far away, but he did never the less.

– Can you hear them speak? He asked Bob.

– Who? Bob was very busy loading his rifle.

– Linda, Betty and the girls.

– No. Bob shook his head, clearly indifferent. – Too far away. This isn't a natural amphitheater like in Greece, amplifying sound, you know.

Ted didn't say anything more. He had heard the admiration in Betty's voice. It wasn't exactly an unknown quality to him, after all. And he turned, if possible even more confused.

– There is a melody, a tune here, Betty sang, – one of the wilderness, of the desert.

She still sat there, among the other girls, but she didn't speak to them.

– I know you can hear me, she told him. – I just wanted you to know that I know you know. You can hear all the cries from the mountaintops, all the ghostly whispering in the desert.

She stretched, displaying herself to him. The others might think she was just being forward, that she enjoyed showing off, but it was for him, only for him.

– Can you feel it? I know you can. The land here is resonating very much like a desert. It is your fate. There will be a time when you remember my words and know their truth.

They placed targets in the terrain, boxes and also boards with numbers from one to ten. Ted tried to get the feel of the rifle in his hand, to remember what he knew by heart when being much younger. After standing there for quite a while he fired at the nearest box - and missed. Bob fired at the box the farthest away, and it jumped joyously in the air. Helen hit her box, too. John missed his, but he had never been very good with a rifle.

Ted recalled the shooting contest shot by shot, how every shot felt like an extension of himself. He recalled every single lash of the whipping hitting his skin in the windy cabin.

He almost sat down, right there, in the mud. He almost threw away the rifle. His hand held on to it for dear life, clutching it so hard it almost broke. He remembered the shot he had fired in that other, bigger cabin, remembered the blood when the bullet hit another human being, the scream, the fire. He hit some boxes, missed others. There was no sense of release, of triumph when he hit something.

They fired at the boards, in series of five each. Bob got fifty points every time. The others around forty. Ted beat John once. But when they stopped after five tries he had finished last, with a lot of points up to third place.

– Well, let's try something different then, shall we?

Bob produced his 357 Magnum and wanted to hand it to Ted. Ted shook his head. Bob meant well, but Ted couldn't do it. He just couldn't.

John and Bob, especially John did a show nothing short of remarkable. And he was even better on moving targets. They threw boxes in the air, and he hit every single one. Bob missed most of the time. Eventually John kept it going alone. The revolver seemed to come alive in his hands. He was just as good with both hands. They had seen him perform before, but he had never been quite this good, this great.

– I love the old westerns, he admitted, very modest.

– This gun is a bit to the left, though, he added, perhaps not so modest, before returning it to Bob with an apologizing smile.

There was a kind of uplifted mood afterwards, the kind Ted had basically had in mind when prompting this exercise. It would do. It would have to do.

– You should all become members of the club when we return to Denver, he told them. – We should start doing this on a regular basis. One never knows what may be needed one day.

They did listen to him. He wasn't sure if they understood the implications of his words, but they did listen.

The twenty and three sat around the dinner table, most of them in a clearly exalted mood.

– Let's have a feast… Bob rose and raised his glass. – For no other reason than to have one.

Laughter. Raising of glasses, meeting and parting of glasses.

– And in honor of the winner by default… I give you the champion of the foggy mountains…

John reddened. More laughter, exalted and rich.

– Hello, there, Helen nipped Bruce in the collar. – Didn't we talk about this? Nothing but soda during daytime.

– This is men's soda, girl, he grinned. – It's the occasion, right? Besides, it won't be more than this one glass.

– Promise? The dark-haired girl nailed him with her eyes

– And hope to die, he solemnly swore, and held up his hand like a president sworn into office.

Tilla didn't laugh much or even say much. She just kept close to Ted in very much the same way she had done with Mike. Ted pretty much ignored her, just as he knew Mike would have done.

– It's weird, Jane giggled. – It's broad daylight. I can see outside, see the rest of the living room, but just now it is as if the rest of the world beyond this table… doesn't exist.

It was true. The images of the chairs, the tables, the carpet, the trees and the rocks did seem two-dimensional, didn't look real.

Iris drank a lot, and laughed a lot.

– I have heard lab rats feel that way, Liz said.

– Well, the human ability to deceive oneself is astounding, Dennis said.

Ted wanted to address that, to correct him and her somehow. He agreed, but not in this context. This wasn't self-deception. This was real. Something was happening, something horrible, something unique and great.

– I mean… Dennis kept up. – Unless something truly bad happens, we basically think of childhood as a happy time. But it isn't, not really, not if you think about it.

– We're all a bunch of pathetic nostalgic assholes. Bruce spoke up. – Cheers!

– Cheers, Dennis cried.

Their glasses met and parted, and they drank, drank a lot.

– Behold, two nascent philosophers, Linda said, not unfriendly.

– Something is being… born, Ted told Tilla.

Or perhaps it was Betty. Betty was on his other side, and just for a moment he couldn't tell them apart.

– Yes, she said.

Ted kept to the soda, without the *spiced* version most others were consuming. He felt no rush at overcoming the contempt he felt against alcohol. It still burned in his stomach, as he had heard, as he imagined wine would have done. Or even exploded there, like Liquor. He felt… he felt so much.

He still smelled it on him, from the moment he had almost drowned in the stuff, drowned in the pool outside Forester Minor Mansion. Drowned in the kids' contempt, nasty words and actions they probably didn't even remember anymore. It hadn't been such a big deal… to them.

– Bob is taking the defeat in quite an outstanding way, Glory said to Linda.

– He has been such a prick lately, the White Rose replied. – So I guess he decided to lighten up a bit.

Ted heard that. Everybody heard that.

Bob whispered, just loud enough in Veronica's ear:

– Girls having their monthlies should be careful expressing themselves.

Veronica threw her head backwards, laughing, kissing him passionately.

Ted felt like he was drunk. Everything turned indistinct. The room whirled and whirled before his eyes, subtle but real. He tasted the soda carefully, to see if anyone had spiked it, but no. It was just soda. Pretty poisonous, generally pretty devastating on the human body and mind, but just soda.

They had left the table, and circulated in the various groups forming.

John struck Ted on the shoulder, shaking him out of his

pondering.

– We will rise early tomorrow and leave the stupor behind, to fish trout, right Ted?

Distractions, all over the place. Damn. Ted left John without replying, rushing into the corridor, into darkness and clarity, but clarity still eluded him. Information, process information calmly, Stewart had said. Find out what you know and don't know. Think it through.

There was shouting, from one of the rooms. His. The door was open. The one he «shared» with Tilla. He stopped and listened. Suddenly it did no longer matter if he was silent or not. Loud voices assaulted his ears. He heard Linda's hateful voice:

– YOU'RE LYING. Tell me the truth. BITCH!

Ted walked through the doorway and watched it happen. To emphasize her words, her accusations Linda slapped the other girl, leaving a visible mark of a hand on the other girl's cheek. Ted grabbed Linda and pulled her away.

– You jealous witch, you couldn't stay away, huh? So, what is your excuse?

He let her go, ready for anything, really, raising his arm, ready to strike.

Linda stared at him, shock and disbelief filled her eyes. She was years back in time, to their twelfth birthday.

– Why did you do that? You should have helped me, you should…

– I'm waiting.

– Betty knows, Linda snarled, seething in wrath and fear. – Knows what happened in the cabin. And Tilla told her. She denies it, but I know she did it.

– What if she did? Ted sighed. – What difference does it make? Is it the end of the world, do you think?

Linda just looked at him, looked at him, turned and left.

He turned to Tilla, looking at her.

– I didn't tell her, Tilla said. – I didn't!

– Okay. He sat down on the bed, trying to find something, anything to hold onto. – As I said it's no big deal anyway. I never thought it would remain a secret.

– That's good, she mumbled. – That's very good.

Then she took one step forward, and there was suddenly a horrible rage in her eyes.

– Why didn't you *punish* her? Why didn't you beat her senseless?

He looked up, his eyes turned to glass, and he looked at her, unable and unwilling to hide his feelings.

– I'm not Mike.

And she stared horrorstruck at him.

– And you're no longer Mike's bitch, even though you seem to believe you are.

He rose abruptly and rushed out of the room, wanting to get as far away as possible. He heard her chasing him in a kind of daze, and he stopped, not sure what to expect, not sure what he expected.

She put a hand on his shoulder.

– I'm truly sorry, she whispered.

He turned towards her, to her shaken, tearful expression.

– It is I, now, she insisted. – Not Mike's bitch, not the monster you've been forced to endure today.

She touched his cheek, caressed it softly and tenderly.

– I'm sorry. I let you carry the load alone. All of it. I'm sorry. I love you.

He wanted to stay hard, a part of him did. He relented after holding back a few seconds. She gave away a tiny, soft cry of joy.

They kissed, and he did feel better, a little better, a little worse.

She pulled him with her, eager and sensuous, transformed. He put his index finger to his lips, deliberately, alerting her. She looked inquiringly at him, curiosity tinged with inevitable disappointment. He checked all the adjacent rooms, before entering their room. He checked outside their window, before turning to her. She closed the door. Clever girl. He loved her.

– I've got something to tell you, he said. – It's long overdue.

And he told her everything, straight up, without adding or subtracting anything. Watching how her face, rich in texture, as always changed and shifted in shadow.

She walked to him, forgiving him, signaling that there was nothing to forgive, and she was no longer this meek, sycophantic creature doing so. That, he thought, pleased him more than anything.

– There's something going on, he said, agitated, straining to keep his voice low. – There's danger, here, in this place, and no matter where we choose to go. Because it's connected to us, not places.

She tried to speak.

– The world is our enemy, he said, sending waves of frost through her.

– But what about Stewart? She insisted.

– Do you know what the last thing he said to me was? Ted Cousin spoke emphatically, with a voice cutting into her, cutting through diamond. – «Have a nice trip», he told me. «Enjoy yourself». I haven't seen him since.

Ted mimicked Stewart's voice to an uncanny degree. To Tilla it was as if the cop was there, with them, totally useless, as they both knew he would be.

– We're on our own, she said. – We will always be.

– Yes, he rose, – even though there might be moments where there might be alliances, we will always, in moments of absolute truths be alone. This is who we are.

– We will tell some of them, she said. – Iris, Bob, John, Linda… and…

– Jane, he completed.

– One by one, she said. – To make them see it our way.

He looks at her face, her aggressive stance, her closed fist, taking her hand.

They grabbed Iris when she left one of the restrooms.

– You'll come with us, he said brusquely.

– It's no big deal. Tilla comforted her, pushing one index finger at her lips. – We'll just have a little chat, that's all.

– You guys have gone nuts, right? Iris grinned, and didn't cry out.

Her speech was slurred. Her face filled up with the mask of joy, but despair desaturated her eyes.

They pushed her into the bathroom, the girl's room. She stumbled and almost fell.

– What are you up to? She complained in a loud voice. – What are you doing?

– You've been drinking heavily since dinner, Ted said icily. – If we had let you keep it up you would've been dead by nightfall.

– What concern is that of yours? Her voice became that of a spoiled child. – What do you care? You don't care about *me*.

– So, do you live the night by day, too, or is it just a part time occupation? Sorry about asking, but too many «night people» are merely playing at it, and you look like a prime candidate for hypocrisy, my lovely part-time witch.

She looked confused at him, uncomprehending.

Ted looked at her with obvious, deliberately patronizing curiosity.

– Raise your hands, Tilla told her.

– Huh? The stupid, doll-like look in her face haunted them both.

They knew her, knew what she was going through

– Your arms. Raise them above your head. This is a hold up.

Iris didn't get the attempt at levity. She just obeyed, dully and just as out of it.

Tilla undressed her, piece by piece. Eventually she stood before them, completely nude.

– We're so kind to you, Tilla pointed out. – I want you to know that. We didn't have to remove the clothes first.

She pushed her into the shower and turned on the cold water. Iris screamed, and jumped back out again. Tilla grabbed her and pushed her back in. Tilla raised her hand, ready to strike. Iris remained in the booth, shrinking before their eyes, and she started crying. She fell to the floor, while the cold water kept raining down on her.

Finally Ted turned off the water. She looked up at him, at his foreboding figure.

– I feel sick, she sniveled.

Subsequently puking on the floor and on herself. Dinner and wine decorating soft skin and hard floor. She crouched in fetal position for some time, bathing in her own vomit.

– Get up, Tilla commanded. – Get up, you lazy bitch!

It took some doing, but she finally got up on all fours. Then she puked again.

– I'm sick, she complained. – So very, very sick.

She got up… somehow, returning to the shower, turning on both cold and hot water, taking a shower.

– Why don't you join me, she offered, smiling sickly. – Why don't you both join me…

They didn't reply. Not with words. Even reduced the full, writhing body made feverish images dance before his eyes. He got a hard-on to end all hard-ons, and he almost scared himself with the level of self-control he displayed.

Tilla shrugged.

– It isn't up to me. You fuck her. I don't mind sharing you.

– She's just a child, wanting her father to return to her, he said viciously.

Iris whimpered then. She concentrated on cleaning herself up. There was no more fight left in her. She turned off the water and stepped out from the stall. Tilla handed her a towel, and she started drying herself thoroughly and extensively.

– I'll get you new clothes. Tilla left. She closed the door behind her.

Iris didn't «try» anything. Ted looked at her all the time. She bowed her head in shame, and he wanted to kick himself, but the rock-hard self-control persisted.

Tilla returned with a bundle of clothes, and handed them to the other girl. Iris dressed in stiff, mechanical movements. She stood there before them, fully dressed, asking with a dull, weak voice:

– Is the game done, now, Ted? Please, Ted.

– It is, Tilla confirmed. – There's no need for it anymore, is there?

Iris shook her head.

Ted took a stone, or rather a pebble out of his pocket, and put it on the floor.

– Do the trick, he said lightly.

– I can't do it when I'm drunk, she said ashamed.

– Then don't get drunk, Tilla said softly.

– I know I shouldn't, okay. The minor display of anger faded quickly, and the despair and self-contempt returned. – But it keeps the visions away, too. The visions are… ugly.

– Do it! Ted insisted.

Nothing happened for a long time. Iris looked at Ted. He gave her an encouraging look.

The pebble shook, before floating a bit, just a bit. Then it fell, and rolled across the floor. Ted and Tilla stared absolutely astonished at the uncanny sight.

– That was nothing. Iris brightened visibly. – I can do much more.

And the three slowly started smiling, as they slowly gained some common ground, a reason for not being alone in the world.

Evening came, dark came. Day finally turned to night.

They gathered in the living room. On Ted and Tilla's quiet, shrewd insistence the party sort of ended early. It hadn't been much of a party anyway. Those who had been drinking heavily, except Iris, who had an early start recovering, were long since dead to the world.

– Bruce should be here soon, Helen assured everybody present.

– My god, it is true. John shook his head in disbelief.

– And what might that be. Helen cut through him with her razor-sharp voice.

– Love makes blind, the boy grinned.

Laughing with the others she looked like she wasn't ready to let the subject go completely, when she was interrupted in whatever her intent was.

Bruce stumbled a few steps into the living room… before falling and hitting the floor hard. He didn't move.

– He's dead, Helen shouted, as she rushed to his side. – HE'S DEAD!

And everybody covered their ears.

– He's dead, all right, Ted grinned. – Dead drunk.

He lifted up the boy's head, and Bruce started to snore like a storm.

Everybody breathed easier. Someone applauded.

– That scoundrel, that liar, Helen screamed. – Just wait until he wakes up.

– Hit yourself, Iris grinned, still a bit shaky, – he crossed his hidden fingers. I saw it.

Ted and Dennis carried the wreck to bed, careful not to dump him on the bottle left there.

– Are you coming? Dennis wondered when Helen knelt by her
unconscious boyfriend.

– You two go first, I'll stay here for a while.

– You'll come with us this moment, Ted told her. – You can't
do anything for the dumb shit here.

They both looked at him, unused as they were to the steel in
his voice. Helen hurried after the two boys without thinking
twice about it.

They gathered in the living room, gathered around Ted
Cousin. It was a quiet, subdued, but intense mood in the room.
He started speaking without waiting for the last sounds to fade,
and the last sounds did fade.

– Last night something happened, he said. – Some of you may
deny that it did, but that doesn't change facts. Reality doesn't
stop existing just because some don't believe in it. It wasn't
altogether pleasant, but that's beside the point. And yesterday is
immaterial anyway. It just confirmed what we've seen before:
We're bound all of us, by fate and circumstances. Our lives are
connected in ways that will only slowly reveal themselves, as
we journey into the world *together*.

The voice was cutting them in a way quite different then what
Helen's had done. This one was smooth and sharp at the same
time, sneaky and clear. They felt as if he was invading them,
and they listened.

– Tonight, we'll just talk, Tilla said. – No ceremonies, no
experiments. We talk, about whatever is on our mind.

Tilla sat down in the ring. Ted did, too. They all sat there,
looking at each other for a while, clearly restless.

– Any takers?

Jane stood up. They could all see it, how she seemed to grow,
as she climbed to her feet. She held a book in her hand, very
determined.

– I will read from Modern Slavery, by Sheila Ashcroft, Jane
said. – I have tried to raise this subject in conversations before,
but I've always been ridiculed and rebuffed.

– This time, you won't be, Ted said.

Jane was the political radical among them. He had known that
beforehand, and had been right about her, in more ways than
one. That certainty sent a pleasant sensation through his body.

That, and what meeting Tilla, Iris, Jane and Betty's eyes did to him.

Jane opened the book.

– *I woke up in a cage.* She began her reading hesitatingly, picking up strength as she read. – *A huge one, where there were other women keeping me company. The men were in another cage across the steaming hot room. We were all naked and we were chained hands and feet. Our captors had kept us drugged off and on for days after our capture and gleefully explained our circumstances to us: We were to be trained, trained as docile slaves, and then be sold off to the highest bidders for whatever sick purpose they had in mind for us. We no longer had any rights, any human dignity, for we no longer had any value, beyond what our masters happened to place on us.*

She read for some time. It had turned absolutely quiet. Veronica sniffed a bit in Bob's arms. Others shifted their position a bit. Aside from that horror ruled them all, growing the longer Jane kept going.

She finally stopped, too angry and too distraught to continue.

– It's bull, Liz finally stated.

– No, it's not, Ted countered. – Stewart knows this woman. It was he and three others, among them Lieutenant Clarke, who rescued Sheila and others from their captivity in southern France, just before they were about to be put on the block and sold off. Many others weren't rescued and vanished completely, never to be seen again.

– That's the way of the current world in general, isn't it? Jane spoke again, subdued rage showing in the subtext of her fairly modulated speech. – Everything is for sale, including humans and life in general.

– Fortunately, we live in America, Frank said. – We're far away from such things.

– Are you KIDDING? John exclaimed. – You speak of a country where the only value is money, and everything and everyone can indeed be bought or bought off. You should know.

– A nation built on slavery and genocide, a nation that was one of Adolf Hitler's foremost «inspirations» for his machinations and ideology, Jane spat. – The blacks were

463

enslaved for a long time after America's «independence». They were property of the white, both in Europe and America, and...

– What are you talking about? Frank shook his head, still on his high horse, and they heard something as rare as anger in his voice.

– You don't know, do you, don't know about it at all? I suspected as much. You don't know about all the native tribes, «Indians», either, eradicated one by one during «our» illustrious history?

– Sure, he shrugged. – But that was long ago, wasn't it. It was all so very long ago.

– I grew up on a reservation, Helen shouted. – A result of American «integration policies». Only the coincidence, the good fortune of my voice made me escape living conditions you most certainly wouldn't have lived through.

Glory stepped forward, a figure of rage.

– I grew up in Memphis. Black girls are routinely *raped* by white policemen there, you shithead, without the government doing anything about it. The cops see it as part of the salary. They usually get away scot free.

– You think today's America is lily white, huh? Betty smiled ironically, perfectly calm. – Last year, September 11th they did the military coup in Chile, and that's merely one of many similar atrocities the government, supported by the CIA and bunch, and a braindead population, has committed all over the world, both domestically and in foreign countries. Members of the Black Panthers, a black community organization, have been persecuted for years by various government organizations, most notably the FBI. Everybody seeking information on their own, seeking to think and act for themselves, knows these things.

Frank just shrank further and further in his tracks. His skin turned gray and dead.

The deluge finally paused. Ted smiled, a smile burning them all.

– Most people are sadly ignorant. There is clearly a need for the most basic information, but generally speaking these things and others are *known*. Most people, though, are so dehumanized that they don't care, they just don't care, and are thereby setting themselves up as victims.

He turned towards Frank, grabbed him, grabbed him hard. Frank gasped.

– Listen, where people come from doesn't mean shit. It's what they do with their lives that matters.

A shocked expression filled the fat boy's face.

– Yes, your father has said that, on more than one occasion. It's one of America, the current world's major deceits, illusions, is it not? Your father, and people like him either don't know the meaning of their own words or they don't want others to grasp their true meaning. We may all be a result of generations of genetic and cultural breeding, but we're in no way bound by it. We're our own masters.

A thrill shot through the room, through him. He sensed it in his gut, sensed it in their gut.

– Current society is… destruction personified, Jane said slowly, painfully. – Hell, sometimes, in my despair I think even civilization itself is just plain wrong.

– The stick and carrot thing is prevalent everywhere today, Iris grinned, regaining a bit of her old self. – Civilization is in a state of constant repair, or disrepair, if you will. It needs constant maintenance because nature is *constantly* attacking it. We're surrounded by artificial constructs, both actually and figuratively.

– We need to use stronger reinforcements, Bob said. – Or nature will reclaim everything.

– Use more artificial constructs alienating us even further from ourselves, you mean, Iris countered. – Use the problem to solve the problem, that makes sense…

– Return to the caves, Bob countered. – Sure, that makes sense.

– Why not? Iris stretched playfully. – It would be fun.

They laughed. It was a good joke. Bob, too, laughed, clearly strained. At least to Ted it was.

Ted sensed the rage in his friend, and wondered if Bob realized how primal his emotions truly were. Ted could hardly believe how sensitive he had become lately. It was as if all the anger and countless emotions in the room… lived on in him, a living thing crying for release.

– Suffering has become an epidemic state, John sighed sadly.
– The rule, instead of the exception.

And Ted felt it then, too, the subtle change, both at that moment, and what had changed during the course of the evening. He had done it, with a little effort and minor input, changed their direction. Pride coursed through him.

– Most people today are slaves, Linda said, suddenly, unexpectedly, violently. – Jim Morrison was right, taunting his audience from the stage. They didn't enjoy it very much, because they knew his words to be true. Some people are differentiating between slavery and wage slavery. That's just another artificial construct.

– Yeah, isn't it *obvious?* Jane bristled. – Slaves are fed and kept warm… occasionally, to be better able to work and serve, lulled into the illusion that they are properly «compensated». And do you know what really riles me? Most of the «leaders» and «rebels» of the sixties' «counterculture movement» are already joining the society they profess to hate, in the misunderstood notion they will be able to change it from within. It's sick.

– They have just realized that Order is preferable to chaos, Bob emphasized. – So will you.

– Everyone goes through a period of rebellion in their youth, Veronica insisted. – Before realizing the error of their ways.

– Except Bob and Vernie, Tilla joked, not unfriendly.
More laughter.

- One of Ulrike Meinhof's main theses is that society is becoming more and more like a machine, Jane said. – That we, as parts, pegs of society become machines ourselves. And that it alienates all of us from our natural surroundings, and even from ourselves. The only way to become real, to become *human* is to liberate ourselves from the Machine.

Dennis looked at another of the books by her feet.

THE CONCEPT OF THE URBAN GUERILLA

- Where the hell did you get that one? He wondered, absolutely fascinated.

- Are you kidding? She laughed. – They're everywhere these days.

Then more somber, sad:

- At least they used to be.

Words, and emotions ran like water. Time flowed, until one second just as well could be an hour or the other way around.

Here, in this limited space and time, at least they were somewhat free, to be what and whom they truly were.

The heated discussion faded eventually, but what it had made them feel didn't, and it did feel great. The thrill of excitement didn't leave Ted.

He walked to the kitchen. He was thirsty… and hungry, and ate and drank a lot, not that long after dinner.

– You usually never eat between meals, Tilla commented.

– Never. He shook his head. – I even skip meals occasionally. And we haven't even exercised today. The shooting hardly counts, does it.

– Is it… nerves?

– I don't know what else it could be.

She sat down in his lap, caressing his hair.

– I love it. I love it when you're normal…

It was a bittersweet statement, and she realized that the moment she said it, but it couldn't be retracted. He just returned her smile.

The sounds, the voices from the living room faded in their awareness, faded from attention. They just sat there for a while, relaxing, breathing, doing nothing else.

Iris entered the kitchen, so quietly that they hardly heard her. She walked to them shyly.

– Thank you, she said to him, kissing him on the cheek.

– Thank you, you too, she said to Tilla, giving her, too, a kiss on the cheek.

– You're welcome, Tilla said curtly.

Pieces, Ted thought. Everyone is just pieces of the whole in this world, shards of what we can be. Everything is merely flashes of what is truly happening.

He found himself outside, looking at the stars.

– What do you see? Betty wondered.

– Infinity.

– Me, too, she said excitedly.

– I can feel it, he wondered, – the desire in the night. I can almost grasp it, the shadow in the mirror, what I've been looking for my entire life.

She stepped forward, stopped in front of him, grabbing both his hands. Her eyes were shining, her face flushing.

– You did it, she exclaimed. – You set them in motion. A temporary rise of awareness, at least. Congratulations.

– Thank you. I think…

– When people say to you, many years from now that your accomplishments are a result of fate I want you to know it is horseshit. You have done it all. You have created your own fate.

– Now or then? He wondered teasingly.

– Yes… She disappeared into the night. He watched her hair fade like dying embers.

He stared at the stars.

He saw eternity.

*************/

Dark, a sword cutting through the light. The small group of humans was traversing even higher up in the Rocky Mountains, on the edge of the ice sheet covering a peak. It was raining hard, and they were soaked through every piece of cloth they wore. But the intense activity had warmed them, and only occasionally they felt the cold from the ice. Ted took in the wild beauty. He took in everything. Tired and even stumbling he felt the joy, the joy of the wild.

Everything worked better out here. Thoughts raced so fast through his mind that he could hardly catch them. That in itself wasn't unusual, but now he also saw everything clearer. Ideas came to him, and more. Everything suddenly turned negative on him, and what he saw wasn't the waterfall before his eyes, but another place, in the dark. He stopped, wide-eyed. The others looked at him. He moved on.

They were on their way back to the cabin, after a strenuous trip, far longer than they had anticipated and wanted. They had (as usual) taken the wrong turn at least twice. Jane and Liz, the exercise nuts among them took it in stride. John and Linda supported each other. Ted and Tilla managed to walk on their own, but that was just about it. Bob had been carrying Veronica the last few minutes.

– I can't do this often, Helen moaned. – My voice cracks and I won't have dry clothes to wear.

– Join Iris' nudist club, Ted joked. – Then you won't have to worry about clothes, at least.

Tilla clutched his hand. The others did something that perhaps could pass for laughter. It wasn't for lack of will, but rather sufficient strength.

– Where the fuck has Leadville disappeared to? Ted wondered.

– Haven't the foggiest, Bob replied.

– Sometimes, John wailed, – in my nightmares, I imagine that the fucking guide guided us to South America or something, and that this is only a reasonable facsimile of the Rockies. All mountains look the same, right?

They wanted to laugh.

But couldn't.

There was a flash, obscuring Ted's vision, but he couldn't identify it. It was only there for a moment and then fading once more.

Heavy feet thundered on his grave. He saw the grave. He felt the weight of the feet, and he realized it was the cemetery in Denver, Mike's grave.

Just within the door, they fell on the floor. Only Bob and the two spry girls stood on their feet.

– You've turned soft, Teddy. Bob taunted him.

– I don't feel so bad, Ted replied lightly.

And it was true. He usually had limbs like lead after hard exercise, but now they were still supple. He was exhausted, but he felt good.

– This is nothing, Liz assured them. – After doing this for a week I guarantee you'll be able to not only walk, but actually run twice today's distance.

She was practically overrun with insults and told in many various ways what to do with herself. And they all laughed, laughed a lot.

Iris approached them, giving them a patronizing snarl.

– You guys stink. What a way to join a party.

But Ted didn't smell alcohol in her breath.

After her rather charged salvo she enjoyed the sorry sight a bit longer, before turning on her heels and vanishing into the girls' restroom.

– She's turning crazier by the minute. Bob shook his head hard.

– Is she? John wondered, clearly countering Bob.

And then there was the ritual again. The boys went to the boys' room and showered. The girls went to the girls' room and showered. The water, the hot water rained into Ted's eyes, and made him see clearer than ever. What happened, what followed wasn't really any conscious decision on his part.

– Hey, you forgot something. John called after him when he was about to open the door.

– No, I didn't, he called back.

And went out in the hallway without a towel or anything covering him. Tilla, Helen and Jane appeared from the girls' place. Two of them reddened and turned away, hurrying into their rooms. Tilla just smiled and let her towel fall as well, and when the boys went to the door to look at the spectacle they saw her in all her glory. The two of them walked arm in arm and slowly, naturally into their room, as if they were on their way to a Prom Ball or something.

Betty waited inside. She sat on the bed, dressed, with a tray of food in her lap. She didn't react at all, except for greeting them with one of her enigmatic smiles, which she probably would have done anyway. Ted sensed a strange mix of joy and triumph in her.

– I made some food for you guys. I knew you would be hungry.

She walked to the table and set the tray down there.

They sat down in the chairs, and started eating. He felt it, the hollow rooms in his stomach, like a void sucking everything in. He studied Betty without making any attempt at hiding it, hide his interest. She returned the favor, but she wasn't visibly influenced, and she was certainly not blushing.

– Your Change has begun, she told him. – And nothing can stop it.

She turned to Tilla.

– Yours, too, but you won't need his enormous amount of energy.

The darkness exploded in his eyes. This time it lasted longer. It faded, and he felt empty.

470

– What did you see? Betty asked him anxiously.

– A house, a castle outside Denver…

– Where you went with Stewart, right?

He looked at her, just looked at her.

– Oops.

She said.

Ted wolfed down the remaining food. Tilla wasn't really hungry, but she ate about one fifth of it.

– Dinner will be ready in half an hour, my lord and lady, she enlightened them. – It's very important to eat quickly, to build muscle mass after such a strenuous trip.

– I thought we had just eaten?

– Yes, Betty replied.

And she left.

They remained silent in the chairs for a while, facing each other, touching across the small table.

– She gives me the creeps, Tilla said. – But I no longer believe she's out to harm us, at least not yet.

– She's playing a game, Ted pondered. – The question is what she will do when the game is over.

He struck the wall with his fist, making a visible dent in it.

– There's something out there, he despaired. – A huge monster out to get us. And I can almost see it. It's right there, in front of me, and I can't see it. Why can't I see it?

– Hush. She took his head in her arms and embraced it. – Hush.

They dressed, choosing the lightest part of their light wardrobe. She giggled.

– I can still see the girls' faces when you walked out of the bathroom stark naked. It was priceless. Priceless!

– As were the boys' faces when seeing you. Hey, we must have made some impression on them…

They walked into the living room with a slight smile on their lips, nodding to people, completely ignoring the others' wide-open eyes.

The twenty-three had dinner again. Together. More lively talk. More life. And Death.

– So, in your opinion something… profound happened two nights ago? Bob asked Iris.

– It did indeed, she said lightly, meeting his eyes stubbornly.

– And what was that, if I may ask?

– We touched something out there, she said, both anxious and excited. – And it touched us. We were Changed, and we will never be as we were.

– And do you have any… proof of this experience of yours, proof that you or Betty or whoever didn't put something in our tea, making us see things?

– Proof is an interesting concept, she said. – Do you have, for instance any proof of your own existence? Can you prove to me that you exist?

He scowled at her, and the look was so nasty that she almost stopped

– Your statements are meaningless, she said. – We shared an empathic, empiric experience. We all saw pretty much the same, even though we didn't speak about it at the time. The collaborating evidence is overwhelming. And we're just one group anyway. Millions of people have had similar experiences. This is reality. Get used to it.

– You know… Ted stated to Bob. – Your denial is almost as bad as people attacking witches and such. In their zeal they're attacking everybody not fitting into their perception of reality.

– You're all *sick*. Bob rose and left the table, turning as he opened the door, raising a finger. – All of you.

Veronica ran after him.

Ted sighed and glanced at Iris.

– He will get over it, she insisted.

But she didn't truly believe that, and neither did Ted.

Music played, both from the speakers, and inside the youths' hearts. They sat by the table, eating, having dinner. Suddenly it was evening again, night again. Ted and Tilla danced. Or rather she danced, and he tried to, as usual. She drank, but only wine. She knew he couldn't stand the close stink of Liquor, so she kept away from it. It didn't really matter if their movements on the floor didn't match. They still moved to the same beat. Yesterday had been bad, but once they got past that everything went smoother. They got closer with every new step, every recent heartbeat.

– Bob is really serious with his usual «culture versus nature» thing, Tilla giggled.

– I'm afraid so, Ted said with regret. – We have always disagreed on a few key issues, though. No big deal.

They heard John and Dennis speak by the couch. Dennis courted Jane, but was caught up in a deep-going philosophical conversation.

– I remember it like it was yesterday, Dennis said. – Two people had just set foot on the Moon. And it… meant nothing, and it should… shouldn't it?

– I agree completely, John nodded. – Human Space exploration should be very important, but it's just one more vehicle for the rich and powerful to distinguish themselves. Everything is so fucking wrong today, you know, no matter from what perspective one is looking at it. Everything!

Dennis turned to the couch to get Jane's opinion, but she was gone.

– I think I should keep Glory company a bit, Ted said.

Tilla turned to look at the black girl, the only black girl in the assembly.

– I think that's a very good idea, Tilla said.

Ted kissed her, and approached Glory. Two pairs of brown eyes met.

– Hi, he grinned, – would you like to dance?

– Thanks, she replied. – But I don't dance.

– Well, neither do I, as you've probably noticed… He reddened a bit. – I just thought you could dance, while I keep trying…

She hesitated. She clearly hesitated.

– Thanks, but no thanks. I like you, but… no.

– She doesn't like me, he reported to Tilla.

– Her loss.

– Or she didn't care much for my dancing.

– I wonder why…

Ted saw everything in the room so clearly right then, the people, the joy, the dislikes lingering.

But he couldn't see past it, past the corner, to the darkness on the other side.

It was later, much later. He couldn't remember much that had happened in the interim. He remembered nothing or everything.

He and Tilla were still «dancing».

– Have you looked at yourself in the mirror in a dark room?

– No. She shook her head. – Can't say I have.

– I think it is then you see your true Self, he said.

– What a strange thing to say, she said lightly, – but then again that's not unusual for you. Fortunately not.

She looked excited at him.

– Do you know what? I think you're finally glimpsing it, what's hidden, the very step before truly seeing it.

He closed his eyes, as he began talking, feeling the girl around him, feeling himself around her.

– There's very little light. The door is closed. The light is turned off, even in the hallway outside. It's daylight and the tiny amount of light is gray. You stare into the mirror. You have very little sense of yourself, except in the mirror. There's nothing there, really, except the dark of the room. There isn't even the room. You're elsewhere. You stare straight ahead, and that's when you see it, you sense it, seeing its outline… the dark shape.

– Cold is trickling down my spine. She shuddered.

She kissed him, wasn't content with it, wasn't pleased and kissed him again, a bit anxious, a bit desperate.

Come let's go.

She whispered in his ear.

Without a sound.

She danced in front of him, and he danced in her tracks, into the darkness. The lights in the hallway didn't seem to matter. They walked to the restroom, the one furthest from the living room, closest to the exit. She pulled him inside and closed, locked the door behind them. He wanted to grab her, but she slipped away. Giggling softly and hardly audible she placed him in front of the mirror. She rushed to the switch by the door, and everything turned dark. Not just the room, but everything. Right after that he sensed her hands on his shoulders.

– There's no weak daylight here, she said, – but it will have to do.

There was no crack under the door either. The light from the hallway didn't reach them. There was no light anywhere.

– Concentrate, she whispered. – *Focus*. Discover what's

hidden.

He stared into the mirror, he knew he did. He saw nothing. The dark was a swarm of nothing in front of him, around him. The music of her breath played in his ear. She was good at this. She made him relax, made him breathe, emptying his mind for thoughts. A line of faces paraded before his blind eyes, indistinct, unrecognizable.

– Reach deep within yourself, he heard the siren song. – You're a *witch,* an ancient being of power and knowledge. Nothing is beyond you, beyond your reach.

There, it was said. He felt cold and warm all over when he heard the warmth in her voice. She accepted him, accepted the monster inside him, fully and unconditionally.

Flashes. Flashes of black in the black, differentiated by shadows. And in the shadows, there were faces. Stewart's. The hooded figures in the castle outside Denver he and the lieutenant had «paid a visit». He saw them reveal their faces one by one, relived the ceremony in a filed away part of his memory.

Then... then...

In one flash, repeating itself, the image of a millipede, one with a human face, poison flowing from its feet.

He saw the Shadow in the mirror. A massive human shape, seemingly the same size as himself, but that was just... just because he couldn't see the rest, see everything behind, beyond. There were no details, no... features. He blinked and gasped. There was more whispering, but he couldn't hear the words. He stared into the mirror. Tilla was... gone. He knew she stood behind him, looking over his shoulder, but there was nothing where her head was supposed to be, and when he took one step to the side, there was no body either. He turned and looked at her, able to see in the dark, and there she was. He saw her face and body in a sort of pale bluish, silvery light, water from the moon. But when he turned towards the mirror, she wasn't there. He could see the room, see the Shadow, slowly gaining features, gaining his face, but she wasn't there.

– What is it? She asked anxiously. – What's wrong?

He gasped and fell to his knees.

– Pain, he gasped, saliva flowing from his mouth, gasped the

Shadow, liquid darkness flowing from its mouth. – It hurts.
Being born hurts.

A flash - slow and long-lasting. As he and Stewart was about
to leave, a glimpse of a face, words, a voice reaching them
from afar.

– Bob…

– Bob? Tilla wondered. – Should we speak to him? It's about
time, I guess.

– He's with them.

– With…

– He's on their side.

She helped him up. Light faded. It turned dark once more.

– Are you sure? Her voice was anguish, feeling his anguish.

– I saw my memory in a clearer light. I felt its undeniable
truth. I'm sure.

He sensed the power, the power of the dragon rise from the
depths.

– It was unbelievable, he said, shaken, exalted. – The
power of deduction… It was like I was Sherlock Holmes or
something.

He laughed, a short, shrill laughter.

– Come.

He told her to her face.

They stumbled out in the hallway, its lights flooding their
minds, obscuring their sight.

– It was so obvious, Ted said. – Everything was. I should have
seen it earlier, much earlier.

– What was? Tilla panted at his heels. – I don't understand.

– His smug behavior when Jane read from the book. He has
always been smug, but… Gidman's craft, for fuck's sake. It's
Gidman's fucking craft.

His voice shook in rage and fear. Tilla paled. Her brown skin
turned pale as milk.

– The Guide, he ventured. – Fitzallan. He said the proprietor
of the bar, of the Silver Dollar had told him we had gone in the
wrong direction, that the guy had seen us at the crossroads, but
we couldn't see the place from the crossroads and he couldn't
see us. No way! Fitzallan lied.

Everything just flooded him now, small things gaining

476

importance in hindsight, pieces of the horrible puzzle.

– We should run away, he said. – Slip away unnoticed in the dark. Go for help.

They both stopped, looking at each other, considering their chances, the options.

– No. He shook his head. – They're probably already outside somewhere, waiting for the right moment… whatever that is. Perhaps they do see this as a kind of social experiment. They would be into that.

The living room again, so different. Bob was there. Rage and fear guided Ted Cousin, making him cold as ice. He stopped in front of Bob, right in front of him.

They were all present, every single one of them. Good, let them watch. Let them *see*.

– «Welcome to the Brotherhood of the Thousand Feet, you no longer nameless one, welcome, Robert Tremblay».

He spat it out, the venom in his voice almost tangible.

Bob shook.

– «We have with us tonight the few, the proud we have chosen to initiate into our fold, the new generation chosen to start as our squires, at the lower floors of the pyramid of power. We are those illuminating the shadows, those shining a light in the night. We shall persevere. We were present at King Arthur's table, at the church meeting in Nicaea, at the last supper of Christ. Our ways are unchanging, eternal».

Bob smiled, a sickly, vicious scowl.

– Seems like you got me good, doesn't it, old friend?

– So, you're not denying it? Ted cried.

– Why should I DENY it? I'm PROUD of it. Of course I am.

He reached inside his jacket, for his gun. Ted grabbed his arm. Bob shifted position slightly, and threw the other's body into the wall. He stepped back, waving his gun around, pointing it at the charging Tilla. She froze.

– You see, we learn a few tricks in the Order, too.

He was a completely different person. During those few, critical moments he had gone through a complete transformation, if not in actual appearance, then in expression.

All the others stood there frozen, uncomprehending.

– What's going *on?* Frank yelped. – Have you two… or

477

three…

He nodded weakly to Tilla.

– … taken a leave of your senses?

– He's in league with David Gidman, Ted said aloud, drying blood from his jaw. – You know who Gidman is, don't you, what he is? He was in that book Jane read from.

– He's *Illuminati,* Jane stated, thunderstruck.

– Hah! Bob barked in contempt. – A story for small children. Nobody can control the entire world anymore. It has long since grown too complex, too big for that.

– But one can steer, one can shepherd the flock, right, Bob? Ted's voice was perfectly calm.

– Yes, Bob said triumphantly. – Those who are worthy rule the world. Those who are not serve. It's really that simple. And you…

– You, Bob said icily, – are the kind keeping Order from the world.

– B-bobbie… The weak, shrill voice came from the door. – W-what's w-wrong, Bobbie?

Veronica rushed towards him. Tears flowed down her cheeks. He struck her down with the gun hand. Instantly afterwards he was about to point the gun at Ted. Tilla jumped at Bob, kicking the hand. The gun fell on the floor. Tilla struck him on the jaw. He hit the wall hard. She grabbed his hair and pulled his head down, and his head on the way down met her knee on its way up. Blood flowed from his nose. He went down. She kicked him in the ribs, and then gave him another kick in the head. He lay still. She stood above him, breathing a bit harder, looking enraged at him.

Ted picked up the gun, and rose.

He grabbed Bob's hand, showing them all the ring on its finger.

- This is a sign that he belongs to the Brotherhood of the Thousand Feet, the proof of his elevated standing in society, the proof of his right to fuck with us lowly mortals.

- So what? Frank said, voice shaking. – My father is a «foot». He has a ring like that, too. It's just a harmless club. The Coalition of Concerned Citizens I think they call themselves. They're mostly doing social work and shit.

- Thank you for telling me that, Ted said. – That makes Forester Senior even a worse greasebag than I thought. You can be very glad your father hasn't found you «worthy» to become a member yet, like Bob's loving father obviously did with him.

Frank stood there, like a dustbin, a statue of eroding soil.

– Find a rope someone, Ted ordered.

No one moved.

– Will someone PLEASE find a rope and tie the fucker up?

– I'll do it, Liz whimpered. – I'm good at it. I was a girl scout.

– Good. Those of you that brought guns, get them. All of them.

– I'll get yours. Betty smiled and ran off.

The others started moving slowly, very slowly. Ted stopped John when the boy was on his way out, handing him the gun. John froze, absolutely mortified.

– I can't shoot anyone. He shivered. – You take it.

– You have to, Ted said. – I can't shoot straight with a revolver. I have a phobia against it, too, but I would have handled that if I could have used it, but I can't. Every single one of you is probably a better shooter than I with this shit.

– You were about to fetch your rifle, John, Iris said.

– I'll just… fetch it, John said. – I won't use it.

– You coward, Linda said. – You spineless coward.

His face turned immeasurably sad, and he vanished out in the hallway.

– Give it to me, Linda said. – I'll use it.

He handed it to her. Their eyes met briefly.

Liz returned with rope, a lot of rope, and tied Bob up, tied him up hard. Anger dominated her every move.

– What will happen, she complained. – What will happen to us? What shall we DO?

I don't know, Ted didn't say. I don't have the slightest idea.

Betty returned with a rifle in her hands. The others, too. Dennis was the only one who had brought a gun they didn't know about.

– You were prepared, Ted acknowledged. – That's good.

Ted sensed the panic, sensed it crawl under the skin of everybody present. They all turned to him, as he had hoped and feared they would. If not for that they would have been running in panic from the cabin right now. He wasn't entirely sure that would have been a bad thing. He thought so, but he wasn't sure.

– We must kill. He spoke direct, evenly. – Kill to survive, kill to escape the fate planned for us. Those who don't have guns get yourself a knife, a kitchen knife or a screwdriver if necessary. And when they come for us, and they will, you go at them with everything you've got. Cut, cut, and never stop cutting. Do you *understand?*

They mumbled. They nodded.

– I'm not... not certain about this. Helen mumbled.

They had never before heard her mumble.

– What are you not certain of exactly? Tilla asked her.

– What happened here? Bruce stepped forward, supporting his mate. – What did we see?

– I can explain it to you, in detail, Ted said, – but I'm not sure we have the time.

He looked at Betty. She looked like she was enjoying herself, studying him, studying everything.

– This is the... wrong cabin.

Nobody heard him. At least it seemed that way.

– This is the WRONG cabin, Frank shouted.

– What the hell are you TALKING about? John exploded, clutching the rifle in his hands, his shaking hands.

– It looks like the right cabin, Frank said nervously. – It even smells like the right cabin, exactly as I remember it, from years ago, but it is in a completely wrong place. I'm sorry. I should have told you earlier, but I didn't want you to be... angry at m-me. I told you. I told you we somehow took the wrong turn at the crossroads. Everything looked okay at first, but it wasn't. Somebody must have turned one of the pointers around deliberately. I FUCKING TOLD YOU!

He just sat down in the middle of the floor and started crying, totally out of it.

– Fitzallan, or whatever his name is did that. Tilla enlightened them enraged, fairly unnecessary. – And then he waited, until we were very needy little children, and came and rescued us, leading us by the nose, and finally, so cleverly switching Frank's keys with his own.

They went through it in their mind. Their thoughts were practically visible in their eyes.

– You are, I trust aware of what this means? Tilla continued, hammered them relentlessly. – Those standing against us have gone to insane lengths to place us here, to the point of copying Frank's dream cabin piece by piece.

– But why didn't they just take us the first night? Frank sniveled. – They could have. At the very least if they are capable now, they would have been then… so why didn't they, why all the extra… bother?

– This is a laboratory of a social experiment, Betty stated, nodding in acknowledgement to Tilla. – We're the mice, running through the maze.

– There you have it, people, Ted said, a fist raised above his head. – Do you need any further incitement?

They shook their head, mumbled a denial. Not very convincing, but it would do.

It would have to.

Linda handed John the revolver, and this time he accepted it.

– We stay together, Ted said. – We don't post guards. Here we stay, here we fight.

Jane placed herself before Ted, standing straight.

– We should protect ourselves from potential teargas-attack, she stated. – We need to cover our mouth and nose.

– Excellent thinking, he praised her, making her blush. – Get to it.

Seconds passed. Minutes passed.

Veronica sat on the couch, crying. Iris comforted her or attempted to do so, in vain.

Ted stood by the window, looking out, as if in defiance of what might be lurking out there. Was that the worst, that they didn't know for sure?

– You're worried.

He turned and saw Betty, precisely where he reckoned she would be.

By his side.

The red hair was fixed in a bun marking the form of the face. It once more struck him how alike she and Tilla were.

– I can understand that, she said. – It's not like you don't have a reason.

And then her stare turned pointed, toxic, or at least slightly so.

– Jack, your father also had that, I'm told… before he wised up.

He was hardly surprised. Only a slight shaking of the hand holding the rifle revealed the shock he felt.

– Being new at this you did an excellent job, though. You took the offensive, took charge, before panic set in among your nascent warriors.

– And have you seen everything you need to see, now? He wondered. – Will you slip away in the night?

– Where you go, I will go…

He grabbed her jaw in a provocative gesture. She did nothing to pull away. He looked at Tilla. She returned the look. He turned to Betty once more, letting the hand fall.

Bob woke up, bristling with agitation almost instantaneously.

– HEY! He yelled. – Untie me.

– Someone put a gag into that yapping gap, Ted snarled.

He could hardly believe it. They had forgotten. He had forgotten.

– You think you've won anything, Bob said completely relaxed, not yelling anymore. – You haven't won anything, except given me one more reason to treat you *badly* when the time comes.

– I'll give you reason, Ted mumbled.

Two steps, and he was right in front of Bob Tremblay. He smeared his foot on his former friend's face. He bent down and started to beat him up, enraged and methodically. He struck and kicked, alternately, attacking the prisoner with all the pent-up rage he possessed.

And then, finally, by an act of will, he stopped, stopped cold the red haze shrouding his mind, and his face turned hard and frozen, like a mask. He disregarded his friends' shocked expressions; like he did Bob Tremblay's beaten to a meatball face.

– There's a lesson here, for all of you, Betty said. – This is the world. This is who we are.

There was silence then, finally silence again. They opened the door to the hallway, kept it open, and looked down the bright lit dark path, to the entrance.

– Windows are closed, Linda reported, as she and Dennis returned some time later. – All doors are closed and locked. I checked them personally.

– Good, Ted said, not quite satisfied with the answer and repeated it. – Good.

He felt very tired. The fiery blood that had kept him going had cooled down. All the released adrenaline made his head hurt.

Nobody said much. They clutched their guns, their forks, their knives.

Darkness descended on them all, between them like something physical. Everything that had happened was like a series of continuous blows to the skin, attacking their minds like worms. There was no let up, and there was no rest. Everything just kept happening, kept hurting.

Blood leaked from open wounds.

Minutes passed. Minutes turned to hours, and bloodshot eyes started to close.

– We sleep on shifts, Ted said, – the half of us to the north first. We will wake you in four hours.

Or if something happened they wouldn't have to.

Those standing closest to the northern wall fell right to the floor, to the nearest spot on the floor, and slept their restless sleep in less than two minutes.

They had been tired, as dead tired as those still standing felt.

– I'll make coffee, Glory said, and hurried to the kitchen.

Ted sent her a grateful look. Another idea one shouldn't need a crystal ball to realize.

– They won't burn down the cabin, will they? Jane wondered anxiously. – They don't want to call any attention to themselves.

– No, Ted agreed. – I don't think they will.

– And they don't want to kill us either…

Betty butted in, just as smug.

– They want to do far worse.

She looked in contempt at those of them cringing at her words.

Glory returned with the coffee. They removed their masks and drank. It tasted like shit, like most homemade coffee, but the half not sleeping drank it straight up, emptied at least two cups. Betty, too. Ted noticed the bags under her eyes, and her shaking hands, and that she noticed that he noticed, and she lowered her eyes in shame.

– It's natural to be afraid, he said to her.

– Yes, Ted. Her eyes glowed in gratitude.

Minutes passed. Hours passed. And time stood still.

Those standing sat down on the remaining chairs and stools. Ted looked around him, immeasurably tired. He saw how Jane's head fell down, how her jaw met her chest.

Let her relax a bit, Ted thought. Let her rest.

Bruce crawled across the carpet, until he stopped moving altogether. Tilla rested in Ted's arms. He shook her. She slept. He saw how Betty tried to rise from her chair, and failed. She fell off the chair and hit the floor.

He realized he was on the floor himself. He hadn't noticed. An enormous dread overwhelmed him. A switch was turned and he was gone.

Chapter twenty

Ted sat up, unable, for a moment, to open his eyes. They slid open, like rusty doors. John touched his shoulder, shaking it, shaking him. Dark gray light seeped through the windows.

– You fell asleep, John said. – You all fell asleep.

Impressions of the room started crawling into his brain. The sounds, the sights, the smells. It flooded his mind. After seconds like hours it flooded his mind.

– Bruce is drunk again, Iris reported giggling. – I can't get him to wake up.

– I woke up the rest of my half first, John said. – We decided to rouse you, too, from your slumber. We have all slept well, haven't we?

Careful laughter. Ted shook his head and smiled.

Bob remained by the wall, still tied up and gagged, probably still unconscious. There was no movement to read in his beaten to a pulp face.

Betty moaned as she cautiously lifted her head. Eventually everybody sat upright, yawning. It was almost like a ritual, the yawning. Everybody was expected to do that, after a night's sleep. Bruce puked, vomited all over himself and the carpet in front of him.

– CHRIST, Frank shouted, in a not very logical moment. – Are you aware of what it will cost to clean that carpet?

Ted wanted to point that out to him, but decided not to bother.

Everything felt muted, dislocated.

– It will be morning soon, Liz said.

– And still no sign of any… intruders, Helen continued pointedly.

– They will be here when it gets light, Ted said, horror stuck in his throat. – We are at our lowest ebb, and we can't sneak away, *slip* away in the night. Damn.

He struck the wall. It didn't hurt really.

Even the rage felt muted, dislocated, like it wasn't even a part of him anymore, and the dread overwhelmed him.

– How can you say that? Helen cried. – How can you say they will be here at all? We have been doing this… *wake* for God knows how long, done it for nothing.

He picked up his rifle.

– Because phase one has ended. Damn it.

Betty puked.

– Christ! Frank whispered.

– This is so lame, Liz said, – so Ted, the little boy screaming for attention.

And Ted, the boy looked at her, his skin and bones bathed in her contempt, in her fear and loathing. He realized now she had always disliked him, but had never bothered to give voice to her contempt before.

He cocked the rifle, and then, in a fit of rage, threw it at the wall.

– What's the matter with you? John rushed forward and picked it up. – That thing is a gem and is guaranteed worth...

He held his tongue. They saw him turn pale, actually saw it, and they understood. Unbelievably enough they all got it.

The firing pin was gone. Sometimes during the night the deadly weapon had been reduced to a useless toy.

John hurried around the room, grabbing all the guns. The others just stood there, allowing him to take them, to convince himself of what they and he already knew. The guns were all useless, one way or another.

– My body can fight off most poisons, Betty gasped, pale and sick. – Those it can't usually cause a very violent reaction, making me queasy or worse.

Bruce, still on the floor opened his mouth, but he never managed to speak.

The entrance door was opened, just plain opened. One by one men and women dressed in uniform charged inside. The door hit the wall silently. All steps began as silent thuds against the floor, but grew quickly to a howling march. Ted looked at the veranda. People were coming in that way, too. They were surrounded. They were sitting ducks.

Panic spread like wildfire. Many started screaming. Terrified they ran back and forth, going nowhere.

Ted was filled with an insane rage. The attackers were suddenly right there, in their midst. There were those who fought back, those who fell to their knees begging for mercy, all in vain. Ted kicked one woman in the face, landed on his feet, turning towards the next enemy. He was afraid, he was enraged. He wasn't petrified, and it felt so good, felt so good to let go. A huge man grabbed Tilla. He started tying her up, quickly and expertly, as if he wasn't bothered by her struggle at all. Ted picked up one of the useless guns and struck the tall man in the head, making a big hole in it. The man fell dead to the floor. Tilla tumbled into Ted's arms.

The attackers forced the youths down on the floor, and then they tied them up. It happened so fast, and so efficient, showing that they were clearly professionals. Ted and Tilla jumped through the window with their feet first. There was nothing here, nothing for them. No battle not already ended, no hope already dead. They landed on their feet outside and they ran. He saw Betty deck two attackers with two swinging, ruthless kicks, but then she was forced to the floor, moving her lips.

Run, she screamed.

To him.

He saw Iris run towards the exit. Two men blocked her way. Suddenly it was like a sledgehammer hit them both. Their chest was pushed in. Ribs broke like dry twigs, and Iris had a clear path. She ran like a deer, her face filled with shock, fear and triumph, catching up with the other two unbelievably fast.

– I've never used *it*… that way, in an… aggressive manner before, she gasped. – It was horrible. It just came to me. It felt *wonderful*.

They ran, so hard they couldn't breathe.

– I saw Liz be forced down on the floor and bound in a matter of seconds, she choked. – It was horrible.

They looked back, fear choking their mind, no longer able to see the cabin. Fog surrounded them. Wild hope coursed through them. And they ran.

It felt… incredible, like every bit of fatigue he had ever experienced had vanished, had completely and utterly been eradicated from his body. He flew like the wind.

– I can't do it again anytime soon, Iris said in despair. – My head feels like it's about to burst.

Feet hammered against the ground, hard and soft treacherous ground. They ran. Down, down, down. Tilla wanted to say something. He silenced her with a finger to his lips.

Where do we go? She asked. Where is safe?

Leadville. Was Leadville safe? He had recognized several people from the Silver Dollar in the attack force. They were in the middle of nowhere, ten thousand feet above sea level. The Sheriff's office in Leadville. Could they do anything against between twenty and thirty professionals... even if they wanted to?

He sent the girls an encouraging look. Tilla returned the smile, very set on not revealing her fear. How the sound of motorbikes came closer and closer. He would never know.

Then, before she could once more concentrate on the running she stumbled in a root sticking up. She cried out in pain and fell hard to the ground.

He stopped, ran back and grabbed her, pulled her on her feet. She cried out again, pain twisting her face.

– I can't run. She turned her hands into knots. – You must go on without me.

He stared at her, paralyzed.

– But we can't do that. You'll be... I...

She returned his stare, calmly, intensively.

– You must. Remember what we talked about? If only one gets away it will help those captured. And you can't carry me. Then we will soon have all of us as prisoners, instead of just me.

Iris had stopped, also paralyzed. Ted freed himself first from the paralysis and dragged her with him. Something inside him, long cold turned that much colder.

Tilla was gone, faded away in the mist.

The white dots floated by them, ghostly and wet, cracks in the gray revealing a rock there, a field here. They slowed down, tried their best to get a handle on the terrain, where they were heading. They kept doing down, in the certainty that this fixed tactic wouldn't fool them into going in circles, turn back to the cabin. Both were breathing hard now and muscles burned. They knew desperate people could keep it going for hours, if they had to, but not flat out. There had to be breaks. They slowed down even more, to something more like fast walk, constantly turning their heads.

He heard her anxiety before he saw it. She grabbed his arm and pointed, and up there, on a rock, perhaps thirty steps away they saw a man in uniform scouting the terrain, making no indication he had spotted them, but the sight still made them shake like leaves.

It was no use running anymore. Minutes of straight out running from the cabin, and they hadn't shaken the pursuers. These people were so experienced. They had known the prey would be heading down the valley. Despair descended on the two kids. They would have to walk quietly, sneaking off.

Both tried, but to them every step sounded like thunder. Knowing fully well they heard it better than people further away did nothing to lift their spirits.

Shaking overwhelmed them both, and they had to stop, for a while. Both were crying, silently, drying each other's tears. Ted tried to use his mind, tried to make it work, but everything was just wool buzzing silently between his ears. Move, he thought. Keep moving. We're talking about an enormous territory here. We have the entire Rocky Mountains to hide from these bastards.

They walked through the gray blanket and down a ravine, a passage to freedom. Three uniforms blocked their path, standing motionless at the ravine's exit, waiting for them. Ted and Iris stopped indecisive, frozen in limbs, frozen in mind. A lasso descended on Iris. The rope tightened, and she was pulled away from the boy.

Ted twisted away from the loop meant for him. Since that night three years ago he had trained, trained hard on avoiding lassos. A grinning soldier dragged Iris away. Blood and brown hair remained on the sharp rocks. Ted turned and turned his head, from her, to the unmoving awaiting figures, and back to Iris, unable to decide upon a course of action.

– Don't think about me, Iris cried. – Run. *Escape*.

He remained undecided a moment too long. Iris shouted a warning, and he looked up, steeling himself, but there was no lasso falling on him now, but a huge fine-woven net. One of its heavy corner weights hit him in the head, and he fell dizzy to the ground. He struck out, attempting to free himself, and in doing so only entangled himself further. He struck out again.

The net surrounded him like glue. The more he struggled the worse it got. He shouted in desperation and his movements turned completely erratic. His mind shut down, and there was nothing more, no more impressions or thoughts, until he lay completely wrapped up in the net, exhausted and defeated, crying out his defeat and suffering, making Iris stare in horror.

– Behold the ensnared wild beast, how all the fight has left it.

And then, for the first time he faced David Gidman, saw him clear as glass, through tears and blood of pain, an enormously tall, broad and imposing figure, towering above him, above everybody, above the mountains itself.

– We finally meet, white boy. You have no idea how long I have been looking forward to this.

– I'm not white, Ted mumbled. – Is the Cyclops color blind as well as dumb?

One Eye kicked him in the belly. He hadn't imagined the pain could grow any worse, but it did. The cords of the net cut into his skin, his lips, his clothes. He could hardly speak.

– I'll bet you think you know what pain is, white boy. But I'll show you that you're dead wrong. I and my associates will be educating you all. You'll be so grateful when we're done, so very, very grateful.

Iris was beaten until she could hardly breathe. Then she was bound hands and feet.

– You will be a good girl, won't you? Gidman pulled her up by the hair.

– Yes, she whispered.

– You won't even think of rebellion, of doing anything to displease your masters… right?

– No, I won't, she whimpered. – I'll be good, so very, very good. Please, don't hurt me anymore. Please, please, please…

– See? Gidman turned back to Ted. – See how easily she is cowed, how quickly she submits to her betters?

The boy wanted to close his eyes. He couldn't. Everything just flooded him, unedited, and it hurt.

One Eye grabbed his hand, and he started to squeeze, and his squeeze was so much harder than what anybody else could muster. Ted started breathing faster, wanted to clench his teeth, but couldn't, couldn't, couldn't. One Eye *squeezed*.

Ted *screamed*. The sound was so primal, so horrible that Iris blocked it out completely. She cringed there, staring at the boy's bloated face, unable to hear the slightest sound.

– You will be a good boy, won't you? Gidman pulled him up by the hair.

– Yes, he whispered.

– You won't even think of rebellion, of doing anything to displease your masters… right?

– No, I won't, he whimpered. – I'll be good, so very, very good. Please, don't hurt me anymore. Please, please, please…

– Of course, I will hurt you, you dumb shit. Gidman shook his head in contempt. – But I won't injure you… much. You're much too valuable for that. I didn't break a single bone in your body, none of your bodies. You are all my property now, and only a fool ruins his own property.

Grinning he put his huge paw of a hand around Ted's neck, squeezing. He kept doing it, until the captive turned gray blue. And it didn't end with that either. After he had let go and the boy attempted to breathe Gidman hit him hard in the abdomen. The boy hit his head on the rock and lay still.

In a terrible moment Iris feared he was dead, but then his head turned, and vomit erupted between the shivering lips.

– Now, white boy, I believe you've learned your place, Gidman said harshly. – Your first lesson of many.

They were lifted up and carried away on two of the men's shoulders.

Everything has been taken away from us, Iris thought dully. Everything!

Even though she feared there was yet more, more left to lose. Both she and Ted moaned in pain and bottomless despair all the way back.

The cabin, like a grotesque monster it appeared in the fog. He saw its eyes, its ears and its hungry mouth, its hungry, hungry gap. It swallowed him, digested him, and spat him out like nothing. There was no escape, no life, only existence. He choked, couldn't stop choking.

From the living room rose heartbreaking howls of suffering, the stink of fear. The youths had been thrown in a heap on the middle of the floor. Ted and Iris joined them. The others hardly registered it. After a few seconds, eternities it was like they, too, had always been there.

Ropes cutting into skin. The heat, the weight of bodies, both below and above. Everything hurt. Everything was boundless pain. And they knew nothing more, nothing less.

– We never had a chance.

No one recognized the voice of he or she who said that, and they couldn't, wouldn't consider the further implications of it. They couldn't think, couldn't reason. The world was pain, and nothing besides.

Nothing was said beyond this. Beyond this were only the wails.

Piss and feces mixed with the stink of blood and vomit in the endless hell they had been condemned to.

A man stood there, by Gidman's side. A masked man, smoking a cigar.

– You're right, my friend. They're ready. Prepare for transport.

The voice was nothing, only a barbwire pretending to belong to a human being.

– Cut them loose, Gidman laughed. – Give them their reward.

The command was executed with the subordinates' usual efficiency. The wails increased to insane levels when the blood returned to hands and feet, a torture certainly on par with everything else the youths had endured.

Buckets of ice-cold water were thrown at them. The shock focused the pain, made the prisoners even more pliable.

– ON YOUR FEET!

One of the subordinates. Nothing special with that voice. Just an ordinary, ten on a dozen voice. The youths obeyed, the sound of cracking whips, the sting on their skin making them desperate to obey the command.

– In line, you lazy shits. You're going on a long journey.

Men and women with whips and clubs surrounded the boys and girls.

– You first. Gidman pulled Veronica from the formless mass.

She stumbled forward with dead eyes. The others shuffled in her tracks.

Glory waited for them, in full uniform at the end of the

hallway, a very different Glory, one with cold, hard eyes.

Two tall, muscled black men were by her side, piles of... of chains and bracelets at her feet. Ted had believed there was nothing that could bring him lower, but he realized now these were merely the early stages of a long and horrible degradation road, one there was no end to. He wanted to scream, shout his pain, but no sound erupted from his sore throat.

Veronica was pushed brutally before Glory.

– You are the least, Glory said viciously. – You'll have the honor of being first.

She slapped the short girl on her cheek. Veronica remained in place, staring blindly at the black girl.

Glory fitted the bracelets around wrists and ankles. One chain between the wrists, one between the ankles. One long chain with collars to unite them all around the neck.

Veronica stood displayed before her friends. The shame made her bow her head. Jane resisted far less when it was her turn and John even less than she did. Eventually the youths only took one mechanical step forward when it was their turn, like sleepwalkers.

One by one they all joined the long chain and as it happened the final glimpse of defiance died in their eyes. The collar around the neck made it difficult to breathe. They stumbled forward, ever forward. It happened quickly, without notable resistance.

When it was Tilla's turn she stepped on her injured foot and stumbled, and Glory started slapping her, slapping her repeatedly, before sending her further on her way. Then it was Ted's turn. Glory grabbed him around the jaw, laughing scornfully.

– So you wanted to play nice with the poor, lonely nigger bitch, HUH?

She scratched the skin under his ear.

– I've marked you now. You're mine.

There was no change of expression, no reaction.

– No fight left in you, huh? I figured as much. You're no better than the rest of these wretches, these dumb beasts.

Gidman moved an arm, holding up something, a gun. Ted recognized it. Now, there was a reaction, a fleeting flare of reaction in the soil-like eyes. He knew to whom the gun had belonged.

– It's hopeless, right, white boy? Your great protector can no longer protect anybody. He fell down a deep ravine, and I doubt anybody will even recognize him if the body is ever recovered. I, personally am convinced he will be one of those people that will quite simply, quietly disappear. Just like all of you. Never to be seen again.

Ted's brain was no longer wool. It was an empty space. There had been a shock of sorts. Now, he was no more than an empty shell. He stared at the floor as if the surroundings weren't in any way real.

When they fitted the bracelets and chains on him the boy felt something break inside him, something infinitely precious that might be called humanity, something that could never be recalled.

Walls, floor and ceiling dissolved around them. They were on their way, marching to the singing of whips, the striking of clubs, up hills, down hills, up hills, down hills, up hills. Everything was just about one thing: To put one foot in front of the other, to not fall, to not be deluged by the sharp pain of the whip when one stumbled and fell.

The man leading the procession shouted and cursed endlessly, constantly.

– You're just dumb beasts in chains, and nothing more. What do you think you are? Do you believe you have value, your own worth, that you're deciding your own fate? I'll tell you something: If we haven't reached the shipping station by nightfall you will know how truly worthless you are.

It was just words, masking the truly horrible realities behind it. Ted was shocked to discover that he was still able to think, to reason. It came to him in flashes, off and on, and he wished it hadn't. Tilla walked in front of him, Betty behind. He glimpsed Tilla's dead, gray eyes… and then Betty's green. The green was dull and pale, too, but there was something there, something to hold onto.

Growth is pain. Being born hurts.

– My father is rich, insanely rich, Veronica had screamed sometime, long ago. – He can pay.

494

- It's almost funny, isn't it? One of the slavers chuckled. – Just about any kid of rich parents in America has probably learned those two, crucial sentences.

The consequences of his words dawned on the youths, making hopelessness descend on them even more than before.

There would be no ransom demands. These people had different plans, different goals. They would take them far away, possibly to another country. Life had led them here, unsuspecting and defenseless.

Defenseless? Wasn't everybody? Didn't virtually all people close their eyes to the world's reality unless it struck them? And when it happened it was too late to reopen them.

Now, his eyes were open. Now, they were closing.

Apathy descended on him once more, the black cloud of gray, one foot in front of the other. That was all there is. All in all this chain gang looked perfectly similar to a slave transport at the start of the nineteenth century, except now there were predominantly whites being chained and driven like cattle.

They hardly noticed when the ground beneath their feet changed from soil to shingle and asphalt. A truck seemingly growing from the road itself awaited right ahead. Its back wall opened and created a ramp for them to walk up. They did, encouraged by added incentives of whipping and beating.

– Arms above your head, the whip barked.

They obeyed the order the same way they did every order, instantly and without thinking twice about it. The Voice was everything. The Voice was All.

There were hooks hanging from the ceiling in the truck's storage room. They were pushed forward. The chain was fitted to the hooks, one for each of them. Their feet were chained to the floor. They were trapped. The hooks were raised further up by whirring machinery to fit individual height, until everybody had their hands high above their heads, and had to stand on their toes. Everything happened with the usual speed and efficiency. Black masks were pulled over their heads, fastened by straps around their neck. Something hard and unpleasant pressed against their ears. There was an opening for the mouth, but no light reached their eyes. They were blind.

– You will remain here for a while. They heard Glory's Voice tight by their ears, through their earphones. – When you leave here you will be home.

The door closed, and the engine started, but they hardly heard it. A pre-recorded Voice had started speaking through the earphones. The truck moved. They moved. Everything floated. They floated in a pool of blackness.

Listen, the Voice told them. Learn.

Obey, it commanded. Serve.

– SPEAK, they heard Betty far away. – Resist the Voice.

Some did. Some didn't bother.

They heard Betty's guttural speech mixing with the Voice. For a short while, until she started screaming and throwing fits.

Then they heard the unmistakable singing of the whip, and Betty screaming in frustration and pain.

– I knew you were a clever girl, they heard. – No matter, you will learn to serve like the rest of them.

The singing of the whip and Betty's angry screaming, fading into whimpers and begging, and declaration of obedience continued for a short while, followed by a short period of crying. Then there was only the sound of the Voice.

Repeat after me, the Voice said, and everybody did. Nobody dared resist its call.

Very good, the Voice praised them. Good boys and girls. Open your mouth.

They did, and the taste of sweets was found on their tongue.

Swallow, It said. And they so did.

The words continued in a steady flow, uninterrupted. The Voice was everything and everything was the Voice. They listened. They couldn't help it. And they heeded the Voice. Learned what It wanted them to learn.

You have been good, It told them. It's bedtime now.

(And it was bedtime).

Time to sleep, good boys and girls. Time for listening and learning.

Ted suddenly felt unimaginably tired. He couldn't help it, and he wanted to cry, but couldn't.

Embrace the cold inside you, someone or something said, and he couldn't tell if it came from outside or inside. Embrace the fire.

Sleep overwhelmed him fast. There was nothing he could do. Nothing. Certainty came, in a flash. He was fully asleep, but he had the ability to think (he thought). He faded. Ted Cousin faded. And no matter what happened next, he would be no more. Another would take his place, he knew that, and he wondered.

Who it would be.

They were all still, still as death. The enticing voice kept whispering to them, kept teaching them. And the truck drove a long way, passing townships and cities, inevitably approaching the end of the journey. The nightmare had just begun.
***/

It didn't hurt anymore.

Details, details flooded the boy's mind, but nothing registered. All the youths had been undressed. They didn't wear chains anymore. No watches, jewelry or ornament of any kind. John's glasses had been taken from him. Suddenly Ted wasn't sure whether or not John had ever used glasses. There was a terrible black hole of uncertainty within him.

Room wasn't big. It was circle-round, and they were all placed along the wall, the wall without corners. Everything had a soft quality in here. Carpets covered floor, wall and ceiling. They saw no sharp edges. No windows, no visible light, no furniture. Light reached them from somewhere, but they could not say from where.

They had no recollection of waking up, only of being awake. Nobody would look at anybody else, ashamed about their nudity, ashamed about everything. They looked at themselves or unidentified nude skin, because there was nowhere else to look. Ted noticed no blood anymore, no vomit, no wounds, no bruises, no pain, no thoughts. No more chafes, no marks after the chains. They had all been bathed, smelling of soap and perfume. The girls' nails had been cut.

– They don't want us to hurt ourselves, someone stated.

Ted had no idea whom.

Bars. I can feel bars in my hands.

There was the image of a cage, of bars surrounding him on all sides, no matter where he turned, and he felt the cold metal at his palms.

We've still got teeth, he didn't think.

They walked through a long, badly lit corridor, walked endlessly with no end in sight, stumbling, skin against skin, dead skin.

Soft carpet. He hardly felt it under his butt, his heel, his back. Soft skin. Dead as doornails.

A circle in the room's middle section descended downwards. They saw it lower itself, staring at the black hole. The circle-round piece reappeared and brought with it piles of fruit. They stared at the fruit. Suddenly they were all on the move, rushing towards the fruit.

Hungry. Sooo hungry.

Everybody attempted to reach it first, jumping forward, totally disregarding everybody else, pushing and pulling. The smell of food filled their nostrils, spread through the body and to their soul, making them go totally insane. The spectacle filled the room, the screams and groans, and the sound of chewing. There was blood, and bruises and cuts, but no pain. The dull fever dominating them overwhelmed everything else.

Like children in a sandbox like children in a sandbox like children in a sandbox

Afterwards they heard crying. At least they thought so. Nothing happened in here. Nothing real.

They heard the sound of chewing long after they once more sat quietly on the carpeted floor, and the fruit was gone from sight, as if it had never been. When they looked fearfully at the center of the room they spotted no remains, no traces of anything ever having been there. Ted sensed skin against his skin, glimpsed red hair at the edge of his vision. Tilla was gone. There was nothing there. Even though she sought close to him, like a little child in the night, all fire had left the staring, empty glare. He stroked her hair, attempting to comfort her somehow, but there was nothing there. She shivered constantly, as if someone had placed a vibrator on her skin somewhere and it spread all over the body. He hardly felt it. He wished he had.

Soldiers surrounded them, pushing them through dark passages and hallways, beating up on them for every minor perceived disobedience or transgression. Noise, screams, suffering bombarded them, so much they could hardly stand it. But everything just kept coming, beaten into them like nails. Helen *screamed*. They recognized her voice, shockingly, horribly.

They stumbled into a room with many strong lights, unable to make sense of the jumbling images surrounding them. Wide eyes glimpsed poles, horizontal and vertical poles. Horizontal poles hanging from the ceiling. Vertical going from floor to ceiling. Some of them were made to kneel and were chained to the vertical poles. Others were chained and hung upside down, from metal poles, thick metal poles flashing in wet red. They whipped Jane and made everyone watch. Those who attempted to look away were instantly punished with their own beating and whipping. This room was dirty. Dust and shit floated everywhere. It couldn't have been cleaned for months. It was a square room, contrasted in light and dark, softened in mist, a mist made of sweat and blood, and tears. This - this was the torture chamber.

Ted's back burned. Welts created by the whip weren't deep (they didn't damage the skin), but they stung, oh, how they stung. His back burned and there was no escape from the pain.

One of the soldiers, a woman stopped before them. She held up a prod, waited until she had their complete attention, and then scratched it against the wall. It sparked and blazed. They stared horrified at her.

– Yes, this is an electric prod, she said proudly. – Used well and extensively in Chile and other experimental laboratories these days. Who will be first? Who among you will be first to be honored by its touch?

She walked among them, before and behind them. They stared at nothing, and wanted for nothing.

– It's a wonderful all-purpose tool, the woman recounted. – So versatile for teaching purposes, so simple to make, so simple to use. Let me tell you a secret: Your existence has always been that of two extremes. This is a truth we're merely formalizing in this place, in this your new home, to honor you, to show you beyond doubt, beyond fear, the truth of the world. ONE is *punishment*. TWO is *reward*. The world is this simple, and that is all you will ever need to know. Oh, there are skills and nuances to be sure beyond this, but these are the basic tenets in which you will live your lives from now on.

– You people are CRAZY!

The powerful voice cut through the room, silencing everything.

The boys and girls looked at Helen in horror. The woman smiled.

– Thank you, my dear. I will now be rewarding you, give you your devoirs, show my appreciation for your eagerness, your eagerness to *learn*.

Helen's face hardly had time to change from expressive anger, to protest, to paralyzing fear before the prod was pressed at her thigh. She hung horizontally, facing the floor, arms and legs stretched up, hanging from the pole. She screamed. The prisoners had believed they had heard the worst kind of screams lately, heard it penetrate deeply into their flesh and bones...

But they had heard and seen nothin'.

Helen screamed, until she screamed herself hoarse, and had no voice left. The entire body shook. Eyes bulged. Face was distorted into a demonic mask. Her voice, like a knife, a blade sharpened and tempered forever and ever cut into the absolutely horrified captives. The woman pulled back a bit, before a second later renewing her effort, pushing the prod into Helen's groin, and then... then the screaming began in truth.

The woman pulled back the prod and pressed it at Dennis' testicles.

Everybody screamed now. They could no longer discern between their own scream and that of others'. There were more soldiers with prods, all casually and randomly using the prod. No reason, no rhyme.

One series of treatment ended, hours later. There was a short recess. But pain didn't end. Pain reigned forever. Pain coursed through them as the woman spoke, teaching them about the world.

– You're all such beautiful children. It is pure pleasure teaching you.

And it continued, as if it had never stopped.

Then something... happened.

A male, when once more being treated with the kindness of

500

the prod started shaking, shaking in cramps.

– STOP!

All the uniformed men and women obeyed instantly. The boy hanging from the pole continued shaking in violent cramps.

– Oh, FUCK AND FUCK. The woman threw her hands up in exasperation. – Where is the fucking *physician?*

A woman in white coat rushed into the room and at the boy. She put a stethoscope to his chest.

– HEART ATTACK, she cried calmly. – He needs treatment at once. Let's get him out of here.

Just a few seconds more, and he was freed from the chains and carried out of the room.

The Teacher paraded among them, not really shaken either. They stared at her through tears, saliva and blood, very attentive children.

– Probably a genetic defect, she shrugged. – It happens. Not often, but occasionally. It's good. He was *weak,* not fit to aspire to a place among the Abraxas Omega, and was weeded out before he could diminish our great order.

She stopped by another male.

– But you're fit, aren't you? You want to join our ranks?

– Yes, Teacher, he stated eagerly, tears of horror, of gratitude flowing down his face.

(You will be given a teacher, one to teach you the secrets).

– Repeat the Oath.

– I'm born inferior, he shouted. – Born to serve, born to obey the Abraxas Omega in all things. I'm the lowest of the low. I'm a slave, and a slave I will remain until the day I die.

– Good boy. She petted his cheek. – And now you.

Everybody repeated the words. It flowed from their lips as if had always done so, as if they had recently been born, and they had.

– It isn't necessarily true, of course, she said lightly. – You might one day rise above your low station, if one of the masters sees a potential in you, if you are eager enough, obedient enough, strong enough.

She walked to a female, slapping her.

– YOU! What is your purpose?

– To obey and serve the masters, the girl said promptly. – To live and die for the Abraxas Omega, for the Purpose, the All.

Teacher smiled, stepping back a little, giving the sign. Everybody choired the words.

– You've passed the test, she declared. – School may begin. You've been born. Now it's time for the first class.

They were released from their chains, slow movements, dull eyes, memory failing they followed the Teacher and her entourage out of the room, scared to death to take a wrong step, making a wrong turn.

This was their life now, and they hardly remembered anything else.

They entered a hall. At its center was a large bathtub.

– You will now wash yourself, wash each other, make yourself presentable. Get to it, and make a good effort, or I will flay the skin from your bones.

They jumped into the pool. Water splashed around them, slowly, the world moved so slowly. They grabbed the pieces of soap by the edge, and started to wash each other, to clean each other, and there was nothing there, nothing in their actions except the Master's will.

I want to live, Helen told Bruce. I want to serve. Please help me.

He washed her breasts. The nipples hardened in his palms, but there was nothing beyond that, no arousal beyond the need for serving, for obeying.

Dim memories of no consequence played in their minds, echoes of the nothing they had emerged from.

Ted saw something, more glimpses at the corner of his eyes, the edge of consciousness. He saw Gidman, Glory and Bob far up there on the stand, a small outgrowth of the wall, a VIP stand. He got Goosebumps. In the hot water it covered his entire body. He saw Bob's face covered in bandages, the hateful look in the eyes.

He washed Tilla. She washed him. There was no contact, no intimacy.

The world, he whispered into her ear. I will scour the world for you.

There was no reaction. She made no sign that she had heard him. The face, the eyes, the body remained impassive. He wasn't sure he had said anything, anything at all.

They won't break me, Liz shook so hard that she was unable to stay still

She stayed still.

They already have, Linda said with a twitch in her doll-like face.

Ted saw Tilla and Betty side by side. They were the same. There was nothing there, separating them. They smiled to him. They cried with him. There were no more tears left.

He had dim memories of more dark corridors, more hallways, of kneeling down before the Teacher, of being clothed, of being unclothed, and everything was like a dream, a handful of dust in the desert. They were ordered out of the pool, and bid to dry each other, scrub each other raw. Body hurt. Every piece of skin was pain. Skin was sensitized, he realized. It was the masters' will. Teacher touched his manhood. He felt nothing. She smiled.

What was that again? He didn't remember.

Four. They were no more than four, now. Ted, Betty, Helen, Bruce. Not one name. Four. One Master in front. He led. They followed.

The big cage turned. The pyramid of bars and air turned. Master pushed a button with his foot, and it stopped. The door opened. He commanded them to step inside and they did.

– This is a display, Master said. – Masters will come here and look at you. No words will be spoken, and you will perform for them, show yourself, display the eagerness to serve.

Marionettes, puppets on invisible strings. Four places in the cage.

Ted (of Ted, Betty, Helen, Bruce) remembered Glory being here, remembered displaying himself before her. She studied him with a cold, compassionate smile. He felt desire in her eyes.

In the pool they had been divided into groups, groups of four. Esthetic, very esthetic. Red and black, black and red. Similar height and build. Pyramid turned, the pyramid cage.

Sleep now, the Master said, the Voice said. Listen. Learn.

School is a place of learning. School is a place of joy.

They slept. They learned.

Chapter twenty-one

The Pyramid turned, whirling like sand in the desert. The desert whispered to him, whispered to her.

Consciousness is Deep, he recalled. Levels within levels within levels. What seems like a smooth surface of a sea may boil below. Hope boiled. Embers burned.

– I'm cold.

He knew it was Betty's voice, but he didn't recognize it.

– I never thought it would be like this. I'm cold.

Ted wanted to reach out to touch her. He didn't move. But he kept looking at her. He drowned in the green fire of her eyes, and it felt indescribably good.

– This can't be happening. She looked desperately at him.

– We must keep resisting, keep fighting, he insisted, attempting to comfort her.

And he said it. He knew he said it.

– No, you don't *understand*. She half raised a hand. – I'm trained to resist it, trained to withstand anything like it. And you…

She stopped. Hand fell. She returned to be a doll again. The sound of steps was heard in the hall again.

Round and round the pyramid turned, and all sides were the same.

Learn to bow, learn to perform. You are pets. You've been pets all your life, and will remain pets for the rest of your days, useful perhaps, but pets none-the-less.

He remembered. School here, school there, write nicely, behave yourself, earn the teachers' favor, and you will be well fed and taken care of.

This is a small pyramid. The room outside, perhaps the entire building is one bigger pyramid.

They are fed. They cannot eat without help, cannot do anything without aid, without explicit permission. Teaching is all. Teaching makes the wheel turn.

Bug. Dead bug. The bug is dead. The man is dead. Man is dead. Fire. I want the fire back. I want all the fire back. Let the ashes burn. And fire consumes the world. All of me, I am falling into a black hole. I am the black hole. I am the fire.

Betty was breathing faster.

– I can hear you, she hums. – I can hear your song. It has begun.

– See how it jumps, they said outside the cage. – See how the puppets dance.

Wings are torn apart. Blood and feathers are spread across the Earth. But each feather keeps dancing in the wind. I am lost. I am lost. I am lost. I find myself. In the deepest, darkest corners of the Abyss

I find myself.

The puppets dance, and the entire world is applauding, applauding the mindless dance.

He shook his head. The sound of burning is fading, fading, embers into ashes. Betty is smiling.

They are dressed, sitting in a classroom, and are being fed information. What is needed to serve. Nice boys and girls fading. Shining faces. Attentive boys and girls doing what they are told. Taught how to be useful, learning nothing.

His hand rolled into a fist, didn't roll into a fist.

They walked, the four of them, led by the Guide walking in front, through dark hallways and corridors. Everything looked alike, a labyrinth, a labyrinth of fear. They knew they could walk forever, without ever returning to their point of origin, without ever finding their way.

Until they spotted a door. They hardly recalled what a door was. It had been so long since they had last seen one. The door flew open. A nude, unknown black girl stumbled outside while supporting herself on the wall. Blood flowed from her groin and down her thighs. Face and body both had turned pale from fear, from boundless fear, and they were unable to imagine what made her display this fear, what she had experienced in there they hadn't already been subjected to.

– HELP ME! She shouted. – IS THERE NO ONE WHO CAN HELP ME!

Before she managed to take another step, she was caught, and pulled back in. The desperate howl echoed in the deepest recesses of their minds.

– Silly girl. We can't even help us.

Ted didn't get who said that. Perhaps nobody did. It no longer mattered.

The four stood there, straight for a while, waiting, not waiting. The door opened, a mirror opened. Two girls and two boys marched through it. Betty walked first, then Ted. He stamped on her foot, and she cried out in pain. Both fell on the floor. Bruce, unable to stop fell on top of them. Helen panicked when Betty screamed, and ran off. Whiplashes bit into sore skin, and they got to their feet in a raging fervor. Ted stopped then. His eyes stopped. His mind stopped.

David Gidman towered above them.

Gidman didn't seem to notice them, was totally indifferent to their presence. But they noticed him, noticed his. It penetrated them, surrounded them like anesthetic gas, paralyzing them.

Not that long afterwards as they didn't measure time, Helen was returned to the room. Thrown brutally on the floor, she lay there gasping, whimpering. Gidman prodded her with a stick.

– You will be severely punished for that one, girl. We're way past the point of accepting the slightest disobedience from you.

Ted saw the room. He didn't see it. He wasn't ordered to do so. It reminded him of a doctor's office, sterile, purpose-oriented, and filled with instruments and apparatus. The ball grew in his throat and he could hardly breathe.

Three people entered through another door. Bob, Glory and another man. Ted noticed the other man. He made a bigger impression than Glory's sadistic, expectant smile and Bob's bandaged face. He was white, both in hair and skin. He wasn't old, in spite of the hair, about forty. The hair was thicker than on most twenty-year-old people. He had no wrinkles, but a long, white scar ran from his left eye to his jaw, making the face appear rough and brutal. The four youths felt straight out ill. Betty reacted uncommonly strong. Ted sensed her shivering.

This, the little boy thought, is the bogeyman.

Daddy. I want daddy.

– My name is Meinz. He spoke evenly, indifferently. – Kurt Meinz. It is I who will take you on your final journey. You may feel you have endured much in terms of tutoring already, but that was just the preparations. This is the real thing.

He enjoys listening to his own voice.

That alone gave little Ted the willies, the fear that the man would hear his thought actually making him want to run, tempting him with Helen's fate.

He didn't care about them at all. The talk was for his own benefit, only for him.

– I, with the help of my assistants, my eager students will make sure your value reaches optimal level.

Value. There was always the talk of value.

Stewart appeared to Ted's inner eye, dead Stewart, Stewart the corpse, the bloated, stinking corpse, lying somewhere on a rock, a rock red and rosy.

– Honey, Gidman called.

They turned to him in disbelief, but then their eyes turned from him, and to the half-naked woman entering the room. Ted recognized her. He didn't recognize her. From the times she had served him dinner, lovely, delicious French cuisine. He saw Jean Stewart through eyes of the past, and noted only what hadn't been there before: The sweet and dead smile, the red fist burned into her left thigh, the symbol of fear and subordination. She carried a whip and was dressed in black. Ted sensed nothing of what she had been.

– Greetings, slave, Gidman said. – You may reply.

– Greetings, Master, she replied huskily.

Voice was dead and submissive, her entire aura a rotten sort of violet. Something inside Ted just shriveled to garbage.

– Jean will be your aide, your kind helper. She will help you adjust, as she has adjusted. She knows her place now, and so will you.

Gidman had left. Jean remained, standing rigid against the wall, awaiting commands.

Hatred remained in Ted. He clung to it.

Glory grabbed his hair and pulled, pulled hard. Pain, not much, enough to make him notice her.

– The nigger-lover, she said softly.

– You will learn to serve, Meinz said. – Certainly, as you already have, through fear, but also, in time enthusiastically, craving your Masters' approval, our recognition, as proof of your existence. You do not exist, you know. I will make you real. I will give you purpose in life. I am Doctor Fixit. I fix things, and I am very, very good at it.

He walked to Helen. She pushed herself at the wall, eyes hard as glass. He sat down on his heels, brushing a bit of hair from her face.

– You're all sweaty, aren't you, slave?

– Y-yes, she stuttered.

– Yes, *Master*.

He corrected her with a snap of his voice.

– Yes, Master. YES, MASTER, PLEASE MASTER

– You will be punished for that, too, of course. A slave is supposed to be pleasing to the Master, and sweat isn't very pleasing at all. Not during the initial *presentation,* at least.

Sick. Ted felt sick.

All those sick thoughts tumbled around in his head, and he wasn't human anymore.

Meinz cleared his throat while fingers played with her long, dark nipples. For a while he remained there, sitting on his heels, reviewing and examining her.

– Hmmm, Indian, ain't you?

– Yes, Master.

– Okay, that should do it for a cursory examination. Go and lay down on the bench.

She obeyed, eagerly and fearfully. Bob and Glory fastened and tightened straps round her neck, arms, wrists, thighs and ankles.

– All of you, Meinz snapped. – And be quick about it.

No mind, no thought, but the Voice. They didn't protest and didn't oppose the command, the will of the Master. Ted saw himself strike Bob's bandaged head, saw it having no effect, saw Bob enjoy beating him to a pulp, punishing him for his transgressions, laughing at him and scorning him. Died. The entire him died, a flower falling to the ground, absorbed by the greedy soil.

Glory slapped Bruce with a belt, slapped him on his manhood. Bruce screamed in despair, in everything. They had hit bottom on degradation road eons ago, and they just kept falling.

– Yes, Meinz said. – You are little children, desperately desiring to return to your mother's womb. And you are, you will. We are your womb now, your mother, and when you are born we will care for you, and teach you what is important in life, teach you everything you need to be a good slave. We are Alpha to Omega, and you are nothing but an extension of our body, our will.

They were all strapped to benches, lying still, waiting for the inevitable.

– They're ready, Doctor, Bob reported triumphantly. – The examination may begin at any time.

– In a moment, Meinz grinned. – My not so cooperative bladder is giving the subjects a momentary continuance.

He left the room.

– Why? Ted whined, hating himself, – Why, Glory?

Her playful fingers touched his thigh, moving to the center of the body. She grabbed his cock, grabbed it playfully. Hatred coursed through him, when he realized he reacted to her touch, and he almost cried in gratitude.

– You don't get it, but you will. You're our beasts of burden, created to do menial tasks, all menial tasks, and I know, being the eager beasts I know you to be, you will perform admirably.

– Don't bother him, Betty said. – Come to me.

Glory grinned and took the two steps towards the girl, lifting her hand to strike, but never made it. Ted saw. He witnessed how Betty's face, Betty's dead face changed into radiant life. He knew what was happening.

And it did. Bob joined Glory expectantly.

– You're the slaves, Betty snarled, in a low, intense Voice. – You're hardly more than dirt under my feet.

They shook and stiffened like statues.

– And now you will free us, free us all.

Bruce looked incredulous at what was happening, as the two freed Betty.

– NO! Helen howled. – He will punish us. I can't stand it. I can't take anymore. PLEASE!

Meinz returned from the bathroom, somewhat composed, strangely composed.

– On your *knees!* Betty thundered.

There was no effect. Ted witnessed, as suspicion in her turned to certainty how panic and horror returned to Betty's eyes, fear he had hardly noticed in her before.

– I know who you are, she whimpered. – You are…

– Shut up, WHORE, Meinz shouted, also unusually agitated, a completely different personality compared to the Kurt Meinz they had learned to know these long minutes.

He slapped her on the mouth. The slap was so hard that her head seemingly jumped a bit to her right. Before she fell he grabbed her neck and held her up. Blood flowed from her slack jaw, but her eyes were still alive and burning.

– May you burn in hell, *traitor,* she spat. – They will find you, they will give you your just reward, and you will wish you never had been born.

– Your Masters think they have everything figured out, he snarled to her. – *He* certainly thinks so. But I'm going to stop it. I'm going to put a stop to all of it.

He struck her, harder, and she was unable to keep her head high. It slipped from shoulder to shoulder as he threw her back on the bench. He fastened the straps unnecessarily tight. When she cried out in despair and pain the sound cut through the boy. He wondered about Meinz' loss of composure and his sudden rage, he did. It cleared his mind, rekindled his fire. There was deep, unmistakable fear in Meinz' eyes. Ted knew. This concerned him, concerned the mystery surrounding his life. Betty Morgan knew. She knew who he was.

– Do what you want with me, she said, strangely indifferent. – I'm not important. You will pay. If not before, so during The Final Days. You will suffer a thousand deaths.

– You may not be, he grinned, – but *he* is.

Both turned to Ted. He felt strangely detached from it all. For a small moment true horror was visible in Betty's eyes, but then she relaxed, smiling scornfully at the man towering above her, smiling in blinding fervor at the boy.

– Foolish man, she laughed. – Believing you can stop the rivers from running, the wind from blowing, the earth from moving and the fire from Burning.

– That might be, Meinz snarled, absolutely beside himself. – But you won't live through it. I will take particular pleasure in breaking your will.

Meinz shook his two students hard. Slowly life returned to their eyes, and they started moving.

– What *happened?* Bob complained in a confused and sorry state.

– Never mind, Meinz replied curtly. – Let's get going. Fetch the equipment.

They hurried off. Meinz opened a drawer, slowly putting on two thin skin-like gloves.

– Sterilized, he told them. – Slaves must not be sick.

The hate sent pangs of frost through Ted. He welcomed what was coming, welcomed the coming transformation, the embracing of hatred.

Slaves paraded through the great hall. One of them wondered what he had thought a second ago, something important, but no matter how much he pondered it he couldn't remember, and he felt tears flow inside, joy flow everywhere. Slaves are bundles of joy, the girl with the red fist on her thigh had said during her lessons. They are born to please the masters.

Come to me, she had said, and I will show you great wonders.

She was regal, obedient and docile. They listened to her.

Helen shook when the Doctor approached her. Saliva flowed from her mouth.

The first few minutes he did nothing an ordinary physician wouldn't do. In fact, it was more than clear that he had been one once. He examined her body, took blood samples and studied her teeth. But then it started. He split her thighs with practiced ease and without warning pushed a hand inside of her. She screamed, and her scream had grown even a few notches in quality and strength.

– Jolly good, he exclaimed with regret. – We have a virgin here. That won't do. That won't do at all.

He pushed even harder. The scream was cut short. She shook and the body slackened.

– Good girl. He petted her cheek.

He kept talking, as if he was a professor at a faculty.

– You may think your flashes of lucidity and anger are signs of your strength, of your indomitable will, he commented, – but you would be wrong. That happens to virtually all of you, and is expected, as a part of the process, as the last few quakes until both the surface and the deep turns calm, forever. We are erasing you bit by bit, until nothing remains, but putty in our hands. And telling you this is of no relevance, since shortly you won't remember any of it anyway.

It lasted well and long until Bob and Glory returned. The four almost saw it as a relief. Betty, Ted and Bruce looked away from each other, filled with familiar bursts of shame.

This was not their first stop, was it?

This was… just a stop.

Bob and Glory pushed a box on a table. It had wires attached to prods, too, but looked… different, somehow. The shakes were permanent now, an integral part of their personality. Frost and fire, fast and furry, fast and furry. Ted laughed. He wasn't sure he had, in truth been laughing.

Glory stopped by his side.

– You did something to me, didn't you? She said hatefully, made me lose my wits, my Self

– Pan - kettle - black, he spat in contempt. He did it, managed to put strength into his voice, knowing fully well it wouldn't last, scared shitless of the Void awaiting him.

She grabbed his cock and started massaging it, cruelty glowing from her very skin. It hurt. She made sure it hurt. And she was good. She could make it hurt, could make the pain sweet. He smiled. It did something to him. Dread rose like death in him, and mind faded. This was teaching. He was a pet. This had happened earlier. He was petted, given his reward, being a cute pet, a docile slave. He ejaculated all over himself. She slapped him, slapped him until the blood flowed freely.

– You pathetic, clumsy wretch, she scorned him. – See what you have done to yourself. You stupid *beast*.

Tears. She dried his tears. She was kind. Kind as a nanny, cruel as a sister.

Sister, he thought.

And forgot.

– We are still experimenting, Meinz lectured, – walking different paths to perfection. We have a control group, of course. There must always be a control group. All ways lead to Rome, and all ways lead from Rome. This is what you know.

– Know? Helen whispered.

– Precisely, my dear. – Good girl, good slave.

He pushed the table with the box a little closer to Betty's

bench.

– This is a slightly different method from what you have
been subjected to earlier, more refined, so to speak. They are
butchers. I am an artist.

While he made the final preparations, Glory put a hand on
Ted's belly.

– Here you are. She smiled sweetly to him. – Unable to lift
a finger. I can do whatever I want with you. You're my pet
already. You will be in my stable, and I will own you forever.

She scratched him all the way to the chest. He clenched his
teeth and stared at the ceiling. She was right. She could scratch,
beat and kick, destroy him. He was already destroyed. He
wasn't human. While the heat from her thigh broke through his
skin something happened inside of him. What had previously
ruptured now dissolved completely. It was a process taking
many years, from the twelfth birthday, to Mike's death, to the
little red house, to now, the completion.

He existed no longer. Ted Cousin didn't exist. If he ever
escaped he would no longer be Ted Cousin. The Ted he had
been had no place in today's world. For that he was too naive,
too innocent and not cruel enough. He was *weak*. And weak
and dumb people were stamped on in today's society, stamped
in the dirt, staying there for the rest of their lives.

Horror and hatred, frost and fire kept flowing through him and
from him. Meinz' horrendous machine was switched on. There
was a weak hum, creating vibrations in the prod the Doctor
lowered at Betty.

– This will hurt, he told her graciously.

He pushed it at her right nipple. Tears jumped from her eyes,
and the sound rising from her throat was in no way anything
as benevolent as a scream. He laughed and moved over to the
other nipple. Her eyes seemed to turn inside out, and the body
twisted insanely on the bench, pulling wildly in the straps. He
repeated his works, constantly on the breasts. Betty just faded
as Ted watched, as Ted saw nothing, as he felt the dread grow
to a black hole inside. Meinz repeated his thing ten times,
before nodding in satisfaction, and handed the prod to Bob.

Betty lay still. Now and then she shook, as if there was
another shock, originating from nowhere but her own

nightmarish imagination.

– You haven't broken me yet. You haven't broken me yet. You haven't broken me… yet.

Sweat poured from her skin. She was so weak, and her mouth flickered so much she had serious problems forming words.

– She doesn't present a very convincing show, does she now? Meinz turned to Helen. – How does she sound to you, my dear?

– Like she's begging, Master, Helen said eagerly. – She will come around.

Meinz stroked Betty's body, touching her nipples and they hardened instantly.

– No, Betty moaned. – No, please.

– You like that, don't you? So much better than the bad current.

– Don't… do… it. Go… away.

– Good girl, the Doctor soothed her. – So eager to please. So eager to submit, to please her Master.

Betty sobbed softly. Meinz patted her cheek. Bob pushed the prod into her groin. The girl twisted wildly with her mouth open. She was unable to close her mouth. Bob did her soles and the open palms. Betty screamed continuously at this point. Bob tortured her with rising savagery and her voice slowly faded. The electricity made her fade, reducing her previously strong will to ashes.

Glory approached with a drawer from the medicine storage locker. Meinz pulled a syringe from there, already prepared.

Bob was done and pulled back. Ted looked for some kind of regret, some soft spot in his former friend's eyes and stance, but there was none.

– Now listen carefully, Betty. Meinz spoke in a low, intense voice.

The girl's eyes were closed now. A bit of saliva, just a bit flowed from her mouth. It looked like all her strength had left her, all her vaunted strength.

– You have been disobedient, Betty. That is why you are being punished. You are being punished because you are not obeying and serving your betters, your Masters.

The doctor's strictly formal speech made the captives feel even worse, added further to their woes.

514

She didn't even move a finger when he set the needle in her arm. The only small move she made was to release a throaty sound that could pass for a whimper.

He pulled out the needle.

– Relax, Betty. Time for sleep, Betty.

Just a few seconds passed before her eyes started closing. A few more seconds and she lay there like a statue, rigid and pale.

– You are asleep, but you are still able to hear me, understand what I am saying… Now, you will lift your right arm, and when you have done so you will open your eyes.

Her right arm moved to his specifications. The strap snapped. Mechanical as a machine the girl raised her arm until it pointed ninety degrees straight up. Her eyes opened. There was no blinking, no pupil dilation. They were a doll's eyes. Meinz twisted his mouth in a triumphant grimace.

– You recall the electricity and pain, don't you?

– *Yes*.

– You don't want to be punished anymore, right?

– *No*.

– You will be obedient from now on, won't you?

– *Yes*.

– Good…

He patted her cheek, and started to caress her body, massage her breasts.

– *You like this, don't you?*

– *Yes*. She started writhing and moaning in a low voice.

– *This is the opposite of punishment, you see. This is the reward for obedience and servitude. You will do this often, do you understand?*

– *Yes*.

– *Good*.

Ted didn't recall anything more then. Sight failed him. Memory failed him. Everything just… disconnected. He had no idea how long they kept it going with her, since he slipped into a condition where he was more asleep than awake. Jean was there. They had food and drink. Jean fed them.

I will be your support in harsh times, she told them softly. When things go bad, I will be here to guide you, as my Master has instructed. There is a strict protocol you must adhere to, to avoid unpleasantness. I will guide you through it all. I can teach you. I have been taught well.

And he wanted to laugh, to cry, when listening to her childish voice, but he just sat there, attentive and with a stupid grin in his face. He could see himself from the outside, as if he had left his body.

They were training, exercising and learning martial arts. They learned social skills. They were being taught all the skills their Masters wanted them to have. It was drilled into their psyche, their soul.

– You'll be excellent guards, commandos and killers, the female instructor told them. – For the glory of Abraxas Omega, for the glory of the Masters.

– You'll learn the skill of seduction, of conquest, male and female instructors taught them. – To be predators, to approach and devour the prey. You'll bring glory to your ranks, your clan.

Everything mixed in his chaotic mind. The imagery he saw was no more than mist. The sounds merely noise. Was he under treatment, too, now? Did they electrocute him in… Had they injected him with anything? They would. They would. He swallowed. He swallowed hard.

– *See how it grows. You like this, don't you?*

– Yes. Ahh.

– *This is the opposite of punishment, you see. This is the reward for serving and being obedient. You will do it often and enjoy it. Do you understand?*

– *Yes.*

– *Good.*

When he once again was somewhat lucid everything remained the same. Meinz and his… assistants remained by Betty's bench. He writhed a bit, but noticed no sores or anything implying he had been there for a long time. It didn't matter. During Sleep the kidnappers could have moved them a thousand times, treated them for sores, wounds, anything. Days might have passed since the first time they had been taken to this room. He exchanged looks with Bruce and Helen. There was no hope in their eyes, and he didn't believe it was more prevalent in his own.

516

– Release the slave, the Doctor ordered. – She is ours, now.

Bob and Glory obeyed eagerly, and released the transfixed girl.

– Sit up, Betty, Meinz told her softly, like he was talking to a child.

She obeyed. With eyes just as empty as Jean's she sat there unmoving on the bench. It was a horrible sight. There was nothing there, anymore, no will left. Meinz waved a hand in front of her face. Her eyes didn't move.

– You see? He turned towards the three other captives. – Such a cute doll, right? Rejoice, soon you will join her.

He pulled out a drawer in his desk, and found four metal collars there. It looked like the ring they had worn around their neck earlier, but was clearly different. It made them shiver.

– This is for registration, but also for other, harsher teaching purposes. You name and number is on it… and it carries a powerful electrical charge.

Betty's eyes were just as dull when he fitted the collar around her neck.

– Stand on the floor, Betty.

She stood on the floor, dead and blind.

– Walk slowly around in the room.

She obeyed instantly, without a twitch in the lifeless face.

– Run, he said casually

And when that order reached her the same happened. She didn't increase her speed evenly as most people would have done, but accelerated into marching speed in a second. She walked, and a moment later she ran.

Ted noticed that Glory looked at him. The brown eyes seemed huge and scary. She grabbed the prod, the electric needle. He wanted to move, keep fighting, but he couldn't even twist his body there on the bench. He was defenseless, condemned.

– I can see your mind working, Meinz said. – Quite amazing, really, but believe me, useless. No matter how much you struggle, how much you fight against the inevitable, it won't help you.

Glory petted him.

– You're troubled, I can tell, but don't be. It's so counterproductive. If you should manage to escape, against all odds, where will you go? We are everywhere. Where are you gonna go, where are you gonna run?

Condemned, yes, from birth. A failure his entire life. All the bad things happening had been seemingly preordained.

Betty still ran. Sweat covered her body and she was breathing hard, but kept going at exactly the same speed... until Bob kicked her legs away from her. She fell, and didn't make any attempt to get up. It was a dog lying there, not a human being.

– You are disobedient again, Betty, Meinz scolded her. – We told you to run and you did not. You must be punished.

He pushed a button on a little box he held on to. Betty grabbed her throat, but couldn't do it for long. She twisted and turned on the floor like insane. The electric needle had been bad. This was... this was...

Meinz turned off the current. Bob reached out a hand, his face twisting under the bandages. Betty grabbed his hand, kissing it.

– *What are you?*

– I'm a slave, Master, I live to serve.

Betty Morgan was no longer present, just a creature of codependence coincidentally called Betty.

Ted shook, shook and couldn't stop shaking.

– This is you, slave, Glory snarled to him. – In just a little while.

Ted wanted to say something, anything. He tried, tried moving his lips, but they moved by themselves, and he heard nothing. Fear constricted his throat. He didn't want to close his eyes, wanted to look at his executioners as long as possible. Glory moved the prod slowly down his belly, towards his groin.

– Enjoy your last moments, old dog. Say hello to new dog.

And then everything was screams and pain.

EPILOGUE:
THE MASTERS

On the American east coast it was the evening of August 8th 1974. In Washington DC a man sat down behind a special desk for the final time. Coming tomorrow it would no longer belong to him. He was perceived as one of the world's most powerful men. He was the president of the United States of America.

He waited there for while with the manuscript in his hands while the TV-people put on makeup, so his skin wouldn't look too pale on the screen. Then everybody pulled back. He drew breath and shifted in the chair. A signal and the cameras started running. The stage was set.

– *Good evening.*

– *This is the 37th time I have spoken to you from this office, where so many decisions have been made that shaped the history of this Nation. Each time I have done so to discuss with you some matter that I believe affected the national interest.*

– *In all the decisions I have made in my public life, I have always tried to do what was best for the Nation. Throughout the long and difficult period of Watergate, I have felt it was my duty to persevere, to make every possible effort to complete the term of office to which you elected me.*

Richard Nixon made an effort to not appear too stricken by the event, but all the millions watching him on TV couldn't avoid noticing the bags under his eyes, another visible sign of massive worries and little sleep, the rounding of his shoulders revealing how exhausted he truly was.

– *I would have preferred to carry through to the finish whatever the personal agony it would have involved, and my family unanimously urged me to do so. But the interest of the Nation must always come before any personal considerations.*

– *I have never been a quitter. To leave office before my term is completed is abhorrent to every instinct in my body. But as President, I must put the interest of America first.*

– *... Therefore, I shall resign the Presidency effective at noon tomorrow.*

In another room, far from the Oval in the president's residence three men sat and followed the speech with interest on a large screen built into the wall. They didn't speak. One of them smiled ironically occasionally.

– *We have ended America's longest war, but in the work of securing a lasting peace in the world, the goals ahead are even more far-reaching and more difficult. We must complete a structure of peace so that it will be said of this generation, our generation of Americans, by the people of all nations, not only that we ended one war but that we prevented future wars.*

*– We have unlocked the doors that for a quarter of a century
stood between the United States and the People's Republic of
China.*

*– In the Middle East, 100 million people in the Arab
countries, many of whom have considered us their enemy for
nearly 20 years, now look on us as their friends.*

One of the three, definitely an Arab brushed cigarette ash off
his knee and exclaimed irritably:

– What an idiot!

*– I pledge to you tonight that as long as I have a breath
of life in my body, I shall continue in that spirit. I shall
continue to work for the great causes to which I have been
dedicated throughout my years as a Congressman, a Senator,
a Vice President, and President, the cause of peace not just
for America but among all nations, prosperity, justice, and
opportunity for all of our people.*

*– To have served in this office is to have felt a very personal
sense of kinship with each and every American. In leaving it, I
do so with this prayer: May God's grace be with you in all the
days ahead.*

A click, and the screen turned black. Silence reigned for a
while in the room. Sheik Kurman Al Rashid looked nonplussed
at the two on the other side of the table. David Gidman, and the
man only known as The Mask. He wore dark glasses and hid
his face behind a mask of cloth.

– As I said: The guy is an idiot and what are you two doing
after having witnessed his demise? You look like schoolboys
having been reprimanded by an old and respected teacher.

The last word the sheik spoke as if he had something stuck in
his throat.

Gidman turned towards him. The large man smiled indulgent.

– Kurman, my good Kurman, I'm a bit disappointed by your
opinion here. Didn't you in fact study mass psychology at
Harvard?

– I don't get it. What does mass psychology have to do with
this?

– A lot, I would say, Gidman replied dryly. – Let's take your
less favorable description of departing President Nixon…

He grabbed a fruit from the large basket on the table before continuing.

– Your claim that Nixon is an idiot isn't only stupid, but also shows you can never reach as high as he on the peaks of democracy.

– Most politicians in trouble uses standard phrases like his, the Mask said. – Before the people they give the impression that certain troubles are merely trifles. Other troubles are, on the other hand vastly exaggerated. Notice that he plays up the sense of «national pride». He isn't the first and won't be last doing that… And the final sentence: «May God's grace be with you in all the days ahead». Oh, yes, religion is important.

The sheik was a faithful Muslim. That, combined with the fact that someone dared to hide his face to him, irritated Al Rashid enormously.

– Nixon has been piling up mistakes for years. Gidman shook his head. – The belief in his own infallibility was his downfall. In spite of this he remained in office for five and a half years. He managed to get himself re-elected. Amazing, if you ask me. Even though you can chalk that one up to people's gullibility as well.

– I understand you're having great fun with such analysis, Al Rashid said rigidly. – But I didn't come here for that…

– You're worried, right?

– Well, yes…

– We have good news.

Gidman grabbed another fruit. He ate enormous amounts of food.

– Quite a few of our associates are leaving the White House with Nixon tomorrow, The Mask shrugged.

– But that can't be good news. We'll lose influence in one of the major chambers in the world.

– As far as I recall we will earn one more extra associate when Ford moves in tomorrow. The various Rockefeller Institutes and others are giving us a steady flow of new blood.

Even though the Arab had risen quickly in the Order he was a fairly new member. He had yet to grasp its true significance. One Eye grinned and the other face moved under the mask. Al Rashid's gesture of apology ended the discussion.

The Order and its various partly independent branches recruited «people of good standing» from all over the world. They were the spiders weaving or rather maintaining the web. Al Rashid was loath to admit it, but he had been close to awe when it dawned on him what he had actually joined.

– And you had a pleasant journey, I presume?

The previous conversation had evidently been forgotten. By changing the subject The Mask showed that he «forgave» Al Rashid his «indiscretion».

– What can happen with your men as sentinels? The sheik wouldn't be any less generous.

He spoke excellent English. His father had sent him to Harvard, and also to prestigious business schools before dying, and leaving Kurman as one of the wealthiest men in the Middle East, and after last year's oil crisis - the world.

– You're so right, the other laughed.

Gidman clapped his hands twice. Al Rashid hadn't seen him use that one in particular before, but it was obviously a signal.

A platinum blond woman clothed partly in velvet, partly in nothing entered the room, kneeling before them.

– Is everything ready, Jean? You may reply.

– Everything is ready, Master. What is Master's wish?

– Put things in motion. When we're done you may go to the red room and wait for me there.

– Yes, Master, she curtseyed and retreated.

Al Rashid had an eye for such thing, and he had seen instantly that the woman belonged to Gidman, exclusively. She was not available.

– Amazing isn't it? The Mask commented. – People who are free their entire lives are reduced to sniveling goats.

– It certainly is, the sheik nodded.

– Or perhaps it isn't that amazing. Perhaps they haven't truly been free. Perhaps they're taught the role of sniveling goat from day one.

There was a snarl in the voice, a rage Al Rashid easily recognized. He didn't respond verbally to the last statement. He agreed, of course, but something about it made him uncomfortable.

The Mask walked to a drawer and fetched one bottle of wine

and three glasses. The way he poured the glasses suggested he was quite experienced in such matters.

– Chateau Margaux Pillet Will 1969. He raised his glass.
– Though not yet fully realized a very good year. Let's have refreshments before turning our attention to other matters.

Al Rashid raised his glass calmly. He had never cared much for the Muslim prohibition on alcohol.

– To us, he cheered. – To the Thousand Feet.

– To us, the other two cheered. – To the Thousand Feet.

He wondered a moment, if he didn't hear a bit of irony in their voices.

They emptied the glasses, put them down on the table, and left the room. An aide and Al Rashid's personal servant waited outside the door. The aide was a young woman in uniform.

– Good evening. She bowed. – My name is Sandra. I will be your Guide tonight. Please follow me.

The three and Achmed, Al Rashid's servant followed her. Al Rashid shook his head, amused. Achmed was surely a typical Arab, seen from Westerners' point of view, with his shaved head, and his many scars. His height and build was quite impressive, but when walking next to Gidman he looked like a dwarf. The sheik was very amused by that.

The room they entered was luxurious from all point of views, even though Kurman was used to such things and wasn't impressed by that. But the setting did impress him.

Among the plush couches, chairs, beds and oak furniture two rows of naked, collared youths knelt in a half moon formation on the carpet. The sight, the layout almost took his breath away.

– Brilliantly arraigned, he said. – Give my regards to the interior architect.

– Thank you, sir, Sandra said softly. – I will relay your appreciation.

He didn't have a lot of appreciation for the general Muslim view on women either. He was all in all quite the modern man.

Another group of men and women entered the room from the opposite side. The sheik had just met them a few times, but the sight of them brought a thrill to his consciousness, in spite of his pride. He knew their presence here signified an important event. They had accepted him among their ranks.

Kurt Meinz entered through a doorway behind them. He slipped almost undetectably to their side.

– Yeah, these are our new batch, he offered casually. – None of those left have any notable flaws.

– How many were… rejected?

– Only three, three of fifty all in all, a very low number. One heart defect and two other unfortunates.

Sandra looked at Gidman. He nodded.

– RISE! She commanded. – Display yourselves.

Everything jumped to their feet simultaneously, a mini-ballet turning Al Rashid's throat dry.

Sandra filled a glass of water from a jug, and handed it to him. He accepted it, ogling her intensively. She blushed. He drank, drank greedily.

One by one the slaves displayed themselves for the masters, the inviting smiles never leaving their faces. The Arab shook his head in disbelief.

– These are ordinary Western children?

– The ultimate scoundrels of the Earth, Meinz confirmed.

– So how is it possible to make them this obedient in such a fairly short time? It takes years in the harem before the white bitches are completely freed of their ignorant ideas of equality.

– Oh, you may say we are using fairly harsh means.

– What type? Brainwashing, hypnosis, torture?

– I think you can safely assume all of the above and more. But seriously, Kurman, I feel your view is generally too simplistic. Behavioral modification techniques have taken major strides and even leaps forward, the last decades, and I have perfected it with my own brand of control measures. My treatment cannot be described in short or simple terms. It is a masterpiece.

Al Rashid couldn't completely avoid the slight shiver. Meinz seemed more than a bit insane when standing there, speaking in a low, emotional voice. There was something sick and disgusting about him that could make even the hardest react.

– We are partly, initially at least using the technique of hypnosis, of suggestion and learning during sleep or better; non-consciousness, force-feeding them the desired attitudes. Later we are slowly but surely erasing their personality. The electric ring around their neck is certainly effective, but if that had been it, they would only have been physically restrained. It would not have kept them from thinking. Now, they are so dulled I very much doubt all of them remember their last name.

– Some do then? The sheik spoke with unavoidable malicious pleasure, directed at Meinz, not the slaves.

– Some do. The Doctor shrugged. – But it doesn't really matter, does it? What matters is the blind obedience engraved on their souls. They love us and will do anything for us. We *are* drugging them lightly during the first period of time. Later it will not be necessary. Then they will have lived so long in degradation and humiliation that they will be broken for all time. Then they will be slaves through and through.

Al Rashid raised his hand when a big girl with red hair and gray eyes was about to pass him. She stopped, kneeling down. He signed again and she rose, keeping her head low.

– What are you? He snapped. – You may reply.

– I'm a slave, Master. I live to serve.

– Who are you?

– I'm Tilla, Master. I'm a slave. I'm a good girl. I've been taught from an early age what a man wants.

Al Rashid looked bemused at Meinz.

– Sometimes these things happen, Meinz shrugged. – Unexpected things. They add spice to life, do they not?

The Arab Sheik turned away from Meinz, dismissing him.

– Achmed.

Al Rashid commanded.

Achmed stepped forward. Tilla smiled in anticipation. She performed for Achmed now, knowing fully well whom she truly had to please. Achmed grabbed her. She stroked his organ carefully, licking her lips. The Arab let his pants fall. He put her down on the nearest couch. She was wet already, uncannily so. One could see it, not only on the humid inner thighs, but in her features, moves and laidback eagerness.

– By the Prophet, Kurman whispered.

Sandra handed him another glass of water. He accepted it in a daze.

Tilla rested unmoving on the couch. Achmed got up, pulling up his pants.

– She knows the tricks, Master, he reported in halting, hardly understandable English, – and it's all coming from the inside, it's all real.

Another sign, and Tilla jumped up and rejoined her fellow slaves kneeling on the floor, her skin flushed in a healthy color.

– Yes, this is good, Kurman said hoarsely. – This is very, very good.

– These are the early stages of this particular project, Meinz said pleased. – We have been waiting for years to start its development. The time has finally come. This and the few other batches we have acquired so far is just the pale beginning. They don't even begin to cover the need and the potential.

David Gidman nodded pleased, nodded to the men and women at the other side of the room. They nodded back, hardly able to contain their excitement.

This was surely an event of major magnitude. Plans put on hold for decades could finally be implemented, and thus, inevitably, in a few years, the batch of slaves kneeling before them tonight would only be one group of many.

«Approximately a million people are every year sold to forced labor, prostitution or quite simply slavery. It's a common myth that slavery is abandoned in our time.

It's shameful that we in 1993 are faced with a world encompassing slave-trade, from Brazil to Bangladesh, in China, Thailand, Pakistan and Europe, in San Francisco, San Diego, Chicago, New York, Boston…»

Excerpt from speech held by
Joseph P. Kennedy III
In the American Congress, Thursday, July 15th 1993

AUTHOR'S WORD

It is a special pleasure for me to publish this novel. It is my first, and thus it has been rejected most times by established publishers…

This is the first book of ten (or eleven) in **the Janus Clan** series: Ten stories (or so) about the wild man in the modern world, forty years of wandering before the Phoenix is rising from its ashes.

It usually takes me about ten years to complete a book, from start to the final finishing touch. But with The Defenseless it has taken me thirty-seven years. It has been a long, long Journey, from the moment I first glimpsed the story in my fevered dreams when I was twelve.

My first version was about 50 000 words. I quickly grew dissatisfied with that one. My second was about 150 000 words. The main difference between those, written in the late seventies and early eighties, and this, final one is that I know more, now, much more, about everything, and that I've learned to write dialogue. The dialogue in the two first versions sucked, quite frankly. I have strived to keep the original mood, though, the fact that the story was originally written by a teenager, which is manifesting in a number of ways. It's the same story, in spite of the minor and major changes in approach when it comes to telling it. I also remember it all, the context and my state of mind when I wrote it.

This book is very different from all others I've written, even different considering that I always strive to make each new book I write different from the previous, to always and passionately seek new ground. I see that in every sentence, every paragraph, perspective and inclination.

Ted isn't me, even if he is fairly close, at least in some aspects, and all major characters I write or wrote are usually both demonic and idealistic versions of myself. Like any writer and artist, I use what I experience and observe, both good and bad.

This novel is me, like every story I tell is me.

I longed for humanity's savage past already as a child, of course, the freedom and the unblemished nature, and I have always strived to recapture what was misplaced, also through my art.

Well, this is it, Wild Man. I greet you and hope we will meet out there, on the true Freedom Road.

It's a long, hard and brutal path, also within the story, but know that it *will* be worth it.

Amos Keppler

1977
1982
2003
One Sherwood Forest 2010-06-16

Paperback:
One Sherwood Forest 2019-01-20
The Sherwood Forest isn't a place, but a state of mind.

The paperback is published after four amazing years of publishing for me. During that time all my novels and poems ready for publishing were published, and published without me making any concessions or suffering any censorship.
Every single word in the books is mine and my aspiration fulfilled.

Other published and upcoming novels and collections of poetry by Amos Keppler from **Midnight Fire Media**:

The Janus Clan - (ten chapters about the Wild Man in the modern world, a world balancing on a razor's edge):

The Defenseless
The Slaves
Birds Flying in the Dark
At the End of the Rainbow
Lewis of Modern York
The Werewolf of Locus Bradle
The Valley of Kings
Eye in the Sky
The Iron Cage
Phoenix Green Earth

The Slaves

Civilization needs slaves, needs cogs in the machine, a braindead population in a world filled with shame, for the machinery to keep working. Everybody is defenseless in a certain sense in present day society, bred to be servants, to be victims, to be slaves.

A group of youths was kidnapped, broken and brainwashed to fit the needs of the Cabal of people calling themselves Abraxas Omega, a clandestine organization working behind the throne, the seats of power on present day Earth.

On the passenger liner M/S Aphrodite, a playground for the rich and powerful. The streets and houses of London. In the American desert. In the highest political and executive offices around the world.

A ghost is hunting the slavers, a specter from the past thought long dead, slowly gaining substance, gaining life. In the city of London the spark is struck, the Burning begins, one that in time will engulf everything, from the deepest sewer to the highest tower.

Ted Warren is born in that seething cauldron.

ISBN 978-82-91693-09-5

ℰhadow 𝐖alk

The world is changing. They know this, in their core of cores, where everything moves and shifts. Night and fire have followed them all the days of their lives.

What they carry inside has always scared them, always intrigued them...

They have always felt different, apart from the crowd. And here, now, they get the confirmation they have always wanted, always yearned for, that they are truly different, a breed apart. The metamorphosis begins. Their minds, their bodies are changing in shocking and unpredictable ways, as what's on the inside is brought to the outside. And as they themselves are changing they are also changing the world.

Danger awaits them, Life awaits them, in the small, backward New England town. Magick and Mystery may be found beneath unturned stones.

People, young and old, are descending on the small, insignificant town of Northfield, New England.

Boys and girls, students at the school of Life, Seekers, yearning for what's different, what's hidden.

They're seeking within and without, high and low.

And here, in this dusty, remote place they're finding it, turning the stone, finding the strength within themselves to be themselves, to break out of confines, to the world beyond. And in time, after the initial, tentative steps, pushing down paths new and undreamed of.

And the present-day order sees them for what they are... Agents of Change, a threat to any establishment, any imposed reality. The heatwave, the worst in living memory, is nothing compared to the boiling within the human heart. The Indian Summer heralds the twilight of mankind.

ISBN 978-82-91693-12-5

Your Own Fate

In boca al loco - in the mouth of the wolf.
Italian salutation

From The Book of Fate:
In the Book of Fate there is everything. Every incident,
all times, everything that has been, that is, that will ever be,
everything that might be, everything that could have been.
But who is writing it? Who is penning it? Who is turning
page by page, too many to be counted, blowing in the wind?
Does it perhaps write itself, with a pen moving across the
yellow sheets? Or is it a hand moving the pen, one unseen, one
stretching back into the past, back to the time before everything
was created, creating itself from nothing?

Timothy Joyce is an enigma, a man without a past, appearing
from nowhere, to go on a rampage in an astonished world.

Jeremy Zahn is hunting Timothy Joyce. It seems like he has
always been hunting him, from old London, from the island of
angels, where it is said they met for the first time, to the city of
angels, California, the new world.
Here, on this shaky ground, following confrontations
spanning the globe, its time and space the two will fight for the
last time.
And the world is watching, its people shivering in their frozen
hearts.

ISBN 978-82-91693-05-7

www.ingramcontent.com/pod-product-compliance
Lightning Source LLC
Chambersburg PA
CBHW061326050726
47504CB00013B/262